About

Stephen Leather was a journalist for more than ten years on newspapers such as *The Times*, the *Daily Mail* and the *South China Morning Post* in Hong Kong. Before that, he was employed as a biochemist for ICI, shovelled limestone in a quarry, worked as a baker, a petrol pump attendant, a barman, and worked for the Inland Revenue. He began writing full-time in 1992 and has written 14 novels. His bestsellers have been translated into more than ten languages, and *The Stretch* and *The Bombmaker* have been filmed for television. He has also written for television shows such as *London's Burning*, *The Knock* and the BBC's *Murder in Mind* series. Stephen Leather now lives in Dublin and you can visit his website at www.stephenleather.com.

STEPHEN LEATHER

Hungry Ghost
The Chinaman

CORONET BOOKS

Hodder & Stoughton

Hungry Ghost copyright © 1992 by Stephen Leather
The Chinaman copyright © 1992 by Stephen Leather

Hungry Ghost first published in Great Britain in 1992
by Hodder & Stoughton

The Chinaman first published in Great Britain in 1992
by Hodder & Stoughton

This omnibus edition published in 2003 by Hodder & Stoughton
A division of Hodder Headline

The right of Stephen Leather to be identified as the Author
of the Work has been asserted by him in accordance with the
Copyright, Designs and Patents Act 1988.

A Coronet Paperback
1 3 5 7 9 10 8 6 4 2

A CIP catalogue record for this title is available
from the British Library

ISBN 0 340 83077 8

Typeset by Palimpsest Book Production Limited,
Polmont, Stirlingshire

Printed and bound in Great Britain by
Clays Ltd, St Ives plc

Hodder and Stoughton
A division of Hodder Headline
338 Euston Road
London NW1 3BH

Hungry Ghost

For Angela

The door opened with no sound on well-oiled brass hinges. Two men and a girl came in on tiptoe like students on a Rag Week stunt. The girl was dressed in a nurse's uniform, starched white with a pocket over her right breast, and white shoes. On her head was a white cap and she carried a small, black leather bag. She was barely five feet tall, but perfectly in proportion, so that standing alone and from a distance it was hard to judge her height. But with a man either side of her in the gloom it was obvious that she was petite, far too small to ever be a model but pretty enough to break hearts.

She moved over to the bottom of the bed and beckoned the men to move to either side. They wore dark business suits, but they wore them badly as if unused to the feel of heavy cloth and long sleeves. While the girl had the soft, well-cared-for skin of a city creature, the men looked weather-beaten and worn as if they'd spent their lives in the fields. And while the girl looked as if she'd never had to lift anything heavier than a lipstick, the men were well-muscled and strong.

The girl gently placed her bag on the foot of the bed, close to the sleeping man's feet and silently opened it. She nervously licked her upper lip, a quick showing of her small, pink tongue, and she took a deep breath, the soft mounds of her breasts pushing the uniform up. She nodded, once, and the two men moved at the same time to grab an arm each. The man on the left, the slightly smaller of the two, reached across and clamped a hand firmly across the sleeper's mouth. He woke with a start and began kicking his legs up and down and twisting his shoulders, his eyes wide with fright and shock. He tried to scream, to force air out of his heaving chest, but the bitter-smelling hand muffled all sound except for a pig-like grunt, too quiet to be heard outside the room. He tried to thrash his head from side to side but the hand held him steady. He tried to bare his teeth to bite the flesh but the thumb was under his chin and painfully squeezing his mouth shut. The men, neither of whom he could see, pulled his arms to the side so that he lay crucified, rigidly held to the bed above the waist but still kicking his legs and grunting. They held him until his legs tired and the grunting stopped. The panic eased somewhat as he realized that they hadn't hurt him. Maybe they just wanted to give him a message, didn't want him to disturb the rest of the party. Perhaps if he lay quietly they'd move the hand and allow him to speak, perhaps they'd tell him what they wanted. He relaxed, let himself go loose to show that he wasn't struggling anymore. But they kept his arms outstretched and the hand stayed where it was, forcing him to breathe noisily through his nostrils.

He became aware of the girl then. He could just make out the top of her head, the white cap and below it two oval-shaped eyes. He felt a weight press down on the bottom of the bed and then saw her face clearly as she climbed up and knelt down with her knees either side of his legs. She had high cheekbones and finely arched eyebrows, and she watched him with a look of quiet amusement. She was gorgeous, no doubt about it, and he couldn't take his eyes off her pouting lips. Her tongue came out and she licked them, slowly and sensuously, like a cat, and began to move up his body, moving one knee at a time. It was a hot night and he was naked under the sheet and he could feel the coolness of her thighs through the cotton. She looked like a nurse, he thought, but what was a nurse doing in his room in the middle of the night and who were the men? For a wild moment he thought he might be in hospital, suffering from amnesia or something, or perhaps he'd had a breakdown. But he knew he was still in the Embassy compound, in the bed he'd occupied for the past three nights. He wasn't in hospital and this wasn't a dream.

She reached his thighs and settled back, nestling her firm buttocks on his knees. Her lips drew back in a teasing smile and he saw white even teeth and behind them her small pointed tongue. Her ears had no lobes, he noticed, and her skin was flawless. She wasn't flat-chested like many Chinese girls, he could see the swell of her breasts under the white dress. His gaze wandered down the line of studs on the front of her dress, down between her breasts to her lap. The dress had ridden up her thighs and he could see her knees by squinting his eyes. Then he saw the hypodermic in her hand and he froze. It began to move upwards and he watched it like a rabbit hypnotized by a snake. The girl held it in front of her face, needle upwards. In her other hand she held a small vial, containing a colourless liquid, which she pushed onto the needle and extracted fluid from.

The man groaned and began to buck up and down and rock from side to side. The girl gripped him tightly with her thighs as if riding a horse, then she slid up his body

3

until she was sitting on his groin. The dress rode higher up her legs and he caught a glimpse of suspenders and white lace panties. She finished filling the syringe and then popped the empty vial into her breast pocket. The man felt himself grow hard under the sheet, and the girl felt it too. She pressed down against him and smiled, enjoying the feel of his maleness, so close to her, just a sheet separating them. She reached down between her thighs and stroked him, just once. To tease him. Then she removed her hand and tapped the glass with a long, red-painted fingernail and watched the bubbles closely as they rose to the top, under the needle. She gently squeezed the plunger at the bottom, creating a miniature fountain that played over her hands.

The man panicked then, he thrust up and down, trying with all his might to throw her off. He shook his head violently from side to side, eyes rolling with fear, but the hand round his mouth tightened and locked him still. Her cap fell off and black hair tumbled down over her face and across her shoulders, a solid curtain of blackness. She flicked it back and it cascaded around her face. He tried rolling his hips but she just gripped him tighter and moved with him. She reached forward with her left hand and ran her fingertips down his cheek.

'I'm not going to hurt you. I promise,' she said in unaccented English that took him by surprise. He began to sob quietly but lay still, and then she leant forward and injected the contents of the hypodermic into his right arm. Tears rolled down his cheeks and trickled along the side of the hand that kept his mouth clamped shut. She put the empty hypodermic on the bed and he felt a coldness travel up his arm, like pins and needles. She moved forward, placed her hands on the pillow, and kissed him softly on the forehead. He caught the fragrance of jasmine and then it hit his heart and his chest exploded in pain and he died, no sound because his jaw was still locked tight.

The girl shuddered, either with pleasure or relief, and then slid off the bed, gathering up the hypodermic and replacing it in the bag. The men arranged the dead man's arms under the sheet, and then the three left the room as silently as they'd entered just three minutes earlier.

Sunday was a hell of a funny day to be summoned down to Suffolk to see your boss's boss, but it wasn't the sort of invitation that Donaldson could turn down. In fact invitation was the wrong word, he'd been ordered down by Grey, even though the order had come in a very obtuse form. Grey was his normal soft-spoken self on the phone, but there had been no doubt in Donaldson's mind that something was worrying the man.

When Donaldson took the call his first thought had been that he was about to be sacked, that the latest round of positive vetting had uncovered his little secret. He'd been careful to cover his tracks and whenever he met others who shared his tastes he'd used a false name, but these days you could never be sure; it was always a risk. And perhaps it was the possibility of being caught that added to the excitement. But Grey had simply said that he'd needed his help and that it was something that had to be dealt with out of the office.

He'd been given quite a complicated set of instructions

to follow to reach the house and once he'd left the main road he'd had to stop a couple of times to read the scribble he'd jotted down on the back of an internal memo. It had rained for a while, which hadn't helped. It was the height of summer but the weather owed more to November. It was almost chilly, and had been for the best part of a week. A freak north wind, said the forecasters. Bloody typical, thought Donaldson.

He was ten minutes late and Grey was waiting for him at the entrance to the drive. He was holding open a wooden gate which he closed behind Donaldson's Toyota as it pulled up in front of the thatched farmhouse.

As he climbed out of the car Donaldson instantly felt over-dressed in his light blue suit. Grey had swapped his customary Savile Row pinstripe for baggy cord trousers and a thick white fisherman's sweater. With his greying temples and weather-beaten face he looked more like the head of a farming family than an off-duty civil servant. He shook Donaldson limply by the hand and took him along the hall past a selection of tasteful hunting prints and into a sitting-room packed with plush settees and Victorian furniture. It was very much a woman's room, with pretty lace things on the backs of the chairs and a collection of old perfume bottles on a circular table in one corner. On top of a large television set was a collection of brass-framed photographs of the Grey clan. A fire was burning merrily in a white-painted metal fireplace that looked original and Grey gestured towards the two floral-patterned easy chairs either side of the blaze. In between the chairs was a low coffee table on which stood a fine bone china tea-set and a silver teapot. There was also a plateful of crumpets dripping with butter.

The two men sat down and made small talk while Grey poured. The conversation turned towards the office, and workloads and politics. Donaldson felt uneasy; Grey wouldn't normally even say hello to him if they passed in a corridor. Donaldson was a Grade 2 admin assistant, albeit with a high security classification. His main job was to keep track of expenses of agents in the field, he was always at arm's length from operations. The nearest he got to the sharp end of intelligence work was to read thrillers by Brian Freemantle and John le Carré.

The fire crackled in the grate, the logs moving against each other like uneasy lovers. A gust of wind blew down the chimney and a plume of smoke bellowed under the rim of the fireplace and wafted gently towards the ceiling, filling the air with the fragrant scent of burning pine.

'There's nothing like an open fire,' said Donaldson, settling back in the chair and enjoying the warmth but wishing that his host would just get on with it. Men of Donaldson's rank didn't get social invitations for tea and crumpets in deepest Suffolk.

'It's worth the effort,' replied Grey.

Sure, thought Donaldson. Grey probably kicked his wife out of bed in the morning to empty the ashes, fill the grate and blow on burning newspapers until the bloody thing was lit. Either that or he'd have a servant to do it. Grey wasn't the sort of man who'd be caught dead with a dustpan and brush in his liver-spotted hands.

'More tea?' asked Grey, proffering the silver teapot.

'Thank you, no, sir,' Donaldson replied politely. He already wanted to visit the toilet.

'I suppose you're wondering why I asked you here,' said Grey, as he poured himself another cup.

Of course not, you silly old fool, thought Donaldson, but he merely smiled and nodded, once.

'We have a problem in Hong Kong,' continued Grey. 'Or to be more precise, we have a problem over the border, in China.' He stirred his tea thoughtfully, the spoon clinking gently against the cup. 'You are of course aware of the massive loss of confidence in the colony, especially after what happened in Tiananmen Square. There has been a rush to get out, businesses are thinking twice about investing there, the place is a shambles. The British Government is struggling to make the transition in 1997 as smooth and painless as possible.'

He replaced the spoon in the saucer and sipped the tea with relish.

'The Government has already made it clear that we cannot offer sanctuary to all the six million Chinese who live in Hong Kong, so it's vital that we keep the lid on things, if you follow me. Once Hong Kong is part of China, of course, it is no longer our problem. Until then our intelligence services are doing everything they can to nip any trouble in the bud. We are actively seeking to dissuade those local politicians and businessmen who are trying to delay the handover, or to impose restrictions which we know the Chinese will find unacceptable.'

Grey gave his pale imitation of a smile and leant forward to place his cup and saucer on the table between them.

'That is background, background you are no doubt aware of. Now to the problem in hand. There is a nuclear power station in China, some six miles away from Hong Kong. The authorities in Beijing have received a threat to destroy it, to blow it up.'

'My God!' said Donaldson. 'A nuclear explosion six miles from Hong Kong?'

'Strictly speaking, it wouldn't actually be a nuclear explosion,' said Grey, clasping his hands and resting them in his lap. 'As I understand it, a conventional explosive device has been placed in the foundations, close to the reactor. If detonated it will crack open the reactor and lead to the sort of thing we saw at Three Mile Island and Chernobyl. Not a nuclear explosion, but the release of a cloud of radioactive material. Hong Kong, I should add, tends to be downwind of the power station.'

Donaldson fell silent as his mind tried to grasp the enormity of Grey's revelation. There were so many questions to ask that he didn't know where to start and he was relieved when the old man began speaking again.

'MI6 tells us that the ultimatum was delivered to Beijing by one of the triads in Hong Kong, the Chinese mafia if you like. They are especially fearful of what will happen when the colony comes under full Chinese jurisdiction. They execute criminals in China, you know. In football stadiums. Parents take their children to watch.' He shook his head sadly. 'It's a simple matter for the big hongs like Jardine Matheson to switch their domicile to Bermuda, or for the Hongkong and Shanghai Bank to invest money overseas and transfer its capital around the world, but the triads are firmly rooted in Hong Kong. They cannot afford to give up their illegal activities in the colony. They simply have too much to lose. So with only a few years to go before the British pull out they have decided that their only hope is to delay the handover. They want the *status quo* to continue, for fifty years at least.'

'Why fifty years, sir?' asked Donaldson.

Grey smiled thinly at the man's lack of knowledge. 'In 1997 Hong Kong will be given back to China, but for fifty years after handover it will operate under its own rules and regulations. It will have its own Government, including its own elected representatives, and its own laws, which are currently being drafted. It will be part of China, but at the same time separate from it. Special Administrative Region, I think they're going to call it. It will stay that way until 2047 when it will become just another part of China. But during those fifty years the policing of Hong Kong will be the responsibility of the Chinese. And it is that which is worrying the triads.'

'I thought they were bailing out along with anyone else who can afford to buy a passport, sir,' said Donaldson, and was rewarded with a nod from the older man.

'Yes, but it's not as simple as that. Any sort of criminal record will stop them getting into Canada, Australia or the United States. The middle classes and the rich have no problems buying second passports, but it's standard practice in most Western countries to cross-check with Special Branch in Hong Kong to ensure that applicants don't have triad connections. I've no doubt they could buy a passport from Andorra but most of them have nowhere to go. Some have managed to get out and as a result many of the triads are active overseas. They operate anywhere where there are Chinatowns . . . or Chinese restaurants. But the bulk of their income comes from vice, drugs and extortion in Hong Kong. And they are naturally reluctant to lose that revenue.'

'But surely, sir, contaminating Hong Kong is no answer?'

Grey shrugged and reached for his cup and saucer

again. 'It seems to be a sort of scorched-earth policy. If they can't have it, no one else will. But I suppose they assume that their demands will be met.'

'All they want is for the police force to remain British, you say?'

Grey drained his cup and sighed. 'You know what happens when you give in to blackmail, particularly where terrorists are involved. You submit once and the stakes are raised next time. The Chinese are not stupid. They know if they give in to this demand then more will follow. And to be frank, there is not one hope in hell of the Chinese – or the British – agreeing. The British Government just wants a clean withdrawal and the Chinese want complete control. No, their demands will not be met. The men behind it must be stopped.'

Donaldson nodded.

'That's why I need your help,' said Grey.

'I don't follow, sir,' said Donaldson, feeling out of his depth.

'On no account must the Chinese be aware that we know of the blackmail threat. We haven't been approached officially, nor will we be. That is why we cannot deal with this through normal channels, as news would soon filter back to Peking.'

'I hardly think we have any Chinese double-agents, sir,' said Donaldson smugly.

'If we have I wouldn't expect you to know about them,' said Grey, and Donaldson winced at the reprimand. 'No, our department cannot be involved officially. Or unofficially for that matter.'

'So you want me to arrange a freelance, sir?'

'No,' said Grey, carefully putting his cup and saucer

back on the table and looking wistfully at the now empty teapot. 'No, not a freelance.' He looked up at Donaldson, eyes shining like a ferret's. 'We want to use Howells.'

Donaldson stiffened as if he'd been plugged into the mains.

'Howells is dead,' he said.

'Retired,' stressed Grey.

'That's what I mean,' said Donaldson.

'No,' smiled Grey. 'I mean he really *was* retired. Pensioned off. He's alive, and available.'

Donaldson sank back into the easy chair, his mind whirling as it tried to come to terms with what he'd heard.

'Howells is a psychopath,' he spluttered.

'Actually, I think the phrase the psychologists use is sociopath, admittedly with homicidal tendencies. Though you'll have to take it from me that Geoff Howells is a changed man, for the moment at least. Have you seen the garden?'

The change in subject caught Donaldson by surprise. 'I'm sorry, sir?' he said.

'The garden, have you seen the garden? Come on, I feel like a walk.'

He led the younger man down along the hall to the back door where he pulled off his slippers and donned a pair of green Wellington boots. He gestured towards a matching pair.

'The grass is still wet. Try those for size. They're my son's, he's up at Oxford.'

He would be, thought Donaldson. The boots fitted, though.

Grey hauled open the door to be greeted by two heaving

12

Labradors, one black, one golden-brown, tongues lolling out of the corners of their mouths, tails wagging madly, overjoyed to see their master. Donaldson had seen similar reactions from section heads going into Grey's monthly think-tank meetings. Not that Donaldson had ever attended one. The black dog leapt up and tried to lick Grey's face and he pushed it away, though obviously pleased at the show of affection.

'Down, Lady,' he said, but there was no harshness in his voice.

The dogs ran in circles around the two men as they walked along the edge of the lawn which sloped gently down towards a small orchard. The grass formed a triangular shape with the base at the house and the clump of apple trees filling the apex. The garden was bordered by a thick privet hedge some ten feet high and between it and the lawn was a wide flower bed packed with plants and bushes. The air was cool and moist and Donaldson breathed in deeply, savouring its freshness.

'Do you live in the country?' asked Grey.

'Ealing, sir,' replied Donaldson.

'Ah,' said Grey quietly, as if he'd just heard that Donaldson was an orphan.

'I have a garden, though,' Donaldson added, and then inwardly squirmed as he realized how lame that sounded. They walked in silence for a while until Grey sniffed the air and turned to peer upward at the roof.

'Damn chimney's smoking too much, I'll have to get it swept. Have you any idea how much it costs to have a chimney swept?'

Donaldson didn't; his three-bedroomed semi had radiators in every room.

13

They wandered into the orchard, a dozen or so trees twice the height of a man, a mixture of apple, pear and plum, and Grey carefully inspected each one.

'Do you think they need spraying?' asked Grey, but Donaldson guessed it was rhetorical.

You never knew with Grey, that was the problem. He was often so subtle, so obtuse, that it was easy to miss what he was trying to say. He'd once called in one of his departmental heads for a half-hour chat and the poor man had walked out of the office without even realizing that he'd been sacked. It wasn't until Grey passed him in the corridor a week later that he discovered he was still on the payroll. It wasn't unusual for group meetings with Grey to be followed by a flurry of phone calls along the lines of 'what exactly did we decide?' Donaldson was on edge for any hint, any clue as to what it was that Grey wanted. All he knew so far was that it involved Geoff Howells, a man he thought had been dead for more than three years.

That was the last time one of his expense sheets had passed over his desk. Ridiculously high, as usual. Donaldson had enjoyed wielding the red pen, often slashing them by half. Until the day Howells had burst into Donaldson's office. Jesus, he'd been terrified. Damn near pissed himself.

'Did you ever work with Howells?' asked Grey.

Donaldson shook his head. 'No, but I followed his career with interest.'

'Short but eventful,' said Grey. 'He managed to gain quite a reputation in a relatively short period of time.'

'Captain in the SAS, wasn't he? Trained to kill.' And the bastard damn near killed me, thought Donaldson. He'd grabbed him by the throat and pinned him to the wall.

That's all Donaldson remembered until he woke up in the empty office with one of Howells' expense sheets shoved between his teeth. That was the last time he'd used the red pen.

'Special Boat Section, actually. One of the best. Did a superb job during the Falklands War, led one of the advance reconnaissance teams sent in to identify the Argentinian positions. Recorded nine kills during a four-day mission.'

'Impressive,' said Donaldson.

'Problem was,' said Grey, studying a small patch of green mould on the trunk of one of the plum trees, 'two of them were SAS troopers. That's when he came to our attention.'

'What!' exploded Donaldson.

'We hushed it all up of course, we were getting enough bad publicity at the time as it was.'

By 'we' Donaldson assumed he meant the British. 'What happened, sir?' he asked.

'He joined one of our more low profile departments.'

'No, sir, I mean what happened to the SAS men?'

'Howells was sitting in a hole a hundred yards or so from an Argentinian artillery unit when two SAS soldiers practically fell on top of him. According to Howells one of them was about to shoot and he reacted instinctively, killed one with a punch to the throat and knocked the other to the ground and broke his neck. It was over in seconds, apparently, and the Argentinians didn't hear a thing. He left the bodies in the hole. One of life's little tragedies.'

Donaldson thought for a moment that Grey had made a joke, but realized that he was serious.

'We took him in and trained him. He was good, very

15

good. One of the best, in fact. Ten clean kills in a two-year period. Never any problems, not as far as the technical side was concerned, anyway. I am going to have to speak to Perkins about this.'

'Perkins?' said Donaldson, totally confused.

'My gardener. He's going to have to do something about this mould. It can kill the tree if it isn't treated, you know.'

Donaldson didn't know, and frankly he didn't give a toss. He had only one tree at the end of his pocket-handkerchief of a garden.

'He started to enjoy the work, that was the trouble.' Donaldson realized Grey had switched back to Howells, though he was still studying the mould intently.

'The psychologists picked it up during his monthly check-up. He was fretting when he wasn't working and they discovered that he'd put a little too much, shall we say, effort into his last job. His target was a Libyan student who planted that messy bomb in Manchester some time back, you remember the one? Killed three people. Nothing we could prove in court so Howells' department was told to arrange a termination. Howells decided to make it look like a car accident. And he did, too. By the time they cut the Libyan out of the wreckage there was barely an unbroken bone in his body.'

'So?' said Donaldson, though he knew what was coming.

'So that's the way the Libyan went into the car. Howells killed him with his bare hands – slowly and very painfully.'

That was one of the crazy things about their line of work, mused Donaldson. You could do the job, and do it professionally, but once you started to enjoy it, you were finished. The psychologists reckoned that only a madman could enjoy killing, but they never asked if a truly sane man would do the job in the first place. Going by the names and expense sheets that went across Donaldson's desk, three years was as long as they normally lasted in the job, though some could go on for much longer. The CIA was rumoured to have a grandmother on their books who'd been active for nigh on thirty-five years.

'You know why he wasn't transferred?' Donaldson didn't, of course. 'We tried to shift him over to a desk job, but Howells wouldn't have any of it. Said he wanted to carry on doing what he was good at, what we had trained him to do. Said he wouldn't accept a transfer.'

That happened sometimes, when operatives got so addicted to the adrenalin rush that they couldn't bear to lose it. And if they were forcibly moved into another job they'd find another outlet for their frustrations and innocent bystanders would get hurt. It happened, but when it did the man, or woman, was swiftly retired. And retirement didn't mean a pension and a cottage in Devon. Retirement meant permanent. It was never spoken about openly, not at Donaldson's level, anyway. But every now and again a name would just disappear from the approved-expenses list and the file would be recalled by Personnel and never seen again. Donaldson had breathed a sigh of relief when Howells' name and file had gone. The man was a nutter, a dangerous nutter.

The two men walked out of the trees and back along the lawn towards the house. Grey picked up a small dead branch and threw it for the dogs. They rushed after it, barking and barging into each other. They reached it at the same time and grabbed an end each, pulling it and grunting with pleasure. Donaldson knew exactly how the stick felt.

'Where is he now, sir?'

'Bali.'

'Bali?'

'Indonesia.'

This was becoming bizarre, thought Donaldson. In the space of a few minutes the conversation had gone from a threat to destroy a Chinese power station to a retired killer lying on a beach in Indonesia. And somewhere in the middle, like the stick caught between two dogs, was Donaldson himself.

'We want to use Howells to clear up this Daya Bay business,' said Grey.

'Daya Bay?'

'That's where the nuclear reactor is. We want Howells to defuse the situation.'

He didn't seem to realize the pun. The black Labrador had won the tussle over the stick and came running over to Grey to present the trophy, and receive a pat on the head for her trouble. The other dog pretended to lose interest and wandered among the trees, sniffing at roots.

'Why Howells, sir?' asked Donaldson, hoping it didn't sound like criticism.

'We need someone who can't be traced back to us, someone who isn't on our books, and that rules out staffers and freelances. The Chinese mustn't know that we know, if you see what I mean. So any action we take must be completely covert.'

'But surely that would also rule out Howells, sir?' Donaldson though he knew what was coming and he prayed to God that he was wrong. He didn't want to meet Howells again – ever.

'Because he used to work for us? That isn't a problem. He's never worked in Hong Kong or China, so it's unlikely he would be recognized. His mental problems and his retirement are no secret, and if anything goes wrong it would be assumed that he'd just gone on the rampage. I can't think anybody would believe that the British Government would use such an agent.'

Donaldson agreed with that one. And his own involvement was starting to give him an uneasy feeling in the pit of his stomach. His urge to go to the toilet was increasing by the minute. Maybe it was the tea, maybe it was the cold air, or maybe it was the thought of working with Howells. That seemed to be what Grey was suggesting.

'I must repeat that it is crucial that the Chinese do not find out that the British Government is involved. The negotiations between the triads and the Chinese are being conducted at the highest level in Peking and there is only a handful of people involved. If they discover that we know what is going on, there is a good chance it will expose our source. There must be no connection at all seen between Howells and my department.'

Which, thought Donaldson, is why I'm here. To provide the distance.

'Howells isn't the man he was,' continued Grey.

'In what way, sir?'

Grey thought for a while, oblivious of the dog shuffling backwards and forwards at his feet waiting for the saliva-smeared stick to be thrown.

'Have you ever had a tooth capped?' he asked.

Donaldson shook his head. What the hell did teeth have

19

to do with this? There were times when he wondered if the older man really was starting to go gaga.

'It's worth doing if you've got a tooth that's so badly rotted that it can't be repaired with a normal amalgam filling. You build another tooth out of porcelain and metal and bond it to what's left of the original tooth. It looks real and it functions as normal.'

He threw the stick hard and high and the dog hurtled after it as it curved through the air. The dog in the orchard pretended not to notice, but its tail wasn't wagging.

'Howells had a personality that was rotten to the core. For whatever reason, he'd got to the stage where he enjoyed inflicting pain, enjoyed killing. He spent six months in a private sanatorium while some of the best psychologists in the country tried to undo the damage – but to no avail. Their conclusion was that Geoff Howells could never be returned to society. He was facing a lifetime in a Broadmoor cell weaving baskets.'

The dog was back, stick in mouth, but Grey ignored her. The two men had returned to the back door of the house but Grey made no move to open it. Donaldson's bladder was starting to hurt.

'We decided instead to try a different method, which brings us back to the dental analogy. They produced a new personality and in effect grafted it on to the old one, just like capping a bad tooth. They used deep hypnosis and God knows what drugs to suppress all his killer instincts, dampened his feelings and emotions and overlaid them with a new set. He has the memories of what went before, but it's as if they belong to someone else. To all intents and purposes Howells is now a confirmed pacifist, as docile as a lamb. We've done a few favours for the Indonesian

Government over the years so we arranged for him to live there.'

Until he was needed again, thought Donaldson. Until now.

'If he's been neutralized, surely he's no good to us now, sir,' said Donaldson, more in hope than belief.

Grey smiled. 'The conversion isn't permanent. In the same way that a cap can be pulled off a tooth, the new personality can be removed to reveal the man he used to be. And it's that man we need.'

'I still don't follow why it has to be Howells, sir. Surely we could use any freelance and just make sure our tracks are well covered.'

God, that sounded like a whine. Would Charlie Muffin have said that? Would Quiller refuse to take an assignment because it meant dealing with a psychopath/sociopath? If he had any bloody sense he would.

Grey shook his head. 'No, you know how they work. They all keep safety deposit boxes with envelopes to be opened in the event of their deaths. And they don't take kindly to being used, it can have a nasty habit of backfiring. No, Howells is perfect. He has no living relatives, he will follow instructions to the letter and he is . . .'

'Expendable?' asked Donaldson hopefully.

'Exactly. I am glad we understand each other.' He seized the doorknob and pushed open the wooden door, careful not to allow the panting Labrador in. He ushered Donaldson inside where they removed their boots, then led him into the sitting-room and picked up a manila file off a small mahogany side-table. 'Sit down and read this. It goes without saying that I don't want you to take notes.' If

21

it goes without saying, thought Donaldson, why mention it? 'Come and see me when you've finished reading the file. I'll be in the garden.'

Grey closed the door gently. A minute or so later Donaldson heard him let himself out of the back door and call for the dogs. He settled down into the chair and began to read, all thoughts of his bladder gone.

Donaldson spent the best part of an hour reading and re-reading the report. It was sketchy in parts, but when he'd finished Donaldson felt he knew a lot more about what made Howells tick. And it didn't make him feel any easier about meeting the man.

The remoulding of his personality had been done by two top psychologists, one as part of a Government-sponsored research project he was doing at Bart's in London: the other was a young high-flyer on attachment from the CIA.

As Grey had said, it had taken some six months to make Howells safe, if not sane, but the trigger to reactivate him consisted of just three colour-coded cards which had to be produced in the correct order. According to the detailed instructions which came with the report, Donaldson was first to ask Howells if he was ready to take on the assignment, to appeal to the man's loyalty to his country. Then he was to offer him money. If the psychologists had done their job properly, Howells would spurn both offers. Donaldson was then to show him the cards which were contained in a white envelope. There would be little visible change but Donaldson was then to hand him a second envelope containing a full briefing. Simple, thought Donaldson. He slipped the two sealed envelopes into his inside jacket pocket and concentrated on memorizing the instructions. When he'd finished he took the file out into the back garden. This time he didn't bother with the Wellingtons.

Grey was at the bottom of the garden, to the right of the orchard, gathering up dead grass and fallen twigs with a rake. As Donaldson approached Grey sprinkled lighter fluid over the damp pile and dropped on a lighted match. He stepped back with a satisfied smile on his face as the bonfire flared into life.

'I've read the file, sir,' said Donaldson, handing it over. Grey reached into his back pocket and pulled out a third envelope.

'This contains your tickets and travelling expenses.'

Donaldson took it and put it into his pocket with the other two. He was starting to feel like a postman.

'Your flight leaves tomorrow, Cathay Pacific to Hong Kong and then Garuda to Bali. I suggest you phone in sick first thing tomorrow morning. On no account are you to tell anyone where you are going. You're not married, are you?'

'No, sir.'

'Family?'

'My mother and father live in Cheshire. They won't miss me.'

'Good man,' said Grey. 'Can you see yourself out?' he added, dismissing Donaldson with the rhetorical question.

When he heard the man's car start up and drive off

Grey dropped the file on top of the bonfire and watched as its edges browned and curled in the heat. As the pages shrivelled and burnt he absent-mindedly patted the black Labrador on the head.

'Two birds with one stone, Lady,' he said softly. 'Two birds with one stone.'

Much the same thought was going through Donaldson's mind some forty-eight hours later as his Garuda flight approached Denpasar airport. There were two things he liked best in the world. One was immersing himself in a good thriller and the other was having sex with small boys. Preferably small boys that were tied down and whimpering. The assignment from Grey looked set to satisfy both passions. He'd heard that the boys in Indonesia were simply gorgeous, big brown eyes and soft, smooth, brown bodies. Just the thought gave him a hard-on.

The Garuda Airbus looked new, the blue and grey interior trim sparkling clean. The plane seemed to be a cheap version, though, with none of the optional extras, no movie screen and no music. It was cold, too, bitterly cold. But instead of turning up the heat the cheerful stewardesses doled out blankets soon after they'd taken off from Hong Kong. His legs were cramped and he cursed Grey for only providing him with economy-class tickets. Cheapskate, he thought. It wasn't as if getting the expenses approved would be a problem.

It was pitch dark outside and there seemed to be hardly

any lights on the island below as the plane descended. He took a last look at the Garuda brochure, which told him that Indonesia consists of 165 million people spread among 13,677 islands. Half of the population are aged under twenty and, thought Donaldson eagerly, half of them are boys. The 300 ethnic groups speak 583 different languages, but he didn't plan to do much talking. His palms were sweating, despite the cold in the cabin.

Donaldson didn't see the airfield until the plane slammed into the ground, bounced fifty feet or so back into the air and then landed properly. Third bloody World, he thought sourly.

The Airbus came to a halt a hundred yards from the terminal building and Donaldson was annoyed to discover that he and his four dozen fellow passengers were expected to walk. God, it was hot, and humid, and before he'd even descended the mobile stairs to the tarmac he felt beads of sweat on his face and was gasping for breath. The air was filled with the sound of crickets and other night insects proclaiming territorial rights or offers of marriage or whatever it was that insects found so important to communicate after dark. A gaggle of Hong Kong Chinese tourists overtook Donaldson on his right and left before regrouping in front of him like fish passing a reef, talking incessantly.

The sweat was now pouring off his back and he could feel rivulets of water dripping down the backs of his legs underneath the lightweight grey Burtons suit he was wearing. He shifted his shoulder bag, wincing as the narrow plastic strap bit into his flesh through the thin material.

He reached the terminal building and gratefully sucked

in lungfuls of cold air which immediately made his skin feel clammy. Immigration and customs were a breeze; Bali was obviously well geared up for tourists, and Donaldson saw two uniformed teenagers who he'd quite happily have died for. Or paid for. They both had skin the colour of polished mahogany, and beautiful brown eyes that looked as if they were brimming with tears, though they both returned his smiles with pleasant grins. Down boy, thought Donaldson. Later, in Jakarta, on the way back. A couple of days of R&R, a well-deserved reward for a job well done. Christ, he was getting hard again.

As he walked from customs and into the arrivals lounge he was accosted on either side by Indonesian men, dressed in shabby T-shirts and frayed jeans and nowhere near as attractive as the uniformed youngsters from whom he'd had to tear himself away.

'Taxi? Taxi? You want taxi?' they chorused.

'Yeah, yeah,' said Donaldson, starting to sweat again. 'Which of you speaks the best English?'

He took off his glasses and wiped the condensation off with his handkerchief for the tenth time since leaving the flying fridge.

'I speak good English, sir,' said a man on his left, about the same height as Donaldson but much thinner and with a drooping moustache. Like Donaldson it appeared to be wilting in the heat.

The man seemed bright enough so Donaldson walked with him through the open doors towards a line of battered cars. Now that Donaldson had been claimed the rest of the drivers moved away in search of fresh blood. The Indonesian took Donaldson's bag for him and led him to an ageing car of indeterminate make that could have been green, or blue, or black. It was parked some distance away from the terminal and there was no lighting so it was hard to tell. Twice Donaldson slipped into holes in the road as he walked behind his guide and he swore loudly.

'Sir?' said the driver, opening the rear passenger door and throwing in the bag.

'Nothing,' said Donaldson, sliding into the car. It appeared to be lined with some sort of fur, and brass chimes dangled from the driving mirror.

'Go where?' asked the driver.

'Shit,' said Donaldson, suddenly remembering he had no local money. 'Wait here, I'll have to change some money.' He lurched out of the car and back to the terminal.

The driver, unwilling to let his fare out of his sight, scampered after him.

'No problem, hotel can change money,' he said to Donaldson's back.

'We're not going to a hotel.'

That worried the driver and he waited anxiously while Donaldson changed a handful of ten-pound notes. The Mickey Mouse money had a hell of a lot of zeros and it looked to Donaldson as if he had instantly become a millionaire in local terms.

On the way back to the taxi he explained to the driver where he wanted to go; to head for the Hotel Oberoi but to drive one mile past the hotel's entrance to a crossroads, then to turn left. Howells was living in a villa close to the beach where the road petered out.

'You want Oberoi Hotel,' nodded the driver and started the car.

'No, you idiot,' snapped Donaldson, and he repeated the instructions to the smiling driver.

When he'd finished the driver grinned even wider and said, 'No problem.'

'I bet,' said Donaldson.

The driver grated the car into gear and moved off, humming quietly to himself. It was sweltering. Donaldson tapped him on the shoulder. 'Switch the aircon on,' he said.

The driver turned and said smilingly, 'No aircon. Sorry. Open window.'

'Terrific,' said Donaldson, and flopped back into the seat. He wound the window fully down and let the breeze blow across his face. It felt like a blast from a hair-dryer and if anything it made him sweat even more.

They soon left the airport lights behind and drove along a double-track road with no pavements, the car constantly swerving to avoid pedestrians. God knows why so many people were out this late at night, thought Donaldson. Maybe the television was bad. There were women with brightly coloured dresses carrying sacks on their heads, children running around parents, kids walking hand in hand. The darkness beyond the headlights of the car was absolute, and the driver seemed to have some sixth sense that allowed him to hit the horn and start moving the car before they came into vision. Motor-cycles buzzed past constantly, young men without crash helmets crouched low over the handlebars with girls riding sidesaddle behind, hair flying in the wind and tears streaming from their eyes.

Donaldson closed his eyes and tried to relax, and when he opened them again the car was alone on the road.

Through the open window he could see the star-packed night sky, but there was no moon and the countryside to either side of the road was totally dark.

'How far?' he asked the driver.

'Not far. Soon,' the driver said. He pointed over to the left hand side of the road. 'Monkeys. Many monkeys.'

Donaldson peered into the blackness. Nothing. He squinted. Still nothing. He tried opening his eyes wide. Nothing. The driver was looking expectantly over his shoulder, waiting for some reaction.

'Super,' said Donaldson. The driver nodded, obviously pleased.

A few minutes later he gestured to the right. 'Rice fields,' he said.

Donaldson looked. Pitch black. 'Fantastic,' he said.

The driver took a left turn and the road narrowed, still supposedly a double track but with passing places every half mile or so. He pointed to the left. 'Very old temple,' he said to his passenger. 'Very famous.'

Donaldson didn't even bother to look. 'Marvellous,' he said, and settled back in his seat with his eyes closed. Maybe the guy would shut up if he thought he was asleep.

He didn't. He continued his guided tour, and Donaldson alternated between 'Super,' 'Fantastic,' and 'Marvellous.'

At one point in the journey they drove along a line of shops that seemed to stretch for miles, all of them open. They were a mixture of cheap and cheerful restaurants, boutiques selling T-shirts and cotton dresses and shops with no fronts that contained racks upon racks of cassette tapes. Obviously pirates, thought Donaldson, cheap counterfeits selling for one tenth the official price. The only customers seemed to be tourists, blonde women with chunky thighs and bra-less breasts and men with long hair and burnt skin uniformly wearing scruffy T-shirts, shorts and sandals. There were no food shops, no sellers of the essentials like soap powder or salt or vegetables. An Asian Golden Mile, without the funfair.

'You want to stop here?' asked the driver.

Donaldson shook his head. 'Are we nearly there?'

'Soon,' said the driver, honking his horn at a yellow jeep trying to push in from a darkened side-road.

The car slowed to a walking pace behind a queue of Land Rovers, jeeps and bicycles that seemed in no hurry to move any faster. Probably the heat, thought Donaldson, wiping his glasses again. A thin balding man with John Lennon glasses bought a bowl of noodles and pieces of meat on little wooden sticks from a street vendor and leant against the bonnet of a parked car to eat while his companion, a broad-hipped woman with cornflower hair tied in braids, watched. 'Don't you just love this food?' he said in a mid-Western drawl and she smiled. One case of hepatitis B coming right up, thought Donaldson. Serves the Yank right.

The air in the car was starting to stink of exhaust fumes but it was so hot that Donaldson didn't want to wind up the window. Instead he took his handkerchief out and held it over his mouth. It didn't seem to make any difference. He tried holding his breath but that made him feel even dizzier than the fumes.

Eventually they left the strip of shops and plunged into darkness again. The headlights picked out three roadside signs pointing the way to hotels on the left and then they stopped. The driver pointed through the windshield. 'Oberoi,' he said.

'OK,' said Donaldson. 'Drive straight on.'

'Straight on?'

'Just drive,' he said, waving his hand towards the bonnet of the car. He peered at the speedometer. It was in kilometres and Grey had said to drive for one mile past the hotel turn-off. They hit the crossroad at 1.4 kilometres and Donaldson told the driver to turn left. The man was starting to get uneasy, but he remembered the pile of foreign money Donaldson had changed. Just another crazy tourist. Probably just had a bit too much to drink on the plane.

The road quickly became a single track, and from what Donaldson could see in the lights of the car there were fields on either side with a scattering of tall trees. It felt a little cooler and once or twice he thought he could smell the sea, and then he saw thirty yards or so to the right of the track, a pointed roof atop what looked like a square building, silhouetted against the stars.

Donaldson tapped the driver on the shoulder. 'Stop here,' he said.

'Here?' echoed the driver, but saw from the look on Donaldson's face that the answer was yes so he slammed on the brakes.

'How much?' asked Donaldson, suddenly realizing that he hadn't agreed a price before getting into the cab. The driver's eyes lit up, too, as he remembered the same thing. The driver mumbled a figure with a lot of zeros on the end and Donaldson was too damn tired to try and convert it into real money. He quickly counted out a handful of notes and threw them on to the front seat.

'Thanks a bunch,' he said.

'Don't mention it,' said the driver, nodding his head in time with each word. 'Good English, yes?'

'Marvellous,' agreed Donaldson, grabbing his bag and staggering out of the car. His right leg seemed to have gone to sleep.

The car did a jerky four-point turn and then lurched back down the track, leaving Donaldson alone in the dark with his sleepy leg. He limped towards the house.

As he got closer to the house he noticed that the bottom of the roof was illuminated with a warm glow, though the top was shrouded in darkness. Then he realized that what he was looking at was a wall, half as tall again as a man, which ran around the house itself. The light was inside. There was no doorway in the side of the wall he was approaching, so he followed it around to the left. Still no door. He was walking towards the sea, the waves breaking on the shore like thunder. He was walking on grass, but as his eyes became more accustomed to the starlight he could see a strip of white that must be the beach.

Donaldson stopped and listened. In between the watery crashes he could hear music. Pink Floyd. Dark Side of the Moon. God, that took him back.

He turned right and found the door, two slabs of weathered wood set into a stone arch. To the left was a brass bell-pull, like a stirrup attached to a long rod. Donaldson reached out his hand, then noticed that the door wasn't closed; light was shining through a two-inch gap. He pushed gently and the gap grew silently wider. He could hear the music more clearly now. Facing the doorway was another wall made of the same rough-hewn stones as the outer barrier, but about five feet tall. Sitting on top of it was a stone eagle, or chicken, or angel. Or perhaps it was a combination of all three, it was difficult to tell with the light behind it.

Donaldson had to turn sharp left for three yards or so and then right, into a small courtyard, surrounded by lush green plants. At the opposite side of the stone-flagged square was a small pool into which trickled water from the mouth of a stone lion set into the wall. Lily pads floated on the surface, moving gently around the dribble of water. Somewhere a frog croaked, but quietly, as if afraid to draw attention to itself. The pool was illuminated by three spotlights set into the wall and by a soft glow that came from large french windows that led into the house. Donaldson moved into the centre of the courtyard, sidestepping a brown-shelled snail that was meandering towards the water. From somewhere above his head a bird called into the night, a high-pitched whine that grew louder and deeper and then stopped, like incoming mortars in a war film. His right hand was tightly clenched around the strap of his shoulder bag, drenched in sweat. The heat, he told himself, ignoring the smell of fear that was pouring off him, the smell that dogs can scent and which raises their hackles and starts them growling and snarling. It was just the heat, thought Donaldson, just the heat. *Christ, what are you doing here?* asked a small voice inside, the voice of a threatened schoolboy. *Howells is an animal.* He ignored the whining voice and moved forward again, towards Pink Floyd and the window.

He could see into the room now, the french window framing a scene of domestic bliss, a man and two girls. The three were sitting at the far end of the room around a small table, the man with his back to the window, the girls to his right and left. The man's hair was tied back in a short ponytail by a rubber band, and his head bobbed forward and back as he spooned in food from a small bowl. He was sitting cross-legged on the floor, wearing faded jeans and a white shirt, sleeves rolled up past the elbows. The girls could have been twins, pretty in a boyish way, giggling to each other and with the man as they ate. They both had pageboy hair cuts and seemed achingly young, with smooth and unlined skins and bright, wide eyes with dark, fluttering lashes. Occasionally, one or the other would reach out to touch the man, or to ladle rice into his bowl or hand him a piece of meat. They were talking, Donaldson could see their mouths moving, but the music drowned out the words. The girls wore simple flowered print cotton dresses, open at the neck but covering their arms. One wore a thin gold chain around her neck, but other than that Donaldson wouldn't have been able to tell them apart. He found their boyishness over-poweringly provocative, but at the same time he was repelled by their obvious femininity. He took out his handkerchief and mopped his brow again. He replaced the wet square of linen and knocked gently against the glass with his knuckles.

Whatever the psychologists had done to Howells, they hadn't affected his reactions. In one smooth, flowing movement he'd replaced his bowl on the table, uncurled his legs and moved three paces to the side, away from the girls, side on to Donaldson but looking straight at him. Donaldson knew with a tight feeling in his stomach that if Howells had had a gun in his hand he'd have been dead. It was Howells, he was sure of that, but he'd changed. The face was thinner, and the soft beard and moustache were new. He'd lost weight, too. Not that Howells had ever been anything other than hard muscle, but now he looked almost emaciated. Donaldson could see his stomach was dead flat, and he had a marathon runner's backside and legs. Howells spoke quickly to the girls and they slowly moved away from the table, away from him, worried frowns on their faces. Howells seemed to be looking through Donaldson with impassive hazel eyes and for a moment Donaldson wondered whether reflections meant he couldn't see through the window. No, that couldn't be right, there were lights outside. He reached out and knocked again.

Howells walked forward slowly, balls of the feet touching the ground first, as if ready to spring at the slightest shock. He didn't look like a former SBS officer, or a professional killer, more like a junkie itching for a fix, but there was something in his cat-like walk that was unnerving. The room was still filled with music, but Donaldson knew that Howells was moving silently.

He stepped back as Howells slid the window open and Pink Floyd swelled out. Howells didn't say anything, but he reached up and gently smoothed the underside of his chin with the back of his hand as he studied Donaldson. Donaldson's bladder was suddenly heavy. His mind was whirling, wondering exactly what he should say. *Hiya Geoff, remember me?* Perhaps *Mr Howells, I presume?* How about '*I'm sorry I must have the wrong address*' and then getting the hell out of here said the voice in his head. He coughed quietly, trying to clear his throat. How could his body be soaking in sweat while his mouth was so dry, he thought.

'Geoff Howells?' he said hesitantly.

Howells nodded slowly, still stroking his beard.

'Er – can I come in?'

Howells said nothing.

'Grey sent me,' Donaldson added, almost as an after-thought. 'From London,' he continued lamely.

Howells smiled, a lazy confident smile that revealed white, even teeth. It seemed like a real smile, the smile of a friend, not the plastic version of a used-car salesman. Donaldson immediately felt easier and relaxed. Howells stood to one side and opened the french window further.

'Come in,' he said, and Donaldson was surprised at how soft and gentle the voice was. 'I'm afraid we don't get many visitors.'

Donaldson stepped over the threshold. He shivered as he passed Howells. Did he remember him? Probably not. Something to do with the brainwashing, maybe.

The room was square, about twenty feet by twenty. To the left were two doors of a dark red wood that looked as if it would be warm to the touch. There was no aircon, though a fan set into the white-painted ceiling was doing its best to keep the air moving. The walls were white, dotted with framed prints of what looked like Balinese gods. Tasteful, thought Donaldson, but somehow sinister. They weren't gods to help the unfortunate and protect the weak, they were vengeful gods who would kill and maim. Between the two doors was a large carved wooden chest with a big brass lock set into the front and a stack of newspapers and magazines on top. The furniture was made of the same red wood as the doors: a long, low sideboard, a bookcase full of paperbacks, and a rattan three-piece suite with cream coloured cushions. The girls were standing together behind one of the wooden chairs, holding hands and looking at Donaldson from lowered eyes. To their left was a racked stereo system, matt black and expensive with waist-high speakers. He jumped as the window thumped shut behind him. He turned to find Howells watching him with an amused smile on his face. 'Sorry,' he said. 'Can I get you a drink?'

'No,' replied Donaldson. 'No, thanks, I'm fine.'

There was a sickly sweet smell in the air. Incense. It was coming from some sort of shrine set into the wall between the doors, a wooden box open at the front and painted a garish crimson. There were three sticks of incense smouldering away, and in front of them there seemed to be pieces of rotten fruit and a small garland of yellow flowers. Howells sat in one of the chairs and stretched his long legs out in front of him.

Donaldson sat down on the settee and balanced his bag on his knees. That felt uncomfortable so he put it by his side. 'Well,' he said, and Howells raised his eyebrows.

The album was almost finished, the second to last track, *Brain Damage*, and the words echoed through Donaldson's head. '*You raise the blade, you make the change, you rearrange me till I'm sane.*' Very apt, thought Donaldson, except that it hadn't been a surgeon's scalpel that had changed Howells' personality, it had been deep hypnosis and drugs, and in his pocket he had the colour code sequence that would bring the old Howells back to life. Howells the sociopath. Howells the killer.

'Well,' said Donaldson again. How to start, that was the problem. Grey had been quite specific; first he was to check how effective the programming had been, before showing him the cards. But what the hell was he supposed to say? There's a man we want

37

you to kill? To eliminate? To terminate with extreme prejudice?

The girls had grown bolder now and they scurried over to sit either side of Howells on the floor, looking up at him like adoring poodles. They were lovely. God, what must the young boys be like, thought Donaldson.

'Could I speak to you in private?' he asked.

'Sure,' said Howells, and he spoke quickly to the girls in some sing-song language. They looked as if they'd been whipped but he smiled and said something else and they nodded excitedly and, holding hands again, went through the other door. Probably the bedroom, Donaldson decided.

'Do I know you?' Howells asked, gently stroking his beard and studying Donaldson with what appeared to be quiet amusement.

Donaldson swallowed. 'I think we met a couple of times in London. You probably don't remember.' The smell of incense seemed to be getting stronger, filling the air and threatening to choke him.

'And you say Grey sent you?'

'Yes,' Donaldson replied, and then cleared his throat noisily. 'Do you remember him?'

'Of course.'

'I have a message from him.'

'Well?'

Donaldson was confused. 'Well what?'

'What is the message?' Howells asked patiently.

'He wants you to work for him again.'

'Like before?'

Donaldson nodded. 'Exactly.'

Howells looked pained. He slid down the chair and

rested his neck on the cushion, looking up at the ceiling.
'I don't do that sort of thing any more.'

'What sort of thing?'

'You know what I mean. I'm different now. I'm a
Buddhist.' He fell silent for a few minutes, eyes closed.
'I can't do it. It's a part of my life that I'd rather forget.
I just can't kill any more. I'm practically a vegetarian.'

Donaldson reached for his bag, and unzipped it. 'Grey
asked me to give you something, he said it might make
you change your mind.'

'Nothing can do that. Go back and tell him, thanks, but
no thanks.'

Donaldson's hand groped around the bag like an
inquisitive ferret until he located the two sealed envelopes
Grey had given him back in England. The thicker of the
two he left on top of the bag and he tore the other open.
Inside, as Grey had said, were three coloured cards the
size of beer-mats: one was lime green, one blue with a
yellowish hue, and the third was a sort of silvery beige,
but it seemed to change colour the longer you looked at
it. On the back of each card was a number: 1, 2 and 3 in
blue ballpoint.

'Grey said I was to show you these,' said Donaldson,
getting to his feet. He stood in front of Howells, the cards
in his hand, like a conjuror preparing to perform. With a
weary sigh Howells raised an arm and took the card with
number one written on the back.

'What is this supposed to be?' he asked, squinting at the
green card. He turned it over and examined the number.
Donaldson licked his upper lip and handed down card
number two, the blue one. Howells frowned, and forced
himself into a more upright sitting position, confused

rather than worried. He shrugged and made to give them back to Donaldson.

'There's one more,' he said, and handed it down.

Donaldson wasn't sure what he expected to happen, though he'd played the scene through his mind time and time again on the journey from Heathrow. A minor epileptic fit, maybe, fluttering of the eyes, fainting, the look of a sleeper awakening, maybe a confused 'Where am I? Who am I?' Howells was a big disappointment; he did none of those things. His frown deepened, he examined all three cards again, turned them over and handed them back.

'And what is that supposed to mean? Is it some sort of code?'

Now it was Donaldson's turn to be confused. What had gone wrong? He checked the cards, confirmed that he'd passed them over in the correct order, and put them back into the envelope.

'Do you feel any different?'

Howells snorted, the sound of a cat sneezing.

Donaldson shook his head, trying in vain to clear away the thick smell of burning perfume. He weighed the second, bulkier, envelope in his hands and wondered whether it was worth giving it to Howells. The experiment had obviously failed dismally. Whatever Howells had been like before he now had the killer instincts of a pet rabbit. He dropped the sealed envelope on to the knees of the sitting man and walked dejectedly back to his own seat.

'What is it?' Howells asked.

'It's a letter. From Grey. My orders were to show you the cards and pass that envelope on to you.'

'Mission completed,' said Howells, opening the envelope.

'I suppose so,' said Donaldson. He watched Howells take out a sheaf of papers and what looked like a wad of currency. Howells sat and read in silence, once raising his eyebrows and snorting again.

'I suppose I'd better be going,' said Donaldson. 'Can I call a taxi from here?'

Howells shook his head without taking his eyes from the papers. 'No telephone,' he said. 'Let me finish this and I'll run you into town.'

Donaldson settled back into his chair, toying with the strap of his travel bag. Eventually Howells finished. He refolded the papers and replaced them in the envelope and placed it, and the money, on the table alongside the remains of the meal.

'Very interesting,' he said. 'And Grey expects me to do this for him?' He got to his feet, shaking his arms by his side as if restoring the circulation to cramped limbs. 'The callous bastard doesn't change, does he?'

Donaldson smiled nervously. 'He doesn't, but I think he expected you to have.' He stood up and slung the bag over his shoulder. 'Have you got a car?'

'A jeep, round the back.'

'It's very kind of you.'

Howells smiled and stepped forward, his right arm swinging quickly sideways and then twisting up, fingers curled back so that the heel of the hand made contact first, shearing off the cartilage that was Donaldson's nose and driving it into the centre of the man's brain. His legs gave way and he slumped to the floor, a trickle of blood running down his chin. It was a good clean kill, thought Howells, a move he'd practised ten thousand times but never used, until today. He felt a glow of satisfaction at how easy it had been, the feel of the nose breaking, the speed of the blow, the fact that Donaldson hadn't had time to react or to make a sound. As he looked down at the body the glow turned into something else, something almost sexual, a shiver that ran down his backbone making him gasp. Like an orgasm. Only better. Howells wished he had more time, time to play, to prolong it, but the girls were in the bedroom and he didn't want to disturb them. The tremor of enjoyment passed, as it always did, leaving him with a sense of loss, an itch that he wanted to scratch again. He opened the chest, hefted the body on to his shoulder and dropped it in. Later, when the girls were asleep, he'd bury it. But first, he was hungry. He wanted a steak, a thick one, medium-rare. It had been a long time.

The road that Howells drove along to the airport was quieter than when Donaldson had arrived. It was light, but only just, and his jeep was the only vehicle to be seen. Hardly surprising, it was 4.30 in the morning, two hours before his flight was due to leave for Hong Kong. The rice fields were deserted, criss-crossed with lines of string to keep the birds away. Every hundred yards or so were small wooden platforms under roofs of reeds where farmworkers could shelter from the hot sun. The strings ran from platform to platform so that they could be pulled from the shade but at this time of the morning there were no sudden movements, just gentle swings in the wind. The wind blew through tin cans nailed to wooden posts making an unearthly wailing noise, another way of keeping the birds at bay.

It was three days since he'd killed Donaldson, now safely buried three feet below the courtyard, close to the pool. Howells had sent the two girls back to their village, promising them that he'd return in a few days and knowing it wasn't true. It felt good to be working again, to be following orders, to be able to use his initiative and his skills. He felt free. He stroked his chin, enjoying the feel of the bare skin now that he'd shaved off the beard and moustache. His hair was still longer than he liked, but he'd change that when he got to Hong Kong.

He'd been to Hong Kong twice before, but both times en route to other destinations. He'd never worked there, just visited a few bars and toured the shops. He remembered buying a camera there, a Pentax, but for the life of him he couldn't remember what had happened to it. Not that it mattered any more. Howells began whistling to himself quietly, his face a picture of contentment.

In his back pocket was the envelope from Grey that Donaldson had so faithfully delivered. It contained two photographs of a man called Simon Ng, three closely typed sheets of background information on him and ten thousand American dollars in large bills. Slightly less actually, because he'd used some of the cash to buy a ticket to Hong Kong. A one-way ticket.

Howells started smiling as he whistled, and the smile quickly widened into a grin. He began laughing out loud, an unnerving, disjointed sound.

It was eight o'clock in the morning when the *QE2* dropped its anchor above Patrick Dugan's head. That's what it sounded like anyway. The rattle of metal links against hard wood went on for twenty seconds or so and then stopped dead. God knows what they were doing, but whatever it was they did it every morning. And last thing at night it was furniture-moving, or footsteps, or the shower running. And sometimes it was at three or four o'clock in the morning. But always the anchor dropped at eight, on the dot. Dugan groaned and stuck his head under the pillow. He felt, rather than heard, the sound of lift doors closing several floors below him and knew that he wouldn't be able to get back to sleep.

His block was twenty-eight storeys high, and there were eight flats on each floor. If each flat had a average of one point five wage-earners, and most had two or three, then that meant 336 people would be leaving for work of a morning. And assuming they all left between 7.30 a.m. and 9.30 a.m., that meant an average of one every twenty seconds or so. And each departing resident meant a lift door opening and closing twice. There was no way he'd get back to sleep, not with the noise and the sun streaming in through the bedroom window.

'Shit,' he said with venom. He decided to make an effort to blank out the sound of the lift but the more he tried to ignore it, the more the vibration through the pillow annoyed him. He tossed on to his front and tried resting his forehead on the mattress. No good. He tried lying on his back. No good. 'Shit,' he said again. He decided to get up and groped for a towel to wrap around his waist. It was a thick blue and white striped one he'd stolen from the Shangri-La Hotel in Bangkok and he tied it around his thickening waistline. He'd never got around to buying curtains for his shoebox of a flat and he could be observed by the occupants of at least three dozen other homes during the short walk to the bathroom. He'd got used to the lack of privacy very quickly; it was just the noises which annoyed him now.

When he'd first moved into the flat the one above him had been empty and he'd actually enjoyed waking up in the mornings. Six months after he'd taken on the mortgage his peace and quiet had been rudely interrupted. The new occupants had embarked on a renovation programme that had taken the best part of twelve weeks, drilling, hammering and banging that started at daybreak and went on until early evening. God knows what they did because the biggest flats in the block had only three rooms, small ones by UK standards though fairly spacious in Hong Kong terms.

Then the building work stopped. Bliss. Then the *QE2* started docking every morning, bright and early, and the furniture began moving at night. And someone began arriving home in the early hours, pacing up and down in high heels before spending half an hour in the shower. A hooker, maybe, with carpenters for brothers. And shipbreaking parents. For a time he'd thought there might be a drugs ring operating from the flat and he'd toyed with the idea of flashing his warrant card and demanding a look inside, but thought better of it; not without probable cause, and there'd been no telltale vinegar smells. He had been up once, months ago, when the furniture moving had gone on for what seemed an interminable time, screeching and groaning and scraping until he hadn't been able to stand it any more. He'd rung the bell and it had been opened by a pretty Chinese girl in sweatshirt and jeans. Behind her were two young men holding opposite ends of a small wooden table.

'Please, it's very late,' he said in his very best Cantonese, not the street talk and triad slang he used at work but polite and all the tones spot on. 'I am trying to sleep. What are you doing to make so much noise?'

'We finish now,' she said in fractured English, smiled and closed the door.

They stopped. But the following night they were back at it again. Dugan had given serious thought to moving. Finding another flat wouldn't be a problem in Tai Koo Shing, there were thousands of them and a steady stream of vacancies as families packed up and emigrated to Canada or Australia. Trouble was he'd got a ninety per cent mortgage and the rest had taken every cent he had in the bank. There was no way he'd be able to raise the legal fees, stamp duty and estate agent fees to move again. And chances were he'd end up in exactly the same position. It was Hong Kong, when all was said and done. Six million people crammed into a few square miles. You had to expect noise, he told himself.

He'd spent almost ten years in rented flats before deciding to buy, encouraged by the fact that the mortgage costs were actually less than the rent he'd been paying for his flat in Happy Valley with half a view of the racetrack. He'd seen prices plunge before, in the 1980s when the thought of what would happen when the colony was given back to the Communists had put the shits up everybody, but there was an air of confidence in the place when he decided to buy. Sure, there were still queues to get out but for every family selling up there was another eager to get its first step on the home ownership rung, a huge Chinese middle class with money to spend. He'd done all the sums before he'd bought this place, but he had miscalculated on the costs of furnishing it even though it was tiny. In London it would have been described as a compact studio flat but in Hong Kong it was sold as a family-sized home. He'd had to arrange an overdraft to buy the air-conditioners which he'd foolishly assumed the previous owners would leave behind free of charge. He should have known better. When they moved out they even took the lightbulbs and shower curtain, and unscrewed the towel rail at the side of the washbasin.

Dugan had invested every cent he had in the flat and then the geriatric lunatics in Peking ordered the massacre of unarmed students in Tiananmen Square and the bottom fell out of the property market, and for a few agonizing months Dugan's flat was worth about a fifth less than his mortgage. It had climbed back since, but there was still an air of unease in the colony, based on a total mistrust of the Chinese Government and their trigger-happy soldiers.

The bathroom floor was damp again but he still couldn't work out if it was condensation or a leak. At least it didn't smell like piss. He reached for the flush handle but it swung uselessly in his hand and he realized with distaste that the water had been turned off again. It happened every week or so, every time someone in the block needed plumbing work done. The toilet supply was separate from the drinking water; all flushing was done with sea water held in a big tank on the roof, so at least he'd be able to shower and make a coffee – though sometimes they switched off the main water supply as well. He watched two turds gently circle each other like wary otters in the toilet bowl and he cursed quietly. What if he brought a girl back tonight? Great aphrodisiac, a toilet full of stale shit.

He walked into his galley kitchen and put the kettle on the single gas burner. That and a microwave were the only cooking gear he had. Usually he ate out, and all the fridge contained was milk, a few frozen TV dinners and a bar of Cadbury's fruit and nut chocolate. He spooned some Gold Blend granules into his 'I'm The Boss' mug and went back to the bedroom to put on a CD. He'd moved the CD player into his bedroom after the night noises started, using music to cover the sound of moving furniture, high-heeled shoes and opening and closing lifts. It almost worked. By the time he'd chosen Orchestral Manoeuvres In The Dark his kettle was starting to whistle feebly. He poured the water on to the brown granules and showered while it cooled. Mould was starting to grow in the cracks between the tiles and he groaned inwardly – another Sunday morning to be spent scrubbing the walls with an old toothbrush. As usual the hot water laboured to crawl out of the shower head and he had to move his broad back around to rinse off the suds. He shaved in the shower, being careful not to damage his moustache. He'd been growing it for three months now and it was in good shape, almost oblong with just a slight downturn at the edge of his lips. It made him look more serious, he reckoned, and also went some way to make up for the thinning thatch on top of his head. He checked his teeth at the mirror. At least they were OK. Dugan didn't look at himself through rose-coloured glasses: he knew all his faults; the thickening stomach, the thinning hair, the nose that had been broken once too often playing rugby for the police team. He wasn't good-looking, and he looked five years or so older than he really was, but his deep blue eyes and warm smile attracted more than enough girls. Girls rather than women; his escorts were usually at least ten years younger than he was, and usually Chinese. The blue eyes and fluent Cantonese usually won them over without too much trouble. Like plucking apples in an orchard. A frustrated gweipor had once asked him what it was about Chinese girls that attracted him so much. 'There are so many of them,' he'd answered, only half joking. He relaxed the bared grin into a gentle smile and winked at himself in the mirror.

'You smarmy bastard, you,' he said. He walked barefoot back to the kitchen, leaving behind a trail of wet footprints on the polished wooden floor. The hot coffee gave him a boost and the energy to dry himself and dress. His grey suit was sombre enough for a senior inspector in the Royal Hong Kong Police Force but it could do with dry cleaning. It was crumpled, but not stained, so he could live with it for a few days longer. His white shirt was clean and he wore his second-best rugby club tie. He stood in front of the fitted unit that stretched from the floor to the ceiling and used his reflection in one of the mirrored cupboard doors to help comb his hair over his bald patch. It didn't look too bad. A hell of a lot better than it looked in the changing-room after a game of rugby, that was for sure. Not that baldness worried him, but there was no harm in making the most of what he had left.

He switched off the CD player, double-locked the front door behind himself and waited for the lift. There were three, computer-controlled so that you never had to wait more than thirty seconds. There was a note in Chinese taped to one of the lift walls. He couldn't read it, his fluency was confined to spoken Cantonese, but he knew that it meant the water had been switched off.

Dugan's office was in Wan Chai, close to the bar area and the quickest way this time of the morning was to go by MTR, the Mass Transit Railway. Dugan could walk from his flat to the MTR station under cover every step of the way, thanks to the interlinking design of the Tai Koo Shing complex; tower blocks, schools, restaurants, department stores, all linked by covered walkways.

A small group of elderly women were practising t'ai chi on the podium, watching the moves of a white-haired frail grandmother in black silk trousers and white shirt and trying to copy them. The moves had started life as one of the most effective of the Oriental martial arts but through centuries of teaching, of being passed from instructor to pupil, they had lost all purpose and were now no more than a slow-motion dance, useful for keeping old folks supple but of little use in a fight. Dugan smiled as he imagined the grandmothers trying to fight off a mugger and wondering why they couldn't disable their attacker by standing on one leg and waving their hands in front of them.

Blankets and mattresses had been spread out around the fountains to air in the morning sun and he threaded his way through them to the entrance to Cityplaza, the estate's main shopping complex which also contained the MTR station.

It never ceased to amaze Dugan how clean it all was, the lack of litter and graffiti. If it had been in England the vandals would have long covered every flat white surface with spray-painted obscenities, but Tai Koo Shing looked pretty much as it did when Swires first built it on reclaimed land more than a decade earlier.

Dugan remembered the pictures in the *South China Morning Post* of the queues to buy flats in the first block, and ever since it had been a place where middle-class Chinese aspired to live, the two- and three-bedroomed flats often representing the pinnacle of a lifetime's work or the launch pad to emigration. And because it was a middle-class dormitory town and not a working-class dumping ground, and all the residents had to pay a fairly hefty monthly management charge, it was always well cared for and repairs were usually done promptly. It was an OK place to live, once you got used to the crowds. It was busy even first thing in the morning, and on weekends it wasn't worth trying to do any shopping there it was so crowded. They came from all over Hong Kong to wander around and window-shop, to gaze at the displays of high-priced fashion and state-of-the-art consumer electrical equipment. Some bright entrepreneurs had even started running bus trips from the villages in the New Territories, and on weekends you'd see lines of old men and women with dirt-encrusted hands and worn clothes being taken around in groups, wide-eyed at the bright, shiny affluence of it all. The MTR station was mobbed, as usual, and Dugan had to fight to get on to the first train that stopped. A small man in stained T-shirt and shorts called him a 'gweilo prick' but Dugan didn't let on that he'd understood. No point.

Dugan's only blessing being that he was virtually a head taller than most of the rush-hour crowd, at least he had the illusion of space from the neck up. The underground train was like a huge snake as it rumbled along, one long continuous chain of carriages. On the straight sections of track he could see from one end of the train to the other, every inch occupied by the great unwashed public. He tried to breathe through his nose as much as possible because he worried about catching flu or something. There must have been at least two dozen people within breathing distance and any one of them could have had something contagious, he thought.

Standing on the MTR and swaying as the train braked to a halt, he made the effort to concentrate his mind on the work that was piling up on his desk. There were at least ten cases that had to be treated as urgent, but there were two that he was particularly interested in. One was a complicated fraud case involving a small Chinese bank – a case of cheque kiting that involved three Hong Kong deposit-taking companies and banks in Texas, Geneva and the Cayman Islands. The stream of cheques, each one covering another, had totalled 160 million dollars before anyone had noticed, and the twenty-three-year-old cashier who looked as if butter wouldn't melt in her mouth had netted herself a cool $12 million with the scam. Dugan was putting a case together and, just as importantly, was trying to track down the missing money. The girl was out on bail, her passport confiscated, and Dugan was sure that at any moment she'd disappear into the mainland or to Taiwan. God, what he'd give to go with her – and the money.

The other case concerned a company that sold computers and then stole them back a couple of months later. Over a dozen firms, most of them in Sha Tin, had been hit, the same computers in each case. Dugan reckoned there'd be a triad link somewhere and privately nursed the hope that it would bring him to the attention of the top brass in the anti-triad squad. He was getting bloody nowhere, though. How was he expected to, for God's sake, when he was practically chained to his desk?

He brooded about the unfairness of it all as he got off the train and took the escalator to the surface of Wan Chai MTR station. The hot air took him by surprise as it always did when he left the air-conditioned station and stepped into the bright sunlight. By the time he got to his office he was sweating. He slumped into his chair, glared at the pile of pale green files on his desk and sighed deeply. Coffee, he thought, and wandered out into the corridor. His boss, a beanpole by the name of Chief Inspector Christopher Tomkins – Chief Inspector to his friends – was by the machine, gingerly removing a liquid-filled cup.

'Why the hell does this machine always fill right up to the brim?' he asked Dugan.

Dugan shoved a two-dollar coin into the slot. He pressed the button marked 'black coffee with sugar'. The machine vomited dark brown liquid into Dugan's plastic cup. It stopped half an inch from the top.

'It likes you,' said Tomkins, jealously.

Dugan took his coffee back to his laden desk and slumped down in the chair. It rocked dangerously; one of the wheels was loose – again. At least once a week he upended it and screwed the five castors in as tight as he could but it seemed to make no difference. Sometimes he worried that Tomkins might be sneaking into his office late at night and unscrewing them. As he sat down he realized that Tomkins had followed him. He seemed to have something on his mind, so Dugan looked at him expectantly.

'The computer case,' said Tomkins.

'It's going well,' said Dugan. 'I thought I might visit a few of the computer shops in Tsim Sha Tsui, rattle a few cages and see what falls out.'

'Actually Pat, I've had a call from the anti-triad squad. They want the file sent over.'

'What!' Dugan snapped. 'How the hell do they know about it?' It was obvious from the look on Tomkins' face that he'd told them. Dugan shook his head, lost for words. His big case. His chance to be noticed.

'Come on, Pat, you've got a heavy case load as it is. You should be glad they want to help.'

'Help?' said Dugan. 'You mean they'll let me work on the case with them?' Tomkins looked embarrassed at the hope in Dugan's voice.

'No,' he said. 'They'll handle it, but I guess they'll want to talk to you about it.'

'It's not fair!' said Dugan.

'Life's not fair, Dugan. Don't be dumb. You've plenty of cases.' He nodded at the stack of files on the desk.

'This one's different. It's a big one.'

'It's triad-related.'

'I know it's triad-related, that's why I want to work on it.'

'Look, Dugan, that's what the anti-triad unit is for.'

'There are plenty of guys in Commercial Crime working on triad cases, you know that.'

'Yeah, but they don't have relatives running one of the biggest triads in Hong Kong, do they?' said Tomkins, beginning to lose his temper.

'Is that what it's about, my brother-in-law?'

'There's nothing I can do, Pat. The word has come down from on high. You're to be kept off this case.'

'Christ! He only married my sister,' said Dugan. 'It's not as if I sleep with him or anything! What do they think I do, go over all my cases with him? Is that what they think?'

'Don't fight it, Pat, you'll be pissing into the wind.' He held out his hand and with a snort Dugan thrust the file at him. Tomkins took it and started to say something but Dugan waved him away.

'Forget it,' said Dugan. 'Just forget it.'

Howells booked into the Holiday Inn Harbour View. The hotel was about ten minutes' drive from the single runway of Kai Tak airport, on the mainland, close to the bustling shopping arcades of Tsim Sha Tsui. It was a modern, comfortable room with light teak furniture and a picture of a golden peacock on the wall.

It was early evening and Howells lay on the bed, his legs crossed at the ankles, slowly rereading the three sheets of papers that held the life, and death, of Simon Ng. Chinese name Ng Chao-huang, but to his friends and associates he was Simon Ng. Simon Ng was the Lung Tau – Dragon Head – controlling a drug and vice empire that pulled in tens of millions of dollars every year. Simon Ng, who lived with his family in a closely guarded complex in the New Territories, surrounded by triad soldiers. Simon Ng, who had to die. The two black and white photographs lay by his side. They showed a good-looking Chinese man in his early forties, smooth-skinned with a small dimple in the centre of his chin. The face was squarish, the hair closely cropped so that it stood up almost straight on the top of his head and was shaped around his ears. He had thin lips that didn't look as if they had the habit of forming a smile. Simon Ng looked hard. And if Grey's notes were to be believed, he was hard.

The triad leader had a wife, an English girl called Jill, and a daughter, eight years old, called Sophie. He had two brothers, one in San Francisco, the other in Vancouver, and a sister who'd stayed in Hong Kong and married a Chinese banker. Father had retired to a large house on the Peak where he spent his time polishing his collection of jade. The father used to be the head of the organization, but now the power lay with Simon Ng.

Howells rang down to reception and asked if he could hire a car through the hotel. It was easily arranged, said the girl who answered, and yes, the hotel could supply him with a road map, she'd send one right up.

He'd travelled on his own passport but booked into the hotel under Donaldson's name. He'd brought Donaldson's passport with him, and his credit cards, and his glasses, just to be on the safe side. He didn't look much like the man buried under the flagstones of the villa in Bali, but neither did the picture in the passport, and with the glasses on he was close enough.

The map arrived and he studied it until the phone rang and the receptionist said his car was downstairs. It was a blue Mazda, almost new, with a pine air-freshener fixed to the dashboard. The agent who'd delivered it to the hotel had left the aircon running so it was pleasantly cool. He dropped the map on to the passenger seat and edged out into the afternoon traffic of downtown Kowloon. The car was a right-hand-drive automatic and the traffic drove on the left so it confused him for a while. He'd been in Bali too long and grown accustomed to driving on the right. Cars and vans were bumper to bumper for the first mile or so as he drove past the tourist shops packed with cameras, electrical goods and clothes. Hong Kong looked a prosperous city, with none of the obvious poverty he'd seen in Indonesia, where the pavements were full of beggars and children in tattered clothes and the roads buzzed with motorcycles. Hong Kong had few bikes, all the cars seemed new, and the crowds on the pavements were well-dressed and affluent. The buildings were as clean and new as the cars, blocks of glass and steel and marble. Howells drove out of Tsim Sha Tsui, through the industrial areas of Kowloon and past towering residential blocks, thirty storeys high. He glanced at the map a couple of times, but only for reassurance. His sense of direction was unfailingly good and he'd been trained to memorize routes. He left the built-up areas behind him and was soon driving through countryside that reminded him of the Brecon Beacons, rolling hills and thickets of wind-stunted trees.

It was an hour's drive from the hotel to where Ng lived, halfway up a hill that looked down on the South China Sea. The house stood alone, a single storey H-shaped building, two long wings connected by a third block in which was set the main entrance. It was surrounded by green, well-kept lawns on all sides and enclosed by a ten-foot-high stone wall. That was what the file had said, anyway; all that Howells could see from the main road as he craned his neck out of the Mazda's window was the imposing wall. A single track side-road linked the main road to the compound, winding its way left and right up the wooded hill to a pair of black metal gates. The nearest houses were about half a mile away, red-roofed three-storey blocks that would have looked at home in a Spanish seaside town, but they were served by a separate road. There was only one way up, and there seemed to be no way of getting the car to the top of the hill from where he could look down on Ng's house. He'd be able to make it on foot, but he'd have some explaining to do if he got caught.

He drove the car off the main road and headed up the track but he'd barely travelled a hundred yards before the way was blocked by a horizontal pole painted in bright red and white. There was a large sign covered in foot-high Chinese characters and Howells didn't have to be a linguist to work out that it meant 'Halt' or 'Private Property' or 'Trespassers Will Have Their Balls Removed'. He stopped the car, but before he could open the door a man came out of a wooden gatehouse, hand moving towards the inside of his brown leather jacket. The hand didn't reappear, it lingered around his left armpit as if idly scratching. Howells wound down his window and grinned. 'I'm trying to get to Sai Kung,' he said to the guard. The man was about fifty, but stockily built and in good condition. He shook his head.

'Not this road,' he said, and pointed at the barrier. 'Private.' He took his hand away from the shoulder holster, confident that he was talking to a stupid tourist who'd just lost his way. He rested both hands on the car door and leant forward, smiling at Howells with yellowed teeth. 'You must go back.'

'Whatever you say, sunshine,' said Howells, conscious that another guard had moved out of the trees behind him and was standing at the rear offside wing of the car. Security was good, and he had no reason to doubt that there would be more men scattered through the woods. He reversed the Mazda back down the track and on to the road before driving around to the far side of the hill.

So far as he could see the road was the only way he'd be able to get up to the compound. And even if he got there, what then? This wasn't a James Bond movie, one man couldn't storm a fortress alone, no matter how heavily armed. The thought of free-falling in from 25,000 feet made him smile, bringing back fond memories of his days with the SBS. But even then it wouldn't have been considered without a team of four and stun grenades and Uzis and whatever else they could hold on to at 120 mph during the long drop. No, while he was at home, Ng was safe. Howells drove back to Kowloon deep in thought, whistling quietly to himself through clenched teeth.

Hot Gossip was jumping. It was one of Dugan's favourite bars and a hangout for many of the unmarried cops, gweilo and Chinese. A bar where you were reasonably sure of picking up a girl and reasonably sure of not picking up something contagious, where the food wasn't bad and the music was loud and the drinks were expensive enough to keep out the rabble. It was on two floors in Canton Road, the bar and dining area above and a trendy disco below. Dugan was upstairs, priming himself with half pints of lager before diving into the flesh market below.

He was standing by just about the longest bar in Kowloon, a polished black job that could seat a couple of dozen people without looking the least bit crowded. And behind the bar, at intervals of ten feet, were wall-mounted television screens all showing the same music video. At the far end of the bar, where it curved around to the left to the nook where the barmen mixed their high-priced cocktails, was a cluster of tables with pink tablecloths. They too were surrounded by television sets. No matter where you stood or sat you could see a screen without moving your head.

Dugan had left the office early and had walked in on his own but soon found friends in the form of three officers from the anti-triad squad who were also on the police rugby team. They'd begun teasing Dugan about his work, as they always did, and asking when his next quarry would be taking a one-way trip to Taiwan. Dugan was used to the ribbing, in the same way that he was used to suspects disappearing from Hong Kong as soon as the Commercial Crime boys got anywhere near ready to make an arrest.

'It's all right for you bastards,' he said, waving his half-filled glass at them. 'You can catch them with a gun in their hand or a pocket full of dope. Or you can kick down the door to a fishball stall and catch them with underage girls.'

'Chance'd be a fine thing,' howled Colin Burr, a hefty scrum-half with shoulders that looked as if they were made for bursting through doors.

'Deny it,' said Dugan. 'Deny it if you can.'

'You pen-pushers ought to give it a try some time,' said Nick Holt, a lanky Scot with a Hitler moustache who'd only been in Hong Kong three years.

'Yeah, have a go at real police work for a change,' echoed Jeff Bellamy, the oldest of the group and, like Dugan, starting to lose his hair. Unlike Dugan, though, he'd given up trying to comb what he had left over the bald patch and instead had it cut short, a brown fringe that ringed the back of his head.

'Real police work?' sneered Dugan. 'Don't make me laugh. When was the last time you put away one of the Dragon Heads? Name one.'

'Cheung Yiu-chung,' suggested Holt. 'He went down for seven years.'

'Bastard,' conceded Dugan. 'OK, name five. Go on, name me three.'

'Oh piss off, Dugan.'

'You know what I mean. Sure, your arrest records look better than ours, but almost all yours are small fry. Foot soldiers. But we go after the big fish. The real criminals, the ones who steal billions at a time.'

'Yeah, but Dugan, how many do you actually catch?' sniggered Burr as he drank.

'It takes time to build a case,' said Dugan. He fell silent and watched Patsy Kensit prance around on one of the screens behind the bar. She was gorgeous. What made him so argumentative was that he knew they were right. In the first place it often required months of painstaking research that owed more to accountancy than to police work before they had enough evidence to make a case. And by the time they'd got enough evidence together the suspect or suspects had usually had plenty of warning, and they were usually rich enough to be able to buy themselves an escape route. It could be frustrating. Bloody frustrating.

Dugan looked away from the screen and scanned the diners, taking in the whole restaurant area with one easy glance. He realized with a jolt that he too was being studied, by a petite Chinese girl with beautiful eyes. She was sitting at a table with two other girls, wearing a dress every bit as black and shiny as her hair. She seemed small, even for a Chinese girl, but the eyes were knowing and teasing. The eyes of a woman, the body of a young girl. She smiled at Dugan, catching him off balance. He looked away, embarrassed, as if he'd been caught peeking through the window of a schoolgirls' changing-room.

He shrugged. 'Downstairs?' he said.

'Now he's talking sense,' said Bellamy. They emptied their glasses and walked the length of the bar and down the stairs that led to the disco. The throbbing beat enveloped them like a clammy mist and they had to push their way through the crowd to reach the bar. Holt ordered a round of drinks and they stood together, watching like predatory sharks preparing to carve through a shoal of fish.

'What about those two?' said Holt, nodding at two girls dancing together.

'Tasty,' agreed Burr. 'Very tasty.'

The girls moved well together, obviously used to dancing with each other.

'Want to give it a go?' Holt asked Burr.

'Sure,' he replied, and the two men placed their glasses on the bar and edged their way on to the crowded dance floor, towards the girls.

'See anything you fancy?' Bellamy asked Dugan.

'Not yet,' said Dugan, 'but it's just a matter of time.'

Across the disco he saw three girls walk down the stairs and stand at the edge of the lights. One was the small Chinese with the beautiful eyes. She seemed to be looking right at him, though he knew he must be obscured in the gloom.

'You're staring,' laughed Bellamy.

'Pretty, isn't she?'

'The short one? Exquisite. But a big gweilo like you would tear her apart. Pick on someone your own size.'

Dugan looked at him and laughed and when he looked back to the stairs the girls had gone.

The two men stood by the bar, scanning the dance floor and tapping their feet to the beat. Burr and Holt seemed to be doing OK, they'd moved in on the two girls and now were gradually edging them apart like sheepdogs with nervous sheep.

Dugan thought about asking Bellamy how his application for a transfer was getting along, but decided against it. Wrong time, wrong place. God, he wished they'd pull their finger out. He was going slowly mad in Commercial Crime's A Division, even before today's disappointment. It wasn't police work, it was clerking, pure and simple. The straw that had broken the camel's back was the Carrian affair, a three-year investigation followed by an eighteen-month trial, the longest in Hong Kong's history, and the most expensive. It had ended abruptly when a single judge had decided that the defendants had no case to answer. Almost five years of hard work down the drain. Dugan had worked his balls off on that case, ten or twelve hours a day. He'd eaten, slept and breathed the Carrian case, only to see it dismissed by one man.

The night after the judge had stopped the trial Dugan

went out and got seriously drunk. A week later he'd put in his first application for a transfer, to switch from A Division to C Division. A Division handled the long, complex fraud cases, split into four taskforces to handle the big ones. B Division looked after general fraud; a move there would have been seen as a step down, a demotion. C Division had more kudos, chasing up counterfeit cases. That meant a lot of foreign travel, undercover work, the real *Miami Vice* stuff. Trouble was there were only forty officers and the competition to get in was cut-throat. When Dugan had applied he'd been told it would be three years at least until there'd be an opening. Dugan reckoned they were giving him the brush off, that they thought he was too valuable for A Division to lose.

Eventually his patience had snapped and he'd decided to break with CCB completely and try to get back to real police work. But nobody seemed to take his application to join the anti-triad squad seriously – and now he knew why.

Bellamy noticed his silence, and reached over to clink glasses with him. 'How's life?' he asked.

Dugan shrugged. 'Nothing changes. I'm still pissed off with CCB.'

Burr and Holt were back to back now, moving the girls further and further apart. They'd pulled, all right, and done it without talking, too, because they couldn't be heard over the driving beat. Dugan drank deeply. He didn't care any more that it was the wrong time, wrong place.

'I've got to get out,' he said.

'Music too loud?' said Bellamy.

'You know what I mean,' said Dugan. 'Out of Commercial Crime.'

Bellamy shook his head slowly. 'You're better off where you are, Dugan.'

'No,' hissed Dugan. 'I want out.'

The two men looked at each other over the tops of their glasses. Dugan wanted to push it, even though he knew by the older man's silence that he was going to be disappointed. Like phoning to ask a former lover if she'd give it one more try, knowing that he wasn't going to get what he wanted but determined to try nevertheless, even though the pain of rejection would be worse than maintaining the *status quo*.

Dugan explained about losing the computer case. 'I want to move to the anti-triad squad. I have to get back to real police work.'

'Commercial Crime is real police work,' answered Bellamy, avoiding Dugan's eyes.

'I don't understand why they're making it so difficult for me to move,' Dugan drove on stubbornly, knowing the answer. He saw Bellamy's lips move, but the words were lost in the music.

'What?' he shouted.

'You know why,' Bellamy yelled. 'Your bloody brother-in-law. That's what's stopping you. Simon bloody Ng and your sister.'

Dugan sighed and felt alternate waves of anger and frustration wash over him. The computer case was the first he'd lost because of Ng, but it was obvious that it wouldn't be the last. And now it was clear that the powers that be would not allow him to move out of Commercial Crime. Bellamy looked away, embarrassed.

'Fuck it,' said Dugan, and forced a grin. 'Let me buy you a drink. And then I want to get laid.'

When he turned to the bar, she was there. Small and cute and looking up at him with an amused grin on her face. Had she heard him? Dugan hoped not. He smiled. 'Hello,' he said. 'I saw you upstairs, didn't I?'

She nodded. 'And I saw you. Small world, isn't it?' She giggled. Pretty mouth, thought Dugan.

'Can I buy you a drink?' he asked, switching into Cantonese and enjoying the look of surprise on her face.

'I'd like a soft drink, something long and cool,' she said quickly in Cantonese and he knew he was being tested.

'How about me, will I do?' he asked, and she laughed again.

'How come your Cantonese is so good? You a cop?'

'Of course,' he said. 'What do you really want to drink?'

'Perrier,' she replied.

Dugan ordered himself a beer and a fizzy water for her, and then felt a thump in the small of his back.

'Don't forget your friends,' Bellamy growled.

Dugan ordered a lager for Bellamy and handed it to him without looking. His eyes stayed on the girl, worried in case she moved away.

'How about an introduction?' Bellamy asked.

'How about riding off into the sunset and letting me and this young filly get acquainted.' He talked in English, quickly, and he used slang so that the girl wouldn't be able to catch the meaning but she grinned and reached past Dugan, arm outstretched, and shook hands with Bellamy.

'My name's Petal,' she said.

'Pleased to meet you, Petal,' said Bellamy. 'I'm Jeff Bellamy. And this young reprobate is Patrick Dugan. A man to be avoided at all costs.'

'You can let go of her now, Jeff,' said Dugan. He took hold of the girl's hand. It was soft and cool. 'Nice to meet you, Petal.'

'Nice to meet you, Patrick Dugan.'

'It's my turn to ask,' he said. 'How come your English is so good?'

'I was a good student. A frightfully good student,' she said, and her accent was pure Cheltenham Ladies' College.

Dugan gestured at the drink in her hand, bubbles bursting against the slice of lime. 'Not drinking?'

'I'm here to dance, not to drink.'

He took the hint and together they moved to the dance floor. She moved well, and she kept close to him as she danced, touching him occasionally, by accident or by design, he couldn't tell. Just a nudge of an elbow, or their hands would meet as she turned to one side, and each time it was like receiving a small jolt of static electricity. He wondered where her friends were, now she seemed to be alone. The DJ switched to a slow ballad and made some crack about it getting to that time of the night; and Dugan made to leave the floor but she stepped forward and linked her arms around his waist and rested her head against his chest, eyes closed. God, she was tiny, like a schoolgirl, though the breasts that pressed against him were those of a woman. He circled her with his arms and he felt big and clumsy. She smelt of fresh flowers.

Howells was sitting at a bar some two miles south of Hot Gossip, in a Wan Chai dive called the Washington Club.

The brash signs above the head of the aged doorman who sat outside on a wooden stall promised topless dancers, but it had been many years since the place had seen a naked breast. The main drinking area was a circular bar surrounding a small raised dance floor where two girls wearing identical black and silver swimsuits and high-heeled shoes did their best to keep in time with the music. Between the dancers and the bar a group of middle-aged women in long evening dresses either served customers or sat on stools with faces like thunder.

When Howells had walked in through the door and past the large ornamental fish tank an hour earlier a woman old enough to be his great-grandmother led him to a stool and asked him what he wanted to drink. While she fetched him his lager two of the overweight women moved towards him like menacing bears. One of them reached for his hand and held it, rubbing the flesh gently. She felt like sandpaper, thought Howells. 'How long you been Hong Kong?' she asked, smiling with twisted teeth.

'Two days,' he answered. His drink arrived and he used it as an excuse to get his hand back. A white bill was folded into a plastic tumbler which the great-grandmother placed in front of him.

The second woman, plump with loosely permed hair and a prominent Kirk Douglas dimple on her chin, blinked and said: 'Where you stay?'

'Mandarin Oriental,' lied Howells.

'Good hotel,' she said, nodding. 'What your job?'

'Salesman.'

'What your name?' said the other woman. Bargirl was not the right description. Barwoman? Barhag? Howells wondered how she listed her profession in her passport.

'Tom,' said Howells, using the first name that popped into his head. The women introduced themselves, each formally shaking his hand.

'You buy me drink?' asked Dimple.

Howells could see a price list fixed to a pillar to the left of the dancers showing that his lager was about the same price as it would be in a five-star hotel and that the cheapest hostess drink was about three times as much.

He shook his head. 'Not tonight, thanks.'

'Not expensive,' she said.

'No,' said Howells, and pointedly ignored them. They spoke to each other in Cantonese, gave him a filthy look each and then walked off. Howells nursed his lager and concentrated on the dancers. One was short with long black hair and a small, upturned nose; the other was taller with a frizzy mane of hair and a curvier figure. Both had skin that was a darker brown than the middle-aged couple who had just tried to mug him. As he watched they moved into a synchronized dance routine, legs kicking and shoulders shaking. They'd obviously done it many times, no need to watch each other's steps. Real troupers. Another four girls with skin the same colour as the dancers' sat together at the back of the bar eating shelled peanuts. They were wearing T-shirts over their swimsuits and chattering in a bird-song language, probably Filipina.

There were a dozen or so customers drinking at the bar, all of them male. Three of them were drinking with hostesses, and they had blue slips in their tumblers alongside their own white receipts. One, a balding guy with horn-rimmed spectacles and the downtrodden look of a man who'd escaped from his wife for a few hours, was being given a real working-over by four of the hags, two in front of him and one either side. They were all drinking from champagne glasses and there was a wad of blue chits in his tumbler. They laughed at his every word and the women on his side of the bar took it in turns to massage his neck.

The two dancers came to the end of their routine and stepped off the stage, their places taken by two other girls. The one with the cute nose rubbed herself with a blue towel and shrugged on an orange shirt and sat on a stool opposite a tall, cadaverous man with slicked-back brown hair and a thin moustache. The great-grandmother placed a hostess drink in front of the girl without waiting for the man to agree. Obviously a regular. Probably in love.

Howells sat with both hands cupped around his lager, head slightly bowed but eyes taking everything in – the TV set suspended from the ceiling showing an Olivia Newton-John video that bore no relation to the Cantonese pop song to which the girls were dancing – the two tall and hefty-looking Chinese men standing together by the gents, obviously on standby in case there was trouble – the small Filipina girl in a black strapless dress whose large eyes switched to the door every time it opened – the bags on the floor behind the bar containing the girls' going-home clothes.

The dancing girls stood back to back, wriggling and rubbing their arses together, laughing as if they meant it. Olivia Newton-John was prancing around in jogging gear and a white headband. A girl came out of what Howells reckoned was probably a staff restroom at the far end of the bar, about five foot four with hair that curled under her chin, and eyes that were big and wide and more Western than Asian. She was wearing a clean white blouse with a lace collar and sleeves, a black string bow and a black skirt that reached to the floor.

Her eyes scanned the bar professionally and she smiled when she saw Howells. She seemed to have too many teeth for her mouth, the lips curled back like a horse about to neigh and they gleamed like ivory tombstones in the flashing lights above the dance floor. Howells raised his eyebrows and lifted his glass to her in mock salute. She laughed, her lips curling back even further showing even more teeth and she lifted a slender hand to cover her open mouth. She should have been taken to an orthodontist when she was a child, thought Howells. Maybe her parents didn't know better. Maybe they didn't care.

She walked over and stood next to him. 'Hi. What's your name?' The teeth flashed white.

'Tom,' he said, sticking to his first story.

She held out her hand and he shook it. It felt cool and dry. 'My name is Amy.'

'Pleased to meet you, Amy,' he said. 'Can I buy you a drink?'

She looked taken aback, surprised at the offer. Probably taken all the fun out of it, thought Howells. Maybe he should have played hard to get. She walked over to get her own drink and put a blue chit into Howells' tumbler.

She clinked her glass against his. 'Thank you,' she said.

'You're welcome. How long have you been in Hong Kong?'

She looked confused. 'I was born Hong Kong,' she said, her brow furrowed.

71

'Where do you live?'

'Tsim Sha Tsui,' she answered.

Howells kept a serious look on his face. 'What is your job?'

Now she really looked confused, and bit her lower lip. She didn't answer.

'You buy me drink?' Howells asked her, and suddenly she got the joke.

'You joking me,' she said, and pinched his forearm, hard. 'You play at bargirl. You very bad man.' She was attractive rather than pretty, her nose slightly flattened, her lips a little too thick, but her eyes were bright and mischievous and her skin was good. She could have been anywhere between twenty-five and thirty-five years old, which put her in a different generation to the rest of the barhags. 'You work in Hong Kong?' she asked.

Howells nodded. 'Salesman,' he said.

'Selling what?'

Death, he thought. 'Fridges,' he said, and she looked at him quizzically. 'Fridges,' he said again. 'To keep things cold.' He drew a box in the air with his hands and mimed opening its door.

She got it and smiled. 'Fridge,' she said, and repeated it a few times, committing the word to memory. That was probably how she picked up her English, thought Howells, talking to customers and getting them to explain the words she didn't understand. Her English wasn't that bad; she had no trouble understanding him so long as he didn't speak too quickly and he wondered how much was the result of pillow talk.

Amy earned her money. She listened carefully to his every word, her eyes never leaving his face, answered all his questions politely and took an interest in him; where did he live, where were his family, how did he like Hong Kong. Occasionally she'd reach across and run her fingertips along his arm and when he flattered her she'd lower her eyelashes and almost blush. She made her small drink last twenty minutes, but as soon as she'd sipped the last drop the great-grandmother sidled up and picked up the empty glass. She showed it to Howells like a detective producing evidence of a murder.

'You buy girl drink?' she asked, tilting the glass from side to side as if to prove that it really was empty.

Howells nodded. 'Sure, why not?'

'Thank you,' said Amy, and put her small hand on top of his as if he'd just done her a huge favour and it wasn't simply a business transaction. Howells wondered how many thousands of times she'd done that, whispered thank you and held hands. Her drink arrived and so did another blue chit.

'What about buy me a drink?' said the old woman.

'Not tonight,' he said. 'Next time.' He turned away from her and concentrated on Amy, asking her about her life.

'My story very sad,' she said.

It was too, a story about a big family and a drunken father who'd assaulted her when she was twelve years old. She'd run away and been befriended by a sixteen-year-old drugs dealer who encouraged her to start chasing the dragon – smoking heroin – and then put her to work in a fishball stall, an underage brothel. She'd escaped from him the day before her fourteenth birthday and fell into the arms of a money-lender who lent her money, set her up in a one-room flat and supplied her with half a dozen customers a night to pay off the interest. She'd eventually met a businessman, a plastic bag manufacturer, who'd promised to marry her but dropped her as soon as she got pregnant. She'd had an abortion but he still wanted nothing to do with her. Now she lived alone and had worked in a succession of bars, on Hong Kong island and over in Kowloon.

She told the story in a flat monotone and Howells wondered how many times she'd told it, and how much of it was true.

She told him how much commission she got from each drink, how many drinks she got a night, how all the girls had to work double shifts – fourteen hours a day – whenever there was an American ship in town. Howells asked her why she didn't dance and she scowled.

'Only Filipina or Thai girls dance,' she said, scornfully. 'Chinese girls not do that.'

That was rich, thought Howells. Mugging drunken tourists for drinks was respectable, going back to their hotels was a legitimate business transaction, but dancing in a swimsuit was beneath her. Amy seemed to have no feelings of shame or regret about her job, it was just business. He asked her how often she left with customers, and she shrugged.

'Depends,' she said. 'Sometimes one month four times, sometimes one month and I not go.'

Again, she had her own set of values. Americans were out 'because they not clean', and she didn't like Germans because a German had once beaten up her friend and stolen her purse. She was wary of tourists and never went with policemen because they wouldn't pay. What she liked best, she said, were married men who lived and worked in Hong Kong. 'They very careful because they not want wife to get sick, and they not stay all night,' she said. You couldn't fault her logic, Howells realized.

'You want to buy me out?' she asked Howells, finishing her second drink. The great-grandmother was by her side before she'd even had a chance to place it on the bar. Howells said yes to the drink, but no to the buy-out offer.

'I've very little money tonight,' he said. 'Maybe another time.'

'No problem,' she said. 'You can use credit card. And we give you receipt.' She pouted and pinched his arm gently, pulling at the hairs. 'I like you, Tom.'

Howells knew it was an act, an act she'd put on thousands of times before, but he was still half convinced that she thought he was special.

He shook his head, firmly. 'I like you too, Amy, but not tonight.'

Her drink and chit arrived, along with a fresh lager for Howells which he hadn't ordered but which he accepted anyway. Amy gently clinked his glass. 'Nice to meet you,' she said. Then she went back to work, talking and laughing and touching.

The dancing girls continued their rota, twenty minutes on and forty minutes off, taking drinks from customers during the rest periods. They seemed to have a different approach to Amy, greedily gulping down their hostess drinks whenever the customers looked away, pouring them into the sink when they went to the gents. Amy was as good as gold, making each drink last a full twenty minutes.

'Do many police come here?' asked Howells.

Amy shook her head. 'No. They go Club Superstar sometimes. It is a disco and you not have to buy girls drinks there.'

Howells smiled. 'Where else do they go? Where Kowloon side?'

Amy pouted again. 'You want to go? You tired of me?'

'No,' he laughed. 'Don't worry.' They touched glasses again. 'Where in Kowloon do they drink?'

'Rick's Café, Canton disco, Hot Gossip,' she said, 'many places.'

Howells remembered the names in the same way that Amy had memorized the word 'fridge'. He left her half an hour later, promising to see her again but not meaning it. She looked mournful as he said goodbye but he looked over his shoulder as he reached the door and saw that she was already on another stool talking to a bearded tourist wearing Union Jack shorts. Just business. Fickle cow, thought Howells.

Dugan was pleasantly surprised when Petal agreed to go home with him. He'd half expected her to play coy but she'd seemed eager and clutched his hand tightly as they sat in the back of the taxi, and when he leaned forward to kiss her, her lips parted and she moaned softly, her small hand gently caressing his thigh.

His luck was obviously in. Even getting the taxi had been fortuitous; normally late at night you had to fight the masses, every man for himself, but tonight one had pulled up just as they walked out into the night air. The gweilo in the back seat had even held the door open for them before disappearing into the disco.

Petal had laughed at all his jokes on the way back to Hong Kong island and she leant against him in the lift. Dugan's heart was pounding and his hands were actually shaking as he slotted the key into the lock and opened the door for her. She grinned as she walked past him, and he was suddenly ashamed of the smallness of the flat. He wanted to impress her and he knew that his shoebox of a home wouldn't impress anyone. God, the bedroom was a mess – and then with a jolt he remembered the unflushed toilet. He pushed past Petal and dashed into the bathroom. He took a deep breath and pushed the handle, sighing out loud as he heard the water flush. When he walked back into the lounge Petal was sitting on the sofa, smiling.

'You seemed in a hurry,' she said. 'Problems?'

'No,' said Dugan. 'When you've gotta go, you've gotta go.' Oh Jesus, had he really said that? 'Can I get you a drink?'

'Hmmm, that would be nice. Do you have any wine?'

Dugan couldn't believe the way things were going. Hiding at the bottom of the fridge was a bottle of Californian white that he'd never got round to drinking. 'Of course,' he said, 'white OK?'

'Fine,' she answered.

Even the cork came out smoothly and for once there were no bits floating on the top when he poured it into two matching glasses. Their fingers touched when Dugan handed her the glass and she smiled again. Dugan sat next to her. The flat was so small there was nowhere else to sit, unless he went into the bedroom.

'Very convenient,' she said.

'I'm sorry?'

She nodded out of the window. 'Very convenient,' she repeated. 'If you get bored watching your television you can always watch the neighbours.' From where they were sitting they could look right into next door's lounge, which was at right-angles to Dugan's. His face fell and she realized she'd hurt his feelings. 'It's a lovely flat,' she said.

'No it's not,' he said, and his voice had a brittle edge to it. 'It's small and it's noisy and if I could afford somewhere bigger I'd move but on an inspector's salary . . .'

She pressed her finger against his lips. 'I love it,' she said. 'Show me the bedroom.'

Howells held the door of the taxi open, not out of politeness but because he found it difficult to take his eyes off the girl who was waiting to take his place, a mixture of small-girl vulnerability and obvious sexuality that he found a little disturbing. She looked like a child but moved with the easy grace of a woman, and her face was that of an angel, albeit an Asian one. He envied the heavily built white guy she was with. She smiled at him as she moved past and murmured a thank you. He breathed in her perfume, the fragrance of jasmine, and then the taxi was gone.

He stood for a moment and then entered Hot Gossip and went upstairs to the bar, where he took an empty stool and ordered a lager. He drank it and looked around with the hungry look of a man on the make looking for a single girl, his eyes flitting from face to face. He made eye contact a couple of times as he checked out the whole bar, hopeful girls without dates, but they weren't what Howells was after.

He watched one of the television sets mounted on the wall, an old black-and-white video of the Beatles, a fresh-faced John Lennon shaking his head in time to the beat. Howells raised his glass to the screen. 'You'll go out with a bang, John,' he said. 'At the top. The best way to go.' He drained the glass and paid his bill and walked down to the hard driving noise of the disco.

He shouldered his way through the sweating crowd, helped by the fact that he was a few inches taller than most of the clientele. His gaze swept back and forth like a fighter pilot on patrol, and he found what he wanted standing by the bar: two Europeans, short haircuts, fit-looking with restless eyes. Howells stood about six feet from them as he ordered another lager, straining to hear them over the music. They looked like coppers and after ten minutes or so Howells had heard enough to know that they were. One was a big bastard, the other was tall and thin with a moustache. They each had a Chinese girl hanging on to their arms but they ignored them, talking over their heads as if they weren't there. They were joined by a third man, also a policeman, and they began discussing another man, something about wanting a transfer. Office politics.

The one with the moustache looked the best yet. Howells was now completely clean-shaven, but it wouldn't be a problem; men shaved and grew moustaches all the time.

Howells waited until he went to the toilet and caught up with him as he banged through the black door.

'Sorry,' muttered Holt.

'OK, no problem,' said Howells, keeping his head down. Holt stood in front of one of the urinals and unzipped his flies. It looked as if they were the only two in the room, but to be sure Howells ducked down and pretended to tie his shoelace while checking the toilet doors. Both unlocked. All clear. Holt had closed his eyes as he urinated. Howells swung his arm round and slammed the edge of his hand into Holt's temple, not hard enough to kill, but hard enough so that the policeman dropped without a sound, urine splashing down his left leg. Howells caught him under the arms and dragged him backwards into one of the compartments. He eased him on to the seat and then undid his belt and pulled the man's trousers down to his ankles. One of Holt's shoes had fallen off and Howells went back for it. He locked himself in with the unconscious man and was just replacing the shoe when the door to the washroom thudded open. Soundlessly Howells sprang up, placing his feet between Holt's thighs and balancing on the seat, arms outstretched against the walls.

When they were alone again Howells finished tying Holt's shoelace before going through his pockets. The warrant card was in a clear plastic pocket in Holt's brown pigskin wallet. Howells took the lot; there was more chance of it looking like a robbery that way. Holt's head had slumped down on his chest. He was breathing heavily through his nose, and apart from a red mark on the side on his head there was nothing to indicate that he hadn't just passed into a drunken stupor. Howells put his hands on top of the cubicle and heaved himself up and over. He stepped down on to the neighbouring toilet bowl and slipped through the door. He kept his head down as he walked back into the disco, nodding in time to the music and pretending to be slightly unsteady on his feet. Two minutes later he was in a taxi heading back to his hotel, gently rubbing his right hand.

Dugan awoke as the morning sunlight shafted through his bedroom window and pinned him to the bed. The aluminium window-frame began clicking as it warmed up and he rolled over in the double bed and opened his eyes. She was gone. For a moment he wondered if he'd dreamt her but there was a dip in the pillow and several long, black hairs, and the smell of her perfume.

'Petal,' he called. 'Are you there?'

There was no reply, and when he walked into the lounge he found a note on the circular dining table. *Pat – you looked so sweet I didn't want to wake you. Call me if you get time – Petal.* She'd left her telephone number and at the bottom of the sheet of notepaper was a flower, hastily drawn.

Dugan made himself a black coffee and sat in his bathrobe as he drank it. Normally he showered first, but this morning he wanted to put if off as long as possible; he knew it was stupid, adolescent even, but he didn't want to get rid of the smell of her.

'God, I'm wrecked,' he said out loud. He grinned stupidly. It had been a long time since a girl had made him feel the way Petal had. There had been a horrible moment when he thought that maybe he'd read the signs wrong and that she was on the game, she'd seemed almost too willing. Dugan was no stranger to hookers; many was the time he'd gone home with one to fill up an empty night, and he didn't begrudge them the money. A couple had even become friends, though he still had to pay them. But he'd wanted Petal as a lover, and as a friend, and anything else would have spoiled it for him. But she didn't force him to shower first, the way that hookers always did, nor did she insist that he wore a sheath. 'I'm on the pill,' she whispered. He'd been overcome by an animal passion that almost scared him with its intensity, but it had been coupled with an overwhelming feeling of tenderness. He'd wanted to squeeze her, bite her, eat her, to dominate her and yet at the same time be completely in her power. He'd stroked and caressed her and he was sure she'd come within seconds of his moving inside her, and eventually he'd cried out her name and afterwards she'd curled up next to him like a cat with his arms around her and he'd fallen asleep with her head under his chin.

He began to grow hard again as he thought of her and when he stepped into the shower he put it on full cold and gasped.

Howells sat in his rented car and yawned. The sky was smudged with the first light of dawn but he'd already been up an hour. He'd bolted down a room-service breakfast and driven out to Ng's house, where he'd parked about a quarter of a mile from the junction of the main road and the track that led up to the triad leader's compound.

There had been three deliveries: the papers, the milk and the post. Nothing else. Howells waited patiently. He didn't read a newspaper, or listen to the radio, or do anything else that might distract him from the job at hand – the waiting and the watching. Twenty minutes after the postman had left, an olive-green Mercedes 560 nosed down the track indicating that it was going to turn right, towards where Howells was sitting. The engine was already running because he'd needed the airconditioner to keep from melting. He waited until the Mercedes passed him, then began to follow it, never getting closer than fifty yards. It headed towards Kowloon and there was plenty of morning traffic so Howells wasn't worried about losing it.

They followed the road into the built-up area and then the car indicated a left turn as it approached a set of traffic lights and Howells did the same. The lights changed to amber as the Mercedes went through and by the time Howells made the turn they were red. The car in front braked suddenly and he had to swerve around it with a squeal of tortured tyres. He had no choice, he knew that, but he also realized that it was a sure way of attracting attention to himself. He should have waited, but he'd reacted instinctively, the way he usually did, letting his subconscious show the way. He stamped on the accelerator and caught up with the Mercedes, twenty feet from its bumper, then fifteen, and then he indicated he was going to overtake and rattled past it. There were three people in the car: a uniformed driver, a heavily built man in a leather bomber jacket in the front passenger seat, and a small girl in pigtails. She had blonde hair, Howells noticed with surprise. The girl was playing with something, her head down in concentration. The driver looked straight ahead but the passenger gave Howells the once-over and then looked scornfully at the rented car.

Howells accelerated until he was about a hundred yards ahead of the Mercedes and then he slowed to match its speed, watching it in the driving mirror. Another set of traffic lights came up and Howells slowed. The Mercedes indicated a right turn and Howells followed suit. They were driving through a commercial area now; shopkeepers were opening their small stores, pushing up metal grilles and sweeping floors. The traffic was denser; there were at least a dozen cars between them, and Howells was having trouble keeping the Mercedes in sight. He came to a busy crossroads and drove straight on, seeing too late that the Mercedes was indicating it was going to turn right again. Howells checked his watch. They'd been driving for twenty-five minutes and he doubted if the girl's school was much further away. He'd pick them up at the crossroads tomorrow morning. Now he had some shopping to do.

He found a diving shop in Tsim Sha Tsui, not far from the hotel. It used up about a third of the cash that had been left over after he'd paid for the ticket from Bali, but he got everything he needed. The guy in the shop must have thought it was Christmas – a customer who didn't bother bargaining and who paid in cash. He carried his purchases back to the hotel in two nylon bags and spread them out on his bed.

There was a single steel cylinder that the salesman had filled with a compressor at the back of the shop, a demand valve, flippers, a mask and a snorkel. Howells had thought about a wetsuit and discarded the idea, because he didn't plan on being in the water for long and the South China Sea wasn't particularly cold. And if he didn't wear a suit he wouldn't need a weight belt; the cylinder would just about balance his natural buoyancy. He'd bought a pair of trunks and a large knife and scabbard to strap to his calf. He already had a diving watch, a gold-plated Chronosport that he'd owned for going on fifteen years, but he'd paid for a good underwater compass. He didn't need a depth gauge.

He'd been prowling among the shelves when he spotted a small metal cylinder with a mouthpiece attached to its mid-point that he'd never seen before. He'd seen one in a James Bond movie once – *Thunderball*, he thought – but that had obviously been faked because it had only been six inches or so long, hardly enough for a couple of breaths even under very high pressure. The packaging on this one said that it was an emergency air supply and could be used for approximately thirty deep breaths. It was, the blurb stressed, only for emergency use. Howells bought one. The shop also sold a range of security equipment: truncheons, torches, Mace sprays and the like. Howells included a pair of handcuffs in his purchases.

He laid them all out on the bed and checked each item again before repacking them and putting the bags in the bottom of the wardrobe. Then he got the Yellow Pages out of the cabinet under the TV and began looking for a firm that hired out boats.

The first one he went to see was moored a couple of hundred yards from the shore of a place called Hebe Haven, about half an hour's drive from the hotel. There were hundreds of boats there, all shapes and sizes, yachts and junks, but the nearest was at least fifty metres away, a small, white and red cruiser that obviously wasn't lived on. He wouldn't be disturbed, he was sure of that, and if pushed he could always move it.

It was built in the style of an old-fashioned junk, shiny teak boards with a raised deck at the back and a single mast, but no sail because down below there was a powerful diesel engine. It bobbed in the water to the sound of ripples slapping against seasoned wood.

'You like?' asked the tall, gaunt Chinese boy standing next to Howells, leaning over the rail and staring at the sea.

'It's a good boat,' said Howells. 'How old is it?'

'Four years,' said the boy. 'Built Kowloon-side. For banker.'

'What happened to him? Emigrate?'

The boy laughed, showing yellowed teeth. 'No emigrate. He steal from bank. Go Taiwan. Bank sell boat. Now I rent.'

It seemed perfect, thought Howells. The hull looked solid, and the portholes were small, too small for even a child to climb through. Below decks was a large master bedroom and a thick, teak door which opened to reveal a small chemical toilet, and there was a lounge area with seats either side that pulled out to form two more beds. A galley kitchen lay to the left of the wooden stairway that led down from the main deck and at the rear was the engine-room.

By the look of the state of the engine it had hardly been used; the banker had probably only bought it for show. The upper deck at the back was perfect for a drinks party, and Howells could imagine a gathering of beautiful people out in the moonlight, drinking pink gins and making small talk.

The boy said that for a price he could arrange a place in one of the typhoon shelters, or even a berth at one of the yacht clubs, but Howells said no, where it was was just fine.

'You sleep here?' the boy asked.

Howells nodded. 'Sometimes.'

'You cannot sail, you must have boatboy to sail. Understand?'

Howells said yes, he understood. He paid a month's charter and a deposit, in cash. Then the boy climbed down to his black and red speedboat and roared off, the boat rocking in his wake. There was a small white glass-fibre dinghy tethered to the back of the junk so that Howells could row himself to the shore. The main landing-place was a large, L-shaped concrete pier that jutted into the water but to either side of it were ungainly, rickety old wooden jetties to which were moored lines of small boats waiting for their owners. Most of them were probably weekend sailors – and by the weekend it should all be over, thought Howells. Bar the shouting.

Dugan's head was starting to hurt, a dull thudding pain behind his left eye. Maybe he needed glasses. Sometimes he had to squint a little when watching television and he had trouble reading the signs down in the MTR stations, but he had no trouble reading, no trouble at all. He rubbed his temples, making small circles with his fingertips, and closed his eyes.

'Sleeping, huh?' said a laconic voice at the door. It was Burr. Dugan kept his eyes closed.

'I'm not sleeping, you wanker. I've just got the mother and father of all headaches.'

'Just behind the eyes, is it?' asked Burr, sympathetically.

'Yes,' growled Dugan.

'A sort of sharp, searing pain, like a nerve pain?'

'Yes.'

'First symptom of a brain tumour,' laughed Burr. 'You're fucked.'

Dugan opened his eyes, but continued to massage the sides of his aching head. 'Can I help you, Colin?' he asked.

'Just popped in to see if you'd heard about Holt.'

'What happened?'

'Stupid bastard got mugged. After you left. In the toilets. They found him sitting on the pan with his trousers round his ankles. They had to break the door down. He reckons somebody walloped him from behind. They took his wallet.'

'He's OK, though?' Dugan was genuinely worried; Holt was a friend.

'Yeah, he's all right. They took him to casualty for a checkup and they gave him the all clear. He'll probably be in Hot Gossip tonight as usual. Are you on for a bevy tonight?'

'I suppose I could be persuaded to force down a pint or two.'

The phone rang and Burr waved goodbye as Dugan picked it up.

'Hi,' said Petal. 'How's your day going so far?'

'It was OK,' lied Dugan. His head was still throbbing. 'Yours?'

'*Ma ma, fu fu*,' she said, Mandarin Chinese for horse horse, tiger tiger – not so good, not so bad. 'Same as usual.'

Dugan realized he didn't even know what she did. But then again, she hadn't asked too many questions about what his job involved. He'd spent what, nine hours in her company, four of them in bed, and yet he knew next to nothing about her. But at the same time he seemed to know everything, a sort of empathy, knowledge by osmosis.

'Are you doing anything tonight?' he asked.

'Nothing planned.'

Dugan cleared his throat. 'Do you fancy going out?'

'With you, you mean?'

Dugan laughed. 'That's what I had in mind.'

'Well . . .' she sighed, but Dugan knew he was being teased.

'Of course, if you've got something else on . . .'

'I'd love to see you,' she said.

'Dinner?'

'Mmm. Where?'

'There's an Italian restaurant in Tsim Sha Tsui, great food.'

'That sounds fine, I love Italian food.'

'OK, I'll meet you opposite the Hang Seng Bank inside the Tsim Sha Tsui MTR station at eight.'

'See you then.'

She put the receiver down first, and Dugan held it

to his ear for a few seconds, listening to the electronic tone.

Howells lay on the bed, flicking the remote control from channel to channel, but there was nothing to hold his attention for more than a few minutes. He'd eaten a room-service sirloin steak an hour earlier. There was nothing in the room worth reading and he didn't feel like sleep.

He'd transferred all the equipment to the junk, and he'd bought a strong lock and bolt which he'd screwed into the toilet door so that it could be locked from the outside. He'd stocked the galley with the bare essentials: bread, milk, and cans of soup and stew. He'd tested the aqualung and spent half an hour snorkelling around the boat, enjoying the feel of the water. But there was nothing he could do now. First he had to find out which school Ng's daughter went to, and he couldn't do that until tomorrow. It wasn't that Howells was nervous; there was no adrenalin rush, just empty hours to fill. He decided to go back to the Washington Club.

The taxi dropped him close to the bar and the moist, humid atmosphere wrapped itself around him like a damp towel as he stepped out of the air-conditioned environment. He was wearing light brown cotton trousers and a dark blue fake Lacoste T-shirt, yet he still felt as if he was overdressed. It wasn't just that it was hot, it was the humidity that made it uncomfortable. He'd spent three weeks in the deserts of Oman a few years back, helping the Government do a favour for the Sultan, and he hadn't felt half as hot as he did now. He wiped his forehead and when he took his hand away it was wet.

At several points along the length of the busy road were small groups of people lighting fires in the gutter. One group was a few steps away from the entrance to Popeye's, and Howells stood for a minute to watch. There was a mother with a young baby strapped to her back, her husband and two small boys gathered around a cluster of joss sticks that had been stuck into a large orange. The man was crouched down, squatting on his heels watching a pile of sheets of paper crinkle and burn. He was holding what at first glance looked like orange banknotes, but there were so many zeros on them that Howells realized they were play money. As the pile in front of him died down, the man fed more notes on to it. To the left of the burning paper was a cardboard plate on which were two pieces of meat, some grapes and a bread roll. The two boys were skipping around their mother, clapping their hands in excitement. Howells couldn't work it out; they were a well-dressed family, and the man was wearing an expensive wristwatch. Some religious festival, maybe. He left them to it.

Amy spotted him as soon as he walked in. She came over and gave him her tombstone smile. 'Nice to see you, Tom.'

She caught him by surprise until he remembered that Tom was the name he'd used the previous night. He was impressed that she'd taken the trouble to remember his name, but then realized that it was part of her job – make the customer feel wanted and important and special and chances are that he'd buy you a drink. Sound commercial sense, nothing else.

'Hiya, Amy. How are you?'

'Happy to see you,' she said, and linked her arm through his, leading him to the circular bar. It was crowded and there were only two empty seats, one either side of a bulky giant of a man with a crew cut and bulging forearms. Amy touched him lightly on the arm and asked him to move to the right, and he did so with a beaming, drunken smile. Amy guided Howells to one of the seats and sat down next to him. 'Beer?' she said.

Howells nodded. 'What's the best local beer?'

'San Mig,' she said. 'You want?'

'Sure, I'll try it.'

There were two girls dancing, with three sitting on stools chattering. The cadaverous man was there talking to his girl-friend, a sheaf of blue chits in the glass on the bar in front of him. Must be love, thought Howells sourly. Most of the men in the bar were soldiers or sailors, youngsters with cropped hair and pimples, laughing and shouting above the pulse of the music, ogling the girls and heckling each other. American accents everywhere. Amy returned with his drink.

'Get yourself one, Amy,' he said.

The girls dancing were Filipina, short and slightly chubby, mahogany skin and black eyes, flirting madly with their adoring audience. The record changed to a Beach Boys number, *Surfing USA* or something, and with whoops of delight three of the young men jumped on to their stools, waving their arms and swaying from side to side in a pretty good imitation of surfing. The girls stopped dancing and stood there pouting with their hands on their hips. Amy put a plastic tumbler in front of him with a white chit for his beer and a blue one for her hostess drink.

'Sailors,' she said. 'Americans.' As if that explained everything.

'Good business,' he said.

'No,' she said, with surprising venom. 'Just trouble. They come from PI. No money left.'

'PI?'

'Philippine Islands. Girls there very cheap. When they come here no money left. And they not buy drinks for girls, just themselves. And usually they very impolite.'

Howells nodded sympathetically. 'How long are they here for?'

'Four days. I think I try to take holiday tomorrow. I ask mamasan.'

'Probably a good idea. What sort of ship are they on?'

'Submarine. Nuclear submarine. They stay about five miles away and come in on small boat. Stay four days and then go.'

'To where?'

'Supposed to be secret, but one of them said they go to Korea. They talk all the time, boasting. See that boy?' She nodded towards the middle of the three barstool-surfers. 'He weapons officer. His job is to fire the missiles.'

He looked to be barely out of his teens, a faceful of freckles and ginger hair, flushed with drink and frowning as he tried to maintain his balance. He whooped and attempted to spin his stool around, his arms windmilling through the air and knocking his two mates over. The three of them tumbled backwards, crashing into the wall behind them and falling into a pile of arms and legs and stools.

One of the girls screamed but they were OK, too drunk to hurt themselves with anything less than a fall from an eight-storey building.

'You look fierce,' said Amy, concern in her voice. 'What is wrong?'

Howells forced a smile. 'Nothing,' he said. 'Just a hard day, that's all. Hey, what's going on outside?'

'What do you mean?'

'Families burning paper and putting food in the street.'

'Festival,' she said. 'Festival of the Hungry Ghosts.'

Howells looked bemused and Amy laughed. 'This is the time of the year when the gates to Hell are opened and all the ghosts come back to earth. You must keep them out of your houses, so you feed them in the street. And burn money for them. You must keep them happy so that they bring good luck.' She lifted her glass and looked at Howells through it. 'Nice to meet you, Tom,' she said. Over the other side of the bar the three surfers had climbed back on to their stools and were busy drinking themselves into oblivion.

The meal had gone well, very well. The pasta had been cooked to perfection, an unusual feat in Hong Kong, the veal was as tender as he'd ever eaten and the bottle of red wine they'd put away had relaxed Dugan completely. The only black spot on the evening had been when the waiter had returned with his Access card and told him that it hadn't been accepted. Dugan realized he hadn't paid the last account from the card company. There hadn't been enough in his bank account to cover it. He handed over his Amex card and smiled apologetically at Petal.

'Let's split it,' she said.

'No, it's OK. It's just an administrative foul-up, that's all. And my salary cheque went in a couple of days ago. Don't worry, I'm solvent.'

Until the bank took his mortgage payment out, and the management charges for his flat, and the electricity, gas and phone bills all got whipped out by the magic of direct debit. And he'd have to pay something on his credit cards or they'd be repossessed this time, he was sure of it. Shit. At least if he was in the private sector he could go and ask his boss for a raise.

'Well, I insist on you letting me buy you a nightcap,' she said. 'How about going back to Hot Gossip?'

'Fine by me,' Dugan answered, though with just a tinge of regret. He wanted to get back into bed with her as quickly as possible. She looked stunning; tight black velvet trousers and a jacket made of some glossy, gold-coloured material, with padded shoulders and a thin collar that was turned up at the back. She had on open-toed shoes and he noticed for the first time that she'd painted her toenails bright pink. God, she was sexy, even more so by virtue of the fact she seemed so small and vulnerable. Still, if the lady wanted Hot Gossip, that's what the lady would get.

They walked through the crowded streets of Tsim Sha Tsui, Dugan taking pride in the fact that Petal turned a lot of heads, Chinese and gweilo. He wanted the whole world to know that she was with him, wanted to label her as spoken for. He made do by holding her hand. It felt small and cool and was lost in his.

95

Most of the shops they walked past were for tourists: electric goods, jewellers, high fashion, with a sprinkling of topless bars, but even here families were out in force with their offerings to the ghosts.

'Do your family do this?' asked Dugan.

Petal nodded earnestly. 'Of course. It's part of our heritage. Even more so on the mainland. I help clean my ancestors' graves each year, I eat moon cake during the moon festival, I feed the ghosts.' He still couldn't get used to the cut-glass accent coming from such an obviously Chinese girl.

'But do you believe in it all?'

'It doesn't matter whether I believe it or not. That's not the point. It's part of being Chinese. You wouldn't understand, and I don't mean that nastily.' She squeezed his hand. 'I'm not explaining it very well,' she said.

'Are your family in Hong Kong?' he asked.

'No,' she said. 'Manchuria, northern China. What about your parents? Where are they?'

Dugan noticed the sharp change in subject, as if he'd touched a nerve. It was understandable, though; many Hong Kong Chinese were sensitive about their origins. Most were refugees, or the children of refugees, and the richer families didn't like anyone taking too close a look at their backgrounds because a great many of the old fortunes were based on opium or drug smuggling.

'They live in a town called Cheadle Hulme, near Manchester.'

'The north of England.'

'That's right. They have a shop there, a bookshop.'

'Are you from a big family?'

Dugan shook his head. 'No, just one sister, Jill.'

96

They'd reached the entrance to the disco, but went upstairs to the bar. Standing at their usual place were Bellamy and Burr, and Bellamy raised his eyebrows as he saw who Dugan was with.

'Petal,' he said, stepping forward to meet her. 'So nice to see you again. It seems like only yesterday . . .'

'It was only yesterday, Jeff,' said Colin.

Bellamy took her elfin hand and kissed it gently. Dugan felt a flash of jealousy but let it pass. Bellamy tried it on with every girl he met. His theory was that the more times you tried, the more often you'd succeed – it was just a matter of statistics.

'How's Holt?' asked Dugan.

'He'll be OK, it's his pride that hurts more than anything,' said Burr.

Dugan put his arm protectively around Petal's shoulders. She smiled up at him and held him around the waist. Bellamy and Burr looked at each other with mock horror on their faces.

'The boy's in love,' gasped Burr.

'Throw a bucket of water over them, somebody,' yelled Bellamy.

'Christ,' said Dugan, and he looked up at the ceiling in exasperation.

Petal seemed to revel in the company of the three men, laughing at Bellamy's corny jokes and listening with rapt attention to Burr's stories of police work. Dugan began to show his impatience; he didn't want to be standing at the bar with just one third of her attention, he wanted one hundred per cent of her, ideally naked and preferably in bed. He kept his arm around her shoulder and occasionally he'd give her an encouraging squeeze, but she made no move to go. The bar was busy, buzzing with its usual night-time mix of off-duty coppers, television starlets, Chinese yuppies and underworld figures. For once Dugan's eyes weren't prowling the crowd looking for possible conquests – he'd got all he wanted right under his arm. Petal was all he wanted to look at. It had been a long time since he'd felt like that about a girl.

'But aren't you frightened, taking on the triads?' she asked Burr.

'What's to be frightened about?' he said.

'Well,' she hesitated, 'don't they try to stop you?'

'Of course,' he said. 'But not with violence. They wouldn't dream of hurting a copper, not a gweilo anyway. The whole force would come down on them like a ton of bricks. They fight each other all the time, hatchets, guns, acid, the works. But it's always in-house violence, the public hardly ever gets hurt. And they leave the cops alone.'

Bellamy nodded in agreement. 'Most of the top triads are OK guys when you meet them socially. Wouldn't you say so, Dugan?'

Dugan grinned, a smile with no warmth. Bellamy was a bit tight, but even when sober he took a malicious glee at picking away at people's sore points, and right now friendships with triads was a definite touchy subject so far as Dugan was concerned.

'Take a look around you,' said Burr, waving theatrically with his arm. He pointed at a Chinese youth, late twenties, in a snappy blue silk suit, who was eating a steak and talking at the same time to a demure girl in a tight-fitting black dress that left little to the imagination. On the table in front of the man was a mobile telephone.

Petal raised an eyebrow expectantly. 'What about him?'

'Triad,' he said. 'Danny Lam. Very big in drugs, and I mean big. Danny Boy drives a very pretty little Ferrari, and he's partial to young Chinese girls – and I mean young. That one he's with now is twice the age he normally goes for. He gets them hooked on cocaine and when he's finished with them he hands them over to one of the fishball stalls.'

Petal wrinkled her nose. 'The what?'

'You've never heard of fishball stalls?' said Bellamy in disbelief. 'Under-age brothels. Chinese only, gweilos are never allowed in. We raid about five a week, charge the organizers and send the girls back to their parents. A few days later the girls run away again and the bad guys are out on bail. And so it goes on. See that guy over there?' This time he gestured towards another young man, this one with slicked-back hair and an expensive leather jacket. Under one arm he carried a small Gucci case from which protruded the aerial of a portable telephone. He was laughing with two teenage girls, one either side. Not exactly twins, but close. Petal looked at Bellamy for an explanation.

'Stockbroker,' he said. 'One of the best. Drives a Porsche. Now, can you tell them apart? Neither can I. They look the same, they drink in the same bars, they're members of the same clubs, they eat at the same restaurants. Chances are they even went to the same school.'

'What are you getting at?' said Dugan, angrily. He felt as if Bellamy was setting him up for something, but he wasn't sure what.

99

'The point I'm trying to make to Petal, Patrick my boy, is that triads are no different to any other local businessmen.'

'In fact,' added Burr, 'we actually get on quite well with some of them.'

'You're friends with them?' said Petal.

'No, not friends,' said Bellamy. 'Never friends. But we drink with them. It's part of the game. They'll stand and talk with us, part of the macho image, it gives them a boost to be seen drinking with cops. And sometimes they'll give you info about one of their competitors.'

'Part of the job,' said Burr.

'Sounds crazy,' said Petal, slipping into Cantonese.

'The world is crazy,' replied Burr, also in Chinese. All three of the men were good enough to be able to flit between the two languages without hesitation.

'Don't your bosses mind you mixing with the guys you're supposed to be trying to catch?' asked Petal, genuinely puzzled.

'There's a line that we don't cross, Petal. We drink with them, we laugh and joke with them, but that's as far as it goes,' said Burr. 'At the end of the day we're trying to put them away.'

'Listen to the Lone Ranger,' laughed Bellamy.

Dugan felt a fingernail run down his spine, and for a moment he thought it was Petal until he realized that her arm was around his waist. He turned to look over his left shoulder and found himself looking into a pair of green, knowing eyes above a slightly upturned nose and a wide, smiling mouth. The smile grew wider and dimples appeared in both cheeks, and as she tilted her head to one side her long blonde hair rippled.

'How's it going, brother of mine?'

'Hiya, Jill. Business as usual, nothing changes. You look good.'

She did, too. The white silk blouse and hip-hugging grey skirt she was wearing had exclusive designer labels and she had several ounces of gold hanging around her neck. The gold Rolex was new, and he didn't recognize the small pearl earrings. It seemed that every time he saw his sister these days she had something new, either clothes or jewellery. She wore her wealth like a badge of office. With pride.

She looked at Dugan's companions. 'Jeff,' she said, 'nice to see you. And you, Colin. Long time no see.'

They raised their glasses to her in unison.

'The lovely Mrs Ng,' said Bellamy. 'Where's your better half?'

'Speak of the devil,' said Burr. 'Here he comes now.'

A tall, well-built Chinese walked along the bar, confidently, like a male model on a catwalk, shoulders swaying slightly, one hand in the trouser pocket of his grey double-breasted suit, the other outstretched towards the girl. He was about forty years old, his hair short and trimmed around his ears, making his face seem even squarer than it was. He looked like a man who was used to wielding power, a man who expected to be obeyed.

He took Jill's hand and smiled, his thin lips pulling back into a smile that would have been cruel if the eyes hadn't been so warm as he looked at her. 'Sorry,' he said. 'He wouldn't let me go.' She tilted her chin up and kissed him on the cheek. Behind him were two men with hard eyes and unsmiling faces. They were never far from Simon Ng or his wife. Bodyguards. Ng looked past his wife at Dugan and nodded.

'Hello Pat,' he said.

'Simon,' he replied.

'And Mr Bellamy and Mr Burr. My favourite policemen. Can I buy you gentlemen a drink?'

The two cops beamed at him, and together drained their glasses. 'I'll have a brandy and Coke. A double,' said Bellamy.

'And I'll have a malt whisky,' said Burr. 'A treble.' It was a game they'd played many times with the triad leader.

A barman had followed Ng as he walked along the bar and was waiting patiently for him to order, ignoring several other thirsty customers. Ng ordered drinks for the two cops and a bottle of champagne and the barman moved off in double time. Ng had that effect on most people.

'What can I get you, Pat?'

Dugan lifted his half-filled glass. 'I'm OK, Simon, Thanks.' Ng looked at Petal, and then back to Dugan. 'I'm sorry,' said Dugan. 'This is Petal. Petal, this is my sister, Jill, and her husband, Simon.'

'Nice to meet you,' she said.

'If you'll excuse me, there's someone I have to see,' said Ng, and he walked over to the table where the blue-suited man was deep in conversation with the girl in the tight black dress. The man practically jumped to his feet and shook hands energetically with Ng, inviting him to sit with them.

'So how long have you known my little brother?' Jill asked Petal.

'Not so little,' interrupted Burr.

'I used to change his nappy, he'll always be my little brother,' said Jill.

'For God's sake, you were three years old at the time,' said Dugan, reddening. Ng was using the man's portable phone, talking and nodding. The girl was watching one of the television screens and pouting.

'Not long,' said Petal.

'Don't worry, he grows on you,' said Jill.

'Like mould,' said Bellamy, and Burr spluttered into his whisky.

Petal smiled at Jill. 'I know what you mean,' she said.

'What do you do, Petal?' asked Jill.

'I'm with the Bank of China. And you?'

'A lady of leisure,' she laughed. 'Bringing up an eight-year-old girl and looking after Simon.'

'You have an eight-year-old daughter?' said Petal, surprised.

'I married young.'

'Too young,' said Dugan.

'Pat didn't approve,' said Jill. 'Nor did our parents.'

'For different reasons,' said Dugan, sourly.

Dugan's objection had been that Simon Ng was a triad member. Their parents didn't want the marriage to go ahead because Ng was Chinese. One of the crueller things they'd said was that they didn't want Chinese grandchildren. Subtle. Jill had gone ahead regardless and she hadn't seen them since. In a way she'd had the last laugh, for when Sophie had been born she'd taken most of her genes from her mother and had curly blonde hair and European features – only the soft brown eyes had come from her father. But it made no difference, because by then the damage had been done.

'Come on, Petal, come and sit down with me and I'll tell you a few things about my little brother,' said Jill, leading her to a table close to where Ng was sitting.

Dugan sighed deeply. It just wasn't turning out to be his night.

The Navy boys were getting frisky. Two of them were on their knees behind the bar forming periscopes with their arms and making sonar noises. Their pals thought it was hysterical, and the dancers were laughing too until one of the glasses of lager was knocked over. The mamasan went over and asked them to be quiet, and the barhags moved away. The boys behaved for all of ten minutes before the horseplay started again, a game of tag with the freckle-faced weapons officer as 'It'.

He ran around the fish tank, feinted to dash out through the entrance and then lurched back to the bar. His mates were hard on his heels as he ran around the bar and ducked into the changing-room, from where he emerged five seconds later chased by two semi-naked dancers, shrieking and hitting him with towels.

He cannoned into the giant with bulging forearms, spilling his drink down the front of his T-shirt. The man growled angrily, grabbed Freckle-face by the throat and banged him against the wall. Amy slid off her stool and moved behind Howells, just in time because the younger man brought up his knee into the giant's groin and pushed him backwards. All the girls started screaming as the giant fell against Howells and overbalanced the stool. They fell to the floor together, Howells underneath, and the weight of the big man winded him. The giant rolled off and went after the weapons officer while Amy helped Howells to his feet.

By the time Howells was up Freckle-face was back with his head being pounded against the wall, his eyes rolling and his neck limp. Two other youngsters were trying to pry the big man's fingers from around their friend's throat, but with little success.

'He's killing him,' gasped Amy.

She was right, Howells realized. There was manic gleam in the man's eyes, a combination of alcohol and bloodlust that by the look of it was only going to end one way. And if the boy was seriously hurt or even killed then the police would come, and that was the last thing he needed.

'Tom, you must stop them,' said Amy, as if she'd read his mind. He looked at her, frowning, and she took him by the arm. 'Mamasan not here, she go to other bar. She leave me in charge.'

Howells realized then that the Chinese heavies he'd seen on his earlier visit weren't there either.

'Please, Tom. I be in big trouble. Some of the dancers do not have visas. Please stop them now.' She practically pulled him off his stool.

Howells decided he'd help; partly because she was so insistent, but also because he could see that Freckle-face was going to get hurt and he knew that if the police did come they'd take names and addresses and ask for identification and he didn't want anyone to know where he was.

Freckle-face's breath was rasping now, his eyes beginning to glaze and spittle foaming on his lips. The big man was breathing heavily through his nose as Howells moved up behind him and slammed his cupped hands against his ears, hard enough to stun but not hard enough to burst his eardrums. He bellowed and released his grip immediately, turning to face Howells with murder in his eyes. Howells smiled, relishing as he always did the way time seemed to almost stop when he was in combat. He could see each drop of sweat on his opponent's forehead, the red tinge to the whites of his eyes, the throbbing veins in his arms. He saw him step forward as if in slow motion and reach out with splayed fingers.

Howells let him come, taking a step backwards and dropping down as he put most of his weight on his rear leg, ready to spring forward. His right hand was clenched and in the ready position on his hip, his left hand slightly crooked, fingertips pointing at the man's face. He was still smiling. Relaxed – Howells had long passed the stage where he tensed up during a fight. There was only one time for tension, and that was when you made contact.

He knew it was a lot easier to kill a man or cripple him than it was to stop him without causing too much damage, and from his cat stance he could put together fifty or sixty combinations of moves that would end the life of the big sailor as easily as stepping on a cockroach. Part of Howells wanted to do it, to bring the side of his palm crashing against the man's temple, to hammer his knee with the side of the foot and then slam his elbow into the man's throat and feel the cartilage splinter. But the rational part of him knew that now wasn't the time. Best bet would be the solar plexus, but he wouldn't risk his fist because too hard and he'd break the sternum. He let the man move until he was almost on top of him, then he went under the outstretched arms, still in his crouch, and threw his right hip forward and thrust his arm towards the centre of the man's chest, dead centre between the base of his ribs. The fist unclenched as his arm moved and when he hit it was with the palm of his hand and it was controlled, but even so the sailor moved back a full yard in small shuffling steps, bent double. He slumped sideways against the wall and then slid down it to the floor, conscious but totally unable to move, his arms clasped around his stomach. The bloodlust had gone from his eyes; now he just looked pained.

Howells gestured to the two young sailors who'd been trying to help their friend. 'Dump him in a cab, now,' he said. 'With any luck, by the time he's recovered he'll have forgotten where he was when it happened.'

The two of them had to strain to lift him, and they half carried, half dragged him out of the bar.

'Thanks mister,' said Freckle-face. 'Thanks a lot.'

He went back to the other side of the bar as Howells picked up his stool and sat on it. Amy stood close to him, and slipped her arms around his waist. 'Thank you,' she said looking up at him. 'Where you learn to fight like that?'

'I had a rough upbringing,' he said, but saw from the look on her face that she didn't understand.

'You looked so peaceful when you were fighting. What style do you fight?'

'No style,' Howells answered. He knew what she meant by peaceful. That's how he felt when he was fighting – at peace. With himself and with the world. Only one thing gave him more satisfaction, more contentment, than fighting. And that was killing.

There was a strong smell of burning as Dugan and Petal stepped out of the lift.

'Jesus Christ,' said Dugan.

'What's wrong?' said Petal. 'Is the building on fire?'

'No,' answered Dugan. 'Just one of the neighbours appeasing his ancestors. It's too much trouble to go outside so they use the stairwell.'

He took her to a wooden door and pushed it open. It led to a small landing where the occupants of his floor left their rubbish to be collected in a large plastic bin. Dusty concrete stairs zig-zagged down to the entrance hall far below. They were supposed to be for emergency use only but Dugan had trudged up and down several times when the lifts had failed. Where the stairs angled to the right at the floor below, an old lady in a blue flowery-patterned trouser suit bent over a chipped enamel bowl, inside which sheets of paper money burnt with a reddish flame. She looked up, startled, like a child caught shoplifting, then relaxed as she saw it wasn't a security guard. She shouted a greeting up to Dugan and he answered.

'Mrs Chan, she lives in the flat directly below me. She's a nice old lady, almost stone-deaf.'

'That must be useful if you want to play your stereo loud,' said Petal.

They left Mrs Chan to it. 'It's a strange place, Hong Kong,' said Dugan as he unlocked the door to his flat. 'Twenty-odd floors up in a modern tower block and a little old lady carries out a tradition that goes back thousands of years without a thought to the fire risk. The management sent around a letter a few days back specifically telling residents not to light fires and joss-sticks inside the buildings and pointing out that there were specific areas on the podium outside where they could do it. But does anyone take any notice? Do they hell. Sometimes I lie awake at night worrying what would happen if one of the flats below went up in flames. You know the ladders of the fire engines only go up eight floors? Any higher than that and you're on your own.'

'I think you worry too much, Pat,' said Petal, flopping down on to the settee.

'Yeah, maybe you're right. Coffee?'

'Please. I liked your sister,' she called after him as he went into the kitchen and switched on the electric kettle.

'Sorry?' he said, popping his head around the door.

'I said I liked Jill. And Simon. They seem a very happy couple.'

'They are. I was a bit worried at first when they married, but it's worked out really well.'

'Worried about what?'

'You know, Chinese guy and English girl. It can lead to problems.'

'It happens all the time,' said Petal.

'No it doesn't. Sure, lots of gweilos take Chinese wives, but not the other way around.'

'Sexist pig,' she laughed. 'Or do I mean racist pig?'

'You know what I mean. A pretty girl is a pretty girl, it doesn't matter where she's from. Wherever in the world she goes she'll be looked at as a pretty girl.'

'And?'

'And it doesn't work the other way. They look at the girl and wonder why she's with a Chinese. Then straight away they'll assume it's for money.'

'Who's they, Pat?' Petal asked in a soft voice. He could feel that he was forcing himself into a corner.

'You know, Petal. Everybody. And I'm not just talking about gweilos, the Chinese themselves are just as bad, just as racist. You know what the Chinese call the children of all mixed marriages.'

'Bastards,' said Petal.

'Bastards,' repeated Dugan. 'Neither one nor the other. And when they die, only the Chinese half goes to Heaven.'

'It's folklore, Pat, just that. Nobody means it any more.' The kettle began to whistle, and Dugan leapt at the opportunity to cut the conversation short. Jesus, second date and already he was arguing with her – over race, of all things.

He put his head around the door again. 'Milk and sugar?'

'Please,' she said. 'Three sugars.'

Dugan brought the coffee in and handed it to her in his Mickey Mouse mug.

'Careful,' he said, 'it's hot.' She took the mug from him.

'Jill invited us to Sophie's birthday party tomorrow evening, and on Sunday for a barbecue at their house,' she said, and sipped the hot liquid.

Just like Jill, thought Dugan, she'd already tagged Petal and him as an item. In a couple of days she'd have them up to the altar and married.

'House?' he said. 'More like a fortress.'

'What do you mean?'

Dugan looked at her through narrowed eyes. 'You do realize what my brother-in-law is?' he asked. He mentally kicked himself, because of course she didn't. He hadn't mentioned it, and Hot Gossip wasn't the right place to start talking about it, certainly not in front of Bellamy and Burr, anyway. He sat down on the couch next to her. 'He's a triad leader, a Dragon Head. Or to be more accurate, the son of a triad leader. One of the most powerful in Hong Kong, Ng Wai-sun, now living in quiet retirement on the Peak and waiting to join his ancestors. Ng Wai-sun has three sons, Simon, Charles and Thomas. Charles is into property development in Canada, legitimate by all accounts, Thomas is in San Francisco looking after the American end of the business, and Simon runs the show in Hong Kong.'

'But what exactly does he do?'

'The same as every other triad in Hong Kong – extortion, protection, illegal gambling, prostitution, drugs. Remember that smooth-looking character that he went up to talk to, Danny Lam?'

Petal nodded. 'The one who likes young girls?'

'That one. He works for Simon. Simon's not a good guy, Petal, don't be deceived by appearances. He's never done me any harm, not intentionally anyway, and he worships Jill and Sophie, but I trust him about as far as I can throw him.'

'What do you mean "intentionally"?'

'I mean he hasn't ever set out to hurt me. But because of him I'm stuck in a job I hate and I can't move.'

'Commercial Crime?'

'Yeah. I want action, Petal, I want to be where the

bullets fly, I want to be a real policeman and not a paper shuffler. But with a triad leader as a brother-in-law they're hardly likely to trust me, are they?'

'Is it that bad?'

'Yes, it's that bad. But what can I do? Jill loves him, she always has done, ever since they met almost ten years ago.'

'You were a cop when they married?'

'Yeah. Just out of my probation. Jill knew the damage that marrying him would do, hell, we talked about it often enough. She loves him, that's the end of it. And the end of my chance of getting involved in real policework. I only got told semi-officially last night, just before I met you. I'd always known it, but I'd always hoped that if I kept my nose clean I'd prove myself. But apparently that's not to be. I stay where I am, or I leave the force.'

'And you don't want to?'

'There's not much else I can do, Petal. Being a private detective looks glamorous on the TV, but real life is different. I suppose I could go and work for Simon.' He laughed bitterly, and Petal placed her mug on a side-table and put her hands on his shoulders. She put her face up close to his, close enough so he could feel her warm breath on his lips.

'I'm sorry, Patrick Dugan. Sorry that you aren't happier.'

She kissed him full on the lips, her small pointed tongue probing between his teeth. She moved against him and slowly straddled him, sitting in his lap and squeezing him with her thighs. Dugan groaned and closed his eyes.

112

Howells looked at his watch and tapped the steering wheel impatiently. There was no way he could have missed the Mercedes; he'd arrived at the crossroads well before seven o'clock and tucked the Mazda into a layby while he waited, but two hours later there was still no sign of Ng's car. Either the girl wasn't being taken to school today, or the driver kept changing routes.

He drove back to the side-road leading up to Ng's house but he couldn't see if the Mercedes was there or not. He couldn't risk hanging around because the guards would be sure to spot him, so instead he began to explore the surrounding area to get a feel of the roads.

He got back to the hotel early in the afternoon. He wolfed down a hamburger and chips in the coffee shop before walking over to the tourist area of Tsim Sha Tsui. He wanted a tape recorder and he found one quickly, a Sony about the size of a paperback book with a decent speaker. He didn't bother bargaining, but got the surly teenage assistant to throw in batteries and a C90 tape for the price. He paid in cash and went back to his room.

He spent the next forty-five minutes lying on his bed with the tape recorder switched on to record, the red light glaring at him accusingly as he read aloud listings from the Yellow Pages, a continuous monologue of names, addresses and telephone numbers. He kept varying the speed and tone of his delivery, but even so he was flagging towards the end of the tape and sighed with relief when it eventually clicked to a halt. He helped himself to a Coke from the minibar as the machine rewound the forty-five minutes' worth of verbal garbage.

For the first time in months Patrick Dugan overslept. Despite the searing sunshine, the clicking window-frame and the echoing lift doors, it was past 10.30 a.m. when he opened his eyes. He was alone, though Petal had left a note saying she'd call him about Sophie's birthday party and underneath it her signature flower.

He'd bought Sophie's present earlier in the week, a big floppy Old English Sheepdog toy with hair hanging over its eyes and a red bow tied behind one ear. He'd wrapped it as best he could and put it on the top shelf of his wardrobe, and after he had shaved and showered he put the parcel on his bed. A paw had come loose and was poking out but it looked kind of cute so he left it as it was. He thought of taking it into the office with him but knew that he'd get his leg pulled so he left it where it was. He'd come back and pick it up after work. Jill hadn't told him where Sophie's party was going to be, but he doubted if it would be at home. Simon Ng would want to be seen to be spending a great deal of money on his daughter and doing it at home would be interpreted as doing it on the cheap, as a massive loss of face. Ng would probably book a function room at one of the big hotels in Tsim Sha Tsui, so Dugan would be able to come back to Tai Koo Shing to change and then get the MTR over the harbour.

He got through most of the morning on autopilot. His headache had returned, with a vengeance. He'd swallowed a couple of aspirins but they hadn't made him feel any better. Maybe it was his eyes – sometimes headaches were a sign that you needed glasses. He closed his left eye and looked at the type-written sheet in front of him. He had no problem reading it. He tried it with his right eye closed and the left open, and he could still read it. He held the sheet at arm's length and squinted at it.

'What the hell are you doing?' It was Tomkins, standing in the doorway with a file under his arm.

'I'm trying to work out if I need glasses or not.'

'Headache again? It could be the airconditioning,' said Tomkins.

Dugan put the paper down on his cluttered desk. 'What do you mean?'

'I read an article somewhere that they put ions into the air, or take them out, or something. Or was that aerosols? What the fuck, who cares anyway. How are you getting on with the kite-flyer?'

'Uphill all the bloody way. I'm still no nearer finding where the money went. Why?'

Tomkins waved the file triumphantly. 'Lee Ling-ling is her name, isn't it?'

Dugan said yes, brow furrowed. 'You on to something?'

'There can't be too many Lee Ling-lings around. And I've just come across one who's a director of a futures trading company that appears to be trading without any clients.'

'Hardly surprising, considering the lack of interest in the futures market here. Hang Seng Index futures aren't actually flavour of the month, are they?'

'Yes, but this firm has been buying Standard and Poors

500 futures quite heavily, so much so that the authorities in New York asked us to take a look. And up crops little Ling-ling. Maybe that's where she's been putting her ill-gotten gains.'

'She's a greedy little cow if she has. If I'd been her I'd have salted it away in a Swiss bank account somewhere.'

'Yeah, well, not everyone is as careful with their money as you, are they?'

'Is that the file?'

Tomkins nodded. 'I need it though, so just photocopy anything you need.' He threw it on to Dugan's desk. 'Let me have it back when you've finished.'

He left the office, walking as he always did as if someone had grabbed him by the back of his belt and was jerking him up and down. His buttocks were clenched, as if he expected at any minute to be the victim of anal rape. Some of the guys called him God because he moved in such a mysterious way. Tomkins outranked Dugan, but they were the same age and had been in the force for the same length of time, so they tended to operate as equals unless Tomkins was in a particularly foul mood. Both men knew that if it wasn't for Dugan's brother-in-law their positions could easily have been reversed.

Dugan massaged his temples with his knuckles. Thinking of Lee Ling-ling reminded him of Petal and he cursed himself again for not getting her office number. The phone rang and he grabbed for it, hoping it was Petal but not too disappointed to find it was his sister. He got a small glow of satisfaction when she told him that Sophie's birthday party was being held at the Regent Hotel.

'Seven o'clock,' she said. 'And I should have told you before, it's a theme party.'

'And the theme?'

'Pirates,' she said.

'Yeah, that'd be right,' he said.

'Behave, brother of mine.'

'Or you'll have my legs broken?' said Dugan, laughing.

'Are your phones tapped?' she said. 'Because I'd hate anyone to hear what I'm about to say to you.'

'I'll see you tonight, you can say it to my face.'

'Be there or be square,' she said, and hung up.

Dugan had barely replaced the receiver before it rang again. It was Petal.

'I overslept,' said Dugan.

'You had a hectic night,' she laughed.

'You should have woken me up,' he said. 'When you left.'

'I didn't have the heart to disturb you. You sleep like a small boy. Anyway, I'm just calling to see what time we're going to Sophie's party.'

'That's a coincidence, I'm just this minute off the phone with my sister. It's at the Regent Hotel. How about I meet you there, just before seven – is that OK?'

'Fine. It should be great fun, the pirate theme is a terrific idea.'

'How did you know?'

'Jill told me last night. I'm really looking forward to it.'

Then she said she had to go and the line clicked off, almost in mid-conversation, as if someone had come near her and she didn't want to be overheard. Maybe they didn't like her making personal phone calls. He bent down over the files. The evening seemed an eternity away.

Howells looked at his watch. Half past six. There was nothing he could do now until the following morning. He had a good working knowledge of the roads in the New Territories and the scuba gear had been tested. He stood at the window and looked across the harbour to the office blocks of Central. There were still lights in many of the windows, and behind the business district towered the mountains of Hong Kong island, dotted with the houses of the rich.

Below the hotel, between the road and the bustling harbour, was a wide walkway that followed the water, dotted with courting couples and tourists taking the evening air. There were fishermen too, old men and teenagers, squatting by the water's edge and throwing in baited lines. He saw one youngster yank in his line and pull up a small, struggling fish. Behind him stood an old man with a walking stick, which he was waving in the air in wide circles as he shifted his weight from foot to foot. At first glance Howells thought that perhaps he was just a senile old man throwing a fit, but as he watched he began to tune in to his rhythm. The stick was being used to block and to strike, and the old man was constantly moving his centre of gravity but was always in a stable position. He flowed from one position to another, and Howells saw the stick strike at head height, then down low as if tripping an attacker, then the man slowly spun around and used the stick in a scythe-like motion. It wasn't a form of martial arts that Howells recognized, but he could sense the purpose of the movements and could differentiate the killing blows from the blocks. He began to mimic the man as he watched, pacing his breathing as he twisted and turned in time with the old master. It felt good.

The adrenalin began to flow as he exercised, and he knew that he wouldn't be able to stay confined in the room all evening. He decided to go for a walk and left the hotel to stroll along the main road, towards the Star Ferry terminal. The pavements were so densely packed that he was constantly jostled and banged. He hated to be touched; it was bad enough that his personal space was constantly being invaded, but physical contact really put him on edge. At the first pedestrian crossing he came to he went over to the other side of the road where there seemed to be fewer people. He walked past a huge shopping complex, the New World Shopping Centre, the air filled with rattling chimes as the warm wind blew through a high-tech chrome sculpture. Cars were turning off the main road to drive up to the Regent Hotel on his left and Howells stopped to let them go.

As the last car accelerated away he stepped into the road, and then a big Mercedes sounded its horn and turned the corner and he stood back on the pavement. His mouth dropped in surprise as he recognized Simon Ng sitting in the back seat, next to the little girl. He couldn't see who else was in the back seat but he was sure it would be Jill Ng. The Mercedes drove up to the hotel, followed by a dark blue saloon car. Howells briskly walked after them and arrived as Simon Ng was helping his daughter out of the car. She was dressed as a pirate and was chattering excitedly, this time without pigtails, her hair loose around her face. A striking blonde woman in expensive clothes waited until a doorman in a gleaming white uniform opened the door for her before stepping out of the car. Jill Ng. The passenger in the front seat was the heavily built man he'd seen last time he followed the Merc, but he'd forsaken the leather bomber jacket for a dark green suit and a black velvet bow tie. The occupants of the saloon car also got out, three of them, young men who looked as if they could handle themselves. Howells could see that they weren't carrying guns but he had no doubt that they'd have knives concealed under the expensive suits. Two of them walked into the hotel lobby and looked around as the little girl slipped her hand into Ng's and tried to pull him along. He waited until one of the bodyguards turned and nodded before allowing her to drag him inside. Jill Ng walked with him and they were followed in by the other two men with watchful eyes. One of them slipped the doorman a tip as the two cars drove off, and then looked at Howells as he too walked into the lobby. Howells knew they wouldn't regard him as a threat – they'd be on the lookout for rival triads, not a gweilo.

Howells' mind was racing. All his planning had been based on catching Ng alone, and he knew it would be foolish to risk an attack when Ng had so many bodyguards around. But he also knew how often in the past he'd been able to take advantage of luck, to deviate from a set strategy because an opportunity presented itself. The group walked across the lobby, heading for a large white marble staircase. Howells walked at an angle to them as if heading for a newspaper counter to the left of the reception desk.

He saw Jill Ng say something to her husband, who nodded and smiled and freed his hand from the small girl's and came back down the stairs, heading for where Howells stood flicking through the newspapers. The bodyguards stood on the stairs and watched as Ng walked across the lobby. Howells dropped his left hand slightly and clenched and unclenched his hand, controlling his breathing. *Yes or no?* his mind screamed. The lack of a weapon didn't worry him: a fist to the temple, or the side of the hand to the throat, or the neck, one blow would do it. He wanted to, God he wanted to, he could feel the blood-lust rising like a sexual urge. Why was Ng on his own, what was he doing? What were his bodyguards playing at?

Ng reached the counter and spoke to the girl in Chinese. She pointed to a bank of phones and smiled and as Ng thanked her Howells stepped back, his mind screaming *Yes! Yes! Now!* He began to move his arm and then over Ng's shoulder he saw two of the bodyguards coming up, concern on their faces; Howells relaxed, picked up a copy of the *South China Morning Post* and paid the girl for it.

Ng's bodyguards walked with him as he went over to the telephones. Howells took the paper and sat down on one of the large leather sofas where he had a view of the stairs and could also watch Ng make his call. Had the bodyguards simply slipped, or were they normally so careless? Maybe they were over-confident, or perhaps they'd relaxed once they'd checked that the lobby was clear. Either way, it was a good omen for what was to come. But God, how he would have loved to have done it there and then, to have taken Ng's life with his bare hands and then slipped away.

Ng finished his call and the three men went back up the stairs after Jill and the girl. Howells decided to stay put for a while. Over the next half an hour he saw a number of children dressed as pirates being escorted up the stairs by doting parents, and he realized that it must be a party of some sort. Perhaps it was Sophie Ng's birthday, which would explain why she hadn't gone to school. Another good omen for the following day. He decided not to push his luck and to go back to the Holiday Inn.

Five minutes after Howells left the lobby of the Regent Hotel, Dugan arrived. He felt a complete and utter prat. The only item of clothing he could find that resembled a pirate's stripy jumper was his rugby shirt, so he'd put that on along with the bottom of his black track suit and tucked the legs into an old pair of black cowboy boots. He'd ripped a piece of black card from a file in the office and back in his flat he'd cut it into the shape of an eye-patch and tied it around his head with string. Then he'd twisted a dishcloth around his head, but one look in the mirror showed him that he'd gone too far so he took it off. He was lucky, he'd caught a cab as soon as he stepped out of his tower block, but the driver kept giving him funny looks over his shoulder.

He stood by a pillar and wished that the ground would swallow him up. Under his arm was the badly wrapped parcel from which protruded a thick, furry paw. Dugan loved his niece with all his heart, but even so he was beginning to have second thoughts. There was a reception to mark the opening of a new range of Dickson Poon boutiques in progress in the main ballroom, and a constant procession of dinner-jacketed businessmen and their glamorous wives and girlfriends walked past and up the huge staircase; it seemed as if every one looked at Dugan and smiled. A couple laughed out loud and one Chinese girl in a tight gold-coloured dress pointed at him and shrieked as if she'd seen a murder.

He pressed closer to the pillar, but his brightly striped rugby shirt was not exactly conducive to camouflage. Every now and then parents arrived with little pirates in tow, but Dugan was dismayed to see that all the adults were wearing normal casual clothes. The children giggled and waved at him and the adults just giggled.

'Oh my God,' said a small voice to his left.

He turned to see Petal, eyes wide and unbelieving, her small hands flat against her cheeks. 'Oh my God, Patrick, is that you?'

Her whole body began to shake with laughter and she bent forward at the waist, overcome with the funniness of it. Dugan was even more embarrassed.

'I had sort of hoped that you'd be dressed as a pirate, too,' he said glumly.

Petal straightened up and there were tears streaming from her eyes. Her large, gold hooped earrings were swinging backwards and forwards as she laughed. She wiped the tears away with the backs of her hands, giggling and snuffling all the time, and fought to get herself under control but failed abysmally. She deteriorated into whoops of uncontrollable laughter, leant against the pillar for support and put her hands over her mouth, turning her head away from him and then looking back and creasing up again.

Under normal circumstances Dugan would have been knocked out by Petal's outfit, a white, slinky dress, demure at the front but cut deep behind so that it showed most of her shoulder blades and back. It made her hair seem even blacker than usual and it ended at her knees, emphasizing the curve of her legs and her petite feet. She looked absolutely beautiful, but she looked nothing like a pirate.

'Patrick, you look fantastic,' she said when the giggles had finally subsided.

'Jill said it was a pirate party,' said Dugan lamely.

She began laughing again, her eyes moistening and her cheeks going red. 'For the children, Patrick. For the children!' She leant back against the pillar, her shoulder next to his and hugged herself as she laughed. She looked down, caught sight of the paw sticking out of the badly wrapped parcel and went into fits of laughter again.

'I'm going,' said Dugan, but she grabbed him by the arm and pulled him back.

'Don't you dare,' she said and held him close, her head up, asking to be kissed. Dugan kissed her softly, full on the lips as she stood on tiptoe. It made him feel a lot better. 'Come on,' she said. 'Let's go and see Sophie.'

They began to walk through the reception area when she suddenly stopped. She removed one of her gold earrings and helped Dugan attach it to his ear. She stepped back to admire her handiwork and with a straight face said it looked perfect, then she linked her arm through his and together they walked to the function room where the party was, guided by signs bearing a skull and crossbones with the words 'Sophie's Boarding Party' underneath.

Jill and Simon were standing at the double doors to greet the guests and Dugan saw with a heavy heart that they had also forsaken the pirate theme. Simon was wearing well-fitting slacks and a Dunhill shirt and Jill had on one of her favourite Chanel dresses and several ounces of gold jewellery.

'Don't say anything,' he growled. 'Just don't say anything.'

Sophie was standing with a group of friends by a large table laden with food set into a mock-up of a pirate ship. She beamed when she caught sight of him.

'Uncle Patrick!' she screamed and came running over, her blonde hair streaming behind her. He picked her up with his free arm and hugged her. She put her arms around his neck and squeezed the breath from him. 'Wow,' she said. 'You look great! Come and see my friends.'

She wriggled out of his grip and slid down his body. She was wearing a red and white silk shirt and black baggy trousers and she had a pink plastic sword thrust into a black leather belt with a big silver buckle. Around her neck was a diamond and gold necklace he hadn't seen before.

She saw him looking at it and fingered it. 'It's a birthday present from Daddy,' she said. 'Isn't it nice?'

'It's beautiful,' he said. It must have cost a thousand times more than his dog. He held his parcel out to her. She grabbed it and ripped off the paper and gasped as she saw the toy.

'Oh, Uncle Patrick, it's lovely.' She hugged it, rubbed her face against the fur and then held it at arm's length to look at it. 'It's so cute, it's my absolutely best present. Thank you.'

Dugan felt better and he allowed her to take his hand and pull him over to her friends.

'I'll stay with the adults,' Petal called after him.

Dugan eventually managed to untangle himself from

125

the mass of young pirates and made his way over to Jill, brandishing a plastic cutlass. She laughed and handed him a glass of lager. 'Thirsty work, being a pirate?' she said.

Dugan drank deeply and grinned. 'This is more fun than I thought it would be,' he said. There was a line of foam along his moustache and Jill reached across and wiped it away with a napkin.

The parents, mainly Chinese but with a sprinkling of Europeans, were standing by the impressive buffet while waiters hovered with trays of drinks, and the children were being entertained by a conjuror who kept producing green and yellow budgies from his clothing. He was dressed as a pirate, as had been the juggler who'd made the children gasp with his sword-juggling and rapier-swallowing. On a table next to the double doors was a display of small wooden chests each containing a parchment treasure map and a gold sovereign, going-home presents for the children.

'Did you arrange all this?' asked Dugan.

Jill shook her head. 'No, Simon found a designer to do it, some sort of professional party planner. You give him the theme you want and he does the rest. Do you fancy something special for your next birthday?'

'Don't even think about it. Where's Petal?'

She pointed over to the buffet. 'There, with Simon. Pat, she's delightful. Were did you find her?'

He shrugged. 'I guess she sort of found me. She is beautiful, isn't she?'

'She's lovely, but she's so sweet as well. She seems so interested in everything and everybody, she's completely different from the bimbos you normally go out with.'

'Thanks, kid.'

'You know what I mean. You've been out with some fantastic-looking girls but their IQs are rarely above room temperature. Petal is very sharp, but so gentle with it. Simon is quite taken with her.'

They stood and watched Petal talking to the triad leader, hanging on his every word as she held her glass with both hands. Dugan fingered his earring. 'She is different, isn't she?' he said quietly. 'To be honest, I can't understand why she does go out with me.'

Jill sighed with exasperation. 'For God's sake, stop being so hard on yourself! All I ever hear you do is complain about how you're getting old and how you're stuck in a rut. Petal thinks the world of you. All the time she was talking to us she kept looking at you and smiling, but you were so busy playing at being the pirate leader that you didn't notice. You should take a good look at yourself, brother of mine. You're tall, goodlooking, and you're a hell of a lot more fun than those deadhead cops you hang out with. All you need is a woman to show you how to make more of what you've got and to get you off junk food.' She looked him up and down coolly. 'And, it has to be said, your dress sense is a little suspect.'

They laughed together and Petal turned and waved to Dugan. She said something to Simon and they came over together. Petal linked her arm through Dugan's and kissed him on the cheek, then leant up, put her mouth close to his ear and whispered, 'Shall we go?'

'Sure,' he said, and he made to go but she pulled him back.

'Promise me one thing,' she said.

'What?'

'That you'll wear your eye-patch tonight,' she giggled. 'It looks really sinister.'

Dugan was suddenly overcome with affection for her and he held her close, resting his chin on top of her head as Jill and Simon looked on. 'We're going,' he said.

'Thanks for coming,' said Simon. 'And for getting into the spirit of it.'

They said their goodbyes and left, and as they walked out of the hotel Dugan didn't care about the looks or the giggles. He was with the prettiest girl in the world and that was all that mattered.

In the taxi Petal leant against him and sighed. 'I saw a different side to you tonight, Patrick Dugan,' she said softly. 'I didn't realize you liked children so much. They adored you.'

Dugan put his arm around her and kissed her forehead. He wanted to tell her that he adored her, but somehow he didn't think it would sound right coming from a man dressed as a buccaneer so he decided he'd save it until later.

The following morning the Mercedes arrived at the crossroads and with a sense of relief Howells slipped in behind it. He could see the uniformed chauffeur, the heavily built bodyguard in the front passenger seat, the girl in the back seat.

Five minutes later the car pulled up in front of a four-storey white-painted stone building surrounded by a tarmac playground. The girl opened the door herself and slipped off the seat, pulling a brown leather satchel after her. She slammed the door shut and ran over to a group of girls in white uniforms and blue belts without even a backward glance. Ng's daughter walked into the building chattering with her friends and the men in the Mercedes watched her until she was out of sight before driving off.

There was a large wooden sign fixed to the railings at the entrance to the playground and Howells noted down the name of the school, its headmistress and the telephone number.

He drove back to the Holiday Inn and ate eggs and bacon in the coffee shop before going up to his room. He sat on the bed with the phone, and placed two pieces of paper in front of him; one bore the name and number of the girl's school, the other the number of Ng's home. In between them he put Holt's warrant card.

He went to the wardrobe and took out his one suit. It was still a little rumpled after the trip from Bali, and he was surprised at how well it still fitted, considering the amount of weight he'd lost. He wore it with a light blue shirt and a navy blue tie with a yellow crest on it, and with his short hair and cold eyes he knew he'd have no trouble passing for a cop. He combed his hair in the bathroom and checked himself over again.

He had his wallet and he had the car keys. Everything else was on the junk. He sat down on the bed again and dialled the first number, the school. He asked the switchboard girl for the headmistress and was put through to her secretary. He told her he was Chief Inspector Caine and that he had to speak to the headmistress immediately.

He was put on hold and then a crisp female voice came on the line.

'Good morning, Chief Inspector. How can I help you?'

Howells spoke slowly and with a voice deeper than normal, phrasing each word carefully and precisely. 'Good morning, Miss Quinlan. I am sorry to bother you but I am calling in connection with one of your pupils, Sophie Ng.'

'Yes, she is one of my pupils. Is she in some sort of trouble?'

'No, no, she isn't in trouble, Miss Quinlan. But I am afraid there has been an accident involving her parents, a car crash.'

'Oh my Lord, no,' said the headmistress. 'Is it serious?'

'Yes, I am rather afraid that it is. They are both in intensive care and we are in the process of contacting the members of the family. Mr Ng's father is on the way to the hospital now. My reason for ringing you is to let you know that we have been asked to get Sophie to the hospital as quickly as possible. One of my men, an Inspector Holt, has already left and he should be with you shortly. Could you please arrange to have Sophie ready?'

'Of course, of course,' she said. 'Oh dear Lord. The poor girl.'

'And Miss Quinlan?'

'Yes, Chief Inspector?'

'I'd be grateful if you said as little as possible to the girl at this stage. It would be best not to upset her. Better to allow her grandfather to explain.'

'I quite understand.'

'Thank you for your help. Inspector Holt should be there soon. Goodbye.'

Howells replaced the receiver then immediately picked it up again and dialled Ng's home. It rang three times and then a guttural Chinese voice answered.

'*Wei. Wan binwai?*'

'Mary had a little lamb, its fleece as white as snow,' said Howells.

'*Wan binwai?*'

'And everywhere that Mary went, the lamb was sure to go.'

'*Neih daapcho sin la,*' said the voice and hung up. Howells switched the tape recorder on to play and left the receiver next to the speaker. On the way out he put the Do Not Disturb sign on the door handle. Miss Quinlan probably wouldn't bother to call the house to check, and if she did she'd find the phone engaged. Hardly surprising, what with the accident and all. And if the hotel switchboard should listen in to the call she'd just hear a crazy gweilo dictating a list of names and addresses. He retrieved his car from the hotel car park and drove to the school.

Miss Quinlan looked pretty much as Howells had expected from her voice: prim and proper, greying hair and horn-rimmed spectacles. Her features were sharp and pointed and she had a slight moustache of straggly black hairs. Howells didn't have to look to know that there wasn't a wedding ring on her finger. Miss Quinlan was the sort of woman who preferred to be married to her work and God help any of her little charges if they ever let her down. Howells didn't know if corporal punishment was allowed in Hong Kong, but he was sure that Miss Quinlan would be more than happy to administer a few strokes of the cane across bare buttocks.

'Inspector Holt,' he said, and offered his hand. She took it and shook it firmly. He could feel the bones under papery skin.

'I've been expecting you,' she said. 'Sophie is next door with my secretary.'

She walked back behind her large oak desk, seeking the reassurance it offered, something to hide behind. It was a masculine desk and on it there were no feminine touches to indicate that it was used by a woman. There was a brown leather-bound diary, a heavy crystal paperweight, a brass paperknife and two paper-filled wire trays, a black telephone and a grey plastic intercom. No flowers, no family photographs.

'Is there anything I can do?' she asked, tilting her head down so that she could look at him over the top of her glasses.

'No, everything is being looked after,' said Howells. 'The important thing now is to get Sophie to the hospital.'

The headmistress nodded. She pressed a button on the intercom and bobbed her head down like a pecking bird to talk into it. 'Can you bring Sophie Ng in, please.'

There was a double knock on the door and it opened to reveal a young Chinese girl in a charcoal-grey suit who was holding the hand of the little blonde schoolgirl. Miss Quinlan came out from behind her desk and smiled at the girl.

'Sophie,' she said, 'this gentleman is Inspector Holt. He's a policeman. He's come to take you to see your grandfather.'

The girl's eyes widened. 'Is something wrong?' she said.

Miss Quinlan turned to look at Howells and he knew she was going to suggest they tell the girl there and then so he quickly shook his head.

'No, everything is all right,' he said, reaching forward and patting her on the head.

The headmistress followed his example and nodded reassuringly. 'Your grandfather will explain,' she said.

The girl still looked worried, so Howells took her hand and led her to the door. He stepped to one side to let her through first, and as he did so he mouthed 'thank you' to the headmistress.

As the door closed behind them Miss Quinlan sat down and picked up the telephone. She tapped out the number of the Ng house, but it was still engaged.

Howells took Sophie to the car and made sure she'd fastened her seat belt before starting the engine.

'Where are we going?' she asked.

'To see your grandfather,' he replied.

'Why?' She was polite but insistent, her head tilted side-on, resting against the back of the car seat as she watched him and waited for an answer.

'He wants to see you.'

'Why couldn't Daddy or Mummy come?'

'They're busy,' he said.

'There's nothing wrong, is there?'

'No, of course not. Look, your grandfather will explain everything.'

'But why did they send you to get me?'

'What do you mean, Sophie?'

'You're a policeman.'

'Yes. You know I am. Miss Quinlan told you so.'

'So why did they have to send a policeman to get me?'

'Because it was quicker to send me.'

'Why don't you have a uniform?'

'I'm a plain clothes policeman,' he said. 'Not all policemen wear uniforms.'

She thought about that for a while, then she spoke to him in rapid Cantonese.

Howells grinned. 'And not all policemen speak Cantonese, Sophie,' he said.

'I thought they did,' she said. 'And this isn't a police car.'

Howells hadn't banked on this, interrogation from an eight-year-old girl. They were still driving through crowded city centre streets so there was no way he could use force to shut her up. He'd just have to keep talking until they were on their own.

'Where are we going?' Sophie asked, running her fingers along the dashboard and checking them for dust, the way she'd seen her mother do after the amahs had finished cleaning. 'To a police station?'

'No,' said Howells softly, 'to a boat. Your grandfather is waiting for you there.'

'Daddy's boat, you mean?'

'No, another one.'

There was less traffic about now; the nearest car was about a hundred yards behind.

'What sort of boat is it?'

'A junk. Like one of the old-fashioned ones.'

'How big is it?'

'I don't know. Thirty feet or so, I suppose.'

'Ha! My daddy's boat is forty-five feet long. It's an ocean-going cruiser.' She was obviously pleased by this show of one-upmanship and sat back in her seat, arms folded across her chest with a 'so there' look on her face. At least it stopped the torrent of questions.

'Mrs Ng?' Jill would never, ever, get used to the surname. The sound had no real equivalent in English, a sort of nasal grunt that Westerners just couldn't cope with. On the occasions she'd been to America or back home to Britain she'd switched to her maiden name when Simon hadn't been around. It solved a lot of problems.

'Mrs Ng?' repeated the amah.

'Yes, Rose, what is it?' Rose was one of two Filipina maids who lived in the house, cooking and cleaning and looking after Sophie.

'The phone isn't working. There is somebody talking on the line.'

'A crossed line?' said Jill. 'Leave it for a while, Rose, it might sort itself out.'

'Yes, Mrs Ng. Do you have the shopping list for me?'

'It's in the kitchen, Rose. On the table. Is Manny back with the car yet?'

'Yes,' said Rose.

'You might as well go with him, then. And can you buy some more gin, please.' Rose nodded and left Jill alone in the lounge, curled up on the white leather sofa with the *Hong Kong Standard*.

In Howells' bedroom in the Holiday Inn the tape

reached the end and the recorder automatically clicked off.

After a few minutes the switchboard girl came on the line. 'Excuse me, Mr Donaldson, are you still using the phone?' she asked. There was no reply, yet the receiver was definitely off the hook. Probably didn't want to be disturbed, the girl thought. Strange that it was still connected to an outside line, though. She disconnected it without a second thought.

Howells stopped the car and walked round to open the door for the girl. There was one road that led from the Clearwater Bay Road to Hebe Haven pier. It ended at a row of metal bollards so that cars couldn't drive on to the pier, but just before were parking bays. His was the only car there. Sophie ran through the bollards, past a long-abandoned canoe that seemed long enough to seat twenty people in single file, propped against a wall.

'Where is it?' she asked, squinting out across the shimmering blue sea at the forest of yacht masts. 'There are so many.'

'Over there.' Howells pointed to the left of the pier.

'Is that it, the wooden one?'

'Yes,' said Howells, 'that's it. Come on.'

'It's small,' she said. 'Where is Grandfather?'

'He's there. Maybe he's down below.'

Sophie cupped her hands round her mouth and yelled at the top of her voice. 'Grandfather . . . we're here.' Then she called again in Cantonese, her shrill child's voice echoing around the beach.

'Sophie, no,' said Howells, and grabbed her by the shoulder tightly.

'Ouch,' she squealed, 'you're hurting me. Let go.'

'I'm sorry,' he said. 'But you mustn't shout.'

'But I wanted to let Grandfather know we'd arrived.'

She was quiet now, and there was suspicion in her eyes, the mistrust of a hurt child. An old, balding man was sitting on the edge of the pier on a bleached wooden stool, threading earthworms on to a hook. By his side was a small wooden birdcage and as he impaled the worms he was talking to a small brown bird with a bright red beak.

Howells smiled at the girl. 'Come on,' he said, 'that's our dinghy there.'

He pointed to the jetty nearest the pier, where the little boat bobbed up and down where he'd left it. She looked as if she was going to argue so Howells forced a beaming smile and held her tightly by the hand. He took her back down the pier and along the shore, through a boatyard where large gleaming white cruisers lay cheek by jowl with battered old fishing boats that had seen better days. He let her go first along the wooden planks. From a distance they looked spindly and positively unsafe, a ragbag collection of pieces of wood that had been haphazardly nailed together, but close up he could see that the wood was sound and the nails unrusted, and there was very little give as they walked along.

They reached the dinghy and Howells lifted her in. As he pushed it away from the jetty his arm slipped into the water and his jacket sleeve was soaked. Sophie laughed at his comfort, her fear forgotten, for a moment at least.

He tilted the outboard motor into the surf and tugged at the starter until it kicked into life. Sophie sat at the prow, head over the edge, and trailed her hand in the water as Howells guided the boat towards the junk.

When they got close he cut the engine. He tied the boat up and held it steady while Sophie made her way up the wooden ladder, and quickly followed as she ran down the deck shouting for her grandfather. She went down below, past the galley, through the main cabin and into the bedroom, where Howells caught up with her. She turned round and ran into him, then stepped back, a look of panic on her face.

'Where is he? Where is my grandfather?' she screamed, tears brimming in her eyes.

Howells pressed his forefinger against his lips. 'Shh,' he said softly. 'There's nothing to cry about.'

Sophie began sobbing and backed away from Howells until she was up against the bed.

'Who are you?' she said haltingly between sobs. 'What are you going to do?'

'You have to stay with me for a while,' he said. 'Not for long, but you have to stay on the boat.'

He stepped forward and stroked the top of her head. Sophie flinched. She was suddenly furious with herself. Her mother had told her time and time again never to go with strangers, and once a policeman had come to the school and given a talk about what to do if someone tried to make you go with them. There were bad men who wanted to hurt children, he had said, but he'd never said why or what it was that they did. Neither had her mother. They'd never said why, only that she was never to trust strangers – but Miss

138

Quinlan had said it was all right. Sophie began to shake uncontrollably.

She couldn't look up at Howells; she didn't want to see his face. In a quiet, trembling voice she said: 'Please don't hurt me.'

Howells smiled down at her and ran his hand down her soft, blonde hair to the nape of her neck. 'Don't be silly,' he soothed. 'I'm not going to hurt you.'

The phone rang out, the sudden noise surprising Jill. She uncurled her legs and padded over the parquet floor to the black wooden sideboard. So much for the phone not working, she thought, lifting the receiver. God save me from stupid amahs. It was Simon, inviting her out to lunch at the Excelsior Hotel, and she accepted eagerly. It'd give her the chance to take the new Porsche out for a run; at this time of the day there wouldn't be much traffic using the cross-harbour tunnel.

She changed quickly, choosing clothes that she knew he'd like, and three-quarters of an hour later she was in the Grill Room. Simon was already seated at the corner table and halfway through his Perrier water when Jill arrived, slightly out of breath, with the head waiter in tow.

He stood and kissed her on the cheek. 'You look fabulous,' he said in Cantonese.

'You flatterer,' she replied, also in Cantonese. 'You are twice a liar. I look a mess and you have been waiting for some time. But thank you for lying so beautifully.'

The waiter raised his eyebrows, impressed with her fluency, and held the chair for her as she sat down.

'Can I get you a drink?' he said, in English.

'Campari and soda,' she said, her eyes on her husband. For the millionth time she marvelled at how good-looking he was. There really wasn't anything she didn't like about him physically. His hair was thick and black and his eyes a deep brown, his teeth strong and white, his shoulders broad and his skin the same light brown colour as a cocker spaniel her parents had owned in her childhood. His hands were squarish and strong; she could always feel their suppressed strength when he touched her, yet he'd never once hurt her, physically or mentally. He was immaculately dressed as usual, a black light-weight wool suit with a faint grey pinstripe running through it and a white shirt with his Hong Kong Club tie. His shoes were shining and she knew he'd gone to his regular shoe-shine boy, a wrinkled old man whose patch was in an alley near the Mandarin Hotel.

She'd learnt a lot from living with Simon Ng, not the least being the way her dress sense had improved. There was no doubt that was partly because as his wife she had a hell of a lot more money at her fingertips and several gold credit cards and charge accounts, but it was also as a result of going shopping with him. He had a good eye for design, always insisted on buying the best, and he knew what suited Jill. It had been hard for her to admit at first, but after a while she came to realize that on the occasions she met people when she was wearing an outfit he'd chosen the compliments came thick and fast. When she dressed in clothes she herself had chosen nothing was said. Under his guidance she'd gradually changed her

whole wardrobe, and now it consisted mainly of the sort
of names she'd only read about in the fashion magazines
before she got married – Chanel, Kenzo, Charles Jourdan.
She'd also acquired his love of expensive accessories. She
had more than a dozen watches and three times as many
rings, though she wore only one chain around her neck,
a think strand of seamless gold that he'd given her when
Sophie was born.

Today she was wearing a beige silk two-piece suit that
stopped just below her knee; she carried a small matching
Gucci bag and had her hair tied back with a small black
bow, the way he liked it. She enjoyed dressing up for
him. She was even wearing the white suspenders he
liked, though he wouldn't see them. Until later. Her
drink arrived and Simon raised his glass to her, the way
he always did.

'To the prettiest girl in Hong Kong,' he said.

She snorted. 'I wish,' she said. 'I'm way past the age
when I can be called a girl.'

'You'll have to excuse my lousy English,' he joked.
A waiter handed them menus. 'What would you like?'
Simon asked.

'You choose,' she said. 'You know what I like.'

He ordered for her and waited until the waiter had left
before speaking.

'I have to go to Beijing next week,' he said.

'Again? You were there last week.'

He shrugged. 'Business,' he said. 'You know how it
is.'

She knew. Jill knew all too well the business he was
in, she'd known about his triad activities long before
she married him. She'd known of them and she'd

accepted them. She loved the man and so turned a blind eye to the comings and goings at their home, to her husband's frequent absences, the late-night phone calls, the ever-present bodyguards. The papers were filled with stories about triad killings, drug seizures, raids on under-age brothels, the bread and butter of the criminal empires, but even though she knew Simon was head of one of the most successful triads she didn't believe that he was personally involved in the violence. He was always so gentle and considerate with her, and when she watched him with Sophie her heart ached.

She reached over and stroked his hand on the table. 'Must you go?'

He nodded.

'Why Beijing?' she asked. 'Surely there's no business to be done there, not now.'

He pulled his hand away and there was a coldness in his eyes. 'It's business, Jill. Just leave it at that.'

It was always this way, Jill thought. He gave her everything she could want, he protected her and took care of her and he loved her, but there was a part of him that would be always unattainable and sometimes that frightened her. Her link with Simon Ng went back less than a decade, but the Ng family had ruled the triad for centuries. Jill often wondered what would happen if she pushed him to make a choice – her or the triad? She'd never put it to the test, because in her heart of hearts she knew which he would choose – and she could not bear to lose him.

She smiled and stroked his cheek. 'I just miss you so much when you're away,' she said, 'that's all.'

He took her hand and raised it to his lips, kissing

it softly. His eyes warmed and he squeezed her. 'I won't be long. And I'll bring you back a present,' he said.

The room was just as he'd left it when Howells returned. He replaced the receiver and put the tape recorder in the drawer of the bedside table. He stripped off his clothes, dropped them on to the bed and walked naked to the shower.

Later, as he sat on the bed wrapped in one of the hotel's thick white bathrobes, he dialled the number of Ng's house. It was answered on the third ring and a female Filipina voice recited the number in a sing-song voice. Howells asked to speak to Simon Ng and was told he wasn't at home.

'Is Mrs Ng there?' asked Howells.

Again he was told no. When would they be back? She didn't know. Howells hung up and lay back on the bed, fingers intertwined behind his neck, legs crossed at the ankles.

He waited a full two hours before calling the Ng house again. The Filipina girl answered again, and this time she said that yes, Mrs Ng was at home. She asked who was calling and he said Inspector Holt. He waited while the amah relayed the message to her mistress and handed her the receiver.

'Nick,' she said. 'How are you feeling?'

Howells was caught off guard. The last thing he'd expected was for the woman to know the copper he'd taken the ID from. He sat bolt upright on the bed, his mouth open and his mind racing.

'Nick, are you there?'

Part of Howells wanted to slam the phone down while he got his act together, but he realized that wouldn't solve anything, he'd only have to call back. All that mattered was that he spoke to Simon Ng; it didn't matter who he said he was or whether or not the stupid cow knew the copper or not.

'I'm sorry, Mrs Ng, I think you've got the wrong person. I'm trying to get hold of your husband.'

'He's not here at the moment. Didn't you say your name was Holt? Inspector Holt?'

'When will he be back?'

'I really can't say. Look, who is calling?'

'It is important that I get in touch with him, Mrs Ng. Does he have a mobile phone or a pager, or do you know where he is?'

'Is something wrong?'

Everything was going wrong, thought Howells. She was suspicious, Simon Ng wasn't there and in all probability she'd be on the phone to the real Inspector Holt as soon as he was off the line.

'No, nothing is wrong. But this is urgent, Mrs Ng.'

'Well, if you leave your number I'll ask him to phone you when he gets in.'

'Actually, I'm just about to leave the office – better I call him. What time do you think he'll be back?'

'I don't know,' snapped Jill, and she slammed the receiver down.

All Howells heard was the click of the line going dead; he had no idea of the venom with which the woman had cut short the conversation or the way she cursed him afterwards, but he knew that she hadn't been fooled.

Dugan winced as his phone rang. It was Petal. She wanted to see a movie and was Dugan free? Of course, he said, and they arranged to meet outside the cinema later on.

'How's your day?' he asked. That morning she had left without waking him, leaving only an indentation in the pillow and her signature flower.

'Busy,' she said. 'I've been tied up all day, that's why I'm so late calling you.'

'What is it you do for the Bank of China?'

'Marketing,' she said. 'Promoting their financial services. Nothing exciting. I'm sure my work isn't anywhere near as fun as yours. What case are you on today? That woman with the cheques?'

He was pleased and flattered that she took an interest in his work and that she'd bothered to remember what he was working on, but all the same he was aware that once again she'd given him the brush-off as soon as he'd asked about what she did. She'd done it pleasantly enough, but he still got the feeling that she was being evasive, that there was something she didn't want him to know.

'Yeah, but it's an uphill struggle.'

'Think of me and smile a bit,' she said. 'I'll see you tonight.'

After they'd said their goodbyes, Dugan sat with his head down over Lee Ling-ling's file and rubbed his forehead with the palms of his hands. His headache was worse. He drained his fifth paper cup of coffee and was just getting to his feet for another visit to the vending machine when his phone rang again.

'Pat?' It was his sister.

'Jill, how are you?'

'Fine,' she said. 'How about you?'

'Lousy headache, lousy job, and I think the aircon-ditioner in my bedroom is about to pack up. Nothing changes.'

'Pat,' she said, and Dugan could tell by the change in her tone that she was serious. 'Pat, do you know an Inspector Holt?'

'Only Nick, Nick with the wounded pride and the surgical collar.'

'No, I don't mean Nick. Another Inspector Holt. Is there anyone else on the force called Holt?'

'Not that I know of. Why?'

'I've just had a phone call from someone calling himself Holt, wanting to speak to Simon. He was very evasive when I asked him what he wanted.'

'Are you sure he said he was a cop?'

'He called himself Inspector Holt. But he wouldn't give me his phone number.'

'Let me check it out, I'll get back to you as soon as I can.' It wasn't like Jill to get upset at something like that. Dugan was the worrier of the family, and over the years since Jill had married Simon Ng she'd grown increasingly more confident, so much so that occasionally the confidence crossed over to arrogance.

'OK, Pat. Thanks. It'd put my mind at rest. It's probably nothing.'

As soon as she hung up Dugan called Personnel and

asked them to check their files. There was no Inspector Holt, other than Nick. He called the ICAC and they said they'd check and get back to him.

Jill Ng was sitting on her white leather sofa with the phone next to her, and even though she was waiting for her brother to call her she still jumped when it rang.

'Pat?' she said. It wasn't, it was Miss Quinlan, the headmistress of Sophie's school.

'That's not Mrs Ng, is it?' asked the old woman, obviously confused.

'Of course,' said Jill, equally surprised. 'Who did you expect?'

The headmistress stuttered and stumbled for words and for a fleeting moment Jill wondered if she'd been drinking.

'To be honest, Mrs Ng, I'd heard that you and your husband had been involved in an accident. I was calling to see if there was anything I could do. I am rather surprised to find you at home. Inspector Holt said you were in the hospital.'

Jill's heart froze at the name. She gripped the phone tightly. 'Inspector Holt?' she said. 'He called you?'

'No, Mrs Ng. He came round. To pick up Sophie.'

Jill sagged back into the leather sofa, her mouth opening and closing soundlessly.

The headmistress realized that something was badly wrong. Her voice began to tremble. 'He showed me his identification, he was definitely a policeman, I know he was, I had no reason to . . .' Her voice tailed off.

Jill's voice was flat and emotionless when she spoke again. 'Why didn't you call me first, before you let him take my daughter?'

'Mrs Ng, I tried to call, but the phone was engaged. I did try.' The pleading whine annoyed Jill and she felt a red wave of anger.

'You're not fit to be in charge of children,' she hissed. 'You let a complete stranger take my child. Oh God, what have you done? What have you done, you old bitch?'

Miss Quinlan began to cry as she felt her world collapse around her. The sound of her tears made Jill hate the old woman even more, but she was so consumed with anger that words failed her. She quietly replaced the receiver, tears welling up in her eyes. She rose unsteadily to her feet and tottered over to a chrome and glass drinks trolley where, with shaking hands, she poured herself a tumbler full of brandy. She gulped it down, the alcohol making her eyes sting, and then refilled it.

She was finding it hard to breathe, as if there were steel bands around her chest and neck that were being slowly tightened. A thousand images of Sophie flashed through her mind: Sophie on Christmas Eve opening her presents, building sandcastles on the beach, riding piggy-back on Simon, playing pirates with Patrick.

She practically ran back to the phone and tapped out the number of her husband's portable phone, tears streaming from her eyes.

Simon Ng was standing stock-still with his arms out-stretched like a man crucified. Before him a small, portly old man with skin like an old chamois leather ran a tape measure around his waist.

'Same as always,' he nodded approvingly at his teenage assistant. He measured the length of the arms, the shoulders, and then he knelt down in front of Ng and ran the tape up his inside leg, calling out the measurements to the boy, who wrote them down in a small notebook.

They were in a poky room on the second floor of an ageing building in Tsim Sha Tsui, the walls lined with shelves piled with rolls of cloth. Ng was facing a large oak desk on which were stacks of cloth sample books and to his left was a tall, thin free-standing mirror in which he'd be able to examine the finished product. It took Mr Cheung five days to complete a made-to-measure suit, three days for favoured customers. Simon Ng had been taken to Mr Cheung by his father for his first suit the day before his fourteenth birthday. Mr Cheung never took longer than forty-eight hours with his order.

There were two men sitting on high-backed chairs, one by the door and one by the desk, solid-looking men with calloused hands and hard eyes, bodyguards who'd both been with him for many years. They held the rank of Red Pole in the triad, fighters who had proved their worth. Both had killed for Simon Ng.

The one by the door in a brown suit and wearing brown brogues that wouldn't have been out of place on the feet of a Scottish landowner was Ricky Lam, forty-eight years old but with not a single wrinkle on his face. Lam had served Ng's father for more than two decades and still paid regular visits to the old man on the Peak where they would relive old times over a pot of jasmine tea. In the inside pocket of his jacket he carried an ivory-handled stiletto and he had a throwing knife strapped to each arm. Lam could use all three with deadly accuracy, but he could just as easily kill with his bare hands and feet.

The man in the other chair was Lam's cousin, on his mother's side, a twenty-nine-year-old kung fu master called Franc Tse. If Ricky Lam represented the traditional triad way of life, then Franc Tse was positively New Wave. He wore pristine white Nike training shoes, skin-tight Levi jeans and an expensive dark brown Italian leather jacket, the sleeves pulled up almost to his elbows and the collar turned up. Whereas Lam's hair was in the traditional mainland 'pudding basin' style, Tse's was lightly permed and swept back off his forehead. Tucked into the back of his belt was a nunchakyu, two lengths of hard wood separated by a short piece of chain, a martial arts weapon derived from a rice flail. At night, when he couldn't sleep, Tse would stand in the middle of his room and practise using the flail with his eyes closed, enjoying the hard slap of the wood against his hands and hearing it whistle through the air. He was an expert with the spear, the long knife, the three-section staff and the throwing stars, but the nunchakyu was his favourite.

Both men were fiercely loyal to Simon Ng, and would have had no hesitation in giving up their lives for him, or for his family. Ng in turn trusted them completely. It was a relationship that went far beyond employer–employee, or master and servant; it was bound up with the oaths each had sworn to the triad, the triad that existed before them and would exist long after they were gone from the world. Each had sworn a blood oath to put the triad and its members before family, before friends, before life itself, and each knew they had a part to play in the triad. Lam's and Tse's role was to protect the Dragon Head, Simon Ng. And they would – to the death.

Ng had left his portable phone on the desk and he stepped around Mr Cheung to pick it up when it warbled. It was Jill.

'Simon?'

He wanted to chide her for asking the obvious, but he could tell from the tone that something was wrong. Badly wrong. He listened intently as she told him about the phone calls from the gweilo and the schoolteacher.

'Simon, what's happening?' she asked.

'I don't know,' he said. His mind was racing, his brow furrowed, and his two bodyguards fidgeted, picking up his nervousness. Even Mr Cheung walked over to his rolls of cloth and pretended to study them. His assistant stood at Ng's elbow openly listening, until Mr Cheung angrily waved him away with a flick of his tape measure.

'I'm coming home now, stay there until I get back,' he said. 'Don't ring anyone, don't talk to anyone. And don't answer the phone; if Sophie has been kidnapped it will be better if I speak to them. Do you understand?'

Jill didn't answer. All Ng could hear were her sobs.

'Jill,' he hissed. 'Do you understand?'

'Yes,' she said eventually.

Ng broke the connection and weighed the phone in the

palm of his hand as his men looked on anxiously. First things first – he had to limit the damage. He called the school and spoke to the headmistress, who was every bit as distraught as Jill. He calmly explained that there had been a misunderstanding, that the police had indeed been asked to collect Sophie from school, that it was Ng's grandfather who had been hurt in a car accident, and that Sophie was now back with the family at the hospital.

'It was all my fault, I'm afraid, Miss Quinlan,' said Ng. 'I went straight to the hospital and phoned a friend in the force asking them to fetch Sophie before I could get hold of my wife. She didn't know my father was in hospital and she seems to have panicked when you spoke to her. She feels very badly about the way she spoke to you, but I'm sure you understand how upset she was.'

The relief in her voice was obvious now that the old woman believed that her job and her pension and her conscience were safe, but Ng wasn't one hundred per cent sure that she was convinced by his story. With any luck she'd just let it lie and wouldn't contact the police.

Ng realized Lam and Tse were looking at him like dogs waiting to be thrown a bone. He nodded curtly. 'Let's go,' he said, picking up his jacket. 'Mr Cheung, I am afraid I must cut short the fitting.'

Mr Cheung slung his tape measure around his neck and cupped his hands together in front of his chest, bobbing his head backward and forward. 'Not at all, not at all, not at all,' he chanted, following on Ng's heels as the three triads left his shop.

Ng waited on the pavement, Lam watching his back as Tse stepped into the road and waved at the driver of their car. He was another old retainer, Hui Ying-chuen, who still insisted on wearing an old chauffeur's cap that Ng's father had given him thirty years ago. There was no need for Tse to wave; Hui wasn't the sort of driver to sit at the wheel reading a racing paper or to pop into a tea house to yam cha. He already had the Daimler in gear and glided to a halt so that the rear passenger door was exactly opposite Ng. Tse opened the door for Ng and then slid in beside him while Lam took the front seat, eyes ever watchful.

Hui drove quickly but smoothly, his liver-spotted and wrinkled hands light on the wheel and deft with the gear stick. The Daimler was the only one of Ng's five cars not to have automatic transmission, in deference to the old driver who'd never managed to get the hang of driving without a clutch. The four drove in silence, Hui because he never spoke unless spoken to, Tse and Lam because they knew that during periods of stress their boss often retreated into himself, deep in thought while he considered all his options.

The gates to the compound were already open as they arrived and Jill was at the front door of the house to greet them, her face stained with tears, her eyes red. She threw herself at her husband and hugged him hard. 'What are we going to do?' she wailed.

He put his hands on either side of her face and held her in front of him. Her lower lip was trembling and she tried to stop it by gently biting down. 'We're going to start by keeping calm,' he said evenly. 'We're not going to help Sophie by crying. Come with me.' He put his arm around her shaking shoulders and led her through the front door and into the lounge. One of the dogs, he couldn't remember its name, sniffed at Jill's legs in puzzlement and Ng glared at it until it backed away, its tail twitching

153

between its legs. He sat her down on the sofa and stood over her so that he had to raise her head up to see him. 'Tell me again what happened.'

She went through it, the phone call from the man calling himself Holt, and call to her brother, and then the one from the headmistress. He could smell alcohol on her breath.

'Has anyone called since you spoke to me?'

'The phone rang twice, but I did as you said and didn't answer it.'

'Good girl,' he said. 'Don't worry, it's going to be all right.' He tried to sound confident but it belied the cold dread in his heart and Jill knew it. 'Wait here, I have to speak to Franc and Ricky. Do you want another drink?'

She shook her head fiercely. Alcohol wasn't a crutch she needed when he was there.

Lam and Tse were standing in the hall, unwilling to intrude on the family's grief. They'd heard enough from the phone conversation in the tailor's shop to know what was going on but he quickly explained anyway.

'I need Double Flower White Paper Fan. And tell Elder Brother to be ready.' Ready for what, he didn't know. Lam and Tse scurried off.

Elder Brother wasn't related to Ng, it was slang for the triad's Hung Kwan official, the man who controlled the twelve fighting sections, almost 250 fighters in all, Red Poles like Lam and Tse. White Paper Fan meant adviser, and the prefix Double Flower identified Ng's most senior confidant, Cheng Yuk-lin. Cheng had been appointed White Paper Fan by Ng's father and Ng himself had promoted him to Double Flower soon after his father had retreated to the Peak and handed over the mantle of Lung Tau – Dragon Head.

Ng went into the kitchen and helped himself to a Coke from the fridge before joining Jill in the lounge. She was still wearing the silk suit, but the black bow had disappeared and her hair was a mess; yet she was still the most attractive woman he'd ever seen and he loved her passionately. She was looking straight ahead with blank eyes and at first he thought she was in shock until he realized she was looking at Sophie's photograph in the bookcase. He walked over and picked it up, a colour picture of her in her school uniform taken six months earlier. He handed the brass-framed portrait to her and she sat with it in her lap.

Neither of them knew what to say, how to put their grief into words. It had been a difficult birth eight years ago, one that had nearly killed Jill and which had left doctors in no doubt that Sophie would be an only child. To have her taken from them now was more than they could bear. Ng would pay, or do, anything to get her back. He sat down next to Jill and rested his head against her cheek.

'I'm sorry,' was all he could say, and then she started crying again, tears plopping down on to the glass covering the photograph. He reached for her but the phone rang, startling them both.

Ng picked it up. 'Yes?' he said, using English. Jill clasped the photograph to her chest.

'Simon?' said Dugan. Ng cursed inwardly but kept his voice pleasant.

'Pat, how are you?' He'd have checked up on Holt by now.

'Fine, is Jill there?'

'She's upstairs, can I take a message?'

'Er – I'd rather speak to her if she's there, Simon. She rang me earlier.'

Ng knew that if he tried to stop him he'd set alarm bells ringing so he placed his hand over the receiver and said quietly to his wife: 'It's your brother, you'll have to talk to him. Don't let him know there's anything wrong. Understand?'

She nodded and wiped her eyes on the back of one hand. Ng handed her the phone.

'Hiya, brother of mine,' she said. Her voice wavered slightly so she shook herself and sat bolt upright.

'Are you OK?' asked Dugan.

'Of course,' she said brightly. Ng could see the tears were about to start again.

'I'm ringing about that Holt thing. Just as I thought, there is only one Holt. I've checked all the departments and the ICAC.'

'Must be somebody fooling around,' said Jill. She closed her eyes tightly to hold back the tears.

'Maybe, and maybe not,' said Dugan. 'But it seems a bit more than coincidence that someone steals his warrant card and then you get a call from an imposter wanting to speak to Simon. Have you told him?'

'No, I mean yes.' Christ, she was getting confused. 'I just told him. He said it was probably a joke, one of his friends trying to fool him.'

'Simon doesn't have too many gweilo friends, does he?'

'No but, oh I don't know, Pat. I'm sure it's nothing worth bothering about. Thanks for checking but just drop it.'

'OK,' said Dugan. 'I'll see you Sunday then.'

'Sunday?' said Jill.

'Yeah, you invited Petal and me around for a barbecue. It's still on, isn't it?'

'Yes, yes of course. Look, Pat, I have to go. See you.'

She hung up and began sobbing again as she rocked backwards and forwards on the sofa. Ng sat down next to her and held her hands, waiting for the tears to subside. A discreet cough from the doorway made him look up. An old man stood there, dressed in the traditional Mao-style jacket and trousers made from black Chinese silk, plastic flip-flop sandals on his feet. His head was egg-shaped and totally bald, the eyebrows thin and stiffly arched, the eyes pale and watery, the lips bloodless and curling downwards. It was not a friendly face, it was a face that led to some of the younger and more irreverent triad members calling Cheng Yuk-lin 'The Vampire' behind his back. It was a face that had barely changed over the thirty years or so that Simon Ng had known it; there was nothing left to age, no more hair to lose, no smooth skin left to be wrinkled. The only step left in the ageing process for the triad's trusted Double Flower White Paper Fan was death.

'Cheng Bak-bak, thank you for coming,' said Ng, getting to his feet and walking over to greet him. The old man nodded slowly and gravely and Ng knew that he'd already been told about Sophie. Only in private did he call his adviser Bak-bak, or uncle. It would give neither of them face to be so informal in front of other triad members, but there was a bond between them that went way beyond the normal relationship between a Dragon Head and a White Paper Fan. If Cheng hadn't loved Ng like a son he would have retired long ago and Ng had always been grateful for his guidance. Cheng had his own cottage on the opposite side of the compound, screened by a clump of palm trees; there he could tend his small garden and listen to his collection of songbirds in peace.

Ng took Cheng through the hall and into the book-lined study. It was an incongruity in the hi-tech house; old-fashioned, heavy English furniture that would have been more at home in a London club. There were framed hunting prints on the walls and a brass swan-necked lamp on the leather-topped walnut desk. The windows overlooked the gate and guardhouse where Ng could see Lam talking earnestly to the three men on duty. Locking the stable door after the horse had bolted, Ng thought ruefully. He sat on the captain's chair behind the desk and rested his elbows either side of the blotter as Cheng carefully lowered himself on to a generously upholstered Chesterfield.

'Would you care for tea, Bak-bak?'

'No thank you, Chao-huang.' Cheng was the only person, apart from his father, who called Ng by his Chinese name. 'Just tell me what happened.'

Ng went over it for the old man, and when he finished he realized how little information they had.

'Your wife is sure it was a gweilo?'

'Definitely. And he used the name Inspector Holt.'

'Then you realize this is not a brotherhood problem. It is either a simple matter of extortion, or something personal, an individual or organization trying to hurt you, almost certainly from outside Hong Kong. Locals would surely not bring in gweilos, not when help is so readily available from Taiwan or the mainland. I suggest you compile a list of all those non-Chinese who might want to cause you harm. And your fathers and brothers should do the same. Other than that there is nothing to do but wait until he calls again.'

'He might have done that already,' said Ng. 'I told Jill not to answer the phone and it rang before I returned home.'

The old man nodded, and as he did so the phone on the desk rang, giving them both a start. Ng grabbed for it and had the receiver to his ear before the echo of the first ring had faded.

'Yes?' he said. It was the gweilo.

'Simon Ng?'

'Yes.'

'Listen and listen well,' said Howells. Ng scrambled in his right-hand desk drawer for a writing tablet and took a pen from the crystal pen stand in front of him. He gestured towards the door and mouthed the word 'extension' and Cheng eased himself off the sofa and padded out. Before he'd crossed the hall Ng heard a click on the line and realized that Jill had picked it up. He hoped she'd be sensible enough to keep quiet.

'I have your daughter,' said Howells.

'I know,' said Ng.

'This is what you must do if you want her back. Do you have a pen?'

'Yes.' The monosyllabic answers were clipped and efficient. Ng was not a man to waste time.

'I want one million dollars from you. One million Hong Kong dollars. I want it by tomorrow morning, seven o'clock.'

Ng began to protest, trying to play for time, but Howells interrupted. 'Don't insult my intelligence, most of your businesses involve cash. I will call you at six o'clock tomorrow morning. If you do not have the money by then, she dies. Is that clear?'

'How do I know you have her?'

'How many ransom demands have you had today?'

'Then how do I know she is all right?'

'You don't. But if I do not have the money by seven o'clock I can guarantee that she will not be all right.' The connection went dead.

Ng joined Jill and Cheng in the lounge. She was drying her eyes with a white linen handkerchief. She blew her nose loudly. Rose came in and stood by the sofa, wringing her hands, knowing that something was wrong but not sure what it was.

'Sorry to bother you, Mrs Ng, but Manny wants to know if there is anything you want collecting from town when he goes to pick up Sophie,' she said.

'Tell Manny that Sophie won't need picking up today,' said Ng. 'She's going to a party with one of her schoolfriends straight from school. And could you fetch my wife a cup of tea, please.'

When the amah had left, Ng asked Cheng what he thought. The old man held his arms out at his sides, hands wide open, palms up.

'One million dollars is not a lot of money,' he said simply.

The thought had already occurred to Ng. Anyone who knew him would know that he would pay a lot more than that for his daughter's life. Why not two million? Or five? There were a hundred other families in Hong Kong that could just as easily be hit for a million bucks – why risk the wrath of a triad?

Unless it was personal. That was the only thing that made sense.

'What's wrong?' asked Jill. 'What do you mean, it's not a lot of money?'

'Mr Cheng means that we'll have no problems raising it,' said Ng, pacifying her. There was no sense in getting her even more agitated. In fact, he already had at least a million in the safe in their bedroom. Getting the money was the least of his problems.

'I will come back tomorrow morning,' said Cheng, taking his leave as Rose returned with Jill's tea. Ng took it off the tray and lifted it to his wife's lips and waited while she drank. She wiped her eyes again and sniffed.

'I'm sorry,' she said.

'What for?'

'For being so weak.'

'Don't be silly,' he said, hugging her and burying his face in her hair. 'It'll be all right, I promise I won't let anything happen to her.' He wished he felt as confident as he sounded.

'You seem miles away tonight,' said Petal.

Her voice jolted him out of his reverie and Dugan smiled. 'Just tired I guess,' he said. They were in a noisy, boisterous Taiwanese restaurant in Causeway Bay. The cinema had been packed, not a seat to be had, and they had decided to go and eat instead.

'You must be exhausted to daydream in a place like this,' she laughed.

It was true. The restaurant was packed to the red velvet-lined walls with Chinese families, never quiet eaters at the best of times. At the table nearest them were three squabbling children, one playing with a small electronic game that had an annoying 'beep beep' and the others having a shoot-out with plastic guns that flashed lights and whirred. Two old men were shrieking at each other and jabbing their chopsticks into the air as if impaling flying insects while a middle-aged woman lowered her head to the grubby pink tablecloth and noisily spat out a mouthful of chewed chicken bones. A waiter swaggered up and slopped tea into their cups from a stained and chipped teapot, the lid tied to the handle with plastic twine. The air was alive with arguments and laughter, with the clicking of chopsticks and the clunking of bowls, and the rattle of metal trolleys piled high with dirty crockery being pushed to the kitchen. Even the fans overhead grated and shook as they tried in vain to stir the smoky atmosphere.

Petal and Dugan were sitting side by side at a table big enough for six. They'd polished off prawns fried in garlic, sweet and sour soup and beef with green peppers and white cabbage in a creamy sauce and were now filling what little space was left in their stomachs with fried rice. Dugan's chopsticks had been suspended three inches above his bowl of rice before Petal broke into his thoughts.

'I miss the old Berni Inns,' he said.

'Huh?' She made the soft grunt that the Chinese used to mean a thousand different things, anything from 'Pardon' to 'I agree' to 'The Restaurant's On Fire But We've Still Got Time To Finish The Rice.' Dugan guessed that in Petal's case it meant she didn't understand.

162

'A restaurant chain in England,' he explained. 'Steak, chips and frozen peas, a prawn cocktail to start and Black Forest Gâteau to finish. And virtual silence throughout your meal. Bliss.'

'Do you miss England that much?' she asked.

'No, I'm only joking. And the food is one of the best things about living in Hong Kong, being able to choose any one of a hundred sorts of cuisine: Thai, Korean, all the different kinds of Chinese, Japanese, and even British pub food. No, I don't miss England that much.'

'So what happened at work to put you in such a gloomy mood?' she said, pouring beer from a large bottle for him.

'It wasn't so much work, I was just thinking about Jill . . .' He left the sentence hanging and Petal saw his eyes glaze again. Dugan snapped himself out of it, and grinned sheepishly. 'I'm sorry, I was off again, wasn't I?'

'It doesn't matter,' Petal said. 'Is there anything I can do to help?'

'No, I'm probably worrying about nothing. She rang me this morning and said someone had called her claiming to be Inspector Holt, the friend of mine who was mugged in Hot Gossip. She asked me to check out if there were two guys called Holt and when I called her back she said I was to drop it. But she sounded strained, as if she'd been crying.'

'And you think she's in trouble?'

Dugan shrugged and dropped his chopsticks on the table. He leant back in his chair and sighed deeply.

'I don't know. When we were teenagers we were so close that I knew without asking what was troubling her. Once she married that all changed.'

'That happens. A husband has got to be closer than a brother.'

'Yeah, I know.'

'Perhaps she's having problems with her husband, perhaps that's why she was upset. They could have had a row or something.'

'No, he was there with her, he answered the phone. And he didn't sound as if they were in the middle of an argument. They're not the fighting kind, anyway.'

'You said he was a triad leader. That's a violent way of life.'

'No,' said Dugan, his jaw tight with conviction. 'He's never hurt her, and he never will. He loves Jill totally, and Sophie. Outside the family he's a hard man, a killer, and he's got his fingers in some very dirty pies. But he keeps Jill and Sophie right out of it.'

Petal smiled and nodded. 'OK,' she said. 'She's your sister.'

'I'm sorry,' he said. 'I didn't mean to steamroller over your opinions.'

'You didn't, you were sticking up for her, that's all. I wish I had a brother around to stand up for me.'

A waiter was hovering nearby, a teenager in a tatty blue waistcoat and black trousers that he'd outgrown. Dugan made a scribbling motion with his hand and asked for the bill.

'I'll call her again tomorrow, maybe.'

'We could go round and see her if you want.'

Dugan liked the way she said 'we', as if taking it for granted that they were a partnership, a team. But going round to the Ng house wasn't his favourite pastime. Driving past the guards was a sharp reminder that he was

164

entering enemy territory, and the obvious signs of wealth made him nervous and a little angry. What annoyed him most was the way in which Jill revelled in it; the expensive furniture, the works of art and oriental relics that she so enjoyed collecting, the staff at her beck and call. The house didn't feel like a home, not to Dugan anyway. It felt like a cage, a moneyed cage.

The waiter returned with the bill on an oblong aluminium tray. He paid with cash, conscious that both his credit cards were too close to their limit for comfort. The last thing he wanted now was for the waiter to come back with a sly grin on his face to tell him that there was a problem with his card.

'Do you fancy going anywhere for a drink?' he asked, pushing back his chair and standing up.

'I don't feel like drinking tonight,' she said. 'How about we just go home?' It was 9 p.m. Dugan's smile widened, and he took her arm. The waiter came back with a couple of green notes and a handful of coins on the tray and Dugan waved him away as he followed Petal to the door, watching her hips sway as she walked, the way her hair rippled and shone as it moved against her shoulders.

The slight rocking of the boat and the sloshing of water against the hull was soporific and Howells knew that he'd soon be asleep. He was sitting on a wooden rattan chair that he'd wedged against the door that led out of the main sleeping cabin. The girl was sitting cross-legged in the middle of the bed, staring at him. She'd got past the crying stage and Howells had made no move to hurt her so the fear had subsided. She'd stopped whining for him to let her go, she'd stopped promising that she wouldn't say anything. At one point she'd pretended to faint and lay on her back making wheezing noises like an upturned turtle. Now she was indignant. She'd threatened him with the police, with her father, and with his bodyguards, eyes flashing fire. Any moment now and Howells reckoned she'd attack him. The kid had spunk.

'You'll be sorry,' she said.

'I'm sorry now,' laughed Howells. 'If you're not quiet you can sleep in the toilet.'

He'd kept her locked in the toilet while he'd been in Tsim Sha Tsui. He'd thought of tying and gagging her but decided against it in case she panicked and choked. The cubby-hole was wood-lined with no window and the nearest boat was far enough away that her cries couldn't possibly be heard, and she'd soon tire of yelling. But if she didn't let him sleep he was serious about putting her back there.

'Sleep,' he said.

'I don't want to sleep,' she said. 'I want to go home.'

'You will go home. Tomorrow,' said Howells, the lie tripping easily off his tongue. He still hadn't decided what he would do with her. He'd never killed a child before but he knew he was quite capable of it. A lot depended on how well his plan worked out. At the moment he needed her alive in case Ng totally refused to co-operate unless he spoke to her. He shifted in the chair and slipped his shoes off his feet.

'My parents will be worried. They'll be looking for me.'

166

'They know you're with me,' said Howells patiently. 'They're not worried.'

She was persistent. Howells had never married and had no children, and he'd never known his mother or father, he'd been abandoned as a baby and spent his whole childhood in institutions and with a succession of foster-parents. The kids he'd met there weren't like Sophie Ng at all, they were usually one of two extremes, either browbeaten into meek subservience or delinquents who were forever bucking authority just for the hell of it. Sophie's social skills and self-assurance were the result of a childhood where there was no shortage of love or money and he envied her that. Howells spent his life looking forward, not back, and he had no regrets about his lot, but he knew that if he'd had a better start in life things would have turned out differently for him. He wouldn't have had to escape into the Royal Marines, he wouldn't have been selected for the SBS, he wouldn't have fought in the Falklands and he wouldn't have been spotted by a man called Grey at a time when Britain's intelligence services had decided that it was better to use the highly trained killers of the SAS and SBS to do their dirty work than to put their own Oxbridge paper-shufflers at risk.

'Are you hungry?' asked Howells. He'd already made her a mug of oxtail soup and a cheese sandwich but she hadn't finished either.

Sophie shook her head. 'I want to go home,' she said.

'So do I, kid,' said Howells. 'So do I.' He wondered what it would be like to kill a child, to feel his hands tighten around her thin, white neck, to hear her small bones snap and to see the fear in her wide, brown eyes just before she died.

Jill shifted her position for the ten-thousandth time and kicked her legs from under the pale pink silk sheets. Once or twice she'd drifted off into a restless sleep but each time she'd suddenly woken up with her heart pounding and a dull ache in her chest that she knew only the return of her daughter would soothe. Sophie filled her mind incessantly, a labyrinth of thoughts that kept her mind trapped and refused her the luxury of rest. She opened her eyes and looked across at her husband. He was asleep and she felt a wave of resentment. He was lying on his front as usual, head turned to his left, towards her. He was breathing deeply and evenly, his brow untroubled, the sleep of the innocent – the unworried. How could he? How could he sleep at a time like this? As if he were reading her thoughts Ng opened his eyes.

'Can't sleep?' he asked.

'No. What time is it?'

He pulled his left arm from under the sheet and squinted at the slim Cartier watch on his wrist, the one Jill had bought for Sophie to give him last Father's Day. 'It's almost five.' He sat up and rubbed the sleep from his eyes. 'You stay in bed,' he said. 'I'll get you a cup of tea. Are you hungry?'

She shook her head. 'He'll call soon,' she said.

'I know,' said Ng, sliding off the bed. He grabbed his robe and headed for the kitchen. Jill lay on her back and stared at the ceiling, her arm across her forehead.

168

*   *   *

Dugan awoke to the sound of high heels clicking on a wooden floor above his head, pacing backwards and forwards, tap, tap, tap. He groped across the bed but he was alone. He listened, but there was no noise from the bathroom or kitchen. 'Petal?' he called hopefully, but she'd gone. She had a cat burglar's skill for getting out of his bed and the flat without waking him up. He knew without looking that there was a note on the table. All things being equal he'd rather have had a good-morning kiss and a cup of freshly made coffee, but at least the few scribbled words and the flower showed that she'd thought of him as she left.

At first he'd thought it quite cute that she slipped away without waking him, but now Dugan was worried that perhaps she had to be somewhere else when dawn broke. She seemed to be happy with him, and God knows she seemed to enjoy being in bed with him, so what could it be? She couldn't be married, and it wasn't as if she rushed to get home before midnight or anything, it was just that when dawn broke she was never there.

He looked at his watch, and groaned when he saw it was only quarter past five. It had been after two when Petal had eventually flopped down next to him, skin damp with sweat, panting like an exhausted dog. Dugan had felt like he'd been hit by a train at the time and he didn't feel much better now, but he knew he wouldn't be able to get any more sleep. The distant clunking of lift doors opening and closing would ensure that. He switched on his CD player and Ultravox filled the air. He twisted the volume button savagely. If he wasn't going to get any more sleep he was damned if anyone else should.

Howells' internal clock woke him up at 5.20 a.m. Early rising was a habit he'd picked up living in a children's home and which had continued in the Royal Marines, but this was something else, a natural ability to wake up on command that had never failed him. He was still slumped on the chair, though he'd used one of the pillows to support his back. The other was wrapped in Sophie's arms as she slept on the bed, still in her school uniform.

His neck ached and his mouth was uncomfortably dry but he'd woken up in worse positions, in peaty trenches in the Falklands or under the blisteringly hot sun of the Libyan desert. A luxury junk was nothing to complain about. He used the bathroom, leaving the door open so he could keep an eye on the girl. He washed himself with a flannel, and shaved using a can of shaving foam and a disposable razor he'd brought with him, but then realized he'd forgotten his toothbrush. No matter, he'd gone without cleaning his teeth for weeks at a time before when out in the field. Toothpaste was a chemical signature that even humans could detect in the jungle or the desert. Soap, too. He swilled his mouth out with warm water and rubbed his teeth with the flannel to get rid of the sour taste of sleep.

Sophie slept through his ablutions and didn't even react when he opened the door and went into the galley to boil a pan full of water. He made a pot of coffee, put three sugars into hers and made it half and half with milk, the way he used to like it when he was a kid. His own was black and bitter, the way he liked it now. There had to be a moral there somewhere, he thought, as he carried the mugs into the bedroom.

He put Sophie's mug on the floor and gently shook her. She moaned quietly and hugged her pillow tightly. 'Wake up, kid,' he said. She murmured something in Chinese and curled up into a foetal ball. Howells checked his watch. It was five thirty-five and it would take him exactly twenty minutes to get the dinghy to the shore and get to the public telephone. He gathered her up in his arms, pillow and all, and carried her through to the toilet. There was just enough room for her to lie on the floor. He closed the door and locked it, then took her untouched coffee back into the galley and poured it down the sink.

Simon Ng waited for the call in his study, sitting calmly behind his desk with his hands clasped on the blotter. His face was impassive, seemingly unworried; the only sign of tension was the fact that he was unconsciously toying with his wedding ring. His wife's distress was more evident. She sat on the Chesterfield, her face pale and drawn and her hands trembling. Jill was rarely up at this time of the day, she'd always been a late riser and living with Ng meant that a nine-to-five existence wasn't exactly at the top of life's priorities. She'd dressed in an old pair of jeans and a grey sweatshirt, and her hair was dull and lifeless. Ng was immaculate as always in a dark blue double-breasted suit, a crisp white shirt and his Hong Kong Club tie. Dressed to kill, thought Jill ruefully, conscious of the fact that by letting her appearance slide she was causing her husband to lose face in front of his men. She tried to force a smile but Ng seemed not to notice as he sat there, deep in thought. On the left-hand side of the desk was a slim, brown leather briefcase. Ng hadn't opened it but Jill knew it contained one million dollars.

Next to her was Cheng. He was well-used to rising early; he was often up to watch the dawn and listen to his birds proclaiming dominance over the little territory they had. He too seemed untroubled, sitting with his back ramrod straight, his hands resting on his knees.

Standing by the open door was a big bruiser of a man, well over six feet with thick forearms that were a tailor's nightmare. His name was Lin Wing-wah, but for five years or more he'd been the triad's Hung Kwan and everybody called him Elder Brother. He'd started off as a tough street fighter, a basic 49 Red Pole in charge of one of Ng's Mong Kok fishball stalls. He'd spent some time as the Cho Hai official, in charge of organizing the triad's rapidly expanding protection rackets, but when the Hung Kwan slot fell vacant Ng moved Lin into it. His sheer physical presence meant that Elder Brother was rarely disobeyed. His hair was parted in the middle and tied back in a small pigtail and he had a thin, drooping moustache under a nose that had been broken more times than was good for it. There was a black wart with a clump of hairs sprouting from it just above the middle of his lips. He called it his beauty spot. Lin was big and ugly, but Ng didn't pay him to win beauty competitions. He was paid to

172

be the triad's strong-arm man and he did the job perfectly, and enthusiastically.

Lin's soldiers were split into a dozen fighting sections of between twenty and twenty-five men, and he had two of his best units waiting outside. There were four Mercedes in the drive in addition to Jill's Porsche, Ng's Daimler and the 560SEL that Manny drove. There were another six cars lined up on the single-track road leading from the compound. Lin was as prepared as he could be, but he still had no idea who the enemy was, or where the handover was to take place. Howells had told Ng that he wanted the money by seven o'clock and that he would call one hour earlier. That meant that Howells wanted the swap to take place within an hour's drive from the house, but at this time of the morning that just about covered the whole of Hong Kong island, Kowloon and the New Territories. A map of the territory had been pinned to the wall opposite the window and though it was small in area Lin knew there were a million places to hide, even for a gweilo.

There were only four of them in the study, but the room felt crowded, oppressive. They were careful to avoid eye contact with each other, like warring relatives at the reading of a will. Jill couldn't understand it, the crisis should have brought them closer together but instead it seemed to have isolated them, locked each of them into their own private world. Right now what she needed most was physical contact with her husband, his arm around her, the reassuring feel of his flesh, but she was reluctant to show her feelings in front of his men. Worse than that, she was afraid that he would refuse to comfort her, that he would be embarrassed by her and reject her. She could see now the power he had, how hard and controlled he was when dealing with a crisis. It wasn't the Simon she knew, despite the occasional smiles he threw her way. For the first time she was a little frightened of him. She had to be like him, strong and controlled. Public displays of hysteria wouldn't get her anywhere.

The phone rang and they all jumped, even Cheng. Ng let it ring, three times, four times, before he picked it up, so as not to appear to be too anxious. Lin slipped out of the room to pick up the extension.

'You have the money?' asked Howells.

'Yes. I want to speak to my daughter.'

'You can talk to her all you want once I have the money,' said Howells. The line clicked as Lin picked up the phone in the lounge.

'I want to talk to her now,' said Ng, firmly.

'She isn't with me now. Once you have given me the money I will tell you where she is.'

'How can I believe you?'

'You have no choice. Now listen and listen carefully. I will only tell you once.'

'I am listening.'

'You know a place called Hebe Haven, about half an hour's drive from your house?'

'Yes, I know it.'

'There is a pier there, an L-shaped pier.'

'Yes.'

'You are to park your car on the road and walk to the pier. To the right, as you face the sea, is a row of concrete steps that lead down to the water. I want you to wait there at exactly seven o'clock. Alone. With the money. If you are not there the girl will die. If you are not alone, the girl will die. If you do not have the money with you, the girl will die. Do you understand?'

'Yes.' Click. The line went dead.

Ng got up from behind the desk and walked over to the map.

'What did he say? What did he say?' asked Jill.

'Hebe Haven,' said Ng. 'I have to deliver the money to Hebe Haven in one hour.'

Lin walked back into the room. There was a low groan from Cheng as he pushed himself up off the sofa. He massaged his left knee and then slowly kicked his leg backwards and forwards. 'By sea or by land,' he said quietly, as if to himself. 'He could come either way.'

Ng nodded in agreement. He turned to Lin. 'I must arrive alone, but if we are careful we might be able to get one or two men near the pier, maybe even on it. Pretending to fish, or painting, something. No more than two and they must leave now.'

Lin went without a word and less than a minute later a car drove away.

'The sea way will be harder,' Ng said to Cheng.

'Perhaps not,' said the old man, pointing to the map. The cove that was Hebe Haven was about two kilometres long and one kilometre wide, an impossibly large area of water to patrol, but the gap that led to the open sea was only a few hundred yards across.

'Here,' said Cheng. 'Two boats placed between the headland at Chuk Kok and the tip of Pak Ma Tsui would effectively seal off the whole cove. Assuming he comes in by sea we could let him in and then shut the door behind him. You could hand over the money but there would be nowhere for him to run to.'

'Unless he beached the boat within the cove.'

'Station men on the beaches, it wouldn't take many.'

Lin had returned now. 'It wouldn't be difficult,' he agreed. 'They all have radios. But if we decide to send them they'll have to go now.'

Ng nodded and once again Lin went to brief his men. This time three cars left. Jill, sitting alone on the Chesterfield, felt alone and quite, quite useless.

'So,' said the old man thoughtfully. 'He comes in by boat. We close the gap after him. He takes the money. Does he have the girl with him, that is the question.' He sucked his teeth, nodding his head up and down slowly. 'I think not,' he said eventually. 'I think he will come alone.'

'I don't see that as a problem,' said Ng. 'Once we have him he will tell us where Sophie is. I have no doubt about that. No doubt at all.'

The chilling conviction in his voice shocked Jill. It wasn't something she'd heard from her husband before, and for the first time she became aware of the power he commanded, the power of life and death, and pain.

Lin came back into the room, baring his teeth at Ng's words. 'He'll talk all right. We'll make him sing as sweetly as one your songbirds, Master Cheng.'

'The boats will be a problem,' said Ng. 'My launch is berthed at Clearwater Bay. We won't have time to get there and get it to Hebe Haven.' He jabbed a finger at the map, an inch or so above the cove. 'Sai Kung,' he said. 'We can beg, borrow or steal boats from there. Send six men to Sai Kung – they are to choose the fastest boats they can find. And tell them to be discreet about it. We don't know where he's coming from.' Yet again Lin left the study. 'What do you think, Cheng Bak-bak?'

'If he comes from the sea we will have him,' said Cheng. 'But he would also be aware of the danger involved. And we should not assume that merely because he mentioned the pier he intends to come by water. You must also guard the road.'

'There is only one road,' said Ng, 'Hiram's Highway, the one that leads to the Clearwater Bay Road. The road to the pier comes off Hiram's Highway, and if we put one car on either side of it we can seal it completely. There is nowhere else to go. There is a hill behind the road, we can put a man there and he'll be able to see the whole area, from the main road to the pier.'

'I'll be there,' said Lin, who had returned to the room.

'You'd better go now,' said Ng. 'And make sure the cars are inconspicuous, whatever you do. You'll be able to put a few of our men in the boatyards disguised as workmen, but get them in place right away.'

Lin nodded curtly and left.

Cheng and Ng stood together at the map. Jill wanted to join them but she could tell from the strained silence that the two men were deep in concentration and that she would be in the way. She sat on the sofa, legs pressed tightly together, her stomach a mass of nerves. She knew there was no point in even asking Simon if she could go with him.

'Well, Bak-bak, what do you think?' asked Ng.

The old man rocked back on his heels, his hands clasped behind his back. 'If he comes by sea, he will surely be trapped,' he said quietly. 'If he comes by the road he will also be trapped. He surely cannot come by air, unless he can fly like a bird.'

'A helicopter isn't impossible, but air traffic control at Kai Tak would be on his back right away,' added Ng. 'What we must be careful of is a combination, arriving by sea and leaving on land, or vice versa.'

'But even so, once he is at the pier he will be trapped on all sides,' said Cheng, sounding unconvinced.

'You seem worried, Bak-bak.'

'If you and I can so easily see that it is a trap, why did the gweilo arrange to meet you there?'

Ng nodded. 'Presumably because he assumes that he can just as easily get away? But how?'

'I would assume that when you see him, he will not have your daughter with him. He will think that so long as he has her he will be safe. He will want to take the money and release her later, when he is out of harm's way. Sophie will be his way out.'

'But as Elder Brother said, once you have trapped your bird, it is easy to make it sing.'

'But if the bird is not alone, if he has friends, and if the bird does not return to its nest . . .' The old man left the sentence unfinished, hanging in the air.

'We have no choice,' said Ng. 'If we let him escape with the money, there is no incentive for him to release her. Especially as she can identify him.'

'Identification is not such a problem,' said Cheng. 'Do not forget that the headmistress also saw him. I do not think that he will kill your daughter merely because she has seen his face.'

'We cannot take the risk,' said Ng. 'We must hope that he brings Sophie with him, and if he does not then we will force him to tell us where she is. It will not take long.'

'Oh my God,' gasped Jill. 'Please, please be careful, Simon. I just want her back, I just want Sophie back.'

Ng turned round as Jill got up, and took a step towards her and held her close, her head on his shoulder, nuzzling his neck.

'You will have her back,' he said. 'I promise.' Over her shoulder he could see Lin driving through the gates in the Mercedes, leaving the Daimler for him. He looked at his watch. It was 6.25 a.m. 'Time to go,' he said, releasing himself from her clinging grip and holding her shoulders at arm's length. 'You'd better get her room ready, when she gets back she'll be tired and hungry.' He kissed her tear-stained cheek and picked up the briefcase on the desk. He left the house without looking back but knew that she watched him go from the study.

Howells watched them come from his hiding-place below the pier. The water around the supporting legs of the structure was shoulder-deep so he stood next to one, back bowed forward so that he was submerged from the chin down. After making the phone call exactly at 6 a.m., he'd taken the dinghy back to the junk and put on all his diving equipment. He used the snorkel for the first quarter of a mile to save air and only submerged when he got close enough to shore to be seen. As soon as he reached the safety of the pier he switched back to the snorkel as he swayed gently backwards and forwards with the rhythm of the waves. He could see a good chunk of the shoreline and had a clear view of the approach road in the distance, and if he turned round he could see most of the bay, and his junk bobbing up and down in the water.

The first two arrived just after 6.30, a young man in jeans and T-shirt carrying a fishing basket, and an older man with a couple of cans of paint and a tattered holdall. They came one at a time, on opposite sides of the road, but Howells had no doubt that they were together.

The fisherman came first. Howells lost sight of him as he passed through the metal bollards that marked the end of the road, but a minute or so later he heard him walk overhead to the end of the pier. The older man stood by the bollards, pulled out a pack of cigarettes and lit one, leaning back his head and blowing smoke up at the sky. He began to unpack brushes and cloths and after opening one of the tins of paint started to apply unprofessional strokes of red to a bollard.

Five minutes later a white van drove down the road and turned in to one of the boatyards and three men in dark blue overalls climbed out. One of them knocked on the door to the yard's office, and on getting no answer all three moved between the boats until they were out of his sight. Even at this early hour the main road seemed busy, but not so busy that he didn't notice the two big Mercs driving past or see one of them go in the opposite direction a few minutes later. He'd expected them to seal off the road, and knew that the way out to the open sea would be closed off as well.

Howells checked his watch. Ten minutes to go. He shivered, but it was the cold, not fear. The water was colder than he'd anticipated, yet to be warmed by the early morning sun. The harness was starting to chafe against his skin but he knew it would be a mistake to take it off so he ignored the pain. The emergency cylinder was hanging from the harness, occasionally banging against his leg. A plastic bag drifted past, followed closely by a scattering of green leaves from some sort of Chinese vegetable. One piece washed up against his mask and he ducked his head down under the water to clear it. When he surfaced he saw Ng, standing at the top of the stairs, briefcase in hand, shading his eyes as he looked out to sea.

Lin had left his three Red Pole fighters looking under the bonnet of his car, the engine running so they could move quickly if needed, while he climbed up the hill, moving effortlessly through the bushes and spindly trees. He stopped halfway up, not even breathing heavily, and then cut across to give him the best possible view of the pier. He had a pair of powerful binoculars and a walkie-talkie with which he could contact his men who were now scattered around the bay and on two launches just beyond the headland. He spoke to them one by one: the men in the cars on the main road, the team in the boatyard, the man and woman walking their dog along the housing development at Marina Cove on the southern rim of the bay, which overlooked the pier, and the men on the boats. Like Lin they were all armed. His pistol in its leather holster felt heavy under his left armpit.

He put the binoculars to his eyes and scanned the bay. Nothing. He spoke into his walkie-talkie again, asking the men in the launches if there was anything approaching. Nothing. He heard Ng's Daimler tearing up the road before he saw it, then it rounded the bend and indicated it was turning right. Ng accelerated down towards the pier and stopped with a screech of brakes in one of the white-painted parking spaces. The painter looked up, then put his head down and got on with his work.

'Easy, easy,' said Lin through clenched teeth. A flying insect buzzed close to his ear but he ignored it. Ng opened the car door and stepped out, black shoes gleaming in the sunlight. Lin heard the door clunk shut and watched as Ng walked past the painter, briefcase swinging, and headed for the stone steps. Lin knew that Ng's gun was in a holster in the small of his back, under the Italian jacket, and that he had a wicked hunting knife taped to the calf of his right leg. In his inside jacket pocket he had a small walkie-talkie but it was switched off. A blast of static or a careless broadcast could spoil the whole thing. The painter and the fisherman were also under orders to keep theirs switched off. They were too close to the action.

Lin looked at his watch for the hundredth time that morning. Five minutes to go. That surely ruled out a boat, for there was no sign of activity in the bay at all. Lin radioed to the men at the roadside telling them to get ready, that it looked as if the gweilo would be coming by road.

He steadied his binoculars and checked Ng. He was still standing at the top of the steps, looking out to sea.

Howells bit on to the rubber flanges of the mouthpiece and ducked down under the water, the taste of salt on his tongue. He kicked his flippers and hugged the seabed as he headed towards the base of the stone steps. As he covered the fifty yards or so from the pier he unclipped the handcuffs from his belt. The water got shallower and shallower and once or twice his knees banged into sand as he swam, scraping his skin. Then he saw the steps ahead and he slowed to a halt. The water was about five feet deep so he kept his knees bent as he surfaced so that only his head was in the air. Ng was still at the top of the steps and hadn't seen him. Howells removed the mouthpiece and took a deep breath.

'Stay exactly where you are,' he said, firing the words in sharp staccato fashion, like bullets from a machine-gun, knowing that Ng was more likely to obey the authority in a strong voice than a weak-willed whisper. 'Don't look down. Put the briefcase down on the floor.' Ng did as he was told, then stood still with his hands at his sides. 'Now do the same with your gun.'

Ng hesitated. Howells was sure he would be armed, and wired. Neither the gun nor the communications equipment was likely to function under water but it would be safer to get rid of them straight away.

'Do it or she dies,' said Howells, and he saw the fight drain out of Ng. The triad leader reached behind his back and removed the gun, then bent down and placed it next to the briefcase.

'Now the radio.'

Ng took out the walkie-talkie and dropped it on to the concrete steps, where it clattered down and plopped into the dark water.

'Now, walk down the steps towards me,' said Howells.

Lin caught his breath as Ng put the gun on the floor. 'What are you doing, Lung Tau?' he said to himself. Ng straightened up and a few seconds later he took something from inside his jacket and threw it down the steps. Even through the binoculars, Lin could not see what it was. He checked the pier. Nothing – and the road was clear. What the hell was going on? He called up the launches on the radio. No, they hadn't seen anything. There were no boats on the way to Hebe Haven. Ng began to walk down the steps, slowly. Suddenly Lin understood, like a bolt of lightning streaking through his consciousness. He pressed the radio to his lips.

'He's in the water,' he barked. 'He's in the fucking water. Get those boats in now.'

Lin began to run down the hill, slipping and sliding through the undergrowth, not caring about the branches and thorns that tore into his trousers. As he ran he called up the teams by the cars, ordering them to get to the pier, and then he shouted instructions to the men in the boatyard. He didn't wait to hear their acknowledgements, he concentrated on running, on covering the quarter mile to the pier in the shortest time possible. The hillside levelled out and he burst through the trees, vaulted over a wall and crossed the road in three strides, his arms pumping up and down as his feet slapped on the tarmac. As he hurtled down the approach road to the pier he heard the Red Poles hard on his heels.

Ng was confused. He took four steps down and then stopped.

'What about the money?' he asked.

'Keep moving,' said the gweilo. 'Keep moving or she dies.'

Ng took another couple of steps, his mind whirling. The whole point of this was the money, yet the gweilo wanted it left behind. It didn't make sense.

'Where is Sophie?'

The man gestured with his hands; something metallic, a chain perhaps, glinted wetly between his fingers. 'Faster,' he said. 'Keep moving.'

Ng walked down to the water's edge. The frogman stood up, his shoulders rising above the water. 'I'll take you to see your daughter,' said the gweilo. The voice was powerful but controlled, each word carefully enunciated and projected.

Ng was still unsure. Behind him he could hear shouts and the sound of men running. He turned to look up the flight of steps and then he felt a hand close around his ankle and pull. He fought to regain his balance but the pull was too strong and he toppled forward, arms flailing. He hit the water, the shock forcing all the air from his lungs, and as he gasped for air he took in salt water and fought back the urge to retch. The gweilo's arm was round his neck, his face pressed close to his ear.

'We're going under the water,' the gweilo said. 'Put this in your mouth and breathe slowly. The water will sting your eyes so keep them closed.'

Ng saw a silver cylinder with a black mouthpiece thrust towards his face. He didn't want to obey but in his confusion he did as he was told. As soon as his teeth were closed on the mouthpiece the gweilo pulled him under the water and his ears were filled with a roaring noise. The salt water stung his nostrils and Ng reached up to hold his nose. He could feel the gweilo kicking his legs and the sensation of water passing over his body. He opened his eyes, but the salt water burned so he clamped them shut and concentrated on breathing. He felt something hard lock around the wrist of his left hand and then his ears popped as the gweilo continued to drag him down to the seabed.

Lin bellowed like a bull as he ran. The walkie-talkie slipped from his sweating fingers and he ignored it as it smashed on to the tarmac and broke into plastic pieces. One of the Red Poles, Kenny Suen, caught up with him and it gave Lin the adrenalin boost he needed to speed up. The two ran together, chests heaving and arms pounding. The painter looked up and saw the men running towards him, stopped painting and straightened his back. The fisherman at the end of the pier stood up, his line forgotten.

'The water!' yelled Lin. 'The water!' He pointed at the stairs but both men just continued to look at him, totally confused. Suen had pulled ahead and was certain to get to the steps first so Lin stopped and cupped his hands around his mouth. 'Get Lung Tau. He's in the water,' he roared. The painter realized first and he dropped his brush on to the floor and sprinted to the top of the steps. Once he started to move the fisherman followed, running at full pelt down the pier. Lin started running again, and as he passed the bollards he pulled his gun out of the holster. Suen reached the steps first, closely followed by the painter, and both had guns in their hands and were looking down at the water by the time Lin got there.

Lin pushed them apart and looked left and right before he realized they were alone. He opened his mouth to speak but could see that the two men were as baffled as he was. He'd expected the gweilo to be in the water, probably with diving equipment, but there was no way Ng could be under the water. There was no blood, there had been no gunshot, no sign of violence. Nothing.

Suen picked up the briefcase and flicked the catches open. He showed the money to Lin.

'What is happening, Elder Brother?' he asked. Franc Tse and Ricky Lam arrived then, followed by more of the Red Poles in ones and twos until there were a dozen men standing together, all of them armed with nothing to shoot at. They looked at Lin for guidance and he knew with a sickening surety that he had no idea what to tell them.

Ng struggled at first, making it difficult for Howells to make any progress through the murky water. He kept low and kicked the flippers hard, wide scissor-kicks that made his calf muscles ache. Ng's free hand, the one that Howells hadn't handcuffed, groped around, throwing them both off balance, then his head jerked from side to side in panic. But soon he began to calm down, and reached up to hold his nose shut against the water. Howells let go of the small cylinder and allowed Ng to hold it at the same time as pinching his nostrils. At least that way Howells knew that both of Ng's hands were occupied. He rolled Ng over so that he was underneath him, which made it easier for him to swim in a straight line, though it meant that Ng was continually banging against the sea bed. Howells' ears began to hurt and he squeezed the soft rubber either side of his nose and blew gently to equalize the pressure until the pain eased. If Ng was smart he'd do the same, or burst an eardrum. Ng's feet dragged along the sand, clouding the water even more, and first one shoe slipped off, then the other. They were about twenty feet below the surface now so Howells began to level off and the sea bed gradually fell away. The visibility began to improve as they stirred up less sand and in the distance Howells could see the hull of a yacht. He steered Ng towards it.

'Give me your radio,' Lin told Suen. The two launches came round the headland a mile away in a shower of spray. Lin called them up but couldn't make out what they were saying.

'Don't talk, just listen,' he said. 'Head for the pier. Head for the pier now. He's wearing scuba gear, he's under the water. I repeat, he's under the water and he has Lung Tau.'

Tse and Lam were kneeling at the bottom of the steps, shading their eyes and trying to peer through the water but the light reflecting off the surface obscured everything. Lin handed the binoculars to Suen and told him to stand at the end of the pier and watch out for tell-tale bubbles.

'The rest of you come with me,' he said, and he led them towards the boatyards and one of the small wooden piers where there were several dinghies tethered together like goats.

As they got close to the yacht Howells began to dive down, clearing the pressure from his ears again. The anchor was lying on its side, a thick chain leading up from it to the white hull above. He moved towards it, the two men scuttling along the seabed like a crippled starfish. Ng's eyes had become more used to the salt water and he was looking around, his right hand still pinching his nostrils closed and holding the small cylinder. His suit was floating grotesquely around him and his tie had come loose and was drifting over his shoulder. Howells pulled him down hard, closer to the heavy anchor. The motion turned Ng on to his back and his legs rose above his head. He kicked in an attempt to right himself and then Howells tugged him again and locked the handcuffs to the metal ring at the top of the anchor. Howells let go of the cuffs and drifted away from Ng, using his arms and slow kicks of his fins to keep himself standing virtually upright a few feet above the sand. Ng saw him and began trying to swim up to the surface, but realized he was fixed to the anchor. He pulled himself down to it and tried to get free, panic obvious in his movements. He began to breathe faster, his head shrouded in bubbles. Howells doubted if there could be much air left in the cylinder now. There was hate in Ng's eyes, and fear. He put his shoeless feet either side of the anchor and grabbed it with his hands, then heaved up. He managed to get it up to his waist and then tried to push himself up to the surface and its life-giving air. It was too heavy, and dropped back to the side, plumes of sediment scattering around his feet like escaping snakes, while the cylinder swung to and fro from his mouth.

Howells watched, and waited. Getting a gun in Hong Kong would have been difficult, and he hadn't been certain of getting close enough to kill the triad leader with a knife. But here, thirty feet under the waves, he'd know for sure that the man was dead. That's what he told himself, anyway. But in his heart of hearts, in the dark place in his mind where even he was frightened to dwell too long, Howells knew that he wanted to watch, to see the man run short of air, to see water rush into his gasping lungs and to see the eyes milk over as he died.

Ng's chest heaved and Howells knew it would soon be over. He steadied himself with small circular movements of his hands, eyes fixed on Ng's face. Ng bent double, his hand going for the knife strapped beneath his trouser leg. On dry land maybe, just maybe, he'd have managed to do it, to have grabbed the knife and slashed and cut before Howells could have reacted, but with Howells' reactions it would have been a million-to-one shot. Under water it was a non-starter. Howells had all the time in the world to watch as Ng brought out the knife and tried to slash him across the stomach. Howells drifted back in the water, kicked once lazily to move out of range, and then righted himself.

It was better when they fought. Sometimes, when they knew death was inevitable, they gave up, they relaxed and just let it happen. Sometimes they closed their eyes and pretended it was a bad dream and that by wishing hard Howells would go away. Sometimes they called on God for help. Sometimes they called for their mothers. And sometimes they fought to the very end – they were the best. Animal against animal, eyes bright with the fire of life and teeth snarling, one on one. To the victor the spoils, and life. Howells knew how the gladiators of ancient Rome must have felt in the arena, and he knew too why those who were prepared to die gloriously often had their lives spared, while cowards always got the thumbs-down. There was a nobility in dying well that deserved to be rewarded.

Ng tried hacking at the chain with his knife but it was useless. His whole body was heaving as his lungs fought for air, his cheeks blowing in and out as he tried to breathe. He lunged again but the anchor held him back. He turned away from Howells, knowing that it was futile, knowing that it was important to conserve what little air was still in his lungs. His shoulders sagged and then he looked at Howells, straight in the eye. It was impossible to see the look on Ng's face because of the mouthpiece and the cylinder that hung from his face like an elephant's trunk, but it seemed to Howells that the man was smiling. Then the contact was broken as Ng sank to his knees on the sand, as if in prayer.

Even before the knife rose in the water in Ng's fist, Howells knew with a tremor of anticipation what was going to happen, and he moved closer. The knife fell again and again as Ng hacked away at the wrist that was keeping him prisoner, until the water was cloudy with his blood. Howells groaned to himself as he watched.

'Can you see anything?' asked Lin. The men all shook their heads. There were four of them in the wooden dinghy, two rowing while Lin and Kenny Suen knelt at the prow looking down into the water. There were two other rowing boats moving clumsily and noisily through the water in a 'V' formation, gradually moving further and further apart as they splashed away from the ramshackle wooden pier. Out in the bay the two motor launches carved lines through the water, but Lin could see that they were going too fast to be of any use. He called them up on his radio and told them to shut off their engines and drift with the tide.

'How long have they been under?' Lin asked.

Suen checked his watch. 'Fifteen minutes,' he said.

'Anyone know how long a cylinder of air lasts?' said Lin.

Nobody did, and Lin knew it didn't matter anyway. Nobody had seen the diver so they didn't know how many tanks he had or how many more he'd stashed away on the sea bed. One thing was for sure, fifteen minutes was a long time. More than enough time to cover half a mile at a slow walking pace, and a diver with decent flippers and equipment would move a lot faster. But calling off the search would be as good as admitting that the Dragon Head was dead and Lin wasn't prepared to take that responsibility.

Howells watched the triads as they searched, safe inside the main cabin of the junk. Once he was sure that Ng was dead he had swum quickly away, keeping low, hugging the contours of the sea bed, shallow breathing to keep the bubbles to a minimum. Without Ng to slow him down he coursed through the water like a shark, arms loose against his sides, head moving from side to side, all the power coming from his thigh muscles. He'd only slowed once, to check the gauge that told him how much air he had left. He'd made it with plenty to spare.

When he surfaced close to the junk he spent a full minute using the dinghy as cover while he checked that he was in the clear before he slid out of the water and on to the wooden platform at the rear of the junk. He stowed all the gear in the engine-room and wrapped himself in a bathrobe before kneeling down on one of the seats in the dining area and scanning the bay with a pair of binoculars. The men who had been on land were rowing their boats about half a mile away, and there were two powerful launches bobbing in the water a few hundred yards in from the entrance to the bay. Howells knew they'd call off the search before too long. They wouldn't know if he'd swum to a boat, or simply gone ashore at any one of a hundred places around the circumference of the bay and made off in a car. And even if they decided that a boat was the most likely hiding-place, there were still more than a thousand in the bay. Marina Cove alone had spaces for 300 vessels. It would take weeks to search every one, and as it was midweek most of them would be securely locked. All Howells had to do was wait.

'It's ten o'clock, Elder Brother,' said Suen.

'I know,' snapped Lin. 'What do you think we should do? Abandon him? Do you want to explain to his father and his brothers that we left him to die beneath the waves? Do you want to do that?'

Suen lowered his eyes, shamed by Lin's outburst, but knowing that he was right and that he spoke for others. They had been rowing round and round in circles for almost two hours and seen nothing but rotting vegetation, mouldly driftwood and plastic bags. If they were still under water then they were surely dead. If they had left the water then they had done so unnoticed. Either way they were wasting their time.

Lin used his walkie-talkie to talk to the men in the launches and his teams on land. Nothing. He stood at the prow of the boat, his hands on his hips, his chin up defiantly as if daring the frogman to come up and fight him, man to man.

Dugan was reading the *Standard* with his third cup of coffee when the phone rang.

'Good morning, Patrick Dugan.'

'Hiya kid. What's new?'

'Nothing much. Business as usual,' said Petal.

'What's the view like from the tallest building in Hong Kong?' he asked.

'I wish I had a view,' she said. 'I'm nowhere near important enough to warrant an office with a view. Or a high floor. You'd laugh if you saw my cubby-hole. How are you this glorious morning?'

'Knackered,' he said. 'You'll be the death of me.'

'I don't know what you mean, Patrick Dugan. I hope this isn't going to turn into an obscene phone call.'

He laughed, and spilt his plastic cup of coffee across the paper.

'Fuck,' he said angrily, and leapt to his feet.

'I was wrong,' Petal giggled. 'It *is* an obscene phone call. I suppose you want to know what colour underwear I'm wearing?'

'I spilt my coffee, all over my God-forsaken desk,' he said. 'Why does this always happen to me?' He lifted one corner of the paper and carefully poured the brown liquid off and into the waste-paper bin. Luckily it hadn't soaked through to the two files underneath it.

'It's not my day,' he said.

'Cheer up,' said Petal. 'It can only get better.'

'Are you free tonight?' asked Dugan. 'Some of the guys

in the anti-triad squad are having a party at Hot Gossip to celebrate a big drugs bust. You can read all about it on page three of the *Standard*.'

'Sounds great. What time?'

'Fairly late, I've got a stack of paperwork to get through. Say about eleven o'clock. We can eat in the restaurant there, they serve food practically through the night.'

'OK, I'll see you there at eleven.'

'Hey, before you go, can you give me your number at the bank? I've tried to get you a couple of times but the switchboard girls never seem to know where to get you.' Dugan felt that she hesitated, but after a second or two she brightly gave him the number. He wrote it down on the first page of his desk diary. 'One more thing,' he said.

'What's that?'

'Just what colour is your underwear?'

'That is for me to know, and for you to find out,' she laughed sexily, and hung up on him. God, thought Dugan, the night felt like a lifetime away.

Lin eventually called off the search at one o'clock. He radioed the launches and told them to wait at the entrance to the bay and check any boats that left. Wherever possible they were to search the vessels, but if that proved impossible they were to make a note of the name and identification number. He left two Red Poles at Marina Cove and a handful of men scattered around the circumference of the bay, but in his heart of hearts he knew it was too late. The gweilo had been well prepared. He was either safely on board a boat or he'd long since swum to the shore and escaped.

They left the three dinghies tied where they'd found them and walked in disconsolate silence back to the cars. Howells watched them go before allowing the girl out of the toilet.

'I'm hungry,' she pouted.

'Me too,' he said. 'Ravenous. What do you want?'

'I want to go home.' She stamped her foot as she spoke and Howells smiled. Any man who got stuck with this young lady was going to have a hard life.

'To eat,' he said. 'What do you want to eat?'

The look of deviousness that flashed across her face was so transparent that Howells laughed out loud.

'Can I have a look in the galley to see what there is?' she asked as if butter wouldn't melt in her mouth. This was obviously a girl who was used to getting exactly what she wanted from her doting parents.

'No,' said Howells patiently. 'You stay here.'

'A woman's place is in the kitchen,' said Sophie, toying with a strand of her blonde hair. Howells gave her a mock growl and she glared at him. 'You're going to be sorry when my father catches you,' she threatened. Howells said nothing.

The convoy of cars moved slowly up the approach road to the compound like a funeral procession. Lin and Suen were in the lead car, Ng's Daimler. They saw

Jill standing at the front door as they crackled to a halt on the gravelled drive.

'Shit, Elder Brother. Who's going to tell the gweipor?'

'You want to do it?' asked Lin, savagely, and snorted as Suen shook his head. 'I'll tell her. And then I'll speak to Master Cheng. Keep the men by the guardhouse. I'll come and talk to them soon.'

He stepped out of the plush interior of the car and walked towards Jill, his arms out to the side, shoulders low. He found it impossible to meet her eyes as he got close. He had little respect for the white woman, she shared the Dragon Head's bed but not his office and he tried wherever possible to have nothing to do with her. He was certainly not afraid of her, but now she was a stark reminder of his failure, of his failure to protect his boss, her husband.

It seemed to Lin that the closer he got to her, the more his guilt grew, until he could feel it as a heavy weight pressing down on the back of his neck, compressing his spine and making his legs buckle. He tried to straighten his back, to thrust back his shoulders but the pressure just intensified. He stopped, some ten feet in front of her, and looked at her shoes, bright red, the colour of blood.

'Where are they?' she asked quietly. 'What has happened?'

She spoke to him in Cantonese, and as always Lin marvelled at how well she spoke the language that defeated so many gweilos. But when he answered it was in halting English. She was a gweipor and there was no way he could bring himself to speak to a gweipor in his own language. The difference would always be there and in Lin's mind it was a difference that had to be highlighted.

'I am sorry, Mrs Ng,' he said. He forced himself to look at her face. 'The man grabbed your husband and took him into the water. He was wearing diving equipment. We do not know what has happened to him.'

Jill sagged on the doorstep as if Lin had punched her in the stomach. She wrapped her arms around her middle and bent forward, making a low moaning noise like a wounded animal.

'And my daughter?' she asked, still in Cantonese.

Lin shook his head. 'I am sorry,' he said. 'There was no sign of her.'

Jill collapsed in a heap, legs splayed as she slid down the door frame, hugging herself. Lin didn't know what to do; he took an uncertain step forward and then stopped, embarrassed by her show of grief. He was saved by the amah who ran down the corridor and crouched next to her mistress, talking to her softly before helping her to her feet and into the shadows of the house. Lin sighed with relief and turned his back on them. Telling Master Cheng would be no easier, but at least he would take the news better, and he would know what they should do next. He walked around the right-hand side of the house, his feet crunching on the stones. The right-hand wing of the H-shaped house contained the bedrooms, and though it was early afternoon the curtains were drawn. It looked like a house in mourning. The path narrowed and then forked into two, one winding to the left around the back of the house, the other curving away to the right, through a sprinkling of fruit trees and past a small goldfish pool to Cheng's small one-storey house surrounded by its shady palm trees. It was cleverly landscaped so that there was no sign of it from the main house, and Lin heard the songbirds long before he got there. Cheng was sitting on his front doorstep holding a wicker cage in his lap, head on one side as he listened to the deep-throated warble of the yellow and brown bird within.

Lin stood for a moment in front of the old man looking down on his bald head, and then he squatted down, resting his arms on his knees, his backside just a couple of inches from the ground. It put his head lower than Cheng's, and accorded him the respect his age and his position warranted. Lin hadn't adopted such a position for many years; it was a youngster's way of resting, and his knees shrieked with pain and his calf muscles ached but his face remained impassive.

Cheng kept his eyes on the caged bird as he spoke. 'What happened, Wah-tsai?'

The old man spoke to him the same way now that he had more than twenty years ago, using the diminutive of his name. Cheng didn't do it to belittle Lin, or to humiliate him; it reflected the length of time they'd known each other and that theirs was still very much a teacher–pupil relationship. There was a lot Lin still had to learn from Master Cheng if he was ever to get the chance of taking on the mantle of Lung Tau.

'I have failed, Master Cheng,' Lin said softly.

'Tell me what happened,' replied Cheng, his eyes still on the bird. Lin told him in a gentle voice that belied his strength and size.

When he finished the old man carefully placed the cage on a small rosewood table at the side of the door, in the shade of one of the palm trees. He took a small brass watering can and poured a trickle of water into the bird's drinking dish, a reward for a song well sung. The bird dipped its beak into the fresh water then threw back its head and swallowed, shaking with pleasure.

'I shall tell his father,' Cheng said finally. 'You must tell his brother. His brother must come back.'

'He will take charge?' asked Lin. He wanted to lead the triad so badly that he could taste it, but he knew that it was not his time yet. And he also knew that the worst possible thing would be to push himself forward. Such audacity could easily backfire, fatally. He had seen it happen before.

'That will be up to his father. But that does not matter. He must be here. Have you told his wife?'

'I have.'

'How did she take it?'

Lin was going to say 'like a gweipor' but he bit back the words. The bond between Master Cheng and Simon Ng was almost as strong as that between parent and child and unlike Lin the old man's respect and affection included Ng's wife and child. 'Not very well, Master Cheng.'

Cheng nodded thoughtfully. 'She must be watched, Wah-tsai. Her brother is a policeman and she may be tempted to seek his help.'

'It will be done, Master Cheng.'

'We must look for the gweilo. Start with the boats in Hebe Haven, though I do not believe he will be stupid enough to remain there. And send one of your more tactful Grass Sandals around to speak to the headmistress at the girl's school. She saw the gweilo and we need a description. Once we know what he looks like we should begin to check all the hotels. At the moment that is all we can do.'

'Yes, Master Cheng.' Lin straightened his legs with a

grunt and backed away from the old man, taking two steps before turning away. As he walked down the path he could hear the old man talking quietly, either to himself or to one of his beloved birds. Lin couldn't tell which, and he knew it would be impolite to turn and look. He went back to the house to use the phone.

Howells waited until the evening sky darkened before he left the junk. Sophie had demanded that she be allowed to shower and Howells stood guard outside the door to the small shower cubicle until she'd finished. Twice she accused him of peeping and she stayed there until she'd dried herself and dressed again. She wanted to know if he'd get her some clean clothes and he told her that she wouldn't be needing them because she'd soon be going home. He made the girl a cheese sandwich and gave it to her as he locked her in the toilet.

'How long are you going to be?' she asked.

'I don't know,' he said. 'But you'll be going home soon, I promise. I'll call your mother and she'll come and get you. Keep quiet, OK?'

'OK,' she said, taking the sandwich. 'Are you a kidnapper?' she asked, her eyes wide.

'I suppose so,' he said.

'So if you're a kidnapper, what am I?' she asked seriously.

'What do you mean?'

'I mean, what do you call someone who has been kidnapped?'

'A victim,' said Howells, trying to close the door. She put up her small hand and held it open, looking up at him.

'I'm tired of being a victim,' she said quietly. 'I want to go home.'

'I know,' said Howells. 'You're not going to be a victim for much longer. Trust me.'

'OK, I will,' she said, letting go of the door and allowing him to close and lock it.

Howells hadn't decided what he'd do with Sophie when it was over. It would be a simple matter to phone Ng's house and tell them where she was. Or it would be just as easy to kill her. He didn't really care, either way.

He picked up an empty shopping bag from the galley, carried it to the back of the junk and lowered himself down into the boat. It was so dark that he couldn't see the pier or the beach, so he knew that he couldn't be seen from the shore, but even so he rowed the boat across to Marina Cove rather than using the outboard, slowly and taking care not to splash.

He guided the boat in among the luxury yachts moored at the marina and tied it up. Once on land he walked slowly, swinging the bag and whistling to himself. The triads would be there, he was sure, and there was no point in trying to sneak past. His best bet was to be out in the open, just a gweilo sailor going out for provisions. There were several dozen people walking along the marina, and many more sitting on their boats; the triads couldn't stop everyone. He'd left the car at the marina's car park where there were at least fifty others, and he headed towards it. A young man in a faded T-shirt and cut off jeans was filming his pretty, bra-less girlfriend with a small, hand-held video camera as she leaned on a railing at the water's edge. Howells turned to look at her as he walked past, partly to shield his face from the lens but also because he got a good feeling seeing her breasts bouncing under her thin cotton top. She smiled at him as she realized he was looking at her and he grinned back.

The couple with the dog were still there, walking slowly by the moored yachts, occasionally stopping to peer through the portholes. God knows what they thought they were looking for, thought Howells. Wet air tanks and a schoolgirl tied to the bed, no doubt. He reached the car and threw the shopping bag on to the back seat before driving off.

As he drove off he noticed two men in a dirty white Honda Civic, both wearing dark glasses. One of them had a notebook and he started scribbling as Howells turned onto the main road and headed back to Tsim Sha Tsui. They were obviously clocking all the cars that left, and that meant they'd probably be tracing them too. It wouldn't be too long before they tracked down the hire company and it was a short step from there to the Holiday Inn and room 426. No sweat, he was checking out anyway.

Jill Ng sat on the small brass-framed bed with the floppy grey and white Old English Sheepdog on her lap and used one of its ears to wipe her tears. She was in Sophie's bedroom, surrounded by her things, her clothes, her toys, her books. Her Garfield telephone crouched on the bedside table, ready to spring. A poster of a bare-chested rock band that her father had said was too revealing for a girl her age but which she'd begged and pleaded to be allowed to pin on her wall. Her school books piled high, unopened, on her child's size desk. Jill's mind was in turmoil, a jumble of thoughts of her husband and daughter, flashes of the good times, the holidays, the Christmas present openings, the birthdays, the rows, the arguments, the tears.

There was a bottle of tablets next to Garfield, green ones that the doctor had given her to treat the depression that had hit her like a tidal wave during the weeks after Sophie's birth. She'd kept them hidden at the back of the bathroom cabinet like an unsavoury secret, a memory that she was ashamed of but which couldn't be banished. Next to the tablets was a glass of brandy, half finished. She'd used the alcohol to wash down two of the tablets and now she sat and waited for the combination of alcohol and chemicals to numb the pain and allow her to fall into the oblivion of sleep.

Outside the bedroom door sat Rose, squatting on the floor with her back against the wall. She too was crying.

Howells delivered the car back to the hotel and checked out, settling his account in cash. He had no fear at all of being traced as he'd given Donaldson's name and passport details. The trail stopped dead at the Holiday Inn. He walked along Salisbury Road past the Regent Hotel on his left, the grand old Peninsula on his right, to the Star

Ferry terminal. An old man wearing blue and white striped pyjamas and a baggy green pullover was selling English newspapers and he stopped to buy a *Times*. It was only one day old. He paid the man and dropped a dollar coin into the turnstile at the entrance to the ferry terminal and didn't bother collecting his change. The old lady in a blue patterned trouser suit behind him pocketed the unwanted cents without a thought.

He sat in the middle of the ageing ferry on a hard wooden bench seat, listening to the comforting throb of the engines below. Most of the skyscrapers in the island's business district had huge neon advertising signs on the top. Even the futuristic HongKong and Shanghai Bank building, looking for all the world like a Ford Cortina radiator, had the bank's red and white hexagonal logo at its summit. Not one of them was flashing as Kai Tak airport was just across the harbour and it was a difficult enough approach without the hassle of competition for the landing lights.

A ferryman in a dark blue sailor suit and black plastic sandals stood by the upraised ramp that allowed passengers on and off, idly running a thick, hemp rope through his grubby hands. He cleared his throat loudly and spat noisily into the waves.

Howells flicked through the paper. It was the first English newspaper he'd read in more than two years, but there was nothing in it that interested him. The names of the politicians were the same, so were the policies and the rhetoric. Inflation was under control, the pound was strong, the peasants weren't revolting, all was well with the world. None of it mattered to Howells any more. All he cared about was working again, to be given the chance to show what he could do, what he'd been trained for.

He left the paper, half-read, on the bench when he left the ferry. The sailor took it and put it with his collection in his locker. Later that night they would be back on sale.

Howells caught a taxi to the Hilton, where he booked in under his own name. The young man behind the reception desk gave him a big toothy smile and asked how Mr Howells would be settling his account and when Mr Howells said it would be cash the smile tightened a smidgen and he asked for a deposit. The Hilton was used to businessmen and plastic cards, but Howells had plenty of yellow thousand dollar notes left, more than enough to win another gleaming smile.

Howells turned down the offer of a bellboy to show him up to his room. It was on the tenth floor, and not much different from the one he had just checked out of with a colour television, minibar, a big double bed and an uninspiring painting on the wall. It could have been a hotel room anywhere in the world, Hilton circa late 1980s.

It was nine o'clock at night, which meant it was one o'clock in London, lunchtime for the hundreds of thousands of the capital's bureaucrats – not that it would matter. Grey never answered the phone number he gave his agents, or associates as he preferred to call them. Their calls were always routed through to an answering machine which he religiously checked every hour, either manually or with a small coded bleeper that he carried which allowed him to listen to the machine's tape from a phone anywhere in the world. Howells rang through and the machine clicked on after the fourth ring. He heard Grey's sombre voice repeat the number and then there was a high-pitched tone, the signal to talk.

Howells gave his name, the date and time, and said simply that the contract had been signed and that he was now at the Hilton Hotel awaiting further instructions, and then rang off. All that was left to do now was to wait. He thought of calling Mrs Ng and telling her where her daughter was, but decided against it. It would do the girl no harm to spend another night on board the junk, and it would keep the triads doubly occupied, if nothing else. He poured himself a lager from the bar and lay on the bed watching television. He chuckled through an old episode of *The Man from Uncle*, a boyish Ilya Kuryakin and an earnest Napoleon Solo blowing away THRUSH agents with no blood and no recoil from the guns.

Grey was in his office on the ninth floor of Century House when the phone rang, but he made no move to answer it. He sat in his big, black leather swivel chair, his fingers steepled under his chin and listened carefully as Howells dictated his message. When the machine clicked off, he reached for the black push-button phone that squatted next to the brass-framed photograph of his wife, standing in the garden with a basket full of cut roses, the dogs at her heels. He had the number ready on a slip of paper and he punched out the digits that would connect him to Hong Kong.

He waited for the electronic impulses to travel up to the satellite way out in space and back to the few square miles of British soil on the rump of Southern China where it was relayed to an office in the Central business district, to an office with cheap teak-veneered furniture and an answering machine not unlike his own.

A man's voice, guttural with a heavy Chinese accent, carefully repeated the number in English and then the tone signalled that it was time to leave a message.

Grey took a deep breath and in a level voice passed what he knew would be the death sentence for the man he had sent to Hong Kong. 'Geoff Howells,' he said. 'Hilton Hotel.' Then he slowly spelled out the name and hung up.

He had never met the assassin who would get the message, and he hoped he never would. All he knew was that the assassin was called Hua-fan, that Hua-fan had a one hundred per cent success rate and that when Hua-fan's work was done and Howells was dead then the circle would be closed. Strange name for an assassin, he thought. Hua-fan. Chinese for flower petal.

Petal had dressed all in black, and she looked very, very sexy. She had on a pair of cotton trousers that ballooned out over her hips and tapered down to her ankles, like something out of the Arabian Nights. Her top was a close-fitting silk shirt that clung to her like a second skin, the collar buttoned up tight and held in place with a man's black bow tie. Round her waist hung a loose, thick leather belt. The outfit effectively covered every inch of skin below her neck, except for her tiny hands, and what made it all the more sexy was that Dugan knew every inch of her body underneath the clothing – it was as if her body was a secret that she allowed him alone to share. As she walked across the bar to where he was standing, he could see heads turning to watch, attracted by the sway of her hips, the glossy hair and the achingly pretty face, but it was Dugan she slept with, Dugan that she undressed for.

He could see some of the heads looking to see who she was there to meet, and Dugan stood taller and sucked in his gut. Without thinking, he raised his hand to smooth down his hair.

'Hi,' she said, standing on tiptoe to kiss him on the cheek. 'Been waiting long?'

'A lifetime,' he said, and he was only half joking. 'What do you feel like?'

'Just a Perrier water,' she said. 'I've got the beginnings of a headache.'

Dugan ordered her drink and then led her over to the table he'd booked earlier. He pulled the chair out for her and pushed it in as she sat down. Dugan marvelled at the way she brought out the gentleman in him when they were in public, and brought out the animal in him when they were in bed. A waiter came over with two large glossy cardboard menus. Petal ordered a cheeseburger with French fries and Dugan asked for Hainan Chicken – pieces of cold chicken with a selection of spicy sauces, rice and soup. There was nothing unusual in the gweilo choosing from the Chinese menu while the local girl opted for Western food, it happened all the time to Dugan. The girls were trying to prove how modern, how westernized they were, while Dugan simply preferred to eat eastern food.

'Why so late in the office?' she asked, both hands

clasped around the glass of sparkling water. She looked nervous, thought Dugan. Probably the headache.

'A couple of cases that need tidying up, nothing much. One of them comes to court next week so I had to get all the paperwork out of the way. Really boring stuff, but it has to be done.'

'You don't like your job, do you?'

Dugan shrugged. 'It's OK. But I'd rather be doing real policework, rather than just shuffling papers. Life is funny, isn't it? We spend almost one third of our lives doing jobs we don't particularly like, and another one third asleep. That means we only do what we really want to do for one third of our lives, and into that time we have to cram eating, washing, shopping, cleaning the house. Life is so short, Petal. Too short to fill with things we don't enjoy. Don't you think?'

'At least you can change your life, Pat. You can switch jobs, or you can always go back to England.'

'Sure, but I still have to work. But what can I do? No work, no money. And Hong Kong is the last place in the world to be without money. That's what makes the place tick. I wish I'd been born rich.'

'You're not poor, not by any means.' She reached up and touched his cheek. 'Stop feeling sorry for yourself.' She pinched the lobe of his ear, hard.

'Ouch,' he said, surprised at the pain, but at the same time excited by it.

'Well,' she said, 'you need jogging out of your misery. Stop being so morose.'

'Yeah, you're right,' he said grudgingly. The waiter returned, a plate in each hand. 'Do you feel like wine?'

'No, I'm fine with Perrier,' she said. Dugan ordered a

lager for himself, and another Perrier for Petal. She toyed with her food, pecking at it with her fork.

'Not hungry?' he asked.

'I'm OK,' she said brightly. 'I'm just feeling a bit, how do you say it, out of sorts.'

'I'm sorry. Can I help?'

'Just being here helps,' she said. She put her knife and fork down. 'You don't know how lucky you are,' she said earnestly.

'What do you mean?'

'You have so much freedom. You can go anywhere. Do anything. I envy you, and all you do is complain.' Dugan realized he had touched a nerve and reached over to hold her hand. 'Imagine living in a world where you are told what to do all the time: what to study, where to work, what to eat, where to live, what to think. To have no freedom at all. To be taken away from your family, to be made to work on a farm, to be forced into a job you don't want to do just because you show a talent for it. You have so much freedom, Pat, and you fritter it away and moan about what a tough life you have.'

Tears were welling up in her eyes and the couple at the next table glanced over to look at the big, awkward gweilo bullying the small Chinese girl. Dugan hunched forward over his plate, wanting to get closer to her, wanting to comfort her but not knowing the magic words that would make it all right.

'Do you have any idea what life is like in China, Pat Dugan? Have you any idea at all?'

He shook his head. He wanted to tell her that it was OK, that he understood, except that he didn't think he did.

'I'll tell you a story,' she said slowly. 'And maybe

212

when I've finished you'll count your blessings and stop feeling so sorry for yourself.' She sniffed and groped in her bag for a packet of paper handkerchiefs. 'I was born in Shanghai,' she said. 'My mother was a singer, a very famous singer. She could sing Chinese opera, but preferred western music and jazz, and in Shanghai during the fifties and early sixties she was as famous as Anita Mui is in Hong Kong today. Her concerts were packed out, and she was courted by all the rich and famous people, invited to all the best parties. She was a star, a real star, not one of the manufactured Cantonese pop idols of today. She had the pick of all the eligible men in Shanghai, but chose my father, a doctor. One of those crazy things; she sprained her ankle horse-riding, he was there when she fell, he treated her, they fell in love. In any normal, sane world they would have been happy ever after. But not in China.'

'What happened?' Dugan asked quietly, conscious that, for whatever reason, Petal was allowing him inside her shell for the first time.

'They married, they had me, and three years later my brother was born. That was before the days of the one-couple, one-child craziness. For a time we were the happiest family you could imagine; we were rich, life in Shanghai was so good. It was a thriving, bustling city, lots to do, lots of places for children to play. We lived in a big house, with servants, and horses. I had my own pony. You can't imagine how perfect it was.'

Her voice was dropping in volume and Dugan had to strain to hear her over the noise of the videos.

'And then?' he said, gently urging her on.

'The Cultural Revolution,' she said. 'The country went

mad. Anything artistic, anybody with money, anybody who was not prepared to swear total and complete allegiance to the Communists, was treated with such contempt, such bitterness, such savagery. The Red Guards stormed our house one day. Actually that's not true, the servants let them in. The servants joined them. They smashed up everything we had. I have no pictures of my parents, none of my mother's records. They even killed my pony, can you think of anything so horrible, so vindictive? They slit its throat in front of me, screaming that animals were for food or for work, not for pleasure. Patrick, they killed my pony.'

She was crying out loud now, small sobs that she tried to stifle with her handkerchief. Dugan felt totally lost. He had no idea what had brought this on, and had no idea what to say. She blew her nose, pocketed the screwed-up ball of tissue and picked up her knife and fork. She had her head down over her plate as she hacked at her burger, her hair hanging forward like a veil. She looked up with a forkful of meat halfway to her mouth and tried to smile.

'I'm sorry,' she said. 'I didn't mean to sound so upset. I've just had a hard day, that's all. I'll be all right, honest.'

Her eyes looked different, as if a bullet-proof screen had come down behind her pupils, locking her emotions in and Dugan out. He felt cheated; for one blinding moment he had glimpsed the pearl within the shell, and then it had closed. He didn't know how long it would be before she opened up to him again, or if she ever would. He began to eat again, but the chicken had no taste.

Both English-language television channels closed down at about one o'clock in the morning. Howells flicked through the buttons on the remote control. He found a black-and-white Chinese historical drama where the men had pigtails and the women looked like porcelain dolls, and a horse-racing programme presented by two young Chinese men in matching blazers. He switched off the set and got undressed. He'd wake up soon enough when Grey rang. For the moment he was tired, dog-tired. His calf muscles ached from the exertions of the morning, and his knees were grazed where he'd scraped against rocks on the sea bed. He slipped quickly and easily into sleep.

Whatever had upset Petal, it didn't get any better as the evening progressed. She seemed lifeless and withdrawn, almost a stranger. Dugan tried to make light of it, told her a few jokes which were rewarded with a weak smile and did everything short of standing on his head to win her round.

'I'm sorry, Pat, I'm terrible company tonight,' she said, half-way through her third Perrier water.

'No you're not,' he said. 'Perhaps you'd feel better after a drink.' He raised his glass of lager. 'Drown your sorrows.'

She shook her head. 'Drink won't help,' she said.

'Anyway, I've got a headache. A drink is the last thing I need.'

Dugan waved at a waiter and asked for the bill. It arrived on a stainless steel tray and he paid with a handful of red notes.

'I'll take you home,' offered Dugan, pulling out her chair for her.

'No, no need,' she said. 'I just don't feel very well, that's all. I'll just go home and rest. You stay here; your friends will be downstairs, won't they?'

'Of course,' he laughed. 'They never go anywhere else.'

'Well, you stay here with them. You can walk me to a taxi.' She held his arm as they walked out of the door and down the steps to the road. A cab was waiting there with its light on but with a red card with the Chinese characters for Hong Kong covering its 'For Hire' sign. Dugan held the door for her. She stood in front of him, her breasts against his chest, her head tilted back so that she could look at his face. 'Thank you for a lovely evening,' she said. Dugan snorted, but he smiled as he did it. 'I'm serious,' she said. 'I'll be OK tomorrow, I'm sure.'

'I hope so,' said Dugan. He kissed her on the forehead. 'Petal?'

'Hmm?'

'Is there anything I can do to help?'

'Don't be so silly,' she said. She reached up, linking her arms around his neck and pulling herself up on tiptoe to kiss him full on the lips. 'Good night,' she said, and slid into the taxi.

Dugan closed the door and stood on the pavement to watch it drive towards the harbour. He could see the dark shape of her head in the middle of the back seat. She didn't turn round and Dugan felt cold and empty inside. He turned and went back to the lights and noise of the disco.

There were three of them, two men and a girl. One of the men bent down over the lock and inserted two thin pieces of wire, one hard, the other curved and springy with a hook on one end. While he worked, silently pushing the tumblers back one by one, the girl and the second man stood at either end of the corridor, keeping watch. It took him less than a minute, and then he rested back on his heels and nodded to his colleagues. They walked carefully, placing each foot flat on the carpet, heel then toe, arms slightly away from their body so that they didn't even disturb the night air with the rustle of clothing.

There was no need to speak; the three had worked together for many years. They worked as one. The lock-picker slowly rose to his feet and rested his palm against the wooden door. He put his tools in the inside pocket of his poorly fitting suit and slowly opened the door. All three were tidal breathing, their lungs taking in just enough air to breathe, no exertion, mouths slightly open.

The two men entered first, moving as if in slow motion, past the bathroom and the minibar, stopping as the girl gently pushed the door closed, turning the handle in fractions of degrees so that it locked with no noise. She carried a small leather bag in one hand. The room was very dark, the thick curtains blocking any outside light, and the trio stood for a while until their eyes grew used to the room. They could make out the dressing-table, the wardrobes, the television, the bedside table and Howells, lying on his back, one arm across the pillows, the other under the single sheet that covered the lower half of his body. It was hot and airless in the room because he'd switched off the air-conditioning.

They moved quickly then, the two men up on the balls of their feet crossing quickly to opposite sides of the bed, grabbing an arm each. Howells woke as the man on his left grabbed hold of his arm, the nails biting into his flesh. He rolled towards him, freeing his right arm from under the sheet and preparing to slash out, fingers curled to strike when it too was seized and thrust down on to the bed. Howells made no sound, he knew there was no reason to cry out, there would be no one to help him. He tried to lift his shoulders off the bed but a bitter-smelling hand hit him in the face and pushed him back on to the pillow, the palm firmly under his chin, clamping his jaw together and making breathing difficult. The fingers of the hand moved to either side of his nostrils and he was forced to breathe through clenched teeth like a muzzled dog.

He tensed, waiting for the knife or the gun or whatever else they were going to use, testing their strength by pulling his arms in towards him. There were two hands holding his left arm, one holding the right, because it was the man on his right who was holding down his head. That was a mistake; Howells was right-handed and when he moved that would be the way he'd go. He kicked out with his legs, pushing the sheet off the bottom of the bed so that he'd be able to lash out with his legs. He saw the girl then. She was standing at the dressing-table with her back towards him. She was dressed in black and seemed little more than a shadow, and when she turned her face and hands were all he could see, everything else faded into the dark. Even her face was partly obscured by her black hair. She was pretty, very pretty, and Howells had the feeling that he'd seen her somewhere before but he couldn't place it, there was just a niggling feeling at the back of his mind. She had something in her right hand, and as she stepped forward to the foot of the bed he could see it was a hypodermic, the needle pointed to the ceiling. She held it in both hands, pushing the plunger up slowly and expelling a small amount of the liquid. It dripped slowly down the needle and she tilted it so that it wouldn't run down her hands.

She moved to the left side of the bed, stepping on the sheet that he'd kicked on to the floor. Howells moved his legs up the bed, crossing his left thigh across his groin, and she smiled at his attempt to cover himself. She knelt on the bed, slowly, handling the hypodermic carefully as she prepared to mount him. Howells flinched, drawing his legs up to his left side, and her smile grew wider. She flicked her head to one side, throwing the black sheet of hair away from her face and she was still smiling when Howells threw all his weight to the left and swung his right leg round and kicked her full on the side of the face with the ball of his right foot, the toes pulled back, the ankle tense, hard enough to kill if he hadn't been held flat on his back and only able to use the lower half of his body.

Her head snapped away and she crashed off the bed, the hypodermic spinning through the air and hitting the curtains. Howells pulled in with both arms, breathing hard with the exertion, then quickly thrust his right arm to the side, slipping through the man's hand just enough so that he could twist it round. He kicked across with the left leg, missing the head but making the man relax his grip again. He released Howells' head but before he could get both hands to hold the arm Howells twisted again and grabbed the man's index finger. He bent it back savagely, hearing the bone crack. The man screamed involuntarily but then bit back the pain as Howells released him. The man on his left hadn't moved, he'd concentrated on holding the left arm firmly on the bed, and he looked across in surprise as Howells' right arm whipped across, fingers rock-hard, the cutting edge of the hand curving through the air and then arcing up and thrusting hard into his temple. His head jerked back and both hands let go. Howells was on his feet immediately, crouched low on the bed. The man shook his head and his eyes focused just in time to see the second strike coming, a clenched fist that smashed into his windpipe and shattered the cartilage. He collapsed on top of the girl, his eyes wide with panic as he fought for breath, air bubbling through the blood that ran thickly down into his aching lungs.

Howells whirled around, dropping down into his fighting crouch again, but as he did his ears roared with a deafening explosion that stunned him and he felt a crashing blow on his right shoulder that knocked him backwards into the modernistic painting on the wall behind the headboard. He rolled along the wall, smearing blood against the painting, and staggered off the bed. The pain hit him then, a red wave that flashed from his shoulder and made him grit his teeth, swallowing the roar of rage that wanted to erupt from his mouth. He dropped low, forward hand up to block any attack, rear hand clenched at waist height, ready to punch despite the searing pain. It was a reflex action because the strength had deserted his right arm, it ached fiercely and he could feel wetness spreading around the wound. The man with the broken finger was standing with a wicked-looking gun in hand, a wisp of smoke oozing from the barrel. Howells realized that if he hadn't been turning the bullet would have struck him in the middle of the back, instead of hitting him in the shoulder. He knew also that he had to move immediately because he could see the man's finger tightening on the trigger. He was perfectly calm, despite being stark naked and facing a man with a gun. All fear, all hesitation, had long ago been trained out of Howells. The gun was in the man's left hand, the right hand out for balance with the index finger awkwardly crooked, and Howells knew instinctively that the man was right-handed. He ducked to the left, a feinting movement that moved the gun just a fraction, and then dropped his weight back on his right leg and flicked his forward leg out and up, so fast the movement was a blur. It wasn't a killing kick, there was little or no focus, but it moved so quickly that before the man's finger could generate enough force to pull the trigger the foot had reached its target, knocking the gun upwards. Only then did the trigger kick, the explosion making Howells flinch as the bullet ripped over his head and buried itself into the plaster ceiling. Howells dropped his kicking leg to the floor and moved forward, bringing his right knee up and then powering forward, focusing the kick a good nine inches behind the man's sternum, kicking through him rather than at him. As the ball of his foot connected with the chest, Howells twisted his hip into the kick, tightening all the muscles in his legs, the whole weight of his body behind the blow. A killing blow. The sternum disintegrated and the diaphragm collapsed as Howells followed through until the man slammed into the wall, blood frothing from his lips as he grunted and died.

Howells stood over the man as he slumped to the floor, watched as his eyes filmed over and only then did he walk over to the mirror above the dressing-table, to check the damage to his shoulder. The man's gun had been a small calibre, a .22 maybe, not a professional's gun. There was no exit wound, the bullet was still in there; he couldn't feel it, but he knew he would once his body's adrenalin and enkephalin had dropped to normal.

He was lucky, lucky that the man hadn't had a .357, lucky that he'd ducked as he turned, lucky that he'd hurt the man's shooting hand. Lucky that they'd planned to kill him with some sort of an injection and not a bullet. But luck was often all that separated the living from the dead. Luck and training.

He dressed as quickly as he could, knowing that someone was sure to have reported the shot. He pulled on his trousers and his socks and shoes, using only his left hand. He could feel blood dripping down his shoulder, so he shook a pillow out of its case and wrapped the white linen across the wound before gingerly putting on a rust-coloured shirt. It wouldn't stop all the bleeding but at least it wouldn't show if it soaked into the shirt.

He looked at himself in the mirror. The bulky pillow-case was bulging under the shirt, it was as obvious as hell.

He had a black cotton bomber jacket so he put that on, too. That looked better. His wallet was on the dressing-table and he put it in his jacket pocket, using his left hand, and then slotted his passport and Donaldson's into the back pocket of his jeans.

The shock was beginning to wear off and shafts of pain shot through his shoulder, making him wince. He stood with his eyes closed, breathing deeply and willing the pain to go away, then he moved quickly to the door. He couldn't risk taking his bag or belongings in case the front desk stopped him. He checked the corridor, both sides, and then slipped out, locking the door behind him.

Pat Dugan was pissed. Well pissed. He'd stayed in Hot Gossip with Burr and a handful of the anti-triad boys, drinking hard and fast. He was angry at Petal for leaving him, angry with himself for not knowing how to handle the situation, and angry at the world in general. He laughed too loud and drank too much until even Burr told him he'd had enough.

'Fuck you,' Dugan told him.

'Fuck you, too,' said Burr. 'Go home.' He walked off, leaving Dugan standing by himself at the bar.

'Time to go, Pat,' he told himself and then headed unsteadily to the exit, bumping into one of the dinner-jacketed bouncers on the way out.

A cab pulled up in front of a young Chinese couple standing at the kerbside and Dugan grabbed at the handle, getting hold of it a fraction of a second before they did. He yanked open the door and glared drunkenly at them, daring them to argue. They moved away, embarrassed by the open show of hostility, and Dugan tumbled on to the back seat. The driver leant over and pulled the door shut. Dugan lay where he was, face down, and shouted his address in Cantonese. The driver grunted and drove off.

Howells had to stand in a queue outside the Hilton Hotel while a tall, bulky Indian with a gleaming white turban, black and yellow tunic and white breeches went down to Queen's Road and flagged down taxis, directing them up the slip road. As he stood in line he felt faint, his head filled with the throbbing sound of his own heartbeat. He gasped for breath and rubbed his forehead with his sweating left hand. His right arm and shoulder ached horribly. His legs began to tremble and he had to lock his knees rigid to stop himself falling over. Two cabs arrived, then a third, and then thankfully it was his turn. The Indian asked, in impeccable English, where he was going, and only then did he realize that he had no idea, simply that he had to get away from the hotel before the bodies were discovered. He heard himself say 'Wan Chai' before he carefully got into the cab.

The Indian nodded and told the driver, and the driver grinned at him. 'Another fucking gweilo about to get fleeced,' he said in rapid Cantonese.

'They never learn,' agreed the Indian.

'Fuck his mother,' said the driver, slamming the car into gear and lurching back to the road. Howells groaned and kept his eyes shut.

There were certain preparations that had to be made if Dugan was to make it through the night, what was left of it. He made sure the aircon was switched on, and pulled a plastic bottle of distilled water out of the fridge and drank as much of it as he could force down before placing it next to his bed. He took a bottle of orange-flavoured Eno fruit salts and tipped a spoonful into a glass and put that down next to the water. He did it all on automatic pilot, humming quietly to himself, and then he sat down on the bed and undressed, dropping the clothes on the floor before flopping back and passing out. He'd left the light on, but he didn't notice.

The taxi stopped outside the Washington Club and Howells fumbled with his wallet. He handed over two green notes and didn't wait for the change. The driver grinned and used a lever under the dashboard to pull the door closed after him.

The aged doorman heaved himself off his wooden stool and opened the door for him, allowing out the pulsing beat of a Cantonese pop song. Howells caught sight of his reflection in the fish tank as he walked into the bar. He looked terrible. Big deal. He felt terrible. He felt like his shoulder had been put between the jaws of a red-hot vice and was being squeezed, hard. The bar was busy but there were a couple of empty seats side by side and he walked to one, being careful not to bump his arm. On the seat to his left was a small man in a crumpled beige suit with sweat stains under the armpits drinking Foster's lager from a can. He raised it to Howells. 'How's it going, digger?' he asked in a broad Australian accent.

'Great,' said Howells. The Australian had blank eyes, a film of sweat over his skin, and a stupid grin on his face. He was well gone.

Howells looked around for Amy. He missed her at first because she was standing on the opposite side of the bar with her back to him, caught between two men in dark business suits, drinking champagne. One of them had his hand on her hip, the other was looming over her, teeth bared like a vampire about to take a piece out of her neck. She laughed out loud and he thought it sounded forced. Wishful thinking, maybe.

She turned to pick up the bottle of champagne out of a battered stainless steel ice bucket and pour the last drop into her glass. She saw Howells then and instantly smiled at him, then followed it by pulling a face and nodding her head towards the man on her left. He grimaced back and she smiled again. She held her hand up, fingers splayed and mouthed 'five minutes'. She was wearing a lemon-coloured evening dress with white frothy lace arms. Howells nodded and told the barhag in front of him that he wanted to see the wine list.

'Huh?' she barked at him.

'Lager,' he said.

She screamed the order over the top of his head at one of the waiters behind him.

'What's your name?' she asked him, leaning her elbows on the bar and breathing garlic fumes into his face.

'Fuck off,' he said. She glanced at him and cursed in Cantonese. 'Fuck off,' he repeated, quietly this time, and she read the menace in his eyes. She backed away, saying nothing.

The Australian was impressed. 'Jesus, digger, you sure know how to treat a girl.' Howells ignored him.

He left his right hand on the bar, trying to keep the weight off his throbbing shoulder. Occasionally he lifted the glass of lager to his lips but he only sipped at it. His mouth felt dry but he knew alcohol would only dehydrate him and that would make him feel worse.

It took Amy more than fifteen minutes to drag herself away from the three-piece-suited barracudas, during which she drank two more glasses of champagne and allowed them to fondle her breasts, albeit briefly.

She stroked the back of his neck as she passed behind him, then allowed her hand to move across his right shoulder. Howells nearly screamed and he had to clamp his teeth together to keep the noise in. It felt as if she'd stuck a red-hot poker into his flesh and then twisted it round, deeper and deeper. She pulled back her hand as if he'd bit it.

'What's wrong?' she said.

Howells kept his eyes closed but he could still see a red mist punctuated with flashes of bright yellow light. He waited until the waves of pain subsided before he risked opening them. He saw Amy sitting on the stool next to him, one hand covering her wall of teeth.

'Tom, what's the matter?'

Howells kept his voice low so that the Australian wouldn't hear him. 'I need your help, Amy.' The dimpled barhag appeared next to him and demanded that he buy Amy a drink. He agreed and she walked off, a satisfied smirk on her face.

'What do you mean?' Amy asked.

'Can I pay your bar fine?' he asked urgently. 'Can I take you out?'

'Of course. But it is expensive. Are you sure you want to?'

'Yes,' he hissed, the pain returning.

'I'll speak to the mamasan,' she said. She slipped off the stool in a rustle of silk and went over to a wrinkled old woman who was wearing an ill-fitting wig and an equally ill-fitting navy blue dress. She had a lousy dress sense, but Howells could see she was wearing a solid gold Rolex and he doubted that it was a fake.

The old woman looked at Howells and he felt as if he was a side of beef being weighed up by a butcher. Then she nodded and Amy smiled and came back over, her hands clasped together across her stomach.

'Mamasan says it's OK. How will you pay?'

Very romantic, thought Howells, but he knew it wasn't romance he needed. It was help, a place to hide and someone who knew what they were doing to take the bullet out.

Howells gingerly took his wallet out and handed it to Amy. 'Take out what you want,' he said. She looked through it and pulled out a handful of notes before giving it back.

'You stay here while I change,' she said.

'Don't worry,' said Howells. 'I won't run away.'

Thomas Ng couldn't remember exactly when it had happened, but somewhere along the line he'd begun to develop a fear of flying. He could remember the time when he thought no more of making the trip from San Francisco to Hong Kong than he did of driving through the Cross Harbour Tunnel or over the Golden Gate Bridge. The first few times he'd actually enjoyed the flight, relishing time to relax away from ever-ringing phones and the demands of others, time to watch a movie and catch up on some work. Then the trip became a regular chore, something that had to be done to keep the family business running, painless but boring. Not something he gave any thought to. But recently he had started to dread the flight, lying awake the night before, tossing and turning, trying wherever possible to postpone the time when he'd be sitting in an aluminium tube thousands of feet above the earth. He'd begun asking for aisle seats so that he couldn't see the wings flexing, he'd started taking a couple of Valiums an hour or so before checking in at the airport. And whereas in the old days he'd have sipped a tonic water with his meal, now he'd put away a couple of Martinis. Or more. None of it helped; he could still feel his heart beating, the sweat beading on his forehead, the physiological symptoms of his apprehension. To make it worse, this time he'd had to fly United Airlines, all the Asian airlines had been fully booked. So instead of being waited on by the girls of Cathay Pacific he had to suffer overweight gweipors with fat arses, plastic smiles and too much make-up.

First had been full and half the plane seemed to have been given over to Business Class and the treatment he was receiving was worse than he'd ever got in Economy with Cathay or Singapore or Thai. He'd held out his jacket to a blonde with scarlet-smeared lips and over-plucked eyebrows but she just looked at him with contempt and suggested he put it in one of the overhead lockers. He'd asked for a Martini and been told he'd have to wait. He asked for headphones and was told they'd be issued after they'd taken off. Ng supposed it was to be expected with a Western airline, but he'd had no choice, he had to get to Hong Kong immediately.

One of the ways he tried to dampen his newly acquired fear of flying was to concentrate on work for as long as possible during the flight, and he sat with a Toshiba laptop computer in front of him, checking and cross-checking his accounts. At first he'd had great doubts about trusting the micro-computer with information about the family business, the drugs, the extortion, the money laundering, the dummy corporations and bank accounts that now spanned the world. He dreaded to think what would happen if it ever fell into the wrong hands. But one of his programmers had devised a foolproof security system that would immediately delete all the information it contained if the correct password was not keyed in. And at regular intervals the machine would ask questions that only Ng could know the answers to. A wrong answer, or a delay in keying in the information, would also delete the on-board memory and clear the disk. And one of the control keys had been reprogrammed so that if Ng was ever surprised while using the machine he could press it and render it useless. Ng made regular copies of the files on floppy disks which were stored in safety deposit boxes in banks in Hong Kong and San Francisco. It was an empire that Thomas Ng was proud of, one that he'd created. If it hadn't been for him the Ng fortune would still be nothing more than money from vice, confined to Hong Kong, and with little or no future after 1997. His father had given no thought to the future other than to ensure that his three sons were well educated at overseas universities. Thomas had studied accountancy at Columbia University and had spent a year at Harvard, and he'd been keen to put his knowledge to good use. Over seemingly endless cups of insipid tea he'd managed to persuade his father that the way ahead lay overseas – overseas property, overseas investments, preparing for the day when the Communists took back Hong Kong. As far as cash flow went, Thomas had realized that it was the drugs business that was the crux of the whole operation, master-minding the export of heroin from the Golden Triangle and distributing it in Hong Kong. Without too much effort that distribution could be extended to the West Coast of America, especially in cities like San Francisco which had bent over backwards to welcome Chinese immigrants. The growth of Chinatowns also allowed the triad to expand its prostitution and extortion activities overseas, and they, too, were good revenue generators. In fact, it was the huge amounts of money generated in the United States that had led to the legitimate side of the Ng business empire.

Whereas Hong Kong banks and deposit-taking companies were quite accustomed, and happy, to handle cash, the US institutions were bound by law to report all cash transactions of over $10,000. But $10,000 didn't buy much of the white powder, and a half-decent hooker could pull in that amount in one day.

There were a number of ways the cash could have been laundered, and in the early days Thomas Ng had simply used his triad soldiers to pay the money into various accounts in small amounts, but as the criminal empire grew that became too time-consuming. He'd had a team of twelve working throughout the day but it still wasn't enough.

He put money, again always less than $10,000 at any one time, into tax-free bonds through a number of stockbrokers, and then once he'd amassed a sizeable mountain of cash he had the brokers transfer the balance to their bank account. The bank then cashed the bonds and passed the money through to an account in one of several tax havens the Ng family used. But before long that, too, became time-consuming and involved too many people.

Thomas Ng hit on the idea of setting up legitimate businesses with a high cash flow and pumping the dirty money into them. He started off with video rental shops, big operations with thousands of videos in stock. Nobody ever checked on how many of the videos were actually rented out, and nobody cared, but each year the carefully tended accounts of each shop processed hundreds of thousands of dollars. Then he set up a chain of quality car rental outlets, offering Porsches, Rolls-Royces and Ferraris. Nobody knew how many of the cars were actually being driven around by customers and how many were simply parked in garages. Nobody cared, but the books showed a very healthy profit curve. High class bakeries were next, shops selling overpriced speciality breads and cookies at exorbitant prices.

When Thomas set the businesses up, their main role was to act as a conduit for money pulled in from the illegal sources, but before long they were thriving in their own right. The money, legal and illegal, was funnelled through a daisy chain of companies that spanned the world, from bank accounts in Switzerland to a shell corporation in the Cayman Islands to a discretionary trust in Vanuatu, most of them little more than brass plaques on a wall. Thomas moved into property then, first buying the leases on his shops, but soon moving into hotels and residential blocks. And he'd now got to the stage where the legitimate side of the operation was on a par with the vice activities. In fact, Thomas was now giving serious consideration to pulling out of drugs and prostitution altogether. What he really wanted to do was to move into banking and financial services, maybe insurance, that was where the really big money lay – big and legal. But how to persuade his father that that was the way to go? He was a man who was devoted to tradition, to his ancestors, and to his family. A man who humoured his Number Two son by letting him run his own business in America – except that the Number Two son was now Number One son, as of eighteen hours ago.

Thomas Ng sat in the aeroplane and scanned the columns of figures on the screen in front of him, but his thoughts were miles, and years, away. His thoughts were of his older brother, the man who'd stayed behind in Hong Kong while Thomas made his way in the world with the sanctuary of a United States passport. Simon Ng, who had been unable to get US citizenship, or citizenship anywhere outside Hong Kong, because of a criminal record acquired when he was nineteen years old and Thomas had been fifteen. Simon, who'd stood in the dock in front of a gweilo magistrate and confessed to slashing an 18K Red Pole with a machete and Simon who'd paid the fine, in cash. Except that it hadn't been older brother who'd lost his temper and pulled out the knife, it had been younger brother. And it had been younger brother who'd drawn blood and dropped the weapon and run away, and older brother who'd picked it up and been caught by the police trying to wipe off the fingerprints. Simon Ng who'd taken the blame and Thomas Ng who'd got the passport. It was a debt that Thomas had never been able to repay, and now he would not have the chance. His older brother would be avenged, that much Thomas Ng could promise.

Howells had nearly passed out when he bent down to get into the cab outside the Washington Club. His knees sagged and Amy had moved forward to support him; thank God she'd grabbed his left arm. She moved on to the back seat next to him.

'Are you OK?' she asked. Howells nodded. 'Are you still at the Mandarin Hotel?'

Christ, she had a good memory, even he'd forgotten he'd told her he was staying there.

'No,' he said. 'Look, Amy, I really do need your help. Can we go to your house?'

'No,' she said, shocked. 'Of course not. You are gweilo, you cannot come to my home. What would my neighbours think? Aieee yaaa! You are crazy.'

'I'm hurt, Amy. I've been shot. I can't go back to the hotel and I can't go to hospital.'

She looked confused, and frightened, and before he could stop her she put her hand forward and grabbed his right arm to shake him. The pain was excruciating but before he could scream he passed out, his face white. His head pitched forward and banged into her shoulder. She put her arm around him and cradled him. His right hand lay in her lap and for the first time she saw the trickle of blood crawling over his wrist. She wiped it with her handkerchief.

The driver impatiently asked her where she wanted to go.

Amy sighed and told him her address.

Dugan was having a hell of a time, flat on his back with a Filipina each side, one with a mug of warm tea, the other with a glass of cold water. They were doing terrible things to him below the waist, and the alternation between hot and cold was driving him wild, until the jangling bell of the telephone dived down into his subconscious and dragged him kicking and screaming out of his dream.

He opened his eyes a fraction and squinted at his watch. It was six o'clock in the morning. It had to be a wrong number and he was sure that when he picked up the receiver a voice would go 'Waai?' and then hang up.

Phone etiquette was not something they went a bundle on in Hong Kong, where good manners were not one of life's priorities. He tried burying his head under the pillow but the phone was insistent. He groaned and rolled over on to his stomach and groped for the receiver. It was Bellamy.

'Dugan?'

'Yeah. Do you know what time it is?' he moaned.

'Pull yourself together, you drunken bum. Petal's been hurt.'

'What?' The mention of Petal cleared his head a little. He pushed himself up and sat on the bed, his feet on the wooden floor. His stomach heaved but he managed to stop himself from throwing up.

'She's been beaten up, badly,' said Bellamy. 'She's in Queen Elizabeth's Hospital, room 241.'

'What happened?'

'We're not sure, Pat. It's a complete fucking mystery at the moment. She was found in a room at the Hilton, along with two bodies.'

'Bodies?'

'Two Chinese. They'd been killed by some sort of kung fu expert by the look of it, a real professional job.'

'Some sort of triad thing?'

'Fuck, we just don't know. The room was booked in the name of a gweilo, and he's disappeared. At the moment he's our prime suspect, or another victim. At the moment it looks as if they were trying to inject the gweilo with something; the lab is checking it out, but it sure as hell isn't distilled water. Look, I've got things to do, Pat. I just called to let you know where she was. If I were you I'd get down there straight away.

I'll call you later this morning. See if you can find out what happened to her.'

'Sure, sure. Will do.'

He hung up and sat with his shoulders on his knees, taking deep breaths to quell his queasy stomach. If he had the choice between two sexy young Filipinas or the glass of iced water it would be no contest. His mouth felt like a ferret's den. He opened the bottle of water and poured it on to the orange crystals. They bubbled and fizzed and frothed and he drank it in one go before groping his way to the bathroom, a thousand questions fluttering around his skull like trapped butterflies.

The doorman who was supposed to be standing guard over the entrance to Amy's block was asleep as usual, slumped on a rickety wooden chair, his head back, mouth open showing rotten teeth as he snored. She led Howells down a corridor, cracked tiles of dirty-white with a brightly coloured motif composed of bowls of grapes, towards the stairs. At the bottom of the concrete steps she held him against the wall and whispered urgently: 'There's no lift, Tom, and it's four floors up. Lean on me.'

Howells had kept his eyes shut ever since he'd fallen against her in the cab. He was so white, Amy thought, as white as freshly boiled rice, as if all the blood had oozed out of his head and down his arm. His sleeve was wet with blood and it was staining her own clothes. She hoped to all the gods in heaven that her neighbours were sleeping as deeply as the old doorman.

Howells nodded and grunted and put his good arm, the left one, around her shoulders. Together they scaled the stairs, Howells putting first his right foot on a step, then his left, shuffling up one step at a time. At the top of each flight Amy let him rest, encouraging him to take deep breaths to clear his head, but he seemed to get weaker the higher they climbed.

Eventually they were outside her door, and Amy made him stand by the wall as she went through her bag for her keys. She opened the door and switched on the light before helping him in. The living-room was small and square, a tiny kitchen to the left and a bathroom to the right. It took only a dozen of Howells' small steps to cross the room to the bedroom door, which Amy nudged open. His legs began to buckle and she barely managed to support his weight until they reached the bed. It was a single bed with one pillow and a thin quilt. Amy did not bring customers home – ever. She would go to a hotel, or if they were local she would go to their flat. That was all. Howells was the first man she had ever allowed through the door, except for the plumber who once fixed a leaking tap for her.

Howells pitched forward and lay face down on the bed, head turned towards the wall. She felt his forehead. He was very hot, the flesh damp with perspiration. Her small flat did not have an air-conditioner but there was a floor-mounted fan under the window. She switched it on and directed the cooling breeze at the injured man.

Amy went back into the lounge, dropping her bag on the one small sofa there. She closed and locked her front door and slipped off her shoes. In the kitchen she filled a blue plastic washing-up bowl with warm water and took it along with a small bottle of disinfectant and a roll of paper kitchen towel into the bedroom. She tried to get the cotton jacket off Howells but as soon as she moved his right arm he screamed involuntarily. She took a large pair of kitchen scissors from a drawer under the sink and used it to cut off the jacket, piece by piece, and she placed the bits gingerly on to a newspaper on the floor. The shirt was rust-coloured, but the area around his right shoulder was darker than the rest, and when she touched it her hand came away stained red. She cut the shirt along the back, up through the collar, and then down along the seam to the cuff. She gently pulled it away and gasped as she saw the blood-soaked material wrapped around his shoulder. She removed it and put it on the newspaper. Blood seeped out and was absorbed by the newsprint. She used pieces of the kitchen roll to clean up his torso, starting from the waist and working up. She was amazed to find that all the blood had come from one small hole just below his shoulder, about the size of a one dollar coin.

She dipped a fresh piece of paper into the disinfectant and dabbed at the wound. She could tell that it wouldn't heal on its own, Tom would need a doctor. She eased her hand under the front of his shoulder and felt around, but there was no wound there. Tom had said that he'd been shot so that meant the bullet was still inside. She carried the bloodstained paper and cloth through to the kitchen and put it in a black plastic rubbish bag, carefully tying it at the top. She put it in a bucket in the cupboard below the sink.

Back in the bedroom she removed his shoes and socks, his jeans and his underpants, putting them on a small wicker chair at the bottom of the bed. She checked the pockets, finding the wallet and the two passports. Both were British, but only one contained his picture. Howells, the passport said his name was. Geoffrey Howells. The other belonged to a much softer-looking man, a man who looked as if he sweated a lot. His name was Donaldson. Neither of the men was called Tom.

She went through the pockets of the wallet. A few thousand dollars, and a handful of credit cards. Some of them were in the name of Howells, and some of them were Donaldson's.

She took the cash out of the wallet, and put the passports into the top drawer of her dressing-table. From the bottom drawer she took a white sheet and draped it over the unconscious man, careful to keep it off the shoulder. There was a telephone on the wall, next to the kitchen door. She went to it and dialled a number as she rubbed the notes between her fingers.

At first Dugan thought that maybe the nurse at the reception desk had sent him to the wrong ward. There were two beds in the semi-private room, separated by a green curtain. The bed nearest the door was empty and the girl in the bed by the window looked nothing like Petal; the face round and puffy, the lips cracked and bleeding, the nose flat against the face. As he got closer to the small figure on the bed he could see that her head was circled with a bandage and that there was some sort of padding on her left cheek. Around her neck was a plastic surgical collar. Her eyes were closed. It was Petal, all right.

He sat on the edge of the bed and took her hand in his.

Her eyes fluttered open and between clenched teeth she whispered, 'Hello.'

'Hello yourself,' he said.

A nurse appeared at his shoulder, a tall, thin woman with buck teeth and lank hair. 'Her jaw is badly bruised, so she can't talk much,' the nurse said.

'Not broken?' asked Dugan.

The nurse shook her head. 'No, but she has lost two teeth, her neck is badly sprained and her cheekbone is cracked. She shouldn't be talking at all.' There was a look of disapproval on her face and Dugan could see that she was gearing up to ask him to leave.

He opened his wallet and showed her his warrant card. 'I won't be long,' he said. The nurse nodded curtly and left the room, closing the door behind her. Petal squeezed his hand and Dugan leant over and kissed her on the forehead.

'You don't look too bad,' he said and she smiled with her eyes. 'Does it hurt?'

'They've given me something,' she said, keeping her lips still as she spoke. 'I just feel sleepy.'

'Can you tell me what happened?'

She closed her eyes.

'What were you doing in the Hilton Hotel? Who hit you? Who were the men in the room? What is going on?' The questions tumbled over each other, even though he knew she'd have to take it slowly and that talking was an effort for her. But he had to know. Part of it was the copper in him, but it went deeper than that. He was falling in love with this pretty little Chinese girl and he didn't want to be locked out of her life. He wanted to know everything, to knock down the wall of secrets and silences between

241

them. And this she couldn't shrug off with a joke or a deft change of subject.

'You won't like it,' she said, still with her eyes firmly shut. He moved up the bed to get closer to her, so that he could catch the whispered words.

'Try me,' he said.

'I have to trust you, Pat,' she said. 'They'll be coming to take me away soon, so when I've told you you'll have to go. You have a right to know, but you must keep what I tell you to yourself.' She opened her eyes and studied his face. 'Do you promise?'

Dugan nodded. He would promise her anything.

'I was there to kill him,' she said simply.

The confusion showed on his face and he shook his head wordlessly.

'It's true,' she said. 'I work for the Chinese, for their equivalent of a secret service. The two men with me were part of my team. The man we were to kill was a guest in the hotel, Howells was his name. It went wrong – he was so fast, so vicious. I have never seen such a man.' There was admiration in her voice and Dugan was simultaneously hit with anger and jealousy, that she could admire the qualities of the man who had beaten her so badly.

'Why?' he asked. 'Why were you trying to kill him?'

'It's my job,' she said flatly.

'You kill for money?'

'No, Pat. I kill for my country.'

Dugan was totally lost, unable to comprehend what she was saying. All he could think of saying was: 'Why?'

'I have no choice,' she said, her voice faltering. 'They tell me what to do. They tell me where to live. They control everything I do.'

'Not in Hong Kong,' said Dugan. 'And who are they?'

'Beijing. The Government. Oh, you don't understand.'

She'd got that right at least, thought Dugan. He ran his hands through his hair and wiped his eyes with the backs of his fingers. To Petal he looked like a small child, trying to be brave.

'Why do it?' he asked. 'You can get away from them here. This is Hong Kong. I can help you. You can get asylum or something.'

'It's not as simple as that,' she said. Her voice was getting quieter and Dugan leant forward, putting his hands on either side of the pillow and lowering his head so that he could hear better. 'I told you about what happened during the Cultural Revolution. Remember?'

Dugan nodded. 'They killed your pony.'

'They did more than that, Pat. Much more. They took everything we had, they paraded us through the streets. They made us wear placards and stupid paper hats. Then they took me and my brother away from our parents, for re-education they said. I was sent to a farm in northern China. My brother was sent to a village in Manchuria. I never heard from my father again, he was sent away to a commune in the middle of nowhere to work as a barefoot doctor. He's dead now.'

'And your mother?'

'She died, Pat. In prison. They put her in prison for being a singer. They persecuted her for being talented. They made me work in rice fields until I was fifteen and then they put me in the army. I served for three years on the Sino–Russian border and then I was sent to Beijing for what they called special training. Now I do what I do.'

She slowly closed her eyes, either from exhaustion or from the medication.

'Let me tell the police. We can get you away, get you to Canada or Australia where they can't get you.'

'Defect, you mean?' she whispered. 'I can't. My brother is still alive. They let me see him every Christmas. He's a soldier, now. He's about to get married. So long as he is in China I must do exactly as they say. He is insurance that I do not run away. But if I do well, he gets a good salary, his children will go to the best universities, he will have an easy life. And so will I.'

'All you have to do is kill for them?'

'Yes, that's all I have to do,' she said bitterly.

'Is there nothing I can do?'

'Nothing,' she said. She lifted up her right arm and gripped his shoulder. 'Pat, they'll come for me soon, to take me back. They'll say they're from Bank of China or the New China News Agency but they'll be from Beijing and they'll put me on the first CAAC jet out of Hong Kong.'

'And then?'

'I don't know,' she said. 'I've never failed before. I don't know if they'll punish me or retire me or just rap me on the knuckles and send me on another mission. You can never tell.'

'Do me one thing,' said Dugan. 'If you can, get in touch with me. Let me know that you're OK. Tell me where you are, anywhere in the world. I'll come and see you.'

'I will,' she said. 'I promise. And if I can get my brother out of China, who knows . . .' Her voice tailed off again.

There was something niggling at the back of Dugan's

mind, something worrying him but he couldn't pin it down. It kept drifting just out of range. He released her grip from his shoulder and put her hand under the sheet. 'I don't want to lose you,' he said quietly. 'I've known you for such a short time, but . . .' It was there again, a shadowy thought floating around a corner of his mind. He tried to grasp it but it shied away like a nervous animal.

'I feel the same,' she said, through unmoving lips. 'I never thought I would, but I fell for you, Patrick Dugan, in a big way.'

It hit Dugan then, like a wave crashing over his head, drenching him with the horrible realization that it hadn't been an accident, meeting Petal. He'd been pushing to one side the fact that never before had such a pretty and intelligent girl been so keen to go out with him, to be with him, to sleep with him. He'd been frightened to look a gift horse in the mouth, to wonder why a girl like Petal would go out with a balding policeman with no prospects.

She saw the frown on his face and her eyes narrowed. 'Don't think about it, Pat,' she said.

'Why did you go out with me?' he asked, his heart filled with dread, wanting to know the answer but at the same time frightened that he wouldn't be able to handle the truth.

'Don't think about it,' she repeated. 'Don't look back. I love you now, that's all that matters. Why it happened isn't important.'

'I know, I know,' he said, sitting up straight. He began biting the thumbnail on his right hand, a nervous habit he'd had since he was a kid. 'I have to know why,' he said. 'It's the policeman in me.'

She sighed, deeply and sadly. 'Your brother-in-law. I was supposed to get close to him.'

'To kill him?'

'I was a back-up,' she said. 'Somebody else was to kill him. I don't know who. But if he failed then I was to do it.'

'When?'

'The barbecue would have been soon enough. But I was only the back-up.'

'But you would have done it if they'd told you to.' He couldn't hide the anger in his voice.

'I'm a soldier, Pat. I obey orders.'

She made it sound so matter-of-fact, so cold, that Dugan began to wonder if he was dreaming. He couldn't believe it was possible that a girl he'd grown to love could so easily talk about killing the husband of his sister, someone she'd met and seemed to have befriended.

'And this man Howells?'

'They didn't say why, they never do. But they said it had to be done immediately.' She fell silent.

'Why?' he pounced. 'What do you think?'

'I think that maybe he was the one that was supposed to kill Simon Ng.'

'So why were you ordered to kill him?'

'Perhaps he refused. Perhaps he changed his mind.'

'And why would the Chinese use a gweilo to kill a Hong Kong triad leader? It doesn't make sense.'

'It never does,' she said.

The nurse came back into the room and told Dugan he'd have to go. Behind her were two shortish Chinese men in dark suits and behind them was the uniformed constable who'd been posted outside the door. He hadn't seen the

246

two men before but they had the look of policemen the whole world over, hard eyes that had seen too much of the dark side of human nature, faces that looked as if nothing would surprise them any more.

'Don't make it difficult for me, Pat,' said Petal.

He leant forward and kissed her on the forehead. 'Remember what I said,' he whispered. 'Whenever, wherever.'

'I promise,' she said.

As he left the room the two men walked in and closed the door behind them.

Amy was sitting on a straight-backed wooden chair with her hands in her lap listening to Howells snoring when the doorbell buzzed. The sound, even though expected, made her jump. She tiptoed across the floor and looked through the peep-hole in the door. She recognized the distorted features of the man on the other side of the door and she unlocked it and let him in. He was carrying a brown leather bag with a brass clasp.

'*Lam Siu Fe. Neih ho ma?*'

'I am fine, Dr Wu. And you?'

'Getting by, getting by. Where is the patient?'

Wu was not a man who wasted any time, which was probably best considering he charged by the minute. He was called Dr Wu by everyone who knew him, and by everyone he treated, but he had no medical qualification that would be recognized by any decent hospital. Medical knowledge he had, in abundance, but he had learned his trade within the Walled City, the enclosed slum close to Kai Tak airport where the police were frightened to go. The city had been demolished but it left hundreds of doctors and dentists without a livelihood. At sixty, Dr Wu was too old to study for a recognized qualification, and too old to find any other sort of work, so he continued to practise, but illegally. His patients now were those who didn't want to go to private or government hospitals for whatever reason. He treated hookers, junkies and triads, and the treatment they got was as good as in the best hospitals in Hong Kong. He had performed an abortion on Amy two years ago with the minimum of fuss and pain. Amy had always been grateful for the gentle way he had treated her, even coming back to check up on her twice, drinking tea and eating a sweet cake she had baked.

'He is in the bedroom,' she said, and took him through. She moved the chair closer to the bed so that he could sit while examining Howells. She stood at the door, feeling useless, as Dr Wu pulled back the sheet and looked at the shoulder wound.

He looked back at Amy over the top of his gold-rimmed glasses. '*Lam Siu Fe*, this is a bullet wound. This man has been shot.'

'I know, Dr Wu,' she said. 'He came to me for help. He said not to call the police.'

'A gweilo frightened of the police?' said Dr Wu. 'Very strange. He is a friend of yours?'

'No Dr Wu, he is not. I only met him a short time ago.'

'No matter, no matter. First we shall make him well, then we shall discuss what must be done.' He did as Amy had done earlier and checked the front of the shoulder for an exit wound. 'The bullet is still in the shoulder,' he said, and Amy nodded. Wu peered at the bullet hole and gently brushed it with his fingertips. 'A small calibre, I think, possibly a .22. He is a very lucky young man.'

'He will be all right?'

Dr Wu looked over his glasses, this time pushing them up the bridge of his nose. 'He is lucky that you called me so quickly. He has lost some blood, but not so much that his life is in danger. And while the damage appears bad the bullet did not destroy any major blood vessels. Once the bullet is out and I have tidied up the wound, he will recover. He will be in considerable pain for a while, but I can give him something for that. Now, I have everything I need except for clean towels and hot water. And you can get that for me, and quickly please.' He put his bag on the bedside table and opened it. A gweilo who has been shot and who does not want to go to the police, he mused. Very curious.

Dugan waited until he was in his own office before ringing Jill. His stomach was still queasy from the previous night's aggressive drinking spree and he forced down a couple of aspirins with a cup of machine coffee. So much of what Petal had told him didn't make sense, and the bits that did make sense made his head spin.

That she had tried to kill a gweilo in the Hilton Hotel seemed to be beyond doubt, that she was a Chinese agent he could just about accept. But he could think of no possible reason that the Chinese would have for wanting to kill his brother-in-law, or to get involved in any sort of violent action in Hong Kong during the run up to 1997. The colony's six million population was so jittery about being handed over to Communist China that such direct action could easily spark off a violent reaction. Hong Kong was no stranger to riots in the streets and it would only need one more heavy-handed example of a Beijing clampdown to ignite a powder keg of resentment.

He could also think of no reason why the Chinese would kill an assassin who was supposed to do their dirty work, unless, as Petal had suggested, he had backed out. Maybe he'd been paid in advance and had refused to pay back the money. But killing the guy seemed to be a massive over-reaction.

The method that Petal and her two assistants used, or had tried to use, also didn't make sense. Killings over money were usually violent and bloody, a warning to others. Using an injection sounded more like they wanted it to look like natural causes. He'd meant to ask Petal what it was she had been trying to inject into the gweilo but he'd been so upset it had slipped his mind. He'd have to wait until the lab had finished its investigation. For now he wanted to speak to Jill, to check that her husband was all right and to warn him to stay out of harm's way.

He tapped out the number and it was answered on the third ring by a guttural Chinese voice. In English he asked for Jill and was told she wasn't in. He asked for Simon and got the same answer.

'Do you know where they are?' he asked.

'They are out,' replied the voice. Probably one of the bodyguards; he couldn't place the voice, but he recognized the attitude. That was odd; usually Jill got the phone herself and if she was out one of the maids would answer. Jill didn't like Ng's men in the house.

He switched to Cantonese. 'When will they get back?'

'Who's calling?'

'Dugan. Pat Dugan. Mrs Ng's brother.'

'I'll tell her you called,' the voice growled and hung up.

At least they were OK, thought Dugan. He picked up one of the files on his desk and began to read it. He was beginning to feel better.

Thomas Ng stood in front of the immigration officer, tapping his foot impatiently. The man in the uniform looked as if he'd barely left school. He flicked through the pages of the US passport for no other reason than to see how many countries Ng had visited. There were a lot.

'American, huh?' grunted the youngster, and he looked up at Ng. Ng had seen the look before when presenting his travel documents at Hong Kong immigration. It was the sort of look bestowed on the passenger of a jumbo jet with engine trouble, a passenger with a parachute strapped to his back. No one knew for sure what would happen when the colony and its six million inhabitants were handed back to the Communists, but there was always an unspoken envious resentment directed at those who had a safety route already mapped out by those who feared they would be left behind. The rush to emigrate had been frantic enough before the killings in Tiananmen Square. Now it bordered on hysteria.

'Yeah, American,' said Ng, using his very best San Francisco accent.

The boy stamped the passport as if he was burying a hatchet into Ng's neck.

Ng walked past the desk and when he had collected his single suitcase walked unheeded through customs, turning left towards the greeting area. The electric doors swished open and the babble of three hundred voices washed over him, Cantonese, Filipino, English, Indian, an international potpourri that reflected the racial mix of Hong Kong. He walked slowly down the ramp, looking right and left for a glimpse of a face he recognized.

He heard his name called and saw Lin Wing-wah waving at him. Standing either side of him were Franc Tse and Ricky Lam, looking grim. So they fucking well should be, thought Ng. Their job, their sole *raison d'être*, was to protect Simon and their failure was written all over their faces. He nodded at them, masking his anger, but Lin's was the only hand he shook.

'Elder Brother, you look fit and well,' said Ng. Like all triad members he referred to Lin as Elder Brother, rather than by his rank or his given name.

Lin's grip was strong and dry. '*Ho noy mouh gin.* America has been good to you, Mister Ng.'

'What is this, Elder Brother. You have forgotten my name?'

Lin looked awkward. 'Now you are Lung Tau, the Dragon Head. You are to be accorded the respect that is due.'

Ng looked at him levelly. 'Have you found my brother's body?' he asked.

'No,' said Lin.

'Then my brother is still Lung Tau. Come, tell me everything that has happened.'

Lin walked by Ng's side as they headed towards the waiting Mercedes, talking quietly, while Tse and Franc walked behind, nervously checking faces. They had lost one Dragon Head – they would not be caught wanting again.

Ng didn't recognize the driver but nodded to him as he climbed into the back seat after Lin. Lam moved in after him while Tse took the front passenger seat. As the car pulled away from the pavement Lin told him about the handover of the money, how his brother had disappeared under the water, how they had searched for hours but found nothing.

'We have no idea what the gweilo looks like, or who he is?' Ng asked.

'We do not know his name. And the only person who has seen his face is the headmistress at Sophie's school.'

'So we can get a description from her?'

'We should be able to do better than that,' said Lin. 'Once it became clear that we had lost your brother I arranged for men with video cameras to cover the whole area, filming everyone around Hebe Haven for hours afterwards. We might have him on film.'

'How many cameras?'

'Three,' said Lin. 'And they filmed for about ten hours. So we've got about thirty hours of tape. If he left the area that day we should have his picture.'

'A big if,' said Ng. 'But a good idea.'

Lin smiled broadly, but in the front seat Franc Tse glowered. It had been his idea but he could see that Elder Brother was going to take the credit. Fuck his mother.

'So now you will show the tapes to the headmistress?'

'That is the idea.'

'Good. She a gweipor or Chinese?'

'Gweipor.'

'Best to pick her up and take her to the house. She'll be able to concentrate there. And it'll cause less fuss.'

'It shall be done, Mister Ng. But what if she refuses?'

'I shall come with you and explain to her how important it is she helps us. If that fails I shall offer to buy her school the latest computer. And if she still doesn't help us you can hold her down and I will break every bone in her body until she changes her mind.'

Lin nodded. He could tell from the man's voice that he was serious. He had not gone soft in the United States.

'We'll go to the school first, drop the gweipor off at the house, and then I must go and see my father. He has been told?'

'Yes,' said Lin. 'Master Cheng visited him yesterday.'

'How did he take it?'

'Not well, Mister Ng. Not well at all.'

Howells dragged himself out of a dreamless sleep. He was lying on his front, his head to one side, the pillow beneath his cheek damp with saliva that had dribbled from his mouth. The room swam in and out of focus, but even when his vision had cleared he did not recognize the place. He tried to lift his head but winced and dropped back. The pain passed quickly and he realized he'd been drugged, and so long as he didn't try to move the injured arm he felt relaxed and slightly light-headed. There was a bandage around his shoulder, too, but he wasn't in a hospital bed. From where he was lying he could see a bookcase filled with toy animals, a fluffy white cat, a green crocodile with gaping jaws and a long red tongue, a monkey with cross-eyes, an elephant with floppy tusks, and on one wall was a framed cinema poster advertising some sort of Cantonese gangster movie.

He remembered the fight in the hotel, and the shooting, he remembered the pretty Chinese girl and the hypodermic and the way she smiled as she moved on top of him, and he remembered getting into a cab, but that was all. Amy walked through the door then and it all came back to him.

'Thank you,' he said.

She smiled, and quickly moved her hand up to hide her teeth. 'I thought you would never wake up,' she said.

'What time is it?' he asked.

'Midday.'

'Where am I?'

'My home,' she said. 'You said you didn't want to go to hospital so I brought you here.' She held up a white carrier bag. 'I bought you a new shirt. Your old one was ruined,' she said.

'Thank you,' he said again.

'No need,' she said.

'Who put the bandage on? You?'

'No,' she laughed. 'A doctor friend of mine. He took the bullet out, too.'

'You can keep it as a souvenir,' smiled Howells. 'How good a friend is the doctor?'

'I don't think he will tell anyone,' she said. 'He is used

to dealing with patients who can't go to hospital. Besides, I have only paid him half his fee. I promised him the rest later, once you are on your legs.'

'Feet,' said Howells. 'On my feet.'

'On your feet,' she repeated. 'Thank you for English lesson, Geoff.'

'No need,' he said, before he spotted the trap. 'How did you find out my name?' he said quietly, but smiling. She'd already demonstrated her loyalty; if she was going to betray him she'd had plenty of chance while he was unconscious.

'Your wallet,' she said. 'And the passports. Don't worry, many men not give me real names.'

'I'm sorry, Amy. My name is Geoff Howells.'

She nodded. 'Pleased to meet you. You buy me drink?'

They laughed together, Howells ignoring the pain in his shoulder as it moved.

'Howells,' she repeated. 'Like a wolf.'

'Yeah,' he said. 'Like a wolf. But a different Howells – not the same spelling.'

'Do you want water?'

'I'd rather have coffee.'

'Doctor said only water.'

'What does he know?' said Howells. 'Coffee, black with no sugar. It'll give me strength, I promise.'

'OK,' said Amy, and she went to the kitchen to boil the kettle. The smile faded as she left the bedroom. She liked this man, this Geoff Howells who smiled so easily but whose eyes seemed to belong to a long dead animal, but she could sense that he would bring trouble to her ordered life.

Behind her Howells closed his eyes and let himself be sucked back into the black clouds of sleep.

Rosemary Quinlan was worried, more worried than she had ever been in all her fifty-four years, and if the truth were to be told it was her own future that preyed most on her mind. To be sure, she was frightened for Sophie, but in the scales of her mind it was her own career and pension and reputation, and the loss of it, that were tipping the balance. She sat behind her large oak desk and polished her glasses as Thomas Ng followed her secretary into the office.

'Mr Ng,' she said, and offered her hand limply. Ng shook it and nodded.

He quickly explained what had happened to his brother, and to Sophie. She interrupted once to say that Simon Ng had called her to explain that it was all a misunderstanding, but Ng told her that things had changed. His brother had not told the truth because he hadn't wanted to alarm her. Now they needed her help.

The headmistress looked at him gratefully. It wasn't going to be as bad as she had feared, he wasn't angry, and she thanked God he hadn't arrived with the police. Or worse, a lawyer. God knows what would happen if it became known that she had handed one of her charges over to a man claiming to be a policeman. Why, oh why, hadn't she checked with the police station? Why hadn't she examined his identification? Why hadn't she spoken to Mrs Ng first?

'Miss Quinlan, I need your help.'

'Of course; I will do everything I can to help,' she said, the words coming out in a rush. 'Anything, absolutely anything. Have the police been . . .'

Ng held up his hand to quieten her, shaking his head. 'No, the police have not been notified. And, Miss Quinlan, I must have your assurance that you will not call the police, or tell anyone what has taken place. It is very important that the authorities are not notified, and I am sure that you would prefer that the authorities do not find out what has occurred. Do we understand each other?'

The headmistress took a deep breath and replaced the glasses on her nose. The man's threat was veiled, but it was a threat nevertheless, and her stomach churned. She looked at him steadily and nodded. She picked up the brass paperknife and rubbed the blade slowly back and forth.

'I understand completely, Mr Ng. And I repeat that I will do everything I can to help put this right.'

Ng smiled, and he tried to put some warmth into it. It wasn't the old gweipor's fault and there was no point in being unduly hard on her. And at the moment she was the only one who could identify the gweilo. He explained about the video cameras, and that he wanted her to go back to the Ng compound to watch the videos and identify the man.

'Now?' she said.

'I am afraid so. It is important that we act quickly. If we can identify the man we might be able to get to him before he can hurt Sophie.'

The headmistress hesitated for less than a second. She reached for the intercom and called in her secretary, explained that she had to go out and that she would phone later that afternoon to say when she would be back. She collected her coat from a rack next to the door and went with Ng to the Mercedes outside the school gates, engine purring.

The phone on Dugan's desk rang and he grabbed at it, his heart soaring with the thought that it might be Petal, but even as he put the receiver to his ear he knew it couldn't be her. It was Bellamy.

'What the fuck's going on, Pat?'

'What do you mean?'

'What did she tell you?'

Dugan knew he'd have to be very careful from now on. He was in unchartered waters, not knowing exactly how much Bellamy knew, not even sure how much of what Petal had told him was the truth. He didn't want to lie to Bellamy, but there was a bond between him and Petal that he didn't want to break, a trust he didn't want to betray.

'She said she was kicked by a gweilo in the hotel room, and that he attacked the two men she was with.'

'And?'

'And what?'

Bellamy's voice hardened and Dugan was glad that he was at the other end of a phone and not across the desk in an interrogation room. 'Don't fuck me about, Dugan, what was she doing in the hotel room? And who were the two heavyweights with her? And why were they trying to inject a stimulant into him

259

that was powerful enough to give a carthorse a heart attack?'

'You've got the results from the lab?'

'What do you fucking well think? Look Dugan, you've had a rough ride as it is in the force. But it's nothing compared to the shit that's about to hit the fan over this one.'

'She told me nothing, Jeff. Honest. She's doped up to the eyeballs and in deep shock. She's in no fit state for anything.'

'That's not what the nurse said. She said you spent a good fifteen minutes talking to her.'

'She was rambling,' whined Dugan. 'Delirious. She wasn't making any sense. The best thing would be to leave her for a day or two until she's more coherent.'

'It's too late for that,' said Bellamy and a cold fist grabbed Dugan's heart and squeezed.

'Oh God,' he moaned, 'she's not . . .'

'No, you daft bastard, she's not dead. But she's not in hospital anymore. A group of Xinhua spooks turned up and took her to the airport and a CAAC jet left thirty minutes ahead of schedule with her on board. There's something bloody funny going on, and I've got a feeling you hold the key, Dugan.'

'I'm as confused as you are, Jeff.'

'You better had be, old lad.'

'Is that a threat?'

'Take it any way you want. But I'd forget any ideas you have about a long-term career with Hong Kong's finest.' The line clicked quietly but Dugan could tell that Bellamy had slammed the phone down.

Lin and Tse waited in the car while Ng took Miss Quinlan into the house. The television and video recorder had been moved out of the lounge and placed on the desk in the study. On the couch were a handful of videocassettes and Ng slotted one into the recorder.

'Would you like to sit on the couch, Miss Quinlan, or would you like me to bring in an easy chair?' he asked the headmistress.

'This will be fine, thank you,' said Miss Quinlan.

The maid came into the study and asked for her coat and she handed it over with a murmur of thanks.

'Can I get you a cup of tea?' Ng asked, wanting to put the woman at ease. If she was tense she might miss something.

'Thank you, no.'

She took her glasses off and began polishing them. Cheng walked in and Ng introduced him to the head-mistress.

'Mr Cheng will stay here with you,' explained Ng. 'If you recognize anyone on the tapes then please tell him.'

Cheng picked up a wooden chair, removed its red cushion and put it down next to the Chesterfield. He sat down with his hands in his lap, smiling at Miss Quinlan.

'Ready?' asked Ng.

The woman nodded and Ng pressed the 'Play' button. The recorder whirred and after a few seconds a view of the pier jerked across the screen, scanning right and left, homing in on faces, seemingly at random, pulling in and out of focus before moving on. Watching the screen made Ng feel nauseous, like riding a big dipper, and he didn't envy the headmistress the hours ahead.

In Cantonese Ng told Cheng to make sure that she concentrated – any lapse and he was to rewind the tape. And if after viewing all the tapes she recognized no one, then she was to sit through them all again. As he turned to go Ng almost bumped into Jill, who had appeared at the doorway. She looked rough, her face pinched and drawn, dark rings around her eyes, her hair lifeless, her eyes dull.

Her lips drew back in an animal snarl. 'What the fuck is that old bag doing in my house?' she hissed. 'Get her out. I want her out of my house now.'

Ng reached for her, holding her shoulders. 'She's here to help.'

Jill glared at him wildly. She threw up her arms and knocked his hands away, then pushed him savagely in the chest so that he had to take a step backwards.

'Get her out of my house,' she screamed. Ng tried to grab her again but Jill's hands lashed out, fingers curled, and one of them caught Ng on his cheek, tearing the skin. She kicked him on the shins and pushed him again and then he lost his temper and slapped her hard across the face, left and right. She collapsed then, keeling against the door-frame and holding it for support, her body convulsed with sobbing.

'She gave away my daughter,' she gasped.

'I know, I know,' soothed Ng, stepping forward and taking her in his arms. She reached around his waist and held him tightly, like a lover, her wet cheek against his as she cried. He led her out of the room and across the hall to the lounge. Cheng looked across at the headmistress, his face a mask.

'Mrs Ng is under a lot of strain,' he said quietly. 'Please forgive her.'

'I understand,' said Miss Quinlan. 'I wish there was something I could say to her to show her how sorry I am.'

'Identifying the man will be help enough,' said Cheng. He stood up and walked over to the recorder to rewind the tape back to where it had been before Jill's outburst.

'And I will concentrate, I promise,' she said. 'I have no desire to go through the tapes twice.'

Cheng nodded. The gweipor spoke Cantonese – he would not forget.

Ng closed the lounge door and helped Jill on to one of the settees.

'Do you want a drink?' he asked, though he could already smell alcohol on her breath.

'Brandy,' she said.

He splashed some into a balloon glass and handed it to her. She gulped it down and handed it back, empty. Ng didn't refill it. He put the empty glass down on the drinks cabinet and went to sit down next to her.

'What's going to happen?' she asked.

'Miss Quinlan is looking at some videotapes that were recorded soon after Simon disappeared. We hope that the man who took him might be on one of them. She saw the man when he took Sophie. If we can find out what he looked like we should be able to catch him.'

'Unless he's already left Hong Kong.'

'That is a possibility,' admitted Ng. 'We are hoping that isn't the case. But we have already made arrangements to

identify all gweilos who fly out as of today. We have a
number of our own men in the immigration department,
and while we cannot prevent anyone flying out we will at
least have a record of anyone who leaves. Once we have a
picture it will not be too difficult to track him down. But
we are assuming he is still in Hong Kong. For one thing,
he still has Sophie, and there is no reason why he would
want to hurt her.'

At the mention of her daughter's name, Jill began to
cry again, and she pressed the palms of her hands against
her temples as if she had a migraine.

'We will get her back, I promise that,' Ng said, but even
as he said it he knew it was not a promise that he was in a
position to make.

'And what about Simon? What about my husband?'

Ng didn't know how to answer that. He went into
the kitchen to get the maid and told her to take Jill
to her bedroom, and to give her some hot milk and
make sure she took one of her Libriums. She'd be
less of a liability sedated than drunk. 'Anyone who
calls is to be referred to Master Cheng,' he said to
the maid. 'Anyone. Once you have put Mrs Ng to
bed I want you to remove the phone from her bedroom so that she is not disturbed. Do you understand?'

The maid nodded, her eyes wide. She understood; Mrs
Ng wasn't to speak to anyone outside the house. The maid
didn't know what had happened, but she knew it was bad
and she knew enough about the Ng family to know that
it was best not to ask any questions. Ng watched as she
led Jill upstairs, before going out to rejoin Lin and Tse
at the car.

'OK,' said Ng, more relaxed now that he was away from Jill. 'Let us go and see my father.'

Golden Dragon Lodge was an anachronism, every bit as out of date as the old triads were in today's hi-tech society, and Thomas Ng hated it. It was two-thirds up the Peak, some distance below the palatial mansion called Sky High which belonged to the chairman of the HongKong and Shanghai Bank, at the end of a small private road. The grounds were surrounded by a stone wall built without mortar, three times the height of a man, and the only way in was through two huge wooden doors, painted scarlet and peppered with black metal studs as if someone had fired them from a giant sawn-off shotgun.

The wall surrounded six or seven acres of prime residential land that Ng knew could be redeveloped into a huge tower block worth millions upon millions of dollars. He'd made enquiries some years ago and found that planning permission would not be a problem and that the site had a plot ratio that would allow them to build more than twenty storeys high. He had broached the subject with his father, but only once. He made it clear in no uncertain terms that Golden Dragon Lodge was not to be touched and the matter was not to be raised again.

The grounds sloped at a twenty-degree angle, with the house somewhere in the middle, with breathtaking views of Victoria Harbour and the skyscrapers of Central and Admiralty, and beyond to Tsim Sha Tsui. In the distance, shrouded in mist, were the eight hills that hemmed in Kowloon.

Two guards opened the huge doors to allow the Mercedes in, and it drove slowly along the gravelled track which twisted along the contours of the hill until it ended in front of a double garage with a circular turning area. Although the house itself was built on foundations which cut into the hill, much of the grounds sloped and the site was criss-crossed with wandering paths and stepped walkways. Getting from the garage to the house involved walking up a dozen stone steps and then along a wooden bridge that curved over a man-made pool in which the humps of a stone dragon, twenty yards long at least, rose and fell in the water, leading to a massive head with gaping jaws and staring eyes that glared over at the Bank of China building. In the waters swam huge goldfish which his father fed every morning. Ng stopped on the bridge and looked at the dragon's head, remembering how he had played around the water with his brothers when they were children. Lin and Tse stopped behind him, fidgeting, not wanting to intrude.

The grounds were tailor-made for games of hide and seek, full of secret places: caves made from concrete with hidden shrines inside, groves of exotic plants that his father had imported from all over Asia, walkways that led to small pagodas with stone seats and tables, there for no other reason than for you to sit and admire the view. There were statues of giant birds and animals, objects that his father had bought on a whim and spent hours deciding where to place in the wonderland of a garden. There was a Japanese rock garden, dotted with tiny stunted trees, a banana plantation, an orange grove, a waterfall that was powered by a giant pump which cascaded over a secret place where Simon, Thomas and Charles used to sit and eat rice cakes and drink lemonade when they wanted to get away from their young sister. At the bottom of the site, screened from the house, was a swimming pool with its own changing-rooms, tiled like a school's pool with the depth marked off at intervals and lanes marked in blue tiles on the bottom, with a high-diving board and a springboard. There was another man-made pool to the left, behind a clump of pine trees in which their father had built a stone junk that could only be reached by walking along a stout plank. They used to play pirates there with wooden cutlasses, fighting for possession of the ship for all they were worth, sometimes allowing Catherine and her dolls to play the part of hostages.

Ng began walking again, over the bridge and up the path that zig-zagged to the front of the building. It was a traditional three-storey Chinese house, but so traditional that it looked like a mockery of what a Chinese house should be. It looked as if it belonged to one of the Cantonese soap operas where warriors with pigtails flew through the air and wizards disappeared in puffs of purple smoke. The roof was pagoda-shaped, with orange tiles that curled up at the edges, and at the four corners were dragon-heads with flaring nostrils and forked tongues. The windows were small and all had shutters. The house had no air-conditioning; it never had and it never would, not so long as his father lived there. The shutters were closed in summer to keep out the searing heat, and closed in winter to keep out the cold, and as a result the house was dark and gloomy all year round, except for a few glorious weeks in spring and autumn.

There was a flagstoned area in front of the main doors to the house where his father waited for him, hands locked behind his back as he looked out across the harbour.

Tse and Lin stopped at the end of the path, leaving Ng to walk alone across the flagstones to his father. Only at the last minute did the old man take his eyes off the ships in the harbour below and smile at his son.

'You look well, Kin-ming.'

'And you, Father.' The old man steadfastly refused to use his sons' English names, and they had given up trying to persuade him otherwise.

The old man had reached the age where the passing of the years seemed to have no effect on him. His hair had all but disappeared and his skin was mottled with dark brown liver spots, but there were few wrinkles on his face. He was a small man, with round shoulders and slightly bowed legs, the sort of man who always received poor service in shops and hotels until people discovered who he was. It was partly the old man's fault; he had never been one to wear his wealth. His clothes were always cheap and off-the-peg, his watch was a simple wind-up steel model that was at least thirty years old, and he preferred sandals to shoes. The only jewellery he wore was a thin gold wedding ring. At a conservative estimate his father was worth US$250 million, but he looked like a hawker, spoke guttural Cantonese with a thick mainland accent and could only manage broken English.

The old man kept his hands clasped behind his back and made no move to touch Thomas. That was his way. He could barely remember the last time they had touched, let alone hugged each other. His father was not a physical man, not a toucher, and he always hid his emotions. Even now he seemed placid and at ease, despite the reason for the visit. He had looked the same way at his wife's funeral some ten years earlier and had looked scornfully at the tears in the eyes of his sons. Thomas had heard him later that night though, alone in his bedroom on the top floor of the house, crying softly and repeating his wife's name over and over again. Thomas had felt more love for him then than he had ever done before, but he stayed where he was at the bedroom door, unable to walk in and hold his father. He knew that if he had, the old man would never have forgiven him, and he had crept silently back down the stairs.

'Walk with me,' his father said, and turned along the path that ran by the side of the house. The path was narrow and it wasn't until it reached a flight of steps set into the hillside and reinforced with slats of wood that they could walk side by side. The steps led to a wide strip of grass surrounded by ornate flower beds. In front of one knelt one of the six old gardeners who toiled to keep the estate in pristine condition. They were paid a pittance, and were now at the age where they worked out of loyalty to the old man and love of the gardens. They lived in a small row of huts behind the pool changing-rooms, along with the three Filipina maids who looked after the house. There were also half a dozen Red Poles assigned to look after the old man. Ng had only seen the two at the gate but he knew that at least two more would be close by, shadowing them as they walked.

They moved in silence through a circle of alternating stone herons and turtles, all looking up at the sky, and clumps of bushes that gave off a heady perfume that made Ng's head swim.

The path led to the two flights of steps, one meandering down to a tarmac tennis court at the far side of the house, the other angling sharply up. The old man gripped the wooden rail of the steps that went up and began to climb, rolling slightly from side to side like a sailor unused to dry land. Ng followed behind, out of breath.

'Not tired, are we, Kin-ming?'

'No Father,' said Ng. The old bastard was doing it deliberately, to show how fit and strong he was.

There were eighty-eight steps, a lucky number – unless you were out of breath and had a rapidly expanding waistline. At the top were two red and gold pagodas, left and right, each containing a large circular stone table surrounded by four stools. Beyond the pagodas were two long single-storey buildings, red-painted wood with tiled roofs, where the old man would play mah jong or cards late into the night with his cronies, or table tennis with Thomas, Simon and Charles when they were young. The buildings were either side of a courtyard the size of a basketball court where the old man practised t'ai chi every morning, and where the boys had learnt kung fu with a succession of teachers. It was a play area, a training area; and a place to come and enjoy the view. It was the highest point of the estate, bar a few yards of sloping hillside which ended at the boundary wall, and it had been Thomas' favourite spot, until their mother had died, and his father had decided to put her grave on the edge of the courtyard, facing the steps. And not just a grave; the edifice he had built was a monument to her, a huge stone dome inscribed with gold Chinese characters standing on a metre-high podium. It dominated the area, and while it could not be seen from the house below, Ng was constantly aware that his mother was buried there. What made it worse was that his father had decided that he also wanted to be buried there, next to her in the tomb. His father had stipulated so in his will, but Thomas knew that once the old man had died the site would be redeveloped as soon as possible if he had his way.

The old man ambled over to the right-hand pagoda and sat on one of the stools, motioning for Thomas to take the seat next to him. They were both facing the harbour and they sat in silence watching the ships, junks and ferries criss-crossing the blue waters and the stream of planes landing and taking off from Kai Tak.

'You are watching the airport,' the old man said eventually, and it was not a question.

'And the ports,' said Thomas. 'We are photographing every gweilo who leaves. Once we know what he looks like we will check all the pictures, and we will know whether or not he has left. If he has left there is nowhere in the world where he can hide.'

The old man nodded. 'But you think he is still here?'

'Yes.'

'Because of Sophie?'

'Whatever has happened to Simon, and we are still not sure exactly what has happened, it is the work of a professional. And professionals do not kill children.'

'In the past, maybe. But the world is different now. They blow up planes, they plant bombs in shops.'

'Terrorists, Father, they are terrorists. What has happened to Simon is different. The man who attacked him was a professional. That is another reason we think he will still be in Hong Kong.'

'The fee?'

Ng nodded. 'He is a gweilo so it cannot be personal. He must have been paid to do the job, and killers are not usually paid in full in advance.'

They lapsed into silence again, and despite the unlined and unworried features of his father's face Ng knew that he was deeply troubled. Once more he wanted to reach out and hold him, to offer comfort, but the fear of rejection preyed on his mind and he held himself back. In the gardens below a peacock screamed, the sudden noise making the old man jump.

'Are we sure the gweipor will be able to identify the gweilo?' he asked.

Ng shrugged and admitted that there was no way they could be certain that the man had been captured on videotape or that Miss Quinlan would be able to spot him. 'But it is our best hope,' he said.

'And when we know what he looks like, how do we find him?'

'We search for him, Father. We search every house, every hotel, every boat, every single place where he could hide. There are only 50,000 or so gweilos in Hong Kong, plus tourists. It will take time, but it will not be impossible.'

'There is one thing you seem to have overlooked, though. It will mean moving into territories controlled by other triads, areas where we are not allowed to operate. You must move carefully, Kin-ming. Large numbers of our men in other triad territories could start a war.'

'Unless we tell them first.'

'That is what I was thinking,' said the old man, smiling for the first time. 'I have arranged for the triad Dragon Heads to come here tonight, to Golden Dragon Lodge. I will have to explain what has happened, and ask for their understanding.'

'And will you get it?'

'We will have to,' said his father. 'Tonight I will ask them to take part in the ceremony of Burning The Yellow Paper. I do not think they will refuse.'

A cat stalked out of the undergrowth behind the pagoda and began rubbing its back against the old man's legs. There were dozens of cats roaming virtually wild on the estate. All were fed each morning, but were not allowed inside the house. Ng's father reached down and picked it up and placed it in his lap where he stroked its head. The cat purred loudly and closed its eyes, pushing up against the hand and arching its back, tail upright.

'Father, do you have any idea why anyone would want to kill Simon? Is the triad in any sort of conflict here in Hong Kong?'

The old man kept his eyes on the cat and said no, each triad was now concentrating on its own dominion, and apart from the occasional power struggle or territorial dispute, most were simply getting on with making as much money as possible before 1997.

'At first it looked like a straightforward kidnapping,' said Ng. 'But the gweilo made no attempt to take the money. I think we must assume that it was Simon he wanted.'

The old man sighed deeply through his nostrils. 'Your brother did not tell me everything he was doing. He still had the impetuosity of youth, and there were some things I had to find out for myself.'

'Such as?'

'Things that were outside the normal business of the triad.'

There were times when the old man could be infuriatingly obtuse, but Ng kept a tight grip on his impatience. He resisted the urge to keep asking questions and waited for his father to tell him in his own time.

The cat had tired of being stroked and it jumped to the ground and disappeared into the bushes.

'It used to be so much simpler,' the old man said. 'So uncomplicated. You took what you could, you defended what you had, and you made money. Now everything is political: the Government, China, you and your businesses overseas. The British should never have given Hong Kong back to China. A benign dictatorship it might have been, but it was a system under which everyone prospered.'

'The British have been good, that is true,' agreed Ng. 'They even introduced us to the opium on which our fortunes are based,' he added with more than a touch of irony.

'And they have given it all away. A curse on them.'

'They had no choice, Father. The lease ran out in 1997.'

The old man snorted. 'Only the lease on the New Territories. The island was theirs for ever. The Chinese could never have taken it back. It belonged to the British legally, by treaty.'

Ng couldn't see where this Form Five history lesson was heading, but he played along with his father anyway. 'Hong Kong island cannot survive without the New Territories, it is too small; all it has are houses for the gweilos and office towers. The British got the best deal they could. Fifty years of stability after 1997.'

'That is what your brother said. And look what happened to him.'

Ng was confused now, he could see no connection between 1997 and his brother. Simon had never been one to get involved in politics, he was a triad leader pure and simple.

'Your brother kept telling me that there was only one way for us to survive after 1997, and that was for us to forge links with Beijing now, to gain favours from the Communists that would be repaid after they took control of Hong Kong.'

'The Communists are not to be trusted,' said Ng flatly. 'They make easy promises but rarely keep them.'

'I told your brother that, but he would not listen. Even after what the madmen did in Tiananmen Square. Even after the children were butchered. He had begun travelling regularly to Beijing, meeting highly placed cadres, and he entertained them when they came to Hong Kong – entertained them like kings; the best food, the best wine, the best of our girls. But that wasn't enough for them.'

'What did they want from him? From the triad?'

'Information. Intelligence. On the police, on the triads, on Special Branch. On the drugs business, the protection rackets, everything. The Chinese want to know how Hong Kong operates, the good points and the bad.'

'And Simon told them?'

'Not everything, of course. He was playing a dangerous game, telling them enough to win their trust but trying not to give away our secrets. He argued that

275

someone would give them the information, so it might as well be us.'

'He had struck a deal with them?'

The old man cleared his throat noisily and spat on to the grass. 'Not a deal. "An understanding" was how he described it. He understood that if he helped them now and co-operated with them after 1997, the triad would be allowed to prosper.'

Ng snorted. 'And he believed them? He is so naïve.'

'He was doing what he thought was best for the triad and for the family.'

'How many times have I told you, the way to go is into legitimate businesses, to turn our backs on the old ways. We should be moving into retailing, to transport, to property. At least property developers do not have each other killed.'

His father turned to look at him with cold brown eyes. 'Now who is being naïve, Kin-ming,' he said softly. Ng flushed, he was not used to being spoken to as if he were a child. He waved his hand in front of his face as if to brush away an annoying insect.

'You know what I mean, Father.'

The old man's face softened into a smile. 'I know what you mean. You must forgive an old man's tongue. Today has not been a good day.' That was the nearest he would come to admitting the pain he was feeling, Ng knew. He reached out and put his hand on top of his father's; the skin felt wrinkled but soft and cold, like a piece of tripe. Ng squeezed his father's fingers gently, then withdrew his hand before the old man had the chance to show disapproval or otherwise at the show of affection.

'You think that Simon might have been killed because he was passing information to the Communists?'

'It is a possibility.'

'But what could he possibly know that would make somebody want to kill him?'

'There is much happening in Hong Kong at the moment that people would not want the Communists to know about. Business deals that are not in the mainland's interest, smuggling of antiquities from China, illegal immigrants crossing the border, agents of foreign governments who are acting against China. There are a host of possibilities.'

'And the most probable?'

'I do not know, Kin-ming. Your brother was being very secretive about the ways in which he was helping the Communists. I do not think we will get anywhere by pondering the reasons why he was killed. Find the killer and we will solve the puzzle.'

It seemed that the old man had already decided that Simon was dead, despite the absence of a corpse. Ng had been constantly reminding himself that there was a chance that his brother had simply been kidnapped, but in his heart of hearts he knew that he was fooling himself. The gweilo already had Sophie, and there were easier ways of kidnapping a man than taking him under water.

'You are right, of course,' said Ng. 'I must go.'

His father nodded. 'You will be here tonight for the ceremony? I suggest nine o'clock.'

'I will be here.'

The old man remained seated while Ng got up and walked back down the steps towards Lin and Tse. He heard a cry somewhere behind him, but it could have been one of the peacocks.

Dugan was swallowing another couple of aspirins when Tomkins appeared at the door.

'How's the brain tumour?' he asked, and Dugan grimaced.

'This one is drink-induced,' he said.

'You have my sympathy then.' He walked over to the desk, buttocks clenched, and looked over Dugan's papers. 'Was it any use to you?'

'What?' said Dugan, his mind a blank.

'Lee Ling-ling's futures dealing. The papers I gave you.'

'Oh shit, I'm sorry. I forgot all about them.' Dugan didn't like the look that flashed across Tomkins' face. It was a look that said 'amateur' and 'incompetent' and 'why the fuck did I bother?' Dugan opened his desk drawer and took out the papers.

'I was just about to go through them,' he said.

'Perhaps you'd better just photocopy them,' said Tomkins. 'Then you can read them at your leisure.'

Dugan was too tired to argue, so he walked with Tomkins along the corridor to the photocopying room. Tomkins stood with his arms folded across his chest like an impatient executioner as Dugan copied each sheet, and then took the original version off him when he'd finished.

'Are you OK?' he asked Dugan. 'You look as if you've got something on your mind.'

'I'm OK,' said Dugan. 'Just a hangover.'

He didn't want to tell Tomkins about Petal, but there was no point in lying because Commercial Crime was a close-knit family and he'd find out before long anyway. 'And I think I need glasses,' he added lamely.

'I've always said you needed your head examined,' agreed Tomkins and tottered stiff-legged down the corridor to his office.

Dugan kept his head down as he walked back to his own desk, deep in thought. He rang Jill again. This time the phone was answered by a Filipina, obviously one of the maids. She said the same as the bodyguard who'd answered earlier, that Jill was not home but was expected back. Dugan asked if Mr Ng was at home.

'Which Mr Ng is it you want, sir?' the maid asked.

'Why?' asked Dugan. 'Is Simon's father there?'

'No, sir, but his brother has returned today from America.'

'Thomas?'

'Yes, sir, Mr Thomas Ng.'

'Can I speak to him?'

'No sir, he is not here right now.'

Despite all his years in Hong Kong, Dugan could still get annoyed by the way Asians could be polite, precise, and at the same time so infuriating that he could quite happily bang their heads against a wall. Secretaries would insist on him spelling his name three times and asking him for a detailed explanation of his enquiry before politely telling him that the person he wanted wasn't in the office. Or they'd tell him four or five times that the person he wanted was not in the office, but not mention the fact that he was on long leave and wouldn't be back for a month. They weren't being deliberately unhelpful, just unimaginative. He thanked the maid and said he'd call back.

The fact that Thomas Ng was back in Hong Kong was a surprise, and a worry. His visits were few and far between, and planned well in advance. According to Jill he was frightened of flying and as a result it was usually Simon who flew over to see his brother. It was too much of a coincidence that he was back in town at the same time that somebody in China was trying to kill Simon.

'Jill, where the fuck are you?' he said under his breath, glaring at the phone. He picked up Tomkins' papers and read them, but his eyes only passed over the typewritten words, they didn't penetrate and he had no idea of the content. He was too busy thinking about Petal and when he'd see her again. Or if he would see her again.

The headmistress saw Howells on the second tape. She leant forward like a retriever that had spotted a downed bird, blinking her eyes. Cheng stood up and walked over to the video recorder.

'You have seen something?' he said.

'Him,' she said, and pointed to a casually dressed gweilo, white cotton trousers, sandals and a red sweatshirt, swinging a shopping bag. He looked directly into the camera for a fraction of a second and then turned sharply to look at a young Chinese girl, then the camera was focused on a family heading towards the pier.

'Let me play it back for you,' said Cheng, and he rewound the tape. 'Watch very carefully.' Miss Quinlan stood up and walked closer to the television screen, and peered at it as Cheng pressed the play button.

'It is him,' she said, after watching the few seconds of film.

'Are you sure?' asked Cheng. 'Let me play it for you one more time. Don't just look at the face, look at the way he moves, the way he holds himself. Look at the whole man, not just the face.'

After the third viewing Miss Quinlan was just as certain, and Cheng allowed a smile to pass over his lined face. The headmistress smiled back, relief flooding over her like a warm tropical rain. At least she'd been able to do something to put right the damage she'd done.

A car pulled up outside, and Cheng and Miss Quinlan heard doors open and close and footsteps crunch along the gravel to the front door. It was Ng. As he walked into the study he could see the triumphant look on Miss Quinlan's face and he raised his eyebrows.

'You have recognized him? Already?'

The headmistress nodded quickly. 'I am sure it's him. Look.'

Cheng had frozen the film at the point just before Howells turned his head. It was a thin face with deep-set eyes, clean-shaven, and with a longish neck. Cheng pressed the advance button and Ng watched the man jerk his head around and walk past the camera. He moved well; there was a fluidity in his walk that suggested he was a man used to sport, or physical exercise. Ng had trained in many dojos in Hong Kong and America, and the gweilo moved like a martial arts expert, relaxed but ready to move fast and hard at the merest hint of aggression or danger.

'We need photographs, close-ups,' Ng said to Cheng.

'I will arrange it. We have a brother who is an editor at one of the local television stations. He will be able to enhance the picture and make prints for us.' Cheng spoke to Ng in rapid Cantonese but he noticed that the gweipor was listening. He turned to her and said: 'Would you do me a great service, Miss Quinlan?' He ejected the cassette and slotted in another. 'Could you watch this third tape, just in case the man returned, or you recognize anyone else?'

What Miss Quinlan really wanted to do was to get back to her school, her office, and her desk, but she knew she could refuse them nothing. She meekly said yes and sat down again and watched the dizzying images on the television set while Cheng ushered Ng across the corridor and into the lounge.

'The gweipor speaks Cantonese,' he explained to Ng.

'A rarity,' said Ng. 'So few of them bother.'

'A teacher. It would be useful in her job. But a rarity nonetheless. I will arrange for the tape to be delivered to our man. What shall we do with the prints?'

'First we must rush copies out to our men at the ports and the airport. We must know whether or not he has left Hong Kong. If he has left, then we must go after him. But for the moment we will assume he is still here. Distribute copies to our men, all of them. Then they are to begin checking all the hotels and guest houses in the territory.'

'There are many.'

'I know there are many, but we must start somewhere. He is a gweilo and he must be staying somewhere. I also want some prints sent up to Golden Dragon Lodge.'

'How many in total?' asked Cheng.

Ng thought for a while. 'One thousand,' he said eventually. 'I think one thousand will be sufficient.'

The normally inscrutable Cheng could not prevent his surprise showing on his face. 'One thousand?' he snorted.

Ng laughed and put his hand on the old man's shoulder. 'My father is going to ask the other triads for their help. And I do not think they will refuse him. It will save time if we have photographs ready to distribute this evening.'

'Asking for favours can be a double-edged sword,' warned Cheng.

'He is aware of that, Master Cheng. But we have to find the gweilo, and to do that we will have to search more than our own territory. Better to ask for their co-operation than to be caught unexpectedly in areas we do not control.'

'Your father knows best,' said Cheng quietly, but it was obvious from his tone that he was far from happy. Ng made a mental note to mention to his father to have a talk with Cheng, to smooth his ruffled feathers. Cheng was too valuable an adviser to upset. He had to be treated with kid gloves, and Ng was out of the habit of being delicate with people's feelings.

'You want to leave the gweipor in there watching the tapes?' he asked Cheng.

'I think it best to keep her here,' he answered. 'I doubt he will be filmed more than once. The shopping bag will have been to confuse any watchers. But better we know where she is. And while she is here she cannot talk to anyone else about what has happened.'

'I doubt that she will tell anyone. She values her job too much,' said Ng.

Cheng inclined his head slightly, a half nod that let

Ng know that he had once again offended the old man. Shit, he thought, and before he could stop himself the thought that Chinese were always so fucking easy to upset flashed through his mind. There were times when he no longer thought of himself as Chinese, he thought like an American, he talked like an American, and in most things he acted like an American, and he now found the Asian sensitivity, 'face' as they called it, infuriating at times. Patience was one of the virtues he had left behind him when he moved to San Francisco.

'But best we do not give her the opportunity,' he added, hoping that would mollify Cheng. He patted the old man on the back and watched as he went back into the study.

He called Lin and Tse in from the outside and went with them back into the lounge. He explained to them about the photographs and told Lin to speak to Cheng about the tape and the prints and to handle it. The phone rang as he was talking and Tse picked it up, listened, and then cursed loudly. He banged down the receiver hard enough to jolt the table and his eyes were glaring as he turned back to face Ng.

'Some prick reporter from the *South China Morning Post* saying he'd heard a rumour that Lung Tau had been killed.'

'Tell him to go fuck his mother.'

Tse grinned. 'Already done,' he said.

Ng pointed his finger at Tse, stabbing the air as he spoke. 'And tell everyone to keep their mouths shut. There's only one way a reporter could have found out what's happening and that's if one of our brothers spoke out of turn. No one, repeat no one, is to discuss this outside the triad. Spread the word round.'

The grin vanished from Tse's face and he nodded and grunted, avoiding Ng's glare.

'About the pictures, Mister Ng,' said Lin.

'What?'

'How do we get so many printed so quickly?'

'Make sure we get several negatives, and then take them to the developing shops that we control. They have machines for such things. Give five hundred to the Red Poles and have them show them at all the hotels and guest houses. Take five hundred to my father's house.' He couldn't bother explaining why and dismissed Lin with a wave of his hand. He hadn't forgotten that it was Lin who was supposed to be guarding his brother when he was taken. Tse stood by the door, shifting his weight from foot to foot, before deciding to go with Lin.

Ng called for the maid and she practically ran out of the kitchen, nervous hands clutching at her white apron.

'Get me a martini,' he said.

'I'm sorry, sir?' she said, looking close to tears.

'A martini. Make me a martini, please. A very dry one.'

Now there were tears in her big, brown eyes. 'I'm sorry, sir,' she said in a small voice. 'I don't know what a martini is.'

'For God's sake, can't anyone do anything here!' Ng yelled. 'I'll make it myself then.'

The girl backed away from him and Ng suddenly felt sorry for her. She was a pretty young thing, nineteen years old or so, long lean legs, firm breasts that moved under her blue uniform as she breathed and skin that matched the colour of the parquet flooring. Her lips were full and red even without lipstick, and her eyelashes had no need of mascara.

'I'm sorry,' he said, smiling. 'I did not mean to shout.'

'I'm sorry, sir, I'm sorry,' she repeated, and continued to back away until she reached the kitchen door, then she whirled around and was gone in a flurry of brown, white and blue.

Filipinas were every bit as sensitive as Chinese, he thought ruefully. He was going to have to get used to operating under Hong Kong rules again.

Sophie sat on the toilet, the lid down, her knees up against her chest, rocking slowly from side to side. Her throat was aching, and she felt hot all over. She'd waited until she was sure that the man had left the junk and then she'd screamed for all she was worth, but no one had come and eventually she'd given up. She'd kicked the door until her feet hurt and she'd tried rattling it to see if she could loosen the lock but it had been no good. She drank a little water from the tap above the tiny triangular washbasin but her throat still hurt. There was no airconditioning and the air in the confined space was hot and stuffy. There was a pink flannel on the side of the washbasin and she ran cold water over it and then used it to wipe her face.

For the hundredth time she looked around for a way out, but with the door firmly locked and no porthole she could see that she was trapped. She was hungry. She'd eaten the cheese sandwich an hour after he'd left. Surely the fact that he'd given her so little food meant he was coming back soon? Or perhaps it meant that he'd left her to starve. She sobbed but no tears came; she was all cried out.

Howells opened his eyes to see the huge tongue of the crocodile, spilling out of its mouth between padded teeth. He knew exactly how the beast felt, his own tongue felt furred and far too big for his own mouth. There was a mug of coffee on a small table by the side of the bed. He raised himself up and reached for it with his left hand, ignoring the burning sensation in his right shoulder. It was cold but he drank it, swilling it around his mouth before swallowing to get rid of the bitter taste that made him think of chewed aspirins. He moved to put the empty mug back but the strength failed him and it clattered down on the table and fell to the floor.

Amy came running into the bedroom. 'What's wrong?' she asked, kneeling by his side.

'Nothing,' he grinned sheepishly. 'I dropped the cup, that's all. I'm sorry.'

'The doctor say you will be weak for some time, Geoff. You must relax until your strength comes back.'

'I'll be OK,' he said. 'I heal fast.'

She ran her hand along the back of his neck, rubbing the small, curly hairs there.

'He said someone shot you before. Many times. He saw the scars. And a knife scar on your leg.'

'Old ones,' Howells laughed. 'I'm faster now.'

'Not so fast,' she said. 'Or you not be lying in my bed.'

287

'I can't argue with you there, Amy. I think the doctor was right.'

'What do you mean?'

'About water being a good idea. Could you get me a glass?'

'Of course.' She walked behind him, out of vision, and he heard a door open and the sound of running water. She came back and lifted a glass to his lips and held it there until he'd emptied it.

'More?' she asked.

'No thanks, that's fine. What time is it?'

'About seven o'clock.'

'At night?' The curtains were drawn and the window was behind him, so he had no idea if it was day or night.

'Yes,' she said. 'Listen, Geoff. I have to go work.'

'Work?'

'The Washington Club. I have to be there at eight o'clock or big trouble for me.'

'Tell them you're sick.'

'I can't.'

'You can.'

'You don't understand. If I don't go to work they will fine me double my bar fine. And mamasan fine me for every hour I am late. It is a rule.'

'Even if you're sick.'

She nodded. 'Unless I have a letter from the doctor. And anyway, they saw me leave with you last night. They will not believe me. They will think I am with you and not charging you bar fine. It will mean big trouble for me. Better for me to go.'

Howells didn't want her to go – not that he was worried about being left alone; he was worried that while away

288

from him she might have second thoughts, and he was in no fit state to take care of himself, just yet. He healed fast, but not that fast. 'Can't I pay your bar fine?' he asked.

'You do not have much money left, Geoff,' she said quietly.

'You checked,' said Howells, allowing the bitterness into his voice.

She looked crestfallen, and bit her lower lip. 'No,' she said. 'You gave me your wallet to pay bar fine last night. There was not a lot left after I paid. I did not check on you.'

'I'm sorry,' he said. 'I take that back.' The last thing he needed now was to get her angry at him. He reached over and held her hand. 'I really am grateful to you,' he said. 'When I'm well I'll make it up to you, I promise.'

She stood up, and smoothed down her jeans. In casual clothes she looked an unlikely hooker, more like a student or playgroup leader, a cheerful, bouncy girl, in faded denims and white training shoes. She walked behind him again and refilled the glass with water. This time she sat on the bed, and ran her long fingernails down his back, gently scraping the flesh, and being careful to keep away from the injured shoulder.

'I won't be long, Geoff. The doctor will be back early tomorrow. I will be here before then.' Howells sighed, too tired to argue. 'No need to worry,' she said. 'I not tell anyone.'

Grey thought long and hard before ringing the American. Like a grandmaster considering all the options to the nth degree, he replayed countless scenarios in his mind: coming clean and telling his superiors what he'd done; early retirement under a cloud; relying on the notoriously inefficient Chinese to track Howells down and try again; recruiting another freelance and buying his way out. Unpalatable as it was, asking Greg Hamilton for help seemed to be the only way of salvaging the situation, and his career.

Hamilton was his opposite number in the CIA, equivalent rank and status and three times the salary with a former model for a wife and a lawyer for a son. They arranged to meet in Hyde Park on a day when the wind was cold enough to keep the Trafalgar Square pigeons huddled on ledges with their heads tucked under their wings for warmth, but not harsh enough to deter the scavenging ducks on the Serpentine. So much for summer. Grey had a perfectly adequate office halfway up Century House but he rarely used it to meet contacts from outside the Service. He preferred to meet people on their own territory, or on neutral ground, and he made it a rule never to brief his operatives in his office. Both men wore overcoats, Grey in a dark blue Savile Row wool overcoat and Hamilton in standard CIA issue Burberry. Hamilton was six or seven years younger than Grey, but the age difference seemed wider thanks to the American's all-year-round tan and snappy dress sense.

Grey kept his head down as he walked, his chin thrust hard against his chest. He looked to be deep in thought but Hamilton knew that all the thinking had been done long before he'd got to this stage. Grey wanted something, something that couldn't be discussed in his office, something that embarrassed the man. Grey wanted a boon, a favour that at some point Hamilton would be able to call in, so he waited patiently as they walked along the side of the lake. A handful of inquisitive ducks paddled over, backsides twitching furiously, eyes alert for food as they kept pace with the walking men.

'I have a problem,' said Grey eventually, talking to his tie. For a moment Hamilton wondered if the man might be wired, but disregarded the thought. If Grey had wanted to record the conversation he could simply have arranged it to have taken place in his office. He kept silent. The ducks gave up and paddled over to a couple of secretaries sitting on a wooden bench and eating sandwiches.

'Do you remember an operative of ours called Howells?'

'The psychopath?'

Grey sighed into his jacket. 'I do wish people would stop calling him that. The psychologists labelled him a sociopath.'

'With homicidal tendencies.'

Grey looked up and smiled thinly. 'Whatever.'

'Howells is your problem? I thought our headshrinkers had solved that one for you.'

'They did. They did a first-class job, too. He was as docile as a lamb by the time they'd finished with him. We put him out to grass.'

'So what's the problem?'

Grey took a deep breath. 'He's back.'

'Back?'

'In action.'

'That couldn't happen.'

The two men walked in silence again. Hamilton didn't

want to press Grey, it had to come in his own time. Any pressure and he'd be frightened off.

'We brought him back. And now it's gone wrong.'

'He's dead?'

'No, no. Quite the opposite in fact. He's the one doing the killing.'

'But I thought our boys had put a stop to that. They neutered him, no?'

'Yes, they did. But we needed him for a job. In Hong Kong.'

'Jesus Christ. You started him killing again? Howells?' Anger flared in Hamilton's eyes but he dampened it quickly. He'd never seen Grey like this before, and if he played it right it would give him an edge over the Brits that he'd be able to use to full advantage.

'One of our own psychologists was on the team that treated him and he'd left a trapdoor in their programming, a way of reactivating the Howells of old. And we used it. We turned him back into a killer.'

'But to kill who?'

'A triad leader in Hong Kong.'

Hamilton didn't need to mention the fact that the colony was outside Grey's normal jurisdiction. The Brits' activities were supposedly confined to internal security, the British Isles, and, on one occasion, Gibraltar, but that had required special authorization from the PM. In fact, the more Hamilton heard of this story the more he was sure that when Grey said 'we' he actually meant 'I'. Grey had been running some sort of maverick operation which had come unstuck. And whatever it was, it was serious enough for him not to be able to use his own people to put it right. He could feel the excitement mounting inside as he realized that if he played his cards right he was going to end up with his own man inside British Intelligence. A man who owed him.

'Did he do the job?'

'Perfectly. As usual.'

'So what's the problem?'

Grey lifted his chin off his chest and turned to look at the American. They stood stock-still, facing each other like gunfighters about to draw their six-guns.

'Let's sit down,' said Grey, and he waved Hamilton towards an empty bench. A young girl with long blonde hair wearing a scruffy sheepskin jacket and faded jeans ran past with an unkempt spaniel tugging at a lead. Grey wished he had his dogs with him. You could rely on dogs, they wore their loyalty and their trust on their faces. Dogs couldn't disguise their emotions; if they were happy their tails wagged and their eyes sparkled, if they were sad or guilty they wouldn't meet your gaze and they'd slink around. A dog couldn't lie even if it wanted to.

He sat with his legs pressed together, his hands resting in his lap. Hamilton crossed his legs and reached into his inside jacket pocket for a pack of Silk Cut.

'Do you mind?' he asked. Grey lied and said no, he didn't. The American's lighter was gunmetal grey, one of the old-fashioned type where the top of it opened and flicked into life with hard downward jabs of the thumb. A Zippo. Grey looked at it and wondered if the CIA man was bugged – the lighter looked big enough to hold a full stereo system. Not that it mattered. The American was Grey's last hope and to enlist his help meant putting himself completely in his power. Grey had resigned himself to that and to all its implications, and having it on tape wouldn't make a blind bit of difference.

Hamilton drew deeply on his cigarette. Smoke blew across Grey's face and he stifled the urge to cough with a gloved hand. It was time to take control, Hamilton realized. 'Tell me what happened,' he said quietly. Grey told him. Everything. About Donaldson. About the mission. About Howells' phone call from Hong Kong. About the attempt to kill Howells and how it had all gone wrong.

'And now he's going to be after you?' The question was obviously rhetorical but Grey nodded.

'And what is it you want? Protection?'

'More than that. I want him taken care of.' Grey looked down at his gloves. 'You understand why I can't do anything myself?'

'Sure.' Hamilton blew a plume of smoke through clenched teeth and it formed a veil in front of his face. 'I can't get over the way you used Donaldson like that.'

'He was a paedophile. A grade A security risk just waiting to be uncovered by someone. And don't tell me you haven't done the same in the past.'

'I can't argue with that,' said the American. 'It's becoming a shitty business.'

'It's always been a shitty business, as you so eloquently put it.'

'Yeah, but it seems to be getting worse. Dirtier.'

'Don't delude yourself,' said Grey. 'It's always been this way. Have you ever read *The Art of War* by Sun Tzu?'

'I'm waiting for the video to come out,' said Hamilton, but his attempt at humour was lost on Grey.

'He was one of the world's greatest military strategists.

He wrote his book in China in 500 BC, almost two and a half thousand years ago. Just think about that. Two and a half thousand years. His book is a classic on the subject of warfare, and the use of secret agents.' He was warming to the subject now, his gloved hands clenching into fists in his lap. 'He realized that any army's main purpose was to administer the *coup de grâce*, to go in for the kill when the enemy has been weakened. That still applies today. There's nothing more futile than a battle between two equally matched forces. It's only worth fighting if you are sure to win.'

Hamilton let the Brit talk, calm on the outside as he drew on his cigarette, but inside he was in turmoil, as excited as the yapping spaniel.

'He defined secret agents as being in five classes: native, inside, double, expendable and living. And he tells a story of an expendable agent, a condemned man who was taken on to the payroll, disguised as a monk and given a ball of wax containing a secret message to swallow before being sent into an enemy stronghold. He was captured and told them everything as soon as they started to interrogate him. They waited for the wax ball to make its appearance and opened it to find a message from the monk's spy master to one of their generals. It was fake, of course. The completely innocent general and the expendable monk spy were both executed. And that was two and a half thousand years ago.'

Hamilton nodded and dropped the butt of his cigarette on to the path, grinding it with the heel of a highly polished shoe. No laces, Grey noticed.

'Sounds like a smart guy. What was his name?'

'Sun Tzu. I'll send you a copy.'

'I'd appreciate it. How did you come across it?'

'I studied Oriental languages at Oxford. And I was in our Beijing embassy for four years during the Sixties.'

'We were practically neighbours,' said the American.

'I don't follow,' said Grey, annoyed by Hamilton's tendency to go off at a tangent.

'I was in Vietnam.'

'Of course,' said Grey, dryly. He would have been – probably enjoyed it, too.

'You've thought through the ramifications of this?' said Hamilton.

'Of course I have. There is no need to rub my nose in this. I need your help and I'll pay you back. You'll get your pound of flesh, don't worry.'

'Just so we understand each other,' replied Hamilton. 'What you are asking me to do is every bit as wrong as what you did. It's my head on the block, too. Even the CIA doesn't go around killing at random.' Grey chuckled like a contented grandfather and Hamilton laughed along with him. 'Not recently, anyway,' said the American.

They watched the teenager unleash the enthusiastic dog. It barked happily and jumped up, pawing at her crotch and she pushed it away giggling. It was getting over-excited, running backwards and forwards, barking at her, barking at the ducks, the trees, the sky, at life.

'You've told me the what, when, how and who,' said Hamilton, 'but what you haven't told me is why. Why you wanted this triad leader killed and why you didn't do it through the normal channels.'

Grey folded his arms across his chest defensively. 'I had to protect an agent. As Sun Tzu would have said, an agent in place.'

'In Beijing?'

'In Beijing.'

'Highly placed?'

'The top.'

'Jesus H. Christ. You've had a mole in Beijing since the Sixties?' Grey nodded. 'All through the negotiations over Hong Kong's future, the talks between China and Russia, the Sino–Israeli arms deals, Tiananmen Square, you've had your own man there. Jesus H. Christ.'

'I recruited him after I'd been in Beijing for a year. That's why I stayed so long. He was nervous, kept saying he'd deal only with me. It took a lot of time and work to reassure him, before I could leave, but still he'd deal only with me. Not often, but it was always gold. Top grade. And one hundred per cent accurate. But always insisting that I remained his handler.'

'It would have been nice if you'd shared some of the gold with your friends,' said the American.

'You must allow us some secrets,' said Grey. 'But we did share much of it, but in such a way that you'd never know where it had come from.'

I bet, thought Hamilton. I just bet. But he smiled and nodded. 'And where did Howells come in?'

'A month or so ago my man got in touch with me; he was frantic. He was already in a state of near-panic following the 1989 purges. He'd survived by distancing himself from Zhao Ziyang early on, and there was a rumour that he'd had a hand in the death of Hu Yaobang. Heart attack, they said. Anyway, he'd managed to stay in favour with Deng Xiaoping and the hard-liners, but this time he said he was sure that he was about to be exposed and that I had to get him out. He wanted me to arrange for his defection, urgently. I calmed him down and went to see him.'

'You?'

'I told you. He was mine. Throughout all the years I was the only one he'd deal with. I was the channel through which all his information passed – it had to be me. So I went and talked him down, and got to the root of his fear.'

'The triad leader?'

'Yes – Simon Ng. Drugs, prostitution, extortion. A nasty piece of work. Married to an English girl of all things.' It seemed to Hamilton that it was the mixed marriage rather than the threat to his agent that caused Grey the most discomfort. 'It seems that this Simon Ng is, or was, also an agent.'

'For whom?'

'Freelance. He worked for the highest bidder. His criminal connections have gained him access to some very useful information. It was information that we were happy to pay for, and I'm sure that if you check you'll find he was on the CIA's books as well.'

'I'm sure. We generally pay better than the British.'

Grey gave him an exasperated look. He was starting to tire of the American's college-boy humour.

'According to my man, Ng had begun to deal with the Chinese. And in a big way, too. But this time it wasn't money he was after, it was political.'

Hamilton looked curious, and lit another cigarette with the Zippo.

'He wanted a guarantee that his triad organization could continue to operate after 1997, when Hong Kong becomes a Special Administrative Zone, part of China.

298

The Chinese refused, of course. They've been cracking down on organized crime in a big way on the mainland. Ng said he could deliver them a deep penetration mole. He'd say nothing more than that, but my man went hysterical. He was sure he was about to be uncovered.'

'How had this Simon Ng found out about your agent?'

Grey shrugged. 'I don't know. Personally I'm not even sure that his cover was in danger of being blown.'

'There was no reason for Ng to lie. Not if he was planning some long-term relationship with the Chinese as you said.'

'It could have been a first offer, just to make them think he had something big, a way of upping the stakes. He might well have been after money when all was said and done, and the agent could have been one of Taiwan's. The mainland is riddled with Taiwanese agents.'

'But your man didn't think so?'

'He was panicking. I could see only one way of keeping him in place.'

'Howells.'

'Yes. Howells.'

'Why not use one of your own men?'

'You can see why. Ng was an agent we used ourselves from time to time. We could hardly be seen killing one of our own. Even a freelance.'

Grey seemed to have conveniently forgotten that Donaldson had been one of his own, mused the American.

'Plus, it wasn't a normal sort of operation. Ng was very well protected, his place was practically a fortress. We needed someone good, someone very good.'

'And you needed someone expendable?'

Grey's upper lip curved up in a smile, a smile without warmth. 'You do understand then?'

The American blew a stream of smoke from his nostrils and a gust of wind blew it across Grey's face.

'I think so. Once Howells had done the job your agent could expose him as the killer. That would do his credibility no end of good. He'd have Howells killed, Howells who was known to be a headcase and no longer used by the British. I suppose they'd assume he'd gone freelance. Maybe they'd even think he was working for us?'

'Hardly,' said Grey.

'But the end result would be the removal of Simon Ng and a pat on the back for your man.'

'Two birds with one stone,' agreed Grey.

'Except the Chinese missed him.'

'They lost two of their best men, and a woman was injured.'

'They'll try again.'

'Of course they'll try again. But now Howells knows they're after him. And he must know by now that I told them where he was. Nobody else knew.'

Caught between a rock and a hard place, thought Hamilton. Grey could hardly use his own people to hunt down Howells, not without answering a lot of very sticky questions. So the Brit needed help, and Hamilton knew the price of his help.

'I'll handle it,' promised Hamilton. 'It won't be a problem. I'll be in touch.'

The two men stood up, shook hands, and walked off in opposite directions. The deal had been struck without even being discussed. Hamilton was elated and was humming quietly to himself as he waited for a cab. It was a good exchange, he reckoned. The life of the psychopath for a share of the Beijing goldmine.

Thomas Ng arrived at Golden Dragon Lodge an hour before the ceremony was about to start. With him in the back of the car was Cheng Yuk-lin, who as well as being the triad's most trusted Double Flower White Paper Fan was also Heung Chu, the Incense Master, guardian of the ceremonies and initiation rites that bound the organization together.

Ng had decided to take the Daimler and he'd given Hui the chauffeur the night off. Lin Wing-wah was driving, and next to him was Kenny Suen, but they were told to remain in the car. The Burning of the Yellow Paper ceremony was only for the triad leaders. Strictly speaking Ng himself should not have been there as, for this meeting at least, his father had once more assumed the role of Dragon Head.

Lin's small pigtail waved from side to side as the car powered up the drive to the garage and stopped smoothly. Without a word Cheng and Ng got out of the car and walked up to the house in the gathering gloom. Cheng carried a green sports bag which he swung backwards and forwards in time with his steps. Suen remained in the car but Lin went back down to the gate to supervise the guards as they admitted the guests. Tonight would not be a night when any mistakes would be tolerated.

Ng Wai-sun was waiting to greet them at the entrance to the house wearing his red robe of office, a white belt loosely around his waist and a red band with several ungainly knots tied around his head. On one of his feet was a plain, black slipper but the other was adorned with a hand-made fibre sandal. He looked ridiculous, a small, balding man about to go to a fancy dress party, but Ng knew better than to smile.

'My son,' said Ng Wai-sun, stepping forward to shake his son's hand. He turned to face Cheng and put both hands on his shoulders. 'Cheng Yuk-lin. My good friend. I will need your help and support tonight.'

'You have it,' said Cheng. He raised the sports bag. 'I have my things here,' he said. 'The ceremony will be in the usual place?'

'It has been a long time, but yes, the usual place.'

Cheng nodded. 'I shall go upstairs and change.'

He walked into the house, the interior of which was lit by small, oil-burning lamps that gave off an orange glow. The house had electricity, but the old triad leader wanted the lamps on.

'It seems an eternity since you were in this house wearing the triad robes,' said the old man to his son.

'Most of our business these days takes place in board-rooms,' admitted Ng.

'The ceremonies have their place,' said his father. 'They are the glue that binds the triad together. They make us a family. Come into the house.' He took Ng by the arm and led him over the threshold, as if it was the son who was the weaker of the two. 'Who came with you?'

'Lin Wing-wah and Kenny Suen, but they will stay with the car.'

'That is good; there must be as little tension as possible in the house tonight.'

It was a warm evening and the lack of air-conditioning and the orange light gave the house a hellish feel, but Ng could never remember being frightened in it. It was an anachronism now, but it still had the friendliness of home, the reassurance that he knew every nook and cranny, every hiding-place. The house had many dark corners but they had all been explored long ago and held no fears for him.

The main room was very formal, with hard chairs and low tables, ornate gilt screens on the walls and two of his father's priceless jade carvings on rosewood tables either side of an antique wooden fireplace. The room was purely a reception area, the family rooms were all upstairs along with the bedrooms and the bulk of Ng's jade collection. To the right of the reception room were a pair of teak doors, dragons carved on to each, rearing back on their hind legs, flames spewing from their mouths and noses. The old man pushed them, one hand on each, and they grated inwards revealing the room beyond. It was a square room, each wall ten paces long, dominated by a huge circular table that could comfortably seat sixteen but which on some hectic family celebrations had seen more than twenty squabbling over laden plates. Tonight there were places for twelve, sheets of notepaper and gold pens spaced evenly around the circumference. There were no name cards; with a circular table there were no feathers to be ruffled by insensitive seating arrangements.

The shutters had been closed and locked and the only illumination came from four brass oil lamps, one in each corner of the room, casting orange orbs that met in the middle of the table and the centre of the ceiling. On the wall to the left of the twin doors was a framed portrait of the Kwan Kung god. The other paraphernalia of the triad, the banners, the sacred objects, the wall hangings, were missing, and Ng realized it was because this was a meeting of many triads and his father did not want to make it appear that his guests were on enemy territory, even though that was the case. The triads rarely indulged in the gang wars of old, but they were still fierce competitors and they would be insecure enough coming to Golden Dragon Lodge, never mind being surrounded by the artefacts of a rival. In front of the portrait was a rough wooden table, the surface notched and hacked like a butcher's block. On it stood a black ceramic bowl.

The room served two functions. It was used for the most important triad ceremonies and initiations, usually those that involved close family members. Thomas, Simon and Charles had all been initiated there, and it was in the room that Thomas had promoted Cheng Yuk-lin to the rank of Double Flower White Paper Fan. But it was also a family room, where Ng Wai-sun held court over the generations, at Christmas, Chinese New Year, and at birthdays and weddings, enjoying the feeling of heading a dynasty, patting heads and passing out red Lai See packets.

The room was also a record of the Ng family. Around the walls, starting on the left of the doors and running along three and a half of the walls was a series of family photographs that spanned two thirds of the life of Ng Wai-sun and all of Thomas Ng's. The first photograph, and one nearest the door, was of Ng Wai-sun and his bride on their wedding day, he in a grey morning coat, holding a top hat, back stiff and face unsmiling, she a radiant young woman in a European-style white wedding dress looking up at him with unashamed adoration.

There followed almost forty pictures, each taken on the anniversary of their wedding day, children starting as small babies, growing into toddlers and then teenagers, and finally men. Walking along the line of photographs was like watching a flickering black-and-white movie, as Ng Wai-sun changed from a whipcord-thin youngster with black straight hair to a balding old man and his wife from a radiant bride to a stooping old lady with clawed hands and parchment skin, the two of them surrounded by three middle-aged men and a woman, and a clutch of small children, including one with blonde hair and pale white skin.

The changes between consecutive pictures were small, other than when babies appeared, but in their totality they made Ng all too well aware of his own mortality. When he was younger it was different; the series of pictures gave him a sense of history, of tradition, and it gave him a feeling of security seeing his parents stretching back across the years. But the fact that his mother had disappeared and no longer took her yearly place at her husband's side made Ng realize that no one lived for ever. And in next year's picture there would be no Simon, standing there with his hands on Thomas' shoulder, and maybe no Sophie either.

He looked at the last picture in the series, taken some three months earlier, the three brothers and sister and a scattering of children, most of them belonging to Catherine, the youngest of Ng Wai-sun's children but by far the most productive. Still in her twenties, she and her banker husband had produced five children, one boy and four girls. Charles and his American-born Chinese wife Sandra had two boys, and Simon and Jill only had

Sophie. Thomas caught his father looking at him as he studied the picture.

'No Father, I have no plans to marry,' he said quietly, without turning his head. Ng had plenty of girlfriends, and no shortage of female company when he was between regular companions, but he had never wanted to marry, and he had no plans to get hitched just to satisfy an old man, especially one who was already a grandfather eight times over. Or seven, if they lost Sophie. Ng Wai-sun tut-tutted, but his eyes were smiling.

'I have had a robe prepared for you in your old room,' he said.

Ng nodded. The robes were just as much an anachronism as the house, but he knew that the other triad leaders, the old ones at least, put as much store by the ceremonies as his father did. The request he was about to make tonight was unusual, unusual enough to warrant them appearing in what, when it came down to it, was little more than fancy dress. Ng went upstairs to change, leaving his father looking wistfully at the last photograph.

The bedroom door was on the first floor, and it was exactly the same as when he'd last seen it some three months earlier, save for the black robe lying on the bed. Ng knew that the room was dusted every day and the bedding changed every week, even though it had been at least ten years since he had actually slept there. It was his room and it would be until he died. There were rooms on the same floor for Simon, Charles and Catherine, though it had also been more than a decade since they had been slept in.

Ng took off his suit and shirt and pulled the robe over his head, draped the scarlet scarf around his neck, the ends reaching past his knees, tied and untied the white belt until it looked right and then he put on the headband with its single knot. At the end of the bed he found a brown shoe and a rope slipper and he put them on over his socks. He checked himself in the large free-standing mirror by the window and couldn't help grinning at his reflection. He looked absurd, and he wondered what his banker friends in San Francisco would say if they saw him in the outlandish outfit, the ceremonial dress of a Pak Tsz official, the adviser.

It was one o'clock in the morning and every girl in the Limelight Club was a virgin. That's what they all told Jack Edmunds, anyway, as he sat on his stool nursing a tumbler of Jack Daniels and watching the dancers sway in time to the music. The Limelight was on the ground floor of Pat Pong One so all the girls were dressed, albeit scantily in bikinis or cutaway swimsuits. You had to go up to one of the first floor bars to watch nude dancers or sex shows but after four days in Bangkok he'd just about seen it all: girls putting safety-pins through their breasts, burning themselves with candles, using their vaginal muscles to shoot darts through blowpipes and to write with large felt-tipped pens. He'd seen full sex and lesbian sex and sex with a German Shepherd dog. Now he was jaded and preferred to sit and drink in the Limelight, where at least there was something left to the imagination. The girls seemed prettier too, though after half a dozen beakers of the amber fluid they all looked good. The bar was a large oval surrounding a raised dance floor on which there were ten or so Thai girls dancing; few moved enthusiastically, but they were all smiling. They were just tired; most of them had been on their feet for the best part of four hours. They danced in twenty-minute shifts, once an hour. The rest of the time they sat around the bar or at the tables around the edge of the room, groping customers' thighs and hustling drinks, much as the girls sitting either side of Edmunds were doing. Small hands, moving inquisitively around his groin. Neither looked much more than seventeen years old but Edmunds knew just how difficult it was to pinpoint accurately the age of an Asian girl. Sure, you could tell the ones that were obviously underage, flat-chested and no pubic hair, and you could spot the old hags, the over-the-hill hookers who still toured the bars looking for a tourist so drunk that he couldn't see the wrinkles and the scars. But in between the two extremes there was no way of telling – they all had the same jet-black hair, smooth brown skin and shining brown eyes.

The one on his right was called Del; her long hair was twisted into a single braid which had been wound around her head like a crown, and she wore a bright green swimsuit. She had two cigarette burns on her left thigh, healing nicely. Edmunds had asked her what had happened but she'd just smiled and shaken her head. There were three cuts on one of her wrists, an inch long and half an inch apart. Not deep enough to be suicide attempts, and obviously done at different times. One was a white scar, the middle was still red and the skin raised, and the third was covered with a thin scab.

The other girl had short, pageboy-style hair and a

rash of acne badly disguised with make-up. She wore a scarlet bikini that barely restrained her lemon-shaped breasts between which nestled a small chunk of jade on a thin gold chain. Her name was Need. Edmunds knew enough Thai to know that Need was a common name for girls or boys – it meant small. For the tenth time that night she looked at Edmunds, stroked his thigh and said: 'You make love now?' She had the sort of teeth that would drive a dentist into bankruptcy. Not a single filling. Edmunds' mouth contained five thousand dollars' worth of bridgework. The first time she'd asked he'd shaken his head and said 'not tonight', the fifth time he'd said 'no money' but now he'd reached the stage where he said 'maybe later'.

'I want now,' she pouted. She pointed to Del. 'Two girls, good price.' Del nodded enthusiastically and her hand joined Need's, gently rubbing up and down his prick. Edmunds took a deep breath and drained his glass. He waved at a waitress behind the bar and gestured at his glass and those in front of the two girls. They were drinking lemonade at twice the price of his Jack Daniels. That's how the girls earned their money, commission on the non-alcoholic drinks plus whatever they could screw out of the customers as tips or payment for sex.

'I want make love,' insisted Need, bouncing up and down on her stool. She did have a cute arse, Edmunds decided. Beautiful firm breasts. And the acne wasn't that bad.

'I love you,' said Need.

'No shit?' he said.

'No shit,' chorused the girls and they giggled. He was

almost three times their age, he realized, but that didn't make him feel any less aroused.

'Now? I very tired,' said Del, resting her forehead on his shoulder and playing with his zip.

'Soon,' said Edmunds, his mouth dry and his mind made up. He reached for his drink and closed his eyes as he swallowed. He wanted the two girls but he hadn't drunk enough yet to dampen the feelings of revulsion in the pit of his stomach. It happened every time he came into one of the Pat Pong bars. He'd sit by himself, intending only to watch and drink, feeling nothing but scorn and contempt for the middle-aged men who sat in the gloom and fondled girls young enough to be their daughters. He'd look at the girls and chat to them, buy a few drinks and watch the shows, knowing that he wouldn't be tempted, feeling anger at the obscenity of a German businessman with an expense account gut and three chins bouncing a sixteen-year-old Thai girl up and down on his knees and slipping his wrinkled hand down the back of her swimsuit. He'd talk to the girls as best he could, ask them where they were from, how long they'd been in Bangkok, and he'd buy them drinks. It happened every time. The alcohol relaxed him, their hands began to wander, and before long the thought of being in bed with a girl young enough to be his grand-daughter didn't seem too abhorrent.

'How much?' he asked Need and she beamed, knowing that he was hooked. 'How much for you both?'

She told him. About the same as a decent bottle of whisky would cost back in the States. Economic rape, he thought. Del's hand grasped his prick through the material of his trousers.

'Now?' she said, looking into his eyes.

'Not here,' said Edmunds. He'd taken one of the girls into a back room a couple of days ago. 'Short time,' she'd called it, down a corridor and into a small square room big enough only for a double bed and a sink. The bed was covered with a sheet stained with God knows what. No pillows, no blankets. A room designed for one thing and illuminated by a single red light-bulb hanging from the ceiling. The girl had looked young, very young; she said her name was Orr but he'd called her Number 11 all evening. That was the number on the badge pinned to her black and white swimsuit and it was about how old she'd looked. She'd taken the money off him and squatted over the sink and cleaned herself, and then insisted that he did the same. She helped him and as he grew hard she'd opened a foil packet and expertly slipped on a condom and pulled him down on the bed, on top of her and into her. Her legs came up either side of his arse and her heels had hooked behind his thighs as she thrust herself against him, hard and fast and tight. Her face was turned to one side, blank and expressionless and he remembered how cheated he'd felt. He started moving, harder and faster, trying to get some reaction from her, some sign that she was enjoying it, but she just gritted her teeth. 'Look at me,' he'd said but she'd just continued to grind into him, wanting it to be over. Wanting to get back to the bar, to the next customer. He'd begun pounding into her then, wanting to hurt, to make her feel pain if nothing else, wanting her to acknowledge that he was there, inside her. She'd winced and closed her eyes but said nothing, just kept moving her hips until he came. Edmunds had felt disgusted with himself then, ashamed at the violent feelings he'd had towards the girl, the way sex had got mixed up with pain in his head. He'd washed himself in silence and given her another note as he left the room.

'No short time,' he said to Need. 'You come back to hotel with me.' The girls smiled. Back in his room he had a king-size bed and clean sheets and more booze. And he'd have time, time at least to feel he was being treated like a human being. Getting the girls in wouldn't be a problem, the hotels in Bangkok knew which side their bed was buttered. Sure, the girls had to be checked in at reception and have their identity cards recorded, but that wasn't to hassle the guests, it was to make sure that they weren't ripped off. And there'd be no snide, knowing smiles from the staff, just polite acceptance of the way the system worked.

'We go now?' asked Del. 'Me horny.'

Jesus Christ, thought Edmunds, where the fuck do they learn their English? But he knew the answer to that – in bed. On their backs. Their hands were fondling him, probing, rubbing, insisting. Two more hands began massaging his neck, slowly and sensually. He dropped his head forward and sighed.

'Mmm,' he said. 'That's good. So good.'

He closed his eyes and concentrated on the cool, strong hands on his neck. The girl was good, very good. She knew what she was doing, all right, he could feel the tension being pulled from his muscles. God, what could she do to him in bed? He'd be putty in her hands, she'd be able to do anything to him. With him.

The hands slid around his neck, stroking the sides until they found the carotid artery and then they tightened, cutting off the blood supply to his head. His eyes bulged and he gasped for breath and he tried to unclasp the fingers around his throat before he passed out. Then they were gone and he fell forward on to the bar, knocking over his glass which spun on to the floor and shattered. As he gasped for breath a decidedly masculine voice behind him said: 'You want massage, you randy bastard?'

Edmunds didn't have to look round, he could think of only one arsehole who'd behave like that.

'You're a cunt, Feinberg. A grade-A motherfucking cunt.'

'I love it when you talk dirty, Edmunds. It gives me a hard-on.'

Del slid off her stool to make way for the second man and he patted her backside as she moved behind him and then stood between them, her hand finding its way back into Edmunds' lap.

'I suppose you want a fucking drink?'

'Jack, I thought you'd never ask,' said Feinberg, in a drawling imitation of W. C. Fields. 'And what about one for your wife here?'

Feinberg had a puerile sense of humour, but the business with the neck hadn't been funny, thought Edmunds. Feinberg could kill with his concert pianist's hands. And had done. Edmunds massaged his neck muscles.

'What do you want?'

'Rum and Coke, thanks.'

Edmunds ordered a round of drinks, and as he waited he remembered the last time he'd seen Rick Feinberg. It was at CIA headquarters in Virginia, eighteen months ago, at a debriefing following a very messy job in South America, and it had been Feinberg's fault that it had been so messy. A bomb that was to have taken out a general with a nasty line in torture also blew three passing schoolchildren into a million bloody fragments. Strictly speaking the two Americans weren't to blame; the bomb had been set off with a simple electric timer and they were back in their hotel when it went off, but Feinberg had decided how much explosive to use.

'I love a big bang,' he'd said as he slipped the carrier bag containing the bomb under the rear passenger seat of the general's Mercedes. Not that Edmunds had told the investigators that when they got back to Langley. Edmunds was a team player – always had been, ever since he played college ball. Always would be.

The drinks arrived and Feinberg leant forward, sipping from the glass as it stood on the bar, like a lion drinking from a water-hole. Del began to rub Feinberg's thigh and she whispered in his ear.

What the hell was Feinberg doing in Bangkok? It was too much of a coincidence to be drinking in the same bar; Feinberg must have been looking for him, even though he still had more than a week's leave to go. He studied him as he drank. He was tall and stringy enough to be a marathon runner but not enough for basketball, with sharp features, a slightly pointed chin and an angular nose between hooded eyes that forever looked as if they hadn't had enough sleep. Since he'd last seen him Feinberg had grown a Mexican-style moustache that drooped down either side of his thin, bloodless lips. It was wilting in the heat. Feinberg was wearing a white short-sleeved Lacoste shirt with green stripes, and jeans held up with a green and red Gucci belt. Edmunds looked past the younger man to a mirrored wall and saw himself. Christ, he looked old. His paunch was spilling over his trousers and though he still had a full head of hair it was all grey. It had been that way for a good ten years, but whereas before he could tell himself it was prematurely grey, now it was just grey. His face, like his body, was fleshier than Feinberg's, the features all smoothed out by subcutaneous fat, though he had the same world-weary eyes. Edmunds' was a temporary condition, though, the result of too much booze and too many late nights. A few days back in the States and he'd soon be bright-eyed and bushy-tailed.

He sucked in his gut, which seemed to take a good five years off the age of his reflection but it was too much of an effort to hold it in and he exhaled with a mournful sigh. He realized that Feinberg was watching him in the mirror with a knowing grin on his face.

'You're putting on a bit, Jack,' he said. 'Stopped the old morning exercises, have we? Not keeping fit any more?'

'You wanna step outside and find out just how fit I am?' snapped Edmunds. 'I can still take you out, and I don't need a kilo of high explosive to do it.'

Feinberg raised his hands in a gesture of surrender. 'Whoa, touchy, touchy,' he said.

'What do you want, Rick?'

'Enough money to be comfortable, a loving wife, peace on earth. Just the normal sort of shit we all want,' said Feinberg. 'And a couple of hours with this pretty young thing.'

Edmunds felt a flare of irrational jealousy burst somewhere inside him. Del seemed to have forgotten he existed, though Need's fingers were as insistent as ever.

315

'What are you doing here, Rick?' Edmunds pressed.

'Just passing through,' sighed Feinberg, his eyes on Del.

'From where?' Need's nails bit into his thigh.

'Langley.'

'To where?'

'Hong Kong.'

'And?'

'What do you mean?' he asked. Need sighed deeply and Edmunds felt the warm breath from her nostrils on his neck.

'I get the feeling there's something you're not telling me.'

Feinberg sniggered. 'Oh yeah, I forgot to tell you. You're coming with me.'

'I'm on leave, Rick. Rest and recreation.'

'More recreation than rest, I'd think.'

'I can't argue with that. What's the game plan?' Need slid off her stool, resigned to the fact that she'd lost Edmunds' attention. And his money. But it was still relatively early and there were plenty of customers in the bar. Del saw her go but decided to continue trying her luck with Feinberg.

'A small problem that our masters want taken care of.'

'Anyone we know?'

Feinberg turned to look at him at last. 'Geoff Howells – a Brit. You know him?'

'Doesn't ring a bell. What did he do?'

'Hey man, ours not to reason why, et cetera et cetera. Since when have we been interested in the whys and wherefores?'

'Since I'm getting pulled off my well-earned leave,' Edmunds smiled.

'He killed one of our men in Hong Kong.'

'Who?'

'A chink. I'd never heard of him, a guy called Ng. A freelance.'

'So why would a Brit kill one of our men?'

'There you go, asking why again.' He began toying with Del's young breasts, fingering the nipples to make them hard. 'We make love?' she asked him. Feinberg grinned wolfishly and pinched her until she winced. 'Never in a million years,' he said. He continued to pinch until tears welled up in the girl's eyes but she wouldn't cry out, didn't try to remove his hand.

'Leave her be,' said Edmunds.

'You're getting soft in your old age,' said Feinberg, but he stopped hurting the girl. She rushed off to the toilet and Edmunds knew she would cry there, away from them. His heart went out to her. Maybe Feinberg was right, maybe he was getting soft.

'Seems a bit strange, that's all.'

'Apparently he's gone loopy. History of psychological problems. You sure you've never heard of him? I thought you knew everybody in this business, the length of time you've been around.'

'I'm getting a bit fed up with all the cracks about my age,' said Edmunds.

'Hey, no offence meant.'

'I bet. So, what do we know about this Howells?'

'Full biog, pics, the works. No details of location but Hong Kong is locked up tighter than a frog's arse. He's not going anywhere.'

'Sounds cool.'

'Cool? Hey, nobody says cool anymore. Cool went out with flared trousers.'

Feinberg saw the anger in Edmunds' eyes and immediately held up his hands. 'For fuck's sake, man, don't be so goddamned sensitive.'

Edmunds laughed, finished his drink and got unsteadily to his feet. 'I'm going back to the hotel. What time's our flight?'

'Just before noon. I'll call you. I'm in the Sheraton as well.'

'OK. You staying here?'

'Sure. I'm going to have me that little girl there.' He gestured at one of the dancers, a tall girl in knee-high boots with long hair tied back in a ponytail. 'I'm going to make her do terrible things to me with that hair. I'm going to make her wrap it . . .' Edmunds didn't hear the rest, it was lost in the pounding music as he headed for the door. On the way he passed the toilets and saw Del leaning against the wall. Her eyes were red but she beamed when she saw Edmunds. 'We make love?' she asked hopefully. 'I love you.'

Edmunds felt a wave of sadness wash over him, sadness mixed with guilt in about equal parts. He pulled out his wallet and thrust a couple of brown notes at her. 'I'm sorry,' he said, and walked out into the hot night air, thick with the smell of spices and motor-cycle fumes.

The twelve triad leaders sitting around the circular table controlled the lion's share of drugs, vice and illegal gambling in Hong Kong, as well as a good chunk of the colony's legal business, but to Thomas Ng they looked like a group of pensioners being told about a forthcoming outing. They sat quietly, occasionally nodding or grunting, as Ng Wai-sun stood in front of the framed portrait of the fierce Kwan Kung god and put before them the events of the previous forty-eight hours. He spoke quietly, his voice steady as he looked each of the men in the eyes in turn.

They had all arrived in separate cars with their own bodyguards, but all had walked alone to the entrance of the house to be greeted by Ng Wai-sun. Some had worn expensive suits, some came in designer casual clothes and one, a man who appeared to be even older than Ng's own father, had turned up in a traditional black silk Chinese suit with ivory toggles, and each had carried a small bag containing his robes of office. One by one they had gone upstairs to change and then taken their place at the table. Ng stood to the left side of the double doors, his arms folded across his chest, and Cheng stood at the right.

The old man told the triad leaders about the kidnapping of his grand-daughter by the gweilo, the abduction and assumed murder of his son, and how they now had a photograph of the man they believed was responsible. Then he paused and slowly looked from man to man before speaking again.

'In days gone by triad often fought against triad in the battle for territory, and for profits, but we have put those days behind us. We have only a few years ahead of us before the Communists take over Hong Kong, and we know what that will mean.' The elderly men nodded in

319

unison. One cleared his throat noisily and looked around for somewhere to spit but decided against it. 'In recent years we have learned the benefits of cooperation rather than confrontation, each maximizing the profits from his own territory and not wasting resources in conflict; the Sun Yee On in Tsim Sha Tsui, the 14K in Mong Kok, the Tan Yee in Wan Chai and Causeway Bay.' He nodded to the respective leaders as he mentioned their triads.

'Today I have to ask you for your consideration during this difficult time for me and for my family. We wish to conduct a search for this gweilo, and it is certain that the search will involve my men going into areas over which you have authority. I do not want our actions to be misunderstood, nor do I wish to cause you any offence; therefore I stand before you and ask your permission.'

He clasped his hands over his stomach and waited.

The Dragon Head of the Luen Ying Sh'e was the first to speak after slowly getting to his feet.

'Ng Wai-sun, I offer you my condolences for the tragedy that has befallen your noble family, a tragedy that is all the more insidious coming as it did at the hands of a barbarian. I offer your men safe passage through Luen Ying Sh'e territory until you have found the man you speak of.'

He was followed by the man who had wanted to spit at the thought of the Communists; he too stood up and pledged his support. But Ng knew that the two were small fry, eager to please and to grant a boon to his father because they knew at some time the favour would be returned. Between them they probably controlled less than ten square miles, and most of that in the New Territories. Despite that Ng Wai-sun bowed to each of them and thanked them profusely. There was silence then, and the remaining triad leaders looked at each other, faces carved from stone, wondering who would be next to speak.

It was the Dragon Head of the Tan Yee who rose first, a bull of a man standing a head and a half taller than Ng Wai-sun and double his width. In his youth he had been one of the most feared of Tan Yee's fighters, and had served a sentence for manslaughter in Stanley for hacking off the head of a Red Pole from a rival triad. It should have been a life sentence for murder but the triad had flown in a top London QC and killed two witnesses, one of them a police sergeant. Mok Shih-chieh had mellowed a bit since then, but not much. Despite his seventy years he still had a full head of hair, though every strand was now pure white, and though most of his muscle had long since run to fat, he was still an impressive sight in his red robes. Five years earlier he'd had half a lung removed and his breath rasped in his throat in time with the movement of his huge chest.

'I echo the sentiments of those who have already spoken, Ng Wai-sun. And I agree with what you have said about our organizations, our families, using our resources wisely. No one here can deny that since we devoted ourselves to business and stopped petty squabbling we have all prospered.'

The men at the table grunted and nodded in agreement.

'Despite one or two minor territorial disputes,' – he gave a knowing look at one of the younger Dragon Heads, who bowed his head under the scrutiny, 'we have concentrated on cooperation rather than confrontation.' He paused and took deep wheezing breaths, leaning forward and placing his hands on the table for support. 'I think the time has come for us to show that this co-operation can be extended even further. You are right, Ng Wai-sun, when you say that we have little time left in Hong Kong. Life will be different here in Hong Kong when the Communists take over. It will not be impossible, but it will be difficult. I myself am glad that I will not be here to see it.'

The men shook their heads at that, but it was generally known that the cancer had reappeared and that Mok Shih-chieh was refusing to have another operation.

'You have shown us the advantages of moving into businesses overseas, Ng Wai-sun, though we have not all the benefit of such an able son as you have.' He nodded at Thomas Ng who smiled, pleased and surprised at the recognition. 'As we move out into the world, away from Hong Kong and the Communists, I think we should do so together, as business associates, rather than as competitors. We are, after all, Chinese, despite our differences. It should be us against the world, taking strength from each other. This is something that I am sure will happen the closer we get to 1997. But I wish tonight to take a step in that direction, to forge the bonds of co-operation. What I am offering, Ng Wai-sun, is not just unhindered passage through Tan Yee territory. I am offering help. The Tan Yee triad will help search for this barbarian, and if we find him we will deliver him to you. I make this pledge in the name of friendship, and trust that it will be accepted as such.' He grunted and sat down heavily, his chair scraping along the floor.

Ng's father bowed to the Tan Yee Dragon Head. 'I am grateful for your assistance, Mok Shih-chieh.' He nodded at Cheng who quietly opened the door and slipped out. 'I accept your offer, and the spirit of friendship in which it is made. And I look forward to closer co-operation between our organizations.'

In quick succession the remainder of the Dragon Heads stood and pledged their help to Ng Wai-sun, and Cheng came back into the room as the last one was sitting down. Cheng had twelve bundles of colour photographs and he walked slowly around the table, placing a bundle in front of each of the Dragon Heads.

'These are the best photographs we have of the gweilo,' Ng's father explained. 'We know what he looks like and we know that he has not left Hong Kong, or at least he has not to the best of our knowledge left through the port or the Kai Tak. But we do not know his name, nor do we have any idea where he is. Master Cheng will be co-ordinating the search, and he can be reached here, any time, night or day.'

Cheng left the room and returned with his bag. He carefully closed the double doors and walked to the table behind Ng Wai-sun. 'I ask you now to join me in the ceremony of Burning The Yellow Paper,' the Dragon Head continued. Behind him Cheng unzipped the bag and took from it a piece of yellow paper and placed it next to the cast-iron bowl. From the bag came a soft, clucking sound. Cheng handed the Dragon Head a black writing brush and unscrewed the top of a small bottle of blue ink. With careful, measured strokes Ng Wai-sun began to write on the paper, speaking each character out loud as he finished it, spelling out the oath of allegiance and the agreement the Dragon Heads had reached. The men around the table nodded their heads in agreement as he spoke. When he had finished he walked over to the Tan Yee Dragon Head and gave him the paper and brush.

'If you would do me the honour of signing first, Mok Shih-chieh.'

Mok smiled in acceptance and wrote the three characters of his name below the oath. The paper and brush were then passed clockwise around the table, and when there were twelve signatures Ng Wai-sun added his own before taking it back to the portrait.

Cheng produced a box of matches and a bottle of port from the bag and while the Dragon Head held the paper over the bowl Cheng lit a match and set fire to it. Flames licked at the paper and smoke curled above it, forming a cloud as if it came from the mouth of the Kwan Kung god. The red-faced warrior seemed to glare through the smoke, and his hands appeared to tighten on the war sword he held across his armoured chest. The old man held the burning paper until there was nothing but ash, ignoring the pain, his teeth clenched tightly. The flame flickered and died and he dropped the burnt sheet into the bowl. Cheng uncorked the port and poured it into the bowl, playing the stream of liquid over the ashes. He placed the empty bottle on the table, and from inside his robe took an ivory-handled curved knife, the blade wickedly sharp, which he handed to the Dragon Head. He leant over the bag once more and pulled out a black chicken by its feet. The bird's wings had been tied tight against its body with string, and Cheng held it out towards Ng Wai-sun so that he could cut the bonds and allow the chicken to flap freely. The Dragon Head seized it by the neck with his left hand and drew the blade across its neck with one firm stroke. Blood splattered into the bowl, some of it spilling on to the table, and then it poured out as the chicken thrashed and shook. Cheng waited until

324

the bird was still before dropping the corpse into the bag and taking the bloodstained knife from Ng Wai-sun. The Dragon Head picked up the bowl and held it close to his chin as he swirled the contents around. With his eyes fixed firmly on the men sitting at the table he raised the black bowl to his lips and drank deeply. When he'd finished he handed the bowl to Mok Shih-chieh. The mixture of blood and wine had given him a red line above his lips like a parody of a smile, a hellish clown's grin. Mok took the bowl almost reverently and then he too drank before passing it to the man on his left.

The bowl went round the table, as the yellow paper had done previously, each man drinking from it in turn until it returned to where Ng Wai-sun was standing. He took it and walked back to the table and held it up before the framed portrait.

'Whosoever breaks the oath and betrays the trust of those who signed the yellow paper, may he perish as the chicken has perished,' he said, before turning to face the men at the table. He threw the bowl down and it smashed into small pieces, the rest of the sickly-sweet mixture spilling on to the floor where it lay in slowly spreading pools, unable to soak into the polished wood.

'And may their families be broken as the bowl has been broken,' he said.

The Dragon Heads nodded agreement, as one.

The anchor chain dropped above Dugan's head at dead on six o'clock, and it was followed by the sound of one dollar coins being dropped into a tin bucket from a great height. For once it didn't annoy Dugan, not overmuch anyway, because he hadn't been able to sleep for more than half an hour at a time. Thoughts of Petal kept riding roughshod over his subconscious and he kept playing his last conversation with her over and over in his mind.

The key to what had happened, he was sure, lay with his brother-in-law, but according to the maid he and Jill hadn't been in all day. The last time he'd phoned, at eleven o'clock at night, he'd left his number and asked that Thomas Ng give him a call. The telephone had remained stubbornly silent all night.

He was in the office at half past seven, drinking coffee with his feet on the desk and he waited until eight before ringing Ng's house. The Filipina maid answered. No, Jill and Simon Ng were not at home. No, she didn't know if they had come back last night. No, Thomas Ng was not there. No, she did not know when he would be back.

Some 30,000 feet above Vietnam Feinberg handed a light green file to Edmunds. 'That's our boy,' he said. 'A real pro. I'm looking forward to this job.'

He was too, Edmunds could see it in his eyes, a manic gleam that he'd seen all too often during his days with Special Forces, when he had been down in the jungle below, killing and torturing and serving his country. He'd believed in what he was doing then; even among the blood and the pain and the shit he knew he was doing the Right Thing, serving God and Country and the President in the best way he could. He'd seen the thousand-yard stare in the eyes of grunts coming to the end of their tours, short-timers who'd seen too much death and lost too many friends, young men who would never be the same again. He'd seen the look and understood it, but he could not fathom how a man like Feinberg, who'd still have been in short trousers when the last helicopter lifted off the roof of the US embassy in Saigon, could have the same cold fury in his eyes. Somewhere along the line Feinberg had just stopped caring. Feinberg would never be sorry for anything he did – no regret, no remorse, no feeling. In a way Edmunds envied him, not for the thousand-yard stare or the eagerness for combat, but for the way he had come to terms so easily with what he did.

Maybe he would change as he got older. Edmunds had. He didn't have flashbacks or anything the documentary-makers described when they went to interview the Vets living rough in the wilderness or locked up in institutions. He didn't wake up screaming in the middle of the night and he didn't flinch at loud noises. It was just that he kept getting overcome with a deep sorrow, a suffocating sadness for what he'd done in the past that dogged him even during his happiest moments. It was there, like a tumour, and like cancer it seemed to grow over the years until now it had almost filled his whole body and was now preparing to burst out of his skin and into the open where everyone would see what he had contained all these years.

'Are you OK?' asked Feinberg.

Edmunds nodded. 'Yeah, I'm just a bit hung-over.'

Feinberg grinned. 'You should have stayed till the bitter end.'

Edmunds forced a smile. 'Did you get her in the end?'

'Who?'

'The dancer. The girl with the ponytail.'

'Fuck, no. She left just before the bar closed, ran out and jumped on to the back of a motor-bike. Her boyfriend, I suppose. Or more likely her pimp. Bastard. No, I picked up two really young ones; Jesus, they couldn't have been more than fifteen, hardly any hair on them at all, if you know what I mean. God, I was up all night with them. Outstanding.'

Feinberg liked using phrases like 'outstanding', words that he'd picked up from books and films about the Vietnam War. In many ways it was a pity he hadn't had a chance to serve in the early Sixties, thought Edmunds. Perhaps if he had he wouldn't have been so keen to use the jargon.

The two men were sitting in the almost empty Business section of a Thai International Airbus where two Thai stewardesses in long purple dresses were about to serve breakfast from a trolley. Edmunds just took coffee and a plate of fresh fruit, but Feinberg took the works, scrambled eggs, bacon, mushrooms and tomatoes, and three bread rolls spread thickly with butter. Edmunds peeled a banana and began to eat but he had no appetite.

The file lay on the tray in front of him, unopened. It was the same green as the fatigues they'd worn when they went into the jungle at night on the sort of operations that would never get into the history books. Edmunds had killed men, women and children in the name of duty, usually with a knife or his bare hands, often at night, and always with the aim of terrorizing the enemy. Edmunds had been all of twenty-five years old then, not much younger than Feinberg was now, and he had been one of the older ones. They were sent into the tunnels where the North Vietnamese rested up between raids or to the thin jungle trails where they sat for days waiting for a VC patrol. Then they killed. And when they'd finished killing they mutilated the bodies to serve as a warning to the rest. No, not as a warning, there was precious little to warn the VCs about; it was to serve as a lesson. This is what will happen to you if we catch you. So keep away. They gutted children and they castrated the men and defiled the women with their hunting knives. On several occasions they'd been helicoptered into friendly villages that had been attacked by the VCs and told to mutilate the bodies of the civilians, dead but still warm, still bleeding. Then just as quickly they were flown out before the Army took in the Press Corps to show them what it was they were up against.

Edmunds thought now as he thought then, that he had been doing the Right Thing. But whereas then he had gone in hard and cold, now he felt sorry for what he'd done, and he wished he'd just been a grunt fighting cleanly with an M-16 in the mud rather than as an assassin with a knife. He couldn't remember how many he'd killed, but there were some he could picture clearly in his mind, as if etched into metal by acid. There was a teenage boy with a rifle whose throat he'd slit from behind, only to find that it was a girl with a broom, there was a woman he'd disembowelled who turned out to be pregnant, a toddler who crawled out from under a bed while he was on the floor hacking away at its mother, an old man who had smiled when he stuck a knife through his ribcage and into his heart. He could remember all their faces, and he knew he would remember them at the moment of his own death, when it came. He sighed deeply and picked up the file, hoping that reading about the man called Howells would take his mind off the memories.

Inside the file were three faxed sheets, two of them containing lines of type; the third was a photograph. It was of a man in his thirties, with a thinnish face, deep-set eyes and a hard-set mouth. It was a face Edmunds recognized, a face he'd seen once, four years earlier, in the Lebanon.

He looked across at Feinberg but he had his head down over his plate, concentrating on his eggs. He scrutinized the picture, but there was no doubt. Howells had saved his life. Edmunds had been working out of the embassy in Beirut when he'd been kidnapped by one of the militia groups. They'd locked him away in the basement of a whitewashed house in the suburbs and told the embassy that if they didn't pay a ransom of US$100,000 they'd kill him. They'd kept him in the room for three months, blindfolded for most of the time, with nothing stronger than water to drink and food out of tins. He'd almost gone mad from the sheer monotony of it all. The threat of death had been nothing new, that he could deal with, but over the whole twelve weeks they had said not one word to him after the initial kidnapping, in any language. They'd refused to give him a television or a radio and the only time they showed him a newspaper was when they ran stories saying that the authorities were refusing to pay the ransom.

Over the three months he had six different guards, with

never less than two on duty at any one time. There were three of them in the house the day Howells came. One of them, a middle-aged swarthy thug with a wicked zig-zag of a scar under his left eye that had distorted the skin and given him a permanent leer, was the leader of the group. With him was a girl with long black hair who always had an automatic rifle in her right hand, and a young man barely out of his teens, a good-looking boy with a crew cut and fair white skin. They took it in turns to guard him, two sitting in the room while the other stayed upstairs. The basement had only one way in and out, a sturdy wooden door with a peep-hole, bolted on the outside and inside. All the room contained was a camp bed and a couple of army blankets for Edmunds, a plastic bucket for him to use as a toilet, and two easy chairs for his guards. Every second day they brought in another plastic bucket, this one half full of lukewarm water, and a rough cotton towel so that he could wash himself. Everything he ate or drank was brought in through the door on paper plates or in polystyrene cups. Twice they took photographs of him sitting on the camp bed holding a newspaper. Both times one of his guards stood by his side with a gun pointing at his temple.

He was nearing the end of his tether by the time Howells came on the scene. He was blindfolded so he wasn't sure who was in the room with him but he'd guessed that one of them was the girl by the way she'd padded across the floor. He heard her walk to the door and pause as she checked the peep-hole. He heard the rattle of the bolt and then he heard the crash of a foot against the wooden door and then a scream and two shots. Edmunds had panicked, rolling off the camp bed on to the floor clawing at the blindfold, scared shitless that at any second he was going to get a bullet in the head. A third shot barked and he heard a simultaneous thud and grunt and he blinked in the light as the middle-aged man slumped to the ground. By the door was the young man, blood pumping from a gaping wound in his chest. The girl was lying at the foot of the bed, her long black hair spreading like a pool of oil behind her head. One of her eye sockets was filling with blood and as he watched he saw red flow among the black tendrils of hair. Her legs twitched as if she was sleeping but the bullet had cauterized most of her brain tissue.

Only then did Edmunds see the man at the door, the man who had done so much damage in a few scant seconds. Lean and wiry with a long face and deep-set eyes, two or three days' stubble on his chin, he held a large handgun in both hands, moving the barrel slowly from side to side, covering the three corpses in the room. Cancel that. Two corpses. The older man was still alive, breathing heavily and clasping his hand around his groin where he'd been shot. Howells looked at Edmunds and aimed the gun at him, face totally relaxed, no sign of the tension that he surely must have felt. Edmunds realized that he must have forced the young man to stand in front of the peep-hole and then pushed him into the room, probably shooting him in the back. One against three, crazy odds that no one in his right mind would go up against. The man didn't look crazy, he looked very, very cool. His voice when it came was cold and hard.

'Who are you?' The accent was English.

'American,' said Edmunds, looking into the barrel of the gun and wincing as he saw the man's finger tighten on the trigger.

'I didn't ask what you are.'

'Ralph Simmonds. I'm a businessman, I sell computers.' Edmunds knew instinctively that it would not be a good idea to tell this man that he was with an intelligence agency.

'Good answer. Stay down on the floor.'

He walked over to the man who was groaning on the floor and stood over him. He fired at the man's right leg and smiled as the bullet smashed through the kneecap and bit a chunk out of the floor. The man screamed and Howells shot him through the other leg. The man stopped screaming then, probably passed out, and Howells leant down and placed the barrel in the man's mouth before pulling the trigger for the sixth and final time. He stood up then, stretching like a cat in the sun, his eyes closed. He exhaled deeply and then turned to look at Edmunds. 'Tell nobody what you saw,' he said, lifting the barrel of the gun to his lips. 'Tell them you had your blindfold on all the time.' Edmunds nodded quickly, acting the part of the frightened businessman.

Afterwards, when he was being debriefed in Langley he was told that the man who'd been keeping him prisoner had been one of the most dangerous terrorists on the loose in the Lebanon; he'd killed three hostages and had been involved in at least half a dozen bombings. They told Edmunds how lucky he'd been. Two of the hostages had been killed after ransoms had been paid. They'd shown him countless pictures but he hadn't been able to identify the man who'd freed him, the man who'd taken such pleasure from torturing his captor. And, to be honest, Edmunds wasn't sure if he would have identified Howells even if he had been shown his photograph. He owed him. And as he looked down at the same deep-set eyes, and read the background information on the man called Geoff Howells, he knew that was as true now as it had been all those years ago.

Dugan waited until after lunch before calling Bellamy in the hope that he'd be in a better mood than the last time they'd spoken.

'Jeff. It's Dugan.'

'What the fuck do you want, Dugan?' Bellamy barked into the phone. Dugan held the receiver away from his ear. So much for his theory that a full stomach would soften his temper.

'Give me a break, Jeff. I just want some information.'

'Dugan, the way I feel at the moment I wouldn't piss on you if you were on fire.'

'I suppose this means you won't pass me the ball during the Rugby Sevens.'

Bellamy snorted and Dugan knew that he was smiling despite himself.

'Business is business, you bastard, but rugby is something else. I'll tell you what, Dugan, I'll give you one minute. For no other reason than the fact that you've got one of the best pairs of hands in Hong Kong. And the clock's ticking.'

'Petal?'

'She's gone. And be careful, Pat. She's trouble.'

'In what way?'

'Special Branch are on to the case. One of the dead

334

guys is some sort of Chinese intelligence agent, he was expelled from Taiwan a few years back and he'd been photographed a couple of times at Kai Tak. I think you're going to get a call from them today.'

'You think?'

'All right, I'm fucking certain you will.'

'You told them I knew her?'

'It wasn't a secret, old lad.'

'Yeah, I know. They think she was one of them?'

'What do you think?'

'It doesn't look good, does it?'

'For you? Or for her?'

Dugan ignored that. 'The gweilo,' he said. 'What's happening about the gweilo?'

'We've got his name and his passport number, and we're lifting his prints from the room. We've got a rough description from the hotel staff but no photograph. We've put a stop on him at the airport but if he's got a false passport we're buggered.'

'But he's hurt?'

'Yeah, there was plenty of blood so the chances are that he's gone to ground. We're checking all the hospitals and the surgeries, but that takes time. And anyway, there are plenty of underground doctors who'll treat him.'

'The question is, why did he run? If they were there to kill him, why run?'

'You tell me, Dugan. Maybe he thought they'd try again. Maybe he's got something to hide. Maybe he went out to buy a pack of cigarettes.'

'What's his name?'

'Howells. Geoff Howells.'

'Have you run a check on him?'

'We checked the name and it matches with the passport number and we're checking with the UK. There's no record of him in our files. He's never been to Hong Kong before, not on that passport, anyway. Your minute's up, Dugan. And we never had this conversation.'

'Understood. I appreciate it, Jeff. Next time I see you I'll give you a big, sloppy kiss.'

'My arse you will,' said Bellamy, laughing.

'Wherever you want it,' Dugan said and put the phone down. So the gweilo was still in Hong Kong, probably in need of medical treatment. His name was Geoff Howells, and for some reason he'd been hired to kill his brother-in-law. He sat staring out of the window, absent-mindedly drumming his fingers on the desk, as he tried to work out what to do next.

You could tell a lot about a country from the way the taxi system was organized, thought Edmunds, as he walked with Feinberg out of the arrivals area and through the electronically operated doors that led to the taxi rank. In a highly developed country only a fool would pay for a taxi – getting from Gatwick to London or from Narita to Tokyo cost an arm and a leg, and anyway it was quicker by train. If you arrived at some god-awful Third World country like Indonesia then the drivers attacked like jackals, grabbing at you and undercutting each other in an attempt to get you into their cab. The Thais were a bit more polite, but the taxis that waited outside Bangkok's airport were every bit as ramshackle and the meters, when they had them, never worked and you had to haggle over the fare before getting in. But they were still cheap. At Kai Tak the cabs queued patiently and the meters worked, but the fares were still affordable. The Jack Edmunds Theory of Economic Development in Relation to Taxis – the poorer a country, the cheaper and less efficient the taxi system. The richer it became, the better the quality of the taxi service until the standard of living of the drivers reached such a point that their cabs became priced out of the reach of most people. London was getting that way. The last time he'd been there he'd had trouble getting his expense sheet through; the accounts department had said he was only supposed to hire cabs, not buy one.

'What are you thinking about?' asked Feinberg as they joined the queue.

'Taxis.'

'Yeah, a bitch, aren't they? Them and death, the only two things in life that are certain. Who said that?'

'You did, Rick.'

'I meant originally.' Edmunds knew what Feinberg meant, but he couldn't be bothered to get into a long conversation about it so he just shrugged.

'Where did you book us into?' he asked the younger man.

There were a dozen or so people in front of them, businessmen in dark suits carrying briefcases and overnight bags, a German family sweating in the heat and a couple of turbaned Sikhs. Edmunds was dressed casually, cream linen slacks and a fake black Yves St Laurent shirt and a pair of brown leather moccasins that he'd picked up for next to nothing in Bangkok. Feinberg was wearing a pale blue safari suit and Nike training shoes and his Ray-Ban sunglasses. Edmunds knew that what the younger agent really wanted to do was to parachute in from 10,000 feet with an M-16 between his teeth, but the Ray-Bans would have to do. Christ, where did the CIA get him from? Obviously rode in on the gung-ho tide of Reaganism which gave the intelligence services back most of the kudos and glamour that they'd lost under Nixon, but which had allowed in a lot of men who would have been more at home in large institutions with bars on the windows and jackets with long sleeves.

'The Victoria Hotel, on the island.'

'We're doing this on the cheap?'

'We're not here officially,' said Feinberg quietly.

'What do you mean, we're not here officially?' said Edmunds, aware that a taxi queue outside an international airport wasn't the most secure environment for a conversation like this.

'Don't panic, for fuck's sake. When I say it's not official, I mean we've just got to keep away from the local office. They're not supposed to know we're here. Nobody is. In and out before anyone realizes we're even here.'

'But it's from the Company?'

'Of course it's from the Company. Do you think I'd take you on a freelance operation without telling you?'

Too right I do, thought Edmunds. Too fucking right. 'So?'

'Greg Hamilton is running this show. I was going to tell you when we got to the hotel.'

'It might have been nice if you'd told me before we got here.'

'Fuck it, Jack. Hamilton called me because he couldn't

get hold of you, that's all. I answered the phone and I got the briefing. I'm just passing on the information, that's all.'

They had got to the front of the queue and they walked across to the taxi. They had one bag each; Edmunds' was a folding job that doubled as a suit-hanger, while Feinberg carried a bright blue nylon holdall. They took them into the back with them rather than using the boot. They were both travelling light. Like Feinberg had said, in and out before anyone knew they were there. Anyone but Greg Hamilton. Feinberg told the driver where they wanted to go but he didn't seem to understand.

'Huh?' he grunted and screwed up his eyes.

'Victoria Hotel,' Feinberg repeated slowly. 'Hong Kong island.'

The driver shook his head. 'Me not know. Me not know.'

'Oh fuck,' said Feinberg. 'Now what are we going to do?'

'You could waste him,' suggested Edmunds dryly.

Feinberg slapped the headrest of the driver's seat. 'Victoria Hotel,' he said again. 'Victoria Hotel.'

Edmunds wound down his window and called over to a well-dressed Chinese businessman, forty years old or thereabouts with horn-rimmed glasses and a crocodile skin briefcase.

'I'm sorry to bother you but we're having a little trouble with the driver. Can you help?'

The man smiled and walked over, leaning down to get his head level with Edmunds. 'Sure,' he said, with a mid-Western drawl. 'Where do you folks want to go?'

'Victoria Hotel,' said Edmunds. The man spoke to the

339

driver in Cantonese and he nodded and grunted. 'Thanks,' said Edmunds.

'No sweat,' said the man. 'Enjoy your stay in Hong Kong.'

Edmunds wound the window back up and sat back as the air-conditioner did its best to cool the cab.

'Hamilton is in London,' he said.

'Right.'

'So why is he running an operation in Hong Kong?'

'He didn't say, and I didn't ask. You can call him if you want to, I suppose.'

'Sure. So what's the game plan?'

'According to Hamilton this guy Howells is injured, he's been shot, so it won't be too long before the police track him down.'

'You didn't tell me that.' Edmunds was starting to get annoyed. He didn't like going into an operation without a full briefing, but he hated even more the fact that the information had to come through a shithead like Feinberg. The least Hamilton could have done was to have spoken to him. He had seniority, when all was said and done.

'Like I said, I was going to sit down and discuss it when we got to the Victoria. Look, Jack, don't worry. This is going to be a piece of cake.'

'I still don't understand why the police shot him.'

'Not the police. He was attacked in a hotel room. Hamilton says he's killed an agent of ours and we have to even the score, but without offending our cousins. This is still British territory, even if there are more of us here than them.'

'So it's a revenge hit?'

'That's all there is to it. Howells hit one of ours, we hit him.'

'But Howells is a Brit. There's something not right here.'

'The Brits retired him, you read the file. Howells is a maverick, he's gone on the rampage. He's the disease and we're the cure.'

'You've been watching too many Sylvester Stallone movies.'

'Sly's my hero,' said Feinberg, grinning like a kid.

He would be, thought Edmunds.

'Look,' continued Feinberg. 'The local police are after Howells. Once they get him we hit him. There's no way he can leave Hong Kong and it's not an easy place for a white man to hide. Especially not with a bullet hole. But I think we can speed things up a bit.'

'What do you mean?'

'He's wounded and he's in an unfamiliar environment. He can't go to hospital so he'll need someone to hide him. He's working alone and as far as Hamilton knows he has no friends here.'

'*Cherchez la femme?*'

'It's the obvious, isn't it. Find a girl to shack up with.'

Edmunds nodded in agreement. 'So we check the bars and nightclubs. There must only be a few thousand of them.'

Feinberg raised his finger and waved it in front of Edmunds' nose. 'Hong Kong has changed since the days of the Vietnam War, you know. There are plenty of bars for the Chinese but he wouldn't go there, he's more likely to have gone to one of the tourist bars, Wan Chai or Tsim Sha Tsui. There's a few dozen of

341

them at most. We can check them out in one night, just show his picture around and say we're looking for an old friend. We might get lucky. And even if we don't the police will get him eventually. Either way he's history.'

Feinberg seemed to relish the idea, and all but licked his lips Edmunds watched him, wondering who really was the psychopath, Geoff Howells or Rick Feinberg.

Amy was stiff all over when she woke up. There was only one bed in her tiny flat, and the gweilo was in that. She had no qualms about sharing her single bed but didn't want to risk hurting him. She came back just after four o'clock in the morning and Howells had been in a deep sleep, snoring soundly. She'd kissed him on the back of the head, and after placing a fresh glass of water by the bed she'd slept curled up on the small rattan couch in her lounge, covered with a woollen blanket.

Normally she slept until the late afternoon, but Dr Wu had said he would come round sometime after midday, so she set her small travel alarm for eleven o'clock. She made herself a pot of jasmine tea and sat on the couch drinking it as she thought about the night before. She had been lucky, a visiting businessman from Sydney had taken a fancy to her and had sat with her for almost three hours buying her drink after drink as he tried to slip his hand down the back of her dress. After he'd bought her a couple of drinks she'd taken him into one of the booths at the back of the bar where the lights were dimmer and the prices higher. There she'd let him kiss her and touch her breasts, outside her dress, and she'd stroked his thigh and speeded up her drink rate from one every twenty minutes to one every twelve. He'd smelt of stale sweat and tobacco and the whisky on his breath made her want to retch but she'd smiled and laughed at his stupid jokes and hung on his every word as his bill rose higher and higher.

As midnight approached he began asking her to go back to his hotel room with him but she'd coyly turned him down. He'd offered to pay her bar fine but she'd said no, and then he said he'd pay double the fine. It wasn't that she was averse to going out with customers, she did that at least once a month to boost her earnings, but the man disgusted her and she was choosy about who she'd go to bed with. Maybe as she got older she'd be less selective and grab each opportunity as it was offered, but she was still young enough and pretty enough to command a high price and while she was quite prepared to let the foul-smelling barbarian fondle and kiss her she'd rather die than spread her legs for him.

He called the mamasan over and told her that he wanted to take Amy out and the mamasan had asked her in Cantonese if she wanted to go and Amy said no, he was a pig. The mamasan gently explained that Amy was having her period, maybe next time, and that if he wanted a girl there were plenty more in the bar. The Australian decided to go instead. He paid with a credit card which meant that Amy wouldn't get her commission for at least two months. Her basic salary was about the same as a typist's, but she got to keep about one-third of the cost of every drink a customer bought her. The more drinks

343

they bought, the more she earned, with the cashier giving her a handful of cardboard tickets at the end of each night signifying how many she'd had. If the customer paid in cash she got the money at the end of the week; if they paid with plastic then she got it when the credit card company settled the bill, and that usually took a minimum of two months.

She'd asked him to pay with cash, he had plenty of notes in his wallet, but he swore at her, called her a cock-teasing bitch. Amy walked away and told the cashier to add two more hostess drinks to his bill. The cashier grinned. 'Fuck the gweilos,' he cackled. 'Fuck the gweilos and fuck their mothers.'

Amy drank her tea, watching the leaves swirl around the bottom of the china beaker. There was more to it than money, she realized. Even if the Australian hadn't been such an ugly bore, even if she'd been attracted to him she wouldn't have gone with him. It was something to do with Geoff Howells, but she wasn't exactly sure what it was, something to do with being faithful – but that didn't make any sense. She hadn't even slept with the gweilo, she knew nothing about him other than the fact that he'd asked for her help and that something inside her had compelled her to agree.

All her life Amy had been used by people: by her father when she was barely into her teens; by a succession of boyfriends who had varied from cruel to callous; by the customers, and by the people who ran the bar. All had simply assumed that they had a right to use her and throughout her life she had gone along with them, taking the easy way out. And now this man was also using her, but in a different way. He needed her, it wasn't just that he

wanted her help, he needed it, and that made a difference.
It made her feel special.

She showered and dressed in a faded denim skirt and
a white cotton blouse with short sleeves before making
Howells a coffee. Without any effort she remembered
how he liked to drink it, black with no sugar. He was
awake when she went into the bedroom, but still lying
face down. He twisted around and smiled up at her as she
knelt down beside the bed.

'Good morning,' he said.

'Good afternoon,' she corrected.

'I can't tell with the curtains drawn.'

'To help you sleep. Dr Wu said best thing for you was
to sleep as much as possible. And to drink water.'

Howells looked at the coffee and smiled. 'Thank you
for the coffee,' he said. 'How do I say thank you in
Cantonese?'

'*M goy,*' she said.

'*M goy,*' he repeated. '*M goy* for the coffee.'

'You better drink it soon, Dr Wu is coming and he will
scold me if he sees I have given you coffee.'

Howells rolled slowly on to his left side and Amy
helped raise him into a sitting position, pushing the pillow
to support the small of his back.

'It'll be our secret,' he said.

For some reason that pleased Amy immensely, and she
blushed. Howells raised the steaming cup to his mouth
and drank.

'Lovely,' he said. 'How do I say delicious?'

'*Ho sik* for food,' she said. '*Ho yam* for drink.'

'*Ho yam,*' said Howells. '*M goy.*'

'*M sai m goy,*' said Amy. 'No need.'

Howells studied her over the top of the cup as he drank, wondering what he was going to do with the girl. For the moment he needed her to hide him, but what then? She knew who he was, and before long she'd know what he'd done. The shooting in the hotel would surely get into the newspapers and he'd used his real name. That was stupid, but he had trusted Grey completely. Still, no point in looking back, it was the future that counted.

'How you feel?' she asked.

'Much better,' he replied.

'Good,' she said. 'I am pleased.'

She looked it, too. Howells wasn't sure if it was because she was glad he was on the mend or because it meant he'd soon be getting the hell out of her flat. The doorbell rang, startling them both.

'Dr Wu,' she said, grabbing the cup and running into the kitchen before opening the door and admitting the elderly doctor. He greeted Amy and then walked into the bedroom.

'You seem much better than the last time I saw you,' he said.

'I heal quickly,' said Howells.

'I will decide that,' said the doctor, putting his leather medical bag next to Howells' feet. 'Lean forward, please.'

Howells leant forward while the doctor removed the dressing and peered at the wound over the top of his glasses.

'Hmm, it seems you are right,' he said. 'I see no problems. I will just change the dressing for you. Do you feel any pain?'

'A dull ache, unless I move the arm suddenly.'

'Do you want anything for that?'

'No injection,' said Howells. 'But if you have any tablets that I could take if it starts to hurt, I'd appreciate it.'

Dr Wu took a small plastic bottle from his bag containing half a dozen white tablets.

'I will leave these,' he said. 'Take one if the pain gets very bad, but on no account take more than two over a three-hour period. They are painkillers but they will also help you sleep. But if it hurts so much that you feel you need to take three tablets then you should call me anyway.' He put the bottle down by Howells' glass of water. 'And drink lots of water.'

'I am doing, Amy is looking after me very well.'

Amy came into the bedroom and stood behind the doctor, fidgeting nervously. Wu turned to her and spoke in Cantonese. She nodded and answered. Seeing the curious look on his face, Amy hurriedly said to Howells: 'Dr Wu is saying you can get up in two days, but he will come see you before.' There was no need to translate, Dr Wu's English was much better than hers, but she didn't want Howells to think she had been betraying him.

Howells looked at the doctor and nodded. '*M goy*,' he said.

Dr Wu smiled. '*M sai m goy*, he said. 'Your Cantonese is very good.' Behind him, Amy smiled with pride.

One of the best things about being a chef was the fact that you always had afternoons free. André Beaumont knew there were plenty of drawbacks to the job: long hours, the pressure of always having to be on top form, the fact that he never got away before eleven o'clock at night, but he relished the free time between the lunchtime rush and the preparations for dinner.

Beaumont was the head chef at one of the top Kowloon hotels and whenever the weather was good and he didn't have a banquet to organize he'd drive his Golf GTI to Hebe Haven, the sunroof open and the stereo full on, and take out his yacht for a couple of hours.

He loved Hong Kong and the lifestyle it gave him: a salary almost double what he'd earn back in France, a 3,000 square-foot flat rent-free that was decorated every year to his specifications, the car, two first-class flights home every year, free hospitality in the hotel and a chance to be head chef at an age, twenty-eight, when his friends who had stayed behind were still *sous-chefs*.

Today was perfect for sailing; a cloudless sky, a fresh wind from the north, and in the seat next to him Caroline Chang, the hotel's public relations manager, who'd sneaked out of her office on the pretence of visiting their advertising agency. She had an easy-going boss and fancied André something rotten and she had no regrets about skipping off for a few hours. She reckoned that she gave the hotel more than enough in terms of hours, dealing with cantankerous customers, checking menus, sending out press releases and handling VIPs.

She raised her face to the sky and let the breeze play through her long black hair as André turned off the main road and drove towards the pier. There were plenty of parking spaces, as there always were on weekday afternoons. It was only at weekends that it got crowded, and then André stayed away.

'Which is yours?' Caroline asked as André closed the sunroof and locked the doors.

André pointed. 'The one with the white hull and the two masts,' he said.

'What's she called?'

'*Katrina*,' he said. 'It used to belong to a lawyer. He named it after his wife and she ran off and left him. He had to sell the boat to raise the money for his settlement. I haven't got round to changing the name yet.'

He walked behind her and slipped his arm around her waist. He rubbed his nose up against the side of her head, breathing in the warm fragrance of her hair. 'Perhaps I should call her *Caroline*.' She was the fifth girl he'd promised to name the boat after, and three of the previous girls had all ended up making love to him in the main cabin. For some reason the promise of having their name on a yacht seemed to act as an intense aphrodisiac. To be honest, André was quite happy with *Katrina*.

Caroline pressed herself against him. 'I'd like that,' she said, and turned to slip her arms around his neck and kiss him full on the lips. He was the first to pull away.

'Come on,' he said. 'We'll get one of the boatmen to row us out.'

They found a grizzled old woman with a dinghy and after a minute of bargaining she agreed to take them out to the *Katrina*.

'It's fabulous, so sleek, so feminine. I love her already,' said Caroline.

'Wait until you see inside,' said André, and held her gaze for a couple of seconds before smiling. She laughed and he knew she was his. For the afternoon, at least.

He climbed on board first and then helped her. 'Ask

her to come and collect us when we get back,' he said and Caroline spoke to her in rapid Cantonese. The woman cackled and rowed away.

Caroline leant over the side and watched the water below as André began to operate the winch to pull up the anchor. It seemed to need more effort than usual; maybe it was caught in something on the sea bottom. That was all he needed. Slowly, painfully slowly, it heaved the anchor up, at about half its normal speed. As he waited André admired Caroline's backside and her long legs. She had unusually long legs for a Chinese. When she screamed it was a blood-curdling yell that caused the old woman to drop one of her oars and wiped all thoughts of sex from André's mind.

Tomkins walked into Dugan's office as if he had an unpeeled banana up his backside. Dugan was eating Kentucky Fried Chicken and had grease all round his lips.

'Bloody Hell, Dugan, you're a pig,' said Tomkins.

'You should be glad I'm working through my lunch,' said Dugan.

'Yeah, yeah, I'm grateful, the Commissioner is grateful, the Governor is grateful, hell I bet the Queen herself will get to hear about this devotion to duty.'

Dugan reached for a sheet of typing paper and used it to clean his hands. The red and white cardboard box was full of chicken bones and a sprinkling of cold French fries. Dugan began to spoon coleslaw into his mouth with a

white plastic spoon, the sort you used to feed babies.
'What do you want?' he said between mouthfuls.

'Me? I just want you to clear your caseload so I can
dump another dozen or so on to your desk. But the boys in
Arsenal Street seem to have other plans for you. I've just
had them on the phone. They want you to go right over.
What have you done to attract the attention of Special
Branch, Pat?'

'Fucked if I know,' answered Dugan. 'They want me
right now?'

'That's what they said. You're to ask for a Chief
Inspector Leigh.'

'I didn't think there were any high-ranking Chinese left
in Special Branch.'

'There aren't. He's a Brit.' He spelled out the name
for Dugan.

Special Branch were also in Wan Chai, in a squat office
block not far from the one where Dugan worked, so he
walked over. The roads were crowded and noisy, trucks
pouring out black exhaust smoke, chauffeur-driven limou-
sines with high-powered businessmen on mobile phones
in the back seats, taxis with impatient drivers banging
their horns, bare-chested deliverymen on bicycles, one
carrying dead, plucked chickens, another with large green
gas cylinders, a mixture of old and new that typified
Hong Kong.

The shops too were a rag-bag of ancient and modern:
a herbalist with shelves full of glass bottles of mysterious green and brown plants and roots, sacks of dried
mushrooms and deer antlers in display cases, a coffin
maker with his wares stacked from floor to ceiling, an
electrician's store with portable colour televisions and

boxes of Japanese cameras, a noodle shop with five cluttered circular tables where Dugan sometimes bought beef noodles when he tired of gweilo fast food, a shop selling nothing but cosmetics. Some of the blocks were twenty years old or more, less than ten storeys high with flats above the shops and entrances blocked with ornate metal grilles, but gradually they were coming down and being replaced with glass and marble towers two or three times taller as the developers moved away from the Central office area in search of big profits.

The pavements were as busy as the roads, and there too could be seen a cosmopolitan mix: gnarled old housewives making their way home with pink plastic bags containing enough food for a day, businessmen with sharp suits and thin ties, the occasional poser walking along talking into a hand-held phone, shouting to make himself heard over the roar of the traffic and the blaring horns, schoolchildren with crisp white shirts and white socks, rucksacks full of books distorting their frail shoulders, mothers with babies on their backs.

Dugan walked slowly, partly because the crowds were so thick but also because he didn't want to arrive for an interview with Special Branch sweating like a pig. Occasionally he had to move off the pavement and into the road and he took care to avoid stepping in the piles of ash and rotting fruit left over from night-time ghost appeasing.

Chief Inspector Leigh looked to be a kindly man; greying hair, soft green eyes and folds of loose skin that gave him the appearance of a tired, but loyal, bloodhound. He seemed ill at ease in his light blue suit as if it had been the only thing hanging in his wardrobe when he got out of bed this morning. He smiled benignly when Dugan walked into his office and took him completely by surprise by offering to shake his hand.

'I've always been a fan of yours,' said Leigh. His voice had the lilt of a Welshman's and made Dugan think of congregations singing in frost-covered stone churches.

'I'm sorry?' said Dugan, flustered.

'You played a blinder during the last Sevens. That last try you scored, sheer magic. I remember telling my wife; Glynnis, I said, that boy could play for Wales.'

'I'm afraid not, sir,' said Dugan. 'I'm not Welsh.'

Leigh looked hurt but it was too late for Dugan to add the word 'unfortunately' without appearing to take the piss.

'Never mind, never mind. Please sit down.'

He waved Dugan to one of the two comfortable seats facing the desk. Leigh's office was much the same as Dugan's, albeit a bit larger. In one corner was a large metal safe, and on it was a brass bowl containing a bushy green plant with bulbous leaves. Leigh's desk was as cluttered as Dugan's though he merited a small table lamp. Dugan could see the back of a silver picture frame and guessed it contained a picture of Glynnis Leigh and probably a couple of children, too. Leigh was no doubt a devoted husband and family man, and a pillar of the church. God knows what he was doing in Special Branch. It must be a soul-destroying job, trying to stop Communist infiltration in a place which was gearing up to be handed over to Red China. Talk about a job with no prospects. Special Branch was due to be disbanded before the Communists took over and all their files gutted or destroyed. Most of the Chinese members had been promised British citizenship, unlike most of the other six million inhabitants, because even the British Government accepted that such men would not last long under the new regime.

Special Branch had other tasks, sure, they monitored CIA activity and any other intelligence agencies that tried to operate in Hong Kong, and they kept tabs on the local members of the Kuomintang, the hardline anti-Communist party that controlled Taiwan; but their main purpose was to identify Communists in Hong Kong and for that they had a network of contacts and informers throughout the colony, whose lives would also become dispensable after handover. That was one of the reasons there were so few Chinese in Special Branch, and none in top positions. The job was too sensitive to be trusted to locals.

'So,' said Leigh, steepling his fingers and leaning back in his chair. 'Tell me about this girl.' It felt for all the world like he was Dugan's father asking about his latest girlfriend.

'What is it you want to know, sir?'

Leigh smiled and his eyes wrinkled. He was obviously a man used to smiling. Dugan could imagine him on Christmas morning, helping grandchildren to unwrap their presents and basting the turkey while his wife looked after the vegetables. 'How long have you known her?'

'A few days, just a few days,' said Dugan.

'What was her name?'

'Was?'

He smiled again. 'A slip of the tongue, son. Of course, I mean *is*. What is her name?'

'Petal.'

'Her Chinese name?'

'I don't know. I only knew her as Petal.'

'You never asked for her surname?'

'It never came up.'

'She knew your name, though?'

'Sure.'

'Both names?'

'Both names,' agreed Dugan.

'Well, at least one of you knew what was going on,' said Leigh, and he laughed. 'Seriously Pat, how well did you know her?'

Dugan noticed the slick way the older man had dropped in his first name, trying to make it a chat between rugby fans rather than an interrogation.

'We were friends.'

'Do you know where she worked?'

'Bank of China. I called her there a couple of times.'

'And you got through to her?'

'Once or twice, yes.'

'You went to see her in hospital?'

'Yes.'

'What did she tell you?'

'She said she'd been attacked by a gweilo.'

'Did she tell you who her friends were?'

'Friends?'

'The two corpses in the room.'

Dugan shook his head. 'No sir, no, she didn't.'

'What else did you talk about?'

'That was about it, sir. She seemed pretty much out of it, she was badly hurt and she didn't make much sense.'

'She wasn't delirious?'

'No, but she seemed confused. I don't think she was sure what had happened.' Dugan could feel himself

355

gradually enveloping the truth in layers of lies, building protective walls around the secret that Petal had given him, that she had trusted him with.

Leigh leant forward and put his arms on the desk. He adjusted his cuffs and studied Dugan.

'We have a problem here, Pat. This girl was in the company of two men, one of whom has already been identified as an agent of the Chinese intelligence service who we have tentatively linked to at least three assassinations in Taiwan. A syringe was found in the hotel room containing a drug that would have given an elephant a heart attack and her fingerprints were on it. She was taken out of the hospital, badly hurt as you pointed out, by a group of spooks from Xinhua, the so-called New China News Agency. Now while the rest of the world fondly imagines that the New China News Agency does nothing but put out press releases on the latest grain harvest, you and I know better, Pat. You and I know that they are Peking's official, and unofficial, representatives in Hong Kong. And we know that out of their offices in Happy Valley walk some of the meanest sons of bitches from China. And it is starting to look as if your friend is one of them.'

Leigh paused, looking Dugan straight in the eye as if his gaze could pierce the layers of lies. Dugan could feel his hands start to shake and he put them on his knees to try to steady them.

'So, what exactly did your friend tell you, Pat?'

'Like I said, sir, nothing.'

Leigh reached over and picked up a file from the left-hand side of his desk. He opened it and casually flicked through it.

'This is your file, Pat. It's not a bad record you've got. If it wasn't for your brother-in-law there's no doubt you'd have made chief inspector by now.' He put the file back on the desk. 'If there's one thing worse than having a triad leader as a brother-in-law, it's not being honest with your superiors, Pat. I would hate to see a career like yours come under any more pressure.'

'It's not as if I'm going anywhere now, is it?' asked Dugan, feeling the resentment grow inside, burning like a flame. He tried to stay calm, knowing that Leigh was just trying to rile him, trying to get him to open up.

'Believe me, it can get a lot worse. A lot worse. Now, what exactly did this Petal tell you?'

The senior officer was smiling still, but it seemed to Dugan that the green eyes hardened and that the kindly lines on the face were a mask. This man was not a friend, not to be trusted, and probably wasn't even a rugby fan. The rugby would be in Dugan's file. Dugan owed this man nothing. Fuck it, he owed the police nothing. They had killed his career, now they wanted his help. Dugan knew for sure then that his loyalty was with Petal. He would protect her and help her. He would lie to this man, he would lie all he could and he would enjoy doing it.

Dugan grinned sheepishly and rubbed his hand over his bald spot. 'It's a bit embarrassing, actually, sir.'

Leigh raised his eyebrows. 'What do you mean?'

'She wanted money.'

'Money?'

'For her hospital bills. She said she didn't think she had enough.'

'And why would she ask you for money, Pat?'

Dugan fell silent, and tried his best to look guilty and embarrassed.

'Why?' pressed Leigh.

'I'd given her money before, sir. She wasn't what you'd call a regular girlfriend.'

'She was a hooker?'

Dugan kept his eyes looking at the floor. 'Yes, sir. I met her at one of the bars the guys go to. I picked her up. At first I didn't realize she was on the game, it was only afterwards that she asked for money.'

'But you said she worked at the Bank of China?'

'That's what I told everyone, sir. I didn't want to admit that I'd had to pay for it. The guys would never have let me forget it.'

'And that's why you never knew her full name,' said Leigh.

'Yes sir,' said Dugan. 'That's why I can't understand why you think she's working with Chinese agents. She wasn't the brightest of girls, sir. A great body, but not a lot between her ears.'

Leigh nodded. 'I see,' he mused. 'I see.'

Dugan looked Leigh straight in the eyes, trying to keep his gaze even and his breathing steady. He kept his hands firmly on his knees, fingers rock-solid, trying to keep all the tension down below the level of the desk, out of sight.

Eventually Leigh seemed to reach a decision. 'OK, Pat, that's all for the moment. Let's call it a day. I'll give you a call if we need anything more from you.'

He didn't offer to shake hands when they parted, but stayed put in his seat and watched Dugan leave and close the door behind him. Leigh drummed the fingers of his right hand on Dugan's file.

'Senior Inspector Patrick Dugan, I don't believe a fucking word you told me,' he said quietly.

Thomas Ng was standing outside the house, looking at the harbour below when he heard the phone ring and then stop as Master Cheng answered it. Cheng had arranged for a large desk to be brought down from one of the bedrooms upstairs and placed in the main lounge. On it he had put the old-fashioned black Bakelite phone and a stack of typing paper, a series of large scale maps of Hong Kong and a couple of felt-tipped pens. Now he sat in a chair taken from the set around the circular table answering the phone which had been ringing non-stop since first light. The maps had come from a property developer who owed the triad a favour, several favours to be exact, and included every single structure in the territory. As each tower block, hotel or house was visited and the doormen questioned the searchers rang back to inform Master Cheng. Cheng noted down the building, the names of the men who had visited it, and the time, which he took from a gold pocket watch he kept by the side of the phone. Sitting by his side was a young Red Pole who had formerly worked in a large estate agents and was helping the old man identify the properties.

The search had started early in the morning, and had been going on for almost eight hours, and Cheng had insisted on answering every call himself, pausing only to drink cups of chrysanthemum tea, and once he ate a small bowl of plain white rice. Ng would insist that he rest soon. This was only the first wave; every building was to be visited three times to speak to all the doormen who usually worked eight-hour shifts. There was no point in just speaking to the men on the morning shift when the gweilo might have been seen late at night. A half-hearted search was worse than no search at all.

He heard footsteps behind him and then Cheng was at his shoulder, face grave.

'They have found him?' said Ng.

'They have found your brother. He is dead, Kin-ming.'

Ng had expected as much but the news still hit him hard. He tightened his hands into fists and slammed them against his thighs, cursing in English. Cheng put his hand on his shoulder.

'Where?' asked Ng.

'Hebe Haven,' said Cheng. 'He had been chained to the anchor of one of the yachts there.'

'He drowned?'

'Yes. And his wrist had been cut. It seems as if your brother tried to escape in the only way he could. He tried to cut off his own hand.'

'Oh no,' muttered Ng. 'No, no, no. Who found him?'

'The owner of the yacht, about half an hour ago. In a way it was fortunate, not many take their boats out during the week. At least we know that he is dead.'

Ng nodded. 'Fortunate is a strange term to use, but I know what you mean, Master Cheng. Can we keep this a secret?'

'I am afraid not, the police are there now. Our men at Sai Kung say they have stopped checking the boats, for a while at least. There are police everywhere and it would not be wise for our men to attract attention to themselves. I told them to withdraw, they can continue again tomorrow.'

'You are right, of course,' said Ng. 'Besides, the gweilo is unlikely to be keeping Sophie so close to where he killed my brother.'

The two men stood together, looking at the mist-shrouded hills of Kowloon. To their left a peacock shrieked as if in pain.

'You must tell your father, Kin-ming.'

'I know, Master Cheng, I know. I will also go and tell Jill. She will not take it well.'

'Neither of them will take it well. Your father is at your mother's grave,' said Cheng, and walked back into the house. The phone rang again.

Ng slowly climbed the eighty-eight steps up to where his father was, his hands dead at his side. The old man was sitting on one of the stools under the pagoda where they had sat together the previous day. This time, however, he had his back to the harbour and his eyes were on the stone dome. He turned to look at Ng as he reached the top and stood there, breathing heavily and not just because of the climb. Their eyes met and the old man knew at once.

'He is dead?' he said quietly.

'He is dead,' repeated Ng, tears stinging his eyes. 'Father, we must get the man who did it. We must, we must, we must.' The words degenerated into a series of sobs as the tears spilled down his cheeks.

'We will, Kin-ming. I promise you we will. Come and sit with me.' His voice was unsteady and he held out his hand towards Ng, palm upward like a beggar pleading for change.

'At least the budget runs to separate rooms,' said Edmunds. He was standing in Feinberg's room in the Victoria Hotel watching a hydrofoil set out for Macau.

'Too right – sleeping with you would cramp my style a bit,' said Feinberg as he flicked through the television channels. 'You hungry?'

'I guess so.'

'We might as well hit one of the hotel restaurants. It's what, four o'clock now? I say we shower, eat, and then hit the bars. We'd better change our money here, and for God's sake keep the receipts. Hamilton said he'd reimburse us but it's not to be done through official channels. And we're not to make contact with the local office.'

'No back up? No support? And our handler eight thousand miles away? It doesn't feel right, Rick.'

'Piece of cake,' said Feinberg. 'And Greg Hamilton is a good guy to keep in with. He's on the fast track and I could go a long way with him.'

Edmunds noticed how the young agent had slipped from the plural into the singular but he was past the stage of being annoyed by petty politics. If Feinberg wanted to jump a few rungs on his career ladder that was up to him. As for Edmunds, he'd long ago resigned himself to not going any higher within the CIA. He hadn't kissed the right arses and he'd been involved in too many dirty operations to ever be allowed a high-powered administrative position. In fact, during his more morose moods he sometimes worried about exactly what would happen to him, whether or not the CIA would actually allow him to retire and collect his pension. He knew where too many bodies were buried. He'd started taking precautions about five years earlier and compiled a diary of some of the murkier episodes of his career on a Macintosh computer and given three floppy disks to his younger brother in Chicago and sworn him to secrecy. Edmunds wasn't sure if it would do him any good, or if it was paranoia in the first place, but it made him feel a little more secure. He knew plenty of CIA operatives who'd taken early retirement and joined private detective agencies or joined law firms or even just opened a bar, but he was also aware of a few who had disappeared on missions that were, as Feinberg would have described them, pieces of cake. Edmunds had only three years to go before he could retire on full pension and spend more time with his wife and he was determined to make it. Like the short-timers in Vietnam he was starting to count the days before he would be back in The World, and that, he knew, made him vulnerable.

Feinberg sat on the bed and opened the telephone book. 'Police,' he said in reply to his partner's raised eyebrows.

Feinberg identified himself as a reporter with the *International Herald Tribune* and asked for the duty officer, eventually got through to someone who could speak English and again said he was a reporter.

'Anything new on the double murder at the Hilton?' he asked and was told there wasn't. 'What about the Brit who was shot? Has he turned up yet?' Again he was told no. Feinberg thanked the officer and hung up.

'Power of the Press,' he said. 'Howells is still on the loose. If he was in hospital they'd have him now. I feel lucky about this. Which side of the harbour do you want, Kowloon or Wan Chai?'

Edmunds shrugged. 'I'm easy.'

'OK, I'll take Kowloon. It's been a few years since I've been to Red Lips and Bottoms Up.' He passed the faxed picture of Howells over to Edmunds and said: 'Can you get a decent photocopy of that? It's pretty sharp so it should reproduce OK. I'm going to take a shower; I'll meet you downstairs in the lobby in half an hour.'

Edmunds agreed, though he was far from happy.

Dugan grabbed at the door handle of the taxi a second before the leather-jacketed Chinese youth who had raced across the road in an attempt to beat him to it. When Dugan pulled the door open the guy tried to slip into the back seat but Dugan side-stepped to block his way.

'Fuck your mother, gweilo pig,' the man cursed in Cantonese.

Dugan grinned at him as he got into the cab. 'Your mother was too ugly but your sister screwed like a rabbit,' Dugan shouted back in Chinese and slammed the door shut.

'Wah! Good Cantonese,' said the driver in admiration as he slammed the taxi into gear and drove off. 'Where to?'

When Dugan told him that they were going to the New Territories the driver began to whine. The tunnel traffic was too heavy at this time of night, it'd take almost an hour to get across the harbour and then he'd have to come back and he was supposed to be finishing his shift soon and had to hand the cab over to his replacement in Tin Hau. Please would the honourable gentleman mind switching over to a Kowloon taxi?

Dugan was too tired to argue, and it was such a long trip there was no point in going with an unenthusiastic driver. There were several unofficial ranks on the island where taxis from Kowloon waited to pick up passengers who wanted to cross the harbour. The driver took Dugan to a petrol station opposite the Excelsior Hotel where there were three taxis waiting, their roof lights on but with red cards covering the meter flags bearing the two Chinese characters Gow Lung, meaning Nine Dragons, the Cantonese name for the area which the British had transliterated to Kowloon.

The driver thanked Dugan profusely and drove off into the dusk. Dugan got into one of the Kowloon taxis and this time he met with no resistance when he said he wanted to go to the New Territories. They pulled out of the garage forecourt and forced their way into the queue of traffic edging its way to the tunnel entrance.

Dugan sat back and closed his eyes, massaging his temples with the palms of his hands. During the course of the afternoon he'd tried several times to get through to Jill, but without success, and he'd decided that the only way to find out for sure what was going on was to go round in person. It was a bitch of a taxi journey but the MTR didn't go anywhere near Ng's house and Dugan's salary barely covered his mortgage payments, never mind a car. They crawled along for the best part of half an hour before Dugan saw the tunnel mouth. They picked up speed once they were under the bright fluorescent lights and the tyres were singing on the road surface. The cars erupted from the end of the tunnel like water from a shower head, spraying out to pay their tolls at the line of booths where the money collectors were wearing white surgical masks to filter out the worst of the exhaust fumes, and then accelerating again, the harbour at their backs.

Dugan still wasn't sure what he'd say to Jill, or to Simon Ng if he was there. He would protect Petal, of that he was certain, but he would have to warn his brother-in-law that his life was in danger. He could tell them about the gweilo who had been attacked in the Hilton Hotel and tell Ng that the police had learnt that the man had been planning to attack him. He'd just have to be vague about the whys and wherefores and hope that the fact that the family would be on guard would keep them immune from harm. Assuming that is that they hadn't been harmed already. What was it Petal had said? She was to be the back-up, the second line of attack if the first failed, and that she thought that maybe the man Howells was the real assassin. He could tell them about Howells, but Petal's involvement would remain a secret.

He was so busy rehearsing in his mind what he was going to say that he missed the turn-off to the Ng compound and he leant forward and tapped the driver on the shoulder.

'We have to go back,' he said, and gestured the way they'd come.

'OK, OK,' said the driver, and he slowed the taxi and

did a reasonable approximation of a three-point turn. Dugan pointed at the side-road which angled off into the woods and the driver headed up it, switching his headlights on for the first time. He drove at full pelt up the track and had to slam on the brakes when he saw the barrier and its warning sign. The tyres squealed angrily and two men came out of the gatehouse before the car had even stopped. Dugan didn't recognize them but they were typical Red Pole thugs, wide shoulders, casual clothes and expensive jewellery; they were chewing gum and their hands swung at their sides as they walked. One of them approached Dugan's window and he wound it down, allowing the hot evening air to balloon into the cab. He could feel beads of sweat forming on his forehead almost immediately.

'Private road. You must go back,' the man said in English. He had a portable phone in his hand. His partner kept some distance away from the car and seemed to put a lot of effort into adjusting the buttons of his cotton jacket. There was probably a gun under it but Dugan wasn't on official business and under the circumstances he wasn't going to make an issue of it.

In Cantonese Dugan explained that he was Simon Ng's brother-in-law and that he wanted to go up to the house. The guard shook his head emphatically.

'Nobody home. You must go,' he said, still in English. He turned to the driver and switched to Cantonese, saying: 'Take the gweilo prick to wherever he came from or it will be the worse for you.' The driver grunted and put the taxi into reverse. Dugan flung the door open and got one foot on to the ground before the guard put his weight against it and tried to slam it shut on Dugan's leg. Dugan resisted and kicked it open with his other leg, knocking the guard off balance. Dugan grabbed him by the neck of his shirt and pushed him against a tree.

'Listen, you prick, don't you dare threaten me again or I'll stuff your balls down your throat. Understand?' He edged his forearm up under the man's chin and forced his head back so that it scraped against the bark. He tried to nod but the pressure on his throat stopped him so he groaned and blinked. The second guard began shouting at Dugan in English. 'Let him go! Let him go!' Dugan swung round, keeping his grip on the first guard so that he formed a barrier between them.

'Keep your fucking hands away from your jacket or I'll break this pig's neck,' Dugan warned and tightened his grip. The second guard looked confused, reached his hands up and then dropped them, then took a step forward.

'And don't move, just listen,' shouted Dugan. The taxi driver had stopped to watch, but he had a pretty good idea what was going on and didn't want to be around when this stupid gweilo got the shit kicked out of him so he began reversing down the track.

The second guard reached inside his jacket and pulled out a gun and held it unsteadily with his right hand, trying to aim at Dugan's head. Dugan kept moving from side to side, keeping his captive in front of him. He squeezed his neck tighter, wanting to keep him quiet but not so much that he'd pass out. He was fairly stocky and Dugan doubted if he could hold him up if the guard's legs collapsed.

'Listen to me,' said Dugan, speaking in Cantonese but speaking slowly, not because he wasn't fluent but because most Chinese couldn't get used to the fact that he could speak it; they just saw his white face and assumed that whatever language came out of his mouth would be English. 'I am Simon Ng's brother-in-law. Jill Ng is my sister. It is important that I speak to him.'

The guard with the gun kept it pointing at Dugan's head. 'We tell you already, he not here,' he said in halting English, refusing to acknowledge that Dugan spoke Cantonese.

'Can you reach him?' Dugan began backing away, step by step, trying to get a tree in between them. His prisoner's chest began to heave in spasms so he released the pressure, just a fraction.

The man shook his head.

'Look, I'm with the police. And I'm a good friend of Simon Ng's. That's two fucking good reasons why you can't shoot me. You put the gun away and I'll let go of your friend. Deal?'

'You let go first, then I put gun away,' said the guard. Dugan didn't trust him one bit, and he guessed that it was mutual.

He pressed his mouth close to his prisoner's ear. 'Throw him the phone,' he hissed. He did as he was told and it fell on the grass by the guard's feet. 'OK, listen to this. Call Simon Ng now and tell him I want to speak to him.'

Dugan could see by the confusion on the man's face that something was wrong and he realized suddenly what it was. Ng was already dead. Oh sweet Jesus, what about Jill?

'Where is my sister?' he yelled.

The guard pointed the gun up at the compound. 'She is in the house,' he admitted.

369

Dugan thought frantically. 'Who is the Dragon Head now?' he asked. The man remained stubbornly silent and aimed the gun at Dugan again.

Dugan was half-hidden by the tree now, and he leant against it for support. His prisoner wriggled but he swiftly yanked his arm tighter round his neck and the movement stopped. Dugan's arm was starting to throb and his elbow screamed in pain.

'Call Thomas Ng,' Dugan shouted. 'Tell him Pat Dugan is here and that I want to talk to him.'

The guard looked hesitant but eventually he knelt down and picked up the phone. He tried pressing the buttons while holding the gun but couldn't manage it so he tucked the gun under his arm while he dialled. Dugan couldn't hear what he was saying but after a few sentences the man held the phone out to Dugan. 'Throw it,' said Dugan. It landed at his feet and he pushed the guard he was holding forward towards the road and grabbed the phone before ducking back behind the tree.

The two guards stood together, his former prisoner massaging his throat. Dugan's right arm had practically gone to sleep so he held the phone to his ear with his left hand.

'It's Dugan here. Is that you, Thomas?'

'Patrick, my old friend. How are you?' There was not a trace of Chinese accent left in Thomas Ng's cultured American voice. They had met several times since the huge wedding almost a decade earlier, but calling him an old friend was pushing it a bit far. Dugan had never really liked him. Simon Ng had always been up front about what he did, take it or leave it, but his brother was always trying to pretend to be a legitimate businessman, acting as if the family fortune was based on hard work, initiative and enterprise rather than on extortion, prostitution and drugs. You knew where you were with the man Jill had married but Thomas was harder to read and Dugan had always kept away from him.

'Thomas, I heard you were back.'

'You should be a detective,' laughed Ng, but it was a harsh metallic sound as if knives were being sharpened.

'Yeah, very funny,' said Dugan, keeping a wary eye on the two thugs. They were whispering to each other but at least the gun was now directed at the ground rather than at his head. 'Look, have you called off your dogs?'

'They won't hurt you, Patrick, don't worry.'

'Hey, I'm not worried. I just didn't want to damage them,' replied Dugan, but he didn't feel anywhere near as cocky as he sounded. Whistling in the dark. 'They're trying to stop me talking to Jill.'

'They are protecting her.'

'From her own brother?'

'We are not sure what we are protecting her from.'

'Presumably from the man who killed Simon.' Ng didn't say anything. 'Simon is dead, then?' pressed Dugan.

'You haven't heard? I'd have thought the police would have told you already,' said Ng.

'Nobody is telling me anything at the moment, Thomas. What happened?'

'It's a long story, Patrick. Come round and we'll talk.'

'Where are you?'

'Golden Dragon Lodge. My father's house.'

'I know it. But I want to see Jill first.'

'I understand. Let me speak to my men again and I will

371

tell them to take you to her. But I must warn you that she is being sedated at the moment. Her husband has been killed . . .'

'Don't worry, I'll be gentle with her,' interrupted Dugan.

'Let me finish,' continued Ng coldly. 'There's something you don't know. Sophie has been kidnapped. At the moment we don't know if she is alive or dead.'

The news stunned Dugan. He didn't know what to say.

'Are you still there?' asked Ng.

'I'm here. I'm here. Christ almighty! Look, I'll be right over after I've seen Jill. Can you get your men to lend me a car? They've scared off my taxi already.'

'They'll drive you,' said Ng. 'Put them on.'

Dugan popped his head around the tree again. The gun had gone back inside the guard's jacket so he stepped out and handed over the phone.

'He wants to talk to you,' he said in Cantonese.

'Thank you,' said the armed guard, in English, and took the phone. After listening and muttering a few words he led Dugan up the track to the black iron gates where half a dozen more guards were standing, two of them with machine guns. Artillery like that was very unusual in Hong Kong, most triad soldiers stuck to knives and hatchets and when they did resort to firearms it was usually handguns. They opened the gate and two of the guards escorted Dugan to the house. Dugan rang the doorbell and it was opened by a Filipina maid whose name he couldn't remember.

'I'm Mrs Ng's brother, can you tell her I'm here please.'

'Mrs Ng is not to be disturbed, sir,' said the maid, her lower lip trembling.

'It's OK,' said Dugan. 'I've already spoken to Thomas Ng and he has said it's OK.'

The magic words 'Thomas Ng' seemed to do the trick and she stepped to one side to allow him in.

'I'll get her for you, sir,' said the maid, turning to go up the stairs.

'No, that's all right. I'll see myself up. Is she in the main bedroom?'

'No, sir, she's sleeping in Sophie's bedroom.'

Dugan left her at the bottom of the stairs and went up alone. He found Jill curled up on a single brass bed with pink sheets and pillowcases, cuddling the dog he'd bought for Sophie. On the bedside table was an empty brandy glass and a bottle containing green tablets. She moved in her sleep when he sat down on the bed and put his hand on her shoulder. She moaned and squeezed the dog, hugging it close and rubbing it with her nose. She looked terrible, her face drawn and pale, dark shadows round her eyes and puffy bags under them, lips cracked and dry. For a moment a picture of Petal lying in the hospital bed flashed through his mind; two girls that he loved, both of them normally so pretty and vibrant, both so full of life, both reduced to shells by the man called Howells, beating one almost to death, killing the husband of the other.

'Jill,' he said quietly. 'Are you awake?'

She murmured something and a hand appeared from under the sheet and brushed a lock of damp hair across her lined forehead. He called her name and her eyes opened slightly.

'Simon?'

'It's me, kid, it's Pat,' said Dugan, leaning forward and stroking her tear-stained cheek.

'Oh Pat, Pat,' she moaned and then she closed her eyes and slept again. Dugan tenderly put her arm back under the sheet and switched off the light before closing the door. On the way out he handed the bottle of tablets to the maid.

'Be careful with them,' he warned. 'Give them to her one at a time, and only if she asks for them. Whatever you do, do not leave them by her bed. Do you understand?'

She nodded and put the bottle in a small pocket in the front of her apron.

Outside two of Ng's men were waiting in a blue Mercedes, the engine running.

After visiting his third Wan Chai bar Edmunds had put together a workable model of the Jack Edmunds Theory of Economic Development as Related to Bars – the poorer a country the cheaper the booze and the younger the girls.

The cab had dropped him at a set of traffic lights on Lockhart Road and he'd gone first into the San Francisco Bar, followed by Popeye's and the Country Club. The layout varied but the music and the prices of the booze were the same, and the girls all had bored looks as if they'd rather be somewhere else, with someone else, doing something else. In each of the bars Edmunds had allowed himself to be shown to a stool and had sat there with a whisky on the rocks. Not one of the three stocked Jack Daniels and occasionally he grimaced as he drank.

Within seconds of his drink arriving he was joined by one of the hostesses with slackly-applied lipstick and bad breath, smiling like a simpleton and asking him his name, his job, how long he'd been in Hong Kong and if he would buy her a drink. In each case he lied to the first three questions and said yes to the last, which earned him an even bigger smile, usually one showing yellowed teeth encrusted with plaque, and twenty minutes of what passed for conversation.

Edmunds waited until they hit him for a second drink before he began to talk about his good friend Geoff, how he was supposed to meet him in one of the bars but couldn't remember which, and then he'd hand over the black-and-white picture and ask if she'd seen him. Three times he showed the picture and three times they'd said no. The women had all been keen to help and had passed the picture around for their friends to examine, but nobody remembered seeing Howells. It was a long shot, Edmunds knew that, but he also knew that Feinberg was right, a wounded man on the run in a hostile environment had few options, and they lost nothing by looking. They might even get lucky. Once he'd drawn a blank Edmunds would gather up his bill and the chits from the plastic beaker in front of him and ask for the check, paying in cash. Both he and Feinberg had changed a stack of traveller's cheques in the hotel before going their separate ways.

The Washington Club was the fourth bar Edmunds tried. As three others had done before him, the doorman jumped off his stool and held the velvet curtain open for Edmunds, waving him inside and promising 'many girls, full show.' A fattish woman in a too-tight black dress who barely came up to his shoulder gripped him by the arm and virtually frog-marched him to an empty stool. Edmunds ordered a Jack Daniels, and received a confused look so he asked for a whisky instead.

'Whisky Coke,' said the woman, and walked away.

'No, whisky with ice,' he called after her but she didn't seem to have heard. What the hell, he was in no mood to drink it anyway. He looked around the bar but it had little to distinguish it from the ones he'd already visited, except for a large fish tank by the door. A boy barely out of his teens was admiring his crew cut in his reflection, smoothing it and patting it down. One of the fish was dying, swimming on its side and sinking to the bottom each time it stopped waving its fins. One of its bigger companions was nudging it, or biting it, Edmunds couldn't tell which.

A short girl, with an impish brown face and short black hair in a pageboy cut and wearing a lime-green cheongsam appeared next to him and smiled up at him, head on one side.

'Good evening,' said Edmunds, and motioned for her to take the stool next to his.

'You American?' she asked.

'Yeah, do you want a drink?'

'Thanks,' she said and gave her order to one of the women behind the bar.

'You're not Chinese, are you?' he said.

She pulled a face as if she had a sour taste in her mouth. 'Filipina,' she said. Edmunds chatted with her for the best part of an hour, during the course of which she racked up four blue chits in the tumbler in front of him. She seemed to enjoy herself, laughing at his jokes and asking question after question about his life, ninety per cent of which he answered with lies; but every time the curtain was pulled back to admit another punter her eyes flicked to the door. She was always alert, and Edmunds knew that as soon as he paid his bill and left she'd be by someone else's side.

He started telling her about his friend Geoff and took the black-and-white picture out of his jacket pocket and showed it to her.

'Have you seen him?' he asked.

She studied it carefully and said no, she hadn't. Edmunds wondered how many customers she fleeced in a night and how many she remembered ten minutes after they'd stepped out of the bar. He asked her if she'd show the picture to her friends and she went from girl to girl, mostly getting quick uninterested shakes of the head, occasionally pointing to him.

Edmunds pretended not to look but as he toyed with his tumbler of adulterated whisky his attention was focused on the girl and the reaction she was getting. He struck gold when she had gone to the far side of the bar, directly opposite where he was sitting. She handed the picture to a young Chinese girl with sleek black hair that curled above her shoulders, a small silver brooch at the neck of a peach-coloured blouse. She was talking to an overweight balding man in a cheap grey suit, laughing with her hand over her mouth, but when she saw the picture her lips closed like steel gates slamming shut. She glared at the Filipina and although he couldn't hear them over the pulsing beat of the dance music he guessed that she was demanding to know where the picture had come from. He looked down as the Filipina pointed and then checked them out in a long mirror above one of the booths. The Chinese girl's eyes narrowed as she studied him across the bar and then she began to question the Filipina.

Edmunds looked at her as she glared down at the shorter girl, hands on her hips. The Filipina kept shaking her head and then the Chinese girl put a hand on her shoulder and spoke to her. Edmunds could see the urgency on her face, and he wasn't in the least bit surprised when she came back and said that none of the girls could remember seeing the man in the bar. Edmunds put the picture back in his jacket pocket and thanked her anyway.

'Why don't you give me your card and write down where you're staying and I'll give it to him if he comes in,' said the Filipina, and Edmunds was one hundred per cent certain then.

'No,' he said. 'No point. I'm leaving Hong Kong tomorrow. I'll catch Geoff next time.' He yawned and stretched. 'I'd better be going,' he said.

'What hotel are you staying at?'

'Hilton,' he lied. 'Can you get me the check, please?'

She didn't seem as friendly now; there was an edge to her voice and a wall behind her eyes, but the smile was still there and she swung her hips as she went over to the cashier. Edmunds suddenly realized just how much he missed his wife. He wanted to be back home with her, sharing a bed with her, no matter how cold it was.

He paid the bill and walked through the curtain out into the hot night air. A couple of hundred yards down the road he flagged down a taxi and got into the back.

'How's your English?' he asked the driver.

'English or American?' he replied with a grin.

'You'll do,' said Edmunds. He opened his wallet and

handed the man two $500 notes. 'I want to hire you for the rest of the night.'

The driver took the notes and examined them under the dashboard lights. 'Where do you want to go?' he said suspiciously.

'At the moment, nowhere,' he said. 'Drive a little way down the road and park. I'm waiting for someone.'

The red doors swung open as the Mercedes approached, and the twin headlights cut through the night, swerving from side to side as they drove up the path to the double garage and parked. The two men escorted Dugan up the steps and over the wooden bridge to the house. The stone dragon scowled at him, illuminated by hidden spotlights under the water, and he scowled back.

Thomas Ng was waiting for him in front of the house and they went inside together. Two men, one old and one young, were sitting at a large desk in the centre of the main reception room, drawing lines on large maps.

'Do you want a drink?' asked Ng, and Dugan shook his head. Ng took him through into the room where only twenty-four hours earlier the triad leaders had pledged their loyalty to Ng Wai-sun. All trace of the ceremony had been removed, now it was a family room once more. Even the lamps had been taken away and the room was now illuminated by the electric lights set into antique brass fittings around the room. Ng sat down at the circular table and told rather than asked Dugan to sit down. Dugan took a seat three away from where Ng sat. He didn't like the way Ng was trying to dominate him so he decided to go on the offensive.

'What the fuck's going on?' he asked.

'My brother is dead,' said Ng. 'And whoever did it still has Sophie, though at the moment we don't know if Sophie is alive or dead.'

'What happened?'

Ng told him how Sophie had been abducted from her school, how the gweilo had demanded a ransom, and how instead of taking the money he had taken Simon Ng instead, and left him to die handcuffed to the anchor of a yacht at Hebe Haven.

'And what happens now?' asked Dugan.

'Now we find the gweilo. And then we find Sophie. We know what he looks like. We have a photograph. We have men at all the ports and at Kai Tak, and we are now searching every block in Hong Kong.'

'Every block in Hong Kong?' said Dugan, surprised. 'You don't have enough men.'

'We do now,' said Ng, but he didn't elaborate.

'It'll be like finding a needle in a haystack,' said Dugan.

'Not at all,' said Ng. 'There are fewer than six million people here, and ninety-eight per cent are Chinese. There is a finite size to this haystack, Patrick, and the needle is different enough to make it clearly visible. It is just a matter of time.'

'Do you know who he is? Or why he killed Simon?'

'No,' said Ng. He did not trust the gweilo cop enough to tell him about his brother's contact with the mainland or the fact that he had begun spying for them. What he wanted from Patrick Dugan was information about how the police were getting on with their investigation. Nothing more.

'If you catch him, what are you planning to do with him?'

'First we will get him to tell us where Sophie is. Then we will ask him why he attacked our family.'

'And then?'

Ng smiled coldly. 'We are not planning to hand him over to the police, if that is what you mean.'

'I suppose not,' said Dugan. He sat with his elbows on the table and ran his hands through his hair. God, it was hot. His hair was damp with sweat and he could feel it running down the back of his neck and soaking into his shirt. Why didn't Ng switch the air-conditioner on?

As if reading his mind Ng said: 'I am sorry about the heat. My father doesn't believe in air-conditioning.'

'Is he here?'

'Upstairs. Polishing his jade, he said, but really he just wants to be alone. He is not a man to share his grief.'

'He has caused enough in his time,' said Dugan bitterly.

'Now is not the time for that,' answered Ng.

'I suppose not,' said Dugan. He looked at Ng, his jaw set tight. He had to help Jill and that meant helping Ng catch the gweilo so that they could get Sophie back, but he was worried about how far he would have to go. He had little loyalty to the police force that had treated him so badly because of his brother-in-law, that wasn't what was troubling him. What was playing on his mind was Petal and what would happen to her if Ng found out that she would have killed Simon Ng if the gweilo had failed. He breathed out, long and deeply, and looked at Ng.

'His name is Howells. Geoff Howells.'

Ng looked shocked. 'The police know who did it? Already?'

'There's more,' said Dugan. 'He's been shot. Some-body tried to kill him in his hotel room at the Hilton. They shot him but he got away.'

Ng stood up and walked up and down the room, past the lines of photographs.

'Do you know why?'

'Why they shot him? No. Nor do the police. Two Chinese guys were behind it. Robbery maybe.' He knew that it didn't sound too convincing, and he knew too that Ng would have his own informers within the police. Hopefully, if he told him as much as he could he'd be too busy going after Howells to bother checking up on what actually happened in the hotel room and that there had been a girl there, a pretty girl with jet-black hair and soft lips.

'When?'

'Last night. He killed the two men and got away before the police arrived. They've put a stop on him at the airport but as they don't know what he looks like they think he might get out using a false passport. They don't know that you have his picture. But they are checking all the hospitals and doctors. They don't think he's going anywhere without medical treatment.'

Ng laughed. 'The police are stupid,' he said. 'Do they imagine he will just walk into a Government hospital with a bullet wound? This man, this Geoff Howells, is a professional killer, an assassin.'

'So what do you think he will do?'

'If he does need medical attention he will get it from

an underground doctor, one without the necessary quali-
fications to practise legally, from the mainland perhaps.
They are not too difficult to find.'

'If they are not difficult to find, then the police will
find them too.'

'There is a big difference between finding them and
getting them to talk. Such men have no reason to tell the
police anything. But they will tell us.'

'I bet,' said Dugan. 'I just bet they will.'

Ng sat down again. 'There is one thing I do not
understand. How do they know this man Howells killed
my brother?'

That was the question Dugan had been hoping Ng
wouldn't ask, because for the life of him he didn't know
what to say because as things stood at the moment the
police had no way of connecting Howells with the death
of Simon Ng; that connection had come from Petal.

'I don't know,' Dugan lied. 'They won't let me anywhere near a murder investigation, you know that. I'm
stuck in Commercial Crime. I only got the information
second-hand, but it's kosher.'

'I'm sure it is,' said Ng. 'Look Patrick, what you've told
me is going to be a big help, a really big help. But can you
do me a favour? Will you keep tabs on the police end for
me, and if anything comes up, let me know?'

'Sure,' said Dugan, and he practically sighed with
relief. If he wanted him to act as a source of information
on the investigation into Howells then the chances were
that he wouldn't start asking anyone else. So long as they
depended on him to keep them informed then he could
make sure Petal stayed out of it.

'I want something in return,' Dugan added. 'I want to

be in on this. I want to be there when you catch him. And I want to help get Sophie back.'

'You will be more use to us staying at work and keeping tabs on the investigation,' said Ng.

'I can do that on the phone. I want to help,' insisted Dugan.

Ng looked at Dugan thoughtfully, weighing him up, and then nodded.

'OK, Patrick, I don't see why not. So long as I have your word that nothing you see or hear will ever be used against us, as you cops are so fond of saying.'

'To be honest, I think my days with the police are almost over anyway,' said Dugan. 'But I'm not switching sides. I'm doing it for Jill, and for Sophie.' And for Petal, he thought. Especially for Petal.

'I'll have a room made up for you upstairs,' said Ng. 'We're controlling the search from here. I'll get on to the men and tell them that we are now looking for a man who has been shot. There is also an outside chance that he will call again about Sophie. If he does he'll call Simon's house and the call will be transferred here. Either way all we can do now is wait.'

'I'll wait,' said Dugan. 'I'll wait for ever,' he added as Ng left the room.

Edmunds had thought he'd have to wait until closing time before Amy went home, and he almost missed her when she came out of the Washington Club at about two o'clock in the morning. She looked different in her jeans and

leather bomber-jacket. Younger. He knew that his visit
to the bar and Howells' picture had upset her and she was
in a hurry to warn him but even so he'd assumed that the
mamasan would have made her stay until the end of the
shift, and he knew from asking the girls that they didn't
shut their doors until after four o'clock.

She waved goodnight to the doorman and stood at the
side of the road and hailed a taxi. Edmunds kept his head
down until her cab drove off and then he pointed after it.

'Follow that taxi,' he said.

'Like in the movies?' said the driver.

'Yeah, just like the movies. Hurry up before you
lose them.'

The driver laughed and jerked the car away from the
kerb. There was something hanging from the driver's
mirror, a sort of upturned horseshoe, a gold-coloured
ingot hanging beneath it, and below that brass rings tied
to a red cord that swung back and forth with the motion
of the cab. Every thirty seconds or so it emitted a couple
of bars of disjointed metallic music. Edmunds had no idea
what purpose it served, whether it was religious or just to
bring good luck, but it was as annoying as hell. The roads
were fairly clear and they had no trouble keeping the taxi
in sight as it headed towards the harbour and through the
tunnel. More than half the vehicles on the road were red
and grey taxis so Edmunds knew that there was no chance
of their being spotted and he relaxed a little.

The traffic was thicker in Kowloon and Edmunds' cab
moved closer, leaving just two or three cars between it
and the one they were following. They passed by the
airport, its runway lights switched off, and then they
burrowed through a maze of housing and commercial

blocks, until they were the only two cars on the road and Edmunds told his driver to drop back. Eventually their quarry stopped and they waited at a distance while Amy paid her fare and got out of the cab. She walked to the entrance of a grimy, soot-stained building, shops with their shutters down on the ground floor, a dozen floors of flats above with tiny metal-framed windows, some with clay plant-pots standing ill at ease on fragile-looking wrought-iron balconies that appeared to have been tacked on to the outsides of the flats as an afterthought.

'Wait here,' said Edmunds, and he opened the door quietly and ran down the road to the building where she had entered. The metal gate at the entrance was not locked and though it was rusting and the purple paint was peeling off it opened easily. An old man in a white vest that had seen better days was slumped over a wooden table, snoring and spluttering in his dreams.

Edmunds slipped past him. A quick look round confirmed that there was no lift so he headed up the stone stairs on the balls of his feet, pausing at each turn to check that the next flight was clear. He moved quickly up to the second floor but then he heard her footsteps and he began to move more slowly. She passed the third floor and by then he was one flight behind her and breathing with his mouth wide open and taking extra care whenever he put his feet down. When she got to the fourth floor he heard her open her handbag and heard metal jingling as she took out her keys. As he heard the key being slotted into the lock he risked a quick look around the stairwell and saw her push open the door. He ducked back, his heart pounding in his ears, but she hadn't seen him; he waited until he heard her step across the threshold and then ran up to the door and followed her inside, grabbing her shoulder and pressing his hand across her mouth.

Before she could scream or struggle he hissed: 'It's all right. I'm not going to hurt you, or him. Do you understand?'

She nodded, her eyes wide with fear, but she didn't look as if she was going to struggle so Edmunds slowly took his hand away.

'Where is he?' he asked.

She looked at the bedroom door, her reflexes taking over, so Edmunds didn't wait for an answer. Amy followed him in. Howells was asleep, lying on his front.

'How badly is he hurt?' asked Edmunds, keeping his voice low. Howells came awake immediately and began rolling off the bed, hands moving to fighting position, ignoring the pain. Edmunds stepped back, holding his arms out to the side, showing he was unarmed. 'I'm here to talk, Howells, that's all. Back off.'

Howells carried on moving, oblivious to the fact that he was stark naked. He looked behind Edmunds to the room beyond, and then when he saw that the man was alone side-stepped across to the doorway so that he was between him and the exit. His face was calm and relaxed, the same as it was when Edmunds had last seen him, when he had killed three people and saved his life. Howells had no weapon but if the file was right then he didn't need one – even with a bullet wound he'd still be fast and strong enough. He knew his own limitations and hand-to-hand combat with someone almost half his age was one of them, unless Howells was a lot weaker than he looked.

'Who are you?' Howells asked, his voice rock-steady, his feet evenly spaced on the wooden floor, toes digging in for balance, heels up ready to move fast, hands poised to strike. The bandage was on his right shoulder so Edmunds knew that if the attack came it would be from Howells' left side so he drew back his right leg, ready to block with his own left hand, shifting position slowly so it wouldn't alarm the Brit. One of the first things they taught you about interrogation was that when you take away a man's clothes you take away his confidence and his identity, but Howells was no less of a killer naked, and it was the American, clothes and all, who was the more nervous.

'Edmunds. Jack Edmunds. CIA.'

'What does the CIA want with me?' His eyes narrowed. 'Do I know you?'

'You saved my life a few years back in the Lebanon,' explained Edmunds, keeping his hands low and avoiding any gesture that could be interpreted as threatening. 'I was being held hostage and the Company was dragging its feet on the ransom.'

'I remember,' said Howells. 'You said you were a businessman.'

Edmunds smiled. 'Yeah, you were a bit slow in identifying yourself. And Americans didn't have friends in too many parts of the world just then. I saw what you did to the three bastards who were guarding me, remember?'

Howells nodded. 'Yeah, you never know who to trust in this business, do you?' He seemed to relax a little. But only a little.

'So you've come all this way to thank me?' Howells asked.

'You wish,' said Edmunds, dropping his hands completely. 'Look, can we sit down and talk about this, you're making me nervous.'

Howells weighed up the American and then shrugged. 'Sure,' he said, turning away and walking into the lounge. He realized for the first time by the way Amy looked at him that he was naked. He opened his mouth to ask her for his trousers but she nodded before he could speak and half ran to a cheap wooden wardrobe and took out his pants and his new shirt. The pants had been washed and pressed. He sat on the sofa and she helped him on with the trousers and then draped the shirt around his shoulders.

'*M goy*,' he said, and she beamed at him.

'*M sai*,' she said. 'Is everything OK?'

'Everything is fine,' he said. 'This man is a friend. Amy, I have to talk with him alone, do you mind?'

She shook her head, eager to please. 'I'll go in the kitchen.' She kissed him on the forehead. 'Do you like coffee or a cup of tea?' she asked Edmunds, who said no, neither. Howells also declined and she left the two men, Howells sitting on the sofa, Edmunds standing by the bedroom door, arms crossed across his stomach.

'Is the bullet out?' asked Edmunds.

'How did you know I'd been shot?' asked Howells quickly. There was no way of telling from the bandage whether he'd been shot, stabbed, burnt or attacked by a swarm of killer bees.

Edmunds began pacing up and down, walking slowly between the bedroom door and the window that overlooked the street below, three paces there, three paces back, his head hung in thought as if he'd forgotten that the Brit was there. Edmunds wasn't one hundred per cent sure just what the hell he was doing alone with the man he'd been sent to kill, but he knew it was something to do with honour, about a debt that deserved to be repaid.

But it was more than that. It was about a lifetime spent doing things he regretted, that made him feel sad and unclean, and that when all of it was behind him and he was retired or dying, he wanted to be able to look back at some things and to think that maybe, just maybe, he'd really done the Right Thing, whatever that was. This man had saved his life; now he was hurt, and it was obvious that he had been betrayed by his own organization. He was a Brit and the CIA operation was being run from London. Maybe that was part of it too, the fact that one day Edmunds might also be betrayed by his own masters and that he'd open his door to a couple of grey-faced men with cold eyes, young men who didn't have bad dreams. Men like Feinberg.

Edmunds continued to pace up and down. Howells sat and watched him, knowing that whatever it was the CIA man wanted, he was no threat. Not just then, anyway. He'd had ample opportunity to take Howells out, so the best thing to do was to let him walk, and talk, in his own time.

Eventually Edmunds seemed to come to a decision; he stopped pacing and stood in front of Howells, linking his fingers and pressing them outwards until the knuckles cracked like breaking bones.

'The man who sent us wants you dead,' Edmunds said quietly.

There were two things Howells wanted to know immediately – who was the man and what did Edmunds mean by us? But he kept quiet, and waited.

'They told us you had killed one of our agents. Is that right?'

'I was doing what I was told to do,' said Howells.

'By who?'

Howells sneered. 'You show me yours and I'll show you mine.'

'I don't freelance,' said Edmunds. 'I'm working for the Company.'

'I haven't done anything that would cut across the CIA,' said Howells.

'What about London?'

'What do you mean?'

'Feinberg said that our operation was being run from London rather than from the States.'

'Feinberg?'

'My partner. And you're lucky it was me that found you first, believe me.'

'How did you find me? The girl?'

'How else? You'd been shot, you couldn't stay in a hotel and you obviously wouldn't want to go near a hospital. You'd have to go to ground, and you needed someone to take care of you.'

'That easy,' mused Howells, looking at the ground. 'Fuck it.'

'Partly luck, partly carelessness,' said Edmunds. 'You should have kept her home.'

'You knew what hotel I was staying at? And you knew I'd been shot?' asked Howells.

Edmunds nodded and Howells knew for sure then that Grey had set him up. But he still couldn't make sense of the sequence of events. First he was attacked by three Chinese, shortly after telephoning London. And then when he'd escaped two CIA agents came after him. What next? The fucking KGB?

'Do you know why?' he asked Edmunds.

'Because of the man you killed, our agent,' said Edmunds.

'Nobody told me he was one of yours,' said Howells. 'I was told he was about to betray one of ours.'

'Life's a bitch,' said Edmunds. 'You never know who to trust.'

'Only yourself,' said Howells.

'Only yourself,' agreed Edmunds.

'So where do we go from here?'

'I go back to the Victoria Hotel and tell Feinberg that I couldn't find you. I owe you one for what happened in the Lebanon. But then we're quits. The rest is up to you. You've got to get out of here, out of this flat and out of Hong Kong. If I can find you so can Feinberg. So can the police.'

'Easier said than done. They're sure to be watching the airport, my passport is fucking useless.'

'You don't need a passport to get on a boat out of here, not if you've got enough money.'

'Yeah, well there's the rub. I've got a few thousand dollars and that's not going to buy me a ticket out of here, is it?'

'That's your problem,' said Edmunds, but as he said it he reached into his back pocket and pulled out his wallet. He gave Howells a handful of notes. 'That's still probably not enough, but it's the best I can do. It's all I can do.'

Howells took the money. 'Thanks, Jack.' He tucked the notes into his own back pocket, using his left hand.

'I'd better go,' said Edmunds. Howells got to his feet unsteadily and called Amy out.

'Jack is going,' he said to Amy. She opened the door for the American and said good night as he left.

'He seems nice,' said Amy as she closed the door and carefully locked it. 'He came to the club and showed your photograph to the girls. I didn't tell him I knew you. I thought perhaps he might want to hurt you. How did he know where I lived? Did y u tell him?'

'No, Amy. I think he must have followed you. But it doesn't matter. He only wants to help me.'

'I thought perhaps he was the man you call Grey.'

Howells looked at her, stunned. He'd never mentioned Grey to her. 'You talked in your sleep,' she explained. 'You were shouting, saying he had betrayed you.'

Howells nodded. 'No, that wasn't Grey. Grey is a man I used to work for. And yes, he is the man who betrayed me. He's the one who had me shot.' He wasn't sure why he was telling her, but part of it was because he was so bitter about the betrayal that he wanted to share it.

'Is Grey a bad man?' she asked.

'Yes. I was very loyal to him, but he wanted to have me killed. He works for the Government in a place called Century House in London.'

Amy slowly repeated the words, Grey and Century House, as she'd memorized the word 'fridge' in the bar.

She sat down on the sofa next to him and rested her head against his shoulder, his good shoulder. 'Can you tell me what is wrong? Can I help?' No and yes, thought Howells. The problem was, how could he get her to help him? And how far would she go?

'I have to go out soon,' he said. 'Jack promised to give me some money so that I can get out of Hong Kong.'

'You can't go out,' she said. 'You are still weak. Let me go.'

He stroked her hair with his left hand, curling it around

his fingers. 'No, I have to go. I won't be long. You can help by making me some sort of sling to support my arm. Do you have some spare material?'

'I'll use one of my old pillowcases,' she said. She went into her bedroom and he heard the sound of a wooden drawer being opened and closed and then she walked through to the kitchen and came back with a plastic-handled butcher's knife that she used to carefully slit it down the seams.

'Help me put the shirt on first,' he said. Together they eased his bad arm through the sleeve and pulled the shirt down, the pain making his eyes water. She folded the cotton material into a triangle and knotted it behind his neck.

'How's that?' she said.

'It's fine. It's really fine,' he said and she smiled.

'Do you want one of the tablets that Dr Wu left you?'

'No, no thanks. They'll only make me sleepy. Maybe later.' She rested her head back on his shoulder and stroked his left thigh. 'Amy?'

'Hmm?'

'Do you have any friends who can get me out of Hong Kong? Secretly?'

She sat upright and looked at him seriously. 'I know somebody who might help you. But he is not a good man. He is a smuggler. I used to work for him.'

He frowned. 'Worked for him? How?'

'I was a, what is the word, a courier?'

'Courier, yes. Carrying what?'

'Drugs sometimes. Sometimes taking gold into Thailand. I didn't do it many times, I wasn't very good at it. I looked too nervous, I always used to feel very sick. I needed the money, Geoff. I didn't do it many times.' It was suddenly important for her to convince Howells that she wasn't a criminal, she didn't want him to think badly of her.

'But the man you worked for, you know how to get in touch with him?'

'Sometimes he goes to Washington Club. But Geoff, he is not a good. He will want a lot of money.'

He smiled easily and kissed her on her forehead. 'Amy, there's no need to worry. Jack will give me more money later tonight. Can you do me a favour and make me a cup of coffee?'

She smiled again, pleased that she could do something for him. As she went into the kitchen Howells slipped the knife into the sling.

Sophie drank a little water from the tap, scared to take too much because her mother had always warned her against drinking tapwater. She'd done it sometimes and never got sick but her mother always made her drink bottled water. She was ravenous, the thoughts of food crowding out everything else except the fear of what was going to happen to her. Occasionally she'd start to panic when her imagination ran riot – what would happen if the boat caught fire? If it sank? If the man never came back and she starved to death? Once she'd almost gone into a fit, screaming and kicking at the door until she'd collapsed exhausted on the floor. It was hot, so hot that she felt as if she was going to melt. Despite being born in Hong Kong she lived most of her life in an air-conditioned world; her house, school and the family's cars provided a stable environment that protected her from the colony's often stifling heat and humidity. Now, locked in the junk's washroom, she was hot and sweaty and uncomfortable. She couldn't sleep for more than an hour at a time before she'd wake up, gasping for breath, her throat dry and aching. She kept soaking a towel in cold water and rubbing it over her face, sometimes sitting with it draped over her head, enjoying the coolness of it. She tried chewing it slowly to see if that would make the hunger pains go away, but it seemed to make it worse, she could feel her stomach rumbling and groaning. She wished her dog was with her, the one Uncle Patrick had given her, at least then she'd have someone to talk to. But most of all she wanted her mother. And her father. She wanted to go home.

Edmunds was in the shower when the doorbell rang. 'Is that you, Rick?' he yelled above the sound of the water. He grabbed a bathrobe hanging on the back of the door and padded across the carpet. He opened the door and his eyes widened as he saw Howells standing alone in the corridor, his arm in a sling.

'I need your help,' said Howells. 'Can I come in?'

Edmunds stood to one side and let him in. Howells walked over to the window, slowly as if in pain, while Edmunds shut the door.

'You shouldn't have come,' he warned. 'If Feinberg sees you . . .'

'Is he here?'

'Not at the moment.'

'Where is his room?'

Edmunds nodded at an adjoining door next to the bathroom. 'Through there. If I know Feinberg he's having a whale of a time in the bars of Tsim Sha Tsui. But he could be back at any time. You said you wanted help?'

'I need money. I have to get out of Hong Kong. I know someone who can get me out but he'll need money. More money than I have. And it's not as if I can go out and stick up a bank in my present condition, is it?'

Edmunds shivered. He'd tried adjusting the aircon earlier but it had made no difference, and now the combination of cold air and water on his skin chilled him. He took a thick white towel from a metal rack above the bath and began to rub it through his hair. 'How much do you need?'

'Five thousand dollars, US.'

'To go where?'

'That'll get me to the Philippines. I can hide out there for a few months until I'm fit.'

'I don't know how much I've got on me,' said Edmunds. He went to the dressing table and opened the top drawer to get his wallet. Howells came up behind him as he rifled through the traveller's cheques. Edmunds felt rather than saw the arm go across his throat because he was looking down but he lifted his head in time to see the knife being drawn across the throat of his reflection in the mirror, and saw the blood pour down his neck and chest. So much blood, and yet no pain, just a spreading coldness around his throat. He opened his mouth but it felt numb and the wallet dropped from his hands and a red film passed over his eyes. The last thing he saw before the red turned to black was the smiling face of an old Vietnamese man, grinning with chipped and stained teeth, laughing silently as he went to his death.

It wasn't quite light when Rick Feinberg returned to the Victoria Hotel, humming to himself as he paid off his taxi and rode the lift up to his floor. He'd had no luck showing the picture of the Brit in the dozen Kowloon bars he'd visited, but he'd enjoyed himself, chatting up the hostesses and touching them up whenever they'd let him. It didn't come close to Bangkok or Manila, they all kept their clothes on for one thing, and they were a darn sight more hard-faced, but it was still better than drinking in the States. He wondered how Edmunds had got on and thought of banging on his door and waking him up but then in an uncharacteristic gesture of friendship decided that he'd let him sleep instead. The old guy needed all the rest he could get. Feinberg couldn't imagine why a guy as old as Edmunds, he must be fifty-five at least for fuck's sake, was still working as a field agent. He must have got somebody back at Langley mighty pissed at him, or there must be some deep dark secret in his personal file that kept him from going any higher.

He unlocked his door and switched on the light. He'd left his curtains open and he switched the light off again and stood for a while watching the harbour. Even at such a late hour the harbour was busy, with motorized sampans chugging to and fro, a couple of large freighters, stacked high with containers, sounding their horns, a floating crane being nursed along by an ancient tug, and two American frigates bobbing silently at anchor, light bulbs outlining their superstructures.

Watching the black water made Feinberg realize how much he wanted to go to the toilet. The last time he'd taken a piss he'd felt a slight burning sensation, nothing too painful, a slight smarting, but it had been uncomfortable and he wanted to put off going through it again. He hoped it was just something he'd eaten. Please God don't let him have the clap. Or AIDS. If those fucking whores had given him the clap he'd go back to Bangkok and give them hell. They'd asked him to wear a condom but he'd insisted on going without, told them that he didn't wear boots when he went paddling. They hadn't understood and they had tried several times to open a packet and slip one on him but he held one of them face down on the bed and forced himself inside her as she yelled at him in Thai. Once he'd had her the other one gave in without a struggle and when he took them both again a few hours later they didn't even bother asking him. Now he regretted it. Not the fact that he'd taken them to bed, but the fact that he hadn't bothered to wear protection.

Edmunds was so lucky. When he'd been screwing his way around South East Asia the worst you could get would be a dose of VD and a couple of jabs of penicillin would put paid to that. This AIDS business had taken a good deal of the fun out of fucking.

A police launch carving through the water below sounded a blaring siren and drew alongside a fishing boat in the middle of the harbour. As he watched two policemen climb from the launch into the junk he became aware of somebody standing behind him. Reflected in the window was a thin clean-shaven face, short hair and deep-set serious eyes. It was the face in the photograph. Feinberg didn't move. There was no point.

'You're Howells?' he said.

'And you're dead,' said the reflection, and it smiled.

The Red Pole assisting Cheng was asleep, his head on the maps, when the phone rang. The phone had been silent for three hours and Cheng had gone upstairs to rest, to gather his strength for the coming day. Ng was also upstairs, but unlike Cheng he was wide awake, lying fully dressed on his bed. Dugan had taken an upholstered chair out of the house and was sitting in it, deep in thought. The phone made him jump as it shattered the silence.

The boy answered sleepily in Cantonese and then switched to English. He listened and then went running up the stairs, calling for Ng. Dugan walked into the house as Ng came down the stairs, rubbing his forehead. 'The gweilo,' he said to Dugan. The two men stood together as Ng put the receiver to his ear.

'Who are you?' said an English voice.

'Thomas Ng. I am Simon Ng's brother.'

'I tried to speak to Mrs Ng but I was told to ring this number. Is she there?'

'Mrs Ng is not taking any calls. You can talk to me.'

'OK. Then listen to this. I still have the girl, and I am prepared to release her if you do exactly what I tell you. I want thirty-two ounces of gold and I want a quarter of a million US in diamonds – stones, not jewellery. I will call you tomorrow afternoon to tell you when and where you are to hand them over. Do you understand? Thirty-two ounces of gold and $250,000 in diamonds. I will phone this afternoon.'

'I understand,' said Ng, but before he could say anything else the line went dead.

Dugan caught some of the conversation but not all, so Ng repeated it for him.

'What do you think?' asked Ng.

'Did he ask specifically for you to carry the ransom?'

'No. But that might come next time he phones. You think he might be after me?'

'It's possible. We still don't know why he killed Simon. If he asks for you to deliver it then I think we can assume he's after you. Look, I think you should suggest that I hand over the money. There's no way he could want to hurt me.'

Ng nodded thoughtfully. 'I agree,' he said. 'It's good of you, Patrick. It's good of you to help.'

'Sophie's my niece, too,' said Dugan.

Ng put his hand on Dugan's shoulder. 'You'd better get some sleep,' he said.

'I'm OK,' said Dugan. 'I'll stay outside for a while longer.'

Ng Wai-sun appeared at the top of the stairs wearing a dark blue silk kimono and Ng went up to tell him what had happened.

Howells knocked on the door and within seconds Amy was there, a worried frown on her face.

'Is everything all right?' she asked as she let him in.

'Everything's fine,' he said. 'He gave me some money, but I still don't think it'll be enough.'

'Does your arm hurt?'

'It's fine,' he said, sitting on the sofa. 'Can I have a cup of coffee, please?'

'Of course,' she said, and went to the kitchen. While she was out of the room he slipped the knife out of his sling and placed it on the floor, next to the sofa, where she was sure to find it at some point. She'd probably think it had fallen there after she'd cut the pillowcase apart. The knife was spotless now, he'd cleaned it carefully after phoning Simon Ng from Feinberg's hotel room.

He leant back and rested his head. God, he was tired. He closed his eyes and breathed deeply, listening to Amy opening and closing cupboards and the sound of the gas hissing under the kettle. There was no doubt that he was going to need her help later on when he went to collect the ransom. But he was having second thoughts about using her contacts to get out of Hong Kong. Better to drop her as soon as possible, he decided. With US$250,000 in diamonds he'd have no trouble buying a passage on a ship, any ship. Howells knew that when he left the colony it would be vital that he left no one behind who knew where he was going – or at least that he left no one alive behind. He had no choice.

She came back into the room and handed him a yellow mug of coffee.

'*M goy*,' he said.

'*M sai*,' she replied and sat down next to him, one leg curled underneath herself so that she could face him. She rested her arms on the back of the sofa and placed her chin on them, looking up at him with wide eyes.

'What is happening, Geoff?' she said.

He reached across with his good arm and brushed her cheek. He had already worked out how he was going to get her to help him. He'd told her about Grey but from here on he'd have to be careful, because there was no way she'd help him if she found out that he'd kidnapped a child. He'd have to lie.

'That man who gave me the money tonight, Jack Edmunds, is a thief. And he's a friend of mine. He's what they call a safe-breaker, do you understand?'

She shook her head.

'He opens safes, sometimes in banks, sometimes in offices. He is one of the best in the world. And I'm a friend of his.'

'You help him steal?'

'Not steal. But I help him get rid of what he has stolen. I help him sell the things he steals. That's why I was attacked. The man Grey thought I had some diamonds and they were going to kill me and steal them. But I didn't have them. Jack had given them to another friend of his. This afternoon Jack wants me to collect the diamonds and to get them out of Hong Kong. It's very dangerous, Amy, because if they find out I have the diamonds then they are likely to attack me again.'

She nodded, her brow furrowed. 'My friend can help you leave Hong Kong.'

'Good. I'll be able to pay him in gold. Will that be all right?'

'Of course. In Hong Kong gold is better than money. But how will you get gold?'

'It was with the diamonds. Jack said I was to use it to pay for my fare. Thirty-two ounces.'

'Wah!' she said in surprise. 'So much.'

'Amy, I am going to need your help. I cannot do this on my own. I will need your help. Will you help me?' He looked at her earnestly and gave her a half-smile, trying to look as if it was the most important thing in the world to him.

'Of course I will help you, Geoff,' she said. 'What do you want me to do?'

'Thank you,' he said, and leant forward to kiss her softly on the lips. Her mouth opened immediately and she pressed herself against him, careful not to put pressure on his right arm. She moved her head from side to side as she kissed him on the mouth, and then she moved to kiss him above each eyebrow, the way she'd soothe a child. She looked deep into his eyes then and solemnly promised that she'd do anything he wanted, and then she kissed him again, opening her mouth wide to allow his tongue to move between her teeth and she moaned and said his name.

Howells tentatively reached for her breasts with his left hand, gently smoothing them with his palm before beginning to unbutton her blouse, slowly because he didn't want to frighten her; he wanted this to be perfect, he wanted her to enjoy it like she'd never enjoyed it before.

Because then she really would do anything for him. And because it would be her last time.

Getting the diamonds and the gold was no problem for Ng Wai-sun. The old man had some fifty taels of gold in the safe set into the floor under the wood panelling at the foot of his bed, and he could call in plenty of favours among the colony's diamond dealers to lay his hands on $250,000 of good quality stones, especially when he was paying for them in cash. The first dealer he woke up was around at Golden Dragon Lodge half an hour later with a selection. Ng Wai-sun held them in his palm and looked at them in the early morning light.

'What do you think?' he asked his son.

'I think we should use fakes rather than risk real diamonds,' said Thomas.

'They are a small price to pay if they get back my grandchild,' said Ng Wai-sun.

'It will not come to that, Father. This time we will catch the gweilo.'

'Beware the over-confidence that comes from under-estimating the enemy,' said Ng Wai-sun, carefully pouring the diamonds from his hand into a small green velvet pouch with a draw-string at the top. He handed the bag to his son.

The two were standing at the round table, on which were lined up thirty-two small oblongs of gold bearing the imprint of the Hang Seng Bank. Thomas Ng put the gold and the diamonds into a small brown leather attaché case. He zipped up the top and passed it to Dugan, who was sitting at the opposite side of the table.

'Be careful with it,' he said. 'That's a lot of money.'

'I'll try not to lose it,' said Dugan. He looked dead tired, bags under his bloodshot eyes, his clothes rumpled. He'd fallen asleep in the chair outside and had been woken up by screaming peacocks just before dawn.

Lin Wing-wah appeared at the double door wearing brown cord trousers and a green and brown camouflage jacket over a white polo neck. He'd carefully arranged his small ponytail so that it lay over the collar of his jacket.

He nodded at Ng Wai-sun. 'Good morning, Lung Tau.'

'Good morning, Lin Wing-wah,' the old man answered. Thomas noticed how easily his father had slipped back into the role of Dragon Head. It was as if he had never stepped down. 'Come in and sit down.'

When all four of them were seated, equally spaced around the table, Ng Wai-sun said: 'There must be no mistakes today. None at all. I have lost one son to this gweilo, there must be no more deaths.' He spoke in Cantonese, knowing that Dugan was fluent. 'We must continue the search this morning; if we wait until this afternoon then he will have the advantage of surprise. Cheng Yuk-lin, can you relay this to the other triads and ask for their co-operation?'

'I shall, Lung Tau.'

'Mister Dugan has brought us valuable information. We know that the gweilo has been shot and must be receiving medical attention from somebody.'

'We have already checked the hospitals, Father. Today we begin to question the legal and the illegal doctors,' said Thomas Ng.

Ng Wai-sun nodded. 'Good. Again, we must move quickly. I think we must assume that once the gweilo has the ransom he will leave Hong Kong. That brings us to the next problem. If we do not track him down before we are due to hand over the ransom, then we must decide how we handle it. At what point do we try to take him? Do we do as your brother planned to do and try to seize him when the ransom is handed over? Or do we follow him after we have given him the diamonds and we have Sophie back? Or do we simply give him the ransom and assume that he will keep his word?'

'The gweilo did not keep his word last time,' Cheng said slowly. 'We must not trust him on this occasion.'

'I agree,' said Thomas Ng. Dugan did not know whether or not he was supposed to contribute to the discussion, but he nodded in agreement with Cheng and Ng.

'That is also my feeling,' said Ng Wai-sun. 'Do we agree therefore that we try to capture the gweilo and then force him to tell us where he has Sophie?'

They all nodded.

'So be it,' said Ng Wai-sun. 'Lin Wing-wah, you must have our Red Poles prepared. I think it best that we do not involve the other triads in the actual ransom, I think we must keep that firmly under our control. It would be best if we have our men spread around Hong Kong so that we are sure to have some men close to where the handover is due to take place. As soon as we know when and where you must be able to contact our men and get them in position. This time there must be no mistake.'

There was no malice in his face but Lin flinched at the subtle reprimand and he was overwhelmed with shame at having failed Simon Ng. This time there would be no mistake, he swore to himself. He would have the gweilo, or die in the attempt.

'I have a suggestion,' said Dugan, speaking for the first time. Ng Wai-sun raised his eyebrows in surprise, but then smiled and asked him to speak.

'I think you should have a fallback position,' he said. Though they had invited him to sit in on their war council, he was still reluctant to say 'we' while in their company.

'What do you have in mind?' said the Dragon Head.

'Bearing in mind what happened last time, I think you should bug the ransom. Place a transmitter, a homing device of some sort, in the case with the gold and the diamonds. Then if he does get away you still have a chance of following him.'

'But what if he finds it?' asked Thomas Ng.

'We can stitch it into the bottom of the case. The CCB technical department has some ultra-thin models that they've been testing. They use small batteries that are only good for twelve hours or so but they can be detected up to a distance of two miles. You pick up the signal with a radio directional finder, a small hand-held job. It would mean that you could have men in cars close to the handover point and they could follow him at a distance.'

'Could you get us the equipment?' asked the Dragon Head.

'I am sure of it,' said Dugan.

Howells woke up slowly, drifting up through layers of sleep, until he became aware of his arm being kissed, just above the elbow, slowly and sensually, a tongue licking the flesh in small circles, warm and wet. He became aware then of Amy's hair lying across his upper arm, shielding her face as she caressed him with her mouth like a vampire preparing to feed. He became fully awake then and felt the warmth of her lithe body, her legs entwined with his, her shoulder against his hip, her lips on his skin.

'Good morning,' he said sleepily. 'What time is it?'

She looked up and smiled at him, and this time she didn't put her hand up to cover her teeth.

'It's eleven o'clock,' she said.

'That was the sexiest alarm call I've ever had,' he said.

'I don't understand.'

'Kissing me like that. It was a lovely way to wake up.' He was lying on his left side, his left arm up on the pillow, his right lying across his chest. The sling lay on the floor, along with the rest of his clothes that Amy had so carefully taken off him hours before. Her clothes were on top of his, because she'd stripped him naked and kissed him all over his body before undressing and slipping on top of him, careful to keep her weight away from the upper half of his body, so that she wouldn't hurt him. She was a gentle and considerate lover, matching her pace with his, taking him first slowly, then moving faster and harder, timing it so that she came a second or two before him and then slipping off him and lying next to him, exhausted but happy. Happier than she'd been in a long time. Now she was his, body and soul.

'Do you want coffee?' she asked.

'Please,' he said.

She slid out of bed and put on his shirt before going to

the kitchen. Howells sat up and gently rotated his arm, the injured one. It hurt, it hurt like hell, but it was healing, and so long as he didn't put too much strain on it he reckoned he could do without the sling. The painkillers were still in the plastic bottle, untouched.

Amy came back into the bedroom and handed him a mug of coffee. She rubbed her hand through his thick hair as he drank, enjoying the feel of it as it ran through her fingers.

'Do you think I'd look Chinese if I had black hair?' he said.

She laughed. 'Maybe,' she said. 'You want to be Chinese?'

'No. I want to look Chinese. And you can help. I need something to dye my hair black. Can you get some?'

She nodded eagerly. 'I go now. I will buy some food for breakfast as well.' She changed into a clean dress, carrying it from the wardrobe to her lounge and making sure that he couldn't see her, suddenly shy and not knowing why. Then she rushed back to kiss him before going out to shop. Howells watched her go, with a smile.

Dugan got out of the lift at the 26th floor, C Division's territory. He walked along the corridor and passed a stuffed camel, its haughty head almost scraping the ceiling. The camel was one of C Division's little mysteries; nobody knew what it was doing in the corridor, nor how it had got there in the first place. To Dugan's knowledge it had been there for at least four years, possibly longer. He'd asked one of the C inspectors once but he'd just shaken his head mysteriously and tapped the side of his nose. Dugan was damned if he'd give them the satisfaction of asking again.

He found Dave Rogers bent over the innards of some electrical equipment that looked as if it had dropped from a great height and bounced badly.

'Whotchya, Dugan,' he said. They were good friends, drinking partners and both were on the police rugby team.

'Hiya, Dave. Can you do me a favour?'

'Sure.' Rogers was like that, helpful and trusting to a fault. You wanted something, he'd give it you; you needed help, you got it – no questions, no comebacks. He was a lousy copper, but he had a degree in electronics from some Scottish university and after a few years working out of a poxy station in Sha Tin they'd realized that he'd be of more use on the technical side than he was chasing villains.

'You remember those bugs you were telling me about, the slimline model? Can I borrow one for a while?'

'Yeah, little beauties. Expensive little beauties. You won't lose it, will you?' he said.

'Listen to yourself, you daft bastard. How the fuck am I going to lose a homing device?'

Rogers laughed and opened a drawer under his work-bench. 'I suppose you're right,' he said. He took out a small stainless steel cylinder about the size of a lipstick, but slightly thinner. Rogers held it in his palm, turning it from side to side.

'See the black button? Press that and you activate it. Push the one next to it to turn it off.'

'You said the battery lasts for twelve hours?'

'About that.'

'And how do I keep track of it?'

Rogers took out another piece of equipment, this one about the size of a small voltmeter, black plastic with a clear plastic dial at one end. He switched it on, and then pressed the black button on the transmitter. He showed Dugan how the needle on the dial followed the transmitter as he moved it.

'Simple,' said Dugan.

'A child could use it,' agreed Rogers. 'I don't want to pry, Pat, but when are you going to give it me back?'

'Tomorrow. Either that or your money back.'

'You any idea how much that baby costs?' Dugan shook his head. 'About as much as you earn in three months.'

'Fuck me, Dave.'

'If you lose it, I might well do,' warned Rogers, only half joking.

Dugan had taken pains to make sure that no one saw him enter CCB headquarters, and he was equally careful when he left. A Mercedes was waiting for him around the corner.

Howells waited until he was sure Amy had left the building before making the call. The phone was answered by an old Chinese man and he asked to speak to Thomas Ng. When he came to the phone Howells asked him if he had the diamonds and the gold ready.

'It is here,' said Ng.

'You are to take the ransom to the same place as last

time, to the pier at Hebe Haven. At four o'clock this
afternoon. I want there to be just one man there, do you
understand?'

'Yes,' said Ng. 'But you'll forgive me if I don't appear
in person. After what you did to my brother, I'm sure
you'll understand my reluctance.'

Howells snorted. 'I don't care who you have there. My
only concern is the money. And I would have thought that
you would have been more concerned about your niece
than your own skin.'

'Think whatever you like, someone else will be there
with the diamonds.'.

'And the gold.'

'And the gold,' repeated Ng.

'Whoever is there must be alone and unarmed,' said
Howells. 'I want him to be wearing nothing but a pair
of shorts. And the tighter the shorts, the happier I'll be.
I don't want there to be any place where he can conceal
a gun, do you understand?'

'Yes,' said Ng, feeling the anger grow inside. He wasn't
used to being spoken to as a child. He was a giver of
orders, not a taker.

'I will send someone to collect the ransom, a girl.
She knows nothing about your niece or where she is. If
you make any attempt to prevent her leaving with the
diamonds your niece will die. If you attempt to follow her
your niece will die. Only after you allow her to leave Hebe
Haven safely will I call you and tell you where Sophie is.
Do you understand?'

'I understand,' said Ng.

'If anything goes wrong, anything at all, I will kill your
niece and you will never hear from me again.'

The arrogance of the gweilo finally got to Ng, and he snapped. 'And where do you think you can hide, Howells? Where do you think you can fucking well go where we can't get to you? And when we get you the pain we'll inflict on you will be nothing to what you're feeling just now.'

If Howells was surprised that Ng knew his name he gave no sign of it, other than a slight pause before he spoke.

'Just have the diamonds there,' he said coldly and hung up.

Ng could feel his cheeks reddening as he put the phone down, a sick feeling in his stomach. He saw Cheng looking at him and he averted his eyes from the old man's withering stare. Losing his temper had been a mistake. Telling the gweilo how much they knew had been a mistake. Damn the gweilo, damn him for ever.

Dugan arrived back at Golden Dragon Lodge in the Mercedes and walked up the path to the house. Thomas Ng was there to meet him.

'You have it?' he asked. Dugan showed him the homing device and the directional finder. 'It is so small, are you sure it will work?' Ng asked. Dugan gave him a quick demonstration.

'Has he called?' asked Dugan.

Ng nodded. 'He wants the money at Hebe Haven. The pier again.'

'That doesn't sound good, does it? One thing that

diamonds and gold have in common – they're both unharmed by salt water. Makes you think, doesn't it?'

'It gets worse,' said Ng. 'He wants you to wear nothing but shorts. He said that was because he wanted to make sure you weren't armed, but . . .' He left the rest unsaid. Dugan knew what he meant – everything pointed to Howells coming out of the sea. And all the indications were that the ransom, if not Dugan himself, would be taken back into the water.

'So what are you doing about it?' Dugan asked Ng.

'We'll be better prepared this time. I've already arranged for our men to sail a dozen or so boats into Hebe Haven, and we'll have the whole bay sealed off. We've also drafted in four of our members who have scuba-diving experience. They're already on their way; we'll put them on a boat and drop them off a half mile or so from the pier with spare tanks. They're going to sit on the sea bottom until we know where the gweilo is.'

Ng Wai-sun came out of the house behind his son. He greeted Dugan but made no move to shake hands.

'Do not let the obvious blind you to the unexpected, my son,' he said quietly. 'If all the signs are that the gweilo will come from the water, it could be that he plans to come from the road.'

'Yes, Father, we will have our men staking out the pier too. And Patrick has brought his transmitter. I'll have it stitched into the bag.' He took it inside, leaving his father alone with Dugan.

'Thank you for helping us,' said the old man in halting English. 'It cannot be easy for you.'

'I love my sister, and Sophie,' said Dugan, also using English, but speaking very slowly so that Ng Wai-sun could follow him. 'I also liked your son. He was a good husband and father.'

The old man smiled and looked at him with watery eyes. 'Be careful today,' he said.

Chief Inspector Leigh put down the file he had been holding and looked at the photograph of his wife.

'Well now, Glynnis, what are we to make of this?' he said softly. It had long been the Special Branch officer's habit to talk to his wife's picture; it helped him get his thoughts in order, but he was careful to do it only when he was alone in his office. His wife smiled at him as she had done for the past twenty years, when the photograph had been taken, her head tilted to the left, her eyes looking right through him.

The blue file on his desk contained the details of a messy double killing in the Victoria Hotel. Not that murders fell automatically within his brief, but the two barely cold corpses discovered in adjoining rooms were both CIA agents, Jack Edmunds and Rick Feinberg, and dead CIA agents most definitely were of interest. Both had been killed with a knife, both had been attacked from the back by a left-handed man. For more than that he'd have to wait for the coroner's report, and with the way the brain drain was affecting the coroner's office that could take two days.

Robbery appeared not to have been the motive; both men still had their wallets and their passports, and it had none of the hallmarks of a triad execution, just one slash across the throat and not the wicked multiple hackings that the local thugs preferred. There was one item in the report, however, that made the chief inspector sit up and take notice. At about the time of the killings, give or take half an hour, two phone calls had been made from one of the rooms, one to the home of the recently deceased Simon Ng, and one, a few minutes later, to the home of that pillar of the community Ng Wai-sun.

It was almost too much for one day, thought the chief inspector. First two dead Chinese agents in the Hilton, with a third spirited away to China, and two CIA agents dead in the Victoria. And a fifth death, a triad leader found handcuffed to the anchor of a yacht at Hebe Haven. It was like a puzzle, and Leigh took great satisfaction in the knowledge that if the file had dropped on to anyone else's desk except for his, the puzzle would probably never have been solved. But Leigh knew what the link was between the five deaths, knew that the single connecting factor was Patrick Dugan the rugby player, the CCB officer who claimed to be infatuated with a hooker called Petal. Patrick Dugan, whose hooker girlfriend seemed to be an agent working out of Beijing. Patrick Dugan, whose brother-in-law was brutally murdered. Patrick Dugan, whose in-laws were telephoned from the room of a dead CIA agent. Patrick fucking Dugan. Leigh reached for the phone and rang Tomkins.

'Is Dugan about?' he asked.

'No, he rang in earlier. Family problems. His wife's husband has been killed and he said he needs time off to arrange things. Something up?'

'I'm not sure. Have you got his home number?'

Tomkins gave it him, but when Leigh dialled the

number there was no answer. He wasn't surprised; he had a pretty good idea where he'd be. The second call had been to Golden Dragon Lodge, and Leigh would bet a season ticket to Cardiff Arms Park that Dugan would be there.

He called for his car and summoned a sergeant and two armed constables to meet him outside. He checked his own gun carefully before adjusting his holster. 'Times like this when I'm glad I'm not a British bobby, Glynnis,' he said to the picture. There had already been five deaths linked to Mr Dugan and Leigh was going to make damn sure there wasn't a sixth.

There were no problems at all in persuading old Dr Wu to give them the address where he'd treated the injured gweilo, no problems at all. Kenny Suen knocked on the door of the doctor's 14th floor flat in a Mong Kok residential block with two other Red Poles and his wife, a frail sixty-year old, bow-legged and slightly hunched, let them in. Suen did the talking; at twenty-five, he was a couple of years older than his companions, and half a head taller. He was the one carrying a gun, tucked away in a holster under his left armpit, hidden by his American football jacket, but there was no need to show it to the doctor as he sat at his dining-table in stockinged feet, his shirt sleeves rolled up, a glass of hot tea and a racing paper in front of him. He polished his glasses nervously on a white handkerchief as Suen introduced himself and told him what they were after. Wu was just a name on a list, and a long list at that, before Suen knocked on the door, but immediately he saw Wu's reaction he knew that the search was over.

The doctor began trembling slightly, and when Suen described what had happened to the Dragon Head his breathing began to deteriorate into short, rasping gasps. He invited the three visitors to sit at the table and asked them if they would take tea with him. Suen and the two Red Poles accepted his hospitality and waited until the old woman had poured three glasses of tea and retired to the kitchen.

'I had no idea, no idea at all,' muttered Wu, shaking his head and replacing his glasses.

'We understand,' said Suen. He knew there was no need to threaten the doctor. He was not a stupid man, he knew what would happen if he lied or if he did not offer them every assistance. Triad justice was swift and sure. They helped and rewarded those who were loyal, they killed those who betrayed the organization. Wu knew that, there was no need to insult him by stating the obvious. So they took tea and offered him the respect that was due to an elderly doctor. He told them everything, apologizing profusely all the time.

Leigh sat in the back of the black Rover with Sergeant Lam. One of his constables, Chan, was driving while the other, Lau, was in the front passenger seat. The traffic was heavy and they moved at a crawl through Wan Chai, hemmed in by double-decker buses and open-sided trucks laden with goods. A man on a bike, his carrier full of green vegetables, cycled by, making better progress than the Rover. Even with the windows up and the aircon on the car was still filled with the bustling noise of Hong Kong, the rattle of trams, the judder of jackhammers biting into concrete, the shouts of hawkers, the roar of engines, the shrill whistle of a traffic policeman on point duty where a traffic light had stopped working. Wherever you went in Hong Kong there were people, and wherever there were people there was noise.

Leigh sat patiently, knowing there was nothing the driver could do to speed things up. It was one of the first things he'd learnt when he arrived in the colony almost a quarter of a century earlier, that the quickest way to a coronary or a stroke was to waste one's energy fighting Hong Kong. That went for the people, the traffic, and the climate. There was no way any of it could be defeated by confrontation, you had to go with the flow. And you had to learn to relax.

He looked across at his sergeant and pulled a face. 'Wrong time of the day to be driving through Wan Chai,' he said.

'Soon be out of it, sir,' said the man in accented English.

Leigh wondered what would happen to Lam come 1997. If he had any sense he'd be out of it then, out of Special Branch and out of Hong Kong. The Chinese had long memories, bloody long memories, and there would be no favours granted to Special Branch after handover. As early as 1989 they'd stopped Chinese officers having access to delicate or sensitive police files, more for their own protection than anything else.

Part of the reason was that the Government didn't want sensitive information getting into the hands of Beijing, but it also meant that there was less reason to put pressure on any former officers who were still around after 1997. They wouldn't know anything, so hopefully the Chinese would leave them alone. Sure, believe that and you'll believe anything.

The top-ranking Chinese officers had already been promised UK passports or resettlement in other countries where they would be safe, and all had been told that under no circumstances were they to come back after Hong Kong became part of China. They had been promised hefty compensation packages and had been issued with secret identification numbers, memorized and on no account to be written down, which would give them priority in the event of an emergency evacuation, much as the Americans had done with trusted South Vietnamese personnel prior to the pull-out of Saigon. Leigh hoped it wouldn't get as ugly as it had in Vietnam, but he had been working against the Communists for long enough to know that it could still all go very wrong, despite all the promises from Peking. What then would happen to the likes of Sergeant Lam and the two constables? No foreign passports for them, no sanctuary in the UK, or Canada, or Australia. God help them.

They eventually escaped from the traffic jamming up Wan Chai and headed up the Peak, Leigh shielding his eyes from the bright sunlight as they ascended, the car whining up in third gear, the driver's foot flat on the floor. They were about a quarter of a mile from Ng Wai-sun's house when Leigh saw the motorcade heading towards them, eight cars driving together.

'Slow down,' he said to the driver, and he craned his neck as the cars shot past. The third car from the front was a large Mercedes and in the back sat Patrick Dugan, his face set as if in stone, unsmiling and clearly worried. The rest of the vehicles contained enough triad fighters to start a small gang war.

Leigh told his driver to turn around and follow them, but at a distance, and he told the constable in the front passenger seat to radio for reinforcements, three more unmarked cars and officers in plain clothes. Four Speical Branch cops in a black Rover wouldn't be able to tail a triad army for long without being spotted. Leigh didn't feel so calm anymore and his stomach began to churn. He reached down to his side and checked that his gun was there. It was, but its weight provided little comfort.

Grey fumbled for the ringing phone while still asleep, trying to stop the noise before it woke up his wife. He checked the time on the clock radio by the bedside, squinting to make out the red figures because his glasses were out of reach. Half past seven – almost time to get up, anyway. He pressed the receiver to his ear. 'Grey,' he said.

'Grey?' The voice was American.

'Yes,' he said, sitting up in bed. His wife stirred next to him, a shapeless lump hidden under the quilt, snoring loudly.

'It's Hamilton.'

'What's wrong?' asked Grey. If the CIA man was

ringing at this time of the morning it wasn't a social call, and good news would have waited until a more civilized hour.

'Everything,' said Hamilton, and it sounded to Grey as if he was talking between clenched teeth. 'Two of my best men are dead.'

'Howells?'

'Of course it was Howells. I've just heard from Langley that my agents, Feinberg and Edmunds, have been found dead in Hong Kong. In their hotel rooms. Their throats had been cut.'

'Good God!'

'I don't think God had anything to do with it,' said Hamilton.

'I don't know what to say,' said Grey.

'There's something else. The girl who tried to kill Howells before, the Chinese girl?'

'What about her?'

'Her name is Hua-fan, yes?'

Grey frowned. He hadn't told Hamilton her name, or even the fact that the assassin was a girl. 'Yes. She's one of their best.'

'So I gather. She also killed one of my agents in Beijing two years ago during a Presidential visit. We thought it was natural causes, but our technical boys reckon that the same stuff was used to kill him that the girl tried to use on Howells in Hong Kong.' Grey said nothing, but he closed his eyes and cursed silently. 'We don't know why he was killed, but it's quite possible that he was on the track of your agent. And that it was your agent, your so-called goldmine, who got Hua-fan to kill him. Does that sound possible to you?'

'I don't know, I really don't know. But yes, it is possible. But I didn't know, I swear to God I didn't know.'

'Whether you knew or not makes no difference. Look, Grey, all bets are off. Feinberg and Edmunds were acting unofficially – I don't think it'll be traced back to me, though it could get a bit too close for comfort. But you are in deep shit. Howells is still alive and I'd think he's going to be pissed at you. And if he gets caught he's bound to tell everything. But that's not my problem, Grey. You and I never spoke, do you get my drift?'

'I understand.'

'I'm going to do everything I can to protect my own back, Grey, and I suggest you do the same. But if you so much as whisper my name . . .' He left the threat unfinished. The line went dead.

'Who was it?' murmured Grey's wife from the depths of the quilt.

'Nobody,' said Grey. 'Nothing for you to worry about.'

The traffic heading towards the tunnel seemed surprisingly heavy, especially as rush hour was still an hour or so away. Dugan sat in the back of the big Merc feeling a bit exposed wearing his too-tight shorts. Ng had scoured the house for a pair that would fit, but the only pair that came close to accommodating Dugan's expanding waistline were still an inch or so too tight and he couldn't get the zip closed up to the top. He sat looking down at his legs, scarred and mottled from too many bad tackles. At his feet was the leather attaché case containing gold and diamonds worth something like US$275,000. Dugan was very conscious of the fact that it would take him more than ten years to earn that much. The triad had raised it with one phone call. It didn't seem fair, but Dugan had long ago learned that the meek inherited nothing, certainly not the earth. He was wearing a red and black cotton T-shirt, but that would have to come off when they got to Hebe Haven. High fashion it wasn't.

Thomas Ng was sitting next to him, immaculate in a sharp grey suit and white shirt and a red tie, the sort that would allow him to dominate breakfast meetings. In the front seat, next to a driver in a chauffeur's cap, was the old Dragon Head, who had insisted on coming along. Thomas Ng had protested, but Ng Wai-sun had been adamant and that was the end of it.

Dugan had made it clear that when the car dropped him at Hebe Haven it should drive well away from the area; it was far too conspicuous to hang around. Lin Wing-wah would be responsible for tailing the girl until she handed the ransom over to the gweilo, and he would be in a battered old off-white delivery van with Franc Tse and Ricky Lam. They had taken the directional finder and had gone ahead of the motorcade so that they could be in position before Dugan arrived. The car moved slowly along and Dugan rubbed his hands together anxiously. Despite the cold air blasting from the aircon he was sweating heavily.

Ng noticed Dugan's discomfort. 'Don't worry, our men will be all around,' he said. 'There will be four under the water around the pier and we'll have half a dozen small boats close by. There'll be three men in the van up close and they're all armed, and they'll be in radio contact with the rest of us. Nothing can go wrong.'

Dugan nodded, but he didn't feel any more secure.

'You know what your biggest problem will be?' asked Ng.

'What?'

'Not getting arrested for indecent exposure in those shorts,' Ng laughed.

Dugan forced a smile. The entrance to the tunnel came into view and they could see what was holding up the traffic. A lorry had run into a taxi on the approach road and both drivers had got out to wait until the police arrived. They each stood by their own vehicles refusing to look at each other. It was a matter of face, neither wanting to admit they were in the wrong, neither wanting to be the first to pull over to the side and allow the cars behind to pass. They just stood and waited, and to hell with the rest of the world. Eventually the Merc passed the taxi and Dugan looked across. There was no damage to be seen, other than a slight denting of the taxi's rear bumper.

'Face,' laughed Ng. 'The strength and the weakness of the Chinese.'

That sounded great coming from a Chinese, thought Dugan, albeit one with an American passport.

Once the accident was behind them the Merc picked up speed and a few minutes later they were Kowloon-side, heading for Hebe Haven. One by one cars left the motorcade, parking on the approach roads leading to the bay, effectively sealing off the area. By the time they were travelling along the Clearwater Bay Road there were just two cars left accompanying the Merc.

Dugan looked at his watch. Half an hour to go before

the deadline. His mouth felt dry and uncomfortable and swallowing was difficult. He wanted something to drink but didn't want to ask Ng. Face, thought Dugan ruefully, didn't only apply to the Chinese.

Leigh's car kept close to the motorcade until he heard over the radio that an unmarked Special Branch car had Ng in sight. They dropped back then and let the undercover boys do the work. Two elderly Toyotas and a Nissan took it in turns to take the lead, rotating regularly so that the triads wouldn't spot them. Eventually the call came over the radio that the Merc had pulled into Hebe Haven, by the sea. Leigh told them all to drive past and asked his own driver to pull into a side road.

He thought for a while, and then radioed the men in the Nissan, telling them to get into the Toyotas. The driver of the Nissan could then go back to the pier and check it out. One of the Toyotas was to wait about a mile away from Hebe Haven along Hiram's Highway, while the men in the other were to take the high ground and find a vantage point where they could look down on to Ng and the triads.

'Have you got any binoculars?' he asked.

'Negative,' was the reply. Leigh just shrugged; there was no point in getting upset, it was his own fault for not reminding them before setting out. If they could think for themselves they wouldn't be constables.

He waited patiently until one of the men radioed back to say he was in position, overlooking the pier at Hebe Haven. At the same time the Nissan turned into the road and drove down to the line of parking spaces. Both reported that Ng's Mercedes had gone, leaving behind a slightly overweight gweilo wearing nothing but a pair of shorts and carrying a leather case.

'Dugan,' said Leigh under his breath. He told his men to stay where they were. He looked at his watch. Ten to four. None of this made any sense. What the hell was Dugan up to?

Lin Wing-wah was standing on the same spot he had occupied only days earlier when Simon Ng had been waiting at the water's edge. He studied Dugan through his binoculars and sneered at the way the gweilo's stomach bulged over the top of his shorts. He could see that he was sweating profusely under the afternoon sun and already his skin was beginning to redden. Dugan paced up and down slowly, his eyes scanning the horizon.

Lin watched a dirty red Nissan drive towards the pier and park. He checked out the driver. A young Chinese, scruffily dressed, reading a newspaper and eating a chocolate bar. Lin turned the binoculars back on Dugan. As he watched he took a toothpick from his shirt pocket and began to work at the gaps between his teeth. Down below, Tse and Lam were parked at the roadside with the detector. He called Ng on his walkie-talkie: 'Nothing so far,' he said. He called up the teams out in the bay one by one. All had nothing to report. He stopped picking his teeth and looked at his watch. Two minutes to four.

Dugan wiped his forehead with the back of his hand and it came away soaking wet. There was no shade and he could feel the hot sun burning his shoulders. He wasn't used to the sun; he disliked sunbathing and rarely went to the beach, and while his legs and arms were tanned from playing rugby, his upper body rarely saw daylight and was white and pasty, and his skin would burn easily.

He swung the bag by his side, hoping that the homing device was working. He'd switched it on before getting out of Ng's Mercedes, but there was no way of telling if the detector was picking it up. He walked to the top of the steps leading down to the water at the side of the pier and looked down. He wondered what he would do if Howells appeared and demanded that he go underwater with him. Would he go? Dugan didn't know how he would react; he had to get Sophie back, but the thought of how his brother-in-law had died under the waves made his blood run cold.

He heard a car and turned around to see a taxi driving down the road. He shielded his eyes from the sun to see better. There was a girl sitting in the back.

Lin watched the taxi turn off Hiram's Highway and head down towards the bollards where Dugan stood. He spat out the toothpick and called Ng. 'There's a taxi stopping near the pier. Only one girl in it. She's getting out and going over to Dugan.'

'Any sign of the gweilo?' asked Ng.

'No, no. She's on her own – they are talking – she's trying to take the bag from him but he's keeping it away from her. They're arguing. What is the prick playing at? Now they're both walking back to the taxi. This is it.'

Over the radio came Ng's voice, calmly telling him to go back to the van. Lin jogged down the hill, the binoculars banging against his chest. Tse was in the driver's seat and he switched the engine on when he saw Lin. Ricky Lam stayed crouched in the back. 'Here you are, Elder Brother,' he said, and handed over the receiver. Lin thanked him and told Tse to stay on the alert; they had no way of knowing which way the taxi would go when it left with the ransom.

The girl who got out of the taxi and walked towards Dugan was casually dressed in faded denims and she wore wrap-around sunglasses. She had a small canvas satchel, the strap across her shoulder. She kept her hand on the top as if frightened someone would steal her purse. The girl looked nervous, moving her head left and right as she walked, but there was no doubt it was Dugan she was heading for. She stopped a few feet away from him.

'I've come for the diamonds,' she said, and held out her hand.

'Where is Sophie?' Dugan asked.

The girl frowned. 'I don't know anybody called

Sophie.' She stepped forward and tried to take the case from him.

'No,' said Dugan sharply, holding it out of her reach. 'No you don't. Not till I know Sophie is all right.'

The girl seemed totally confused; she moved back, and then stepped forward again, but Dugan refused to let her take the attaché case. The girl looked over her shoulder at the taxi, and then at Dugan.

'You must give me the case,' she insisted. 'You must.'

'Where is Howells?'

'Please,' she said, and he could sense the urgency in her voice. 'Give me the case.'

'Take me to Howells first,' insisted Dugan. 'No Howells, no diamonds.'

The girl began biting her lip and her hands were shaking. She put both hands on top of her canvas bag and gripped it tightly. Dugan wondered if she had a gun. There was enough room.

'Come with me,' she said eventually, and walked back to the taxi. Dugan followed her, sweat trickling down his back.

The plainclothes constable in the Nissan watched over the top of his newspaper as Dugan got into the cab, but made no move to use his radio. He knew that one of his colleagues would already be relaying the information to Chief Inspector Leigh. He waited until the taxi had pulled away before starting his car, and slowly followed them up the road. The taxi indicated left and headed for Tsim Sha Tsui. So did the Nissan.

'They're coming this way,' said Ng. He told Hui Ying-chuen to start driving back towards Tsim Sha Tsui, so that they could keep ahead of the taxi. Hui had practically begged to be allowed to drive, even though Ng Wai-sun had told him it meant handling the Mercedes and its automatic transmission. Hui said he would put up with it. Lin had said the trace was working perfectly so all the triad cars were able to keep their distance until the girl handed over the diamonds to the gweilo.

'Something wrong?' asked his father, twisting his body round in the front seat.

'Dugan was arguing with the girl and refused to hand over the case. He got into the taxi with the girl.'

'Perhaps he wanted to check that Sophie was unharmed before handing it over.'

'That's probably it,' agreed Ng. 'I hope he doesn't get in the way. He is, when all is said and done, still a policeman.'

The taxi driver hadn't waited for the girl to speak; as soon as Dugan closed the door he drove off, turning left on to the main road. He was wearing grubby white woollen gloves with the fingers and thumbs cut off, a black jacket with the collar turned up and a flat cap, the sort that gamekeepers wear when out shooting rabbits. He didn't bother asking for directions so he obviously knew where he was going. The girl leant forward to speak to him, but as she did the driver cleared his throat noisily and accelerated, throwing her back into the seat. She looked as if she was about to burst into tears.

'He wouldn't give me the bag,' she whimpered.

Dugan thought she was talking to him. 'I won't give it to you until you tell me where Sophie is,' he said in Cantonese.

'Speak English,' snapped the taxi driver. 'Who the fuck are you?'

Dugan sat stunned, looking from the back of the driver's head to the girl and to the driver again, trying to work out what was happening. The driver turned round to look at Dugan, the eyes hidden by black sunglasses. With the glasses and hat it was hard to tell what nationality he was, but the accent was one hundred per cent English. 'I won't ask again,' the man said and turned back to concentrate on the road, accelerating out of a curve.

'Dugan. Pat Dugan.'

'The brother-in-law,' said Howells. 'I should have guessed.'

'I'm Sophie's uncle,' said Dugan. He lifted the bag up. 'And you're not getting this until I know she's safe.'

'If you do as you're told she'll be fine.'

'I know what you did to her father.' Dugan was conscious that Howells was speaking very quickly, obviously so that the girl wouldn't be able to follow the conversation. Few Cantonese could keep up with English at speed, especially when native speakers dropped into slang.

'You don't know why I did it. You don't know what you're talking about.' He fumbled in the pocket of his jacket and pulled out a small plastic bottle containing six white tablets which he tossed at Dugan. 'I want you to take three of those.'

'Do you think I'm stupid?'

'I'm starting to wonder, Dugan. Look, if I wanted to put you out of your misery I'd just stick something sharp between your ribs.' He pulled the handle of a knife from the inside of his jacket, just enough to show Dugan that he was serious. 'Look at the label on the side; they came from a doctor, they're not poison.'

'So what are they?'

'They're sedatives, they'll slow you down. I'm not going to hurt you, and I'm not going to hurt the girl. I just want to get away from Hong Kong, and for that I need the stones. What I don't want is to have to fight you. Take the tablets and I'll feel a whole lot easier. And as soon as I know I'm in the clear I'll tell you where the girl is.'

Dugan unscrewed the top of the bottle and picked out three of the tablets. He put one in his mouth and swallowed but his throat was so dry it stuck there until he tried again. He felt like throwing up.

'All of them, Dugan.'

He swallowed the other two with difficulty. He waited anxiously for something to happen, but there was no dizziness, no numbness.

Amy watched as he took the tablets, a frown on her face as she tried to work out what Geoff Howells was up to and why he was giving Dr Wu's medicine to the big, sweating gweilo.

'Can you see them?' asked Leigh.

His car was stuck behind a labouring double-decker bus that ground its gears as it assaulted the hill. Behind them a green Mitsubishi played chicken with their rear bumper.

'No, sir. And at this speed he's going to be leaving us far behind.'

I know that, thought Leigh. He didn't say so, the man was only trying to help. He'd ordered the Nissan to hang back in case they recognized it, so the two Toyotas were taking it in turns to tail the taxi. He radioed his men and was told that they could see it, and that they were some two miles away from the crawling bus. 'Damn this bus,' he cursed under his breath. 'Damn this bus and damn Patrick Dugan.'

Thomas Ng's Mercedes was about as far in front of the taxi as Leigh was behind it. He was talking on his walkie-talkie to Lin, checking that the Hung Kwan official hadn't lost Dugan or the diamonds. He hadn't. One of the Red Poles broke in on the radio to say that there was a carload of uniformed police on the road to Tsim Sha Tsui, heading their way.

'Where are they?' asked Ng.

'Stuck behind a China Motor Bus. We're right behind the police.'

'Keep an eye on them. It's probably a coincidence.'

'Something wrong?' asked his father.

'There are police on the road, but they're some way behind us. I don't think it's a problem.'

'And still no sign of the gweilo?'

'No. Just the girl and Dugan. But the gweilo can't be far away.'

Dugan rested his head against the window. He was starting to feel drowsy and the vibrations made him want to retch – or maybe it was the effect of the tablets on his empty stomach. He opened his eyes wide and shook his head from side to side. He felt like he normally did after drinking six or seven pints of San Miguel. He heard Amy talking to Howells, but it seemed as if he was listening down a long tube that distorted her voice.

'What's happening, Geoff?' she asked. She was leaning over the back of the seat, her arms folded under her chin.

'Don't worry, Amy, it will be all right.'

'Who is he? And why won't he give us the diamonds? You said they would give them to us so we can sell them?'

'We can, Amy. And we will. And then we can both leave Hong Kong.'

She smiled, pleased that he'd said 'we', pleased that he intended to take her with him. She wanted to kiss him, but at the speed he was driving she couldn't risk distracting him. They were racing down Argyle Street, past the grey squarish building that housed the Kowloon Regional

Police HQ. Amy felt a twinge of anxiety, knowing that the building was packed with police and that she was breaking the law, though in exactly what way she wasn't sure.

'Who is Sophie?' she asked.

'A friend of ours,' lied Howells without a second thought. 'He's worried about her, that's all.'

'A girlfriend?'

'No, just a friend.' Over his shoulder he called to Dugan. 'Let her check the stuff, Dugan.'

Dugan did as he was told, not sure if he could resist if he wanted to. He picked up the bag and handed it to Amy. She unzipped it and gasped when she saw the small gold ingots.

'Wah!' she exclaimed. 'So much gold!'

'The diamonds, check the diamonds, Amy.'

She took the small pouch out of the attaché case which she placed on her knees while she poured the stones out carefully, almost reverently, into the palm of her delicate hand. They glittered and shone in the sunlight, and she pushed her sunglasses up on the top of her head while she admired them, open-mouthed.

'They are beautiful,' she said softly. Howells took a quick look over his shoulder as he drove.

'Pick two of the biggest and give them to me.'

She selected two and handed them to him. Howells studied them as best he could with one hand on the wheel.

'They're real all right,' said Dugan. 'I wouldn't let them take any risks with Sophie's life.' Howells believed him. They looked genuine enough.

'I haven't hurt her, Dugan, but I'm quite prepared to. You are going to have to be one hundred per cent honest with me because if I don't get away then she stays locked up where she is. She'll starve to death, Dugan, and take it from me that's not a pleasant way to die. Now tell me, is there a trace on this stuff?'

Dugan closed his eyes and rubbed his forehead. He wanted to sleep, he wanted to lie down in a big, comfortable feather bed. With Petal.

'What?' asked Howells sharply.

Dugan realized he must have spoken her name out loud. He opened his eyes again and looked at the back of Howells' head. He couldn't take the chance of lying; if Howells scrutinized the attaché case he'd soon find the homing device. 'Yes,' he said.

'I'd have been surprised if there wasn't. Amy, put the diamonds back in the pouch and give it to me.' They were driving through a high-rise residential area, blocks and blocks of flats, balconies covered with potted plants and washing, many shielded with ornate metal grilles that bulged outwards as if to proclaim dominance over as much space as possible, even if it was just empty air.

She did as she was told, taking great pains not to drop any. The taxi stopped at a set of traffic lights and she kept her hands low so that the people in the next car couldn't see what she was doing. She gave the pouch to Howells and he put it on the seat next to his leg, then he handed her the two diamonds over his shoulder.

'Keep them,' he said. 'I'll get them made into earrings for you.' She didn't understand so he squeezed his left ear with his fingers. 'Earrings,' he repeated slowly. 'For you.'

Amy protested, but not too vociferously, and then she wrapped them in a paper tissue and slipped the small parcel into her jacket pocket.

The traffic was heavier now as Howells drove through a built-up area; more high-rise housing and a growing number of shops, so he had to concentrate on driving, switching from lane to lane, looking for the gaps and the hold-ups, knowing that the triads wouldn't be too far behind him. They went up a flyover and Howells saw the airport to his left. With a screaming and a roaring a 747 swooped low on its final approach, its landing gear down, so close that Howells ducked involuntarily.

'Do you know where we are, Amy?' he asked.

She nodded. 'Coming up to Yau Ma Tei. This is Waterloo Road. Then it's Jordan and then Tsim Sha Tsui and the harbour.'

'Is there an MTR station close by?'

'Yes, after the YMCA. Not far.'

'OK, listen, Amy. I'm going to drop you there and I want you to go down and catch the first train you see. The men I told you about are after us and I want you to be safe. I'll get away from them and when I've sold the diamonds I'll go back to your flat.'

'I want to stay with you, Geoff,' she said, beginning to tremble.

'I want you to be safe,' he repeated. 'I don't want to have to worry about you. I want you to take the gold and keep it safe for me. It's very important. Will you do it for me?'

Amy nodded, but even Dugan could see that she wasn't convinced.

'I need you,' said Howells quietly, and that seemed to make her mind up for her. She clasped the attaché case to her chest and pointed at the junction ahead.

'There, MTR station.'

'OK,' said Howells. 'Now, when I stop I want you to run, and don't stop running until you're on the train.'

'I will,' she promised. 'Be careful.' She leant forward and kissed him on the cheek, and spoke to him hurriedly in Chinese. Howells slammed on the brakes and the car behind him sounded its horn as he screeched to a halt. Amy flung the door open and ran for the entrance without looking back. Howells reached over the back of the seat with his left arm and closed the door behind her before driving off. Dugan had his head slumped back and he was breathing heavily, almost snoring. As Howells accelerated again Dugan's head rolled forward on to his chest.

'What did she say?' asked Howells.

'She said she loved you. You're a bastard. You know they'll catch her.' He slurred his words as he spoke.

Howells grinned. 'Maybe,' he said. 'But it's rush hour so she's got a fighting chance. And she'll keep them occupied. While they're following her, I'll dump the taxi and disappear into the next MTR station. Then you can go and collect your niece.'

Howells thought it best not to mention the fact that just feet behind Dugan, lying in the boot, was the body of the owner of the taxi, his neck broken. He hadn't told Amy, either. He'd gone out on his own and returned with the taxi, telling her that he'd paid a few thousand dollars to borrow it. He'd considered just knocking the man out but he couldn't take the chance of him coming round and calling the police, so he'd told the driver to take him up a deserted sidestreet behind a foul-smelling dyeing plant and he'd grabbed his head and twisted, feeling the neck crack and enjoying it.

'She's out of the taxi,' Lin screamed into his walkie-talkie.

'What about Dugan?' said Ng, his voice crackling in Lin's ear.

'He's still there. Heading your way.'

'Where are you?'

'Yau Ma Tei MTR. At the junction of Waterloo Road and Nathan Road. She's in the station.'

'With the case?'

'Yes, she's . . .'

Ng didn't let him finish. 'Go after her. Don't lose her. We'll pick up Dugan.'

Lin threw the door open and jumped on to the pavement, the detector in his hand. Lam scrambled over the seat and ran after him. 'Come on,' Lin screamed at Tse. 'Leave the fucking van where it is.' Tse did as he was told and as the three stormed into the entrance of the MTR station the drivers blocked in behind the van began to sound their horns impatiently.

The three triads stood outside the door to Amy's flat. Suen had his gun in his hand, cocked and ready, while the two Red Poles had large knives by their sides. Suen knocked on the door and listened carefully for footsteps. Nothing. He knocked again. Still nothing.

'Break it down,' he said to Ah-wong, the bigger of the two heavies. Ah-wong stepped back and kicked the door hard, just below the lock. It gave a little and there was the sound of tearing wood, then he kicked it again and it sagged on its hinges. It caved in on the third go and the three men spilled into the small flat. It took only a few seconds to see that there was no one there, but they spent some time searching it thoroughly for a clue as to where the girl and the gweilo had gone.

Ah-wong found a blood-stained pillow case at the bottom of a black plastic bag of rubbish in the kitchen and he brought it triumphantly into the lounge. Suen went through the bathroom cabinets. He found a half-empty bottle of hair dye there and he noticed that the sink was stained black in places, though someone had tried to clean it with a cloth. There was a pair of scissors in the cabinet, too, and the drain in the sink was clogged with bits of hair.

'Look at this,' called Ah-wong. 'Look what I've found.' Suen went back into the lounge and Ah-wong waved the blood-stained material under his nose. 'We're in the right place,' he said to Suen.

'But at the wrong time,' replied Suen.

'Let's get back to the car,' said Ah-wong, heading for the door.

'Fuck your mother,' said Suen. 'We phone Ng first.'

One by one Ng called up the cars that had been following behind Lin, told them the girl had taken the diamonds down the MTR station and gave them instructions to get there as soon as possible and follow her down. While he was talking to the Red Poles the car phone rang. Ng Wai-sun leant over and picked it up. It was Kenny Suen.

'We found where the gweilo was hanging out,' said Suen, obviously pleased with himself. 'He was with a girl from one of the Wan Chai bars. She'd let him stay in her flat while Dr Wu treated him. They're not there now.'

'The girl, what does she look like?' the old man said.

'Medium height, high cheekbones, she looks a bit Shanghainese. Dr Wu says she's about twenty-four years old.'

'We have seen her,' said Ng Wai-sun. 'We are pursuing her now.'

'Oh,' said Suen, sounding disappointed.

'She collected the ransom for the gweilo,' Ng Wai-sun explained. 'But we have not seen the gweilo yet. We think she is on the way to see him.'

'Did she look twenty-four?' asked Suen. 'I mean, could she be older?'

'No, she was a young girl, dressed more like a teenager than anything else. Why?'

'There was hair dye all over the sink, it was a real mess. I thought maybe she had dyed her hair. But if it wasn't her . . .'

'Then it must be the gweilo,' said the old man, finishing the sentence for him. 'You have done well. Very well indeed.'

He replaced the phone and waved his finger to attract his son's attention. Ng took the walkie-talkie away from his ear to listen. 'The gweilo has dyed his hair,' said Ng Wai-sun softly. 'Black.'

'The driver!' hissed Ng. 'And he's behind us.'

'How far?' asked his father.

'Less than half a mile.' He told Hui to stop the Merc, no matter how much it annoyed the drivers behind. 'Put the hazard warning lights on, let them think we've broken down. He'll be here within two minutes.' He asked his father to open the glove compartment and the old man reached in and handed over the handgun that he found there. Ng took out the clip and then banged it home again, checking that the safety catch was off. He caught his father looking at the gun with a worried frown. 'It will be all right,' he said. 'As far as we know he is not armed. But we can take no chances. The man is a killer.'

'Be careful,' said Ng Wai-sun. 'I have already lost one son.'

Ng began calling up his triad soldiers, ordering Lin and his team, and one other group of Red Poles who had already arrived at the MTR station, to keep after the girl. The rest were to catch up with the taxi as soon as possible. But from the sound of it the gweilo would reach the Mercedes at least a minute or so before any of the Red Poles would be close enough to make a difference.

Amy was fumbling for her MTR card as she ran into the station, and it was in her hand by the time she got to the barrier. She slotted the plastic card home and then collected it from the return slot at the top of the ticket machine before pushing the barrier and running for the down escalator. As always the Hong Kong commuters seemed reluctant to walk down the moving metal staircase and Amy had to push and shove her way down, all the time repeating '*m goy, m goy*', but even so she was cursed and glared at.

It seemed to take a lifetime before she reached the platforms. The one to the left was for trains heading for Tsim Sha Tsui and on to Central, that on the right was for those going out to the New Territories. She felt a warm wind on her right cheek and knew that that signified a train coming. She ran to the edge of the platform and stood there, her legs shaking and her chest heaving, panting for breath. She looked behind her at the escalator, but all she saw were lines of impassive faces, nobody seemed to be chasing her. She heard the roar of the train and it sped out of the blackness of the tunnel and into the light. It growled to a stop and the doors gushed open, disgorging its passengers. Amy forced her way through before the last of them had got off and leant against the steel pole in the middle of the carriage. From where she stood she could see right along the line of connected carriages, two hundred metres or more. People flooded in, diving to get a place on the long, polished metal seats or a space to the side of the door so they could be first off at their station. The people of Hong Kong treated their mass transit system the same way that they lived their lives – the strong got the best places and got where they were going, the weak were left behind, standing on the platform when the doors closed. That's what it would be like come 1997, Amy thought. Those that pushed and fought would get out, those apathetic or incapable would be swamped by the one billion Chinese on the mainland. Amy knew that alone she would never be able to escape, but with Geoff Howells, maybe, just maybe, she would find a way out. He was strong, he was confident, and he had money. And she was helping him. In return, she knew, he would help her. But first she had to get away from the men who were chasing her.

She saw them then, at the top of the escalator. She heard the driver warning passengers to stand clear of the doors, first in Chinese and then in mumbling English, as three hefty men began shouting and pushing people out of their way as they scrambled down. One of them, a big man with bulging forearms and a small pigtail, almost made it, using his sheer bulk to force his way down. He leapt on to the platform but at the same moment the doors hissed shut. He ran forward and tried to claw his way into the carriage next to where Amy was standing but he was too late; the train pulled away, slowly at first and then picking up speed until the advertisements on the walls blurred. The man with the pigtail screamed and kicked out at the moving train and then Amy was in the black tunnel, heading for the New Territories with the attaché case clasped to her chest.

Behind her on the platform, Lin watched helplessly as the needle on his receiver slammed over to one side. 'Fuck your mother, bitch,' he cursed, and put the walkie-talkie to his mouth.

'They've lost her,' Ng said to his father. 'She got on to the MTR. I've told Lin to catch the next train and go after her, but she could be anywhere by now.' He looked out of the back window at the queue of cars waiting to pass.

'Any sign of the gweilo?' said Ng Wai-sun.

'Not yet,' said Ng. 'But he is not far behind. Hui Ying-chuen?' The elderly driver stopped waving at the cars behind to overtake and turned round. 'When I give you the word I want you to put the car in reverse and ram the taxi.'

Hui's face fell and he looked as if he was going to protest. In all the years he had been driving for the Ng family he had never, ever, been involved in an accident. It was a record he was proud of, but he did not argue. He just nodded and thanked the gods that he was in the Mercedes and not his beloved Daimler.

Ng told his father to make sure he was well strapped in and that his head was against the headrest. 'The Mercedes is much bigger and heavier than the taxi, we'll barely feel it,' he said. 'But better to be on the safe side. Once we've stopped them I'll hold the gweilo until our Red Poles get here.'

He held the gun down near the floor of the car, his finger clear of the trigger so that it wouldn't go off accidentally when the cars collided. The rest of the traffic was now streaming past the parked Mercedes and its flashing hazard warning lights.

Chief Inspector Leigh was becoming more confused by the minute. His men in the Toyota closest to Dugan's taxi had told him how it had stopped near Yau Mat Tei MTR station and how the girl had run into it carrying his case. The Special Branch man had continued after the taxi, but the officer in the Nissan following behind had called in to say that a group of cars had converged on the station and that more than a dozen triads had gone haring down after her.

Dugan was now heading towards Tsim Sha Tsui, alone. Leigh tapped Chan on the shoulder and told his constable to get a move on, to get closer to the taxi so they wouldn't lose him in the rush-hour traffic.

'Get up behind the Toyota,' he ordered. 'Keep that between us and Dugan's taxi and he won't see us.'

Chan put his foot down and began overtaking, thumping the horn as a makeshift siren. He had little trouble making headway and they soon left the green Mitsubishi behind. The Red Poles knew they couldn't follow the Rover without attracting attention to themselves, especially when the police sped past the airport and drove through two sets of red lights before reaching the neon signs of Yau Ma Tei. They drove past the MTR station and the cluster of badly parked cars outside it. The lights at Nathan Road were against them, but Chan edged the car through, carefully because it was one of the busiest roads in Hong Kong. Every second car seemed to be a taxi now and Leigh knew they'd have no chance of spotting the one Dugan was in, but they soon caught up with the Toyota and edged up behind it. The traffic had slowed down to a virtual crawl.

'Where is he?' radioed Leigh.

'Three cars ahead of us,' came the reply from the Toyota.

'What's the hold up?'

'I don't know. Some sort of accident up the road.'

At least it meant they wouldn't lose Dugan, thought Leigh. At last something was going his way.

'I see them,' said Ng. 'Third car behind us. Be ready, Hui Ying-chuen. Put it into reverse now, and as soon as the two cars have passed us, hit him. Hard. Are you all right, Father?'

His father grunted and settled back into the seat, his head pressed against the headrest. Ng lay down, his face against the leather upholstery.

Howells was beginning to get impatient. The traffic hardly seemed to be moving in his lane. Eventually he saw the source of the trouble; a large Mercedes had broken down and in typical Hong Kong fashion the driver had made no move to get it off the road, the passengers just sitting there waiting for someone to come and sort it out for them. During his short time in Hong Kong Howells had seen several accidents but had yet to see a Hong Kong Chinese with his head under the bonnet or pushing his vehicle off the road.

He could see the entrance to Jordan MTR station up ahead and considered leaving the taxi where it was. Then the car ahead indicated it wanted to pass and Howells did the same, but the vehicles in the right-hand lane were reluctant to let them in, deliberately keeping close, bumper to bumper, the drivers keeping their eyes fixed straight ahead. The car in front managed to squeeze in between a delivery van and a minibus and Howells tried to do the same. The reversing lights of the Mercedes came on, shining whitely next to the flashing yellow lights.

'What the fuck's he playing at?' asked Howells.

Dugan leant forward to see what was happening, and as he did the big car leapt backwards, rushing towards them. Dugan yelled and groggily threw himself down on the seat. Howells grabbed at the door handle but realized he wouldn't have time to open it so he dropped across the front seats, the handbrake handle biting into his stomach as he pulled his legs up out of the footwell, his knees up against his chest.

The Merc slammed into the front of the taxi, smashing the lights and crunching the bumper, forcing the air from Howells' chest. The thin metal of the Toyota cab screamed and buckled, the mass of the bigger German car seeming to meet no resistance. Water hissed and spurted from the radiator and still the Mercedes reversed, pushing the taxi back as Ng's driver kept his foot to the floor. There was a second bang then as the rear of the taxi crashed into the car behind it, and only then did the Merc stop. Water flooded around the front of the taxi and bits of metal and glass tinkled to the ground. The distorted car groaned and shuddered like a dying animal. Dugan pushed himself up and looked groggily around, his reactions dulled by the combination of the sedatives and the crash.

He could see startled faces watching from the pavement: an old woman with grey, crinkly hair and her front teeth missing; a young couple in matching T-shirts and stone-washed denims; a man in a grey pinstripe suit with a portable telephone in his hand, a bare-chested teenager carrying a refill for a distilled water dispenser on his shoulder. All were staring at the accident with wide eyes. Dugan smelt petrol and suddenly had a vision of himself and Howells engulfed in flames. With a mounting sense of panic he clawed at the left-hand door, but it had warped in the crash and wouldn't move. He shuffled along to the opposite side of the cab, his legs wobbling as he moved, his arms numb. Howells groaned in the front seat and then pulled himself up, using the steering wheel for leverage. He kicked open his door and fell into the road. He got to his feet to see Ng get out of the Mercedes, gun in hand.

'Stay where you are,' Ng shouted, pointing the gun at Howells' chest, holding it steady with both hands. He was eight feet at most away from Howells, and he knew he wouldn't miss.

'There's been an accident, sir,' said Constable Chan. 'The taxi's hit the car in front.'

Leigh stuck his head out of the window in time to see a well-dressed Chinese man threatening to shoot the taxi driver while Dugan staggered out of the cab into the road wearing nothing but a pair of shorts. The plainclothes officers in the Toyota pulled out their guns, one stepping on to the pavement and steadying his gun arm on the roof of the car, another crouched down behind the driver's door. Leigh's sergeant got out of the Rover and also drew his gun, telling his constables to do the same. Leigh left his in his holster. They had more than enough firepower. The pedestrians began screaming then and running for cover –

the Hong Kong police had a reputation for firing first and asking questions later.

'Drop the gun,' Leigh yelled. 'Drop the gun or we'll fire.'

The surprise showed on Ng's face and his aim wavered. Howells turned to see who was shouting and he too looked stunned to see so many police only yards away. Dugan was the last to turn and he almost lost his balance when he saw Leigh, his stomach wobbling over the top of his shorts. He looked like a drunken bull seal, thought Leigh. Dugan opened his mouth to speak and then shut it again. He was dribbling and he wiped his chin with the back of his hand.

'Drop the gun. This is your last warning,' shouted Leigh.

Howells stepped to the right, getting Dugan in between himself and the police and then stepped up behind him, drawing the kitchen knife from inside his jacket. He grabbed Dugan with his weak right arm and held the blade close to Dugan's neck with his left. 'Don't move, Dugan, or I swear to God I'll kill you,' he whispered.

Howells dragged him over to the taxi. The boot had sprung open in the crash and through half-focused eyes Dugan could see the body of a man inside, his head at an unnatural angle and a wet patch on the front of his jeans. There was no room to get through and Howells didn't want to go any nearer to the cops so he pulled Dugan back, trying to head towards the MTR station. That brought him nearer to Ng, which made him feel equally uncomfortable. Dugan started to complain that the blade was cutting him and Howells told him to shut the fuck up.

Leigh's men looked at him for guidance. In the chief inspector's mind there was no confusion. The Chinese with the gun could kill a lot of people, and the only person the taxi driver was going to hurt was Patrick Dugan. In Leigh's present frame of mind that was no great disaster.

'Keep your guns on Ng,' he ordered.

To Ng he shouted a final warning. Realizing he stood no chance against so many police, Ng threw his pistol to the ground and raised his hands.

Howells saw the gun clatter to the tarmac. He knew he had only seconds to act. Police reinforcements were sure to arrive soon, and he was already outgunned. The roads were too busy so there was no point in trying to hijack a car, and besides, he wasn't sure how effective a hostage Dugan would be. He looked as if he was about to pass out and he wouldn't be much of a shield if he slumped to the ground. His best chance, his only chance, was to get to the MTR and try to do as Amy had done and disappear in the crowds. The Special Branch officer standing by the Rover shouted that he was to drop the knife. He pushed Dugan into the road and dived for the gun, dropping the knife as he moved. Dugan fell to his knees as Howells got the gun in his right hand and then rolled over, howling as he jolted his injured shoulder. He felt the wound open and bleed but he kept on moving, coming up into a crouch, aiming the gun at the police and firing off two quick shots, the recoil burning into his shoulder. The bullets hit Chan in the neck and he fell back, blood streaming down his chest.

'Shoot him,' shouted Leigh, though his men needed no encouragement.

Howells leapt on to the roof of the taxi and rolled over it, dropping on to the pavement in a smooth movement. The crowds of pedestrians scattered like startled sparrows finding a cat in their midst. Sergeant Lam stepped away from the car and aimed at Howells' chest. As Howells raised his gun Dugan staggered to his feet, bellowed and threw himself across the bonnet of the car. He managed to tackle Howells around the waist with his flailing arms and brought him down to the ground. Howells slammed the butt of the gun against Dugan's head but he barely felt it. His grip slackened a little and Howells wriggled away, but Dugan grabbed his left leg and hung on for all he was worth, his eyes closed and his mouth wide open.

'Let go, you stupid bastard!' yelled Howells, but Dugan seemed not to hear him. All Dugan could hear ringing in his ears were the cheers of the crowds at the Rugby Sevens and he hung on for all he was worth, waiting for the ref to blow his whistle.

Howells pointed the gun at Dugan's head and started to pull the trigger, but as he did Sergeant Lam fired. The bullet ripped into Howells' chest and knocked him backwards, the gun falling from his hand. Dugan's eyes opened at the sound of the gun-shot. He drifted in and out of consciousness but kept hold of the leg and crawled slowly up the body as it lay on the pavement. There was a hole the size of a fist in Howells' chest, filling with blood, bubbling in time to his breathing. His eyes were open but seemed not to see Dugan's face.

Ng came running over and shoved Dugan away. He began going through Howells' pockets until he found the bag of diamonds. He waved them triumphantly over Howells' head until Dugan pushed him away angrily. He knelt down beside Howells, conscious that the police were running up and that he didn't have much time. Neither did Howells, that was clear enough.

'The girl,' mumbled Dugan, his voice thick and the words slurring. 'Where is Sophie?' Howells seemed to become aware of Dugan for the first time and he almost smiled. 'Where is the girl?' Dugan asked again, not wanting to beg but knowing that he would if necessary. There was no need. Howells told him and then died.

Dugan sat back heavily on to the road, shaking his head to try to clear it. He felt elated at knowing that Sophie was safe, but he felt cheated too. He had no idea who the killer was, or why he'd wreaked such havoc. Maybe when his head was clearer he'd be able to think and put it all in perspective, but all he wanted to do was to sleep, to curl up in the road and close his eyes and dream of Petal.

Leigh came up behind him and put his hand on Dugan's shoulder. 'Great tackle, Dugan.' Dugan shook his hand away. He got unsteadily to his feet and slowly and carefully went over to see Ng Wai-sun.

The two labradors jumped up and down with excitement as Grey opened the back door to let them out into the night for their last run before turning in. His wife had banned them from the bedroom but had grudgingly allowed them to sleep in the kitchen. While the two dogs did whatever they had to do Grey poked the embers of the fire and looked at the flames. When he was a child he'd spent hours gazing into the fire, making stories out of the twisting shapes; knights fighting dragons, angels against demons. Now when he looked into the fire he saw nothing, just burning coals.

He heard the dogs barking, probably fighting over a long-forgotten bone. Stupid animals – their sole aim in life appeared to be to have a full stomach. Whenever he forgot to put the lid on the dustbin they'd be in, rooting for scraps as if they were strays rather than well-fed pampered pedigrees. Dogs never seemed to appreciate when they were well-off. Neither did people.

Grey's career was finished, he knew that. Less than a week after the abortive attempt to kill Howells, his agent in Beijing had disappeared. There was no trial, no charges, no announcement in the *People's Daily*. With Hong Kong jittery enough in the run up to 1997, the Chinese had no wish to bruise what fragile confidence remained. Already 60,000 of Hong Kong's brightest and most able were flooding out of the colony each year, emigrating to Australia, Canada and the United States. They had no wish to make it worse. A show trial of a British agent, even one who was Chinese, would do more harm than good. He had just vanished, and so had his family. The assassin who had survived would have told them where the order to kill Howells had come from, a trail that led straight to Grey's man. He would have been tortured, Grey was certain of that, and he was equally sure that his man would have told them everything. So what next? There were, in Grey's mind, two possibilities. They would send a man to eliminate him, as an act of revenge. Or they would release the information to the British authorities. Either way Grey was finished. He had decided not to wait and had handed in his resignation, blaming ill-health. It had not yet been accepted, and there would be a long period of debriefing and arranging to hand over to his successor, but his mind was made up. Maybe that would satisfy them. He poked the fire savagely.

One of the dogs had stopped barking, probably the victor chewing on the bone. He straightened his back and put the poker back on its stand. He'd have to get them in. His wife would give him a hard time when he eventually slipped into their bed if he allowed them to bark too long.

He walked through the kitchen, opened the door and whistled quietly. He heard Lady barking but she remained in the darkness, by the sound of it somewhere near the orchard.

'Lady,' he called, but she continued to bark.

He switched on the outside light, set into the wall to the left of the door, but its hundred-watt bulb only illuminated a dozen steps and most of the lawn was still pitch-black. If anything, the light only made the night seem darker. He pulled on his Wellington boots, grunting with the exertion, and then wrapped a red wool scarf around his neck.

He called for the dogs again but they ignored him. One of his collection of walking sticks, a Victorian example with a brass knob on the end in the shape of a swan's head, was leaning against the door jamb. He picked it up and stepped outside.

He stood on the edge of the pool of light and whistled, swinging the stick in his right hand as if it was a golf club. Lady had stopped barking. 'Damn dogs,' he muttered under his breath and headed down towards the orchard. He thought he could hear Lady whining but when he stopped and listened carefully there was only silence.

There was a lump in the lawn to the right of one of the trees, like a pile of wet soil. He headed towards it, the stick held in front of him. He knelt down and reached to touch it. It was warm and wet and when he took his hand away and held it close to his face he could see it was blood. It was Tramp, his brown Labrador. Dead.

He heard a noise, a rustling or an intake of breath, he didn't know which, but he turned round in a crouch to see a man bent down holding Lady's collar with one hand, the other clamped around her muzzle.

'What are you doing with my dog?' Grey asked. The man took his hand from around Lady's mouth and immediately she started barking, her eyes wide and panicking. The man was Chinese, Grey realized with a start. He pulled a wicked-looking curved knife from behind his back. He smiled, and before Grey realized what was happening he drew it across Lady's throat with a jerk and the dog's legs collapsed from under her. She lay on the grass, chest heaving as blood gushed from her neck, her eyes fixed on Grey.

'No!' cried Grey, stepping forward and raising his stick. 'No, no, no.'

Something hit him on the back of the right leg and then on the left; sharp lines of pain burned behind each knee and he felt blood pour down his calves. The strength went out of his legs and he fell on his knees, the pain making him scream. The sound had barely escaped from his mouth when a hand grabbed his chin from behind and stifled his shrieks. He reached up to hit the man with the stick but a man stepped from the side, another Chinese, a cleaver in his raised hand. He brought it down hard, slashing at Grey's forearm. Grey saw in horror the way it sank a good two inches into the arm and then the wave of pain hit him and he almost passed out. The stick dropped from his nerveless fingers. His legs had gone numb below the knees, but he could feel strips of pain and knew that he'd been hacked with knives, probably cutting his tendons. He was going to die. Oh God, he was going to die. He tried to use his left arm to pull the hand away from his mouth and then he felt rather than saw another blow and that arm too fell uselessly by his side. He started to shake as if he had a fever; convulsions racked his body.

The man who had killed Lady stepped over the dead dog and stood before him, the knife pointing at his nose. I'm going to die, was the one thought in Grey's mind. The man stepped forward and the hand round Grey's mouth twisted his head up sharply so that he was looking towards the sky. The man fumbled in his pocket and pulled out a piece of tattered paper. He looked at it for a few seconds before speaking. They were being well paid for this job, and although it had been ordered by somebody more than eight thousand miles away the instructions had been quite specific and the man was determined to carry them out to the letter. The woman who was paying the money, paying in taels of gold, would never know whether or not the instructions had been obeyed. But the man would, and he had professional pride. It had taken more than a week to track down the man called Grey, the man who worked in a building called Century House. Soon the job would be over and he could return to Hong Kong.

Slowly, carefully enunciating every word, he repeated the message on the piece of paper, written there in capital letters. 'This is for Geoff Howells,' he said, pushing his face up close to Grey's. 'For Geoff Howells. Do you understand?'

Grey could feel his life's blood pouring down his arms and pooling around his legs. He felt elated, light-headed, almost happy, as the blood drained from his brain. He smiled. The hand moved away from his mouth and his chin flopped down, saliva dripping from his lips.

The man standing in front of him repeated the words. 'Do you understand?'

Grey tried to speak, tried to say that yes, he understood, that he was sorry he couldn't speak, but his mouth wouldn't work. He felt like giggling. He nodded and groaned, trying to form the words.

The man in front of him looked at his two companions, standing behind Grey, blood-wet hatchets in their hands, to check that they had seen the reaction. They nodded silently and the man smiled. As one they raised their hatchets in the air and brought them down one at a time into Grey's neck.

The flushing water was off again, the handle swinging uselessly in Dugan's hand. 'Piss, fuck and shit,' he cursed.

'Fuck this flat, fuck this place, fuck this whole fucking town.' He didn't feel any better getting it out of his system. He slammed down the lid. There was no problem with the water supply to the shower, thank God, so he pissed gratefully down the plughole and watched the yellow liquid swirl in circles and disappear.

He was in no hurry to get to the office; he'd lost all enthusiasm for the job since Petal had gone. Worse, he'd lost enthusiasm for everything. He'd been out drinking a few times but took no pleasure in it, and he'd spent the best part of the three weeks since she'd gone sitting in his flat watching videos. Not the television, there was precious little point in that, what with the sweeping cuts that took out all but the most innocuous sex and violence and interspersed what was left with adverts every ten minutes or so. He took out three videos a night from one of the Circle K convenience stores and watched them.

He towelled himself dry and put on his grey suit. He couldn't be bothered cooking breakfast, or even making himself coffee. There seemed to be no point – no point at all.

He locked the door behind him and paced up and down the corridor as he waited for one of the three lifts to haul itself up to his floor. On the way down he leant his forehead against the gap between the two doors and sighed deeply. What the hell was he going to do? He'd sent off at least a dozen applications for jobs in the past fortnight, everything from a credit agency in Singapore to an estate agents in Tsim Sha Tsui, but nothing had come of it. An unemployment rate of less than two per cent and he still couldn't get a job. What was wrong with him? 'Oh Petal,' he moaned quietly. 'Where are you?'

He'd never before felt so alone. He didn't even have

Jill to lean on, because she and Sophie had returned to England. Maybe that was the only decent thing to have emerged from the whole sorry episode, the fact that their parents had flown over and re-established contact. They'd whisked Jill and Sophie out of the triad compound into the Mandarin Hotel and flown with them back to the UK, all thoughts of the past forgotten. Jill had been too exhausted to argue, and although Thomas Ng had told her that she was welcome to stay, Dugan reckoned she'd done the right thing. Sophie's prospects would be better in England, too. Hong Kong over the next few years would be no place for children. The tension was building by the week and police riot squads were being trained with tear gas and rubber bullets in the New Territories.

The doors hissed open and he stepped out into the ground floor lobby, turning his face to the large wall-mounted fan and letting the cold breeze play over his damp skin.

Just before the reception desk where a blue-uniformed security guard slept with his head down on his folded arms were the racks of letter boxes, one per flat. He unlocked his. Inside was his electricity bill and a circular from a credit card company. And a postcard, a view of the Oriental Hotel in Bangkok, the best hotel in the world, on the banks of the Chao Phraya River. He'd never stayed there, but he'd had a drink in the Author's Wing once. His name and address were written on the back in a handwriting he didn't recognize. But to the left of the address was something that made his heart leap. No words. Just a flower, carelessly drawn.

The Chinaman

For Nuala

They made an odd couple as they walked together through the store, the girl and the old woman. The girl was beautiful, quite, quite beautiful. Her sleek black hair hung dead straight down to the middle of her back and it rippled like an oily tide as she wandered through the racks of dresses and blouses. She was tall and slim and wore tight green cord trousers and cowboy boots and a brown leather bomber jacket with the collar turned up. She moved like a model, smoothly and controlled, as if used to being watched. The men that followed her with their eyes had no way of knowing where she came from other than that she was Oriental. She could have been Thai or Chinese or Korean but whatever she was, she was beautiful and that was all they cared about. Her cheekbones were high and well defined and her skin was the colour of milky tea and her eyes were wide and oval and she had a mouth that seemed to be in a perpetual pout. Every now and then something would catch her eye and she would take a dress or a blouse off its rack and hold it up and then shrug, not satisfied, before replacing it. Her hands were long and elegant and the nails were carefully painted with deep red varnish.

By the girl's side walked a gnarled old woman, a head shorter and an age older. Her face was wrinkled and pockmarked like chamois leather that had been left for too long in the sun. Her hair was grey and dull and cropped close to her head and her eyes were blank and uninterested in what was going on around her. When the girl asked her opinion on an item of clothing she would barely look at it before shaking her head and then she'd drop her gaze and concentrate on the floor. She wore a thick cloth coat and a faded scarf and she kept her hands thrust deep into her pockets despite the warmth of the store.

It was a Saturday in January and the weather outside was bitterly cold, piles of dirty slush squashed up against the kerb and wisps of white vapour feathering from the mouths of passers-by. The girl looked over the top of a rack of imitation fur coats topped with a sign that promised thirty per cent off, and through the streaked window. She shivered and didn't know why. She'd lived in London for as long as she could remember, and unlike her mother she was well used to the British climate. It was as if someone had walked over her grave, or the grave of her ancestors.

She took one of the coats and held it against herself. A middle-aged man in a fawn trench coat waiting outside the changing rooms with a carrier bag full of packages looked at her and smiled and nodded his approval. She ignored him and studied the coat. The old woman snorted and walked off. The girl looked at the price tag but even with the sale discount she realised she couldn't afford it.

She looked through the large glass window again at the bustling crowds fighting to get into the department store across the road. She wanted to join them and go hunting for bargains but she could see that the old woman was tired and impatient to go home and they had an hour's travelling ahead of them. She put the coat back on the rack.

A large black and red motorcycle threaded its way through the traffic and parked on the double yellow lines in front of the main entrance to the store. It was brand new and gleaming apart from the tyres which were crusted with ice. On the back carrier box was the name of a courier firm. She watched the rider dismount like a cowboy getting off a horse. He was dressed in black leather with a white wrap-around helmet and a tinted visor. There was a walkie-talkie in a leather case hanging from a belt around his waist and a black receiver clipped to his left shoulder. The rider switched on his hazard warning lights and the amber flashing was reflected on the wet road. He looked up and down the pavement as if checking for traffic wardens and then turned his back on the bike and crossed the road towards the boutique. He stepped to one side to let a trio of giggling schoolgirls leave the shop and then came in. As he passed the girl he looked at her, up and down, and she turned to watch him go, his leathers squeaking with every step. The rider was empty handed so the girl

2

assumed he was there to collect something, but he continued to move through the shoppers, passed the pay counter and then he pushed open the doors at the other side of the shop and went out into the street.

The girl frowned and turned back to the window. The bike's lights were still flashing. Her frown deepened and at that moment the twenty-five pounds of Semtex explosive in the back carrier box exploded in a flash of blinding white light, blowing in the window and striking her with thousands of glass daggers. At the last moment she tried to turn towards her mother, to shield her, but they died together in the hail of glass.

The Press Association news desk received the call as the first ambulance arrived at the department store, blue light flashing and siren whining. The reporter who took the call later told the police that the voice was Irish and had given a codeword that the police identified as genuine; the tip-off was not a hoax. The voice was that of a man, he couldn't tell if he was young or old, and the caller said that a bomb had just gone off in Knightsbridge and that the Provisional Irish Republican Army claimed responsibility for it. The reporter hadn't recorded the call, he was new on the job and no one had told him that he was supposed to. The line went dead and he took his notebook over to the news editor who told him to check with the police that there had indeed been an explosion and three minutes later the story went out over the wires as a flash – IRA BOMB EXPLODES OUTSIDE LONDON STORE – AT LEAST FIVE DEAD.

By the time it appeared on the screen of the news editor of the *Sunday World* he'd already had a phone call from a member of the public keen to earn a tip-off fee. He'd assigned two reporters to start phoning the police and their Sinn Fein contacts and was trying to track down their Belfast stringers.

It was 5.30 p.m., the crossing over point when the day shift began to drift off to the pub and the night reporters were arriving. The picture desk had sent two freelances and a staffer to the scene, but Knightsbridge was at least half an hour's drive away from the paper's Docklands offices.

More information was trickling over the wires on PA and Reuters and the death toll kept climbing with each snatch of copy.

"Jesus, now they're saying twelve dead," said Jon Simpson, the news editor. Behind him stood the chief sub and the editor, reading over his shoulder.

"Splash?" said the chief sub, knowing the answer would be yes. The front page lead at the afternoon conference had been a sixties pop star's drug problem.

"We'll have to pull our fingers out if we're going to make the first edition," said the editor. "We'll take the whole of page one, two and three, let me see the pics first. Hold the MP story until next week and hack back the food safety feature. Hang on, no, drop it altogether. And we'll save the splash until next week as well, it's exclusive." The chief sub scurried back to his terminal to redraw his page plans, shouting to the picture editor to send over everything he had.

"You've got two hours until the first edition, Jon. Get everybody on it." The editor wandered over to the picture desk while Simpson picked up the phone.

"Where's Woody?" Simpson yelled at his deputy who was busy scrolling through the PA wire.

"Where do you think?" he shouted back, raising his eyebrows.

"Drunken pig," said Simpson and rang the King's Head, a short stagger away from the office.

As the phone trilled behind the bar, Ian Wood was downing his second double Bells and trying to look down the front of the barmaid's blouse. She saw what he was up to and flicked her towel at him and laughed. "Don't let Sandy catch you doing that," she scolded and he grinned.

"Your husband's too good a guv'nor to go slapping the customers around," he said, finishing his whisky.

"Another?" she said as she picked up the phone. She listened and then mouthed silently "Are you in?"

"Who's asking?" he mouthed back.

4

"The office," she replied, and he realised they looked like a couple of goldfish gasping for breath. He nodded and took the phone off her. She picked his glass up and refilled it.

"Woody, are you on for a double shift?" asked Simpson.

Woody looked at the double measure of whisky in his glass and licked his lips but hesitated for only a second before he told Simpson he'd do it. Woody was a freelance and he needed the money. If he'd been staff he'd have told the news editor where to get off, but it had been a long time since anyone had given Ian Wood a staff job.

"What's up?" he asked.

"IRA bomb. A big one. Knightsbridge."

"Christ. How many dead?"

"They're saying twelve now, no make that thirteen, but they're still counting. Get out there and get the colour. Link up with the monkeys while you're there, they'll need their captions written." Woody heard Simpson call out for the names of the photographers. "Dave Wilkins is the staffer, find him," he said.

"I'm on my way," said Woody and hung up.

He took the glass off the bar and swallowed it down in one.

"You off, Woody?" said the barmaid, surprised.

"Duty calls, darling," he said. "Can you cash me a cheque?"

"Fifty?" she asked.

"Fifty is magic. You're a life-saver. If ever that husband of yours . . ."

She waved him away and counted out the notes as Woody handed over the cheque.

"See you later," he said, and walked down the dimly lit corridor and out of the pub door into the street. He turned right and walked the short distance to The Highway and hailed a cab heading towards the City.

The driver looked over his shoulder when Woody told him where he wanted to go. "We'll never get near the place, mate," he said. "There's a bomb gone off."

"Yeah I know," said Woody. "I'm a reporter."

"OK," said the cabbie and sped off down the road. "Which paper d'yer work for then?"

"*Sunday World*," replied Woody.

"Yeah?" said the cabbie. "What happened? Page Three girl killed was she?" His deep-throated laughter echoed around the cab.

They hit unmoving traffic long before they reached Knightsbridge and though the cabbie tried to find a way through the side-streets they were soon helplessly locked in.

"Best I can do," said the driver apologetically, his professional pride wounded.

"No sweat," said Woody, getting out. He handed a ten-pound note through the window. "I'll walk from here. Call it a tenner and give me a receipt, please."

"Clamping down on expenses, are they?"

"Yeah, tell me about it."

The cabbie signed a receipt and handed it to Woody. Then as an afterthought he ripped off a few blank receipts from his pad. "Here," he said, "fill these in yourself."

"You're a prince," said Woody, and put them gratefully into his raincoat pocket.

He began to jog slowly towards the sound of sirens, his feet slapping on the wet pavement and his raincoat flapping behind him. Despite the cold he soon worked up a sweat. Ian Wood was not a fit man. He was slightly overweight but that wasn't the problem, he was out of condition because he never took any exercise, hadn't since his schooldays.

The police had cordoned off the area around the store and a burly sergeant blocked his way when he tried to duck under the barrier. He fished out his yellow plastic Metropolitan Police Press card and after the copper had scrutinised it he was waved through.

It was a scene from hell. Wrecked cars were strewn across the road, still smoking and hissing. There was an assortment of emergency vehicles, all with their doors open, radios crackling and lights flashing. There were two fire engines though their hoses were still in place, unused. There had obviously been a number of small fires burning but the firemen had used extinguishers to put them out. There were half a dozen ambulances, and as Woody walked towards the police top brass one of them pulled away and its siren kicked into life.

Something squelched under Woody's shoe and he looked down. He was standing on a hand. It was a small girl's hand, the skin white and unlined, the nails bitten to the quick. The hand was attached to a forearm but that was all, it ended in a ragged, bloody mess at the point where there should have been an elbow. Woody's stomach heaved and he pulled his foot away with a jerk, a look of horror on his face.

He backed away and bumped into a policeman wearing dark-blue overalls, black Wellington boots and thick, black rubber gloves that covered most of his arms. The policeman picked up the dismembered arm and dropped it into a plastic bag he was carrying. As he straightened up, Woody saw that the man's face was covered with a white surgical mask and then he saw the blonde wavy hair and realised it wasn't a man at all, but a woman in her twenties. There were tears streaming down her face. She turned away from him, walked a few steps and bent down again. This time she picked up a shoe with a shattered bone sticking out of a green sock. Woody shuddered. There were dozens of policemen dressed in the same overalls and following the girl's grisly example. Woody realised with a jolt why the body count hadn't been finalised. It was at least an hour since the bomb had gone off and they were still picking up the pieces. Ambulancemen were ferrying bodies on stretchers at the run, some of the victims moaning or screaming, others still, their faces covered with blankets. The policemen in their blood-spotted overalls worked at a slower pace, knowing that it was more important to be thorough than fast. They were not in the business of saving lives, simply collecting evidence.

Woody looked around, surveying the damage. All the windows of the store had been blown in, as had those in the shops opposite, and the stonework was pitted and blackened. Lying half on and half off the pavement was the twisted frame of a motorcycle, the back a mass of scorched and melted metal. It was being examined by two middle-aged men in white overalls.

Shocked shoppers and staff were still filing out of the store, urged on by uniformed constables in yellow reflective jackets, as an inspector shouted through a megaphone that there could be another bomb in the vicinity and would the crowds please keep back. Woody knew that he was just saying that to keep the ghouls away. Two bombs would have meant double the risk for the bombers planting the devices, and the IRA never bothered using two devices against civilian targets, only against the security forces in Northern Ireland. Besides, if there was any chance of a second device they'd keep the ambulancemen back while the Bomb Disposal Squad gave the place a thorough going over.

There were a handful of sniffer dogs and their handlers checking the street, and Woody could see more dogs inside the store, noses down and tails wagging, happy to be working. One of the dogs in the street, a long-haired Retriever, lunged forward and seized something in its jaws. Its handler yelled and kicked its flanks and the dog dropped whatever it had been holding. It was an arm. The handler yanked his dog away, cursing. The dog cowered, all the time keeping its eyes on the prize.

Woody went over to the Chief Superintendent and two inspectors who were surrounded by a pack of reporters and photographers. He recognised many of the faces and he knew that all the tabloids and heavies would be represented. If not, some news editor would be getting his backside soundly kicked. The older hacks were taking shorthand notes in small notebooks while the younger ones thrust mini tape-recorders in front of the police. Behind the pack were two television crews trying in vain to get a clear shot. He heard the click-whirr of a motor-drive and he turned to see Dave Wilkins aiming his Nikon at a torso lying in the gutter.

"They won't use it," Woody told him. "Too gory."

"So?" said the photographer.

Woody listened to the Chief Superintendent explaining what he thought had happened. A bomb in the back of a motorcycle, no warning, the streets crowded and the stores packed. No idea yet how many had been killed. Fifteen at least. Yes, almost certainly linked to the recent wave of London bombings, four so far. Correction, five including this one. Yes, the IRA had claimed responsibility.

"And that, gentlemen," he said with the wave of a gloved

hand, "is all that I can tell you right now. Would you please all move back behind the barriers and let my men get on with their work. We'll be having a full press conference at the Yard later tonight." He politely pushed his way through the journalists, and they moved aside to let him go, knowing that the officer had said all he was going to say. There was no point in antagonising him. Besides, they all had their own police contacts who would be a hell of a lot more forthcoming.

Woody went over to the shops facing the department store, noting down the names on the signs. His feet crunched on broken glass and he stepped to one side to let two ambulancemen with a stretcher out of a boutique. They were carrying a girl, her leather jacket and green cords shredded and ripped and dripping with blood. He knew she was a girl because of her long black hair. There was nothing left of her face, just strips of flesh hanging off white bone. Woody felt his stomach heave again. He'd been at accident scenes before, far too many to remember, but he'd never seen such carnage. The area reeked of death, of blood and burning and scorched meat. He fought to keep his emotions under control, knowing that he had work to do. It was harder for the reporters he thought bitterly. The monkeys had it easy. They looked at everything through the camera lens and that insulated them from the reality of it. But reporters had to be there and experience it before they could write about it, they had to open themselves to the horror, the grief and the pain. Sometimes it was almost too much to bear. Almost.

He stood by one of the ambulances and got some snatched quotes from a couple of harassed stretcher-bearers and then he followed a woman in a fur coat that he'd seen leaving the store, ducked under the barrier and caught up with her. Her eyewitness account was harrowing and she had no qualms about giving her name and address. Her eyes were glassy and Woody knew she was in a state of shock and he held her arm gently as he spoke to her and then gestured over at Wilkins, standing to one side so that he could get a head-and-shoulders shot of her.

"Got all you want?" Woody asked the photographer.

"Yeah," said Wilkins. "I'll head back and leave the free-lancers to get the rest. You coming?"

"No, I'll ring the story in, it'll save time. I'll see you back there."

Woody half-heartedly looked for a call box, but knew that he stood little chance in Knightsbridge. He walked to a small Italian bistro and went inside.

"Can I use the phone?" he asked a waiter. The waiter began to protest in fractured English so Woody took out his wallet and gave him ten pounds. The protests evaporated and he was soon through to the office and dictating to a copytaker straight from his notebook. Twenty-five paragraphs, and he knew it was good stuff. When he'd finished he asked the copytaker to transfer him to the news desk and he checked that everything was OK with Simpson.

"Got it here, Woody," he said. "Great read."

"OK, I'm going back to see what else I can get. I'll call you." He hung up before Simpson could order him back to base. On the way out he got a receipt from the waiter.

There was a pub down the road and Woody gratefully walked up to the bar and ordered a double Bells. It was only when the whisky slopped around the tumbler that he realised how badly his hands were shaking.

The intercom buzzed, catching them all by surprise, even though they were waiting for him. There were three of them in the flat, drinking tea and watching television. They were casually dressed – baggy pullovers, faded jeans and grubby training shoes – and looked like sociology students stuck with nothing to do between lectures. One of the men was smoking and on the floor beside his easy chair was a circular crystal ashtray overflowing with cigarette butts. He leant over and stubbed out the one in his hand, pushed himself up and walked into the hall. On the wall by the door was a telephone with a small black and white television screen; he pressed a square plastic button and it flickered into life.

"Welcome back," he said to the figure waiting down below and pressed a second button, the one that opened the entrance door four floors below. As he waited for him to come up in the lift he went back into the lounge. "It's him," he said, but they knew it would be because no one else knew they were there and if they did they wouldn't be coming in through the front door but through the window with stun grenades and machine guns.

There was an American comedy show on the television and canned laughter filled the room. Through the floor-to-ceiling sliding windows at the end of the lounge the man saw a tug struggle along the Thames, hauling an ungainly barge behind it.

He went back into the hall and opened the door as the lift jolted to a halt. The man who stepped out of the lift was in his early twenties, wearing grey flannel trousers and a blue blazer over a white polo neck sweater. He had dark-brown curly hair and black eyes and was grinning widely. "Did you see it?" he asked eagerly, before the other man even had a chance to close the door. He punched the air with his fist. "Did you bloody well see it?"

"Calm down, O'Reilly," said the man who'd let him in.

O'Reilly turned towards him, his cheeks flaring red. "Calm down?" he said. "Christ, man, you should have been there. You should have seen me. It was fan-bloody-tastic." He turned back to look at the television set. "Has it been on yet? How many did we get?"

"Fifteen so far," said the man sitting on the leather Chesterfield directly opposite the pseudo-antique video cabinet on which the television stood. "You did well, O'Reilly." He was the oldest of the group but even he had barely turned thirty. Although he had the broadest Irish accent he had Nordic blond hair and piercing blue eyes and fair skin. His name was also far removed from his Irish origins but Denis Fisher was Belfast-born and he'd killed many times for the Cause. "What about the helmet and the leathers?" he asked O'Reilly.

"In the boot of the car. Just like you said. It was so easy."

"Not easy," said Fisher. "Well planned."

"Whatever," said O'Reilly. "I deserve a drink." He went into the white-and-blue-tiled kitchen and opened the fridge. "Anyone else want anything?" he called, but they all declined. O'Reilly took out a cold can of Carlsberg and opened it as he walked back into the lounge. He pulled one of the wooden chairs out from under the oval dining-table and sat astride it, resting his forearms on its back.

"What next?" he asked, grinning.

"Yes," said the man who'd opened the door and who was now sitting on a flowery print sofa by a tall wooden bookcase. His name was McCormick. "What do we do next?"

Fisher smiled. "You're so bloody impatient," he laughed. He turned to look at the occupant of the chair by the window, the one they called The Bombmaker. "That depends on what MacDermott here comes up with." The Bombmaker grinned.

The comedy show was interrupted for a news flash and a sombre man with movie-star looks reported that sixteen people had died in a bomb explosion and that the Provisional IRA had claimed responsibility. They then cut to a reporter in a white raincoat standing under a streetlamp in Knightsbridge, who said that police now believed that the bomb had been in the back carrier of a motorcycle and that it had been detonated by a timing device.

O'Reilly punched the air again, and The Bombmaker's grin widened.

The police car drove slowly down Clapham Road. Constable Simon Edgington's left hand was aching from the constant gear changing and he cursed the bumper-to-bumper traffic under his breath. It wasn't even worth switching the siren on because there wasn't enough room for the cars and buses to pull to the side.

"It's getting worse," he groaned.

"Sorry?" said his partner, a blonde WPC called Susan Griffin who had joined the Met on the graduate entry scheme. One of the high-flyers, a sergeant had told Edgington, closely followed by a warning not to try anything on because she'd reported the last constable whose hand had accidentally slipped on to her thigh during a hasty gear change.

"The traffic," he said. "We're going to be all night at this rate."

She looked down at the sheaf of papers on her black clipboard. "This is the last one," she said. "Chinese or something. God, I don't think I can pronounce their names. Noog-yen Guan Fong and Noog-yen Coy Trin. Does that sound right?" The names on the sheet were written as Nguyen Xuan Phoung and Nguyen Kieu Trinh.

He laughed. "Sounds like a disease," he said.

She gave him a frosty look. "It's not really a laughing matter is it, Simon?"

Edgington flushed. Griffin was a year younger than him but she acted as if she already had her sergeant's stripes. But his embarrassment came from the fact that he knew she was right, it wasn't the sort of thing to joke about. He wanted to tell her that he was just nervous, that he was trying to relieve the tension that was knotting up his stomach, and that he'd never thought when he signed up three years earlier that he'd have to knock on the doors of complete strangers and tell them that their nearest and dearest had been scattered all over Knightsbridge by a terrorist bomb. He wanted to explain but knew he'd sound like a wimp so he concentrated on driving.

They'd been given three addresses, all south of the river. The first had been a middle-aged couple in Lambeth, a schoolteacher and his wife. Their teenage son had been in the passenger seat of an old Mini that had been fifty feet or so from the motorcycle when the bomb had gone off. Several pieces of wire that had been wrapped around the explosive had burst through the windscreen and torn his face and throat apart. The couple had already seen a report of the bombing on the evening news and before Griffin had spoken the wife's legs had given way and her husband had had to help her to a chair in their cramped kitchen. Edgington had been quite happy to let his partner do the talking, he didn't think that he could have kept his voice steady. He'd joined the police to catch criminals, not to act as some kind of messenger of death. And she'd done it so bloody well, sat them both down, made them cups of sweet tea, phoned their daughter and arranged for her to come round and look after them. She'd sat with them on the sofa until the girl came and then left them to their grief. All the time Edgington had stood by the kitchen door, feeling useless, but Griffin hadn't mentioned it when they got back into the car.

The next call had been at a small flat in Stockwell. No relatives this time, but a boyfriend who burst into tears and hugged the WPC when she told him what had happened. They were going to get married, he'd sobbed. She was pregnant, he said. She held him until the tears stopped and sat him down and asked him if there was anyone she could call, a friend or a relative. Did she suffer, he asked. No, she lied. The sergeant had told them that the girl had died screaming on the pavement with both her legs blown off. "No, she didn't suffer," she said without hesitation.

He wiped his eyes with the back of his hand and she gave him a handkerchief while Edgington telephoned the boy's mother. She said she'd be around in fifteen minutes and Edgington and Griffin decided that he'd be OK on his own until then. They left him hunched over a mug of tea which he clasped tightly between his hands.

"It's coming up on the left," she said.

The traffic crept along and eventually they reached the turning.

"Number 62," she said before he asked.

He drove slowly, counting off the numbers. "Are you sure?" he asked.

She checked the computer print-out on the clipboard and nodded. "That's what it says here."

He stopped the car and they both looked at number 62. It was a Chinese take-away, with a huge window on which were printed gold and black Chinese letters and above it a sign that said "Double Happiness Take-Away". Through the window they could see two customers waiting in front of a chest-high counter.

"That's it," she said, opening her car door. Edgington

caught up with her as she reached the entrance and followed her in.

Behind the counter was an old Oriental man shouting through a serving hatch in a language neither of them could understand. He turned and placed two white plastic carrier bags full of cartons of Chinese food in front of one of the customers and took his money. There was a loud scream from the kitchen and the man stuck his head back through the hatch and shouted and waved his arm.

He came back to the counter and smiled up at Edgington and Griffin.

"What I get you?" he asked. He was a small man, his shoulders barely above the counter. His face was wrinkled but the skin wasn't slack, his cheekbones were clearly defined and there were no loose folds under the chin. It was hard to tell exactly how old he was, he could have been in his forties and had a rough life, or he could have been a well-preserved sixty-year-old. Griffin noticed how sad his eyes were. They were eyes that had seen a lot of suffering, she decided.

"Are you Mr Noog-yen?" she said, and he nodded quickly but corrected her pronunciation, saying his name as "New-yen". The single customer left at the counter stood openly watching and listening to the conversation. Edgington stared at him until the man's gaze faltered and he studied the menu pinned to the wall.

"Is there somewhere we can talk?" Griffin asked the old man.

"I very busy," he replied. "No staff. You come back later, maybe?" There was a thud from the hatch and he went over and picked up another carrier bag. He handed it to the customer. "Come again," he said.

"I'm afraid we have bad news for you," said Griffin. She looked at the clipboard again. God, she thought, how do you pronounce these names? "Mr Nguyen, do you know a Xuan Phoung or Kieu Trinh?" Both names started with Nguyen so she'd guessed that that was the family name and that everything that came after it were their given names.

The man frowned. Another customer came in and stood behind Edgington. Griffin tried pronouncing the names again but still nothing registered so she showed him the computer print-out and pointed to the two names.

He nodded, his eyes wary. "My wife," he said. "And my daughter."

"I'm afraid there has been an accident," said the WPC. "Is there somewhere we can talk?"

The man waved his hands impatiently. "What has happened?" he insisted.

"Mr Nguyen, please, it would be much better for you if we could sit down somewhere."

"No staff," he said. "My wife not in kitchen, so much work to do. What has happened?" He spoke each word carefully, as if stringing a sentence together was an effort, and he had a vaguely American accent. But he seemed to have no trouble in understanding what she was saying.

"Mr Nguyen, your wife and daughter are dead. I'm very sorry."

He looked stunned. His mouth dropped and his hands slid off the counter and down to his sides. He started to say something and then stopped and shook his head. Edgington turned to the customer and found himself apologising, but for the life of him he didn't know why. He felt his cheeks redden.

"Do you understand, Mr Nguyen?" asked Griffin.

"What happened?" said the old man.

"Is there somewhere we can talk?" she asked again. She didn't want to explain about the bomb while she was standing in a Chinese take-away.

"We can go back of shop," he said. He shouted through the hatch and as he opened a white-painted door a balding Oriental with sleeves rolled up around his elbows and a grease-stained apron came barrelling out. He ignored Nguyen and glared at the customer. "What you want?" he barked.

Nguyen led them down a tiled hallway, up a flight of wooden stairs and through a beaded curtain. Beyond was a small room with heavy brocade wallpaper and a faded red patterned carpet. The furniture was dark rosewood, a square table with carved feet and four straight-backed chairs with no cushions. On one wall was a small red and gold shrine in front of which a joss stick was smouldering, filling the air with sickly sweet perfume.

In a corner by a small window was a semi-circular table on which stood a group of framed photographs of Nguyen with an old woman and a young girl. Edgington walked over to the table and studied the pictures as Griffin sat down with the old man. Most of the pictures were of the girl, she was obviously the focus of the family. In the most recent photographs she looked to be in her mid-teens and she was absolutely gorgeous, long black hair and flawless features. She could have been a model. There were pictures of her in a school uniform and even in those she looked sexy. The old woman was obviously her mother, but there was little or no physical resemblance. The girl was tall and straight and the woman was small and stooped. The girl's skin was smooth and fresh and the woman's dark and wrinkled. The girl had eyes that were bright and sparkling while the woman's appeared lifeless. As he studied the photographs he heard Griffin explaining about the bomb. Edgington did the calculations in his head – if she'd had the child when she was twenty she'd be under forty, and even if she'd given birth at thirty the woman couldn't be much older than forty-eight and yet she looked much older. In one of the photographs, the biggest of the collection, the girl was sitting in a chair, her parents behind her. Nguyen was smiling proudly and had a protective hand on her shoulder. They looked more like her grandparents. Something else struck him. There were no pictures of her as a baby or a toddler. In none of the photographs was she any younger than seven or eight. Curious.

"Please," said the old man behind him and Edgington turned round to see him holding out his hands. "Please, the picture."

Edgington took over the big framed photograph and handed it to him. He didn't speak, he didn't know what to say.

The old man cradled the frame in his arms and then hugged it to his chest. There were no tears and he made no sound, but the intensity of his grief was painful to watch.

"Who did this to my family?" he asked eventually.

"The IRA," said Edgington. They were the first words he'd spoken in the room and his voice sounded thick with emotion. He cleared his throat and Griffin looked up, surprised that he'd spoken. "The IRA have claimed responsibility," he said.

"IRA," said Nguyen, saying each letter slowly as if hearing them for the first time. "What is IRA?"

Edgington looked at Griffin and she raised her eyebrows. Was he serious? He sat down next to the old man.

"Terrorists," he said quietly.

"What do they want, these terrorists?"

Edgington was stumped for an answer and he looked helplessly at Griffin. She shook her head, knowing that what the old man needed was sympathy and a sedative, not a political discussion. The man turned to her. "What do they want?" he asked her.

"They want British troops out of Ireland," she said reluctantly.

"How does killing my family do that?" he asked.

She shrugged. "Is there someone I can get to come and take care of you?" she asked. "Do any of your family live nearby?"

"I have no family," he said quietly. "Now I have no family. I am alone. These IRA, will you catch them?"

"Yes," she said, looking him in the eye.

"And will they be punished?"

"Yes," she repeated. Lying was coming easily to her today.

"Good," said the old man. He nodded as if satisfied.

The second edition was coming off the presses when Woody finally got back to the office. He slumped in his chair still wearing his raincoat. He'd spilled something down the front of it and when he dropped his head on his chest he could smell whisky. "What a waste," he mumbled.

The reporter at the desk next to his leant round a potted plant and said: "Simpson is after your arse, Woody." There was more than a hint of sadistic pleasure in his voice as he passed on the bad news. Like Woody he was a freelance and each time a freelance was shafted there was more work to go round for everyone else.

"Thanks," said Woody, determined not to show how worried he was. He needed the work, God he needed the work, and he'd been banned from most of the London papers over the last twelve months or so. He was finding it harder and harder to get through a shift without drinking, and that didn't go down well in the new high-tech world of modern newspapers. In the old days, the days when reporters looked like reporters and they worked on typewriters that sounded like typewriters, then the Street was full of characters – men and women who could take their drink and whose work was better for it, and who would be fondly forgiven if they were found late in the evening, flat on their backs under their desks. The news editors then would call for the office car and have them sent home. If they were really badly behaved then perhaps a just punishment would be handed out, a nasty door-stepping job in the pouring rain or a night-time road accident in the middle of nowhere, character-building rather than malicious. Not these days. These days most of the journalists seemed to be straight out of university with weak chins, earnest eyes and stockbroker voices. Few of them could even manage shorthand, Woody thought bitterly, and it was a common sight in the newsroom to see them plugged into tape-recorders transcribing their tapes and breathing through their mouths. Woody remembered the purgatory he'd gone through to get his own spidery shorthand up to the required one hundred words per minute, and the rest of the shit he'd had to go through before he got to Fleet Street. Now the papers were all staffed by kids, kids who if you managed to drag them bodily into a bar would drink nothing stronger than bubbly water. Ian Wood was forty-two years old but at that moment he felt he was going on eighty.

"Woody!" screamed a voice from the far end of the room. "Where the hell have you been?"

The question was rhetorical, Woody realised, because it was swiftly followed by a torrent of abuse. He heaved himself out of the chair and ambled over to the source of the noise, hoping that if he got close it'd cut down the decibels and reduce the embarrassment factor. Simpson was sitting back in his reclining chair with his expensively shod feet on the desk. The news editor spent twice as much on a pair of shoes as the paper paid its freelances for an eight-hour shift. They were well polished and gleamed under the overhead fluorescent lights and Woody looked down involuntarily at his own soaking wet, brown Hush Puppies. Woody began to explain but Simpson cut him off and told him that he should have been back hours ago and that he was to get the hell out of the building and not to bother coming back, that he'd got pissed on the job once too often and that there would be no more shifts for him on the paper. Woody could feel that he was being watched by everyone in the newsroom, and he could tell without looking around that more than half the voyeurs were grinning and enjoying his discomfort. His face reddened. He knew there was nothing he could do, he'd have to wait until Simpson had calmed down, maybe some time after Hell had frozen over, but he couldn't face the walk to the door, not with everyone staring at him. He opened his mouth to speak but Simpson waved him away and turned his back on him.

Woody stood there swaying for a few seconds and then with every ounce of control he could muster he slowly walked across the newsroom, his head held high and his eyes fixed on the purple door that led to the stairs and the street and the pub. There was only one thing he wanted, other than a double Bells, and that was to get out of the room with what little dignity he had left intact. He almost made it. He didn't notice the overflowing wastepaper bin and he crashed over it and sprawled against the door. He pushed the door but it wouldn't budge so he pushed harder and then he saw the sign that said "Pull" and cruel laughter billowed around him as he eventually staggered out into the corridor.

He headed for the sanctuary of the King's Head but realised that there would be other reporters there, probably knocking back Perrier with the way his luck was going, so instead he walked to the Coach and Horses. They wouldn't cash cheques for him there, not since the bank had bounced one, but at least he wouldn't be laughed at.

It started to rain so he put up the collar of his coat and hunched his shoulders and he stuck close to the wall until he reached the pub. It was fairly busy with closing time fast approaching, but Woody knew that the landlord paid little attention to the licensing laws and that it would be many hours before the last customer left. He took off his coat and shook it before hanging it up by the fruit machine.

"Evening, Woody," said the barman, a teenager whose name Woody couldn't remember. "Usual?"

Woody nodded and the barman poured a double Bells. A woman sitting on a stool looked at the Bells bottle and then up at Woody. She shuddered. "You should try a real whisky," she said. She was sitting next to a man in a brown leather jacket and they both had glasses of amber fluid in front of them. Woody reached for his glass and toasted them.

"This will do me fine," he said, and drained it in one.

"Now I'll have one of whatever they're having, and one each for them, too," Woody said, mentally calculating how much he had in his wallet. They were drinking a ten-year-old malt the name of which Woody didn't recognise but it was smooth and mellow and warmed his chest. He fell into amiable conversation with the couple, talking about the weather, about Docklands, about the Government, anything but what he'd seen that evening.

They asked him what he did and he told them he was a journalist. Her name was Maggie and his was Ross, he sold fax machines and she worked for an insurance company.

As the level of whisky in the bottle dropped Woody began opening himself up to them, about how unhappy he was in his job and his plans for a new life in Los Angeles. An old pal of his had gone out to LA a couple of years ago and had set up an agency specialising in showbiz features and oddball stories for the tabloids, and he'd been pestering Woody to go out and join him.

"You know, I think I will go," Woody said, and they nodded in agreement and Maggie bought a round. Some time later the man slapped Woody on the back and said he had to go.

He kissed Maggie on the cheek, a brotherly peck Woody noticed, and left. Woody was surprised as he'd assumed they were married or lovers, but Maggie laughed and said no, just friends. He slid on to the stool vacated by Ross, even though he generally preferred to stand while drinking. He was quite taken by Maggie. She had shoulder-length red hair and grey eyes, and the freckles of a teenager even though she must have been in her early thirties. She spoke with a faint Scottish burr and laughed a lot and told jokes dirtier than even Woody thought was proper.

"Are you serious about LA?" she asked, and Woody said he was. She told him that she had a friend living there, and that if he did go she'd put him in touch. She asked for his telephone number and he gave it to her. Eventually she said she had to go. Woody offered to walk her home but she thanked him and said no, she only lived around the corner. Woody shrugged and said goodbye, wondering how she'd react to a brotherly peck on the cheek from him but deciding against it. After she went he finished his whisky and left the pub in search of a black cab. Ten minutes later he was back for his raincoat. It wasn't his night.

Sergeant Fletcher's heart sank when he saw The Chinaman walking slowly up to his desk. He kept his eyes down on his paperwork and wished with all his heart that he'd go away. Nguyen Ngoc Minh coughed quietly. Sergeant Fletcher ignored him. Nguyen coughed again, louder this time. The policeman knew he could put it off no longer. He looked up and feigned surprise.

"Mr Nguyen," he said. "How can I help you?" His fingers tensed around his ballpoint pen.

"Sergeant Fletcher. Is there news about the bomb?" said Nguyen slowly. He stood in front of the desk, his head bowed and his fingers clasped together below his stomach. He was wearing the same clothes he'd worn on his four previous visits to the police station, brown woollen trousers, a blue and green work shirt and a thick quilted coat with a hood. His dark-brown boots were scuffed and worn and if Sergeant Fletcher hadn't known better he might have assumed that the man was a down-and-out looking for a warm cell for the night.

The policeman shook his head slowly. "I am afraid not, Mr Nguyen. But we are doing everything we can, believe me."

The look in The Chinaman's eyes suggested that he did not believe the sergeant, but he smiled nevertheless, his face wrinkling into deep crevices. It was an ingratiating smile, an eager-to-please look that for some reason made the sergeant immediately feel guilty.

"Do you know who exploded the bomb?" Nguyen asked.

"As it says in the papers, the IRA has claimed responsibility."

"And do they know who in the IRA is responsible?"

"No, Mr Nguyen, they do not." Sergeant Fletcher fought to keep himself from snapping at The Chinaman, but it was hard, bloody hard, because every time he came and stood in front of the desk he asked the same questions with the same inane grin on his face. He realised that the man must be devastated, losing his wife and his daughter, and God knows Fletcher wanted to help, but there was nothing he could do. Nothing.

"How long will it be, Sergeant Fletcher?" Nguyen asked quietly.

The policeman shook his head sadly. "I wish I knew," he said.

"The lady policeman who came to see me last week said that the men would be caught."

"I am sure they will be."

"She said that they will be punished."

The silly cow. Fletcher wished she'd kept her mouth shut and not raised The Chinaman's hopes. He made a mental note to find out who she was and give her a piece of his mind.

"I am sure that when they are caught they will be punished, Mr Nguyen," agreed Sergeant Fletcher.

Nguyen began wringing his hands as if washing them. "When will that be, Sergeant Fletcher?" The smiled widened, the lips stretched tight across his yellowing teeth.

It was a nervous smile, Fletcher realised. The policeman put his palms down on the desk. "I do not know. I simply do not know."

"I know you and your men are doing their best. I know they want to catch the men who killed my family. But I wonder . . ." He left the sentence unfinished, his eyes fixed on Fletcher's face.

"Yes?" said the sergeant.

"I wonder if there were any other policemen on the case. How do you say, specialists? Policemen who hunt the IRA. The terrorists."

Fletcher suddenly felt the sky open and the sun beam down. He saw a way of getting The Chinaman off his back once and for all.

"There are such policemen, Mr Nguyen. They are called the Anti-Terrorist Branch."

"Where do I find the Anti-Terrorist Branch?"

Fletcher found himself grinning. "Mr Nguyen, stay right where you are. I'll go and write down their address and telephone number for you."

Elliott Jephcott drove the white Rover off the main road and into the small cobbled mews. He switched off the radio and looked at his watch. It had just turned 8.30 a.m. and he didn't have to be in court until 11.00 a.m. He had plenty of time. He checked his hair in the driving mirror and then reached into the glove compartment for his breath-freshener aerosol and gave his mouth two minty squirts. He put the aerosol back and as he did he saw that a streetsweeper was watching him while he attacked the cobbles with a long-handled brush. Jephcott blushed like a schoolboy caught with a dirty magazine and was immediately angry with himself. A High Court Judge feeling guilty under the scrutiny of a roadsweeper in a filthy donkey jacket? Ridiculous, he thought. He locked the car and walked to the door of Erica's cottage. It opened just as he was reaching for the brass knocker.

"I heard the car," she said. She looked ravishing, her blonde hair carefully arranged so that she gave the impression that she'd just got out of bed. She moved to the side to let him in and he smelt her perfume. It was the one he'd bought her last month and he was pleased that she'd worn it for him. She was wearing a purple blouse with a high collar and pockets over each breast, and a purple, green and pink flower-patterned skirt that reached halfway down her calves, and around her waist was a purple leather belt. On her left wrist was a thick gold bracelet and around her left ankle was a thin gold chain. He'd bought her the jewellery, too. And the Alfa Romeo outside. That had been a twenty-first birthday present. She was worth it, God she was worth it.

She closed the door and stood behind him, helping him to remove his jacket. She took it and put it on a hanger before putting it away in a cupboard by the front door.

"What time do you have to go?" she asked. He knew that she wasn't nagging, not the way his wife did when she asked the same question, she just wanted to know how much time they had together so that she could plan accordingly. He turned and smiled and slipped his arm around her waist.

"Not long enough," he said and kissed her.

She opened her lips as their mouths met and he felt her soft tongue and heard her moan. She took him by the hand and led him upstairs. "Let's not waste any of it," she said.

Outside in the mews, the roadsweeper worked carefully, pushing the litter and dust into small, neat piles before using his shovel to scoop it into the plastic bag on his cart. He whistled quietly as he worked, his breath forming white clouds in the cold morning air. The collar of his donkey jacket was turned up and he was wearing thick, woollen gloves. On his head was a blue bobble hat that had seen better days. He stood up and surveyed the area he'd cleaned and nodded to himself. He clipped the shovel to the side of his cart and moved it further down the mews, stopping next to the Rover. Out of the corner of his eye he saw the upstairs curtains being closed.

He began to sweep around the car, slowly and conscientiously, still whistling. He moved between the cart and the car and knelt down to unclip the shovel. As he did he took a metal box, about the size of a box of chocolates, from the rear of the cart and in a smooth motion slipped it up under the wheel-arch of the driver's side of the Rover. There were two large magnets on the box and they latched on to the metal of the car through the underseal and its coating of mud. There was a small chrome switch on one side of the box and he clicked it on as he pulled his hand away.

Inside the box were two batteries, a black plastic alarm clock with a digital display, a small aluminium tube, a tangle of different coloured wires and five pounds of pale-brown Semtex explosive in which was embedded a detonator. As the roadsweeper unclipped his shovel and carefully swept up a cigarette packet and a pile of dust, the clock began ticking off the seconds. The man was in no hurry. The clock was set for five minutes, but even when the time was up the bomb would not explode. The clock merely completed the circuit for the second switch, a mercury tilt-switch which acted as a motion sensor. The design prevented the device going off accidentally. It was one of The Bombmaker's favourite bombs, and one of the simplest. There were no booby traps because it was a small bomb and if it was discovered the bomb disposal experts would dump it into an armoured chest and take it away rather than try to deal with it on the spot.

The streetsweeper left the mews just as the five minutes were up. He left his cart a quarter of a mile away, along with the hat, the donkey jacket and the gloves. Fisher had planned everything down to the last detail. O'Reilly kept on walking until he saw a black cab. He hailed it and took it to Victoria Station where he waited for half an hour before catching another cab back to Wapping.

The front door of the mews cottage in Chelsea opened at the same time as the cab turned into Wapping High Street.

Erica's hair still looked as if she had just got out of bed, but this time her lipstick had gone and as Jephcott kissed her he smelt her sex rather than her perfume. Her classy clothes had gone, too, and in their place she wore a white silk dressing-gown. Something else that he'd bought for her.

"Tomorrow?" she breathed, her body tight against his.

"No, my love, I'm afraid not," Jephcott replied. "I'll call you." Over her shoulder he looked at his watch. Plenty of time. He kissed her again and then pulled himself away. She closed the door behind him with a final goodbye, and he adjusted his tie as he went to the car. He unlocked the door to the Rover and got in. He looked at himself in the driving mirror and smoothed down his hair before using the breath-freshener again. The Rover started first time and as he edged it forward the bomb went off, blasting through the wheel-arch and taking off both of his legs in a burst of fire and exploding metal.

Detective Chief Inspector Richard Bromley was filling his briar pipe from a weathered leather pouch when the phone on his desk rang.

"It's the front desk, sir. He's here again."

Bromley groaned. "Tell him I'm busy."

"I've done that, sir. He says he'll wait."

"Tell him I'll call him when there's any news."

"I've done that, sir."

Bromley groaned again. He'd had the same conversation more than a dozen times over the past three weeks but he always hoped that it would end differently, that Nguyen Ngoc Minh would just give up and go home. It had started with phone calls to the general enquiry office, but somewhere along the line somebody had told him that Bromley was handling the case. Nguyen began telephoning him twice a day, once at nine o'clock prompt and again at five o'clock, asking for Detective Chief Inspector Bromley, always polite and deferential. When he first spoke to Nguyen, Bromley felt sorry for him and when he asked how the investigation was going he did his best to sound optimistic. That was his mistake, he realised, he should never have raised the man's hopes. Nguyen explained what had happened to his wife and daughter, quietly and seemingly without emotion, and he told

Bromley that the men responsible must be caught. Bromley had agreed and said that they were doing everything they could. Nguyen had thanked him and asked that Bromley call him when the men had been caught. He'd said "apprehended" but had pronounced each syllable separately as if reading the word for the first time. Five seconds after replacing the receiver, the inspector had forgotten all about the man with the strange name and the awkward English. Until the next day when he rang again. He was just as polite, always calling him "Detective Chief Inspector Bromley" and never raising his voice. He simply repeated the questions once more. Was there any news? Did they know who had set off the bomb? Were the police about to catch the men? When? He listened to Bromley's replies, which were less optimistic this time, told him how important it was that the men were found, thanked him, and rang off. He rang again the following day. And the day after. Bromley stopped taking his calls and forgot about him.

Three days after the last call he was told that there was someone waiting for him at reception. It wasn't unusual for people to arrive at New Scotland Yard with information that might be useful for the Anti-Terrorist Branch, but he was surprised that the man had asked for him by name because most of his informers wouldn't have wanted to have been seen within a mile of the building. It was Nguyen. Bromley told the man on reception to send the old man away, but he had simply sat down on one of the hard grey sofas and waited. He'd waited until the main offices had closed and then he'd left, only to return the following day. He'd maintained his vigil for more than a week, never making a fuss or doing anything that would justify ejecting him from the premises. He just waited. Bromley had been impressed by the man's stubbornness, but he was also hugely irritated by it. Several times he'd had to walk through reception while he was there and he'd glanced at the slightly built Oriental sitting with his hands in his lap, head lowered like a monk at prayer. Once he'd looked up as Bromley passed and he'd bitten down hard on the stem of his pipe and quickly averted his eyes, but too late to keep the guilt from his face. The old man had called

28

out his name but Bromley didn't look back as he headed for the sanctuary of the lift.

Bromley tamped down the tobacco with his thumb. It wasn't that he was afraid of talking to Nguyen, it was just that there was nothing to tell him. There had been six bombs in all, a total of thirty-two people dead, and the IRA had claimed responsibility for each explosion and assassination. The bombs had been of different types, though Semtex was always used. They were pretty sure it was the work of one IRA active service unit and that they were based in London for most of the time, but other than that, nothing. They were no closer now than they were when the bombing campaign had started ten weeks earlier. Bromley had told Nguyen that during one of the first telephone calls. Maybe what the old man needed was counselling, or a psychiatrist. Bromley held the phone between his shoulder and his ear while he lit the pipe and puffed it until the tobacco glowed. The pipe, and the tobacco, had been a birthday present from Chris, his fifteen-year-old son, paid for from the money he'd saved working on his paper round.

"She was only sixteen," Nguyen had said of his daughter. Bromley wondered how he would feel if Chris had been killed. His stomach went cold at the thought of it and he heard himself tell the man on the desk that he'd come down and speak to Nguyen.

"You'll come down, sir?" repeated the man, not believing what he'd heard. Bromley hung up without replying.

Nguyen was standing by the reception desk and he stepped forward to meet Bromley as the lift doors opened.

"Detective Chief Inspector Bromley, it is good of you to see me," he said slowly and bowed his head. No mention of the countless times that the policeman had refused to even acknowledge his existence. Bromley felt a rush of guilt. He asked the man behind the desk if there was an interview room free and he was told there was. Bromley took Nguyen through a pair of double white doors and along a corridor to a small square room containing a table and two orange plastic seats. He motioned Nguyen to the seat nearest the door but the old man waited until Bromley was seated before he sat down.

Bromley drew on his pipe and studied him through a cloud of smoke.

Nguyen was smiling earnestly like an eager-to-please servant. His clothes were clean but scruffy, as if they'd been slept in, and his hair was lank and uncombed. The hands clasped on the table were wrinkled but the nails were neatly clipped. After twenty years as a policeman Bromley had acquired the knack of summing people up at a glance but he had no idea where to start with Nguyen. Maybe it was because he was Oriental. Certain points were obvious. Nguyen was not a rich man, but he had the look of a man who was used to hard work and responsibility. There was suffering too, but you didn't have to be Sherlock Holmes to work that out, Bromley knew. His English was reasonably good, though he had to make an effort to choose his words carefully, and there was something vaguely American about his accent. He seemed honest and straightforward and he looked Bromley in the eye as he waited for him to speak.

Bromley took the stem of the pipe from his mouth and ran his left hand through his short-cropped beard. "Mr Nguyen, you must realise that we are doing everything we can to find the people who killed your wife and daughter. Everything that can be done, is being done, you must believe me when I tell you that. There is no point in you coming here every day. If there is something to tell you, we will telephone you or we will write to you. Do you understand?"

The old man nodded twice, and his smile widened. Several of his back teeth were missing, and one of his canines was badly chipped. "I understand, Detective Chief Inspector Bromley," he said slowly.

Bromley continued with the speech he'd rehearsed in his mind while travelling down in the lift. "The men are members of the IRA, we think they are living in London, probably moving from place to place, perhaps living in bedsitters or cheap boarding houses. They will be using false names and they will be experts at blending into the background. What I am trying to say to you, Mr Nguyen, is that it will be very difficult to find them. Do you understand?"

Nguyen nodded again.

"In fact, it might well be that we never find them. That is a possibility that you must come to terms with. Sometimes the IRA will mount a bombing campaign and then the political climate changes and the bombing stops. If that were to happen, we might never catch the men. But at least the killing will stop. Do you understand?"

Nguyen nodded. "No," he said quietly. "That cannot be so."

"It is so," said Bromley.

"It is not something I can accept, Detective Chief Inspector Bromley," the old man said, still smiling as if he was afraid to offend the policeman. "You must catch these men."

"If it is possible, we will, Mr Nguyen. That I can promise. But if it is impossible . . ." He shrugged and put his pipe back into his mouth.

"These men in London. They are doing this because they are told to, yes?"

"We believe they are members of the IRA, yes."

"But this IRA is not a secret organisation. You know who is in it, you know where they are."

"Yes," said Bromley doubtfully, not sure where the man was heading.

"Then why cannot you arrest someone else who you know is in the IRA and make them tell you who is doing the killing?"

Bromley smiled ruefully, knowing that there were a good many men in the Royal Ulster Constabulary and even his own squad who would be more than happy to do just that, to pick them up off the streets and take them to an underground cell and attach electrodes to their private parts and squeeze every bit of information out of them. And there were others who'd welcome a shoot-to-kill policy, official or unofficial, so that they could blow them away without bothering about the niceties of evidence and procedure and witnesses.

"That is not how we do things in this country," said Bromley.

"What I do not understand is why the Government allows this IRA to be," said Nguyen.

"To be what?" said Bromley, frowning.

"To exist, to be," Nguyen said. "Why does the Government not arrest everybody who is in the IRA. Lock them up. Then there will be no more killing. And perhaps then you find who murdered my family."

Bromley held his hands up in surrender. "Life is not so simple, Mr Nguyen. It is a question of politics, not policing. You should speak to your MP."

"MP?" said Nguyen, his brow creased.

"Member of Parliament," explained the policeman. "Perhaps he can help you."

Bromley got to his feet. "Mr Nguyen, there is nothing else I can tell you, I am afraid. I don't want to offend you, but you must not keep coming here. I am very sorry about what happened to your family, but your coming here is not helping. It makes it more difficult for us. Do you understand?"

Nguyen pushed back his chair slowly and stood in front of Bromley, still smiling. "I understand, Detective Chief Inspector Bromley. And I thank you for talking to me." He held out his hand and Bromley shook it. The small, wrinkled hand was surprisingly strong, as if there were steel rods under the old skin. Nguyen turned and walked out, leaving Bromley alone with his pipe.

Tempers were flaring on the football pitch. It wasn't that there was anything at stake other than the game itself, it was just that the army team hated to lose and they were two goals down with less than ten minutes to go before half-time. Their opponents, the local police team, had the edge when it came to skill and finesse but the army boys had the aggression. The referee looked at his watch and missed the sharp elbow jab in the ribs that sent the police sweeper sprawling but he heard the cop swear and he blew hard on his whistle. The crowd jeered as the referee fumbled in the pocket of his shorts for his notebook.

There were two groups of supporters, one on each side of the pitch. The police supporters, mainly loyal girlfriends and bored wives, stood with their backs to Woolwich Common, facing Stadium Road. The army supporters, mostly soldiers with nothing else to do on a Saturday morning, were ranged along the other side. O'Reilly was standing with the police wives as he studied the referee through the lens of his Pentax. The man's cheeks were flushed red as he spluttered at the policeman who was waving his arms and protesting his innocence. He moved the lens to the left and the Queen Elizabeth Military Hospital came into focus and then he saw the road sign. Shrapnel Close. He smiled at the irony of it.

The referee blew his whistle to restart the game as O'Reilly walked slowly along the sideline, stopping every now and again to take photographs. Over his shoulder was a black camera bag. Close to the corner flag was a stack of sports bags and towels and two polythene bags full of quartered oranges. The crowd roared as a big, beefy, army striker sent the ball ripping into the net, and as his team-mates rushed to congratulate him O'Reilly dropped his camera bag down among the sports bags. He walked back to the line and took more photographs before checking his watch. Three minutes to go. A red Renault drove down Repository Road and into Stadium Road and came to a halt at the junction with Shrapnel Close. O'Reilly knew that he'd attract attention to himself if he walked behind the goalmouth while the game was on, so he stayed where he was until the referee's whistle blasted out and brought the first half to a close. The players ran across the pitch to where the bags were as O'Reilly walked over to the car. McCormick opened the passenger door for him and he got in. They both looked over at the footballers, clustered around the now-opened polythene bags and helping themselves to pieces of orange.

"Now?" said McCormick, licking his lips nervously.

"No, Fisher said we wait until we're on Shooters Hill Road," replied O'Reilly.

"Let's go then." McCormick put the car in gear and drove to the main junction and indicated before he turned. He pulled the car to the side some fifty yards down the road. O'Reilly nodded and opened the glove compartment and took out a small walkie-talkie. It was an Icom IC2 transceiver, a hand-held model. There was another in the camera bag, though it had been modified. The Bombmaker had attached a relay switch to the loudspeaker circuit which was connected to a second circuit, containing a 1.5 volt battery and a gunpowder detonator. The detonator was embedded in twenty-five pounds of Semtex explosive, around which was wrapped a cluster of three-inch nails. There was no timing device because the bomb would be detonated at a safe distance by the transceiver in O'Reilly's hand. And there were no booby traps because they weren't sure when he'd be able to put the bag down.

O'Reilly saw the avaricious look in McCormick's eye, the pleading of a dog begging for a bone. He handed it over. McCormick handled it reverently like a holy icon.

"Are you sure?" he asked.

"Go for it," said O'Reilly.

McCormick switched the control switch to "send" and held the transceiver to his mouth. "Bang," he said, and they saw the flash of light followed quickly by the thud of the explosion and felt the tremor through the car seats.

"Come on, let's go," said O'Reilly.

They were driving along the A102 heading for the Blackwall Tunnel by the time the first white-coated doctor reached the blood-soaked pitch.

Sir John Brownlow was getting irritable, so Ellen brewed him a fresh cup of coffee and placed it on the desk in front of him. He smiled his thanks and she could read his discomfort in his eyes. Ellen Howard had been the MP's personal assistant for almost three years and she'd reached the stage where she could pretty much judge what he was thinking by the look on his face. Today he was wearing his professional, caring mask but she could tell that he was far from happy. He hated the regular constituency surgeries where the punters queued up to present him with their problems and to ask him to put their lives in order. The ones at the local party office weren't so bad because they were mainly an opportunity of pressing the flesh with the party faithful, it was when he had to go out and about that he suffered. Ellen knew what the problem was, though she would never dare tell the MP to his face. It was that Sir John simply did not care about the man in the street, and he sympathised even less with their trials and tribulations. But he was all too well aware of how narrow his majority had been at the last election, and he had resigned himself to the fact that being seen helping his constituents with their problems was a vote-catcher. Holding the surgery in a local citizens advice centre eased some of the pain as it meant he could usually pass them on to someone else. Teflon Time, he called it. The trick was to make sure that nothing stuck and that the punters went away thinking that their MP had done his best and was worth supporting.

The middle-aged woman sitting opposite him in a thick tweed coat and a fake fur hat had bought her council house by mortgaging herself to the hilt. Her son had helped out with the payments until they'd had a row and he'd left home. Now the building society was threatening to evict her. If she sold the house would Sir John be able to get her into another council house? The MP smiled benignly and told her that there were people at the centre who would help her negotiate with the building society and have the payments frozen or reduced. He motioned at Ellen and introduced her to the woman and then stood up to shake her hand, patting her on the back as he ushered her to the door. Ellen took her down the corridor into another room and left her with one of the advisers there. Teflon Time strikes again, she thought. There were half a dozen people sitting on a line of chairs in the corridor outside the office commandeered by the MP. There was an old couple, a young man in jeans and a motorcycle jacket who looked like he might be troublesome, two house-wives, and a Chinese man in a blue duffel coat. He was muttering something, reading from a small piece of paper in his hands and repeating something to himself over and over again. As she walked past him it sounded as if he said "elected representative".

"Next please," she said, and the old man stood up and

helped his wife to her feet. Sir John greeted them with his hand outstretched and a caring smile on his face.

Ellen sat behind her own desk, to the left of Sir John's and at right angles to it, and watched and learned. She had hopes of one day following him into the House of Commons. Her degree was in political science and she'd been chairman of her university's student union, but what she needed now was hard, political experience. Sir John Brownlow was providing that, even if it meant that she had to tolerate the occasional wandering hand on her buttocks or suggestive remark, but so far she'd been able to fend off his passes without offending him. Besides, he'd stopped being quite so chauvinistic once she'd become a good friend and confidante of his wife and taken his two teenage daughters to the cinema a few times. Ellen knew what she wanted, and how she wanted to get it, and what she didn't want was to get her ticket to the House by lying on her back with the Honourable Member between her legs.

He spent half an hour with the old couple, and then Ellen took them out and called for whoever was next. The Oriental man looked around, saw that everyone was looking at him, and got to his feet. "I think it is my turn," he said quietly.

She asked his name and then he followed her into the office. Sir John was already in position to shake hands and Ellen saw his jaw tighten when he saw Nguyen, but only for a second. Then the teeth flashed and the eyes crinkled into the face that smiled down from the posters at election time. Sir John was nothing if not professional.

"Mr Nguyen," she said by way of introduction. The MP shook the man's hand firmly and he waited until Nguyen was seated before going back behind the desk.

"How can I help you, Mr Nguyen?" he said, steepling his well-manicured hands under his square chin.

In a low, quiet voice, Nguyen told him what had happened to his wife and daughter, about the bomb, and the conversations he had had with the police and the Anti-Terrorist Branch. "My family died more than three months ago," he said. "And still the men responsible have not been caught."

Sir John nodded understandingly. "But what is it that you want me to do?"

"I wrote to you many times, Sir John. Many times."

The MP gave Ellen a sideways look and she nodded quickly. Yes, she remembered his letters now. Carefully hand-written, every word in capital letters. She had drafted sympathetic replies promising nothing and Sir John had signed them without reading them.

"I asked you to help bring the men to justice," Nguyen continued. "Detective Chief Inspector Bromley said that the capture of the men was a political matter."

"Detective Chief Inspector Bromley?"

"He is a policeman who catches terrorists. But he told me that he could not force the men in the IRA to tell him who killed my family."

"That is probably true, I am afraid," said Sir John. "There are many people who probably feel that the police and the army should have stronger powers, but we are, when all is said and done, a democracy. We cannot torture people or imprison them simply because they do not give us the information we seek." He looked concerned, but to Ellen he sounded pompous and uncaring.

"But could not the Government change the law so that such things could be done? So that the police could force others in the IRA to tell what they know?"

"In theory yes, but it would not happen. I am afraid you must allow the police to do their job, Mr Nguyen. I am sure that they are doing their best."

Nguyen smiled nervously. "What I would like, Sir John, is for you to change the law."

Sir John snorted. "Come, come, Mr Nguyen. What makes you think I can do that?"

"Because you are my . . ." The old man seemed to stumble on the words before finishing the sentence. "My elected representative." He seemed to take pride in the fact that he had remembered the words. "You are my MP. I wish you to change the law so that the killers of my family can be brought to justice."

"You have a strange idea of the powers of an MP, Mr

Nguyen. I cannot change laws just because you think justice has not been done."

Nguyen hung his head and said something quietly.

"I'm sorry?" said Sir John, leaning forward to listen.

Nguyen looked up. There were tears in his eyes and Ellen's heart went out to him.

"What am I to do?" he asked the MP. "My family is dead. What am I to do?"

Sir John leant back in his chair and folded his arms across his chest. Ellen recognised his defensive position. There was nothing he or anyone else could do. The IRA was an insurmountable problem. Even if they were to catch the men behind the latest series of bombings, it would not stop, another active service unit would come to life. The killings would never stop, not until the British pulled out of Northern Ireland. And there was little likelihood of that happening.

"How long have you been in this country, Mr Nguyen?" Sir John asked.

"I have been a British citizen since 1982. Very long time." He reached into his duffel coat pocket and took out a passport, the old type, dark-blue with the gold crest on the front. He held it out to the MP but he seemed reluctant to take it and kept his arms folded. Nguyen put it back in his pocket.

"From Hong Kong?" Sir John asked. Ellen realised then why he was so defensive. He had been one of the most outspoken critics of the Government's offer of passports to the colony's middle classes.

"Do you not have family back in Hong Kong? Can you not go back there?"

The old man looked surprised. "Hong Kong? Why I go back there?"

Sir John appeared equally confused. "That's where you came from," he said. "Surely you still have family there?"

"I not Hong Kong Chinese," Nguyen explained. "I am Vietnamese. From Vietnam."

Realisation dawned on the MP's face and he sighed audibly. He was, Ellen knew, even more vehemently against Vietnamese boat people being offered sanctuary in Britain. God, the number of times she'd listened to him address meetings on the difference between political and economic refugees and how Britain couldn't offer homes to everyone in the world who wanted a better standard of living.

"North or south?" asked Sir John.

Nguyen smiled. "Today there is no north or south. Only Vietnam."

"When you escaped," the MP pressed. "Where were you from then?"

Nguyen shrugged. "Both," he said. "North and south."

"And why did you come to England?"

"Because I could not live in Vietnam. Because the Communists persecuted me and my family. I helped the Americans in the war. When the Americans go they put me in prison. So we escaped. To Britain."

"Why Britain?"

"Because here we can be free."

The MP nodded. "But do you not see, Mr Nguyen? The reason that you can be free in this country and not your own is because we have laws for everybody here. Nobody is above the law. But equally nobody is denied its protection. That is what makes democracy work. That is why you wanted to come here in the first place, to be free. You cannot now ask for the laws to be changed, to take away the rights of others."

"Even if they have killed my family?"

"You must allow the police to do their job. You must have faith in our system, Mr Nguyen." He put his hands on the desk top and pushed himself up. Nguyen tilted his head up and for the first time it gave him a more confident, vaguely arrogant look. Then he stood up and he became once more the stooped old man, alone in the world. Sir John patted him on the back as he guided him through the doorway and into the corridor and then he slipped back into the office.

"Christ, Ellen, these people. They come over here, we give them homes, we give them money, and still they want more. If they don't like this country the way it is, why don't they just get the hell out and go back to where they came from?"

"He's still in shock, poor man," said Ellen. "His whole family was wiped out. Think how he must feel."

"That was four months ago, Ellen. And there have been

what, two or three bombs since then. And how many other victims? Yet you don't hear their relatives demanding that we pull in IRA members off the street and pull out their fingernails."

"He wasn't actually saying that, Sir John. He was . . ."

The MP snorted angrily. "Bullshit! That's exactly what he wanted. And can you imagine what the Press would do if they even thought we were considering something like that? They'd scream 'Big Brother' and 'Violation of Human Rights' and you know they would. Remember Gibraltar? They don't think about the people whose lives were saved when the SAS stopped the car bomb from being detonated. All they remember is the IRA being shot while they were on the ground. Remember the uproar over the *Belgrano*?"

Ellen didn't argue. She knew full well that there was no point in taking sides against her boss. She was there to learn from him, not to antagonise him. She smiled and brushed a loose strand of hair off her face. "I'll get the next one in for you," she said sweetly while wondering how such a racist could ever get elected. There was so much she still had to learn, she realised.

Jon Simpson took the call from the uniformed security guard at reception. "There's a chap down here wants to speak to a reporter," he said gruffly.

"What about?" asked Simpson.

"Dunno," said the guard.

"Do me a favour and ask him, will you?" sighed Simpson. The security guards weren't paid for brain power, just for bulk, but there were times when Simpson wished they were a mite brighter. There was a pause before the guard's laconic voice returned.

"Says it's about the bombs."

Simpson felt the hairs on the back of his neck stand up. The IRA bombing campaign had been going on for more than four months and the police seemed to be no nearer catching the bombers. Maybe the punter downstairs held the key, it was amazing the number of times that they came to the paper rather than going straight to the police. Or perhaps it wasn't so surprising – the paper paid handsomely for information. The news editor looked around the newsroom to see who was free and his eyes settled on Woody who was reading the *Daily Star* and picking his teeth with a plastic paper-clip. It had taken Woody weeks of plaintive phone calls before Simpson had allowed him to start shifting again and only after he'd promised not to drink on the job. Not to excess, anyway. Expecting Woody not to drink at all was asking the impossible. And he was a bloody good journalist.

"Woody!" he yelled.

Woody's head jerked up and he came over immediately, pen and notebook in hand. He was still at the eager-to-please stage. "There's a punter downstairs. Something about the bombs. See what he's got, will you?"

Woody nodded and headed for the lift. The man waiting downstairs was Oriental, wearing a blue duffel coat with black toggles, faded jeans and dirty training shoes. He was carrying a plastic carrier bag and was wiping his nose with a grubby handkerchief. He snorted into it and then shoved it into his coat pocket before stretching his arm out to shake hands. Woody pretended not to notice the gesture and herded the old man towards a group of low-backed sofas in the far corner of the reception area. Carrier bags were always a bad sign, he thought, as he watched the man settle into a sofa next to a large, spreading tree with weeping leaves. Punters who arrived at newspaper offices with carrier bags often produced strange things from them. During his twenty years as a journalist Woody had just about seen everything. There were the paranoids who thought they were being followed and who would produce lists of numbers of cars that were pursuing them, or taxis, or descriptions of people who had appeared in their dreams, or lists of MPs who were in fact aliens operating from a base on the far side of the moon. There were the punters who felt they'd had a raw deal from one of the big international companies and had photocopies of correspondence going back ten years to prove it. There were the nutters who claimed to have written Oscar-winning film scripts only to have their ideas stolen by a famous Hollywood director, and they'd open their plastic bags to show their own versions. Sometimes they were written in crayon. Not a good sign.

"How can I help you?" asked Woody, his heart heavy.

"My name is Nguyen Ngoc Minh," the man said, and Woody scribbled in his notebook, just a random motion because he didn't reckon there was going to be a story in this and he didn't want to go through the hassle of asking the guy to spell his name.

The old man thrust his hand into the carrier bag and took out a colour photograph and handed it to Woody. It was a family portrait of the man, an old woman and a pretty young girl. Woody raised his eyebrows inquisitively.

"My wife," said Nguyen. "My wife and my daughter. They were killed this year."

"I'm sorry to hear that," said Woody, his pen scratching on the notebook. He wasn't using shorthand, he just wanted to be seen to be doing something so that he didn't have to look the man in the eye. The brown eyes were like magnets that threatened to pull him into the old man's soul and several times Woody had found himself having to drag himself back. They were sorrowful eyes, those of a dog that had been kicked many times but which still hoped one day to have its loyalty rewarded.

"They were killed by IRA bombers in January," continued Nguyen. He delved into the bag once more and pulled out a sheaf of newspaper cuttings and spread them out on the low table in front of Woody. Among them he saw the *Sunday World* front-page story on the Knightsbridge bombing and the pictures they'd used inside. Strapped along the bottom was a list of the reporters and photographers who'd worked on the story. The intro and a good deal of the copy was Woody's but his name wasn't there, Simpson had insisted that it stay off. Another punishment.

"I remember," he said.

"There have been many bombs since," said Nguyen, and he pointed to the various cuttings. The judge blown up outside the house of his mistress, the bomb at Bank Tube station, the police van that had been hit in Fulham, the Woolwich football bombing. Good stories, thought Woody. He waited for the old man to continue.

Nguyen told him about the visit by the police, of their promise that the men would be caught. He told him about what he'd later been told at the police station, and by the Anti-Terrorist Branch and finally of his conversation with his MP, Sir John Brownlow. "They all tell me the same thing," he said. "They tell me to wait. To let the police do their job."

Woody nodded, not sure what to say. He'd stopped writing in the notebook and studied the cuttings while the old man talked.

"I want to do something," Nguyen said. "I want to offer money for the names of the men who did the bombs. A reward."

Woody looked up. "I don't think the newspaper would be prepared to offer a reward," he said. Too true, he thought. A right bloody can of worms that would open up. It was OK to offer money for the return of a stolen baby, or to pay some amateur model for details of her affair with a trendy businessman or a minor pop star, but he could imagine the response to a request for a reward in the hunt for IRA killers. Put the paper right in the firing line, that would.

Nguyen waved his hands and shook his head.

"No, no, you not understand," he said. "Reward not from newspaper. From me. I have money." He picked up the carrier bag by the bottom and tipped the rest of its contents on the table. It was money, bundles and bundles of it, neatly sorted into five-, ten- and twenty-pound notes, each stack held together with thick rubber bands. Woody ran his hands through the pile and picked up one of the bundles and flicked the notes. They looked real enough.

Nguyen read his thoughts. "They are real," he said. "There is eleven thousand pounds here. It is all the money I have."

Woody saw the guard staring at the money open-mouthed and so he began to scoop it back into the plastic bag. The old man helped him.

"You shouldn't be carrying so much cash around with you," whispered Woody. "Why isn't this in the bank?"

Nguyen shrugged. "I not trust bank. Many people have money in bank when Americans leave Vietnam. They would not give money back. They steal. I take care of my own money. This all I have. I want paper to use it as reward. Can do?"

Woody pushed the bag across the table. "I'm sorry, no. My paper wouldn't do that sort of thing. And I don't think that any newspaper would."

The old man looked pained by what he'd been told and Woody felt as if he'd just slapped him across the face. He stood up and waited until Nguyen did the same, the bag of money held tightly in his left hand. He offered the right hand to Woody and this time he took it and shook it. He felt intensely sorry for the old man, sorry for what he'd been through and sorry that there was nothing that could be done for him. He heard himself say: "Look, why don't you give me your phone number and if I can think of anything I'll call you?"

Nguyen smiled gratefully and told Woody the number, repeating it slowly and checking as he wrote it down. Woody didn't know why but he had a sudden urge to help the old man, to make some sort of gesture to show that he really did care and wasn't just making polite noises. He wrote down his home number on another sheet of paper and ripped it from the notebook. "Take this," he said. "Call me if . . ." He didn't know how to finish the sentence, because he knew there was nothing tangible he could offer. Nguyen bowed his head and thanked Woody and then left. Woody watched him walk down the road, a small man in a duffel coat with eleven thousand pounds in a plastic bag. "And I thought I'd seen everything," he said to himself.

O'Reilly walked up the steps to the main entrance of the police station and turned round so that he could push open the door with his shoulder. He was using both hands to carry a large cardboard box. The box was new and the lettering on it said that it contained a Japanese video recorder. A housewife with a crying child in a pushchair held the door open for him and he smiled boyishly at her.

He took the box over to the enquiries desk and placed it in front of an overweight uniformed constable who looked at him with bored eyes.

"How can I help you, sir?" the policeman asked unenthusiastically.

"I found this in my back garden this morning," said O'Reilly, nodding at the box. "It's a video recorder."

"You surprise me," said the policeman. He opened the flaps at the top of the box and looked inside. He saw a black video recorder, still in its polythene wrapping. There was a blank guarantee card and an instruction booklet.

"You've no idea where it came from?" the officer asked, and O'Reilly shook his head.

"It looks new," said O'Reilly. "I thought of keeping it but my wife said no, it might belong to someone, and besides, you know, there might be a reward or something. So she said take it to the police, you know, and so here I am." O'Reilly smiled like an idiot. He was wearing horn-rimmed glasses with thick lenses, a flat cap and a sheepskin jacket. That was all the disguise he needed because even if they ever connected the delivery of the video recorder with the explosion, all the guy would remember would be the hat and the glasses. People's memories were generally lousy when it came to describing faces, even with the latest computerised photofit systems.

"Very public-spirited of you, sir," said the policeman. "Now, can you give me your name and address?"

O'Reilly gave him a false name and an address in nearby Battersea and explained again how he'd found the video recorder while the policeman carefully wrote it all down.

"Right, sir, that's all. We'll be in touch if it isn't claimed," he said, and O'Reilly thanked him and left. He passed the housewife outside, kneeling by her child and wiping its face with a paper handkerchief. She looked up at him and smiled and he winked at her. "Lovely kid," he said.

45

The policeman lifted the box, grunting as he did so, and carried it out of the office and down a white-tiled corridor to a windowless storage room. He found a space for it on one of the grey metal shelves, next to a set of fly-fishing tackle and a bundle of umbrellas. The room was full of abandoned or forgotten belongings, all waiting to be taken to one of the city's lost property storage centres. The policeman walked back to the reception desk and forgot all about the video recorder and the man who'd delivered it.

The bomb was similar in design to the one they'd used outside the Knightsbridge department store. The Bombmaker had stripped out most of the workings of the video recorder and replaced it with twenty pounds of Semtex explosive. There were no nuts and bolts in this bomb because the aim was to demolish a building rather than mutilate crowds of people but it used a similar detonator and timer. There were two anti-handling devices, though, just in case it didn't go off for any reason. Any attempt to open the casing would set it off, and it was also primed to explode if it was connected to the mains, just in case any light-fingered copper decided to pop it into his car and take it home. The Bombmaker did not have a very high opinion of the police, be they in Belfast or London.

O'Reilly delivered the bomb at four o'clock and it was set to explode an hour later, just as the shifts were changing at the station. He was back in the Wapping flat well before the timer clicked on and completed the circuit which detonated the bomb in a flash of light. The force of the explosion blew out the front and the back walls of the police station and the two floors above it collapsed down, trapping and killing dozens of men and women in an avalanche of masonry and timber and choking dust.

Woody was reading the morning papers when the telephone rang. As usual he'd started going through the tabloids first, and on the desk in front of him he'd opened the *Sun* and the

Daily Mirror. Both had used pictures of the aftermath of the police-station bombing. The *Sun* had the better photographs but the *Mirror* had the edge when it came to eye-witness accounts. He reached for *Today* as he answered the phone.

"Mr Wood?" asked a voice that Woody didn't recognise.

"Yes?"

"It is Nguyen Ngoc Minh. I came to your office three days ago."

"I remember," said Woody. The Chinaman. He flicked through *Today*. Same pictures as the *Sun*, more or less. Plus a line drawing of the inside of a booby-trapped bomb, a Blue Peter do-it-yourself guide for amateurs to follow. And here's one I exploded earlier, thought Woody with a wry smile. "How can I help you?"

"You have seen the newspapers today?"

"The bombing?"

"These people must be stopped, Mr Wood." Woody was only half listening to the man, he had a sickening feeling that he knew where the conversation was heading. Would the paper offer the reward? Would the paper put pressure on the police? The army? The Government? Woody didn't want to be rude to the old man but he wasn't prepared to be used as the paper's agony aunt. Not on a freelance's pay, anyway. He thought of giving The Chinaman the phone number for *Today*. He began turning the pages looking for the number.

"Mr Wood?"

"Yes?"

"You said that you would help me."

"Well . . ." said Woody, about to back-pedal while he hunted frantically for *Today*'s telephone number.

"I want to speak to somebody at the IRA. Do you know anybody that would talk to me?"

Woody stopped turning the pages of the newspaper.

"What are you thinking of doing?" he asked suspiciously, scenting a possible story.

"I want to talk to somebody in the IRA, that is all."

"I don't think they'll help you, I really don't. And it might backfire."

"Backfire? I do not understand."

47

"They are dangerous men, if they thought you were a threat to them, or even just a nuisance, there's a good chance they'd hurt you."

"All I want to do is to talk to them."

Woody sighed. "OK, for a start you don't want to talk to the IRA. You'd be better off trying Sinn Fein, that's the political wing of the organisation. The Sinn Fein spokesmen are well-known."

"Could you give me some names, and tell me where I might find them?"

Woody looked at the photographs of smashed brickwork, broken glass and misshapen metal. What the hell, he thought. Why not?

"I'll have to call you back, give me your number."

"I gave you before."

"I know, but I'm using a different notebook now."

Nguyen read out the figures slowly, and Woody promised to ring him back later in the day. He was about to go over to the cuttings library but had second thoughts and instead decided to call one of the paper's Belfast stringers. Might as well get it from the horse's mouth. For a change the stringer, Pat Quigley, was helpful, sober and in his office, a hell of an unusual combination and Woody took full advantage of it. He gave Woody three names, potted biographies, where they lived, and contact phone numbers, and told him a foul joke involving two nuns and a bar of soap from which Woody deduced that the man wasn't a Catholic.

When Woody called The Chinaman back the phone was answered with a guttural "Double Happiness Take-Away".

"This is Ian Wood," he said, suddenly realising he couldn't remember The Chinaman's name. He had just written "Chinaman" in his notebook.

"Double Happiness Take-Away," the voice repeated.

Woody cursed under his breath, then he heard another voice and the sound of the phone being transferred.

"Mr Wood?" said Nguyen.

"I have the information you wanted," Woody said. He read the notes from his notebook, spelling out the names and repeating the numbers several times until he was sure The Chinaman had got them down correctly.

"Thank you, Mr Wood. I not bother you again." The phone went dead before Woody had the chance to ask The Chinaman for his name. There could be a story in this somewhere. "Heartbroken Father Pleads With IRA Killers". "Bomb Mission Of Tragic Dad". That sort of thing. Good Sunday-paper stuff. Woody was about to ring back when there was a shout from the far end of the office.

"Woody! Call for you. What extension are you on?"

"4553," he yelled back, and waited until the call was put through.

"Woody?" said a girl's voice, soft and with a Scottish burr.

"Yeah, speaking," he answered, groping for a pen.

"It's Maggie." Maggie? His mind raced, frantically trying to put a face to the name and the voice. "How are you?" she asked.

"Me? I'm fine, fine." He closed his eyes and began banging the palm of his hand against his forehead as if trying to jolt his memory.

"You do remember?" she asked, sounding hurt.

"Of course I do." He began flicking through the images in his head, searching for a Maggie.

"The Coach and Horses," she prompted.

Maggie! The girl with red hair and grey eyes and the earthy sense of humour. He remembered how much he'd enjoyed being with her, though for the life of him he couldn't recall what they'd talked about, other than the fact that she'd told him a couple of fairly risqué jokes. Would she appreciate the one about the nuns and the soap? Probably not.

"Of course I remember, how are you?" He tried to recall the name of her partner. Todd? Rob? Ross? It bobbed away on the outer fringes of his memory, just out of reach. Most of that evening was a blank, though he vaguely remembered putting away the best part of a bottle of a very civilised malt whisky. Had he kissed her? He couldn't remember. There was something else as well, something sad, very, very sad. Woody's eyes glanced at the photographs in the *Sun* and it all flooded back as if a dam had burst. It had been the day of the big bombing in Knightsbridge. He'd locked away the sickening images of that day, the pictures that had been too horrific to use in the paper, the twisted bodies, the severed limbs, the blood, the Retriever with its jaws clamped on its gory prize. He didn't want to think about that day, but Maggie had been part of it and recalling her brought everything back into focus. He breathed deeply, trying to clear his head.

"I'm fine, too. Isn't it a lovely day?"

"Is it? We've no way of knowing, here. All the blinds are down so that we can use the terminals." That's what management claimed, but Woody reckoned it was just to stop them looking out of the windows and daydreaming.

"Well, take it from me, the sun is shining and the birds are singing. I was wondering if you fancied going out for a drink again one day this week."

"Sure, that'd be great. What about tomorrow night?"

She agreed, and they arranged to meet at the same pub.

"Woody, are you OK?" she asked. "You sound a bit distant."

"Yeah, somebody walked over my grave, that's all. Nothing to worry about. I'll be fine by tomorrow."

When she'd gone Woody put his head in his hands and closed his eyes, but he couldn't block out the images of death and destruction. He needed a drink. Badly.

The function room had been booked in the name of the Belfast Overseas Investors Club but the dozen men sitting at the long mahogany table had little interest in investment. The man standing at the head of the table in a green tweed jacket and black woollen trousers could have passed as a mildly eccentric provincial stockbroker with his greying hair and slightly flushed cheeks. He was in his fifties and looked like a rugby player gone to seed, which is exactly what Liam Hennessy was. But after playing for his country he'd gone on to become a political adviser to Sinn Fein. Married with two children, Liam Hennessy was one of the most powerful men in the Republican movement.

The eleven listening to him were all high-ranking Provisional IRA officials and they had all been called to the hotel in Belfast at short notice. On the table in front of them were jugs of iced water and upturned glasses, but none had been touched. Each man also had a notepad in a red leather folder and a ballpoint pen.

Hennessy stood with his arms folded across his chest and spoke in a soft Irish brogue. He first thanked them for coming, though a summons from Liam Hennessy was not something that any of them could ignore. The group met regularly, always in different venues and under different names so that the security forces wouldn't be able to eavesdrop, usually to discuss financing or strategy or matters of discipline, but today's gathering was special. They had all seen the television reports of the south London police-station bombing and the pictures of ambulancemen and firemen hauling the rubble away with their bare hands, and they had heard that the IRA had claimed responsibility.

To Hennessy's left was a large flat-screen television on a matte black stand, and underneath it was a video recorder. He took a videocassette off the table and slotted it into the recorder. The screen flickered and then there were shots of the Kensington bombing recorded from the BBC news. It was followed by a report of the Woolwich bombing, the explosion in Bank Tube station and the crop of car bombs that had killed or injured judges, police and army officers. Then the screen dissolved into black and white static and Hennessy bent down and switched the machine off.

"This must stop," said Hennessy quietly. He was not a man who needed to raise his voice or bang his fist on the table to make his anger felt. "Never in the history of the Cause have we been closer to getting a political solution. Look at South Africa. The Government there is now talking to the ANC and that would have been unthinkable a few years ago. The ANC's acts of terrorism go way beyond anything the IRA has ever done. With the Americans withdrawing their troops from Europe and the opening up of Eastern Europe, this

Government is finding it harder and harder to justify its armed presence in Northern Ireland. This Government is getting tired, politically and economically, and it is through the ballot-box and by lobbying in Westminster that this war will be won."

There were grumblings from several of the men at the table and Hennessy held up his hand to silence them. "I am not saying that we give up the struggle, nor that we release the pressure here. What I am saying is that it does us no good at all to take the conflict to the mainland. We have tried in the past and the backlash, both political and from the public, has done us more harm than good. That is why what is happening in England now is so detrimental to our cause."

A few of the men nodded in agreement, but Hennessy could see that others were still not convinced.

"We cannot succeed in our political struggle by using violence in English cities. It must stop. Which brings us to our second problem. Who in God's name is behind this bombing campaign?" He looked at the men around the table but was met with a wall of shaking heads. Over the previous four months Hennessy or one of his associates from the upper echelons of Sinn Fein had met with all of the top IRA organisers in Belfast and in Dublin in an attempt to identify the team behind the bombings. When they'd first been told that the terror campaign was an unsanctioned one they had been astonished – most had assumed that it had been ordered on a "need to know" basis. It was inconceivable, they thought, that a campaign of such ferocity and technical sophistication could be masterminded from outside the organisation. The bombs were all variations of IRA designs and explosives, and whenever the bombers claimed responsibility they always gave the current identifying codeword, but as far as Hennessy could determine they were most definitely not acting under IRA authority. Unless one of the men around the table had been lying.

He studied their faces, most of them in their fifties and sixties, hard men whose eyes looked back at him levelly. Most of them had killed, and the few who hadn't had arranged or ordered assassinations, yet to the outsider they would have looked no more sinister than a group of pigeon fanciers gathered to discuss their annual show.

"After an extensive investigation, we have come to the conclusion that we are dealing with a rogue group, a group that we are sure must have been within the organisation until recently, who are now operating on their own," said Hennessy. He saw one or two frowns. "The fact that they know the codewords, even after they are changed, suggests that they still have connections, and high level connections at that. And the type of explosive devices would indicate that they are IRA trained. It could even be that they passed through one of the Libyan training schools."

One of the older members of the group, white-haired and with rosy cheeks from years on the hills around his farm, cracked his knuckles under the table to catch Hennessy's attention. "If what you say is true, Liam, then it should not be too hard to pin these people down."

Hennessy nodded. "In theory that's so, Patrick. But it will require a hell of a lot of legwork. We are going to have to speak to everyone within the organisation who has bomb-making skills, to find out where they are and if they have been out of the country. Or if they have instructed anyone else. And it cannot be one man, so we'll also be looking for any other IRA members who are unaccounted for. In short, gentlemen, we will have to interview every single member of the organisation."

Patrick Sewell leant back in his chair and cracked his knuckles again. "That could cause some resentment, Liam, especially when many of our younger people are actually in favour of what has been happening. The bombing campaign has its supporters, you know. And it wasn't all that many years ago that you yourself weren't averse to taking the struggle over the water."

Hennessy leant forward and placed his hands flat on the highly polished table. "I'm all too well aware that there are hotheads within the movement who would prefer to see us blowing up police stations in London, but they must learn to understand that there is a time for violence and a time for negotiation," he said.

Sewell grinned. "And if they don't agree?"

"Then, Patrick, you are free to blow their fucking kneecaps off, sure enough."

Hennessy grinned and so did Sewell and the group burst into deep-throated laughter. The two men were best of friends and they went back a long way. A hell of a long way. They both had a powdery dry sense of humour and took great pleasure in winding each other up.

Hennessy waited for the laughter to die away before continuing. "There is a second line of enquiry which we must pursue," he said. "Whoever is behind the bombing campaign appears to have a ready source of explosives and bomb-making equipment. I want every single stockpile of arms checked, both here and on the mainland. And I don't mean that we just check that they are there, I mean every item must be verified. Verified and then re-hidden. It could be that they have access to more than one of our stockpiles and have taken a small amount from each place. You see what I mean? A few pounds of Semtex from here, a detonator there, a transmitter from somewhere else. Hoping that we wouldn't notice."

A thin, angular man with tinted glasses and slicked-back greying hair caught Hennessy's eye with a wave of his hand. His name was Hugh McGrath, and his main job within the organisation was to liaise with the Libyans, providers of much of the organisation's money and equipment.

"Liam, you can't be serious. The whole point of these stockpiles is that they remain untouched until we need them. Disturbing them unnecessarily risks drawing attention to them," he said.

Hennessy took his hands off the table and stood upright. He could understand his concern, McGrath had personally supervised the importation of much of the IRA's ordnance and was all too well aware of what it had cost, in terms of hard cash and lives lost.

"We'll be careful, Hugh. We'll be damned careful. But I think that a thorough examination of all our stockpiles will give us our best indication of who is behind the bombing campaign. I agree it's a risk, but it is a calculated one. It's a risk we must take, right enough."

"If you say so," said McGrath, but Hennessy could tell from his tone that he wasn't convinced. He made a mental note to massage his ego after the meeting.

"What I need from you all is a full list of all your ordnance stocks. And I mean every single one, authorised and non-authorised. I know that we all like to have a little something tucked away for a rainy day, but the list must be comprehensive. And alongside the contents of each stockpile I want the names of all the people who know its location."

There were a few heavy sighs from his audience.

"A list like that will be a very dangerous thing, Liam. In the wrong hands it could be fatal," said Sewell.

"I know that. There will be only one copy, and I will have it. I will arrange for the stockpiles to be checked, and I will arrange for different teams to do the checking. Only I will know all the locations. And the men I get to visit the stockpiles will not be told why. If all goes to plan I will eventually know which have been tampered with, and then by cross-referencing the names I should be able to identify the common links. Now, if you don't object, I suggest we compile the list as best we can. Any omissions can be made good later, but only directly to me."

The men reached for their pens as Hennessy sat down again. He waited until the men had finished writing. It took several minutes until the last man replaced his ballpoint pen on the table. Hennessy asked for the written sheets to be passed to him and he placed them in a neat pile and then carefully folded it three ways and slipped the sheets into his inside pocket. He then asked them to tear off the top half dozen sheets from the pads and he gathered them together and screwed them up before dropping them into a wastepaper basket. He used a silver cigarette lighter to set the papers alight. He realised it looked a bit theatrical, but at least it proved that he was serious about secrecy.

At the end of the room was a table covered with a starched white linen cloth, and on it were bottles of spirits and a selection of mixers, an ice bucket and a row of crystal glasses. Hennessy personally poured drinks for the men in the room, never once having to ask what they wanted. They stood in two groups, drinking and talking, mainly about horse-racing and football, there being an unwritten rule that business was discussed only at the table. Hennessy was the first to leave, shaking them all by the hand as he went.

Outside the room he was joined by his two bodyguards, Jim Kavanagh and Christy Murphy, big-shouldered men with watchful eyes. Even here, on home territory, they were constantly alert. Kavanagh led the way, six paces ahead of Hennessy, while Murphy walked one pace behind, covering his back. Kavanagh pressed the button for the lift, checked it when it arrived, and then he and Murphy stood to one side to allow Hennessy in. They then stood together between the door and their boss. The three men moved smoothly as if their actions were well choreographed, and in a way they were because they had been together for more than a decade and had been through the actions many thousands of times. Murphy and Kavanagh knew without looking where Hennessy was and in which direction he was moving, where the danger points were and where they had to stand to get in between their boss and any attackers. Twice they had saved Hennessy's life, and both bore their scars with pride – Murphy's left shoulder was a mass of tangled scar tissue where a soft-nosed bullet had ripped away a chunk of flesh but thankfully had missed the bone, and Kavanagh's legs still bore the burn marks of a badly placed car bomb that had exploded as he was about to pick up his boss.

Hennessy's car, a black Jaguar, was waiting outside the hotel with his regular driver, a small, intense man called Jimmy McMahon, at the wheel. Hennessy stood patiently while his bodyguards checked the pavements and then the three men quickly moved to the car.

They drove through the Belfast traffic, and McMahon's skilful touch on the wheel had them back at Hennessy's office in Donegall Square within five minutes. Only when Hennessy was safely behind his desk did Murphy and Kavanagh relax. They sat on two large, green sofas in the legal firm's reception area until they were needed again. Hennessy's secretary, a buxom redhead, put cups of coffee down in front of them before knocking twice on Hennessy's door and entering before he had the chance to respond. Like Murphy and Kavanagh, she knew her boss well. He was sitting in a high-backed leather chair, his eyes closed in thought. In front of him on his well-ordered desk was a file of outgoing letters awaiting his signature. Hennessy opened his eyes and smiled.

"I'm getting to them, Beth."

She raised her eyebrows. "We'll miss the post, Liam, sure enough we will," she admonished like a schoolteacher scolding a naughty pupil. She was a good fifteen years younger than Hennessy, but she knew there were times when the lawyer needed a good push to get things done. And she always used his first name, unless there were clients around.

Hennessy sighed and took a gold fountain pen from his inside pocket.

"You're a hard taskmaster, Beth, that you are." She stood in front of the desk, her arms folded across her ample bosom, as Hennessy scanned each letter and signed his name. When he'd finished he scooped them up with a flourish and rewarded him with a smile. She was hellish pretty, thought Hennessy, as he did at least a dozen times a day. If he was younger, and single, and if she wasn't the proud mother of twins, and if he hadn't been married to a woman who made his heart ache. God, there were so many "ifs" that it was laughable. He smiled and her lime-green eyes twinkled as if reading his thoughts.

"Anything else?" he asked, replacing the top on his pen.

"Mr Armytage would like you to call him about his case, and you have a four o'clock appointment with Mr Kershaw. And there's a man trying to get hold of you."

"A man?"

"A foreigner. Calling from London." She saw Hennessy smile and she held up her hand. "No, I don't mean he was a foreigner just because he was phoning from England. He sounded foreign, Oriental. Chinese, maybe."

"And what did he want, this Chinaman?"

"He wouldn't say. Said he had to speak to you. If he calls again, do you want to speak to him?"

"I don't see why not. Right, can you get me Tom Armytage's file? He must be getting nervous about tomorrow."

Beth nodded and left his office. Hennessy watched her hips swing as she went, then caught sight of his wife's smiling face in the brass frame on the right-hand corner of his desk, her arms around their two teenage children. Hennessy grinned at the picture. "I was only looking, darling Mary, only looking. You know that."

The phone on the desk rang, making him jump. It was Beth, telling him that The Chinaman was calling again.

"Put him on," said Hennessy, his curiosity aroused.

Nguyen introduced himself and explained what he wanted, speaking softly and slowly, sometimes so quietly that Hennessy had to ask him to repeat himself. When Hennessy finally realised what the caller was requesting he was stunned, unable to believe that the man could be so naïve.

"What on earth makes you think that I know the men who killed your wife and daughter?"

Nguyen was insistent. Polite but insistent. There was a rustle of paper on the line as if he was reading something. "Because you are a political adviser to Sinn Fein, the political wing of the IRA." The phrase came out so confidently and smoothly that the contrast with his earlier carefully controlled speech and ungainly vocabulary convinced Hennessy that The Chinaman had indeed read it, from a newspaper cutting perhaps.

"I do offer advice to politicians, that is true. But I condemn, as do they, violent acts against innocent members of the public, both in England and here in Northern Ireland." Hennessy realised he had shifted into the standard speech he gave journalists or visiting MPs, the words slipping off his tongue as easily as The Chinaman's when he was reading from the cutting. "You have the wrong man."

"If that is so, Mr Hennessy, could you tell me who in the IRA would tell me?"

Hennessy marvelled at the man's stupidity. "Offhand, I can think of no one who would be in a position to help you. And I would add that the sort of men you are talking about are not the sort who would take kindly to being approached with such accusations." Hennessy kept the threat veiled, aware as always of the possibility that the security forces had his lines tapped. "I suggest that you speak to the police, I am sure they are doing their best to identify the men responsible. But I can assure you that I do not know."

Nguyen fell silent for a while. Hennessy was just about to hang up when he spoke again. "I am afraid I do not believe you, Mr Hennessy. You are their adviser. You know who they are."

Hennessy snorted angrily. "I have already explained, I advise politicians, not terrorists. There is a world of difference."

"I think that IRA politics and IRA terrorism are different ends of the same snake," said Nguyen. "It does not matter which end you seize, you still have the snake."

This, thought Hennessy, was like talking to a fortune cookie. "Using your analogy, I would suggest that it makes a great deal of difference which end you attack," he replied. "One end will fight back." Hennessy felt pleased at the turn of phrase. It had given him the same sort of buzz that he got in court demolishing his opponent's legal arguments.

Nguyen was not deterred. "I have chosen, Mr Hennessy. You will tell me who is responsible."

Hennessy's temper flared. "You are wasting my time. Goodbye." He cut the connection and then buzzed Beth on the intercom.

"Yes Liam?"

"If The Chinaman rings again just tell him I'm unavailable. I don't want to speak to him again. Ever."

Nguyen knelt down in front of the red-painted wooden shrine and lit a stick of incense with an old Zippo lighter. He snapped the top of the metal lighter back in place and then held it with both palms pressed together. He rubbed his hands slowly, caressing the smooth metal. The sweet-smelling smoke curled upwards, drifting in the air, and he breathed it in. He opened his hands and looked at the lighter. On one side there was an insignia etched into the metal. There was a

short-handled dagger, superimposed on a badge the shape of
the blade of a spear, and across the dagger were three bolts
of lightning. Above the badge was a banner containing the
word "Airborne". Nguyen had had the lighter for many years,
but it had never let him down. His wife had carried it out of
Vietnam and had proudly presented it to him when they were
reunited in a refugee camp in Hong Kong. She had never let
him down, either.

He slipped the lighter back in his pocket and sat back on
his heels, his eyes closed and his hands together in prayer as
he emptied his mind of everything save his wife and three
dead daughters. When his first two daughters had died he
had been powerless to help and by the time he was in a
position to do anything the men responsible were hundreds
of miles away. He'd thirsted for revenge then, he'd wanted to
tear the men apart with his bare hands, but there was nothing
he could do. It had been a long time since the two young girls
had suffered, all those years ago in the South China Sea. He
remembered how he'd had to watch. How they'd screamed
and begged him to help, and how something inside him had
died. The urge for revenge had never died, in fact if anything
it was stronger now than it had ever been, though it was
tempered by the knowledge that he had done everything he
could. But this time he would not allow the deaths of Xuan
Phoung and Kieu Trinh to pass unresolved into memories.
He would not allow the men responsible to escape unpunished. He swore to himself he would not. On the souls of his
family he swore it. He didn't move for almost an hour and
when he opened his eyes again they were moist, though no
tears rolled down his cheeks. He slowly stood up, his joints
clicking and cracking as he stretched his legs. He had decided
what he was going to do, but he knew there would be a
thousand details that he still had to work out, so he took a
pencil and one of his daughter's unused exercise-books from
a drawer in the kitchen and sat down at the dining-table and
began writing.

*　*　*

It was dark, so dark that the man could see the car's headlights from more than a mile away, carving tunnels of light through the blackness. He lay down in the grass and waited for it to pass. It was two o'clock in the morning so cars were few and far between along the road connecting the A4008 with the A409 near Bushey Heath, just south-west of the M1. The man was lying face down on farmland, his nose close to the dew-damp soil, listening to the engine noise grow louder and then fade away. He got to his feet, picked up the spade and the metal detector by his side and walked towards a small brook that cut through the fields. He had memorised the location and if he was unlucky enough to be caught he'd say that he was just a treasure hunter out looking for buried coins, but getting caught was the last thing on his mind. He heard the trickling water before he reached the bank of the brook, and turned left and followed its meandering path to a small copse. He pushed his way through waist-high bushes until he came to the base of a towering beech tree. One of its roots, as thick as a man's thigh, crawled along the peaty ground for six feet or so before plunging into the earth, and it was midway along its length where the man began to dig. He was well-built and used to physical exercise, and though he was breathing heavily after half an hour he had dug a hole four feet deep and three feet across. He began to take more care then, and before long the spade clunked into something that sounded vaguely metallic. He bent down and pulled up a long thin package, wrapped in polythene. He laid it on the ground next to the tree and unwrapped it. Under the polythene was a sack, tied at one end with a piece of wire. He undid it and pulled the sack down.

Inside were three Armalite rifles and two handguns, along with several boxes of cartridges. There was a plastic-wrapped package labelled Semtex and a polythene bag containing detonators. The man slowly counted them. His eyes were used to the darkness and he could see enough to identify the contents. He had already memorised the list he'd been shown, the list of what the cache should contain, and he mentally crossed them off one at a time. Eventually, satisfied that nothing was missing, he packed up the munitions and put them back in the hole. He replaced the soil and then stamped up and down to flatten the earth before kneeling down and gently smoothing it over. He walked some distance away from the beech tree and gathered twigs and small branches and placed them haphazardly over the freshly dug soil. It would fool most casual observers and in a day or so it would have blended in perfectly with its surroundings. There was little chance of it being discovered. That's why the hiding place had been chosen in the first place.

Nguyen came out of Charing Cross Tube station and walked to the Strand. He found the shop he wanted and stood looking through the window. It was packed with camping equipment, everything from compasses to water-bottles, a huge range of knives, racks of anoraks, sleeping-bags, dehydrated food in silver-foil packets, first-aid kits, crossbows and a range of martial arts equipment. It was all so different during the war, Nguyen thought. So very different. Equipment then was what you could beg or borrow, or take from a fallen comrade or steal from an enemy. And to think that now you could simply walk into a shop and buy it. If they had been able to get hold of equipment like this thirty years ago, then perhaps none of this would have happened and he and his family would be together in a free Vietnam. He shook his head, trying to disperse the thoughts, knowing that there was no point in dwelling on the past.

He walked into the shop and looked through the racks. A young man tried on an army-type pullover with reinforced patches on the shoulders and elbows as his blonde girlfriend looked on admiringly. A skinhead in a shiny green bomber jacket weighed a small throwing knife in his hand and then ran a finger along the blade. A father and son examined a two-man tent as an elderly shop assistant rolled it out along the floor for them. Nobody gave Nguyen a second look.

He picked a camouflage jacket from a rack and looked at it. It was made of nylon and he heard it rustle even as he held it up. Useless, he thought. You'd hear it hundreds of yards away. And the fasteners were made from the Velcro material that made a ripping noise every time you used it. It was for show, like the knife the skinhead was testing. Pretty to look at, but useless in the field. Just by looking at it Nguyen could tell that the knife had no weight, it would bounce off any live target. He took down another jacket, similar colour scheme of dark and light greens, reminiscent of the tiger-striped fatigues he used to wear in the jungle, made from a soft cotton material that probably wasn't waterproof but which looked warm. He tried it on and the sleeves were about six inches too long, even over his jacket. He looked at the label. Medium it said. European medium, obviously, because Nguyen was not small for a Vietnamese.

"Can I help you, sir?" said a young assistant.

Nguyen held up his arms. "Small size?" he asked, and the youngster smiled and helped him get it off. He flicked through the racks and pulled out a smaller size, pressed it up against Nguyen's shoulders, nodded, and asked him to try it on. It fitted.

"Trousers. Same style," said Nguyen, and the youngster found a pair of trousers made from the same soft material.

"Anything else, sir?" he said, and Nguyen nodded enthusiastically.

"Oh yes, yes," he said. "Many things."

He picked up a pair of binoculars, powerful and covered with thick, green rubber, and asked the assistant if it was OK to try them. The boy said yes, but went with him to the door and waited while Nguyen scanned up and down the crowded street.

"I will take these," said Nguyen, handing them to the boy. He walked back into the shop. So many things to buy. "Bottles," he said.

"Bottles?" queried the boy.

"Water-bottles," said Nguyen, pointing to a canteen, khaki-coloured with a green strap. It looked big enough to hold a quart. "Two of those. No, three."

The boy piled up the purchases by a cash register, sensing that the customer was going to be here for some time. On the wall behind the cash register were a number of replica guns and rifles, dull metal and polished wood. They looked so real, Nguyen marvelled. How could such things be on sale in England? he wondered. Some of the guns he recognised, a Colt .45, a Ruger .22, an M9 9-millimetre semi-automatic. Suddenly he stopped, his heart pounding. It couldn't be, could it? His eyes widened and he walked over to stand in front of an AK-47, a Kalashnikov automatic rifle, perfect in every detail with even its curved ammunition magazine in place. He reached up to touch it, to remind himself how it felt. At the last moment, just before his fingers touched the cold metal, he pulled back his hand and shook his head to clear away the memories.

"Compass," he said, and the assistant took him over to a glass-topped counter. On a shelf underneath were a selection of compasses and map-reading equipment. Nguyen pointed at several and the boy took them out for him to examine. Nguyen chose one. "Knife," he said.

There were so many knives, more than he had ever seen in any one place. There were penknives with all sorts of gadgets attached – nail files, spanners, scissors, bottle-openers. There were throwing knives, useless ones like the skinhead had been playing with, but also serious, properly balanced heavy knives that could kill from twenty yards in the right hands. Nguyen held a pair of the heavy knives, feeling their balance and knowing they were perfect.

"Can try?" he asked the assistant.

"Try?"

Nguyen showed him the knives. "Can I throw?"

"Here?" said the boy. "No, no. God, no." He looked confused.

"Never mind," said Nguyen, putting them on top of the camouflage trousers. There was a big selection of survival knives, big sharp blades, serrated on one side, with hollow handles containing a small compass, a short length of fishing line and a few cheap fishing hooks. Nguyen snorted as he looked at them. Joke knives, not what he was looking for. He was looking for a strong blade, one that he could sharpen until it would cut paper like a razor, with a groove in the blade so that the blood could flow out as it was thrust into a body. No groove and the suction effect would make withdrawing the knife that much harder. The tip of the knife had to be angled, too, so that it could ease the ribs apart and allow the killing thrust to the heart. And the handle had to be heavy enough and sturdy enough so that the blade was kept steady as it was used. A knife was important, your life could so easily depend on it. The choice of scabbard was vital too, the action had to be smooth and silent when the blade was withdrawn and the straps had to be strong and hard-wearing. Nguyen spent a lot of time examining the knives in stock before deciding. The one he eventually selected was expensive, one of the most expensive in the shop, but it was the best. He also took a small Swiss army knife, for its tools rather than its blades.

What else? He looked up and down the shop. There was so much he could use. A tent. A sleeping-bag. A small stove. A lightweight blanket made from foil. A folding axe. A rucksack. A first-aid kit. Nguyen was tempted, but at the same time a part of him knew that equipment was often a trap. It slowed you down, you spent more time and effort carrying it and looking after it than you did fighting. He remembered how he used to go into the jungle in fatigues and sandals, with a water-bottle, a few pounds of cooked rice in a cloth tube tied around his waist and nothing else but his rifle and ammunition. He and his comrades travelled light and covered ground quickly and silently. How they laughed at the ungainly Americans, sweating like pigs under the weight of their huge rucksacks. You could hear them coming for miles as they hacked and tripped their way through the undergrowth. So many were killed before they even had a chance to open their precious backpacks, but they never learned.

"Anything else?" asked the assistant, jarring Nguyen's thoughts.

He walked over to a rack of walking boots but decided against buying a pair. The ones he had back at his house would be better because they wouldn't need breaking in. "I want a small rucksack," he said. The assistant showed him a big, blue nylon backpack on an aluminium frame with padded straps and Nguyen said it was too big and that the colour was wrong. "Too bright," he said. He pointed to a small dark-green rucksack, the sort that children might use to carry their school-books. It had no frame and when Nguyen tried it on it lay flat against his back. He adjusted the straps and walked up and down the shop. It felt comfortable and made next to no noise. He removed it and handed it to the assistant. "This one is good," said Nguyen.

The assistant placed all Nguyen's purchases in a large plastic carrier bag, totalling them up on the cash register as he did. Nguyen paid in cash. As he waited for his change he looked wistfully at the AK-47 replica. So many memories, he thought.

On the way to the Tube station he walked past a photographer's shop with shelves full of cameras and lenses. He went in and asked if they sold flash-bulbs.

"Flash-bulbs?" said the man behind the counter. "Don't get much call for those these days. They all have built in flashes now." He frowned and rubbed his chin. "I've got some somewhere, I saw them a couple of weeks ago. What sort of camera are they for?"

Nguyen shrugged. "Any sort. But not the square ones, the ones they use in the little cameras. I want the single bulbs."

"Yeah, I know the sort you mean. Hang on, let me check out back." He disappeared through a door and Nguyen heard boxes being moved and drawers opening and closing.

"You're in luck," he called. "How many do you want?"

"A dozen," Nguyen shouted back.

The man returned with two packets and handed them to Nguyen. "I can't guarantee they'll still work, mind," he said. "They're old stock and I don't know how long they've been there."

Nguyen examined them carefully and then nodded. "They will be perfect," he said. He paid in cash, put the packets into his carrier bag and left the shop.

* * *

"We need more explosive," The Bombmaker said. Fisher ran his fingers through his hair and sighed. He stretched his legs out and lay back in the leather sofa.

"How much do we have left?" he asked.

"A couple of kilos, no more. We've plenty of detonators, though."

Fisher smiled. "Fat lot of good they'll be to us without the stuff that goes bang," he said. "I'll get us more, don't you worry."

McCormick came into the lounge from the kitchen and put down four mugs of coffee on the table by the side of the sofa. O'Reilly got up from his easy chair and took one of them. He walked over to the french windows and looked over the Thames as he drank.

"Isn't it about time we moved?" asked McCormick.

"Why move?" said Fisher.

"In case they track us down. We've been here for months, sure enough. Normal procedure is to keep moving, never stay in one place for too long."

Fisher shook his head. "No, that's exactly what they'd expect us to do. They'll be checking all the small hotels and bed and breakfast places. A group like us moving around will stick out like a sore thumb. And after the Knightsbridge bombing every landlady in Britain is on the lookout for Irishmen. How long do you think it would take until we were rumbled?"

"I suppose you're right," said McCormick reluctantly. "It's just . . ."

"Look," interrupted Fisher, "we've had this flat rented for almost a year. It's on a long-term lease, paid direct from a dummy company bank account. As far as the landlord is concerned, it's rented to a stockbroking firm who use it for visiting executives from the States. This place is perfect."

O'Reilly tapped on the window. "And if the SAS knock on the front door, we can leg it over the balcony and down the Thames," he said.

"If the SAS find out we're here, we won't be going any-where," said McCormick. "Bastards."

"Nobody is going to find out where we are," said Fisher. "Nobody. So long as we stay right where we are. Our more immediate problem is to get hold of some more Semtex."

O'Reilly turned away from the window, sipping his coffee. He took the mug from his lips and smiled. "You want me to get it?"

Fisher nodded. "Tonight. I'll come with you."

"I can do it."

"I know. But this one is hard to find. You'll need me there."

McCormick coughed. He took a handkerchief from the back pocket of his jeans and sneezed into it. "I'm going down with a cold," he said, but nobody registered any sympathy. He inspected the contents of the handkerchief and put it back into his pocket. "And when we've got the stuff, then what?" he asked.

Fisher's eyes sparkled and he looked over at The Bombmaker. "Something big," he said. "Something very, very big."

Nguyen took the Tube back to Clapham and stored his purchases in the shed at the back of the yard behind his shop. It was a big metal garage but the main door had long ago been boarded up and now it contained three big chest freezers full of frozen meat and vegetables, sacks of rice and bottles of soy sauce. There was also a long wooden bench and racks of tools along one wall. Nguyen placed his carrier bag on the bench, padlocked the door and then went through the shop to his van which was parked outside. He drove to a large do-it-yourself store in south London and spent more than an hour filling a large trolley. He bought sections of plastic drain-pipe, insulation tape, three large bags of fertilizer, a soldering iron and several packs of solder, and other tools that he knew he'd need which he didn't already have in his shed. He paid in cash, and on the way back he stopped at a large filling station. He filled the tank and bought two large plastic bottles of antifreeze, three cans of Shell motor oil and half a dozen cans of white spray paint to match the colour of his van, and a can of black paint.

Pham was washing bean sprouts in the kitchen sink and he grunted a greeting as Nguyen walked by. Pham had agreed to buy the restaurant and had already paid Nguyen in cash. The bank had agreed to transfer the mortgage on the property to him and after a long but good-hearted argument over the value of the kitchen equipment and the food in the fridges Nguyen had agreed to accept thirty thousand pounds. Nguyen didn't ask where Pham had got the money from, but he had relatives in Manchester who had probably helped out. He was planning to switch to Vietnamese cooking, though Nguyen doubted that it would be a success, so far away from the West End. He and his wife had decided when they first moved to London that they were more likely to make money if they kept to a Chinese menu, even though they personally found the cuisine bland and boring. Still, it was up to Pham now. Nguyen had promised to be out by the end of the week but he knew that Pham was keen for him to go as soon as possible so that he could move into the flat upstairs.

After putting the rest of his purchases away in the garage, Nguyen sat at his table and crossed off the list everything he'd already bought. There were three items left: two kinds of acid and glycerine. He knew how to make the acid he needed from other quite innocuous and easily available materials. It was messy, but possible, but there was no need because this was England not Vietnam and here there were firms where you could buy chemicals, no questions asked. He took a well-thumbed copy of Yellow Pages and looked up Chemical Manufacturers and Suppliers. After three calls he had found one firm who would supply him with concentrated acids (for etchings, he'd said) and he arranged to collect a gallon of glycerine from another firm. Nguyen thought it prudent not to buy all three from the same supplier.

*　　*　　*

Fisher stopped the car and switched off the engine and the lights, allowing the darkness to envelop them like a shroud. He and O'Reilly waited until their eyes became used to the blackness, listening to the clicking noises from the engine as it cooled. They were parked at the end of a lonely lane not far from Bexley station, half an hour's drive south-east of central London. Both men were dressed in dark pullovers, jeans and black shoes, outfits that wouldn't stick out at night but which didn't obviously mark them out as burglars. If they were unlucky enough to come across the police then they'd just pretend they were a couple of queers looking for a bit of privacy. That had been Fisher's idea, and O'Reilly hadn't been exactly bowled over by it.

"Look, I promise not to kiss you," Fisher had joked.

O'Reilly had laughed nervously.

"Not on the mouth, anyway . . ." O'Reilly had winced and Fisher knew he'd hit a nerve so he let the joke drop. He mentally filed O'Reilly's over-reaction for future reference, a possible weak point. Fisher did that with everybody he came into contact with, memorising their strengths and weaknesses and the buttons that had to be pressed to get the desired responses.

"Are you right?" he asked O'Reilly.

O'Reilly nodded. They got out of the car and Fisher led the way, climbing silently over a stone wall and walking across the dew-laden grass. O'Reilly's foot knocked against something hard that crunched and rolled, and then he heard a rustling noise behind him, something small scampering through the grass and making snuffling sounds. Hedgehogs, he realised. There were dozens of them, rolling into tight, spiked balls whenever they sensed the two men.

They reached another wall, this one taller than the first, and they had to scramble over. It surrounded a graveyard, close-clipped grass and gravelled paths, the gravestones a mixture of old stone crosses, chipped and weather-worn, and new, clean-cut marble. To their left was a grey stone church with a steeple. In the distance a vixen barked, and her call sparked off a cacophony of howls from dogs in the nearby housing estate. The two men dropped down into a crouch, their backs against the wall, while Fisher got his bearings.

He pointed towards a white concrete angel with spreading wings. "This way," he said, and took O'Reilly along the grass verge, past the angel and between two waist-high tombs, the sort vampires might lie in to sleep away the daylight hours, safe from sunlight. They walked through the drooping branches of a willow and then Fisher headed over to five tombstones lined up in front of the boundary wall like a stud poker hand. He kicked the one in the centre.

"There it is," he said. "Help me get it up."

They knelt down together, scraping away the soil to slip their hands underneath the stone and then they pushed it up, grunting with the strain until it came off the ground with a wet, slurping sound. They stood the stone upright and then leant it against the wall. The smell of damp, stale earth filled O'Reilly's nostrils and made him want to gag. Fisher scraped away the soil like a dog looking for a bone. Less than a foot down his fingers touched plastic and he pulled up a polythene-covered parcel which he handed to O'Reilly. There were two other bundles, one of which was obviously a rifle, but Fisher ignored them. All they needed this time was Semtex. They unwrapped the parcel and took out half the packages of explosive, six in all. They took three apiece, rewrapped the rest and put them back in the shallow hole before pushing the damp soil back and replacing the gravestone. They checked the surroundings to make sure that they were still alone in the graveyard, and then they left as silently as they'd arrived.

Nguyen drove his Renault van down the alley behind the shop, the early morning sun glinting off the bonnet. He'd already opened the two wooden gates that led to the shop's back yard where they usually unpacked deliveries and transferred the food into the freezers in the garage. He parked the van and switched off the engine. He had put on a pair of old overalls after he'd bathed that morning, and he pulled on a pair of plastic gloves. The van was white, three years old and mechanically sound. It had always been parked outside because the garage was used for storage, so it was rusting a little, and it had taken a few knocks from other cars. The name of the restaurant and the telephone number had been drawn in black paint on both sides. Nguyen had painted each letter himself, slowly and carefully, it had taken him hours, but it was the work of minutes to spray over them with a can of white spray paint. He sprayed the paint thinly so that it wouldn't run and he waited thirty minutes before giving it a second coat, and then a third to make sure that the lettering was completely covered.

While the third coat dried he transferred the tool box, bottles and bags from the garage, methodically crossing the contents off the list in his exercise-book so that he was sure he hadn't forgotten anything. It was all there, the acids, the bags of fertilizer, the bottles of antifreeze and cans of oil. He'd forgotten nothing. When he'd finished he used a screwdriver to prise the lid off the can of black paint and, resting a brand new artist's brush against a piece of garden cane, painted on a new set of letters and numbers. As he worked he suddenly felt as if he was being watched and he turned and looked at the upstairs window. A curtain twitched. It could have been Pham wondering what he was up to, or it could have been the wind. Nguyen stared up at the window but saw nothing so he returned to the painting.

When the final letter was in place he stood back and admired his handiwork. It was good. Almost as good as before, even though it had taken him about half as long. "Green Landscape Gardeners" it said, along with a London telephone number he'd taken from the Yellow Pages. The white paintwork around the lettering looked whiter than the rest of the van, but driving through the city streets would soon fix that up. The hairs on the back of his neck stood on end and he whirled around, but this time the curtains weren't moving and there was still no one there.

He went into the house through the back door and up the

stairs. His suitcase was already packed. He picked it up and was on the way to the door when he had a sudden urge to kneel and pray before the shrine. He got down on his knees and used his Zippo to light a stick of incense. He closed his eyes and breathed in the perfume and tried to empty his mind, to steel himself for the trials to come.

The incense filled his lungs. It was the same rich scent that always reminded him of his parents' farm, the room where he'd been born so many years ago. When was it? Could it really have been so long ago? Could it really have been 1943? Where had the years gone, how had they slipped by so easily? He could still picture every inch of the small family farm, close to the Gulf of Tonkin in North Vietnam.

Nguyen shuddered and opened his eyes. They were moist and he wiped them with the back of his hand. It was time to go.

He carried the bag downstairs, not bothering to say goodbye to Pham. He put the case in the back of the van, locked the doors and drove the van out of the yard. He headed north, towards Stranraer in Scotland and the ferry to Northern Ireland. Before he left London he stopped at a garden centre and loaded up the van with bags of peat and more fertilizer, a selection of bedding plants, and a spade and a fork.

It was a long, tiring drive to Stranraer, but Nguyen knew there was no real alternative. He needed the equipment and supplies in the van, so flying was out of the question. He had thought he'd be able to take a ferry from Liverpool direct to Belfast, but he'd discovered that the route had been cancelled some months earlier. The only car ferries now operating seemed to be from Stranraer to Larne in County Antrim, north of Belfast, or from Holyhead in Anglesey across to Dun Laoghaire, near Dublin in the South. Either route would mean hours behind the wheel, but he had reservations about driving through Southern Ireland and across the border. Better, he thought, to go direct to Northern Ireland and not worry about Customs or passports. He drove through the night and slept in the van during the morning before catching the ferry.

73

When he arrived at Larne he saw two men in a Ford Granada being taken to one side and their car searched by four men in bottle-green uniforms while a Labrador retriever sniffed around and wagged its tail, but he wasn't even given a second look. He knew why, it was nothing more than racism working in his favour. He was Oriental and the fighting in Ireland was between Caucasians.

He drove the van from the ferry terminal south to Belfast city centre. It was late evening and he had to find somewhere to stay. He stopped at a filling station and filled up with petrol and then bought a street map. He asked the teenage girl if she knew where there were any guest-houses but he couldn't understand her when she replied. He asked again and this time she spoke more slowly, as if he were a child, but the accent was so strange he couldn't follow what she was saying. He smiled and paid for the petrol and the map and left, none the wiser. He was starting to realise that he was, after all, in a different country.

There were other reminders. The police wore green uniforms and drove around in heavily fortified blue-grey Land-Rovers with metal screens protecting the sides. And there were soldiers everywhere wearing camouflage uniforms and helmets and carrying automatic rifles at the ready, barrels aimed at the ground. The army used green Land-Rovers, open at the top so that the men in the back were exposed but able to react quickly. It made good sense, Nguyen thought.

He drove by what he thought was a prison until he saw a sign that said it was a police station. He was so surprised that he stopped to look at it. He had never in his life seen such a thing, not even in Saigon. Thick metal mesh fences surrounded the building which had what appeared to be a gun turret on one corner. The top of the fence was a tangle of barbed wire and all the windows were firmly shuttered. It was a fortress. He had been considering asking a policeman to suggest a place to stay, but from the look of it the police in Northern Ireland were not geared up for handling general enquiries from the public. They were in a state of siege.

There were posts at each corner of the building, and on the top were surveillance cameras covering all the approaches.

There was a metallic rap against the passenger window of the van and Nguyen jumped. An unsmiling face under a peaked cap glared at him. He knocked on the door again with the barrel of his handgun. Nguyen leant over and wound down the window.

"Can I be of help to you, sir?" the policeman asked. Another officer appeared on the driver's side of the van. In the rear-view mirror he saw two more.

Nguyen smiled and waved the map at them. "I need somewhere to stay tonight. Do you know anywhere?"

The officer was already relaxing. He slid his gun back into his holster.

"Give me the map," he said. Nguyen switched on the small reading light and the policeman jabbed a finger in the bottom left-hand corner. "See this road here, Wellington Park?"

Nguyen nodded.

"There are a few places there, quite cheap." He handed the map back to Nguyen. "You'd best be on your way. And in future don't hang around in front of police stations in a van. We're a touch sensitive about that sort of thing. Understand?"

"I am sorry," said Nguyen. "Thank you for your help."

The policemen grouped together and watched him go, four stout figures in dark-green bullet-proof jackets.

Nguyen followed the map until he reached Wellington Park. He drove slowly down the road, looking left and right. He soon saw a guest-house but it had a sign in the window saying "No Vacancies". Further down the road there was another house with a sign saying "Vacancies" and Nguyen stopped the van in front of it.

It was dark now and the van appeared yellow under the streetlights. Nguyen pressed the doorbell and waited. The front door was wooden with two vertical strips of dimpled, frosted glass. Through the glass he saw a light come on and a figure ripple towards him. The door opened to reveal an overweight elderly woman with close-cropped grey hair and horn-rimmed spectacles. She was wearing a blue and white diamond-patterned dress and a plain white apron and was drying her hands on a red tea-towel.

"Do you have a room?" Nguyen asked her.

She looked him up and down and then scrutinised the van over his shoulder, screwing up her eyes to read the lettering.

"How long would you be wanting it for?" she asked.

Nguyen had difficulty understanding her accent but she spoke slowly enough for him to get the drift.

"Two nights, that is all. A room with a bath."

The old woman sucked her teeth and shook her head. "No baths in the rooms, but I do have one with a shower and a toilet. And a small wash-basin. It's right at the top of the house, very cosy."

Nguyen said he'd take it and the woman seemed doubtful, but then he pulled his wallet from his jacket and offered to pay her cash, in advance, and she smiled and ushered him inside. On the way up the stairs she introduced herself as Mrs McAllister as the notes disappeared behind the apron. He told her his name and she tried to repeat it, but gave up. The room was small with a single bed, an old wooden wardrobe, a dressing-table with an oval mirror, and a bedside table with a brass lamp with a pink lampshade. There was an ornate crucifix above the bed and to the left of the dressing-table was a black-framed photograph of John F. Kennedy. The ceiling sloped down to a window overlooking the street. Opposite the window was a door leading to a tiny bathroom with a tiled floor, a shower cubicle, a wash-basin with a cylindrical gas heater on the wall above it, and a low toilet with a black plastic seat. It was perfect.

The two pirates stood by the bar, tapping their feet to the driving beat of a pop song that Woody only vaguely recognised as they sipped orange juice from tall glasses. One of the pirates was middle-aged with a greying beard and a black patch over one eye, the other was younger with curly blond hair and flushed cheeks, but they wore matching outfits, baggy white shirts, red scarves around their necks, tight black breeches, white socks and shiny black shoes with big brassy buckles.

"Pirates?" said Maggie as she followed Woody to the bar.

"Yeah, they're with the pirate ships," said Woody, squeezing in between two stockbroker types and trying to catch the attention of the young barmaid.

"They would be," said Maggie, still mystified.

Woody pointed over her head, towards the large windows at the far end of the bar. "Pirate ships," he explained. "They're a tourist attraction. A sort of cross between Madame Tussaud's and the Cutty Sark. Those guys are sort of tour guides, cross their palms with silver and they'll take you below decks and tell you blood-curdling tales of life on the salty sea." The barmaid finally saw his plaintive look and came over. She gave him a beaming smile which faded a little when she saw that he was with a girl. Woody tended to attract barmaids, but was never sure why. He was still good-looking, he knew that, though he had allowed himself to go a bit recently. It was his eyes, an old girlfriend had told him. "Your eyes make me go weak at the knees, they're hot. Really hot," she'd said. Woody reckoned it wasn't anything to do with his looks, though. He thought it had more to do with the way he made them laugh. Sometimes he laughed them into bed before they realised what was happening. Woody winked at the barmaid, ordered drinks and carried them over to an empty table, close by the window so that Maggie could look at the sailing ships.

"They're not real, are they?" she asked, sitting down.

"I don't think so, they were built to pull in the punters to Tobacco Dock."

He raised his glass to her and she smiled. He was glad he'd taken her to Henry's Bar in Tobacco Dock because at least they could sit in comfort. Standing at the bar was essential when you were with the lads, but Maggie demanded a higher standard of comfort. No, that wasn't right, she didn't demand it. She deserved it.

"What are you thinking?" she asked.

"Just thinking how pretty you look," he said.

"Why thank you kind sir," she laughed. "You look exhausted."

"Yeah, I'm not sleeping well. It's the heat."

She frowned. "It's not that hot at the moment," she said.

Woody laughed. "No, it's my place. I've a bedsit in a house with about a dozen others, and mine is right next to the only bathroom. The landlord has fitted a hot-water tank as big as a Saturn rocket and my room is always in the high eighties. I have to have the window open even in winter."

Maggie smiled and shook her head. "Why don't you move, you daft sod?"

Woody shrugged. "It's cheap."

"You're not short of money, are you?"

Woody was immediately embarrassed because the answer was yes, he was bloody short of money. Always was. And always would be unless he got a staff job. The shifts weren't coming as often as they used to, he was overdrawn at the bank, yet he still had to stand his round at the pub while he brown-nosed his way back into the good books of the guys on the news desk. "No, it's convenient, that's all." Sure, if you fancied an hour on the bus to get into work.

"So is LA still an option?" she asked.

"Sure. Sure it is."

They drank and sat for a while looking at each other in silence. Woody spoke first.

"Now it's my turn to ask what you're thinking about."

Maggie pulled a face. "I was actually wondering why you didn't get a better job, why you waste your time on a comic like the *Sunday World*."

He sighed deeply, and explained that he didn't even have a job with the *Sunday World*, that he was only a freelance, dependent on shifts, and that even that didn't pay particularly well, not since the print and journalists unions had been broken along with the dockers and the miners and any other groups that had once been able to withhold their labour. She listened patiently and then reached over and touched his shoulder, a friendly nudge that showed she understood. Maybe even cared. She asked him why he couldn't get a staff job. At first he didn't want to tell her, but she pressed, pointing out that he was obviously bright, she'd begun reading his stuff and she could tell that it was good, so what had happened? She wormed it out of him eventually, his time on one of the broadsheets, the investigation into high-level corruption within a north of England police force, the drive home along the motorway, the blue flashing light in his rear mirror, the two surly traffic cops and the discovery of two hundred grams of cocaine under the passenger seat of his office car.

"They framed you?" she asked, wide-eyed.

"Yeah. I managed to avoid being sent down, but I lost the job and for a few years I couldn't get any sort of work. The papers didn't trust me, partly because of the drug thing, but I know for a fact that the cops were putting the word around, too. I stuck with it, though, went to work in the West Country for a while, and then some of the nationals began taking my copy again and now at least I've got my foot in the door. I'm lucky to have that, I guess."

"Jesus, Woody, that's terrible. That's appalling."

"That's life, Maggie."

She forced a smile. "I suppose the *Sunday World* isn't that bad," she said sympathetically. "Do they let you travel much?"

"Oh sure, we get around. There are always lots of freebies to be had."

"And do you get political stuff to do?"

"Sure. That's one of the good things about working on a Sunday paper. They have small staffs so there isn't too much specialisation. I mean, I have to do a lot of showbiz crap and weird stuff, but we get to help out with the big ones too."

"What are you working on at the moment?" she asked.

Woody coughed.

"Pardon?" she asked.

Woody looked shamefaced. "Vampire cats," he said. Maggie collapsed into hysterics.

The man approaching the churchyard was short but powerfully built and even in the dark it was obvious he was not a man to get into a fight with, not by choice anyway. He was wearing a brown leather jacket, scuffed and cracked with age, and dark-brown corduroy trousers. He carried a small sack, tied at the end with a short length of rope, and in one of the pockets of his jacket there was a flashlight and half a dozen metal snares. He'd done a fair bit of poaching in his youth, but he wasn't looking for rabbits, the snares were just cover in case he was discovered. In the back pocket of his trousers was a short-handled knife with a wicked blade which he was quite prepared to use if anyone saw through the poacher's disguise.

Somewhere in the dark he heard a hedgehog snuffle then squeal and he stopped and listened but heard nothing other than the night sounds of the English countryside and an airliner rumbling high overhead, red and green lights flashing.

He swung easily over the wall and landed silently in freshly dug soil. He was standing within inches of a new grave, a gaping black rectangular hole that seemed bottomless. He breathed a sigh of relief, if he'd vaulted the wall just a couple of feet to the right he'd have pitched headlong into it and broken a leg, or worse. The luck of the Irish, he thought with a smile. He stepped off the mound of earth and used the sack to smooth away his footprints before moving on. He skirted around the church and headed for the five tombstones.

He knelt down and lifted the stone that covered the stock-pile, pushing hard with his legs. He carefully leant it against the wall and then stood still, counting off sixty seconds in his head as he listened for anything out of the ordinary, because there was no way a poacher would be able to explain what he was doing lifting a gravestone, especially a gravestone that concealed IRA explosives. Still nothing, even the hedgehogs had fallen silent.

He dug into the earth with his hands and pulled out three polythene-covered packages, working quickly but carefully. If he was surprised to see half of the Semtex explosive missing, his face showed no sign of it. He rewrapped the parcels, replaced the soil and dropped the stone back over the hiding place. He brushed the dirt from his hands, checked that the surrounding area was clean and then walked down the gravel path and out of the churchyard.

Beth McKinstry was on the telephone when Nguyen walked into the office. He stood in front of her desk and waited. He was wearing his only suit, a grey one that was starting to go shiny at the elbows. He had on a white shirt and a blue V-necked pullover with three white skiers across the front. He was holding a white carrier bag in both hands, clasping it to his chest like a baby. Murphy was sitting on the sofa reading a magazine and massaging his aching shoulder. He'd looked up when Nguyen entered, but immediately dismissed him as any sort of potential threat and carried on reading.

Beth watched Nguyen as she talked, frowning slightly. He smiled and nodded at her and she looked down. She didn't look up again until she'd finished the call. As she replaced the phone Kavanagh came out of Hennessy's office and quietly closed the door behind him. He barely glanced at Nguyen before sitting down next to Murphy.

"Yes?" said Beth.

"Please, I would like to speak with Mr Liam Hennessy."

"And your name is?" she said.

"Nguyen Ngoc Minh," he answered.

"Can I tell him what it is about?" She couldn't even attempt to repeat his name.

"It is very difficult to explain," he told her.

She reached for the intercom button but stopped halfway. "Are you the man who phoned last week?" she asked.

"I phoned many times," said Nguyen.

Beth took her hand away from the intercom. "I'm afraid Mr Hennessy is very busy. He won't be able to see you."

"I must see him," Nguyen repeated.

"He's busy!" insisted Beth, raising her voice. Her cheeks flushed red.

Murphy and Kavanagh glanced up. The secretary was

good-natured to a fault and rarely lost her temper. Nguyen said nothing, he just smiled.

"If you leave your number I'll call you to arrange an appointment once I have spoken with Mr Hennessy," she said.

Still Nguyen said nothing.

"You must go!" she said. Murphy and Kavanagh got to their feet and walked over to Nguyen.

"Best you do as the lady says," said Murphy quietly.

Nguyen looked at Murphy and the Irishman could see there was no trace of fear in his eyes. "I must see him," he said quietly.

Kavanagh put his hand on Nguyen's shoulder. "What's the crack?" he asked Beth.

"He's been ringing up at all hours asking to see Liam. He won't take no for an answer."

"Yez heard the lady, Mr Hennessy doesn't want to see yez," said Kavanagh, gripping Nguyen's shoulder and pulling him away from the desk. For a second Nguyen was off balance and he clutched the carrier bag tightly as if afraid that it might fall.

"What have you got there?" said Murphy, for the first time regarding the man as a possible threat. It wasn't likely that the Loyalists would use a Chinaman to attack Hennessy, he thought, but these days you never could tell. He reached for the bag.

"My shopping," said Nguyen.

"Let's see," said Kavanagh. "Let's see what yez got there." At first it looked as if Nguyen would resist, but then the tension in his wiry body eased and he handed the bag to Kavanagh. Kavanagh opened it. It contained two bottles of lemonade, a loaf of bread, a can of Heinz baked beans and a brown paper bag full of new potatoes. Seeing that he was satisfied with the inspection, Nguyen held out his hands for the bag, but Kavanagh kept it away from him.

"Pat him down," he said to Murphy. Murphy moved behind Nguyen and ran his hands expertly up and down his body, checking everywhere that a weapon could be concealed. There was a Swiss Army knife in one of the side pockets of the suit, but other than that there was nothing remotely suspicious – a small roll of Sellotape, a box of matches, some string, a set of keys, a pack of cigarettes and a wallet. The normal sort of pocket junk that anyone might have on them. "He's OK," he said to Kavanagh, who handed back the carrier bag.

"Go," he said. "Before we make yez go."

Nguyen shook his head. Kavanagh and Murphy roughly seized an arm each and were preparing to frog-march him out, when the door to Hennessy's office opened. Hennessy's face creased into a puzzled frown when he saw what was going on.

"It's the man who's been phoning," said Beth, before he could speak.

"Ah . . . The Chinaman," said Hennessy, walking across to Beth's desk. "You're a long way from home."

Nguyen held the carrier bag tightly to his chest. "You would not talk to me on the telephone," he said.

"Out," said Murphy, but Hennessy held up his hand.

"No, if he's come all this way I might as well talk to him, boys."

"Yer man's got a knife," said Kavanagh.

"A knife?"

"A Swiss Army knife."

"Well take it off him. Look at him, for God's sake. How much damage can he do with two strapping fellows like yourselves around? Jesus, Mary and Joseph, let the man be."

Kavanagh took the knife from Nguyen and Murphy took the carrier bag.

"You can pick them up on your way out," said Beth as Hennessy led Nguyen into his private office. He waved him to a hard-backed leather seat in front of his desk while he closed the door behind them.

Nguyen sat with his hands folded in his lap while Hennessy sat down behind the desk and leant forward, his arms folded across the wide blotter which took up most of its surface. "Let me tell you right from the start, you are wasting your time." Hennessy said each word clearly and slowly as if addressing a particularly thick-skulled juror because he wasn't sure how good The Chinaman's command of English was. "I realise you are upset and angry, and I understand how you must want revenge for what has happened to your family, but there is nothing I can do to help you. And you must know that it is very dangerous for you to be in Belfast asking about such things." He pressed the tips of his fingers against his temples as if trying to suppress a headache and studied Nguyen. "It is very dangerous," he repeated.

Nguyen nodded thoughtfully. "I do understand. But if you do not know who the men are, you can surely find out. I want you to find out for me."

Hennessy shook his head, amazed at the man's audacity, or stupidity. Nguyen took the pack of cigarettes and the matches from his pocket.

"Can I smoke?" he asked Hennessy. Hennessy nodded and Nguyen held out the pack to him, offering him one. The lawyer refused and watched as Nguyen lit a cigarette and inhaled deeply. Hennessy noticed how steady The Chinaman's hands were, as steady as the unblinking brown eyes that seemed to look through his skull as easily as they penetrated the wreathes of smoke.

"You will change your mind," said Nguyen, and it was a statement, not a question.

"No," said Hennessy.

Nguyen smiled, and it was the smile of a man who has the sure and certain knowledge that he is right. He stood up and bowed once to Hennessy and then left the office. Murphy and Kavanagh were waiting for him outside, and they gave him his carrier bag and the penknife. He thanked them politely and turned to Beth and thanked her as well.

"Can I use your toilet?" he asked, and she told him there was one in the corridor outside. She pointed at the large sheet of glass at the entrance to the reception and through it he saw the door with "Gentlemen" on it. He thanked them all again and left the office, closing the door quietly behind him. The washroom was small with whitewashed walls and a black tiled floor. There was a wash-basin, a urinal and a toilet in a cubicle. There was a mirror screwed to the wall above the basin and by the door was a paper-towel dispenser and below it a large steel wastepaper bin.

Nguyen entered the cubicle, shut the door and locked it. There was a black plastic lid on the toilet and he closed it and then sat down, placing the carrier bag gently on the floor. He took one of the bottles out and held it between his knees. It contained the antifreeze. He took out the second bottle, the one containing concentrated sulphuric acid. He used the Sellotape to bind the bottles together, wrapping it round and round until he was certain they were secure. He took out the length of string and tied it around the necks of the bottles, making quite sure there was no way it could slip. Individually the bottles of liquid were inert, but together they were very dangerous. He put the bottles on the floor and draped the string over his left leg. He took the box of matches out of his pocket and slid the string through it. He pulled the string to check that it was safely tied and then put his hands under the bottoms of the bottles and stood up slowly. The cistern was high up on the wall and Nguyen stood on the toilet seat to attach the string to the lever which operated the flushing system. When he was sure it was secure he carefully removed his hands. The bottles turned slowly in the air above the tiled floor. He unscrewed the caps from the bottles and slipped them into his pocket. Then he pulled the filter off the cigarette and stuck the frayed end into the matchbox so that the burning tip was about three-quarters of an inch beyond the match heads. Nguyen stepped down, picked up the carrier bag and left the cubicle. He used the penknife to slide the lock closed so that it showed "Engaged".

As he left the toilet he smiled a goodbye to Beth. There was no rush, it would take at least two minutes for the cigarette to burn down far enough to set the matches alight. He walked slowly down the stairs and into Donegall Square. Overhead a helicopter hovered high in the air like a bird of prey searching for a victim.

The intercom on Beth's desk buzzed and Hennessy's voice summoned her into the office. From their sofas, Kavanagh and Murphy watched her hips swing as she walked to the door.

"I would," said Murphy, whispering because he knew what a tongue-lashing he'd get if she heard him.

"Who wouldn't?" replied Kavanagh. "But her old man'd focking kill ye."

Hennessy was standing by his window watching Nguyen walk down the road, swinging his carrier bag full of shopping.

"I'm sorry, Liam," she said, before he could speak. "He caught me by surprise. Next time I won't let him disturb you."

"That's all right, Beth. Just tell Murphy and Kavanagh to take care of it if he turns up again." Nguyen stepped off the pavement, crossed the road and disappeared into a side street. Hennessy turned his back on the window. "I think that man is going to be trouble," he said.

"Don't be silly, Liam," she said as if admonishing a child. "What can a man like him do?"

The sound of the explosion made them both flinch, Beth putting her hands to her face and Hennessy ducking away from the window. Through the open door they saw Kavanagh and Murphy dive to the ground. "Keep down!" Murphy yelled at them.

"What's going on?" Hennessy shouted. They didn't answer. They were as confused as he was.

Beth was already on the floor, crouched by the side of the door. Hennessy went over to her and put his arms around her.

Murphy and Kavanagh were crawling over the carpet to check out the corridor. Kavanagh nudged open the door. The corridor was empty, then a pale-faced young man in a three-piece suit nervously appeared from an office further along.

"Mother of God, what happened?" said the young man.

Kavanagh got to his feet. Smoke was billowing out of the Gents, acrid-smelling and burning as he inhaled. He coughed and his eyes watered as he gingerly pushed open the door to the toilet. Fumes billowed out and the sprinklers in the corridor hissed into life and he ducked back into the office. In the distance he heard a police siren, and then another. He told Murphy to guard the door while he went back to Hennessy's office and helped him and Beth to their feet.

Beth flopped on to a chair and Hennessy went over to his drinks cabinet and poured two Irish whiskies. He didn't offer one to Kavanagh, who was teetotal. Beth gulped hers down and Hennessy followed her example.

Before long, half a dozen green-uniformed RUC officers in bullet-proof vests came tearing down the corridor. A bull-necked sergeant ordered them to stay where they were and left a constable to keep an eye on them. The area round the toilet was cordoned off and then two men in dark-blue over-alls carrying big black cases went in. The phone on Beth's desk rang, startling them all, and she asked the constable if it was OK to answer it. He nodded, his face blank. The men in the RUC had no love for Hennessy and his associates and Hennessy knew that the constable would probably have preferred them all to have been plastered over the walls by the explosion rather than sitting at the desk and drinking whiskey. While Beth was talking on the phone a CID officer in a sheepskin jacket arrived. He flashed his card to Hennessy and introduced himself as Inspector Greig. Behind him stood a young plain-clothes sergeant, a tall, gangly youth with a small, toothbrush moustache. He had the same couldn't-give-a-shit look as the uniformed constable.

"It seems as if you've had a wee bit of bother, Mr Hennessy," said Greig. "Unless it was one of your own boys being a tad careless."

Hennessy shrugged. "These things happen," he said. "Can I offer you a whiskey, Inspector?"

Greig refused, as Hennessy knew he would. "I suppose it's a waste of time asking if you have any idea who might have done this?" said Greig, smiling through tight lips.

Kavanagh laughed sharply but Hennessy threw him a withering look. It was bad enough having the RUC in the office, but if they antagonised them they'd end up being hauled in for questioning and Hennessy didn't want the inconvenience or the publicity.

"Anyway, you'd better take care in future, Mr Hennessy."

"What do you mean?"

"It looks to have been more of a warning than anything else. According to our forensic boys it was a home-made device, in fact device is hardly the right word. They reckon it was a couple of bottles of chemicals that did the damage."

Murphy remembered the bottles in The Chinaman's carrier bag but said nothing.

"An accident?" said Hennessy.

Greig smiled thinly again. "I hardly think they tied themselves to the toilet cistern," he said. "No, it was a simple chemical bomb, the sort we used to make as kids. Sulphuric acid and ethylene glycol. Antifreeze to you and me. Tie a bottle of each together and drop on to a hard surface. Bang! Did you never do that when you were a kid, Mr Hennessy? Great crack." He could see by the look on the lawyer's face that the answer was no. Greig shrugged. "I suppose we went to different schools, eh? Anyway, it would make a big enough explosion to wreck the room, and you wouldn't be laughing if you were in there, but it never stood a chance of damaging the building. It wasn't what you'd call a serious bomb, if you get my drift. Which makes me think that perhaps it was a warning. I don't suppose there's any point in asking if you've got any enemies, is there Mr Hennessy?" Greig was enjoying the Sinn Fein adviser's obvious discomfort.

"I'll certainly keep you informed if anyone comes to mind, Inspector," Hennessy replied.

"I won't hold my breath."

"Probably best," said Hennessy.

"Can I show you out, Inspector?" asked Beth, sensing that underneath the banter her boss was beginning to lose his temper.

Greig hesitated as if loath to let Hennessy off the hook, but then he nodded and followed her out of the office. His sergeant looked hard at Murphy and Kavanagh as he went out, but the two men returned his gaze with easy smiles. They were long past the stage of fearing the police, the army, or anyone else who tried to impose their authority. Greig went into the toilet to speak to the forensic team again. The sergeant turned to speak to Beth but she closed the door firmly in his face.

Hennessy watched her from the door of his office and, satisfied that she wasn't in shock, gently closed the door.

Kavanagh and Murphy tensed, fearing the sharp edge of Hennessy's tongue a thousand times more than hard looks from under-age detectives, but his anger wasn't directed at them.

"I want that Chinaman found," he said with barely suppressed fury. "I want him found and brought to me."

The phone rang and Hennessy picked it up.

"Liam, it's him!" said Beth. She knew that Hennessy had said he wouldn't take any more calls from him, but she was smart enough to know that the situation was now different.

"Put him on please, Beth. Are you OK?"

"I'm fine, Liam. Really." The line clicked and Hennessy waited for The Chinaman to speak.

"Mr Hennessy?" said Nguyen, not sure if he had been put through.

"What do you want?" said Hennessy.

"Mr Hennessy, you know what I want. I telephoned to see if you had changed your mind."

"Why would I have changed my mind?" said Hennessy quietly.

"You know why," said Nguyen.

Hennessy took a deep breath. "I think that perhaps it would be a good idea if we spoke about this again. It might be we can come to an arrangement. Come back and we'll talk."

Nguyen laughed without humour. "I think not," he said. "You will not see me again, Mr Hennessy. But you will be hearing from me."

"It will take a lot more than a loud noise in my toilet to change my mind."

"So be it," said Nguyen, and hung up.

"The bastard," spat Hennessy. "Who the hell does he think he is, threatening me like that?" He slammed down the phone and glared at the two men by his desk.

"Get his description to the boys," he said. "I want him found."

"It might be an idea if yez left Belfast for a few days, just in case," suggested Kavanagh.

"Are you telling me that you can't protect me in my own city?" said Hennessy.

"I'm not saying that, but it would be easier if we went down to yez farm. That's all."

"No," said Hennessy. "He is not driving me out of my own city, he's not going to make me run like a scared dog. Just put the word out."

He waved them away impatiently and flopped down into his chair. He took a mouthful of whiskey, and then another. He knew he shouldn't have lost his temper, but the bombing had shaken him badly. It made him acutely aware of his own mortality, that his own threescore years and ten wasn't all that far away, and the fact that a vindictive Chinaman with a bottle of antifreeze could steal away the years he had left made him very angry. And afraid. The supercilious detective had said it had been a warning. Very well, he would regard it as just that.

Nguyen didn't drive straight back to the guest-house. Once he'd collected his van from the car park off Gloucester Street he headed north along Victoria Street and then cut westwards across the city along Divis Street, past grim blocks of flats, to where it turned into Falls Road. It wasn't that he was worried about being followed, because he knew he was long gone from Donegall Square before the bottles crashed on to the floor. It wasn't that he enjoyed driving, either. He'd always found sitting behind the steering wheel stressful and he'd been looking forward to the day when his daughter would pass her driving test so that she could do all the restaurant deliveries for him. He drove around to get a feel of the city and its people, and at the back of his mind lurked the thought that by understanding the people of Belfast he might be able to understand why the IRA had killed his family. The city centre was prosperous, shiny fronted shops and clean pavements. The cars in the streets were mainly new and well cared for and there were few signs of a city in the throes of sectarian violence. "Belfast Says No" said a banner Nguyen had seen hanging under the green dome of City Hall in Donegall Square, but he didn't know what the city was saying "no" to.

There was a strong police and army presence, with some streets sealed off with metal railings manned by armed policemen and turnstiles to allow pedestrians through one at a time, but there was no air of tension, none that Nguyen could detect, anyway. He had a large-scale map of Belfast and its surroundings spread over the passenger seat, and as he stopped at a red traffic light he scanned it, trying to pronounce the strange names: Knocknagoney, Ballyhackamore, Cregagh, Skegoneill, Ligoniel, Ballynafeigh.

A horn sounded and he realised the light had turned green. He missed first gear and went into third by mistake and the van stalled. The horn blared out again and it was joined by others until he got the engine started-again and pulled away jerkily.

He drove along the Falls Road, the Royal Victoria Hospital on his left, and the city changed character. It took on a brooding, menacing air. He saw burnt-out cars down side roads, rusting hulks that had obviously been there for months, like the skeletons of long-dead animals. There were children everywhere, in push-chairs, playing football on the pavements, walking with their parents, standing on street corners, loitering outside pubs, children with worn clothes and unkempt hair and runny noses. He drove by red-brick houses that had been gutted and never repaired, derelict wrecks like rotting stumps in a mouthful of bad teeth. There were splashes of colour among the drab greyness – extravagant murals on the gable ends of the terraces, paintings of masked men with machine guns, elaborate crosses, memorials to hunger strikers who had died in prison, and the tricolour, the Irish flag. There were slogans too, many of which Nguyen didn't understand, but there were some he could read: "Support The Provisionals", "Troops Out", "Ireland for the Irish". He drove by a pub, windows protected with thick wire mesh. There were two men standing either side of a black wooden door with their hands in their pockets and they scrutinised the van with hostile eyes. Lookouts, Nguyen decided. He would have to be more careful where he showed himself. The city centre had lulled him into a false sense of security. Out here, in the Catholic working-class areas, he could feel the mistrust in the air like the cloying damp of a morning mist. The men saw that Nguyen was Oriental and immediately lost interest in him.

The road curved gently and on his right Nguyen saw a huge graveyard which stretched as far as he could see, and then another cemetery on his left as he followed Glen Road and then turned left at a roundabout and headed south-east on Kennedy Way through the district shown on the map as Andersonstown. He slowed down to look at two depressing rows of flats, precast greying concrete with dirty windows and badly painted frames. The muddy verge of trampled grass that surrounded the blocks was littered with empty crisp packets, tattered pages of abandoned tabloid newspapers, stale fish and chip wrappers and broken bottles, the flotsam and jetsam of inner city life. Nguyen was unable to understand why the people who lived there did not take better care of their surroundings. How could they tolerate such squalor, he thought. Living in poverty was one thing, but that was no excuse for behaving like animals. He shook his head sadly.

He drove towards a place called Malone and the surroundings improved, the depressing neglect giving way to well-kept gardens and freshly painted houses, and then he indicated left on to Malone Road, heading back to the city centre. Just before he reached the city's Botanic Gardens he turned left into Wellington Park, musing over what he had seen. The people who lived in the depressed areas had little to lose, he realised. If his enemy came from the rubbish-strewn slums and the neglected high-rise monstrosities, then surely prison would hold no fear for them. Children reared there would be tough, uncaring, loyal to their own and aggressive against intruders. Their poverty would bind them like iron chains. He wouldn't be taking on one man, he would be going against the whole of the IRA. He switched off the engine and stared out with unseeing eyes. It had to be done, whatever the cost. He had no choice. He owed it to his wife, and to his daughters.

*　　*　　*

Liam Hennessy stood in his garden and looked up at the rocky outcrop they called Napoleon's Nose. Not that it looked like a nose, or any other part of Napoleon's anatomy. Jackie, his red setter, loped out of the house and over the lawn towards him. He bent down and ruffled her ears and let her lick his hands.

He walked around the lawn with his dog, checking the trees and plants. He was a keen gardener but his law practice and political activities left him little time to attend to the half acre or so that surrounded his four-bedroomed red-brick house in Antrim Road. He employed part-time a retired gardener who had formerly helped to tend the city's Botanic Gardens, but he insisted on checking his progress every morning. He knelt down and examined a heather-covered rockery and Jackie ran up and licked his cheek with her sloppy tongue. He pushed her away and laughed.

"She wants a walk," said his wife. He turned and straightened up, brushing his knees.

"You could creep up on the devil himself, Mary," he laughed. She handed him a mug of tea.

"Your dog wants a walk," she repeated. Mary Hennessy looked a good deal less than her forty-six years, tall and slim with dark brown, lightly curled hair in a pageboy cut. Hennessy looked at her appreciatively as he took the mug. She didn't look like a woman who had two teenage children. Her skin was smooth and lightly tanned and the few wrinkles she had made her look all the more beautiful. She still turned the heads of men half her age and she knew it. There were times when he was so afraid of losing her that his stomach churned.

"Our dog," he corrected.

She nodded at the setter as it sat at his feet looking up at him with undisguised love. "Just look at her," she said.

"I can remember when there was a look not unlike that in your own fair eyes," he teased, and she laughed. The phone rang and she ran across the lawn to the house. She runs, for God's sake, thought Hennessy, she runs like an excited child and she laughs out loud. He tried to remember when he'd last laughed out loud. He couldn't recall exactly when it was but it was after hearing Ian Paisley being interviewed on television and it wasn't a gentle, lilting laugh like Mary's, it was sarcastic and biting.

"Jackie," he said, "I am getting old."

The red setter looked up at him and woofed as if agreeing and he reached down and patted her on the head.

"There's no time for a walk, old girl. The car will be here any moment, sure enough."

Jim Kavanagh and Christy Murphy were at Hennessy's side all day and most of the evening, but during the night they went home to sleep and their places were taken by two men from a pool of about a dozen trusted volunteers who stayed outside his house in whatever car they were using. Jimmy McMahon took the black Jaguar to his own house in north Belfast and brought Kavanagh and Murphy with him first thing in the morning. Hennessy looked at his watch. They were late.

Mary appeared at the back door and waved to him. "It's Christy," she shouted.

Jackie's ears pricked up and she romped towards her in the mistaken belief that she was being called in for some titbit. Hennessy walked after her, cursing under his breath and taking care not to spill his tea. The Jaguar had only just come out of the garage after a very expensive service and he hoped it hadn't been in an accident.

Mary handed the phone to him. Murphy sounded short of breath. "The bastards tried to kill us," he said.

"What are you talking about?" asked Hennessy.

"The bastards tried to blow us up."

"Calm down, Christy," Hennessy soothed. "Just tell me what happened."

He heard Murphy take a deep breath before speaking. "We went to get the Jaguar out of Jimmy's garage. He got into the driving seat and was just about to start up the sodding thing when we saw it. Holy Mary, mother of God, if we hadn't spotted it we'd all have been . . ."

"What happened?" interrupted Hennessy impatiently.

"They used a flash-bulb and a couple of wires."

"A flash-bulb?"

"A flash-bulb, and it had been covered in some sort of red powder. It was a home-made detonator, as soon as the ignition key was turned it would have exploded the petrol in the tank."

"OK, Christy. Where are you now?"

"We're all in Jimmy's house."

There was a muttering in the background and the sound of a bottle clinking against a glass. The boys were having a wee snort to calm their nerves, and Hennessy didn't blame them. They'd had two narrow escapes in as many days.

"Listen, this is what you do. Have you removed it?"

"Sure enough, we pulled it out of the tank, but it's still connected."

"Leave it just as it is. Call Willie O'Hara and get him to look at it, he knows what he's doing. And get him to check out the whole car, from top to bottom. As soon as he's given it the all clear, you and Jim come on over. And Christy?"

"Yeah?"

"Take it easy."

He replaced the receiver. The mug of tea was still in his left hand, untouched. He sipped it, a deep frown on his forehead.

"Something wrong?" asked his wife.

He nodded. "Somebody has just tried to blow up the car."

Mary's eyes widened and her mouth opened. He hadn't told her about the explosion at the office because he hadn't wanted to worry her, but he took her into the kitchen and sat her down at the pine breakfast table and told her that there had been two attempts on his life, albeit half-hearted ones.

There was a scratching noise at the door and Hennessy walked over to let in the dog. She scuttled beneath the table and Hennessy realised then how vulnerable he was. He went down the hall, opened the front door and waved over the two men sitting in a blue Ford Escort to the left of the driveway. He told them to be extra careful and sent one of them to stand guard by the back door until Murphy and Kavanagh arrived.

He returned to the kitchen and flashed his wife a smile as he sat down.

"Who do you think is behind this? The Ulster Defence Association?"

Hennessy shrugged and looked down at his mug of tea. A brownish scum was beginning to form on the surface and he poked it with his finger.

"There was some clever dick inspector at the office who said it might be a warning."

"A warning?"

Hennessy looked up and was pleased to see the concern in her eyes. "The bomb in the office wasn't really a bomb, it was a home-made affair that was limited in terms of the damage it could do. And from the sound of it the job they tried to do on the car today was pretty amateurish, too. I mean, they must be pretty stupid not to realise that the first thing we do every morning is to check out the car."

"But why would anyone want to warn you, Liam? The UDA don't normally bother issuing warnings, do they?"

She was right, of course. In recent years there had been an unspoken agreement between the various political groupings not to assassinate the top echelons, an understanding that the leaders had to be able to talk with their opposite numbers without the constant fear of a shotgun blast through the letter-box or a pistol to the back of the neck. The Brighton bombing had shown that no one was safe, not even the Prime Minister, and the whole world had seen a President take a bullet from a lone gunman. The Paisleys and the Adamses and the Hennessys wouldn't last a week if they ever declared open season on each other, but as it was they could move fairly safely through the city. They still kept their bodyguards and trusted the opposition about as much as they trusted the British Government, but the bad old days when a bodyguard had to take a bullet in the shoulder to protect Hennessy were long gone. But if the truce was now over, there'd be no warning, they'd just cut him down with a hail of bullets as he got out of his car. They wouldn't mess around with do-it-yourself bombs. No, this couldn't be political. But if it wasn't political, what was it?

He stood up and put his hand gently under Mary's chin, tilting her head upwards. "There was a man came round to the office yesterday, a Chinaman. His wife and daughter were killed in one of the London bombings. He thinks I'm responsible."

"He came all the way to Belfast to see you?"

"He wants me to tell him who's behind the bombing campaign. I sent him packing and a few minutes later our toilet exploded. Now this."

She shook her head away from his hand. "Why haven't you told the police this?"

"We're not sure it's him. And anyway, it's the sort of thing we can handle ourselves."

"Liam!" she said angrily. "You're playing with our lives here!"

"If it is him we'll soon stop him, don't worry. He's Chinese, he won't be difficult to spot in Belfast."

"I hope you're right," she said. The look of concern had gone now, and it had been replaced by something else, something that seemed to Hennessy to be uncomfortably like contempt. It was a look that his wife was giving him more and more often these days, he thought with a heavy heart. He couldn't seem to do anything right. He decided not to try to win her around, knowing that he was sure to fail.

"I'll be in the study until Jim and Christy get here," he said as he walked out of the kitchen. Jackie rushed out from under the table, her claws clicking against the tiles, and loyally followed him out.

He went into his study and closed the door. Jackie went to her wicker basket by the side of the french window which led on to the small patio and she settled into it with a deep and mournful sigh as if offering sympathy for the rough treatment he was getting from Mary. He knew that she would prefer him to take a tougher line with the Protestant extremists, and on more than one occasion she'd urged him to mount an all-out offensive against the UDA. It was so strange, he thought, the way that he himself had mellowed over the years and she had become more and more committed to an armed struggle. The more he tried to persuade her that the only solution was a negotiated one, the more she seemed to turn away from him, physically and emotionally. But he knew that he was right, that his way was the only way forward. Anything else would only end in bloodshed. Knowing that he was right didn't make him feel any better.

There was a safe set into the wall behind a framed hunting print over a cast-iron fireplace; Hennessy opened it and took out a brown A4 manila envelope. He flicked the open end with a thumbnail as he walked over to the desk. Inside was a sheaf of papers, each a report on an individual arms cache. There were fifteen in all, and he was expecting a further six by nightfall. He spread the sheets out on the desk and examined them. Three of the caches had been interfered with. In all, fifteen kilograms of Semtex had been taken, along with a dozen detonators, two mercury tilt switches, two handguns and a small amount of ammunition. Everything else necessary for the construction of bombs – wires, timing devices, transmitters – could be bought from High Street stores. Hennessy was sure that the maverick IRA team had been stealing from the organisation's munition dumps and he was equally certain that they were being helped by somebody inside the organisation. The trouble was that there was no pattern, no connection between the three dumps. They were the responsibility of three different IRA cells. He grunted and gathered up the papers. Jackie lifted her head and watched him put the sheets back into the envelope.

"Maybe the remaining inspections will supply the answer," he said to her and she chuffed in agreement.

Hennessy heard a car arrive outside and footsteps crunching on the gravelled drive before the doorbell rang. He waited to see if Mary would answer it, but he wasn't surprised when she didn't. He went and opened the door to let in Kavanagh and Murphy and a small sharp-faced man with a straggly moustache and grey, watery eyes, Willie O'Hara. Jimmy McMahon stayed outside in the Jaguar, reluctant to let it out of his sight. Willie was wearing his normal baggy grey suit, the trousers held up by a greasy brown belt, and he was carrying a paper bag. Hennessy took the three men into the study. "Was the car clear?" he asked O'Hara.

"Other than this?" answered the little man, holding up the bag. "Yeah, this was all, but it would've been more than enough." He reached in his hand and took out a coil of black wire and held it out to Hennessy. "Crude, but it would've done the job."

There were two pieces of wire, each about ten-foot long, and both had been soldered to the flash-bulb.

Hennessy pointed to the red powder which covered the flash-bulb. "What's this?" he asked.

O'Hara's eyes shone. "Ground up match-heads," he said. "Mainly potassium chlorate. Just to add an extra kick. Probably wouldn't have been necessary, but it's a nice touch."

"How does it work?"

"Whoever it was had prised open the fuel cap and left the flash-bulb dangling just inside the tank, in the fumes above the petrol. You turn the key and up she goes."

"Guaranteed?"

O'Hara frowned, wondering what Hennessy was getting at. "Pretty certain. I mean, it's not the sort of gadget we'd use because there's always an outside chance that the bulb might fall into the petrol in which case it wouldn't ignite it. And it's also pretty easy to spot."

"A warning?"

O'Hara nodded eagerly. "Yeah, that's exactly what I was thinking. Is somebody giving you trouble?"

"I've an idea who it might be, yes. Willie, thanks for your help." Hennessy shook him by the hand and showed him out, telling Jimmy to drive O'Hara wherever he wanted to go.

Back in the study he sat behind his desk and told Kavanagh and Murphy to make themselves comfortable. He offered them tea or coffee but they declined. He didn't offer them anything stronger because even under stress Kavanagh didn't touch alcohol and he could already smell whiskey on Murphy's breath and they'd all need clear heads.

"I'm coming round to thinking that maybe you were right about what you said yesterday, Jim," Hennessy said to Kavanagh.

"About going to the farm?"

Hennessy nodded. "I think it's best. The weekend's

coming up, and I can just as easily run things from there, for a short time at least. Mary and I will go tonight, Jimmy and Christy can come with us and we'll take another couple of lads with us just to be on the safe side."

"Ye want me to stay here?" asked Kavanagh.

"I want you to organise a search for this Chinaman. He shouldn't be that hard to find, not in Belfast. There can't be that many Chinese here, and this one's a stranger, from London. He's got to be staying somewhere."

"No problem," said Kavanagh.

"And I'm bringing Sean Morrison back."

Both Kavanagh and Murphy smiled. They knew Morrison well and had worked together on many occasions.

"He's still in New York?" asked Murphy. Morrison had left Belfast more than two years earlier.

"Yeah, he's liaising with the various Noraid groups in North America." Morrison had told Hennessy he wanted to get out of Belfast for a while and his request had come at a time when fund-raising in the United States had been going through a rough patch. Morrison had made a difference, not the least because his broad Belfast accent and typical Irish good looks went down so well with the Americans. He looked just like they expected an IRA activist should, tall, broad-shouldered, with curly black hair and piercing blue eyes. He spoke well and with conviction about the aims of the organisation and the Noraid groups had used him to full advantage. Morrison had also been a great help in arranging for forged passports and visas for IRA members who wanted to get in and out of the United States without being identified, and had recently begun to form links with arms suppliers. He had been a godsend. But right now Hennessy needed someone he could trust, and he trusted Morrison with his life.

He told Kavanagh to start the hunt for The Chinaman right away, and asked Murphy to step up security arrangements around the house. He waited until he was alone before picking up the phone and calling New York.

Morrison answered on the third ring, his voice thick with sleep.

"Good morning, Sean. What time is it in the Big Apple?"

Morrison groaned. "Almost five o'clock," he said. "What's wrong, Liam?"

"I need you back here, Sean."

"When?"

"Today."

Morrison groaned again. "You don't ask much, do you?" He didn't ask why because he knew the security forces weren't averse to tapping Hennessy's phone, legally or otherwise.

"I'd like you to come straight here, to my house," Hennessy continued. '"I'll explain everything when you arrive. How long do you think it'll take you?"

"Ten hours or so, Liam, a lot depends on the timing of the direct flights." His voice was clearer now. "I'll call you if there are any problems."

Hennessy thanked him and replaced the receiver. He picked up the wires and flash-bulb that Willie had left on his desk and toyed with them, deep in thought.

Nguyen drove the Renault to a Chinese take-away and bought six portions of plain boiled rice, three of roast pork and three of roast chicken. He told the Hong Kong Chinese behind the counter that he didn't want any sauce or anything, just meat. The food came in the same foil containers with white cardboard lids that he'd used in his own shop in Clapham. He asked for a carrier bag, put the food in the back of the van and then drove to a pub in the countryside to buy ice. The landlord of the first place he tried said he didn't have enough for his own use, never mind to sell to someone who wasn't even a regular. The man behind the bar at the second pub was more sympathetic to Nguyen's story of a wife with an arthritic leg which the doctor said would be helped if she lay with it in an ice bath. He sold him three carrier bags full of ice-cubes shovelled from a large clanking ice-machine for a nominal sum and Nguyen drove back to the guest-house as quickly as he dared. He parked the van, put the packs of ice and one of the bags of fertilizer into two holdalls and carried them inside. Mrs McAllister was dusting the hall and she smiled when she saw him. "Lovely day, isn't it?" she said.

He smiled, nodded and slipped by her. He put the fertilizer on the bathroom floor, dropped the ice into the bottom of the shower and listened at the door until he heard the landlady go into the kitchen. He slipped downstairs and refilled the holdalls. He carried them back up the stairs, walking softly on the balls of his feet close to the wall so that he made the minimum of noise. The less he saw of the landlady and the other guests, the better.

He entered his room and slid back the brass bolt before placing the bag on the bedcover and unzipping it. He unpacked the bag carefully, first removing the two glass bottles of concentrated acids, which he took one at a time into the bathroom and put on the floor by the shower.

He tore open the plastic bags and tipped most of the ice into the shower and then fetched a box of salt and sprinkled it over the cubes before pushing the bottles of acid into the freezing mixture.

While it cooled he emptied the holdall on to the bed. There was the bottle of glycerine, a can of motor oil, several boxes of matches, a tube of glue, a jumble of plastic piping, plastic-coated wire, a box of baking soda, a pair of washing-up gloves, a thermometer, a Pyrex measuring jug, two large Pyrex sauce-pans and a Teflon-covered stirrer. He took what he needed into the bathroom and switched on the light so that the ventilator would start working. The acid fumes would be painful if he inhaled them.

Nguyen had worked with explosives a lot during the war. Whenever possible the Vietcong had bought explosives or used equipment captured from the Americans, but supplies weren't always easy to get and they were quite capable of manufacturing their own blasting gelatine, TNT, plastic or nitroglycerine. Most of the raw materials for explosives could be bought quite legally, though in the later years of the war there were restrictions on the sale of electric timing devices. Not that it mattered, though, because clockwork alarm clocks were just as good.

It took almost half an hour before Nguyen had completed the complex and dangerous series of chemical reations that left him with an oily white substance forming a milky layer at the bottom of the measuring jug.

Nguyen settled back on the cold floor and sighed. His jaw ached and he realised he must have been grinding his teeth with the tension. He was starting to get a headache, a piercing pain behind his eyes that could be a result of the stress or more likely the effect of the fumes. He got to his feet, his knees cracking as he straightened up and walked unsteadily into the bedroom. He opened the window wide and then sat on the edge of the bed, breathing deeply to clear his head.

When he felt a little better he took the bag of fertilizer into the bathroom and tore it open. He spread out one of the empty plastic bags that had contained the ice and scooped handfuls of fertilizer on to it. it was important to get the ratio of motor oil, nitroglycerine and fertilizer right. He added the oil to the fertilizer first, kneading it like dough until it had been absorbed and then carefully poured out the nitroglycerine a little at a time, placing it back in the shower between pourings. The nitroglycerine could be used as an explosive on its own but it was dangerously unstable and would explode if knocked or dropped or if it got too hot. Once it had been mixed with the fertilizer and oil it would be quite inert until detonated but would be almost as effective.

Nguyen worked slowly and methodically and it took him the best part of an hour until all the nitroglycerine had been worked into the mixture and he had a dark-brown gooey paste on the plastic bag. He stripped off the gloves and laid them on the floor and went back into the bedroom. The headache was worse. He looked at his watch. It was six o'clock. He had plenty of time, so he lay down on the bed and rested.

He woke with a start two hours later when the landlady knocked on the door. "Would you care for a cup of tea, Mr Minh?" she called.

Nguyen thanked her but said no and she went back down the stairs. He sat up and rubbed his eyes. The curtains were blowing into the room and the sky was darkening outside. He slid off the bed and turned on the light. There was a lamp on the dressing-table and he put it on the floor, under the window, and pulled out its plug from the mains. He spread a newspaper on the shiny wooden surface and then took the soldering iron, solder, flash-bulbs and wire and put them on the newspaper. He plugged in the iron and while he waited for it to heat up he used the Swiss Army knife to cut twelve sections of wire, each about eighteen inches long, and then stripped a short section of plastic from the end of each piece. He soldered a wire to the bottom of each of the flash-bulbs, and another to the side. He used a battery to test one, touching the ends of the wires to the two terminals. It burst into white light and hissed as it melted. He tossed it on to the bed.

In Vietnam they'd had a plentiful supply of blasting caps, but they were hard to get hold of in peacetime. Not that it mattered, because the home-made explosive was sensitive enough to be detonated by a flash-bulb. Nguyen had decided he would make extra sure. He opened two boxes of matches and emptied them on to the newspaper. He stripped off the red heads until he had a pile of several dozen and then he crushed them with the blade of his knife, one at a time. Occasionally one would burst into flames as he worked and he'd use the blade to extinguish the fire. When he'd finished he had a neat pile of red powder. He smeared glue over the bulbs and then rolled them in the powder until they were completely covered. He left them to dry on the newspaper while he prepared the plastic piping. It was the sort used as drainpipes in cheap housing. He'd cut each piece with a hacksaw so that they were about a foot long. He sealed up one end of each pipe with strips of insulation tape and then took them into the bathroom. He put his gloves back on and half filled each pipe with the explosive mixture, then went back for six of the detonators. He held the wires in his left hand as he carefully eased the sticky mixture around the detonators, two for each pipe, and pressed it down. When he'd filled all three he sealed the ends closed with tape with just the wires protruding. They looked childish and inelegant, but Nguyen knew how deadly and effective they were. Properly planted in a road, they could destroy a car and leave a crater more than six feet across. All that was needed to set them off was to pass an electric current through the wires.

He wrapped them in newspaper and put them into the holdall. He placed the tools on top and zipped up the bag. Everything else he put into a black rubbish bag. He tied the top and lifted it, but realised immediately the thin plastic was in danger of tearing, so he slid it inside a second bag, and then a third, before twisting the open ends together and fastening them with tape.

It was almost ten o'clock. He lay down on the bed and looked for a while at the picture of the former American president. He closed his eyes, knowing that his internal alarm clock would wake him at dawn, but sleep eluded him at first. The face of the man who had first committed the US military to suppressing the Communists in the North floated in front of him and brought with it a flood of memories. He tried to push them away but they were persistent and eventually he surrendered to them.

Nguyen's father was a fanatical Communist but also appreciated the value of money and when Nguyen was nine years old he sent him to live with a cousin in Hanoi, almost 250 miles to the north of their village. The cousin ran a small garage in a back street and there Nguyen learnt how to service cars and each week he sent back half of his meagre wages to his father. In the evenings he went to a night school run by a local Catholic priest where he was taught to read and write and to question the Communist views he had picked up from his father.

He turned eleven on the day that Vietnam won its battle for independence and the French pulled out and he was in the street cheering with his friends when Ho Chi Minh returned to Hanoi. There was no peace, not even when the last French soldier left Vietnam. The struggle then became a struggle between North and South. Nguyen was eighteen when the first American soldier died in Vietnam, working in an armaments factory which manufactured grenade launchers. The factory was in a ramshackle hut in a Hanoi suburb containing little more than rows of metal tables, a brick forge with bellows powered by a bicycle and a lathe run by a rusting Citroën engine that had been fixed to a heavy wooden frame. He spent four years in the factory during which time he married Xuan Phoung and she bore him two children, both girls. They were three good years, the work he did seemed distant from the fighting going on in the south and though the hours were long and the work hard they lived in a small flat in a pretty part of Hanoi and there were occasional supplies of fresh vegetables sent up from his father's farm.

It all changed in 1967 by which time US bombs were regularly falling on Hanoi. Nguyen was drafted into the North Vietnamese Army. There were no arguments, and it didn't matter that he had a young wife and two babies. It would have been earlier if he hadn't been helping the war effort in Hanoi, but now they said his skills were needed down south. After two weeks basic training Nguyen was sent into action as a sapper. Before he left Hanoi he arranged for his family to leave Hanoi and stay at his father's farm. It was a lot closer to the fighting than Hanoi, but he knew that the bombing could only get worse and that in the city there would be no one to take care of them.

Nguyen and his fellow sappers were taken to within twenty miles of Saigon, to an area the Americans called The Iron Triangle, where they spent six months helping to build and equip a network of tunnels that housed hundreds of NVA and Vietcong soldiers. Deep underground were hospitals, training schools, supply stores and munitions factories. For weeks on end he never saw the sunlight. Nguyen was then put to work manufacturing home-made mines from captured US 105-millimetre howitzer shells of which the NVA had an abundant supply. The cash-rich Americans were notoriously careless with their equipment and there were crates upon crates of the shells for Nguyen and his team to work on.

One day when he was supervising a new batch of the mines a VC officer came to watch and began talking to him. The officer had been a mechanic many years before and it turned out that he'd originally worked in a garage in Hanoi not far from where Nguyen learnt his trade. The man complimented Nguyen on his work and after watching for a while longer he went away. The following day Nguyen was called to his commanding officer and told that he was being transferred to a Vietcong guerrilla unit. He'd asked what sort of unit and the officer had shrugged and said that it didn't matter. Nguyen didn't press it because he knew there was no point. He wasn't surprised when he was told that he was ordered to report to the VC officer who'd been watching him earlier. That was when Nguyen had been taught to fight. And to kill.

Nguyen was told that he'd be working in a team of three, setting booby traps on trails used by the American forces. He was given a black uniform to replace his grey NVA fatigues, but he was told he was to keep his AK-47 rifle. And that was that. Nguyen spent almost a year living in fear, creeping out of the tunnels at night, planting mines, setting trip wires and doing everything possible to terrorise the Americans. He became expert at moving silently through the jungle and quickly learned to camouflage himself so effectively that he was almost invisible from a few feet away, even during daylight.

Nguyen himself gave little thought to the politics involved: he was happy to fight for his country and, besides, if he had ever expressed any reservations about what he was doing he would have more than likely been shot in the back of the head. But that all changed one night in the summer of 1968 while he was in temporary attachment to a VC training camp close to Chap Le. The camp was only thirty miles away from Dong Hoi and Nguyen was hoping to be granted leave so that he could visit his family on his father's farm, when word reached him that his father had died. When he officially applied for leave it was refused, with no explanation. He went anyway, borrowing a battered Vespa scooter and driving through the night. When he arrived at the farm he was greeted by his tearful wife and children, and he learnt the full story.

A truckload of Vietcong soldiers had arrived at the farm three days earlier and demanded that they provide them with food and supplies. They helped themselves to rice from the storage sheds and half a dozen chickens. One of them untethered a bleating goat and began pulling it towards the truck. Xuan Phoung had protested that she needed the milk for her children, but one of the soldiers pushed her away and when she tried to take the goat back hit her in the stomach with the butt of his rifle. Nguyen's father went to pick her up and the soldier turned on him, hitting him on the head. The soldiers dragged him to the truck, along with the goat, and drove off. They took him to a nearby hamlet and tied him to a stake and called out all the villagers to watch. They accused him of being a bad Communist and of conspiring against the National Liberation Front and then they slowly disembowelled him as the crowd cheered.

The old man was still dying as Xuan Phoung arrived on foot at the village, and she cut him down and cradled his head in her lap. The VC had left by then and one of the braver villagers helped bury him. No funeral, because that would antagonise the Vietcong and there would be more killings.

Xuan Phoung took Nguyen to the unmarked grave and stood with him in silence as tears ran down his cheeks. He made his mind up then, as he stood by the wet soil, and later that night he took his wife and two children, precariously balanced on the scooter as they headed south. As they got closer to the area controlled by the South Vietnamese forces he took them into the jungle, travelling by night and hiding from all patrols, US, NVA and VC, until he reached a South Vietnamese camp near Hue, on the banks of the Perfume River.

There he gave himself up to the ARVN, the Army of South Vietnam, and applied to join Chieu Hoi, the "Appeal to Return" programme. He'd read about Chieu Hoi in the jungle after a low-flying helicopter had thrown out handfuls of propaganda leaflets. The VCs kept them and used them for lighting fires and as toilet paper.

His wife and children were resettled in a safe village south of Saigon while Nguyen was sent to a rehabilitation camp. He wasn't there long. He'd never had any great love for Communism and the ARVN realised how useful Nguyen would be. When he crossed over he hadn't thought that he'd be fighting for the South, he'd had some vague hope that they'd simply allow him to go back to what he enjoyed doing, working in a garage somewhere and spending the nights with his wife and daughters. He was wrong. The ARVN didn't threaten to put a bullet in his head, but they didn't have to. The South was infiltrated with VC soldiers and agents and if Nguyen and his family weren't kept in a safe village they'd be killed within weeks. Their survival depended on the goodwill of the Government of South Vietnam. And the price exacted for that goodwill was for Nguyen to serve them in the best way he could.

Once he'd satisfied them that he wasn't a VC agent he was sent to the Recondo School, run by the 5th Special Forces Group at one end of Nha Trang airfield, near Saigon. The Recondo School was where the US army trained the men who made up the Long Range Reconnaissance Patrols – or Lurps to the men who served in them. The Lurps operated in six-man teams deep in enemy territory as the eyes and ears of the army, and often as its assassins.

It soon became obvious to the instructors that there was nothing Nguyen could learn from them. Within two days he was teaching them about VC booby traps and camouflage techniques and then the top brass got to hear about his talents and inside a month he found himself seconded to a Lurp unit on the edge of the Iron Triangle.

Time and time again, Nguyen was sent into enemy territory, along the same trails that he'd travelled when he was a VC. He knew many of the hiding places and the supply dumps and the secret trails, and he had a sixth sense for spotting the VC trip-wires and traps.

Nguyen was allowed regular visits to his wife and daughters, and as he drew regular US army pay, life was good fighting for the Americans, until it became obvious that the NVA were going to overrun the South. Nguyen began to worry about what would happen if the Americans pulled out, but he was always assured that he would be taken care of and that his family would be given sanctuary in the United States. He'd believed them.

Nguyen tossed fitfully on the bed, sweat beading on his forehead. His breath came in ragged gasps as he relived in his mind what had happened to his wife and his three daughters, how they'd died and how he'd been powerless to help.

Mary Hennessy was sitting alone in the lounge watching television when the doorbell rang. She got to her feet and smoothed down her dress before going into the hall, but Murphy had got to the front door ahead of her. There were four suitcases by the door, mainly clothes that she wanted to take with her to the farm. Liam had said they were only going for the weekend, but she could see that he was holding something back, and realised that he'd been badly shocked by the two bombing attempts and that they'd probably end up staying on the farm until it had been sorted out.

It was ten o'clock already, but Liam had said he was waiting to see someone before they left and it was a desire to see who the mysterious visitor was rather than a sense of politeness that had taken her to the hall. He was hidden by the door, all she could see was a sleeved arm shaking hands with Murphy, but then she heard his spoken greeting and she gasped, her hand flying involuntarily up to her mouth. The door opened wider and he stepped inside. Morrison was holding a blue holdall in his left hand and he bent down to put it on the floor by her suitcases and it was only as he straightened up that he saw her. He smiled and his eyes widened.

"Mary," he said, in a voice that could have meant a hundred things. He seemed unsure how he should greet her, stepping forward as if to kiss her on the cheek but then holding himself back and offering her his hand instead. Was that because Murphy was watching them, or because he knew Liam was nearby, or was it something else? It had been two years since she had seen Sean Morrison and she couldn't read him as easily as she used to. His hand felt strong and dry and she pressed her fingers into his palm, holding him a little longer than was necessary. He squeezed her gently and he seemed reluctant to take his hand away. That's what she told herself, anyway. She was immediately glad that she'd worn her blue silk dress which showed her figure off, especially around her waist. She wanted to look good for him. He looked wonderful, his hair was longer than when she'd last seen him but otherwise he hadn't changed: smiling blue eyes, his mouth which always seemed ready to break into a grin, and a body that could have belonged to a dancer.

"It's good to see you again, Sean," she said. "How's New York?"

"Hectic," he said. "A lot different to Belfast, I can tell you."

"You're here to see Liam?"

He nodded. "Yeah, is he in the study?"

She wanted to keep him in the hall, to talk with him and find out why he was back, but she knew that she'd already spent too long looking at him, any longer and Murphy would suspect there was something going on. Mary smiled to herself. He'd be wrong, of course. There was nothing going on between her and Sean. There hadn't been for two years, but she could tell from his touch that the electricity was still there between them.

"He's waiting for you," she said. "Perhaps I'll see you later." She held his gaze for a couple of seconds and then turned and went back into the lounge. She poured herself a brandy and held the balloon glass between both hands and breathed in its rich bouquet. "Welcome back, Sean Morrison," she said quietly to herself, smiling.

In the study, Morrison shook Hennessy's hand and sank down into one of the chairs in front of the desk. "The boys seem nervous," said Morrison, and Hennessy explained briefly what had happened, the phone calls from London, the visit from The Chinaman, the explosion in his office and the attempt to blow up the car. Morrison listened without comment, but when Hennessy had finished he was frowning, not sure what was wanted from him.

"You've brought me back to deal with this Chinaman?" he asked.

Hennessy shook his head. "No, no, we'll take care of him. No, Sean, I need your help to stop this bombing campaign on the mainland." He told Morrison about his fears of a rogue IRA unit, and the missing ordnance.

"That explains a lot," said Morrison. "At first the bombings were good news in the States, donations poured in, but some of the recent stuff has produced a real backlash. The Tube bombing especially. The Irish Americans are keen to support us, but massacres like that . . . I've got to tell you, Liam, I'm bloody pleased to hear you hadn't sanctioned it. How can I help?"

Hennessy spoke to Morrison for another quarter of an hour and then the younger man left for the airport to catch the last shuttle to Heathrow.

Mary Hennessy looked up when her husband entered the lounge and tried to hide her disappointment when she saw that he was alone.

"It's been a long time since Sean Morrison was in Belfast," she said. Hennessy went over to the drinks cabinet and poured himself a double measure of whiskey.

"I need his help," he said.

"With The Chinaman?"

Hennessy swirled the whiskey in his glass and shook his head. "Something else. I need someone I can trust, somebody without an axe to grind, and he's been away for almost two years now. He's, how can I put it, untainted. Yes, that's the word I'm looking for. Untainted."

"So he'll be coming to the farm with us?" she asked.

"No, I need him to go to London." He saw from her face that she didn't understand and he smiled down at her. "I need his help to get to the bottom of the bombings. Despite everything that's happened, that's the more important issue at the moment."

Mary's eyes narrowed. "You've got a plan?"

"Something like that." He finished his drink and put the empty glass down on the cabinet. "Are you all packed?"

She said she was, and they went together to the car where Jimmy McMahon opened the door for them and put the luggage in the boot. They sat together in the back while Murphy slid into the front seat. Jackie squeezed under Hennessy's legs and woofed quietly to herself. A red Ford Sierra with three young men waited at the entrance to the drive, its engine running. Four other heavily built men got into a dark-brown Range Rover and followed the Jaguar out into the road. They drove in convoy, the Sierra first, then the Jaguar, and the Range Rover bringing up the rear, down the Antrim Road, through the city centre and on to the A1, the main road south.

Nguyen was jolted awake by a distant siren. He lay for a while on his back staring up at the ceiling and trying to calm his breathing. He was soaking wet, drenched with sweat as he always was when he came out of the nightmare. The visions were always the same: the small boat drifting in the South China Sea. His daughters screaming for help. The helplessness. The anger.

He focused on what he had to do, driving all other thoughts from his troubled mind and gradually his breathing steadied. He sat up slowly and looked around the room as if seeing it for the first time. He checked his watch. It was six o'clock in the morning. Time to go.

The ice in the shower had melted away and Nguyen stepped in and washed himself all over. He didn't use any soap or shampoo because he didn't want any lingering smell of perfume. He towelled himself dry and put on a pair of loose jeans, a faded grey sweatshirt and an old pair of black sneakers before packing the rest of his stuff in his suitcase. He checked the room carefully to make sure he'd forgotten nothing and then he looped the holdall and its deadly contents around his neck and carried the case and the black plastic bag of rubbish down the stairs. He took out his key and left it and a ten-pound note by the telephone and then slipped the catch on the front door and gently eased it closed behind him. He took the rubbish bag down the side of the house and put it in the bin. The case he put in the back of the van, the holdall he slid under the passenger seat. The van started first time and he drove slowly down Wellington Park and turned left into Lisburn Road, the A1. On the seat next to him lay several large-scale maps that he'd bought from a newsagent in the city centre. Ian Wood had told him that Hennessy had a farm between a town called Castlewellan and a place called Haltown in County Down, about forty miles south of Belfast. He hadn't been able to say exactly where, but Nguyen didn't expect to have any problem finding it. The van identified him as a landscape gardener, he'd just drive around claiming to have mislaid Hennessy's address and eventually he'd find someone to point out the right farm.

Sean Morrison had booked into the Strand Palace Hotel late on Friday night so he waited until Saturday morning before calling the offices of the Anti-Terrorist Branch and asking for Detective Chief Inspector Bromley. He wasn't surprised to be told that he wasn't in, because it was Saturday, after all. He asked the duty officer if Bromley was at home or away on holiday and was told that he'd be in the office on Monday.

"Can you get a message to him for me?" Morrison asked.

The duty officer was crisp and efficient, not the least because of Morrison's Irish accent, and he confirmed that he could pass on a message to Bromley.

"Tell him Sean Morrison wants to speak to him."

"Can you give me your number, please, sir?" asked the officer. Nice try, thought Morrison. Either the guy was naïve in the extreme or he had a very dry sense of humour.

"Just tell him Sean Morrison needs to talk to him urgently. I'll call back at noon. Tell him to either be in the office or to have you give me a number where I can reach him. Got that?"

"Yes, sir." Morrison cut the line.

Morrison's next phone call was to Liam Hennessy but a woman's voice answered. "Mary?" he asked.

"Sean? Where are you?"

"London," he said. He wasn't sure what to say to her. Two years was a long time.

"Do you want to speak to Liam?" she asked, and he realised from the edge to her voice that her husband was in the room with her. He immediately felt relieved, as if Hennessy's presence solved the problem of which way the conversation would go.

"Yes," he said.

Morrison heard the phone being handed over and then he heard Hennessy's voice. "Everything OK?" said Hennessy.

"Everything is fine. I was just calling to let you know where I am. I've booked into the Strand Palace . . ." Hennessy interrupted him, telling him to wait while he got a pen and paper. "OK, go ahead," he said.

"I'm at the Strand Palace Hotel," said Morrison, and he dictated the number to Hennessy, who repeated it back to him before hanging up.

Jim Kavanagh had press-ganged a dozen IRA men to help him with the search for The Chinaman, most of them teenagers, but their lack of experience didn't matter because most of their enquiries were done over the phone. They'd moved into Hennessy's office in Donegall Square, the air still acrid from the explosion. Kavanagh divided them into six pairs and distributed copies of the city's Yellow Pages and tourist guides he'd obtained from the Tourist Information Centre in the High Street. The Chinaman had arrived from London, which meant that, unless he had friends or relatives in the city, he'd have to have booked into a hotel or guest-house. He distributed the telephone numbers of all the places where a visitor might stay among the teams, one member to make the phone calls, the other to keep a record. There were more than enough telephones to go round. He hoped they'd be lucky because if not the next stage would be to visit every Chinese family in Belfast and that could take a hell of a long time.

Kavanagh made himself a cup of coffee and settled down on the sofa in the reception area. He was preparing himself for a long wait when a gangly red-haired youth burst into the room, breathing heavily.

"I think we've got it!" he said.

His partner, a head shorter with shoulder-length brown hair, came running after him waving a notebook. "A guest-house in Wellington Park. The landlady is a Mrs McAllister, she says there was an Oriental man staying with her for two nights."

"Is he still there?" asked Kavanagh, getting to his feet.

"She said he left this morning."

"Damn his eyes!" cursed Kavanagh. He called over two men, bigger and harder than the teenage helpers, Roy O'Donnell and Tommy O'Donoghue. He went with them to collect his car and they drove to Wellington Park.

Mrs McAllister showed them into her lounge, a fussy room with a statue of the Virgin Mary in one corner, dozens of small crystal animals on the mantelpiece and lace squares on the backs of the easy chairs. She was a Catholic, a good Catholic, and whereas she didn't have much sympathy for the IRA she knew better than to obstruct them. Kavanagh asked her to describe her former guest and she did her best but found it difficult: not very tall, black hair, brown eyes, rough skin. She was able to give a better description of his clothes and Kavanagh knew she was talking about the same man that he'd seen in Hennessy's office.

"How did he get here?" he asked.

"He had a van, a white van. It was some sort of delivery van, I think, with writing on the side."

"Can ye remember what it said?"

She shook her head. "I'm sorry, son, I can't."

"Not to worry, Mrs McAllister. Can ye show me his room?"

She took him upstairs leaving O'Donnell and O'Donoghue sitting uncomfortably in the lounge. "You keep a very tidy house, Mrs McAllister," soothed Kavanagh as she led him to the bedroom door. She waited outside while Kavanagh checked the room. There was nothing under the bed or in the cupboard drawers. He went into the bathroom but it too was spotless and smelt strongly of pine.

"Yez'll have already tidied up the room, then?" he asked the landlady.

"Aye, son. I dusted and ran the Hoover over the carpet this morning. He was very clean, though, you'd have hardly known the room had been slept in. Except for the bathroom, there was a funny smell in there. Like vinegar or something. I had to spray air freshener around."

"Vinegar?"

"Something like that, a terrible bitter smell."

Kavanagh looked around the gleaming bathroom, not sure what he expected to find.

"I don't suppose he left anything behind, did he Mrs McAllister?"

"No, nothing. He even made the bed before he left. He went early this morning, before I was up. He'd paid the bill in advance, even left me a tip." She was burning with curiosity but knew it was pointless to ask what it was he'd done. If they wanted her to know they'd have told her.

"And ye've no idea where he went? He didn't ask for directions or anything?"

The landlady shook her head. "I barely spoke to him."

Kavanagh tut-tutted to himself, not sure what to do next. The van was a possibility, but a white delivery van with writing on the side wasn't much to go on. Still, it would probably have English plates which would make it a bit easier to find. "OK, Mrs McAllister, thanks for your help. I'm sorry we disturbed yez."

They went back downstairs. O'Donnell and O'Donoghue were already waiting in the hall, expectant looks on their faces. Mrs McAllister opened the door for them and watched them go down the path. She suddenly remembered something and called after Kavanagh. "Oh, son! You might want to check the dustbin round the back. When I was emptying the Hoover I saw he'd left some rubbish there, in a black bag."

Kavanagh's hopes soared and he practically ran down the path to where two dustbins were standing. The first one he looked in contained nothing but kitchen refuse, but in the second, under a layer of carpet fluff and dust, he found a black plastic bag, knotted at the top and sealed with insulation tape. He pulled it out, ignoring the cloud of dust that billowed over his trousers. He opened the bag and looked inside and frowned.

O'Donnell appeared at his shoulder. "Anything?" he said.

"I think so," said Kavanagh. "I want O'Hara to see this."

Kavanagh put the bag into the boot of the car and the three men drove to O'Hara's house, a two-up, two-down terrace in Springfield Road. He was in the kitchen eating bacon and eggs when they were shown in by his wife. His sharp eyes fixed on the bag by Kavanagh's side.

"What have ye got there, Jim?" he asked, wiping a piece of bread across the plate and popping it into his mouth.

"I'm hoping yer'll tell me, Willie. When yez finished your breakfast, that is."

O'Hara took the hint, putting his knife and fork together on the remains of his meal. His wife took the plate and put it in the oven to keep warm and then left the room, knowing that it was IRA business and that the men would want to be left alone. O'Hara wiped his greasy hands on his grey trousers and cleared the rest of the table, a stainless steel cruet set, a bottle of Heinz ketchup and the morning paper.

Kavanagh lifted the bag on to the table and O'Hara gingerly opened it. He took the contents out one at a time: the empty bag of fertilizer, the Pyrex pans, the measuring jug, sections of piping, a burnt-out flash-bulb, empty bottles, empty matchboxes, pieces of cut wire. He inspected each item closely before eagerly moving on to the next one like a schoolboy going through his presents at Christmas, hoping that each one would be better than the last. When the black bag was finally empty and all its contents lined up beside it, O'Hara looked at Kavanagh, a wicked grin on his weaselly face.

"This is from the wee bugger that tried to blow up Liam's car, isn't it?" he asked.

Kavanagh wasn't impressed by the small man's insight – the flash-bulb was obviously the same type that they'd found in the Jaguar's petrol tank. "He left it behind when he checked out of a guest-house this morning. What do yez make of it?"

O'Hara waved his hand at the ragbag collection of items. "This is trouble, right enough," he said. "Big trouble."

Morrison checked his watch for the hundredth time and called the Anti-Terrorist Branch. This time Bromley was there. "I'm sorry to drag you in on a Saturday," said Morrison.

"I'm always happy to speak to public-spirited citizens, Mr Morrison," said Bromley with more than a hint of sarcasm. "The last FBI report that passed over my desk had you alive and well and living in New York. What brings you back to these fair shores?"

"I need to see you," answered Morrison.

"Not thinking of changing sides and working alongside the forces of law and order, are we?"

"Let's just say that I want to make you an offer you won't be able to refuse."

"In what context?" asked Bromley, suddenly serious.

"Not over the phone. I have to meet you."

Bromley snorted. "In a dark alley, I suppose. Come off it, Morrison, why the hell should I put myself at risk? Haven't you been reading the papers in New York? The IRA has declared open season on us here. If you want to speak to me you can come here."

"And how long do you think I'd last if I was seen going into your office, Bromley? I'm not after a bullet in my mouth."

"I suppose that's a Mexican stand-off, then," said Bromley.

"Not necessarily. You can choose the venue, so long as you go alone. Somewhere with lots of people where you'll feel safe and where I can blend into a crowd. Somewhere noisy so I know we won't be recorded."

"When?"

"This afternoon."

Bromley considered the offer for a few seconds. "I can't today. It'll have to be tomorrow. In Trafalgar Square. Be close to Nelson's column at four o'clock."

"Make sure you come alone," said Morrison. "Don't put me under any pressure. I'm not wanted for anything, and I won't be carrying. I just want to talk."

"So you said."

"One other thing – I don't know what you look like. How will I recognise you?"

"Don't worry, Mr Morrison. I've seen enough photographs of you, I'll introduce myself."

"That's maybe so, but don't creep up on me. I startle easily."

"Understood. Until four tomorrow, then."

Morrison hung up. Nothing to do now but wait. He switched on the television and rang down to room service to order a club sandwich and coffee.

Hennessy was walking across Three Acre Pasture with Jackie at his heels when he heard the shrill whistle, two piercing blasts that made the dog jump. He shaded his eyes with his hands and saw Murphy standing by the kitchen door waving his arm high above his head. When Murphy realised he'd caught his attention, he made a miming action with his hand, holding it clenched to his ear. The phone.

It took him a brisk five minutes to get back to the farmhouse, by which time Murphy had gone back inside the cool, oak-beamed kitchen. He held the receiver out to Hennessy, who was slightly out of breath. It was Kavanagh. He described the visit to the guest-house and what they'd found in the dustbin.

"And what did O'Hara say?" Hennessy asked.

"Nitroglycerine," said Kavanagh. "The Chinaman made nitroglycerine in the bathroom. Willie reckons he mixed it with weedkiller and packed it into plastic pipes and is planning to use flash-bulb detonators, the sort of thing he stuck in the petrol tank of the Jag."

"How much damage could they do?"

"Judging by the stuff he left behind, Willie says he could have made three or four devices, each big enough to blow up a car. It's hard to say because a lot depends on the purity of the nitro he made, but Willie says the guy seems to know what he's doing."

Hennessy felt a cold chill run up his spine because the sort of bombs Kavanagh was talking about didn't sound like warnings. It looked as if The Chinaman was raising the stakes. "What are your plans now, Jim?" he asked.

"I reckon the van's the best bet. The landlady said he's driving a white delivery van with black writing on the side. I'll have our lads scour the city. It shouldn't be too hard to find, a Chinaman in a white van with English plates. We'll get him, Liam. Don't ye worry." Kavanagh tried to sound as optimistic as possible because he could sense how worried his boss was.

"OK, keep at it, Jim. And let me know as soon as you get anything."

"Will do," said Kavanagh.

Mary came into the kitchen as he replaced the receiver and asked him if he wanted a coffee. He declined and said he'd prefer something a little stronger. She sniffed, a noise that was loaded with disapproval. She was wearing tight Levi jeans, cowboy boots and a floppy pink pullover that he'd last seen their daughter wearing. He took a bottle of whiskey down from the Welsh dresser and poured himself a double measure.

"I'm driving down to the village to get some bread," said Mary. "Do you want anything?"

He sat down in an old rocking chair and rocked backwards and forwards, nursing the whiskey. "I'm fine," he said.

She turned to look at him, standing with her hands on her hips. "I don't think you should be moping like this, Liam."

"I'm not moping, I'm thinking. And you're acting like my mother."

"And you, Liam Hennessy, are behaving like my grandfather. Now pull yourself together and stop feeling sorry for yourself." She turned on her heels and banged the kitchen door behind her. He heard the car start up and drive off and wondered what it was that was upsetting her so much.

When he first met Mary all those years ago her temper and unpredictability were among her attractions. She was stimulating, she was fun, and there was never a dull moment with her. She'd quietened down after the birth of their children but now that they were at university she seemed to be behaving more and more like she did when she was in her early twenties. Some days she was so gentle and loving that she took his breath away and yet on others she was so cold that he felt sure she was about to leave him. Sexually, too, she had him in a state of constant confusion. When they'd first married they seemed to spend all their time in bed, and it was hardly surprising that they'd had two children so quickly. He'd wanted more children but she'd said that two was enough though even then sex had been good and regular, albeit more calculated and careful. It had been when the children were in their teens, at school, that she had seemed to withdraw from him. She even went through a period when she'd slept in one of the spare bedrooms, claiming that she was having trouble getting to sleep. When he did approach her she would be friendly but insistent: she didn't want to be touched. Eventually she moved back into the main bedroom. He never found out why, but even when she slept in his bed she only occasionally allowed him to make love to her and when she did it was usually quick and unenthusiastic.

Sometimes, though, she would be totally different, she'd wait until he'd switched off the light and climbed into the bed and then she'd reach for him and it would be like it was in the old days, she'd hang on to him tight, biting his shoulder, making him lie on his back as she rode him on top. Those were the worst nights, because she'd close her eyes as she gasped and groaned and he knew deep inside that she was thinking about someone else, that he was being used, but while it was happening he didn't care because her love-making was so energetic and sensual that he wanted to die. Only afterwards, when she flopped down on to the sheets and rolled away from him to curl up with her own thoughts, only then did the revulsion set in. He would lie awake with tears in his eyes, filled with self-loathing, and promise himself that next time she reached for him in the dark he'd refuse her and tell her that he wanted her to make love to him, not to use him as part of whatever fantasy she was enjoying. But he never did refuse her.

Hennessy was genuinely confused by the way she acted in bed, because in every other respect she was a perfect wife and mother. She ran the house like a dream, their children were good-looking, intelligent and well-balanced, she took an interest in his work and his politics, she laughed at his jokes, she entertained their friends, she seemed to thrive in his company. Everyone who knew them said they were the perfect couple, and when they were with friends of their own age he took a particular pride in her apparent youth and vitality. She was stunning, and while her women friends had put on weight and had their hair permed and started to dress like their mothers, she had kept her figure, so much so that she would still go without a bra if the dress warranted it. Over the years Hennessy had tried to talk himself into accepting his wife as she was, to convince himself that the lack of sex was a small price to pay to have her in his life. Sometimes he believed it. He rocked himself backwards and forwards in the chair. The motion was reassuring and he closed his eyes.

The drive from Belfast to the B8 between Castlewellan and Haltown took a little over ninety minutes, but it took another three hours for Nguyen to locate Hennessy's farm. The two towns were about ten miles apart and there were many farms nestled among the patchwork of fields and hills. Eventually a bearded giant of a man in a tractor sent him in the general direction, to the north of the B8, away from the border, and some time later he came across a postman in a battered old van who pointed at a collection of weathered stone buildings and modern barns.

Nguyen spent some time examining his large-scale map of the area. He circled the spot where the farm was. To the east was the Tollymore Forest Park, and to the south-east was a rocky ridge called the Mourne Mountains. Due south was a place called Warrenpoint, which rang a bell in Nguyen's subconscious. He couldn't remember exactly what it was, but he knew something bad had happened there in the past, an explosion or a massacre. The name had cropped up in a news programme on television, he was sure of that much. He'd regularly watched television news with his daughter as a way of helping her to improve her English.

There was a wooded hill a mile or so behind the farm and according to the map he'd be able to get close to it if he took the road to the village of Rathfriland. He started the van and drove to within half a mile of the hill. He parked in a layby, slung the binoculars around his neck, took his compass from the glove compartment, pocketed the map and walked briskly up the hill, following a stony track that zig-zagged through the lush grass. The track was obviously used by a shepherd to round up his flock. There were dog droppings in several places and boot-prints of a man who walked with a stick and all around were sheep and young lambs.

He reached the top of the hill and lay down in the grass, surveying the farmland and its buildings far below through the powerful binoculars. The farmhouse was an L-shaped building, stone with a steep, grey slate roof. Nguyen was looking at it from the rear, he could see the back door leading off the kitchen. The main part of the house was two-storeys high but the shorter section of the L was one-storey and seemed to be made up of outbuildings, the windows streaked with dirt. There was a square tarmac courtyard in the angle of the L where there were several cars parked: a Range Rover, a Jaguar, two Land-Rovers and a Ford Sierra. Nguyen recognised the Jaguar and smiled. He hadn't expected Hennessy to be there. It was an added bonus. Bordering the courtyard, directly opposite the outbuildings, was another single-storey building and behind it was a grass paddock. In the paddock two horses stood nose to nose. At right angles to the stables was a two-storey cottage built in the same solid style as the main house which Nguyen guessed was the farm manager's home.

In front of the cottage was what looked to be a vegetable garden, with tidy rows of cabbages and other green vegetables, and beyond it a small orchard of mature fruit trees. A gravel driveway led from the courtyard, between the farmhouse and the stables, and curved around the front. The fourth side of the courtyard was bordered by two open-sided barns, one full of bales of hay, the other stacked high with sacks at one end, the rest of the space being used as a shelter for farm equipment. Behind the barns were three gleaming white towering silos, like rockets awaiting lift-off.

The driveway led to a single-track road which wound between the fields, linking up with several farms before disappearing to the north where, according to the map, it linked up with the B7. There were passing places every few hundred yards and hedgerows both sides. The fields were mainly devoted to the raising of cattle and sheep but there were crops, too; several of the patchwork squares were yellow with rape-seed and there were green plants growing in a field behind the barns that could have been potatoes or turnips. The area undulated like a down quilt that had been thrown untidily on to a bed and the places that were steep or inaccessible had been left wooded.

Nguyen laid the map on the grass and took his bearings with the compass. With a pencil he drew several routes to Hennessy's farm, from the B180, the B8, the B25 and the B7, following the contours through woodland wherever possible or alongside hedgerows and ditches where there was no tree cover. There was a stream trickling through Hennessy's land, too small to be shown on the map, and with great care Nguyen traced its route as a thin pencil line. He also carefully drew a sketch map of the farm buildings, showing their positions relative to each other, and made a sketch drawing of the farmhouse, including the drainpipes. The soil-pipe was next to the middle of five upstairs windows and the glass was frosted and there was a circular ventilator fan in the right-hand corner so Nguyen marked it as the bathroom. In the distance a twin-rotor helicopter, a Chinook, flew close to the ground, heading towards border country. He waited until it had passed out of sight before walking back down the hill.

His first priority now was to find somewhere to hide the van, because he'd soon be spotted if he kept driving around in the vicinity of the farm. There were very few vehicles around and most of the ones he came across were tractors or army Land-Rovers. Farmers and soldiers both gave him curious looks but neither seemed to regard him as a threat. He could see, though, that they read the signs on the side of his van and he knew that an Oriental landscape gardener would not be easily forgotten. He dismissed the idea of leaving the Renault in one of the nearby villages or towns because being so near the border any strange parked vehicle was bound to attract attention. He needed a place a good distance from the farm, but close enough that he could get to and fro within a few hours. Five or six miles or so would be about right, and ideally with a route that offered some cover from the army patrols and the helicopters which occasionally buzzed overhead. Looking at the map, it seemed as if Tollymore Forest Park offered the best prospects. He drove east along the B8 and then turned left on to the B180 which cut the woods neatly in half on the way to the village of Maghera. He eased the van along the road looking left and right for places to turn off and spotted several possibilities. When he emerged from the forest he clunked the gears through a three-point turn and headed back towards Haltown. He ignored the first three tracks as being too obvious from the road. The first path he'd identified as being suitable went deep into the trees but the Land-Rover tracks in the mud were too fresh and there were too many of them, suggesting that it was used regularly by foresters or possibly by the army. He turned the van round and drove back to the main road. The second track was more what he'd hoped for, a single pathway that was overgrown by ferns and brambles. He drove the van far enough into the trees so that he couldn't be seen from the road and then got out of the car and checked the ground and the overhanging vegetation. The tyre prints in the dried mud were old and flaking and there were fresh green shoots growing through them. The ferns that had encroached on to the track were unbroken and there were no smears of dirt or grease. No one had driven a vehicle down the path for at least a week, and probably much longer, and there were no footprints, none that were human, anyway. He saw where foxes had crossed the path, and rabbits, but that was all.

Satisfied, he got back into the van and slowly drove it down the track, gripping the steering wheel tightly as it jerked like a wild thing. When he'd gone a hundred yards or so further, he turned off the track and guided the van carefully between the trees. When he was sure that anyone driving down the track would not be able to see the van he switched off the engine.

Nguyen spent an hour going back along the route to the path, covering over his tracks as best he could. It wouldn't fool anyone who was searching for him, but a casual observer would be unlikely to spot where he had driven off the track. He gathered armfuls of ferns and dead wood from the forest floor and spread them across the roof of the van. He'd seen enough helicopters flying overhead to know that there was a risk of being spotted from above, albeit a slim one. He picked up handfuls of damp soil and rubbed them over the sides of the van, and the front and back, transforming the white paintwork into muddy smears, and then took more branches and draped them all around it.

He looked at his watch. There were hours to go before dusk so he climbed into the driver's seat and took a portion of rice and another of pork from the take-away carrier bag. He ate slowly, chewing each mouthful thoroughly before swallowing, not tasting or enjoying the food but knowing that it would provide the energy he needed. When he'd finished he settled back in the seat and tried to sleep, saving his strength for the night ahead. In the distance he heard the whup-whup of a single-rotor helicopter, flying low and fast. He slipped into sleep.

The air was filled with the throbbing of helicopters. It was 1975. Nguyen was with his wife and daughters running through the crowded streets of Saigon, sweating from fear and the heat. The roads were packed tight with panicking faces, young and old, families and individuals, all heading towards the US Embassy and the helicopters. Almost everybody was carrying something, a suitcase, a big wicker bag, a bicycle loaded with clothes or electrical appliances. Children barely big enough to walk were clasping bags to their chests, old women were bent double and gasping for breath as they hurried along with bags attached to both ends of bamboo poles. Nguyen had told his wife to pack one bag for the four of them and he carried it while she held the two children. She was crying as they trotted down the street and the faces of the children were drawn and frightened. Nguyen appeared cold and impassive but inside his mind was racing.

He and his family had moved into Saigon because it wasn't safe for them in the country any more. The NVA was walking all over the ARVN and by February Nguyen heard whispers that a helicopter evacuation of Saigon was being planned. Hue fell on March 24 and less than a week later the NVA overran Da Nang and the South Vietnamese were struggling to hold a defensive line north of Saigon. The Defense Attaché Office put together a list of seven thousand or so people it reckoned should be evacuated as the ARVN fought a last-ditch battle at Xuan Loc, just thirty miles east of Saigon. The noise of exploding rockets kept Nguyen's children awake at night. Nguyen went to see his commanding officer and was told that if Saigon fell he would be evacuated along with the American forces.

On April 28 he was told to prepare for evacuation the following day. The NVA attacked Tan Son Nhut airfield on the northern edge of Saigon, preventing commercial aircraft from flying out with evacuees. The plan now was for helicopters to ferry the US forces and their supporters out to ships waiting offshore. Nguyen, along with thousands of other Vietnamese who had served the US forces, was told to wait at home where he would be picked up by a specially marked bus. They waited, but the buses never arrived. Nguyen phoned the US embassy every fifteen minutes but was always given the same answer. Wait. He heard helicopters flying in the direction of the embassy and he waited. He heard the rumble of guns at Bien Hoa and still he waited. When he heard the crackle of small-arms fire he grabbed his wife and children and ran into the street. It was almost 9.30 p.m. and the streetlights were on.

Nguyen dropped the bag in the street and took one of the

girls from his wife, scooping her off her feet and letting her sit with her legs around his neck. She giggled and played with his hair. His wife picked up the other girl. Time was running out. There were fewer helicopters hovering over the embassy. The roads were packed with cars, trucks, bicycles and pedestrians, and everyone seemed to be heading towards the embassy. The crowds were moving faster now, and they had to be careful not to trip over abandoned luggage as they pushed down Thong Nhat Avenue. In the distance they could see the squarish block of whitewashed cement that was the American embassy. More helicopters flew overhead. The crowds were so thick that Nguyen and his family couldn't get any closer than fifty yards or so to the nine-foot wall that surrounded the embassy. The top of the wall was wreathed in barbed wire and protected by Marines with machine guns. The only way in was through the gate, and that was only opened when refugees could produce the correct paperwork and identifying codeword. Nguyen's daughters were crying. Midnight passed and with it came an end to the distant thudding explosions at the airport and still the helicopters came and left after picking up the lucky ones from the landing pads on top of the embassy building. Dawn broke and they had made almost no progress, the solid mass of anxious humanity locked solid. Nguyen's wife almost collapsed from exhaustion but was held up by the pressure of the people around her until he managed to slip his arm around her waist and support her. She looked at him with pleading in her eyes but there was nothing he could do. The papers that guaranteed sanctuary were in his breast pocket but they were useless unless he could get to the embassy gates. It was hopeless. The crowd roared and screamed and Nguyen looked up to see a helicopter lift off from the roof and head out towards the sea where the Seventh Fleet waited. The chopper was alone in the sky and Nguyen realised it was the last one. There were no more guards around the wall, none on the embassy roof. The Americans had gone. Xuan Phoung cried softly. The crowds dispersed quickly, knowing that the T-54 tanks of the North Vietnamese Army would soon arrive. The streets were littered with abandoned ARVN uniforms and equipment.

Nguyen took his family back to their small flat and helped Xuan Phoung put the exhausted children to bed. He held her tightly and kissed her, and she led him by the hand to their tiny bedroom and he made love to her, urgently and with more passion than he'd shown in a long time. It was the night that Kieu Trinh was conceived.

Nguyen jerked awake, his face drenched with sweat. It was dark outside and he sat for a while, forcing himself to relax. He filled his mind with images of the Buddhist shrine at his home – his former home, he reminded himself. He climbed over the back of the seats into the rear of the van and placed the three pipe bombs into the rucksack. He also packed the filled water-bottles and the remainder of the take-away food, along with six coils of plastic-coated wire, two clockwork alarm clocks and a few tools that he reckoned he would need. The batteries which he planned to use to detonate the bombs were zipped into the pockets of the camouflage jacket so that there could be no possibility of them accidentally going off. He also packed the binoculars and the map.

He stripped off all his clothes except for his underpants and socks and then slipped on the camouflage trousers and jacket. He pulled on a pair of thick wool socks and his old, comfortable boots. He rolled up the right leg of his pants and tied the scabbard of one of the throwing knives to his calf. The other knife he tied to one of the straps of the rucksack so that it hung upside down, the handle lowermost where it was accessible in an emergency. He did the same with the big hunting knife.

When he'd finished his preparations he climbed into the front of the van and left by the driver's door. He kept his eyes firmly closed while he opened and shut the door because he didn't want the internal light ruining his night vision. There was no point in locking the door because if the van was discovered it would all be over anyway, but he buried the keys near the roots of a tree he'd be sure to recognise later.

He covered the door with tree branches and stood for a minute taking a bearing from his compass. There was a thin sliver of moon in the cloudless sky and enough starlight to see by. He headed west through the trees, parallel to the B180. He moved at a brisk pace but even so the constant weaving to and fro to avoid trees meant that it took the best part of two hours to cover three miles and emerge from the forest. He kept going due west for another two and a half miles, travelling across fields, sticking close to hedgerows wherever possible, until he reached the B8. After crossing it he took another bearing from the compass and began walking north-west. He changed direction twice to avoid farms and several times he dropped to the ground when helicopters buzzed overhead. Eventually he reached Hennessy's farm. Behind the buildings loomed the empty blackness of the hill which he'd climbed the previous day.

He lay in the sweet-smelling grass for a full thirty minutes before he was satisfied that everyone inside was asleep, then he began to crawl silently towards the farmhouse. He didn't want to risk crossing the road leading to the farm, even in the near-darkness, so he circled around the stables and the manager's cottage and behind the barns until he arrived at the outbuildings. He crept up against the stone wall and slowly got to his feet. He moved on tiptoe through the gap between the wall and the barn, placing his feet carefully so that he made no sound.

When he reached the courtyard and its collection of cars he slowly scanned every inch, his eyes wide to pull in as much reflected light as possible. Only when he was sure that no guards had been posted did he turn right and slip along the rough wall towards the farmhouse. He drew level with a large window made up of four dirty panes of glass in a wooden frame and he peered inside. He could see metal barrels stacked on top of each other, thick wooden benches and a collection of farm tools. He eased himself past the window and reached a wooden door with ornate metal hinges. There was an ancient keyhole and two bolts, one high up and one near the ground. He gingerly pushed back the upper bolt and was relieved that it moved silently and smoothly. Though the door was old and battered, it was obviously regularly opened. The second bolt was similarly quiet. He held his breath, seized the metal door handle and turned it slowly. It grated a little but not enough for the sound to carry and then he pushed the door inwards. It hadn't been locked and it opened with a mild creak. Nguyen slid inside and closed the door behind him.

The room smelt of dust and decay and there was a bitter chemical taste to the air. Nguyen went over to the barrels. Most of them were full and according to the labels they contained weedkillers of various kinds. He was glad that they weren't fuel drums because at this stage he wasn't planning to burn down the house, he simply wanted to prove to Hennessy how serious he was.

He knelt down on the concrete floor and took off his rucksack. He took out one of the pipe bombs, an alarm clock and two of the shortest coils of wire. The glass had already been removed from the clock leaving the hands exposed. Nguyen fastened one end of one of the coils of the wire to the hour hand of the clock, twisting the wire around three times and then spreading the copper strands out into a fan shape. He did the same with the other piece of wire and the minute hand. He cut the length of wire in half with his knife and bared the cut ends. He took one of the batteries from his pocket and connected the wire from the minute hand to one of its terminals, and the loose piece of wire to the other, before setting the clock to twenty-five minutes to five and checking that it was fully wound. He now had about fifty minutes before the two wires came together. He put the pipe next to the wall under the windows and then connected the two wires protruding from it to the timing circuit by twisting the ends together. When the minute hand had crawled round to meet the hour hand and the two bare wire ends touched they would complete the circuit between the battery and the flash-bulb detonator which would in turn explode the bomb.

He repacked his rucksack and put it on before he gently rolled four of the full barrels of weedkiller over and ranged them around the bomb in a semicircle which would have the effect of concentrating the blast against the wall where it would do the most damage. The hands of the clock were forty minutes apart when he edged silently through the doorway and bolted the door.

Nguyen retraced his steps, but he didn't begin crawling when he left the courtyard, instead he ran around the barns in a low crouch, dropping down only when he came within earshot of the cottage. When past the cottage he rose up again and jogged by the stables. The horses were locked inside and he heard snorts and whinnies but no panic. He reached a point in the field where he could see the entire front of the farmhouse and he dropped down into the grass. He took his binoculars out of the rucksack, put them on the grass in front of him, and looked at his watch. Eight minutes to go.

He lay listening to the night sounds: the hoot of a hunting owl, the bark of a faraway fox, the whup-whup of army helicopters. In his mind, Nguyen pictured the clock ticking away the seconds, and his concentration was so intense that it was almost as if he could hear the metallic clicks emanating from the storeroom, getting louder and louder until the air resonated with the beat and he was sure it would wake everyone for miles around.

The blast, when it came, shocked him, even though he was expecting it. From where he was he couldn't see the explosion but the farmhouse was silhouetted by the flash and a fraction of a second later he felt a trembling vibration along his body and a thundering roar filled the night.

He clamped the binoculars to his eyes and scanned the farmhouse. Within seconds a light went on in one of the upstairs rooms and a figure appeared at the window. Nguyen recognised the man as being one of those who had searched him at Hennessy's office. No other lights came on upstairs so Nguyen got to his feet and, keeping low, scurried back along behind the stables. He moved carefully but he was sure that all eyes would be on the shattered outbuilding which was now burning fiercely. He heard the horses neighing in their stalls and the thuds as they kicked out with their hooves. He dropped down and crawled because he realised that someone would probably go in to calm them down. He made his way past the cottage and didn't stop until he was in the orchard. He crouched behind an apple tree and examined the upstairs rooms of the farmhouse. The door of the cottage burst open and a middle-aged man in a striped dressing-gown came running out, shouting, followed by three bare-chested young men. Nguyen checked them out through the binoculars. They were holding guns.

A light had gone on in the window on the right-hand side of the building, the end nearest the outbuildings, and there were lights in the two rooms on the left. As Nguyen watched, a woman came to the window and opened it. She was middle-aged and dark-haired. A light came on downstairs and then the door opened and two figures appeared. One of them was the man he'd seen at the far side of the building, the other was Hennessy They ran towards the flames. A young woman ran out of the cottage and the middle-aged man shouted something at her. She changed direction and headed for the stables.

From the farmhouse four more men emerged, none of whom Nguyen had seen before. One of them was carrying a fire extinguisher and the rest had shotguns at the ready. The flames were flickering out of a jagged hole in the wall where the door and window had been. Most of the roof tiles had been blown off and were scattered around the courtyard and on the cars. The fire extinguisher spluttered into life and the man played foam around the hole. The girl ran out of the stables carrying another fire extinguisher and she gave it to the man in the dressing-gown. He joined in the fire-fighting. The woman shouted down and Hennessy waved at her and yelled something back. Probably his wife, thought Nguyen. One of the men went back into the farmhouse and reappeared with another fire extinguisher and before long the three col-umns of foam had the blaze under control. Nguyen decided he had seen enough. He crawled on his belly, away from the farm and into the darkness. There was a wedge-shaped copse of trees about a mile away that he'd earlier identified as a suitable place to lie up during the day and which would allow him to keep the farm under observation.

* * *

Murphy and Hennessy stepped gingerly over the broken brickwork and peered into the smoking wreckage of the outhouse. Steel barrels had been torn apart in the explosion and they were careful not to tread on any of the twisted shards. The blast had shredded the tough, wooden benches and chunks of wood were scattered around misshapen tools, what was left of them.

A slate from the shattered roof crashed down on to the floor and Murphy pulled Hennessy back. "Careful, Liam," he said. "We'd better wait until daylight before we go messing in there."

Hennessy nodded and followed Murphy back out into the courtyard.

"Jesus, Mary and Joseph, what in heaven's name is going on?" said Joe Ryan, standing with an empty extinguisher in his hand, his dressing-gown flapping around his legs. Ryan had been the manager of Hennessy's farm for more than twenty years. He'd been a little surprised when Hennessy and Mary had arrived with McMahon, Murphy and seven men from Belfast who were now standing around the courtyard carrying various weapons that obviously weren't for shooting rabbits, but Hennessy hadn't offered an explanation and Ryan hadn't asked for one.

Hennessy went over to his manager and put a reassuring arm around his shoulder. "My fault, Joe, I should have told you earlier. But I had no idea he'd follow me here." As they walked to the kitchen door of the farmhouse he explained about The Chinaman.

Mary was waiting for them in the kitchen in a green silk dressing-gown and slippers. She'd made a huge pot of coffee and had placed a bottle of Irish whiskey and a dozen glasses on the table for the men. She poured a generous measure into one of the glasses and gave it to her husband. She told Murphy to fill the rest of the glasses for the men who were filing in behind him. "Are you all right?" she asked Hennessy, touching his shoulder as she spoke, her concern obvious and genuine.

"I'm fine, right enough," he said.

"Another warning?" she said, and he wasn't sure if she was being sarcastic or not.

"He wasn't trying to kill anyone, if that's what you mean, Mary," he said, and took a mouthful of the smooth whiskey.

He turned to Murphy. "Get Kavanagh down here straight-away," he said. "Tell him there's no point in looking for The Chinaman in Belfast. And tell him to bring a dozen or so of his men here. Including Willie O'Hara." Murphy grunted and went out to use the phone in the hall.

Ryan pulled a chair out and sat down, helping himself to a mug of coffee. "Has this Chinaman got hand grenades or what, Liam?" he asked.

"Nitroglycerine," said Hennessy. "He made his own nitro-glycerine in Belfast." The kitchen was full now, men standing or sitting, some of them still coughing to clear the smoke from their lungs. Ryan's daughter, Sarah, stood behind her father, smoothing down his hair, more to calm her own shaking hands than anything.

Hennessy stood with his back to the sink and cleared his throat loudly to attract everybody's attention. "We're all going to have to be on our guard," he said. "I've underesti-mated The Chinaman up until now, and that's not a mistake I intend to repeat. For the rest of tonight I want six of you on guard outside." He nodded or pointed to the six men to indicate those he'd chosen. "Jimmy McMahon can sleep in the kitchen and I'll have Christy Murphy stay by the front door. Joe, you and Sarah should lock yourself in the cottage, and keep Tommy with you. Everyone else try to grab some sleep. By tomorrow I'll have worked out what we're going to do."

The men assigned to guard duty finished their whiskey, checked their guns and went outside. Ryan and his daughter went back to their cottage with Tommy O'Donoghue in tow.

Murphy came back into the kitchen. "Jim's on his way."

"Good," said Hennessy. "Mary and I are going to bed. Jimmy'll sleep here tonight. Can you stay in the hall? We'll get a proper rota fixed up tomorrow after Jim gets here."

"Fine by me," said Murphy.

Hennessy and Mary went up the stairs together. She carried a bright-yellow mug of coffee cupped in both hands. To Hennessy, though, it appeared that she was more annoyed than upset by the disturbance. In the bedroom, she put the mug down on her bedside table and brushed her hair with short, attacking strokes.

"I don't think you should stay here, not with all this going on," said Hennessy, taking off his dressing-gown and hanging it on the back of the door.

"I was thinking the same myself," she answered, watching him through the dressing-table mirror as she brushed her hair. He walked over to the open window and looked down at the courtyard. There were two of his men there, one with a shotgun. They waved and he waved back before shutting the window to keep out the smell of smoke. He drew the curtains with a flourish.

"The house in town isn't safe, even while The Chinaman's here," he said. "Abroad would be best, just until we've solved this problem."

"This problem!" she said, and laughed, her voice loaded with irony. "This problem, as you call it, Liam, is stalking around our farm with nitroglycerine bombs intent on God knows what and you call it a problem. You can be so pompous at times!" She shook her head, sadly, while Hennessy stood confused, not sure what to say. She made the decision for him. "I thought I'd go and stay with Marie." Marie, their daughter, was studying sociology at university in London and there were still some weeks to go before summer holidays. They'd rented her a one-bedroom flat in Earl's Court and Mary had been to stay on several occasions.

"I'd prefer it if you went well away, to America or the Caribbean, London is still a bit close to home," he pressed.

She turned to look at him, still brushing her hair. "Liam, I'll be perfectly safe in London," she said frostily. "In the first place, he's hardly likely to know about Marie's rented flat, and in the second, it's you he's after, not me."

Hennessy couldn't argue with that, so he reluctantly agreed.

"Besides, I'll fly over and I'll make sure I take a very close look at everyone else who gets on the plane. If I see anyone who looks vaguely Chinese, I'll call you," she said. She put down the brush and switched off the light. He heard the rustle of silk against her skin and then she slipped under the quilt. He got into his side of the bed.

"Good night," she said. He felt a light kiss on the cheek and then she turned her back on him, drawing her legs up against her stomach. Liam lay on his back, his eyes closed tight.

The french window was wide open allowing the fresh river air to stream in along with the early morning sunshine. Denis Fisher sat on the white plastic chair, a stack of Sunday newspapers on the circular white table. He was wearing a white T-shirt and faded blue Levis and a pair of black plastic sunglasses. His feet were up on another chair, he had a cup of strong coffee at his elbow, and he appeared to be at peace with the world. He ran his fingers through his blond hair and stretched his arms above his head.

"How's it going?" he called into the lounge.

MacDermott, the one they called The Bombmaker, was sitting at the dining-table in front of a collection of electrical equipment, wiring, batteries and timers, and peering into the innards of a laptop computer.

"Fine. There's acres of space here. More than enough. What I'm trying to do is to use the computer's internal clock as a timer and to connect the detonator to its internal battery. If I can it'll save a hell of a lot of weight. All I'll be adding will be the explosive, the detonator and a few inches of wire."

By the side of the computer was an oblong slab of what appeared to be bright-yellow marzipan, covered in a thick film of plastic. It was less than one inch thick but almost nine inches wide and twelve inches long. On top of the block, under the plastic, was a white paper label with a black border containing the words EXPLOSIVE PLASTIC SEMTEX-H.

The explosive had come a long way. It had been manufactured years earlier in the Semtex factory deep in the woods in western Czechoslovakia in the days when it had been behind the Iron Curtain. Production of the high-performance military explosive stopped in 1980, but between 1975 and 1981 the Czechs sold 960 tons to Libya for six million US dollars through the Omnipol trade agency and several tons of that had found its way to the IRA. The Libyan leader Colonel Gaddafi had filled six brick and sandstone warehouses a few miles outside Tripoli with boxes of the high explosive. The Libyan leader had been a staunch supporter of the IRA throughout the early seventies, but it was after the siege of his embassy in London in the summer of 1985 that he began to help them with a vengeance, as a way of getting back at the British Government.

In October 1986, six months after President Reagan ordered a US bomber strike on Tripoli, a converted oil industry safety ship sailed into Libyan waters and over two nights took on board eighty tons of weapons, including a ton of Semtex. The Semtex was unloaded at a small beach in southeast Ireland and over the next year or so much of it was secretly transferred to caches in Britain. The two packages on the table were from the 1986 consignment.

Fisher put down his *Independent on Sunday* and walked back into the flat. He watched over The Bombmaker's shoulder.

"It looks hellishly complicated," said Fisher.

"I've never done anything like this before," said MacDermott. "I'm testing it with this torch bulb here until I'm sure it'll work. The timing is the crucial thing. The amount of explosive we'll be using is so small that it won't do much damage if it goes off in the wrong place. And there's no room for booby traps or secondary circuits."

"How much will you use?" asked Fisher.

"Two hundred grams is more than enough to blow a hole in the fuselage and cause decompression. It was three hundred grams that brought down the Pan Am jet at Lockerbie. Mind you, it's the Lockerbie fiasco that's making it so hard now."

"What do you mean?"

"You remember that doctor whose daughter died on the flight, the one that took a fake bomb on a BA jet to New York to show how lax security was? He filled a radio with marzipan and a battery but he proved his point and now the airlines routinely check all electrical equipment."

"Does that mean they'll take it apart?" said Fisher, frowning.

"They won't take it apart, but they will ask to see it working, and they'll peer through the grilles and any gaps. And they'll X-ray it. Before the summer of 1990 they'd let you take them on board without putting them through the X-ray machine, but the Secretary of State for Transport changed the rules."

"Won't the explosive show up?"

"It's supposed to on the new models, but I'm hollowing out the transformer and taking out the modem circuit and packing most of it in there. It'll look OK, no matter how good their equipment is, don't worry. Anyway, this is the sort of thing they expect people to take on planes, so if it works OK and the right person is carrying it they won't suspect anything. And it will work, I'll make sure of that."

Fisher put his hand on MacDermott's shoulder and squeezed. "If anyone can do it, you can. How's the Ascot bomb coming on?"

The Bombmaker nodded at a metal camera case on the floor. "That's child's play in comparison. I'll finish it tonight."

Fisher smiled, satisfied.

"Have you any idea which plane yet?" asked The Bombmaker.

Fisher shook his head. "We're going to have to be careful, bloody careful," he said. "We can't hit a flight where there could be Irish on board, or Americans, or kids. What I'm really after is a plane in the Queen's Flight, or one carrying the Prime Minister or any of the Government bastards. Or maybe an RAF plane. I just want to have the bomb ready so that we can use it immediately we get an opportunity. And a mule. We need a mule to carry it on board. Someone with access. A pilot, a journalist, a policeman, someone who can get close without raising suspicion."

"It's risky, mixing with people like that when we're trying to keep a low profile."

Fisher grinned. "I know it's risky, but think of the rewards. Just think about it. It'd be like another Brighton bombing, another Mountbatten."

The phone rang and O'Reilly put down the gun he was cleaning, a Smith & Wesson 9-millimetre automatic pistol, on the coffee-table. "Shall I get it?" he asked, but Fisher already had it in his hand.

"Yes, yes, understood. Yes," he said to the voice at the other end and hung up.

"Interesting," he said, rubbing his chin. O'Reilly and The Bombmaker looked at him expectantly. "The codeword has been changed," he explained. "As of tonight."

"Good of them to let us know," smiled O'Reilly as he picked up the automatic and began stripping it down. "They might not have taken us seriously."

Hennessy was alone in the large pine bed when he awoke. He bathed and dressed and went downstairs to find his wife in front of their stove frying eggs and bacon and grilling toast. Jim Kavanagh, Willie O'Hara, Christy Murphy and Jimmy McMahon were sitting around the table drinking coffee.

Despite the bomb shattering their sleep, Mary looked radiant and seemed to be relishing her role as a short-order cook.

"Right Christy, here's yours," she sang, and plopped down a plate of bacon and eggs in front of him. Willie O'Hara was already halfway through his breakfast, mopping up egg yolk with a piece of fried bread. Kavanagh had finished and was buttering a slice of toast. Liam had heard him arrive in the early hours and he didn't look as if he'd had any sleep, either. Mary broke another two eggs into the pan and put them on the burner, took four more slices of toast from under the grill and slotted them into the toast rack on the table.

"Good morning, Liam," she said cheerfully, and poured him a glass of orange juice. "What would you like?"

"Just toast," he said. He had never been a big eater, and considering the stress he was under just now he doubted if he'd be able to force down much toast. "Thanks for getting here so quickly, Jim," he said to Kavanagh.

"I'm just mad at myself for not getting him in Belfast, then none of this would've happened."

"Where are the men who came down with you?"

"They've relieved the guys who were on duty during the night, and they're over in the cottage having breakfast. We didn't think it fair to all impose on yez good lady wife."

"Nonsense," said Mary, walking over with another plate of food. "Jimmy, here's your breakfast."

Hennessy pulled out a chair and sat down. "How many men are here at the moment?" he asked Kavanagh.

"There's the six that came down with me, plus the seven who came down with ye and Christy. And there's three farmworkers who we can use if necessary. And Mr Ryan and his daughter have offered to help. I think they're a bit reluctant to be out working the farm with this Chinaman on the loose."

Hennessy nodded thoughtfully and sipped his juice. "We can't use the farmworkers, or the Ryans, not for this. If we need more men we'll bring them in from Belfast. So we're talking about thirteen men, plus you four." He saw a look of panic pass over O'Hara's egg-streaked face. "Don't worry, Willie, I won't be asking you to carry a gun." Willie O'Hara was notoriously afraid of firearms, despite being one of the organisation's foremost explosives experts. "And Christy, I want you to take Mary to London later today."

"Och Liam, he doesn't have to go all the way to London with me," chided Mary over her shoulder as she fried more eggs.

"To London," insisted Liam. Murphy nodded. "Jimmy, you'll be driving them to the airport." McMahon grunted through a mouthful of food.

Hennessy asked Kavanagh how many men it would take to make the farm secure.

"Nothing can ever be secure, ye know that," he answered. "Yez could put a hundred men on guard but a determined man could still get through." He could see that Hennessy was not pleased with his answer so quickly added: "Three guards could secure the courtyard, but there's a risk then that he could throw something in through one of the windows of the outside of the building, or get to the barns. Yez'll need a man guarding the barns, two by the stables, one in the courtyard, and three covering the front of the farm."

"So seven men in all?"

"That's at night. During the day four should do it because this place is surrounded by fields and yer'll see him coming for miles."

"That's still eleven men and that doesn't include sleeping time."

"That's right enough. Yer'll need at least twenty-two, and if it goes on for any length of time, Liam, yer'll need as many again because they're going to get tired and careless."

Hennessy slammed his hand down on the table, rattling the breakfast plates. "Damn this man, damn him," he cursed.

Mary put a filled plate in front of Kavanagh and he thanked her. "Are you sure you don't want anything else, Liam?" she asked, and when he said no she took off her apron and put it over the back of a chair. She was wearing tight ski pants and a blue sweater and Hennessy could see O'Hara and McMahon watch her backside twitch as she walked to the door. Did she know that men took such pleasure from watching her move? Hennessy was pretty sure that she did. While he took pride in having such an attractive wife, many were the times that he wished she'd age just a little faster, that she'd look a little less attractive so that men would stop looking at her with lust in their eyes. He wished she'd join him in middle-age and not keep acting like a teenager. Maybe she'd give him more of herself then.

"Christy, get on the plane with her and see her all the way to my daughter's flat. If at any time you even remotely suspect that The Chinaman is anywhere near, get to a safe place and call for help. Don't take any risks. This bastard is out to get me and he might just decide to hurt me through my family."

Murphy put his knife and fork together on his plate. "She'll be safe with me, Liam, I promise you."

McMahon drained his coffee cup and stood up. "I think

I'll take the car to the garage in the village and fill her up so that we don't have to stop on the way. Are they open on a Sunday?"

"The sign'll say closed, sure enough, but sound your horn and old man Hanratty will come out and serve you," said Hennessy.

McMahon wiped his hands on his trousers and went out into the courtyard. They heard the car start up and drive out of the courtyard.

"Willie, I want you to go through what's left of the outbuilding and find out what caused it, whether or not it was one of the home-made bombs you described. Then I think we ought to arrange a . . ."

His words were cut short by the echoing thud of an explosion in the distance, as if a huge pile of earth had been dropped from a great height. Kavanagh got to his feet first and he led the way as they rushed through the hall and out of the front door.

The Jaguar was lying on its side in the field next to the track about fifty yards before it joined the road. There were clouds of steam coming from under the bonnet which had burst open and the engine was racing. Three of the IRA guards were already running down the track to the car and two more came running from the stables, guns at the ready. One of them reached through the side window and switched off the engine.

"Oh God, Jimmy," said Hennessy under his breath as he began jogging towards the Jaguar. By the time he arrived there, with O'Hara in tow, they'd pulled McMahon out of the car and lain him on the grass. His face was cut in a dozen places, there was blood on his shirt and he was mumbling incoherently. Hennessy knelt down by McMahon and held his hand. It was covered in blood.

"Get a car here, we'll have to take him to hospital," he said to Michael O'Faolain, the gangly, red-haired youth who'd come down from Belfast. "We don't have time to wait for an ambulance." O'Faolain ran back down the track towards the farmhouse. "Willie, find out what the hell happened," he said to O'Hara. O'Hara went to look at the car, but Hennessy had already seen the crater in the track and knew what it meant. "The fucking Chinaman," he hissed.

McMahon groaned but didn't open his eyes. His trousers were burnt and ripped and through the slashed material Hennessy could see blood pouring from the injured legs.

O'Hara appeared at his shoulder. "Nitroglycerine bomb by the look of it, Liam, buried a couple of feet down in the track. Detonated by wire."

"That means he was close by."

"Still is, I reckon. Depends how long his wires were." He pointed across the field towards a distant copse. "The wires run in that direction. If you move fast . . ."

"Christ, what was I thinking of!" Hennessy blurted. "We should be after him now." He called Kavanagh over and told him to take all but three of the men and follow the wires and to go after The Chinaman. As an afterthought he told Murphy to stay behind because after what had happened he was even more keen to get Mary out of the way.

O'Faolain arrived in the Range Rover and Hennessy, Murphy and O'Hara helped lift McMahon on to the back seat. There was a large tartan blanket there and they used it to wrap him up in. Hennessy delegated another of the young men to sit in the back and make sure that McMahon wasn't tossed around too much on the drive to the hospital. The Range Rover roared off as Hennessy shielded his eyes and looked at the group of men running across the fields, fanning out the further away they got from the track. Of The Chinaman there was no sign, but he had to be out there somewhere.

Nguyen had begun to crawl through the grass as soon as he had detonated the pipe bomb. The wires had been about fifty yards long which put him about halfway across the field, but he could move quickly on his stomach and by the time the front door of the farm had opened he had reached the relative safety of a hedgerow that cut it off from the neighbouring field where a flock of sheep and lambs grazed and played.

He'd set the bomb in the early hours of the morning before the sky had streaked with red and the sun had made its first appearance. He'd planned to dig down into the track but as it turned out there had been no need. It cut across the field with a narrow ditch on either side to keep the rain running off it during the wet weather. In places, the earth by the side of the track had begun to crumble into the ditch and Nguyen found a spot where he could pull out handfuls of soil with a minimum of effort. He scooped out enough to hide one of the pipe bombs, and he carefully ran the wires down into the ditch and through the grass as far as they would go. The grass was barely tall enough to conceal him but the ground was uneven and towards the road it sloped steeply away from the farm so Nguyen knew that, so long as he kept low, he'd be able to reach the hedgerow without being spotted. He'd lain flat on the ground for about six hours, not moving. He'd seen the sun come up and heard the birds begin their dawn chorus and counted half a dozen helicopters flying overhead before the Jaguar had come down the track.

After he detonated the bomb he rolled under the hedge and found a gap big enough to squeeze through and then began crawling away from the road, back towards the farm. After he'd travelled two hundred yards he peeked through the hedge. He could see Hennessy kneeling on the ground cradling the driver. Nguyen doubted that he would be badly hurt, the bomb had been too far underground to do too much damage. He'd been careful to detonate it just under the front bumper, not so far ahead that the blast would send the windscreen glass spinning into the driver's face, but not so far back that the petrol tank would be ignited. Nguyen didn't want to kill unless it was absolutely necessary, he still hoped to get what he wanted by pressurising and intimidating Hennessy. If that didn't work then he'd rethink his strategy.

A small, thin-faced man was bending over the crater in the track. He knelt down and picked up something and looked at it and then went over to look at the blasted car. He examined the damage to the underside of the car and then walked back to the crater. He looked into the ditch and then jumped over it and began searching the grass. Nguyen knew that he was looking for the wires and that before long he'd find them. He cut away from the hedgerow and ran with his back to the farm-buildings, his rucksack banging on his shoulders. He tramped across a small stream and vaulted over a five-bar gate into a field containing a dozen or so brown and white cattle, breathing heavily because he wasn't used to running. He reached the edge of the copse where he'd hidden the previous evening and slipped into the cool undergrowth before looking behind him. The field was clear, and so was the one behind that, but it was only a matter of time before they came after him. Not that Nguyen was worried. He'd only seen ten men in the courtyard dealing with the fire last night and he doubted that Hennessy would allow them all to go tramping through the fields and woods, leaving the cottage unprotected. Five, or maybe six, that would be all, and Nguyen knew he was more than capable of handling that many because they'd have to spread out.

The copse covered several acres and was on land which was obviously too wet for grazing sheep or cattle. He'd spent several hours getting to know his way around and could move confidently through it, knowing where the best hiding places and vantage points were. The trees were a mixture of oak, horse chestnut and beech, all of them old and draped in moss and surrounded by bushes and brambles. The canopy of branches overhead blocked out much of the sunlight and the air was filled with the chatter of birds jostling for territory. Nguyen made his way towards the middle of the copse, being careful not to break branches or leave obvious signs of his passage. In the distance he heard shouts. They'd be able to follow the wires to the place where he'd lain in the grass and then they'd be able to see where he'd crawled to the hedgerow, but unless they were expert trackers they wouldn't be able to see where he'd gone from there. They'd see the trees but they wouldn't be sure if he'd gone to ground there, or if he'd run through or passed by, so they'd probably split up. Two, maybe three. It would be easy.

A rustling sound to his left made him drop into a crouch, senses alert. A grey squirrel sprinted out from underneath a bush, its tail streaming behind it like a banner, and it ran headlong up a tree with something held in its jaws. Nguyen relaxed and as he did he heard more shouts, heading in his direction. A meandering trail roughly bisected the wood, it was nothing more than a flattening of the soil where countless generations of feet had used it as a shortcut through the trees. By the side of the trail was a huge oak, a centuries-old tree which was gnarled and misshapen with age. It was a good twelve feet across at the base and its roots were as thick as a man's waist before they dived down into the earth. Behind the tree, on the side furthest away from the path, was a deep split where the wood had cracked, half covered with a rambling bramble bush with sharp thorns. Nguyen had marked it out as a good place to hide because anyone searching the copse would probably take the easy way and follow the path. Some fifteen feet or so either side of the tree he'd tossed small, dry twigs along the path which were sure to crackle and break when stepped on so he'd be able to hear them coming no matter how careful they were. He'd prepared traps along the trail in places where it narrowed. Nothing elaborate because he hadn't had the time, just holes dug in the earth, a foot or so deep, with sharpened sticks, smeared with his own excrement, pointing upward. The holes had been covered with a mesh of fine twigs and leaves and overlain with soil, and overnight they had blended in perfectly with the rest of the trail. Even Nguyen himself could see no traces of the traps.

He slipped by the brambles and edged into the hole in the tree, first removing his rucksack so that it wouldn't snag. He unclipped his knife and held it by his side, breathing slowly and evenly. There were more shouts to his left, outside the wood, and then a yelling voice to his right. There were more voices, closer, whispering. He heard someone forcing his way through the undergrowth, but moving away from him, and then a similar noise to his left, also moving away. Two men at least, then. They had entered the copse together and had split up either side of the trail and were moving through the trees. The shouting continued in the distance so he had been right, some of the men had gone by the copse and were probably even now running across the fields and checking the hedgerows.

Nguyen let his mind totally relax so that he could concentrate on listening for his pursuers. They moved like large animals through the trees, pushing branches out of the way, not caring where they trod, and he had no problem in pinpointing their positions. He closed his eyes and let his mind roam the woods. He heard the dry crack of a twig and homed in on the sound, twenty, perhaps twenty-five feet away, someone moving slowly and carefully, somebody who cared how and where he walked. There was a pause of perhaps ten seconds then a second sound, the rustle of a leaf being disturbed.

Nguyen blanked out his mind, wiping away all thoughts and concentrating only on the approaching man. He tried to make himself invisible. Nguyen had once tried explaining it to the instructors from the 5th Special Forces Group at Recondo School outside Saigon, how his sixth sense worked and how he would shield his own thoughts from pursuers so that he could blend into the jungle and not be seen or felt. They'd laughed, thinking he was talking about magic or voodoo, but Nguyen was serious. His talent had saved his life, and the lives of his men, many, many times. It wasn't a case of hearing, or smelling, it was sensing, but even Nguyen didn't know exactly what it was that he sensed. It was as if he could tune into the electrical field given off by a human being or an animal, as if he could detect their auras from a distance. And he believed that the reverse was true, that other animals and humans could detect his aura and home in on it unless he dampened it down.

He heard a small movement and knew that the man was now level with the tree, heading down the trail. Nguyen's mind was empty now, like a placid pool with not a single ripple disturbing its surface. He was no longer aware of the heavy knife in his hand or the pressure of the ground against his left knee as he knelt inside the tree trunk. He was invisible. He flowed out of the tree as gentle as a soft wind, brushing the brambles silently aside. His steps were small and only the balls of his feet made contact with the ground, his legs bent at the knees. The man on the trail was slightly taller than Nguyen. He stood with his back to him, wearing jeans and a dark-blue bomber jacket. In his right hand he carried a gun. Nguyen had planned to silence the man with his left hand and stun him by driving the handle of his knife against his temple but he couldn't risk it now because the man's finger would tighten involuntarily and the gun would go off. Still moving, he slipped the knife into one of the pockets of his jacket and moved behind the man, both hands out. Only at the last minute did the man sense his presence and begin to turn his head, but by then Nguyen was in position. His right hand moved down swiftly and clamped over the gun, fingers splayed so that he caught the hammer and prevented it from being released. His left hand simultaneously clamped over the man's mouth and nose. He pulled the nose between his thumb and the first joint of the opposing index finger while gripping the jaws between the heel of the hand and the remaining finger tips. The man tried to lash out with his left hand but Nguyen twisted away, out of reach. From experience Nguyen knew that it could take up to two minutes for the man to lose consciousness and he gripped tightly until the man sagged and the gun dropped from his nerveless hand. Nguyen put the gun into his jacket pocket and took out the knife. He let the man's dead-weight carry him to the ground. Killing him would have been easy; a quick slash across the subclavian artery would take just three seconds, cutting the carotid artery and jugular vein would kill within twelve. But Nguyen knew that killing the enemy wasn't always the best way, not when you were up against more than one. A dead comrade could be abandoned while the fight continued, but an injured one became a drain on the enemy's resources. He had to be cared for and transported out of danger, with the added psychological damage that a wounded man could do to the able-bodied. Time and time again Nguyen had seen it happen in the jungle. A group of Americans on a mission, the man on point would run into a booby trap, his leg blown off or a poisoned stick through his foot, and his screams and blood would terrify the rest. Not only that but the mission would be suspended while a helicopter was called in or the man was stretchered back to base. And next time a patrol moved down the trail they'd do so with twice the care at half the speed.

He heard a shout far to his right and an answer over to his left. He knelt down by the unconscious man and stabbed him twice in the upper thigh, not deep enough to cut an artery but enough to cause a considerable flow of blood.

The shouting was getting closer and Nguyen ducked behind the tree to pick up his rucksack and began to run down the track, keeping low. A gunshot behind him made him duck and he ran faster. Twice he jumped over places in the track where he'd earlier set spike traps. The man he'd ambushed must have come round because he heard frantic screaming. His screams and the gunshot would bring the rest of the men running to the copse, but Nguyen was still perfectly calm because he had many other hiding-places prepared. It would take a dozen men many days to search the copse thoroughly and they had no way of knowing whether he'd gone to ground or if he'd left the woods. They'd be sure to follow his tracks down the trail but there was a good chance that one of them would fall into one of the foot traps and that would slow them up even more. Everything was going to plan.

It seemed to Hennessy as if his life had been turned upside down. Mary had left with Christy Murphy in one of the Land-Rovers, driving over the fields for a mile or so before turning on to the road just in case The Chinaman had set other bombs. In a few hours she'd be in London where at least she'd be safe. Jimmy McMahon was in hospital where his condition, the doctors said, was as well as could be expected. They'd been told that a faulty generator had exploded because Hennessy didn't want the RUC sniffing around. The man who'd been stabbed in the wood had turned out to have superficial wounds despite all his screaming and they'd patched him up and he was being driven up to Belfast for treatment along with a teenager who'd put his foot through six wooden spikes smeared with what looked like shit. He could barely walk and he'd need antibiotics if the wound wasn't going to go septic.

In the space of an hour, three of his men had been injured and all they had to show for it was a description of a small Oriental man in camouflage gear carrying a rucksack. And if he wasn't armed before, now he had a gun.

Hennessy had posted four guards around the farm and everyone else was now indoors. Joe Ryan and Sarah were staying in their own cottage. With three men injured, one driving the car to Belfast, and Murphy on his way to London with Mary, it left Hennessy with just Jim Kavanagh and Willie O'Hara sitting at the kitchen table. He poured O'Hara and himself measures of whiskey and asked Kavanagh what he wanted.

"I'll make myself a brew, if that's OK with yez," Kavanagh said. He pushed back his chair and put the kettle on the stove.

"We're going to need more men," Hennessy said to his back. Kavanagh shrugged but didn't turn round as he busied himself washing the teapot and preparing a cup and saucer. "Can you arrange for half a dozen good men from Belfast?"

"I'm not sure if that's such a good idea, Liam," said Kavanagh quietly.

"What do you mean?" O'Hara emptied his glass and mumbled something about checking the bombed outhouse and let himself out of the back door. "What do you mean, Jim?" Hennessy repeated.

Kavanagh turned round, drying his cup with a big, white tea-towel. "I'm just not sure that we're going to be able to solve this just by bringing in more people, that's all. There were a dozen here last night and they didn't stop him."

"They weren't prepared," said Hennessy.

"They were prepared when they went into the wood," said Kavanagh. He put the cup and the cloth on the draining-board and sat down, looking earnestly at Hennessy. "Look, Liam, yer know that I'd do anything to protect ye, anything. But this isn't a question of numbers, it's quality not quantity. Yez could bring in a hundred men but they're used to the city, not the country. They're used to fighting in the streets not in the hills."

"So we bring in men from the farms. Come on Jim, that's not what's worrying you. Spit it out."

Kavanagh looked uneasy, as if knowing that what he would say would offend Hennessy. Hennessy found his reluctance to speak embarrassing, he'd always thought that they trusted each other implicitly.

"What's wrong, Jim?" he pressed.

Kavanagh leant back in his chair, as if trying to put as much distance as possible between the two of them. "This man, this Chinaman, has made it personal. It's ye he wants, right enough. Not the organisation. Ye. I just think that if ye use too many of the organisation's resources, it could backfire on yez."

Hennessy nodded. Kavanagh had a point. There were men in Belfast and Dublin who were looking for an excuse to discredit him. They were unhappy at the move away from violence and blamed Hennessy for the switch in policy.

"And the thing of it is, I don't reckon that bringing in more men is going to help. Look at it this way, he could travel ten miles or so in a few hours with no trouble at all. And a ten-mile radius from here will cover about three hundred square miles – that includes Newry, Castlewellan, and Warrenpoint, and most of the Mourne Mountains. There aren't enough men in the whole of Belfast to cover an area that large."

"So we don't search for him. OK. But I have to have guards here. I can't just sit here defenceless and wait for him to attack again."

"But how long do ye keep the guards here, Liam? A week? A month? A year? Round-the-clock protection from one man – think what a drain that would be on the organisation's resources. Think how it would look. I'm telling ye this as yer friend, yer understand? Playing devil's advocate, yer know?"

Hennessy nodded. "I know, Jim. I don't doubt your loyalty, you know that." He reached over and squeezed Kavanagh's arm. "I already owe you my life, you don't have to prove anything to me. And I know you have my best interests at heart. But what am I supposed to do? He obviously means business."

"If ye want my opinion, it was a mistake coming here. It's too open, there are too many places to hide."

"It sounds like you've had a change of heart, Jim. I seem to remember that it was your idea to get me out of Belfast in the first place." He said it softly, not meaning to criticise.

"That was then," admitted Kavanagh. "I thought it was a good idea because I didn't think he'd know about the farm. But now that he does know I think we should go back to Belfast. All yez need there is me and Christy, maybe a couple of others. Now that we know who he is he won't be able to get close to ye. He'll stick out like a sore thumb in Belfast." He held up his hands. "I know what yez going to say, that he managed to blow up yez office while we were there, but yer've got to remember that when he did that we didn't know what a threat he was then. It won't happen again."

Hennessy took a long, thoughtful swig from his glass.

"I don't know, Jim. He got to the car, didn't he? And he's obviously a patient bastard. He'll just wait until he gets another chance, sure enough."

"Yeah, but he'll be waiting in Belfast, not hiding in a wood. In the city we can search for him without worrying where we're stepping all the time."

The two men sat in silence for a while as Hennessy considered his options. He knew that Kavanagh was talking sense, but he knew too that there were advantages in keeping The Chinaman away from Belfast. God knows what it would do to his reputation if it became known that he was being stalked by a maniac with home-made bombs. The Press would have a field day. And so would his enemies within the organisation. Damn The Chinaman. Damn him for ever.

"There is something else yez should think about," said Kavanagh, interrupting Hennessy's thoughts. Hennessy raised his eyebrows quizzically. "The reason he's after yez," Kavanagh continued. "He wants the names of the team who're planting the bombs in London."

"We don't know who they are."

"No, but yer trying to find out. And yer'll find out eventually, they can't keep going for ever. Either we'll find out who they are or they'll make a mistake and the fucking Brits will get them. Either way that'll be the end of yez problem. All we have to do is to keep him off yez back until then. Liam, I know you're handling this yezself, but how close are ye to identifying them?"

Hennessy looked levelly at Kavanagh. He trusted the man sitting in front of him, but it was crucial that only Sean Morrison knew what he had planned. "At the moment we're no closer than we were a week ago," he said. "But if everything works out it shouldn't be much longer. Days rather than weeks. That's all I can say."

"That's good enough for me, Liam," said Kavanagh. The kettle began to shriek and he stood up and poured boiling water into the teapot. "Until then, we'll stick to yez like glue. When is Christy back?"

"I told him to take Mary all the way to London and to hang around for a while to make sure that she isn't followed. He should be back tomorrow night."

There was a scrabbling at the door and Jackie bounded in, her tongue lolling and her coat damp. She careered over to Hennessy and put her head in his lap; he stroked her absent-mindedly.

"I hear what you're saying," Hennessy said to Kavanagh. "Let's wait until Christy gets back until we decide what to do."

"It's yer call, Liam. But if I were ye I'd get a few more men around – not from Belfast but locals, workers from nearby farms maybe, fellahs yez can trust. They'll be used to dealing with poachers and the like and at least they'll be careful where they put their feet."

"That's a good idea, Jim. I'll make a few calls. It shouldn't be a problem."

Jackie growled softly, seeking attention.

* * *

Woody had the mother and father of all hangovers. His head felt twice its normal size, his mouth was dry and bitter and every time he moved his stomach lurched and only an intense effort of will kept him from throwing up. It was a normal Sunday morning. Saturday was always the paper's busiest day and once the presses started running and they'd checked that the opposition papers didn't have any earth-shattering exclusives then all the paper's journalists headed for the pub. The Saturday-night sessions in the King's Head were legendary, but Woody didn't just go for the alcohol and the company, he went because he had to keep in with the news desk and the paper's executives. The paper, along with most of Fleet Street, was cutting back all round, slashing a red pen through expense claims and reducing the number of casual shifts. It was like a game of musical chairs and Woody was fighting like hell to ensure that when the music stopped he'd be one of those left sitting at a desk. The hangover was a small price to pay.

He heard the phone ring on the floor below and one of the other tenants answered it and then he heard his name being called.

Woody groaned and pulled a pillow over his head. Footsteps clattered up the stairs and a hand hammered on his door and the student who lived in the bedsit directly below his yelled that the office was on the phone. If it had been anyone else Woody wouldn't have bothered answering, but a call from the paper probably meant there was a shift going so he coughed and forced himself to sit up, feeling waves of nausea ripple through his stomach. He breathed deeply and groped for a pair of jeans before padding slowly down the stairs, holding his head in his hands.

The phone was hanging down by the wall and he pulled it up and put it against his ear. His head swam and he closed his eyes.

"Ian Wood," he said, flinching as the words echoed around his skull.

"Woody?" said a voice. It was a man, but Woody couldn't place it.

"Yes?"

"Woody, it's Pat. Pat Quigley. I didn't get you out of bed, did I?"

Woody moaned and leant against the wall. "What the fuck do you want, Pat?"

"Jesus, Woody, you sound terrible. Are you sick or something?"

"Pat, you have exactly ten seconds before I go back to my pit. It's Sunday morning, you should be in church and I should be in bed."

"Got you, Woody. OK, listen. Do you remember those Sinn Fein guys you were asking me about a while back?" Woody grunted, but said nothing, so Quigley continued. "Well, there's something funny going on here. I've been told that someone has started some sort of vendetta against one of the men I told you about, Liam Hennessy. He's one of Sinn Fein's top advisers, and a leading lawyer here."

"A vendetta? What the fuck are you talking about?"

"Someone set off a bomb in his office. Just a small one, a chemical bomb I'm told, not high explosive. A warning, maybe. No one was hurt. It seems like a coincidence, you know, happening so soon after we spoke. That's all."

"I still don't see what you want from me, Pat." Actually Woody had a pretty good idea what was going on. As well as stringing for the *Sunday World*, Quigley filed copy for one of the daily heavies and they were probably pushing him for a Sunday for Monday story, what with it being a quiet news week and all.

"I was thinking that perhaps you passed Hennessy's name on to someone, someone who might want to, I don't know, put pressure on him, maybe. I mean, I'm told the attack wasn't sectarian, it was too amateurish for that. Come on Woody, what's going on?"

"Fucked if I know, Pat. Honest. Anyway, my notebooks are all in the office, I can't do anything now. But I'm sure you're barking up the wrong tree, mate. It was just a reader who wanted to contact someone in Sinn Fein, that was all."

"OK, Woody. I thought it was worth a try. Maybe I'll call you in the office during the week." He sounded disappointed, but Woody felt no urge to help him, not in his present weakened state. Besides, Woody could smell a possible story. What was The Chinaman's name? He couldn't remember so he stopped trying and instead concentrated on getting back to his room without throwing up over the threadbare carpet.

The taxi dropped Morrison close to the South African embassy in Trafalgar Square. A group of half a dozen demonstrators were outside, standing on the pavement close to the road. They were dressed like students, pale-faced girls with straggly hair and men with beards and John Lennon glasses. One of the women had a megaphone and she harangued two policemen who stood either side of the door to the building. "End Apartheid now!" she yelled, the electronically amplified shriek echoing off the stone walls of the embassy. Morrison wondered why they bothered. You didn't change things by standing on street corners with faded banners and shouting slogans. You changed things by taking action, by hurting those in power, and then by negotiating from strength. And by being committed to change. The anti-Apartheid movement in the UK had never really learnt that lesson, mainly because they had never experienced the discrimination they were protesting about. The vast bulk of them were from comfortable middle-class backgrounds or were working-class kids with chips on their shoulders. Most of them weren't even black. They'd be a hell of a lot more effective if they couldn't get work because they followed the wrong religion, if they didn't have a fair say in the running of their own lives, and if they and their friends and family could be beaten and tortured by the soldiers of an oppressive regime in a country that didn't even belong to them. The IRA was effective because its members cared and because they all stood to benefit if they were ultimately successful and the British pulled out of Ireland.

He crossed over the road and walked by one of the huge, majestic lions. It was surrounded by a group of Asian tourists laden with designer shoulder-bags and expensive camera equipment. A crocodile of Scandinavian sightseers were following a tour guide and Morrison stopped to let them go by. There were pigeons everywhere, fluttering through the air, sitting around the fountains and waddling along the floor. They had grown fat and lazy and had no fear of humans. On the contrary, they gathered in noisy flocks around the tourists who had paid for little tubs of bird seed and sat on arms and wrists while they fed.

Morrison looked around the square. He normally had a nose for plain-clothes policemen or off-duty soldiers, a sixth sense honed by years of surviving in Belfast. He tagged a man in his forties in a brown leather bomber jacket as one possibility, and he paid close attention to a balding man in a fawn overcoat, but both left the square eventually. Bromley got to within a dozen paces before Morrison realised he was the man he was there to see. Tallish with horn-rimmed spectacles and a well-trimmed black beard, Bromley looked more like a history professor than a Detective Chief Inspector with the Anti-Terrorist Branch. He was wearing a greenish jacket of some indeterminate material with baggy corduroy trousers and a brown wool tie. He was smoking a pipe. Morrison thought the pipe could be cover because it looked brand new, but the man appeared to have no problems inhaling and blew out a cloud of bluish smoke as he drew near.

"Detective Chief Inspector Bromley, I presume," said Morrison. He made no move to shake hands, and neither did the inspector. Each was highly suspicious of the other. Both knew that they could be under observation and whereas a clandestine meeting could possibly be explained, a handshake or any other sign of friendliness would be damning. And in Morrison's case, possibly fatal.

"How can I help you, Mr Morrison?" said Bromley with exaggerated politeness.

Morrison began walking slowly around the perimeter of the square. "It's about the bombs, the bombs on the mainland," he said. "We're not responsible."

"By we, who do you mean?"

"The organisation."

"Well, Mr Morrison, there appears to be some confusion here. The forensic evidence we have suggests that the devices are standard IRA type, and each time responsibility has been claimed they've given the correct codeword. Can you explain that?" Bromley shook his head and puffed on his pipe.

"We think there's a renegade unit behind it. We don't know who."

"Are you trying to tell me there's an active service unit on the loose and you don't even know who it is? Where are they getting their explosives from?"

"They've managed to gain access to several arms dumps in and around London. They have explosives, detonators and firearms. But they haven't been sanctioned by us. We're as keen as you are to see them stopped."

"And the codewords?"

Morrison nodded. "We think they're being helped by someone high up in Belfast or Dublin. But again, we don't know who."

Bromley thrust his hands deep into the pockets of his corduroy trousers and studied the ground as he walked. "You know they've taken explosives, but you don't know who they are?"

"We've checked out all our caches. Some ordnance was missing." Morrison chose his words carefully because he couldn't afford to give away any more information than was absolutely necessary. The IRA was still at war with the British Government, when all was said and done.

"Can't you just identify which IRA members are unaccounted for?"

"It's a big organisation. We're working on it."

"It's a big organisation but I doubt if you've that many bombmakers."

"You'd be surprised," said Morrison. "But with the organisation structured the way it is, it's harder than it used to be to get in touch with people. You of all people should know that."

Bromley grunted around the stem of his pipe. He knew what Morrison meant. Following several much publicised coups by the intelligence services in the late seventies and early eighties, the IRA had undergone a transformation, doing away with the old brigade command structure in favour of a more complex network of cells, each with different but often overlapping functions. Most of the units in Northern Ireland reported to the high command in Belfast, but in the countryside the chain of command was a great deal more flexible, harder to pin down. The cells were graded into four levels. The most important were active service units responsible for fund-raising robberies, assassinations, bombings and weaponry, numbering about one hundred of the organisation's most trusted members. At any one time at least half of them could be found in the H-blocks of Long Kesh.

The second level consisted of about three hundred and fifty men and women divided into small cells, all of them trained and ready to go into action but held in reserve until needed. They were generally less well-known to the security forces and it was members of the second level who were often sent into active service on the mainland or the Continent.

The third level comprised a small number of cells, mainly Dublin-based terrorists who were active during the sixties but who had effectively disappeared from the political scene and who did not appear on any current intelligence files.

The fourth level was made up of what Morrison thought of as the enthusiastic amateurs, usually Belfast teenagers who'd graduated from street fighting or youngsters from Catholic farming families helping with the organisation's smuggling operations. They were useful as couriers or lookouts, or for causing disturbances, but not sufficiently trained for anything more sophisticated. Most were expendable and would rise no higher in the organisation.

The structure had been set up so that if any one cell were exposed, its links with the rest of the organisation would be minimal. The system made the IRA much more secure, but it also made it difficult to run checks on who was doing what. Each cell had to be contacted individually, and that would take a great deal of time. And that wasn't allowing for the IRA members like Morrison who weren't even members of a cell but who worked alone.

"So what are you saying, Mr Morrison?"

"We have a plan," said Morrison quietly.

"We?"

That, realised Morrison, was the problem. "We" meant Hennessy and Morrison and nobody else, so he was going to have an uphill struggle to persuade Bromley to help. And it was made even more difficult by virtue of the fact that the policeman would also have to be sworn to secrecy. It was, whichever way you looked at it, an unholy alliance.

"The Provisional IRA is not responsible for the bombings, that I can promise you. They're using our ordnance and our codewords, but they are acting without official sanction. We plan to change the codeword, but different codes will be given to each member of the high command. When they claim responsibility for the next bombing, we should know who their link is."

Bromley bit down on the pipe, his brow furrowed. "You mean you want the police to tell you which codeword we get?"

Morrison nodded. "That's all you have to do. Give us the word, we'll do the rest."

"That's all I have to do!" exclaimed the policeman. "All I have to do is to co-operate with the IRA! Can you imagine what would happen if that ever got out?"

Morrison stopped walking and confronted Bromley, putting his face close up to the policeman's. "And can you imagine, Detective Chief Inspector Bromley, how long I'd have to live if anyone in the organisation knew what I was proposing? My life is on the line here, so don't give me any crap about your reputation being at risk."

"You're asking me to co-operate with you in a bombing campaign. You're asking me to give you confidential information on an investigation." A pigeon fluttered noisily over Bromley's head, saw he had no seed and flapped away.

"The bomb will go off anyway, whether or not you decide to help, Bromley. I don't know when, I don't know where, but there will be another bomb and people will probably die. There's nothing we can do to stop it, but maybe, just maybe, we'll be able to stop the one after that."

Bromley returned Morrison's gaze with steady, hard eyes. "Who else, Mr Morrison? Who else is involved?"

Morrison swallowed. He had hoped to persuade the policeman without bringing Hennessy's name into it, but he could see that it would not be possible. Bromley wouldn't believe this was a serious operation unless he knew who was running it. "Liam Hennessy," he said slowly. He was rewarded by the sight of Bromley's eyes widening with surprise.

Bromley turned away and Morrison walked with him. They passed a line of tourists queuing up to buy seed to feed the pigeons and neither of the men spoke. Two uniformed policewomen walked by, a blonde and a brunette, and Morrison wondered how they'd react if they knew that a member of the IRA and a Detective Chief Inspector from the Anti-Terrorist Branch were considering working together. Bromley waited until they were some distance from the policewomen before speaking again.

"When do you plan to change the codeword?" he asked.

"It's already done," replied Morrison. "Hennessy did it yesterday. Himself. Only he knows who was given which word. Even I don't know."

Bromley knew of Hennessy, and of his role as Sinn Fein adviser to the Belfast IRA council. He was one of the most powerful men in the organisation, just one step away from the seven-man Dublin-based army council. He was listened to by the council in Belfast but held equal sway over the headquarters staff in Ireland, the men who ran the active service units across Europe.

What Bromley really wanted was the list of men in the high command and the codewords they'd been given, but he knew Morrison would not hand out information like that. He would have to play by the rules Morrison was laying down or not play at all. Could he risk it? Could he afford not to? Morrison hadn't asked him how close the authorities were to catching the bombers. He hadn't needed to. They were no nearer identifying the active service unit behind the bombs now than they were when the campaign started. And it wasn't as if enough resources weren't being put into the investigation. Joining in the hunt for what was in all probability a small, self-contained unit, were the combined resources of Bromley's own Anti-Terrorist Branch, MI5, the Metropolitan Police, Special Branch, the Secret Intelligence Service, the SAS and the Defence Intelligence Service, not to mention the RUC in Northern Ireland. Actually, mused Bromley, combined resources wasn't the correct phrase because all the various anti-terrorist operations tended to work alone and to jealously guard whatever intelligence they collected.

"When I give you the codeword, what happens then?" asked Bromley.

Morrison noticed how the Detective Chief Inspector had said "when" and not "if". The decision had been made. "We'll track down the leak and interrogate him," he answered.

"Which will lead you to the bombers?"

"If Hennessy is right, yes."

"And then?"

"Then?" Morrison was confused.

"I don't think you've thought this through. How are you going to eliminate the unit that is setting these bombs? You can't send another IRA active service unit into London to knock out the first, can you? Or maybe you think you can." Bromley thought for a while. "How do I know that this is Hennessy's idea?" he said.

Morrison shrugged. "You're going to have to trust me on that," he said. "There's no way on God's earth that he can be seen with you. He'd never be trusted again. And that's assuming they didn't just kill him."

Bromley went quiet again and puffed on his pipe. "Very well. I agree. I'll tell you which codeword is given after the next explosion. But on two conditions. And they're not negotiable."

Morrison raised his eyebrows quizzically.

"When you find out where the bombers are, you tell me. You let the authorities handle it."

"The authorities?"

"Whoever it takes. Police. SAS. Whoever. It has to be that way. You can't handle it, not in London."

Morrison nodded. Hennessy had intended from the start that the Brits would clear up the mess, because if it was ever discovered that the IRA had betrayed its own, the organisation would be fragmented beyond belief. It had taken years of diplomacy and compromise to weld the various factions together and Hennessy did not want to undo it all because of a handful of lunatics. "And the second condition?" he asked.

"You give me a telephone number where I can call Hennessy. I'll only give the codeword to him. We'll share the risk."

They walked in silence again until Morrison reached his decision. "OK," he said. He gave him the number of Hennessy's farm and Bromley wrote it down in a small leather-bound notebook.

"I hope I never have to make the call," said Bromley.

"So do I," said Morrison. "But you will."

They parted without a handshake.

Woody didn't usually go into the office on Monday, most of the freelance shifts were towards the end of the week, the paper's busy period, but Quigley's phone call had intrigued him. The security guard on duty nodded good morning over the top of his copy of the *Sun*, he was used to journalists coming and going at all hours.

Woody helped himself to a plastic cup of machine coffee and then began rummaging through the drawer of the filing cabinet where he stored his old notebooks. He found the one he'd used the week The Chinaman had called and flicked through the pages. Among his spidery shorthand he saw "Chinaman" and a telephone number. He couldn't find an address, nor any note of the man's name. There was one name there among the hieroglyphics: S. J. Brown. Or Browning. Woody couldn't make it out.

He racked his memory while he dialled the telephone number. After ten or so rings a sleepy voice answered. "Double Happiness Take-Away," a man said. Woody scribbled down the name.

"My name is Ian Wood," he said. "Are you the gentleman who came to the *Sunday World* about the reward?"

"No," the voice said, and hung up.

"Terrific," said Woody to himself. He picked up a

telephone directory and went through it. There was only one Double Happiness Take-Away, it was in Clapham and the number matched. What he needed now was The Chinaman's name. He rang down to the cuttings library but there was no one there so he went himself and pulled the file on the Knightsbridge bombing. There were two foreign names among the dead: Nguyen Xuan Phoung and Nguyen Kieu Trinh. Woody wrote them down in his notebook and underlined Nguyen.

The knock on the door startled Morrison because he hadn't ordered anything from room service and he wasn't expecting any visitors. He was lying on his bed in a white towelling bathrobe, his hands clasped behind his neck. He sat up and looked at his watch. Ten o'clock. He'd been in no rush to get dressed because he was still waiting for instructions from Hennessy. Morrison had phoned him twice the previous day. The first time there had been no answer, and the second time he'd sounded strained and it was obvious that there were others in the room with him. Hennessy had told him to stay put and that he'd call on Monday. Something was wrong but Morrison realised he'd simply have to wait to find out what it was. The knock on the door was repeated, but harder and faster as if the caller was losing his patience. He felt a sudden rush of fear, thinking it might be the police or even a UDA hit-squad, but realised just as quickly that it was irrational, nobody knew where he was except for Liam Hennessy. Even so, he slid silently off the bed and padded to the door. He placed his hands flat against the wall either side of the door and eased his eye to the peep-hole. Even through the distorting lens he recognised her. She knocked again and he pulled the door open but kept his arm across the doorway as if blocking her way.

"Sean Morrison," she said, grinning.

"Mary Hennessy," he said. Morrison wasn't sure what emotions he felt as she stood in front of him. Pleased, for sure, but worried, too. Worried about what she was doing here. And guilt. Lots of guilt. And desire. Always desire. He'd never been able to look at Mary Hennessy without getting aroused, without wanting to possess her. There were other feelings too, regret, fear, sadness, all mixed up.

"Aren't you going to let me in?" she said.

He stepped to one side to let her pass and then closed the door behind her. She was carrying a white trench coat and she dropped it over the back of a chair before turning to look at him, hands on hips. She was wearing a white blouse with the collar turned up at the back and a soft skirt, patterned with large yellow flowers, and there was a small black bow in her brown hair. She was looking at him with a mischievous smile, her head on one side. Two years, he thought. They'd gone so quickly, so quickly that she hadn't changed one bit. He didn't know how old she was because he'd never cared enough to ask. He knew she was at least a decade older than he was but it hadn't shown two years ago and it didn't show now. Part of him had hoped that if he went away for a few years he wouldn't find her so attractive when he came back, that age would take away the desire, the lust. Her brown eyes sparkled as if she'd read his mind. She walked up to him, slowly, her hands still on her hips. Even with her high heels she had to tilt her head up to look in his eyes. She stood close to him, so close that he could smell her hair, clean and sweet.

"It's been a long time, Sean," she said softly. She reached up and rested her hands on his shoulders.

"I don't think you should be here," he said. The voice didn't sound like his own, it sounded thick and hesitant.

She raised her eyebrows. "Don't you?" she said. She stood up on her toes and put her lips up close to his. Their lips didn't touch but he could feel her warm breath. He swallowed. Even up close her skin was smooth and clear. The only signs of age were the laughter lines around her eyes and they just added to her attractiveness. "Don't you?" she repeated. She moved her head forward, just enough so that their lips touched. She opened hers slightly, but that was all. There was no pressure, no urging. She wanted him to prove how much he wanted her, to take the initiative. Part of him, the guilty voice in the back of his mind that had told him to go to New York, wanted to resist, but he already knew that he was lost. His lips parted too and his hands seemed to take on a will of their own, moving forward to link around her narrow waist. Still she stood on tip-toe waiting for him to make up his mind. He kissed her, once, a quick press of the lips, then he moved his head back and looked at her and then in a rush grabbed her and pulled her tightly to him, kissing her hard, forcing his tongue into her soft, moist mouth. For a few seconds she remained passive, allowing him to invade her, and then she began to kiss him back, returning his passion. He grunted as she kissed him and he closed his eyes as the urge to possess her washed over him again. She slowly put her heels on the ground so that he had to bend his neck to kiss her and she tried to pull away but he put his right hand behind her neck and pushed her head against his.

She used both her hands to push his shoulders away. A strand of hair had come loose, curling over her left eye, but she ignored it. She held him away, bending backwards slightly and pushing her groin against him. He felt as if he was on fire between his legs. Her eyes flashed. "Tell me you want me," she said.

"You know I do," he answered, and tried to kiss her, but she moved her head out of the way, pressing her thighs even harder against him.

"Tell me you want me," she said again. She moved her right hand slowly down from his shoulder and traced her fingernails across the hairs on his chest. He gasped as the sharp nails scratched against his flesh, parting his robe as they moved down between his ribs. She moved her hand lightly across his stomach and then down to his groin. "Tell me," she urged and at the same time took him in her hand. She squeezed him gently and he groaned and surrendered.

"I want you, Mary," he said. She pushed the robe off his shoulders so that he was standing naked in front of her and pulled his head down to hers, grabbing his hair so tightly that it hurt, forcing her body fully against his. He lifted her up and she raised her legs, gripping him around the waist and locking her ankles together. Now there was only one thought in his head. Her.

Nguyen lay motionless and listened to the birds singing in the treetops overhead. He'd made his way back to Tollymore Forest under cover of darkness and found the van exactly as he'd left it. There were a few things he wanted from the back of the van which he loaded into his rucksack, and he took a red can of petrol. He rejected the idea of sleeping by the van in case Hennessy should send a search party to the forest. It was an outside chance but not one worth taking because if they surprised him there would be no escape.

He found a safe place a hundred yards or so away and rested until mid-morning. He sat up and leant against a towering pine tree, the air thick with the smell of pine needles. He was surrounded by thousands of bluebells, shifting listlessly in the wind. He spent an hour or so cutting off the heads of three boxfuls of matches and crushing them into red powder which he carefully poured into one of the boxes. He cut a three-foot length of plastic-coated wire and then stripped off an inch of the plastic midway along it. With the point of his knife he made a hole at either end of the matchbox and threaded the wire through, knotting it so that the bared portion was in the middle, in contact with the powdered match heads. He stripped the ends of the wire clean of plastic and then coiled it up, wrapping it around the box. Nguyen removed the glass front from one of the plastic alarm clocks he'd brought with him and put it into the rucksack with the wired-up matchbox. Connecting the clock, the matchbox and a battery in a simple circuit would give him a basic timed fuse which would be more than sufficient to ignite the can of petrol.

The gun he'd taken from the man in the copse was a Browning HiPower automatic pistol which weighed about two pounds. Nguyen ejected the magazine and counted the bullets. Thirteen. An unlucky number for the Westerners, but not for a Vietnamese. He stripped the gun apart and cleaned it, checking that the mechanism worked. It was fine. The gun had two safeties, one worked by the thumb and one by the magazine, so that it couldn't be fired accidentally. It was a serious weapon. It was too heavy to carry around in his pocket for long so he put it in his rucksack. The smell of roast pork reminded him how long it had been since he had last eaten so he took out a carton of meat and one of rice and ate with his fingers. It had been a long time since he had eaten outside. What was it the Westerners called it? He'd seen the word in one of Kieu Trinh's English story books. Picnic, that was it.

As he ate he worked out what he was going to do next. One thing was for sure, he had to confront Hennessy one last time before he took things a stage further and that meant going back to the farm. Now that Hennessy had seen how much damage he could do, surely he would be more co-operative? Put anyone under enough pressure and they would bend. Not break, perhaps, but certainly bend.

Nguyen sighed and lay back in the pine needles. He took no pleasure in what he was doing. When he'd left Vietnam he'd thought that his days of fighting and killing were over, that he'd be allowed to raise his family in peace. When he saw the last helicopter leave the American embassy in Saigon he still had hopes of escaping from the North Vietnamese and eventually living in the United States. He'd fought alongside the Americans and had seen hundreds of American teenagers die in the fight for a free Vietnam so he didn't regard being left behind as an act of betrayal. He could see what a difficult logistical exercise it was for the Americans to pull out, and he knew that he wasn't the only one to have been left behind. It was only later, when Thi Manh and Mai Phuong died, that the resentment burst like a septic boil and he vowed never to seek sanctuary in the United States. They'd been surprised at the refugee camp in Hong Kong when he'd told them that he would go anywhere in the world but not to America. Officials from the United Nations High Commission for Refugees had interviewed him many times and had explained that because of his war record he would be welcomed with open arms in the United States but he had steadfastly refused and had been equally insistent that he would not explain his reasons. He had told them that two of his daughters had died on the voyage across the South China Sea but never detailed the circumstances. In Nguyen's mind, they had no right to know. They were so beautiful, Thi Manh and Mai Phoung, and even now, after more than ten years had passed, he could picture them clearly in his mind, jet-black hair, high cheekbones, bright eyes and ready smiles, as pretty as their mother had been before the tough years had taken their toll. They had been such well-behaved children and it had been thoughts of them that had kept him going throughout his three years in the so-called "re-education" camps, working fifteen hours a day on a near-starvation diet, until the North Vietnamese were satisfied that he was a good Communist again.

There had been no doubt in his mind that he would be punished by the North Vietnamese but he had no idea of how severe that punishment would be. On the morning of April 30, 1975, he had slipped out of bed, leaving Xuan Phoung asleep clutching a pillow, and stood in the doorway leading to the alcove where his daughters slept together in a single bed, heads touching like Siamese twins. He stood there for more than an hour trying to imprint the scene on his mind, certain that it would be the last time he would see his daughters. The street noises had changed, there were no more helicopters whirring overhead, instead there was the far-off rumble of trucks carrying North Vietnamese troops and supplies into Saigon and the sound of cheering as the bo doi – the soldiers of the people – were welcomed by crowds of onlookers. In the early morning, while he was making love to his wife, Nguyen had heard tanks driving through the streets and the occasional rattle of machine-guns, but whether it was the North Vietnamese mopping up pockets of resistance or simply high spirits on the part of the victorious forces, he had no way of telling.

He dressed casually in washed-out cotton trousers, a faded checked shirt and an old pair of sandals. He'd dropped his army uniform in the street and he'd cleared all evidence of involvement with the US forces from their flat. They had made their plans long before the Americans pulled out, when it had first become obvious that there was no way the South could win the war. They had closed their bank account and transferred all their money into gold, knowing that when Saigon fell paper money would be virtually worthless. They had kept the gold in a safety-deposit box, along with several gold Rolex watches and pieces of jewellery that they had been able to buy on the black market with Nguyen's wages, and two weeks before the NVA arrived at the outskirts of Saigon they had taken everything out of the bank vault. They had already decided that Nguyen should go. It was the only chance the family had of surviving.

Xuan Phoung had friends who would help her to get a job as a kitchen worker and she would hide their savings under the floorboards until Nguyen was allowed to return, or until she got the opportunity to escape with the children. Before he left, Nguyen took a photograph from his wallet, a picture of Xuan Phoung and the two girls, and put it on the bed. He had carried it with him throughout the war but it would be dangerous for them to be caught with it now. He took all identification from the wallet, leaving only a small amount of paper money. It would not be long before a thirty-one-year-old man walking alone would be picked up for interrogation and anything in his pockets would be taken from him, so he left his wedding ring and his watch and his Special Forces cigarette lighter on the bed next to the photograph before kissing his wife once, on the cheek, and then dashing downstairs before he could have a change of heart.

The streets of Saigon were every bit as packed as they had been the previous night, but whereas the rush then had been to escape with the Americans, now the crowds were there to welcome the NVA. Children were waving NVA flags – red and blue with a gold star – and it seemed as if every shop in the city had managed to get a photograph of an unsmiling Ho Chi Minh in its window. Battered lorries covered with thick red mud rattled along loaded with troops, young men with baggy olive-green uniforms and rubber sandals, cheering and lapping up the attention.

He was picked up around lunchtime by a group of five teenage soldiers who prodded him with their guns and demanded his papers. He told them he'd been robbed two days earlier and they slapped him around the face and accused him of lying. They made him kneel on the ground, blindfolded him, handcuffed his hands behind his back and then dragged him roughly and threw him into the back of a truck. Throughout the day more men were thrown into the vehicle. All were blindfolded and manacled and told that if they spoke to each other they would be killed. When the truck was full they were driven for three days with just a handful of foul-smelling rice which they were forced to eat like animals, pushing their faces on to the floor to lick the grains up because their captors refused to unlock the handcuffs. Nguyen assumed they were being taken North and wondered why they bothered because the Communists now controlled the whole country. For a wild moment he thought that perhaps the NVA feared that the Americans would be back but in his heart he knew that could not be true. The evacuation of the embassy was not the action of an army planning to return.

He never discovered the name of the place he was taken to but there was no doubt that it was a prison, and had been for many years. He was thrown into a small cell, two paces by four paces, containing only a wooden bench and a bucket. They took off his blindfold and he saw that the bench was rubbed smooth from the bodies that had slept there over the years. It looked ages old and had obviously been used by the French to hold Vietnamese captives. The bench sloped so that any liquids would run off and there was a small drain hole at the bottom of one of the walls. There was no window in the cell, the only light came from the corridor through the open door and whenever it opened cockroaches ran for the dark corners. Nguyen was forced to lie on the bench and his feet were locked into a set of leg-irons which were fixed to the wall. They put the bucket within reach and took off his handcuffs and left without a word, locking the door behind them. They left him there for two weeks, opening the door only once a day to put down a handful of rice on a banana leaf along with a piece of stale bread. It was stifling hot in the cell and he was always thirsty but he was only given one earthenware jug of water to drink with his food. The cell stank of urine and sweat and decay. The cockroaches did not worry him, even when they ran over his body, but there were mosquitoes and he was covered in itching bites that made him want to scream. His legs were in pain too, rubbed raw by the metal leg-irons.

After two weeks of solitary confinement they dragged him out of his cell and into a room where he saw his first glimpse of the sun through a murky skylight. To the left of the skylight, set into the ceiling, was a large, rusty meat hook. Two NVA officers questioned him for an hour and then he was returned to the leg-irons and the darkness. A week later he was taken out and interrogated again. There was no violence, no threats, just a series of questions, almost identical to the ones he'd been asked on the first occasion, and he was sure that he gave the same answers. The same lies. He was a mechanic, he had never been in the army. He had no family. He had lost his papers. It was impossible to tell from the blank faces of his interrogators whether or not they believed him, and most of the time he could only look through squinting eyes because after the enforced darkness he found even the weak sunlight which managed to get through the dirt-encrusted glass blindingly bright.

They took him back to his cell and left him there for just three days before hauling him back to the interrogation room. By that stage he could barely walk and his gums were bleeding from malnutrition. He had diarrhoea and the backs of his legs and backside were a mass of sores. The older of his two interrogators, a kindly looking major with white hair, told him that they did not believe his story and that they would be grateful if he would tell them the truth this time. He insisted that he was not lying and they nodded, almost sadly. Four NVA soldiers came into the room, holding bamboo canes, and they beat him senseless. Then they threw a bucket of water over him to bring him round before beating him unconscious again and dragging him back to his cell.

For six days the process was repeated. They would ask him for the truth, he would stick to his story, the soldiers would beat him up.

On the seventh day, by which time he'd lost three of his

teeth and they had broken four of his ribs, they changed their tactics. They took a long piece of rope and bound his wrists behind him and then wound it excruciatingly tightly around his arms before hauling him up on the meat hook. It was strange, but he could not remember much about the days they tortured him. He could remember that he had never in his life felt so much pain and he knew that at one point it had been so bad that he'd pleaded with them to kill him, but now, as he lay on the pine needles and looked up through the branches to the clear blue sky above, it seemed as if it had all happened to someone else and that they were borrowed memories. Only one thing had got him through – the images of his wife as he left and his two daughters, asleep with their heads touching. Of all the images that stuck in his mind, they were the strongest, because throughout the torture he'd concentrated on them. They were the reason they could not break him.

He never knew whether or not they believed him, or whether they simply gave up trying to break him, but eventually the torture stopped and he was transferred to a re-education camp where he worked in the fields for fifteen hours a day but where at least there was food. He was forced to write endless self-criticisms which were duly filed away and he spent two hours each day sitting cross-legged on the floor with other prisoners being lectured to on the merits and ideals of Communism and being beaten with sticks if they nodded off. There were other punishments, meted out for the most trivial of offences. Men were shackled upside down and left hanging for days until their legs were weeping with gangrene, locked into cramped steel boxes in the sun or buried up to their necks in the ground. Nguyen was there for three years. Three years of living a lie. Three wasted years.

When he was finally judged to be a good Communist he was released on probation and was assigned to work on an irrigation project to the west of Hanoi. He had to report to a political officer three times a week for further indoctrination. He was lucky, he knew that, because tens of thousands of South Vietnamese were kept in the camps for much longer.

He fled one night and managed to get to Hanoi where he stole identification papers and money and journeyed south to Saigon. He lived rough in the city for several weeks before he dared approach Xuan Phoung and when he did it was at night. He knocked timidly on her door and when she opened it it was clear from her bewildered face that she did not recognise him. It was hardly surprising because he had lost so much weight and appeared to have aged ten years, but she took him in her arms and cried softly. She ushered him into the room and sat him down, knelt in front of him and held him around his waist, crying all the time and whispering his name. He realised then that however badly he had suffered it could have been nothing compared with what his wife had been through. At least he had been able to look forward to returning to her and the children. She had had no way of knowing if he was even alive.

She made him green tea and while he was drinking it she went into the bedroom and brought out a tiny child. A girl. The daughter he had never seen, conceived on the night that the Americans abandoned Saigon and now almost three years old.

"Kieu Trinh is her name," said Xuan Phoung. "But we can change it if you don't like it."

"It's perfect," said Nguyen. He held her in his arms and then his wife woke Thi Manh and Mai Phoung and brought them in to meet the father they barely remembered. He had been away for almost a quarter of their lives. Nguyen was so filled with happiness that he could barely speak, he just held all four of them. His family.

Before he could ask, Xuan Phoung said, "The gold is still here, and I know someone who can get us out."

"We must go soon," he said, his voice thick with emotion.

"I know," she said. "We were only waiting for you."

Nguyen and his wife and children travelled by night to a fishing port in Kien Giang province, all their valuables and papers in two canvas bags. They'd paid a deposit in gold to a middleman in Saigon and were told when and where they were to pay the rest.

They had to spend the night in a dirty hut that stank of

fish, sleeping on small cots with another two families who were also waiting for the boat. During the night little Kieu Trinh developed a hacking cough and when Xuan Phoung put her hand on the child's forehead it was hot and wet. She got worse through the night and kept them all awake. Nguyen stayed by her side, wiping her forehead with a cloth dipped in water and wafting her with a piece of cardboard. She got worse during the day. It was Xuan Phoung who said it first, even though Nguyen had already reached the same conclusion: the child was in no condition for a sea voyage, especially in an unhygienic boat crammed to the gills with refugees. Xuan Phoung suggested they wait in the village until the child was well enough to travel, but Nguyen pointed out that if they did they'd lose their deposit. And it represented a big chunk of their hard-earned savings.

"You must go ahead, with Thi Manh and Mai Phoung," she said. "We will join you in Hong Kong."

He'd refused at first, but eventually realised that what she said made sense. If he went with the two teenage girls, he was sure the captain could be persuaded to accept the deposits of all five of them towards the cost of the trip, leaving more than enough money for Xuan Phoung and Kieu Trinh to buy their passage when the child was well again. When the captain came for them later that evening, Nguyen explained what had happened and eventually he agreed that the five deposits could go towards the three fares, albeit with an extra ounce of gold thrown in. For another ounce he agreed to bring in a doctor to tend to the child.

When Nguyen saw the vessel that was supposed to take them across the South China Sea to Hong Kong, he almost had second thoughts. The boat was about fifteen metres long, its hull rotting and repaired in many places. There were already thirty or so refugees sitting or squatting on its deck and Nguyen and his two children and the two families that had shared the hut had to squeeze between them to find space. The boat was worryingly low in the water.

The captain was joined by a crew of three, men barely out of their teens in ragged T-shirts and cut-off trousers. It took half an hour of patient coaxing to get the engine started and it chugged uneasily out to sea as the huge orange sun sat low in the sky.

There was a hatchway in the deck leading to a hold containing a dozen camp beds where the refugees took it in turns to sleep. There was a small stove there and the women cooked what little food the crew had brought with them: some rice, strips of dried fish and a sack of green vegetables. Some of the men rigged up fishing lines and from time to time pulled in fresh fish to supplement the meagre rations, but mainly they fished to fight the boredom. Most of the days were spent cross-legged on the deck, watching the horizon and hoping that the boat would stay afloat.

Water was rationed and they were each given just a cupful every four hours, carefully meted out by a crewman using stained tin mugs. A blanket had been stretched out from a mast and tied down with ropes to provide some shade during the day and shelter from the occasional rain storm. Conditions were so grim that Nguyen was glad that Kieu Trinh had stayed behind.

They were three days out from Vietnam when they met the fishing boats. There were three of them painted in identical colours as if part of the same fleet. The decks were painted red and piled high with plastic barrels and coils of rope, and the wheel-houses were white. The hulls were pale green and there were lines of white Thai writing on the bows. The crews seemed friendly enough, smiling and waving as they drew close, and they shouted to the captain that they had water and ice to sell. The captain waved them away but a few of the refugees shouted to him that they would pay for it. Nguyen could see that the captain was uneasy and he whispered to the refugees to keep quiet, that the Thais could be trouble, but they ignored him and began calling over to the fishermen. The captain shouted at the man who was on the wheel and the old boat started to turn away but even Nguyen who had little sailing experience knew that there was no way they could outrun the fishing boats if they gave chase. He stood up and as he did he saw one of the Thais produce a rifle and put it to his shoulder. Nguyen yelled a warning but he was too late, there was a loud bang and the captain took the bullet in his chest. More rifles were produced and the wheel-house was riddled with bullets, killing the two crewmen inside. The refugees began to scream as the boat drifted aimlessly. Nguyen frantically looked around for a weapon, but there was nothing at hand. One of the Thai boats drew up alongside and the fishermen used poles with hooks on the end to secure the boats together.

The refugees moved away to the opposite side like cattle shying away from a snake and the boat tilted alarmingly. Women and children were crying, the men shouting, wanting to put up a fight but not knowing how to, not when all they had were their fists and the Thais had guns and hatchets and hammers. Nguyen found himself separated from his daughters, unable to move closer to them because of the crush.

A second boat cut across their bow and half a dozen menacing Thais jumped across, stocky men toughened by years at sea, their faces and bodies darkened by the sun and scarred from fights and accidents with the nets and ropes.

They moved through the refugees, separating the men from the women and the children, killing anyone who protested or tried to stop them. One of the Thais, a swarthy, thickset man with a huge tiger tattoo across his chest, looked down into the hatch. He shouted down in bad Vietnamese that all the women and children were to come up. There were screams and sobs from down below but no one appeared so a fisherman with a rifle jumped over from the boat alongside and fired twice into the hold. There were more screams and shouting and then three women and a young girl came up. One of the women was in her sixties and the fisherman cursed her in Vietnamese and stabbed her in the stomach, twisting the knife right and left before kicking her back down into the hold.

There was an uproar among the refugees and they began to surge forward but a volley of shots rang out and four of the men fell to the deck, screaming in pain. The Thais began searching the men, taking from them their watches, jewellery and any other valuables they had before throwing them down into the hold. Those that put up a fight were killed and thrown over the side. Some of the younger women were grabbed and carried screaming on to the Thai boats where more fishermen were waiting with their arms outstretched to take them. Nguyen watched in horror as the men began tearing the clothes off the women, slapping and hitting them if they struggled too much, before throwing them down on to the deck and raping them. He saw one girl who couldn't have been more than fifteen years old held down by two men while a third climbed on top of her. Her screams chilled him, and then he heard his own daughter, Mai Phoung, screaming for him. Two Thais had her and were taking her to the bow of the boat where more fishermen waited, lust in their eyes.

"She's only thirteen!" Nguyen cried.

"The youngest fruit is the sweetest," said one of the Thais in rough Vietnamese and slammed the butt of his rifle into Nguyen's sternum so that he collapsed to the deck, gasping for breath. Through a red haze he saw Thi Manh dash over to claw at the men in an attempt to save her sister. The men laughed and one of them grabbed her. He seized her shirt and pulled it savagely, the buttons popping off like small gunshots, revealing her small breasts and smooth skin. He was joined by two other men who used large fishing knives to cut away the rest of her clothes. She was screaming hysterically, begging Nguyen to rescue her. He staggered to his feet and pushed his way through the refugees who were still on the deck. Mai Phoung had been thrown across to the Thai boat and was being stripped and beaten by a group of three Thais who were snarling and growling like wild dogs. She too was calling for her father. Nguyen stepped forward towards the men holding Thi Manh but as he moved one of the Thai fishermen appeared in front of him holding a rifle. It was pointed at Nguyen's chest and the man was laughing, his finger tightening on the trigger. Nguyen leapt as the man fired, he felt the blast and a searing stripe of pain across the side of his head and then he was under water, choking and coughing, his head a mass of pain and the taste of blood in his mouth. He surfaced, spitting out salt water and when his eyes cleared he saw the Thais setting fire to the boat and rushing back to their own vessels.

Nguyen trod water, fighting to stay conscious. He would

never forget the horrified screams from the hold, and the howls from the women on the Thai boats. He never saw his daughters again. Part of him wished that he could die too, but his survival instincts took over. There were many bodies floating in the waves and Nguyen used his belt to tie two of them together. He clung to the macabre raft for more than fifteen hours before he was picked up by a British freighter on its way to Hong Kong.

He was told that he was lucky to have been spotted, but Nguyen didn't feel lucky. He felt ashamed, he felt that he'd betrayed his daughters, that he should have saved them or died trying. The guilt of that day had lived with him forevermore. He'd reacted instinctively, without thinking, and not a day went by, not an hour, when the events of the last few minutes on board the refugee boat didn't flash through his mind.

He opened his eyes and looked up through the branches above his head. His arms were shaking and his breath was coming in ragged gasps. He wanted his time over again, he wanted to be back on the boat, because he knew this time he would make the right choice, that he would die trying to save his daughters rather than leaping over the side to save his own life.

He would not fail this time.

Mary Hennessy lay with her head on Morrison's shoulder and made small circles on his chest with her index finger. He kissed her on the top of her head and she smiled up at him.

"It's been a long time, Sean Morrison," she said.

"It has that, Mary Hennessy," he said lazily. He looked at his watch. Eleven o'clock.

"My time's not up, is it?" she said. She ran her hand slowly down through the hairs on his chest. "I bet I could change your mind . . ."

Morrison laughed and reached down and intercepted her wandering hand. "Mary, even you can't raise the dead."

She giggled. "Not dead, just resting," she said, but she put her hand back on his chest. "You're not going to throw me out, are you?"

"I'm waiting for somebody to call me," he said.

"A girl?"

"There's no girl, Mary Hennessy."

They lay together in silence for a while, enjoying each other's warmth.

"You shouldn't have left me, Sean," Mary said eventually, so quietly that at first Morrison thought that she was talking in her sleep. "There was no need for you to have gone."

He sighed. "There was every need."

"Because of Liam?"

"Because of us. Because it was wrong."

She laughed harshly. "The way the world is and you worry about the right and wrong of what goes on between a man and a woman. You amaze me sometimes."

"And you, Mary Hennessy, are a constant source of wonder to me."

"I didn't even know how to get hold of you in New York."

"That was the idea," he said. "Out of sight, out of mind."

She shook her head. "Absence makes the heart grow fonder."

"You were the one who wouldn't leave her husband," said Morrison "You were the one who said that an affair was fine but that it couldn't go any further."

"I've been married for a long time, Sean. A long time."

"I know. I know that."

She sighed and he felt her warm breath on his chest. "If I was free, you know that I'd be with you like a shot. If you wanted me."

"If!" he exclaimed.

"I'm so much older than you, Sean."

He squeezed her and stroked her hair. "It never mattered in the past, and it doesn't matter now."

"But it might in the future. It might."

Morrison closed his eyes. This discussion was a repeat of thousands they'd had before. Sometimes, before he'd left

New York, it seemed to him that they'd spent more time discussing the relationship than living it.

"I wish Liam was more like you," whispered Mary.

"What do you mean?"

"Stronger. Harder."

He laughed and she slapped his chest. "That's not what I meant, idiot. He's changed, he's gone soft. Soft on the Cause. I used to be so proud of him, he had power and he wasn't afraid to use it. Now he'd rather talk, negotiate. He acts like an old man, trying to make his peace with the world." Her voice was becoming increasingly bitter and she spat out the last few words like an angry cat. Morrison didn't know what to say so he lay in silence and concentrated on smoothing her hair, trying to calm her down physically rather than by talking to her.

"I've never forgiven him for Gerry, you know," she said. Her brother had been shot and killed by a Protestant death squad three years earlier. Four men in balaclava masks had forced their way into his house and shot him in front of his wife and three children on Christmas Eve. Mary had been there delivering Christmas presents and she'd been splattered with his blood. Morrison had seen her in the City Hospital several hours later, standing with Liam in the white-tiled corridor with flecks of blood over her dress, a red smear across one cheek, her eyes puffy from crying. That's when he'd fallen in love with her, he realised now.

"He found out who did it, you know?" she said.

"Yes. I know."

"They killed a farmer on the border a month later and got caught, stupid bastards. I begged Liam to have them killed before they got to court. He said no. They're in Long Kesh now, all four of them, and still he won't do anything. One of them is studying sociology with the Open University, Sean, can you believe that? Gerry's dead and buried and he's getting a fucking degree. And Liam says that justice has been done and that the time for revenge is past, or some such philosophical crap. He's lost his fire, and he lost it when I needed it most."

Morrison could feel her heart pounding against his chest and he kissed her softly on the top of her head.

"That's why I'm here, you know. In London. Because he's running away from a bloody Chinaman. One man and he's hiding like a frightened child. And he wants me to hide, too."

"What do you mean?" Morrison asked.

Mary sat up. "Of course, you don't know. He followed us to the farm. He blew up one of the outbuildings and the car. Jimmy's in hospital."

"Is he OK?"

"I don't know, I left right after he blew up the car. Liam thought it would be safer if I came to London. I didn't argue because I knew it would give me the chance to see you." She straddled him and kissed him and then rolled off the bed and skipped into the bathroom. He heard the shower kick into life.

The phone rang and Morrison jumped involuntarily. Guilt? Probably. He reached for the receiver. It was Hennessy.

He told him about the car bombing and the attempt to flush The Chinaman out of the woods and how it had ended in disaster. Morrison expressed surprise and asked who had been hurt even though he'd already been told by Mary.

As he talked, Mary came out of the bathroom wearing a towelling robe that was far too big for her. She was rubbing a towel through her hair. Morrison felt a sudden rush of guilt and he turned to one side so that he didn't have to look at her.

"We're obviously after a man who is used to fighting, some sort of terrorist maybe. Maybe he has jungle warfare experience, you know. Malaysia maybe," said Morrison. Mary had finished drying her hair and she began to brush it slowly, watching Morrison in the dressing-table mirror.

"The area around the farm is hardly a jungle," said Hennessy.

"It's not a jungle, I agree, but there's acres of woodland and a million and one places to hide. A man who knew what he was doing could stay put for weeks, living off the land, hiding during the day and making a nuisance of himself at night. And the more men you send in looking for him, the more damage he'll do."

"That's pretty much what Jim Kavanagh's been telling me. He says we should go back to Belfast. He says it'll be easier to protect me there."

"That's true, but at least you know where he is now. If you can deal with him in the countryside you should be able to keep a lid on it. In Belfast it could turn into a blood-bath." Mary stopped brushing her hair and sat looking at Morrison.

"You have a suggestion?"

"Set a thief to catch a thief. We send in one man, a man who's an expert at tracking, and we let him get on with it. No manhunt, just sit tight and let our man winkle him out."

"Come on, Sean. Where are we going to find such a man?"

"What about Micky Geraghty?"

"Retired," said Hennessy.

"Well un-retire him, Liam," said Morrison, exasperated. "He's the perfect choice. He was a gamekeeper as a kid, his father was one of the best in Ireland." Gamekeeping wasn't the only talent Geraghty had, but his skill as an IRA assassin wasn't the sort of thing to be discussed on an open telephone line. Morrison knew of at least three kills he'd been responsible for, two long distance with a rifle and one close up, a senior RUC officer who'd blinded a young Catholic during a particularly nasty interrogation. The boy had been a second cousin to Geraghty and he'd asked for the assignment. It had been personal, but professional. If he had truly retired, it was one hell of a loss to the Cause. "Doesn't he work as a deer tracker or something in Scotland now?"

"He's retired," Hennessy repeated. Mary stood up and walked over to where Morrison was sitting on the bed. He looked up at her and smiled and she shrugged off the robe so that she was standing naked in front of him. His mind whirled and he fought to keep his voice steady, certain that Hennessy would be able to sense that something was wrong.

"The sort of skills he's got you don't forget." Morrison wasn't just referring to gamekeeping, and Hennessy knew it.

"I don't mean retired from work, Sean, I mean he retired from the Cause."

"Nobody retires from the Cause," said Morrison. Mary pushed Morrison back on to the bed and pulled his robe apart. He closed his eyes and almost gasped when he felt her take him in her mouth. Her soft hair brushed his groin and as she caressed him with her mouth she ran her hands up and down his chest, gently scratching him. She was making small groaning noises and he was sure Hennessy would be able to hear her.

"He was a special case," said Hennessy. "His wife died five years ago. Cancer. It was very, very bad. He lost heart after that. He was no more use to us."

"So who decided he could retire?"

Hennessy didn't reply, which gave Morrison the answer. "It was you, wasn't it, Liam?" Still Hennessy said nothing. "If it was you, he owes you a favour. All you have to do is to make it personal. And let's face it, this is as personal as you can get." Mary began moving her head up and down, running her tongue along the whole length of him. He wanted her to stop but at the same time he didn't, and his confusion was compounded by the overwhelming guilt of it all, talking to Hennessy while his wife knelt naked in front of him.

"He might agree to help track this man down, but that's all. He wouldn't take it any further."

"OK, but that's a start. At least let me talk to him. He might jump at the chance of helping his old friend." A thought suddenly occurred to Morrison. A solution. "In fact, I'll ask him to take me with him. He can find him, I'll do the rest."

Hennessy thought about it for just a few seconds and then agreed. He told Morrison to wait while he rummaged through his desk and dug out an old address book. Morrison could feel himself about to come and reached down with his free hand to stroke Mary's hair and to gently push her away. She slid him out of her mouth and moved over him, licking her lips like a satisfied cat, her eyes flashing. He knew what she was going to do and he shook his head and tried to roll away but she pushed him down and continued to move over his body until her thighs were either side of his hips. She seemed to be revelling in his discomfort, knowing that he couldn't resist too much while he was on the phone, and knowing too that deep down he didn't want to resist, that he wanted her as much as she wanted him. She held him with one hand and positioned herself above him, rubbing him against herself, allowing him inside but only an inch or so and then easing herself away, teasing him and watching his face all the while. Hennessy came back on the line.

"He still does some deer tracking, mainly for Japanese tourists, but he also runs a survival school for executives, based near Thurso," he said.

"Thurso?" replied Morrison and as he spoke Mary pushed herself down so that he was completely inside her. He gasped involuntarily. She moved slowly up and down, grinding her pelvis against him, her eyes half closed, her mouth open and panting.

"It's in the far north of Scotland, about as far north as you can go before you hit the sea." He gave Morrison the address and a telephone number. Morrison told him he had to get a pen and paper. Mary stopped moving and, with him still inside her, leant over to the bedside table and gave him a black ballpoint pen and a sheet of hotel notepaper. He asked Hennessy to repeat the details and he wrote them down, thankful that Mary had at last stopped moving. He felt as if his groin was about to explode.

"And Sean, don't push him, OK? If he doesn't want to do it, forget it."

"OK, Liam," said Morrison. Mary squeezed him with her internal muscles and began to ride him again, throwing her head back and gripping him tightly with her thighs.

"How did the meeting with Bromley go?" asked Hennessy.

"Fine," answered Morrison, closing his eyes and concentrating on his breathing and trying with all his might not to come. "But when he gets the codeword he'll call you direct. He insisted."

"That's OK."

"Everything ready at your end?"

"Yes. I've given out the words. All we can do now is to wait for the next bomb. See you soon, Sean."

"Will do, Liam. Take care." He threw the phone to one side and reached up to caress Mary's breasts. She took one of his hands and placed two of his fingers in her mouth, sucking and licking them as she rode him.

"You, Mary Hennessy, are a bitch. A teasing, dangerous, gorgeous bitch." She laughed throatily and rode him all the harder.

Afterwards, she lay curled up with her back against him, her skin moist with a thin film of sweat. Morrison licked her back, enjoying the salty taste of her.

"That's nice," she whispered.

"I wish you'd come to New York with me," he said.

She sighed, and pushed herself back against him. "Don't start, Sean," she chided. "Just enjoy the time we have together. You already have more of me than anyone else in the world."

"Except your husband."

"You wouldn't want to swap places with him, believe me."

Morrison knew that they were going over old ground, replaying the same arguments they'd had before he left for the United States, but he couldn't help himself. It was like picking the scab of an old wound.

"How did Liam sound?" she asked, changing the subject.

"Worried. Very worried."

"About The Chinaman?"

"Yeah, and the London bombings. I'm not sure which worries him the most."

"Do you think he'll be able to find out who has been setting off the bombs?" She reached behind herself and began stroking his thighs with the back of her hand.

"It's the only chance we've got," he said.

"That's what Liam says, too. But do you really think his plan will work?"

"If there is another bomb, and if the bombers give the codeword when they claim responsibility, it'll lead us straight to whoever's behind it. With a bit of luck, it'll work."

"I hope so," she sighed.

Her hand became more insistent but he pulled himself away from her. "I'm going to have to go," he said.

"Where?"

"Scotland. To talk to a man who might be able to track down The Chinaman for us. What will you do?"

"I'm to stay in London until Liam says it's safe to go back. So if you're not here I'll just have to amuse myself."

Morrison went to the bathroom where he shaved and showered and when he came out Mary had dressed and was brushing her hair. She stood up on tiptoe and kissed him full on the mouth. "It's good to have you back," she said. "Don't stay away so long next time." She turned and picked up her trench coat and blew him a kiss before closing the door behind her.

Morrison shook his head, trying to clear her from his mind. Two years, and it seemed as if he had never been away. If anything he wanted her more now than before. He forced himself to concentrate on the job at hand. He wondered why the normally confident Hennessy was so touchy on the subject of Geraghty and if it really had been the painful death of his wife that had led to his exile in Scotland. He looked at his watch. Two o'clock. He hadn't a clue how to get to Thurso, or how long it would take, but he knew he had to speak to Geraghty in person, it would be too easy for him to decline on the phone. He rang down to reception and told them he'd be checking out and also asked if they'd find out the quickest way to get to Thurso.

"Is that in Cornwall?" the girl had asked. She said she'd phone back once she'd checked with a travel agent and Morrison began to pack his suitcase. He'd just about finished when the girl rang to say that he could go by train but that he wouldn't get there until the following day. The best way would be to fly up to Inverness and go the rest of the way by train or hire a car and drive. Morrison said he'd fly and asked her to arrange for a car to take him to the airport and have it put on the bill.

* * *

Woody was, as usual, short of cash, so he took the Tube to Clapham.

An unsmiling middle-aged Oriental woman was serving behind the counter of the Double Happiness Take-Away, and when it was Woody's turn he asked her for sweet and sour pork and chips. "Is the owner here?" asked Woody.

"Huh?" she said, her mouth dropping open.

"The owner. Can I see the owner?"

"In kitchen," she said.

"Yes . . . right . . . OK . . . could you ask him to come out? Tell him it's Ian Wood, from the newspaper."

"Ian Wood. Newspaper," she repeated. She stuck her head through the serving hatch and shouted. There was an equally raucous reply and she turned to Woody again.

"He busy," she said.

"I know, he's cooking my food," said Woody. "Look, he knows me."

"He say he not know you," she said emphatically and folded her arms across her chest.

Woody waited until his order arrived and she plonked the carrier bag on the counter in front of him. He paid for it and then asked to see the owner again. She glared at him before yelling through the hatch once more. This time a bald, Oriental giant came out carrying a huge carving knife. He stood next to the woman and barked: "I here. What you want?"

Woody looked at the couple, confused. "I'm sorry, you're not the man I wanted to see. I wanted Mr Nguyen." He had assumed that The Chinaman owned the restaurant because of all the cash he had, but perhaps he was an employee. "Does Mr Nguyen work here?" Woody asked.

"No," said the man.

"Do you know where he is?"

"No."

Woody was taken aback. He took his notebook from his pocket and looked at the telephone number that Nguyen had given him. He picked up one of the printed menus off the counter and compared the telephone number there. They were the same. He held the notebook out to the man. "Look, I spoke to Mr Nguyen at this number. Here."

The man didn't look at the notebook. "I own Double Happiness now," he said.

"So Mr Nguyen was the previous owner?"

"He own Double Happiness before. He sell to me."

At last Woody understood. "But you don't know where he went?"

The man shook his head.

"He was very upset about what happened to his family," said Woody. "Do you know if that was why he left?"

"No."

"No you don't know why, or no that's not why he left?"

"No," the man repeated. "I busy, you go now." He made to go back to the kitchen.

"Do you have a photograph of him?" Woody asked.

The man's eyes screwed up. "What do you mean?"

Woody drew a square in the air with his hands. "Photograph. A picture. Click, click!" He mimed using a camera.

The man nodded enthusiastically. "Ah! Picture!" he said.

"You have?" Woody asked eagerly.

"No," he answered, shaking his head.

Woody saw the doorway that led off from behind the counter. "He lived upstairs?" he asked, and pointed.

"My house now," said the man emphatically.

"Can I look?" Woody asked.

"No."

"I'll pay," said Woody, reaching across to lift up the counter.

The man raised the knife and it glinted under the shop's fluorescent lighting. "This my house now. My restaurant. My house. You go now."

Woody held up his hands, admitting defeat. He left the shop, thought about eating the sweet and sour pork but decided against it and dropped it into a rubbish bin before walking back to the Tube.

* * *

Hennessy sat at the kitchen table with Jackie sprawled at his feet and a pile of typewritten sheets in front of him. Except for the dog he was alone. Jim Kavanagh was in the next room, while Willie O'Hara had gone upstairs for a few hours' sleep after volunteering to be on guard duty overnight.

The papers Hennessy was studying were the lists of the munitions supplies that had been secreted in mainland Britain. There were sixteen lists in all. Most had arrived at his office before they'd left Belfast and he'd requested that the few remaining lists be delivered to the farm. Of the sixteen, five had been raided with about thirty-five pounds of Semtex in all unaccounted for. Detonators had been taken, and some ammunition, but no guns or rifles were missing. What worried Hennessy was that there appeared to be no common thread linking the arms dumps that had been tampered with, either geographically or in terms of people who knew about them. Hennessy was starting to think that perhaps more than one person was involved, or that security among the high-ranking IRA officials wasn't as secure as it should have been. And there was the added complication that whoever was behind the bombings could have lied when compiling the list of the contents of his own caches. He slammed the table in frustration and Jackie jerked awake, ears back. To have gone to all that trouble for nothing, cursed Hennessy. Jackie got to her feet and put her head in his lap, whining for attention, and he stroked her flanks.

Kavanagh popped his head around the door. "There's somebody coming," he said.

Hennessy gathered the papers together and put them into one of the drawers of the Welsh dresser. "It looks like Hugh McGrath. It's his car, anyway."

Hennessy went with Kavanagh through the hall to the front door. Two of the guards had already stopped the blue Volvo some fifty yards or so from the house. There were four men in it, including the driver. Hennessy used his hand to shield his eyes from the afternoon sun and recognised the grey, slicked-back hair and angular features of Hugh McGrath, wearing the tinted glasses that gave him what Mary always mockingly referred to as his Clint Eastwood look. McGrath .

owned a farm to the south-west, several hundred acres but little in the way of crops or livestock. Instead he earned a small fortune taking advantage of the price differentials between the North and South. That's how McGrath would have explained it. Hennessy called it by its true name – smuggling.

Price anomalies between the two parts of the divided Ireland meant that McGrath could always make a turn somewhere, be it on wheat, pigs, milk or petrol, or by smuggling things like contraceptives to the south or antibiotics to the north.

Hennessy had always been unhappy at McGrath's smuggling operations but he was a powerful man within the organisation and had many supporters. His role as liaison officer with the Libyans was also vital to the IRA, and he was one of the few men from the organisation who had actually met with Gaddafi. McGrath knew his value and capitalised on it.

The Volvo pulled up in front of the farmhouse and McGrath unwound his angular frame from the back seat. He was a good head taller than Hennessy, even with his slight stoop. He held out his hand and his grip was strong and confident.

"Liam," he said. "How are you this fine afternoon?"

"Fine," said Hennessy. "Come on in." McGrath's driver and his two bodyguards stayed in the car as Hennessy led him into the lounge. Hennessy waved him towards the floral-patterned sofa in front of the unlit fireplace.

"Drink?" he asked, and McGrath asked for a whiskey. Hennessy half filled two crystal tumblers before settling down into a leather wing-tipped chair opposite the sofa. Jackie butted the door open with her head and lay down at Hennessy's feet after first sniffing at McGrath's legs and accepting a pat on the back.

"How goes it?" asked McGrath.

"It's going OK."

"You checked out my arms dumps?" McGrath had been responsible for three arms caches, all close to London, and according to the reports Hennessy had received one of them was missing two packages of Semtex.

Hennessy nodded and told McGrath what his searchers had found. Or rather, what they hadn't found.

"I can't believe that one of mine has been touched. Do you have any idea yet who's behind this, Liam?"

"Not yet, no."

"It makes a mockery of our security, right enough. I know we don't see eye to eye on the question of mainland bombing campaigns, but this looting of our supplies is something else. We have to know who we can trust, Liam. Our organisation depends on it."

Trust and fear, thought Hennessy. In equal amounts usually, though in McGrath's case it was mainly fear. He came from a long line of Catholic landowners. His father was one of the driving forces behind the removal of many Protestant farmers from the border country. His method had been simple and brutal. He had targeted all the farms in the area where there was only one son and he had had them systematically murdered. When the parents became too old to work the farm and they were put up for sale, he made sure that there were no Protestant offers. Those farms where there were several children waiting to claim their inheritance were forced out of business by arson and poisoning campaigns and they, too, were sold to Catholic buyers. McGrath's own farm had once belonged to a Protestant family until their only son was shot through the back of the head as he sat on a tractor eating his lunch one day. The farm was put up for auction a year later and the sealed bid from McGrath's father was the highest, just as he knew it would be. Ironically, McGrath was an only son himself, with three sisters as siblings, but in his case it had been an advantage – not a death sentence.

"I gather you're having a wee spot of bother," said McGrath, stretching out his long legs.

"It's nothing I can't handle," said Hennessy.

"An explosion in your office, your farm and car bombed, Mary whisked off to London, and now Jim Kavanagh is trawling around the farms looking for men to guard you at night. I don't doubt that you can handle it, whatever it is, but I thought I might be able to help."

"I'm working on it," said Hennessy. He was worried about showing weakness in front of McGrath. He was one of the most political, and ruthless, men in the organisation, and always called in his debts. Accepting favours from Hugh McGrath was like doing a deal with the devil himself.

"Do you want to tell me about it?" McGrath asked.

Hennessy knew there was nothing to gain by not telling McGrath, because the man's intelligence network was second to none. He'd find out everything anyway. Hennessy explained about Nguyen and how his questions had turned into threats and how his threats had become reality. McGrath listened, occasionally grunting.

"Would it help if I seconded a few of my men?" McGrath asked once Hennessy had finished.

Hennessy shook his head. "No thanks, Hugh. Jim Kavanagh is getting a few of the local lads in. And I'm hoping to bring Micky Geraghty over. He should be able to track the bastard down, sure enough."

"Geraghty? Will he come back?"

"I hope so. I reckon he'll stand more chance than a group of townies trampling over the fields."

"I hope it works out. But let me know if you need help, OK?"

"I will, Hugh. I will."

McGrath drank his whiskey. It seemed to Hennessy that he had something on his mind.

"Is there something else, Hugh?"

"I don't know, Liam. It's this whole business of bombing on the mainland. Maybe we're going about this the wrong way. Maybe now is the time we should be applying pressure, not pulling back. Now is just the time to show our strength. To show that we're serious. And to give the British public a taste of their own medicine."

Hennessy raised his eyebrows. "What do you mean?"

"Let them have roadblocks on their roads, armed troops in their towns, body searches before they go into shops. Let them feel what life is like under an oppressive regime."

"I don't doubt that the bombs on the mainland will result in an over-reaction from the Government, and I know that'll probably result in a backlash of public opinion, but what about the damage the bombs are doing to our image? They're killing civilians, Hugh. With no warnings. They're not legitimate targets. You know as well as I do what we say in the *Green Book* that we give to volunteers. The only civilian targets that are legitimate are the Establishment, those who have a vested interest in maintaining the present status quo in Ireland: politicians, media, judiciary, business elements and the British war machine. That's virtually a direct quote."

McGrath shook his head. "There are no soft targets, no hard targets. Just targets. The Brits elected their Government, so they're responsible for it. They are all legitimate targets, every bit as legitimate as those in Ulster."

"And no warnings?"

"That's what makes them so effective. You should be embracing these bombers, Liam. You should be grateful to them, for the way they're raising the profile of the Cause around the world."

Liam looked incredulous. "By killing civilians?" he said. "What do you think that does for our reputation?"

McGrath held up his hand as if to calm an impatient child. "It doesn't matter. It never has. That's the big mistake everyone makes, Liam, they assume that when we kill what you call a soft target everyone turns against us. It doesn't happen. We kill a couple of tourists by mistake, we blow up a child, we shoot an old woman, it has no effect. It doesn't affect the votes we get at election time, it doesn't make a blind bit of difference to the amount of money we raise. In fact, you know as well as I do that a big bomb on the mainland, aimed at civilians or the army, often results in more money flooding in from the States, not less. It proves to them that we're serious, that we're prepared to fight for what we believe in."

McGrath shook his head, almost sadly. "Liam, I can't believe we're having this conversation, I really can't. It used to be you who had the drive, the energy. It was you who put the fire into the boys. Have you forgotten? Aldershot 1972? The M62 bombing in 1974? The Guildford pub bombings the same year? The Hilton bomb in 1975? You were with us then, Liam, you were the one who was calling for an escalation of the campaign, right enough."

"That was then, things have changed," said Hennessy. "There's a time for violence and there's a time for negotiation." He sounded tired.

"The Regent's Park bandstand bomb in 1982? The Brighton bombing in 1984? Have you forgotten that you were involved, that you pushed for them? What was it you said then, when Thatcher escaped? They were lucky. They'll always have to be lucky, but we only have to be lucky once. Christ, Liam, you knew what you were talking about then. And it holds true now."

Hennessy said nothing and McGrath continued. "Look what the ANC achieved in South Africa, through violence, look at Israel, founded on bloodshed."

Hennessy stood up and went over to the window. McGrath's bodyguards and driver were sitting patiently in the Volvo. One of them looked up when he saw the movement at the window.

"You've not forgotten what we're fighting for, have you, Liam?" said McGrath quietly.

Hennessy whirled round and jabbed his finger at McGrath. "That's not bloody fair!" he shouted. "I won't have you questioning my loyalty. Not now, not ever. There's no one who's done more for the Cause than me and my family. It's not three years ago that I buried my own brother-in-law, and before that my father and two cousins. My family has shed more than its fair share of blood." He stepped towards McGrath as if about to attack him. "And, I might add, my family hasn't been profiting from the border. We've given our lives in the struggle for a united Ireland, not set out to make fucking money from it. So don't you ever, ever, ask me if I've forgotten what we're fighting for!" He loomed over McGrath, his cheeks red and spittle spraying from his mouth. His fists were bunched and his shoulders quivered with tension.

McGrath looked stunned. He opened his mouth to speak but then seemed to think better of it.

"God damn you, McGrath!" shouted Hennessy. "Get out

of my fucking house. Now!" He stood glaring at the man sitting in front of him and then turned and stormed out of the room. He waited in the kitchen until he heard McGrath leave the house and the Volvo start up and drive down the track. Hennessy stood over the sink, gripping the edge of the draining board with his shaking hands. He felt the acidic taste of vomit in the back of his throat and he retched several times but nothing came up from his stomach. He poured himself a glass of water and was drinking it when Kavanagh came into the kitchen.

"Are ye all right?" he asked Hennessy.

"A wee exchange of words with Mr McGrath," said Hennessy. "I lost my temper with him." Hennessy tried to get his thinking straight. What had upset him so much? Part of it was McGrath's total unwillingness to even consider his point of view, and his almost inhuman eagerness to see innocent bystanders murdered. There was also the bitter memory of the friends and relatives who'd died, deaths that Hennessy had never really gotten over, like Mary's brother, Gerry. That was another reason for the burning anger coursing through his system, Hennessy realised. Mary.

"Jim, did anyone speak to McGrath on the way in?"

"Just one of the men on guard. He recognised him straight-away and let him through."

"No one else? Did you say anything to him?"

Kavanagh looked mystified. "I didn't, Liam. I'll ask the others. What's wrong? What d'ye think might've been said?"

Hennessy took another mouthful of water and swilled it round his gums before spitting it into the sink. The sour taste was still there, washing wouldn't get rid of it.

"He knew Mary was in London," he said quietly. "I want to know how he knew."

Even with the address Hennessy had given him, Morrison had a hell of a time finding Geraghty's house. The village it was supposed to be near was just a sprinkling of stone cottages in a valley sheltered from the biting winds of the North Sea and none of the roads seemed to have names. Geraghty was supposed to be living at Garryowen Farm but there was nothing even remotely like that on the map Morrison had bought in Inverness. It was dark and there were spots of rain flecking the windshield. Morrison decided to try the local pub, a weathered stone building with leaded windows that glowed yellow like the eyes of a wild animal. He parked his hired Rover next to a collection of mud-spattered farmer's vehicles and didn't bother locking his door. Above him the pub's sign – a fox with a dead chicken in its jaws – creaked in the wind. He pushed open the gnarled oak door and more of the yellow light oozed out, bringing with it the hubbub of pub conversation, predominantly gruff, masculine voices discussing sheep prices and football. It all stopped when he stepped over the threshold. It was, Morrison realised, like the scene in a vampire film when the stranger asks for directions to Dracula's castle. At a table near a shoulder-high hearth four old men in tweeds had been playing cards, but they had all stopped and were looking at him, wondering who he was. Under the table lay a black and white sheepdog, its ears up as it sniffed in his direction. A line of four younger men standing at the bar with pints of beer in front of them turned as one to look at him and even the barmaid, blonde haired and rosy cheeked, checked him over as she pulled a pint.

Morrison smiled at no one in particular and closed the door behind him. There was a thick mat just inside the door and Morrison carefully wiped his feet on it.

The card game began again and the dog settled its head down on to its paws with a sigh. Morrison walked over to the bar and put down the map.

"Good evening," said the barmaid. She finished pulling the pint and handed it to an old man wearing a grubby tartan cap. "Here you are, Archie," she said.

The pub was similar to those in farming communities all over Scotland and Ireland, the sort of pub where everyone knows everyone else and strangers are regarded with suspicion bordering on hostility. It was one large room, a handful of wooden tables worn smooth with age ranged against the outer wall and a bench seat either side of the fireplace which was unlit but contained a couple of roughly hewn logs on a blackened metal grate. The bar ran parallel to the wall, the full length of the room, and behind it was a door that obviously led to the landlord's private quarters. The walls of the room had once been painted white but had been stained a deep yellow by years of cigarette and pipe smoke and fumes from the fire. The floor was stone-flagged with a large, rectangular carpet of some long-faded red and blue pattern under the tables. On the gantry behind the bar was an impressive collection of malt whiskies, many bearing simple black labels with white lettering identifying the distillery that had produced them.

"What can I be getting you?" the barmaid asked, and Morrison indicated one of the Islay malts.

He savoured the bouquet of the deep-amber liquid before sipping it.

"Good?" asked the barmaid. She began drying glasses with a white cloth.

"Magic," he said. "Could you help me? I'm trying to find Micky Geraghty's house. Do you have any idea where it is?"

"To be sure," she said. She put down the cloth and reached for the map. She looked at it carefully, frowned, and then giggled. "I can't make head nor tail of this," she said. She held it out to one of the men standing at the bar. "Here Scott, can you show me Micky Geraghty's house?"

The man took the map, studied it and nodded. He put it down on the bar and pointed. Morrison looked over as the man ran his finger along a thin black line.

"Follow the road outside for about half a mile until you get to this crossroad here. Go left and then left again where the road forks, here. About two hundred yards later there's a single track to the right, you'll see a white post each side of the entrance. Micky's about half a mile down the track."

"It's no wonder I couldn't find it," said Morrison, taking another pull of the whisky. He offered to buy the man a drink and quickly extended it into a general offer for his three companions.

"You know Micky?" Morrison asked the man who'd given him directions.

"Sure, he's usually in here a couple of times a week. And every now and then his escapees will find their way here."

"Escapees?"

The man laughed. "He runs one of them Outward Bound places but for middle-aged executives. Teaches them survival stuff, rock-climbing, sailing, things like that. Sometimes he makes them spend a couple of nights on one of the islands, or dumps them miles away with just a compass and a pack of Kendal mint cake. The lucky ones manage to stagger in here to beg Tess for a drink."

The barmaid giggled. "They don't have any money, but we always give them credit. And they always come back and settle up. They're so grateful, bless 'em."

Morrison finished his whisky and said his goodbyes. He followed the man's instructions and ten minutes later he was outside a two-storey grey stone building with a steeply sloping slate roof. There were four cars parked outside the house and Morrison drove slowly past them. The track curved around the house, leading to a large, stone barn which had been converted into flats, and a short row of cottages. There were more cars parked there, all new models, so Morrison reckoned that Geraghty had a group of executives under his wing.

He found a parking space next to a white BMW and walked back to the front door of the house and pressed the bell.

The door was opened by a chestnut-haired girl in tight jeans and a green and white checked shirt. She looked at him with clear blue eyes and raised eyebrows.

"Is Mr Geraghty at home?" Morrison asked.

"Yep, come in," she said, and moved to let him into the hall. She closed the door and led him down a wood-panelled corridor. "My dad's in the study," she said over her shoulder. "Who shall I say is here?" Her accent was north Belfast, as far as Morrison could tell, but soft and with a gentle lilt.

"Morrison. Sean Morrison."

"From Belfast?" she asked.

"That's right." He wondered how come she was so willing

to let a stranger into her house, especially a stranger from over the water. Surely she must know of her father's past and that he'd always be at risk from Protestant extremists? They reached a door and she pushed it open. A grey-haired man with a weather-beaten face was sitting behind a desk talking into a phone. The girl showed Morrison in.

"I'll leave you here," she said. She left the door open and went back down the corridor. Somewhere in the distance he could hear a television set.

Geraghty waved at Morrison with his free hand, indicating a leather chair to the side of the desk, and Morrison sat in it.

"I'm booked pretty much solid now until the end of August," Geraghty said into the phone. He listened, frowned, and looked at a large book on the desk in front of him. "What, the twenty-eighth? Yes, we could do that. Until the eleventh? OK, I'll pencil your group in for that. Can you drop me a letter confirming it? Yes, yes, I'll look forward to it. Take care." He replaced the receiver.

"You'll be Sean Morrison?" he said, taking Morrison by surprise. Geraghty laughed at his discomfort. "Liam was on the phone to me earlier, said he didn't want me worrying overmuch when a stranger arrived on my doorstep. More likely didn't want me taking your head off with a twelve-bore. Good to see you, anyway, Sean. There's a bottle by the table next to you, pour yourself a drink, and one for me, too."

Morrison poured two measures of Irish whiskey. "I'm surprised we never met in Belfast," he said as he poured.

"I was what you might describe as low profile," laughed Geraghty. "I was always kept pretty much in the background."

"I know of the work you did, of course. You were one of my heroes."

"I'm sure you don't know half of it," said Geraghty, raising his glass. "But thanks anyway."

They drank. The study was very much a man's room. Floor-to-ceiling bookshelves lined one wall, every inch filled with a mixture of paperback novels, leather-bound classics and wildlife reference books. The other three walls were wood panelled, much the same as the hall outside, with several framed prints of hunting dogs. The furniture was sturdy, well-worn leather and wood that had long since lost its shine, comfortable chairs, a spacious desk with a brass reading lamp and three small circular tables. It was a room in which Morrison felt secure. To the right of the desk was a small window overlooking the line of cottages. A light winked out and Morrison could imagine an exhausted executive collapsing on to his bed.

If the study inspired a feeling of security, the man himself suggested a quiet confidence, that Micky Geraghty was a man who kept his word, a good guy to have at your back in a fight. He looked to be in his early fifties, broad shoulders and strong hands. His hair was grey but it was thick and healthy and his skin was wrinkled from exposure to the elements rather than age. His blue eyes were set aside a nose that had been broken several times. It was a strong, good-looking face, one that Morrison was sure would go down well with Japanese tourists wanting a set of antlers to take back home.

"Did Liam tell you why I was coming to see you?" Morrison asked, and Geraghty nodded.

Morrison continued: "The idea is for you to go in with me. You find him, I'll do the rest." From the look of it Hennessy's reservations were groundless, Geraghty appeared to be enthusiastic about the idea. Morrison relaxed, settling back in the chair and sipping his whiskey.

Geraghty laughed, his eyes sparkling. "I'd love to help, Sean, God knows I owe Liam a favour or two, but you're going to have to count me out."

Morrison frowned. "I don't understand, what's the problem?"

Geraghty leant back in his chair and swung his left leg up on to the desk. It was covered in greying plaster from his toes to just above his knee. He slapped the cast and pulled a face. "This is my problem," he said ruefully. "I broke it two weeks ago. The Doc says it'll be a couple of months yet before the cast can come off. Until then . . ." He shrugged.

Morrison's heart fell. For a wild moment he thought that perhaps Geraghty was making it up, that the cast was fake and he was just using it as an excuse to back out, but his disappointment seemed genuine, and so did the cast. It had been autographed in several places and the plaster was crumbling a little around his toes.

"How did it happen?" he asked.

"Teaching a group of sales reps to climb. I went up a rock-face to knock in a bit of protection and the guy who was paying out the rope lost concentration. I slipped and he let me fall about thirty feet further than he should have done. Problem was, I was only twenty-five feet above the ground. He was very upset about it."

"I bet," said Morrison. "Who's running things while you're out of action?"

"The admin and the lectures I can handle myself, and I've a couple of instructors working with me. And my daughter, Kerry, the girl who let you in, knows as much as I do."

Geraghty saw the look on Morrison's face and he smiled. "I hope that wasn't a chauvinistic comment I saw forming on your lips," he said. "Kerry knows as much about tracking as I do, and she's been teaching survival courses with me for five years or more. And if the truth be known, she's a darn sight fitter than I am, even without the cast."

"Why, Dad, you've never said that to my face," said a voice from behind Morrison, and he turned to see the girl, standing in the doorway with her hands on her hips and her eyebrows arched.

"How long have you been there, girl?" asked Geraghty. He didn't appear annoyed and Morrison knew that from where he was sitting he could see the length of the corridor leading away from the study so there was no way she could have crept up on them without him seeing her. In fact, the chances were that Geraghty had paid her the compliment knowing that she was within earshot. Morrison wondered how much she knew about Geraghty's past.

"I just came to see if you and Mr Morrison wanted a cup of tea, or something. God forbid I should eavesdrop." She shook her hair back from her face and swept it behind her ears. She had her father's eyes, and the same confident way of holding her head with the chin slightly raised. Her skin was healthy and bronzed and she was wearing hardly any make-up, just a touch of blue eye-shadow and mascara.

Morrison put her age at about twenty-five. Geraghty was right, she looked fit. She caught him looking at her and she grinned at him. He looked away.

Geraghty held up his whiskey glass. "We're doing just fine," he said.

"And I," said Morrison, getting to his feet and putting his glass on the table, "must be going."

"I'll show you out," said Kerry. Morrison shook hands with Geraghty, who wished him well, and then followed Kerry back down the hall. She wasn't wearing shoes and her bare feet brushed against the carpet. "Uncle Liam wanted my dad to do something for him, is that right?" she asked.

"Something like that," said Morrison.

She turned to look at him, stopping so suddenly that he almost bumped into her. Her clear blue eyes bored into his. "What did you want him to do?" she asked. "It must have been important for you to have come all this way. Important for the Cause."

Morrison looked at her, unsure how to react. She had called Hennessy "Uncle" and she was undoubtedly her father's daughter, but he didn't know her well enough to discuss IRA business with her. "We needed his help, but his leg puts paid to that," he said.

Her eyes sparkled and she reached forward, touching his arm. "Don't go yet," she whispered. "Come with me." She took him past the front door and into a comfortably furnished lounge. The television was on but the room was empty. She nodded towards an overstuffed sofa. "Wait there for a while," she said. "Let me talk to my dad. OK?"

"OK," Morrison replied, bemused. He sat down and crossed his legs and wondered what the hell she was up to.

Kerry walked back to the study where her father still had his leg on the desk. He had a knitting needle in one hand and was wiggling it down inside the cast trying to get at an itchy place. He grinned at her apologetically. She was forever warning him that scratching would only make it worse.

She leant against the door jamb and folded her arms across her chest.

"Uncle Liam needs our help, yes?" Liam Hennessy wasn't

a blood relative, but he was just as close. He was her godfather and when they'd lived in Ireland barely a month went by when she didn't see him. He'd taught her to ride on his farm, had given her the run of his rambling library and spent hours just talking with her when her mother was in hospital and dying bit by bit. Kerry loved Liam Hennessy fiercely and would do anything to protect him.

"He needs my help," said Geraghty.

"It's been five years since we were in Ireland, so I guess it's something they think only you can do, something that you can't do with a broken leg? Something to do with tracking, is that it?"

Geraghty sighed. "Why don't you just ask me what it is they want, Kerry? It would save us both a lot of time."

"You'll tell me?" she said, surprised.

"Try me," he answered.

"What is it Uncle Liam wants?"

To her surprise her father explained about The Chinaman and how Hennessy was stuck in his farm. "He wanted me to go with Morrison, to go into the countryside and flush him out."

"And then what?"

Geraghty fixed his daughter with his eyes, suddenly cold and harder than she'd seen them for a long time. "If he's lucky, Liam will hand him over to the police. If he's unlucky, well, you know that some of Liam's friends can play pretty rough, Kerry. It could get nasty."

"But the man's trying to kill Uncle Liam, that's what you said. So he's only got himself to blame."

"Whatever. But it's all immaterial anyway, Kerry. I can't do it, they'll just have to find someone else."

She leapt to her feet and leant over the desk, her hair swinging from side to side.

"No!" said Geraghty before she could speak.

"But I'm perfect for it," she said, exasperated. "You've taught me everything there is to know about tracking, and yet you never let me prove how good I am. You never let me take the hunting parties out on my own."

"You know why that is. The Germans and the Japs pay top

whack to be taken out by a traditional Highland gamekeeper, tweeds and flat cap and all. It's part of the enjoyment for them, it'd spoil it if their tracker was a pretty girl young enough to be their daughter."

Kerry ignored the compliment, realising she'd been side-tracked into an old argument.

"I know about tracking, and I know the area around Uncle Liam's farm, probably better than you do. I've ridden and walked over every inch, I know every hiding place."

"It's several hundred acres, my girl, I doubt if you know every inch."

"It's three hundred and twenty-four acres, Dad, and I know it like the back of my hand."

"It'll be dangerous," he warned, and she knew then that she'd won the argument about whether or not she had the ability.

"Dad, which of us is the best shot?"

"I can't fault your marksmanship Kerry, but I'm not having you trekking around the Irish countryside with a hunting rifle. It's practically a war zone."

"All right then, I won't take my gun. But it's Uncle Liam this man is after, not me," she pressed. "He'll be focused on him, not me." She waved her hand at the books lining the wall to her left. "I've read every book on trapping and tracking on those shelves, and I read most of them before I even went to school."

It was true, Geraghty acknowledged. Even as a child she'd had a fascination for the books, and she'd taught herself to make snares and simple traps and learnt to recognise spoors and tracks from the diagrams they contained. There were other books, too, manuals on warfare and booby traps and explosives, some that he'd bought out of curiosity and others that he'd acquired in connection with his work for the IRA, and she'd read them just as avidly. But unlike Geraghty, almost all her knowledge of booby traps was theoretical and not practical.

Kerry could see that her father was wavering so she decided to raise the stakes.

"It's not just a question of helping Uncle Liam," she said.

"I want to do something to help the Cause. I didn't stop you when you said you wanted to leave Ireland after Mum died, but you know that deep down I wanted to stay in Belfast and help in any way I could. I feel as strongly as you do about getting the British out of Ireland. You know that." Geraghty could feel the intensity of her conviction burning across the desk, and he remembered how, years before, he had felt the same desire to see a united Ireland. "Let me do this, for the Cause if not for Uncle Liam. This is something I can do, something that's a hell of a lot more constructive than throwing petrol bombs at troops or harassing the RUC."

Geraghty closed his eyes and rubbed them with the backs of his hands. He sighed deeply and Kerry knew that she'd almost won. One more push and he'd agree. It was time to play her trump card. She sat back down in the chair, pulled it closer to the desk, and leant her elbows on it so that her head was on a level with her father's. "And," she said thoughtfully, "it would get me away from here for a while." She paused, for emphasis. "From him," she added, just in case he didn't get the message.

"You're not still seeing him, are you?" Geraghty asked.

"I'm trying not to," she answered. For almost a year she'd been having an on-off affair with a British Telecom engineer who lived nearby. He was married but couldn't make his mind up whether to leave his wife or stop seeing Kerry. He'd sworn that he hadn't touched his wife in years, but midway through the affair he'd confessed that she was pregnant and that he couldn't abandon her. "I suppose it'll be a fucking virgin birth," she'd screamed, and thrown an ashtray at his head, but the following week she'd phoned him and their love-making had been better than ever.

Geraghty had made his disapproval plain, but had also refused to interfere, knowing that his daughter was old enough to make her own mistakes. He figured that she'd realise what a hopeless situation she'd gotten herself into and that she'd come to her senses. He was right. It had been almost two months since she had seen him, though she was still at the stage where she had to keep fighting the urge to call him and jumped whenever the phone rang. She knew that if she saw him again she'd end up in bed with him. Geraghty sensed the pressure she was under and thought that perhaps she was right, a spell in Ireland might be just what she needed to get the man out of her system once and for all.

"If you go, you're going to have to be careful," he said.

"I will be," she said earnestly.

"I mean very careful," he said. "It's not a game there, you know. It's not too far from the border. It's a war zone. You don't carry a gun, under any circumstances. You track him, and that's all. You don't take any risks, understand?"

She nodded furiously. "I promise. Can I go?"

Geraghty smiled, but it was an uncertain smile. "Yes," he said. "You can go."

She whooped, and grinned, and reached over the desk to hug him and kiss him on the cheek.

"Go and get Morrison for me," he told her. "I want a word with him."

Geraghty watched her rush down the corridor. He wasn't surprised at her keenness to return to Ireland, or to help the Provos. She'd put up a hell of a fight when he'd first decided to leave Ireland, and she'd come close to staying behind. Kerry had a stubborn streak, and he guessed that she'd got it from him. She had a hard side, too, a tendency to viciousness which went beyond simple devotion to the Cause. There had been times in Belfast when he'd felt she was actually enjoying taking on the army and the RUC, that she was getting some sort of kick out of the Troubles. Despite his apparent change of heart he was still reluctant to allow her to go back to Belfast and its violent influences, but he owed Liam Hennessy. He owed him a great deal. Besides, he knew that if she really set her mind on going back, he wouldn't be able to stop her. He knew his daughter, and he knew that she wasn't above telephoning Hennessy herself and offering her services. And if things were as bad as they sounded, he doubted if Hennessy would turn her down. And if Hennessy asked him if it was OK for Kerry to go back, could he refuse? Could he refuse any request of the man who held his life in his hands? No, he could not. And she knew that, his darling daughter. She knew that full well.

Kerry found Morrison still watching television. "Dad wants to talk to you," she said. "He says I can come with you."

"You?" said Morrison, surprised.

"To help you track down the man who's trying to hurt Uncle Liam."

A bemused Morrison followed her back down the corridor and into Geraghty's study.

"Leave us alone, Kerry, and shut the door this time," Geraghty told her. He waited until she'd gone before speaking. "She wants to help you, Sean," he said.

"Can she do it?" asked Morrison.

"Oh yes, she's a first-class tracker, I've taught her everything I know. She often comes with me out on to the moors after deer. She's a good shot, too. That's what I want to talk to you about. I don't want her carrying a gun out there. Under any circumstances. I don't want her put in any danger."

"I'll take care of her. I promise."

"There's something else." Geraghty scratched his chin and scrutinised Morrison. "I'm not sure how to put this, Sean. Kerry can be a bit, er, overenthusiastic sometimes. Do you know what I mean?"

Morrison shook his head, mystified.

"She's always idolised Liam, and me, and ever since she was a kid she was on the fringes of the Organisation, running errands, taking messages, the sort of stuff we all went through, you know? Throwing stones at the troops, giving the RUC a hard time. But I never wanted her to get drawn into the real rough stuff, the sort of things I was involved in. I mean, she has a pretty good idea of what I did, and I think she wishes she could be more like me."

Morrison laughed. "Jesus, Micky, it's hardly a secret, is it? There's barely a pub in Derry where they don't sing songs about you on a Saturday night when the beer's flowing."

"Aye, Sean, that's right enough. And I'm not ashamed of what I did, far from it. We're at war with the fucking British and I'd do it all over again, the killing and everything. But my family has given enough. I don't want Kerry to get any more involved. I didn't then and I don't now. I promised my wife,

God rest her soul, I promised her before she died that I'd take Kerry away from Belfast before she got in too deep. I don't want her to go back."

"You're going to stop her?" said Morrison, frowning.

"No. No, I can't stop her. But you must make sure she realises that this is a one-off. Don't romanticise it for her, don't pull her back. Just use her this one time, then send her back to me."

"I understand," said Morrison.

"Then good luck, and God bless. And take care of her. She's all the family I've got left." He swung his plaster cast off the desk and it thudded on to the floor. "It's late. You should stay here tonight and make an early start tomorrow. I'll get Kerry to cook us a meal. You might want to telephone Liam and let him know what's happening, if Kerry hasn't done so already." He reached for a set of metal crutches leaning against the wall and used them to clump out of the room.

Maggie linked her arm through Woody's as they stepped out of the cinema.

"Good film," she said. "Bit violent, but fun."

"Yeah, I've always liked a bit of mindless violence," laughed Woody. "You hungry?"

"Mmmm. Sure."

"Italian?"

"Italian would be great."

Woody suggested a place in Covent Garden and they walked together out of Leicester Square and down Long Acre. Maggie asked him how he was getting on at work and he told her about the stories he was working on. She was always interested in what he was doing at the paper and seemed to hang on every word. He told her about the phone call from Pat Quigley and the mysterious Chinaman. She raised her eyebrows when she heard about the money in the carrier bag.

"What do you think's going on?" she asked.

Woody shrugged. "I was thinking that maybe this Chinaman had paid someone to go after Liam Hennessy, some sort of hit-man."

"Wow!" she said.

"Yeah, wow is right. It'd be one hell of a story, if only I can nail it down."

They stood at the roadside and waited for a gap in the traffic before crossing.

"So what's the problem?" she asked.

"He's gone. Vanished. I went round to where he lives and he'd moved. No forwarding address. I don't even have his full name."

"You don't think that perhaps he's gone to Ireland himself?"

"Seems unlikely, doesn't it? I mean, a Chinaman in Belfast on the trail of an IRA leader. It's a bit unbelievable, even for our paper."

"I suppose so."

They walked in silence through the evening crowds, and then stopped to watch a man in a clown's suit juggling five flaming torches.

"Do you get to write much about the IRA?" she asked.

"Depends," said Woody. "I covered the Knightsbridge bombing, remember? The night I met you. Depends when it happens, you know."

"The *Sunday World* usually takes the Government line, doesn't it?" she said.

Woody nodded. "Slightly to the right of Attila the Hun, we are."

"What about you? What do you think?"

"Hell, Maggie, I don't know. I'm a reporter, not a politician." The juggler put down three of his torches to scattered applause and then began fire-eating. "I guess I take the view that we should just pull the troops out and let the Irish sort it out themselves. You know the troops went to Northern Ireland in the first place to look after the Catholics. To protect them from the Protestants. And now it's the IRA who want them out. It doesn't make sense. It isn't something the British

Government can sort out, that much I'm sure. It's an Irish problem. What about you?"

"I suppose you're right. At the end of the day whatever the MPs in Westminster say isn't going to make the slightest difference. Maybe your paper should say that."

Woody laughed. "I don't think many MPs would take any notice of what appears in the *Sunday World. The Times* maybe, or the *Telegraph.*" Something tingled at the back of Woody's mind. Something to do with an MP. He watched the clown blow flaming liquid up into the night sky, a glistening bluish stream which flared into orange and yellow. Of course, thought Woody. S. J. Brownlow, the name in the notebook. Sir John Brownlow. The Chinaman's MP. He'd said he'd written to his Member of Parliament and been to see him. With any luck he'd have The Chinaman's letter on file.

"What are you smiling at?" Maggie asked.

"Nothing," he said. "Come on, let's go eat. I'm starving."

As the darkness crept through the forest, Nguyen opened one of the containers of chicken and ate it slowly, along with a container of boiled rice. When he'd finished he scraped leaves away from the forest floor and buried the remains in the soil. He drank from one of his canteens and put it in the rucksack alongside the components of his firebomb detonator and the stolen gun. The can of petrol was too bulky to fit into the rucksack so he was forced to carry it. He waited until the sun had gone down before moving through the forest. The can slowed him, not because it was heavy but because it was awkward and forever catching in the undergrowth, but once he left the trees and was out in open fields he picked up speed.

He varied his route slightly this time, cutting through different fields and crossing the B8 further north than he'd crossed the previous night. Once he almost stumbled into an army patrol, half a dozen teenage soldiers walking along a narrow country lane, their faces blackened and their rubber-soled boots making almost no noise. They were strung out over fifty feet, walking in two lines. Nguyen was heading in the opposite direction, on the other side of a hedgerow looking for a gap so that he could cut across the track, when he heard one of the men sniff. Nguyen froze and as he did the petrol slapped against the side of the can. The field he was in had recently been ploughed and offered little in the way of cover but there was nowhere else for him to go so he dropped and rolled into a deep furrow and flattened himself down. He was invisible. He heard them go by, and heard the man sniff again. He stayed where he was for a full thirty minutes just in case they retraced their steps.

It was after midnight when he eventually reached the hill overlooking Hennessy's farm. He lay down close to the summit, careful that he didn't break the skyline, and studied the farm buildings through his binoculars for more than an hour until he was satisfied that he had spotted all the guards. The starlight wasn't strong enough to illuminate their faces but he could see that they were carrying shotguns. There was one in front of the cottage, another close by in the gap between the barns and the stables and three standing guard close to the farmhouse. One of them was smoking a cigarette, he could see the small red dot hovering in the air. He sniffed but could smell nothing. There had been times, Nguyen remembered, when he could smell a campfire two days' march away in the jungle, or smell the toothpaste or chewing gum or tobacco of an American who had passed by three hours before, but he was younger then and his senses were more acute.

During the hour he watched, the men walked up and down, occasionally talking to each other, but they did not bother patrolling the perimeter of the farm. Static sentries, thought Nguyen. The easiest to deal with.

He moved slowly down the hill and then crawled across the fields towards the barns, giving a wide berth to the stables and the cottage. He lay in the grass about a hundred yards from the barns and concentrated on them, checking that he hadn't missed a guard, and then began to crawl towards them. He moved only one limb at a time, left arm, right leg, right arm, left leg, keeping his body an inch off the ground to minimise noise while at the same time reducing his silhouette. It took him half an hour to cover the hundred yards to the nearest barn. He hugged the wall and slipped inside among the tractors and farm equipment. The barn was the furthest away from the farm but it would have been his first choice anyway because the other contained nothing but hay and the idea was to cause a diversion not to start a huge blaze that would have fire engines rushing over from the nearest town.

He put the can of petrol under a blue tractor and took off his rucksack. He knelt down and carefully removed the clock, the matchbox and its wire, and from his pocket he took out a fresh battery. He connected short lengths of wire to the hands of the clock and set them at quarter to and quarter past and then connected the battery and the matchbox and its match heads into a continuous circuit. He unscrewed the cap of the petrol can and poured half of it on the floor around the tractor then stood it under the cab. He lowered the matchbox into the can so that it was suspended above the liquid. It was important that the match heads were ignited in the vapour and not swamped with petrol or there would be no explosion. He wound the wire around the handle of the can so that the matchbox couldn't accidentally slip lower. He had thirty minutes to get into position. Plenty of time. He put his rucksack back on and eased himself out of the barn and slithered slowly along the ground, back the way he'd come, and then he crawled clockwise around the barns until he could see the side of the farmhouse and the gap that led to the courtyard.

He waited. The petrol bomb exploded with a whooshing noise followed by the crackle and hiss of the tractor burning. There were shouts and yells and the men at the front of the farmhouse ran towards the barn. Lights went on in the farmhouse and the door to the cottage flew open. When the guards had run through into the courtyard Nguyen made his way to the outbuildings and lay down in the shadows. Hennessy came out of the back door along with two other men, he in his dressing-gown, they in pullovers and jeans and holding handguns. Nguyen had planned to climb the drainpipe and get in through the bathroom window but he saw that Hennessy had left the back door open. The kitchen light hadn't been switched on so the doorway was in darkness. He waited until he was sure that no one else was coming out of the farmhouse and he moved along the wall, hugging the shadows like a cockroach, and then slipped through the door into the kitchen, listening carefully.

He moved on the balls of his feet, knees slightly bent, ready to move quickly if he had to, but it was all clear and he crept into the hall and up the stairs. The stairs turned to the left and he reorientated the map of the farmhouse that he held in his head and when the stairs opened into the first-floor hallway he knew immediately which way to move so that he would pass the bathroom and find Hennessy's bedroom. He unclipped the hunting knife from its scabbard on the strap of the rucksack and held it blade up as he put his hand on the bedroom door and pressed his ear to the warm wood. He hadn't seen the woman leave the house. She might have left during the day but there was a chance she was still in the room. He turned the doorknob slowly and smoothly and eased the door open. The light was on and the bed was empty. He pushed the door and stepped into the room. At the foot of the bed was a wicker dog basket and a brown dog growled at him and then began to bark. Nguyen closed the door as the dog got to its feet and moved towards him, barking and snapping, its tail down between its legs and the fur standing up along the back of its neck.

"Good dog," said Nguyen, holding the knife to his side.

Hennessy stood with his hands on his hips as he watched two of his men spray the burning tractor with fire extinguishers, the foam hissing and bubbling on the hot metal. Joe Ryan had run a hosepipe from the stables and he yelled over his shoulder for his daughter to turn the water on. The hosepipe squirmed and kicked and then water burst from the nozzle and he played it over the walls of the barn.

The rest of the men were busy moving equipment away from the fire, either to the far side of the barn or out into the courtyard. Kavanagh stood at Hennessy's shoulder. In the distance Hennessy heard Jackie bark. "Still think I've got enough guards, Jim?" he asked. Kavanagh remained silent, not sure if Hennessy was getting at him or not. "Any idea what caused it?" Hennessy asked.

"There's a can under the tractor and some melted plastic. It's The Chinaman, right enough. We were lucky that the can didn't explode, it could've been a lot worse. By the look of it the flames came shooting out of the top of the can like a jet engine, spraying fire across the wall and setting light to the tractor's tyres. It's a lot worse than it looks."

"He cocked it up?"

"Looks like it."

"Thank God he didn't set fire to the other barn. If the hay had gone up we'd have never got it under control."

The men with the fire extinguishers put out the burning tractor and moved to help Ryan douse the burning side of the barn. The tractor's tyres had melted and warped and the tractor was blackened and burnt and smeared with bubbly white foam. The smell of burnt rubber was choking and Hennessy and Kavanagh moved back into the courtyard. Hennessy looked up at his bedroom window. Jackie had stopped barking. "Still think we should go back to Belfast?" asked Hennessy.

"No question about it, Liam."

"And if he sets fire to my house? Could you stop him doing that?"

Kavanagh realised that whatever he said he'd be in the wrong, so he said nothing. They stood together and watched the men douse the final flames.

"Morrison should be back tomorrow," said Hennessy eventually. "He's bringing someone with him who might be able to help. Kerry Geraghty."

"Micky Geraghty's girl?"

"Yeah. She's going to try to track down The Chinaman. Micky was going to do it but he's got a broken leg, though from what Sean tells me she's every bit as good. We'll give her a go. While she's trying I'll have to stay here otherwise The Chinaman will just disappear, but if it doesn't work then we'll go back to Belfast and we'll handle it in the city. OK?"

"It's your call, Liam," said Kavanagh.

"You mean it's me he's after," said Hennessy. He smiled ruefully. "And you're right, of course. Look, there's nothing we can do here. I'm going back to bed and I suggest you do the same. I doubt if he's going to do anything else tonight and there's nothing we can do in the dark."

"I'll wait here until the men've finished," said Kavanagh. Hennessy began walking back to the farmhouse. Kavanagh called after him and Liam turned round. "I'm sorry about all this," said Kavanagh.

"Not your fault, Jim," said Hennessy. "And I didn't mean to imply that it was. I'm just a bit tense, that's all. This Chinaman is getting under my skin. I'll talk to you tomorrow."

He went into the kitchen and switched the light on. He poured himself a double whiskey and carried it upstairs to his bedroom. He hung his dressing-gown on the back of the bedroom door and placed the tumbler of whiskey on his bedside table. Jackie lay on the floor at the side of the bed. Hennessy was disappointed that she hadn't welcomed him back with her normal tail-wagging and frantic licks. She was probably sulking because he'd kept her in the room. "Come on, Jackie," he said softly, and patted the bed. Mary didn't allow the dog into the bedroom, least of all on the bed, but when she was away Hennessy reckoned that he should be allowed to give Jackie a treat. He patted the bed again and clicked his tongue, but still she ignored him. He went over to her and knelt down. "Come on, Jackie, old girl," he said, and stroked her neck. There was no reaction and Hennessy began to panic. He stood up and switched on the bedroom light and immediately saw that there was blood pooling around the dog's neck. "Oh God, no," he groaned. He bent down to pick up the dog but as he did he realised that he was not alone in the room. In the gap between the large oak wardrobe and the wall he saw a pair of legs in baggy camouflage trousers and he looked up sharply.

"You!" he said.

Nguyen stepped forward out of the shadows. In his left hand he carried a gun which he pointed at the head of the kneeling man. In his right he held two wires between his fingers and around his neck was hanging what appeared to be a length of grey tubing. He'd used a length of insulation tape to suspend the tube so that it lay against his stomach. Various nails and screws had been stuck to the tube with more tape. To Hennessy it appeared that Nguyen had undergone a complete transformation. It wasn't just the outfit, though the camouflage and the gun gave him a military appearance that was a far cry from the down-trodden Oriental who had turned up at his office, it was more a question of bearing, the way he carried himself. There was a new air of confidence about the man and for the first time Hennessy felt afraid. He looked down at Jackie and ran his hand along her fur.

"You didn't have to kill my dog," he said, shaking his head sadly.

"He was barking."

"She. Not he. And you didn't have to kill her."

"I am sorry," said Nguyen. He walked behind Hennessy and bolted the bedroom door. "Please sit in the chair." He pointed with the gun at a pink armchair in a corner away from the window. The curtains were closed but Nguyen didn't want shadows to be seen by the men in the courtyard below. Hennessy stood up and slowly lowered himself into the chair. From where he was sitting he could see Jackie's head, her eyes nothing more than milky orbs, her tongue hanging grotesquely from the side of her mouth.

"Can I cover her?" he asked Nguyen. Nguyen took the dressing-gown from the hook on the back of the door and draped it over the dog's body.

"What is it you want?" asked Hennessy. He felt naked sitting in the chair wearing only his pyjamas.

"You must talk quietly," said Nguyen. He nodded down at the tube on his chest and held up the hand which was holding the wires. "This is a bomb, the same type I used to destroy the car. If anyone comes into this room all I do is put the wires together. Then we all die." He held up the gun. "And I have this. If we talk quietly nobody will hear us. Do you understand."

"Yes," sighed Hennessy. "I understand. But what do you want to talk about?"

"The names. I want the names."

"I cannot help you."

"You know that I am serious. You have seen what I can do."

"Yes." Hennessy looked down at the dead dog. "Yes, I know now what you can do."

"So you know that I can kill you? That I will kill you?"

"Killing me will make no difference, no difference at all. You see, I have absolutely no idea who is behind the London bombings."

Nguyen looked confused. "They are in the IRA?"

"Maybe."

"I do not understand."

Hennessy sighed because deep down he didn't understand either. "I'll try to explain," he said. "They're saying that they are in the IRA, but I don't know who they are. Nobody in the official IRA knows who they are. You must believe me, we don't want to kill innocent citizens. I'm doing everything I can to find out who's responsible."

Nguyen walked from the wardrobe to the end of the bed and sat down, facing Hennessy. Hennessy could see light glistening on the sweat that covered the man's hands. The wires that would set off the lethal package were less than two inches apart. Nguyen saw him looking at the wires and smiled. "Do not worry," he said. "It will only explode if I want it to explode."

"Killing me won't get your family back," said Hennessy quietly.

"I do not want to kill you, Mr Hennessy. But I cannot allow the men to be unpunished."

"This is getting us nowhere," sighed Hennessy.

"The explosives the men use. Do they make their own?"

Hennessy shook his head. "They've been using our explosives. We have it stored in several places in Britain. It looks as if they've been stealing it."

"Semtex?"

"Yes."

"Which sort? Semtex-H?"

"Yes."

"It would be," said Nguyen. "Everything moves in circles."

"You know about Semtex?"

Nguyen smiled tightly. "I know about Semtex-H," he said. "Hexagen is added, that is where the H comes from. Very stable explosive, but very powerful, more powerful than TNT."

Hennessy's mouth dropped open. "How come you know so much about Semtex-H?"

"I use many times in Vietnam."

"In Vietnam?"

"You do not know your history, Mr Hennessy. Semtex-H was made for the Vietnamese during the war. It is our explosive. They made it for us, the Chax."

"Czechs, you mean. It was made in Czechoslovakia."

"Yes. The Czechs. They made it. Before, when the French were in Vietnam, then we used a French plastic explosive. When the French left we asked the Czechs to make same style for us. They made Semtex-H. Very good for making bombs and for traps. Many Americans were killed by Semtex-H. Now the IRA uses it to kill my family. That is, how do you say, ionic."

"Ironic," said Hennessy. "The word is ironic."

"Yes, it is ironic. Vietnamese explosive kills Vietnamese family."

"I am sorry about what happened to your family. But it is not my fault."

Nguyen pointed the gun at Hennessy's throat. "You will tell me who killed my family. You will tell me or you will die. And when you are dead I will go and ask someone else. I will find out eventually." He said the words in a cold, flat voice and Hennessy knew that he meant it. The gun was cocked and ready to fire and he saw Nguyen's finger tighten on the trigger. Hennessy held up his hands as if trying to ward off the bullet.

"No!" he said.

"Then tell me," hissed Nguyen.

"I don't know," said Hennessy.

"Then die," said Nguyen.

Hennessy turned his head away, his eyes tightly shut. "I don't know but I'm trying to find out," he said, his voice shaking with fear.

"What do you mean?"

"I've set a trap for them. If it works I'll know who they are."

"When will you know?"

Hennessy stopped flinching from the gun, sensing that Nguyen was taking him seriously. Perhaps he had a chance after all. "When the next bomb goes off."

"What is your plan?"

"When they claim responsibility for the bomb they give a codeword that tells the police that they are with the IRA. I have changed the codeword and the one that they use will tell me who has been helping them."

"And then what?"

"We'll give their names to the police. And they will end it."

Nguyen thought about what Hennessy had told him, but the gun never wavered. Eventually he nodded to himself as if he had come to a decision.

"Very well," he said. "I will give you three days. In three days I will come back. But if you do not have the names by then, I will kill you."

"But what if they haven't set off a bomb by then?" protested Hennessy.

"That is your problem," said Nguyen.

"That's not fair!" protested Hennessy.

"Fair? Nothing that has happened so far has been fair, Mr Hennessy." Nguyen stood up and backed to the door. He reached for the light switch and plunged the room into darkness.

"Why are you doing this?" Hennessy asked quietly.

"You killed my family."

"There's something else. Something you're not telling me."

Nguyen moved silently to the window and pulled back one of the curtains. There were only two men in the courtyard below. One was carrying two fire extinguishers, the other was rolling up a hosepipe. He heard the back door of the farmhouse slam shut. The two men in the courtyard walked over to the cottage and Nguyen let the curtain swing back into place.

"I mean, I've lost relatives in the Troubles, my own brother-in-law was killed not so long ago. Almost everyone I know has had someone they know killed or maimed, but I've never met anyone who has taken it so . . . so personally . . . as you have."

"Perhaps if you did take it personally, the war in Ireland would not have dragged on for so long."

"What do you mean?"

"What are you fighting for?"

"To get the British out of Ireland. To be allowed to live our own lives without prejudice or persecution."

"So why do your people not take up arms against the British and drive them from the country?"

"Many do."

"But not enough. Not enough people care. Not enough take it personally. The Vietnamese fought the French until they left the country. And the Communists fought the Americans and the army of the South until the Americans left. They won because the desire to be one country was stronger than anything else. It seems to me that you will never force the British to leave Ireland. Not enough people care. You play at war."

"And you? Why are you doing this?"

Nguyen ignored him. He put his ear to the door and listened. He heard nothing. He turned to Hennessy. "I will go now. Do not shout, I still have the bomb and I will kill anyone who comes after me. I will be back in three days." He slipped the bolt back and opened the door, looked left and right down the corridor before easing himself out of the bedroom, keeping close to the wall. He went silently to the bathroom and put the gun in the rucksack and disconnected the wires before he stepped on to the toilet and climbed out of the window. He held the drainpipe and shinned down, taking care not to scrape his feet against the wall. When he reached the ground he pressed himself against the wall and checked out his surroundings. There was a lingering smell of burnt wood and scorched metal in the courtyard but there was no sound. He crept between the cars, keeping low, and made his way to the stables. Inside he heard the horses snorting and he wondered if they could sense that he was there. He heard footsteps by the cottage so he moved in the opposite direction and left the courtyard between the stables and the far end of the farmhouse.

Hennessy sat in the bedroom, slumped forward with his head in his hands. Part of him wanted to sound the alarm immediately but he knew that The Chinaman had meant what he'd said. He would use the gun and if that failed he would set off the bomb killing God knows how many. He gave him five minutes then switched on the light and went down to get Kavanagh who was stretched out on a sofa in the lounge. By the time Kavanagh had gone out to warn the men on guard duty Nguyen was long gone, slithering through the grass as silently as a snake.

O'Reilly caught the 10.33 a.m. train from Waterloo station and found himself a seat towards the front in a carriage full of men in morning suits and women in long dresses and expensive hats. Two of the couples in his compartment were obviously travelling together and one of the men had produced a bottle of champagne and four glasses and made a big show of opening it. Champagne sprayed out and as the man held it to one side it splashed over O'Reilly's aluminium camera case.

"Sorry old man," said the racegoer.

"No problem," said O'Reilly. He looked out of the window as the train pulled out of the station. Ascot was forty minutes away so he settled back in his seat and let his mind drift. In the inside pocket of his blazer was a badge to get him into the Members' Enclosure, which he'd bought from a ticket agency a week earlier. He'd wanted to get in on Ladies Day but hadn't been able to get a ticket for Thursday and had settled for Tuesday instead. Tuesday or Thursday, it didn't really matter, because a successful bombing at Royal Ascot would be news around the world.

The camera case at his feet was the sort professionals used to carry their equipment, about two-feet long, a foot wide and eighteen-inches deep, with a thick nylon carrying strap. The Bombmaker had stripped out the lining of the case and fitted slabs of Semtex, ten pounds in all, around the sides and the bottom. There were two detonators, each connected to a single timer made from a small electronic travel alarm. The alarm had been set for 2 p.m. and the bomb was armed. O'Reilly was tense but not over-anxious. He'd carried live bombs before and he had complete faith in The Bombmaker. The lining had been replaced over the explosive with alterations made where necessary, and it now contained two camera bodies, a selection of lenses, a light meter and boxes of film. Around his neck was a Nikon with a telephoto lens and a pair of binoculars in a leather case. Attached to the binoculars were a dozen or so badges from earlier race meetings and that, and the trilby hat, marked O'Reilly out as a regular racegoer and not just a social butterfly hoping for a glimpse of a famous face at Royal Ascot.

The train arrived at Ascot station at 11.15 a.m. and O'Reilly joined the crowds flocking to the racecourse. There were plenty of police around but most of them were wearing yellow reflective jackets and were directing traffic with bored faces and aching arms. O'Reilly stood with a group waiting to cross the road. A middle-aged man in a morning suit saw a gap in the traffic and started to cross but a young constable in the middle of the road shouted at him to get back. "Bollocks," muttered the man in the morning suit. He looked to be twice as old as the constable, a roughly hewn face and shoulders that strained at his jacket.

The policeman motioned at the traffic to keep moving and walked over to the man. "Have you got a problem?" he asked, jutting his head forward, his cheeks reddening. He had a thin moustache and the manner of an adolescent with something to prove.

"I think I'm old enough to cross the road on my own," said the man with barely restrained anger. He looked like a man more than capable of looking after himself in a fight and O'Reilly knew he'd be able to handle the copper with one hand.

"That's not what I asked you. I want to know what you said." He was glaring at the man, his teeth clenched together and a vein was pulsing on the side of his forehead. O'Reilly wondered what his problem was because his reaction was out of all proportion to what the man had said.

"Nothing," said the man through tight lips. "I didn't say anything."

The policeman stared hard at the man for several seconds and then nodded slowly as if satisfied. "Good," he said, then walked back into the road and continued directing traffic. The racegoer got a few sympathetic glances from pedestrians around him and he shook his head, exasperated. The Great British Bobby, thought O'Reilly. An angry young man with authority he couldn't handle. It was something he'd grown up with in Ireland, where the Protestant police and the teenage British soldiers would exercise the power of their uniform just for the hell of it, just to feel good. He was used to being stopped on the street and given a hard time from RUC officers who didn't say "sir" and didn't bother to keep their contempt out of their voices, and even as a schoolboy he'd been thrown against walls and roughly searched by gum-chewing soldiers in camouflage jackets. The abuse of authority was nothing new to O'Reilly, and it was with no small feeling of satisfaction that he now saw it spilling over to Britain.

Eventually the policeman held up his hand to stop the traffic and allowed them to cross. He seemed to be glaring at them all, as if blaming them for having to stand in the road.

Despite the strong police presence – there seemed to be hundreds organising the flow of coaches and cars into the carparks around the racecourse – O'Reilly saw no sniffer dogs at the entrance. There were two policemen there but they seemed to be more concerned about eyeing up two pretty blondes in white, figure-hugging dresses and floppy hats. The girls were twins, barely in their twenties, tanned and draped in gold. One of the policemen smiled and touched his helmet in salute. The girls smiled and giggled, and one of them looked back over her shoulder as they walked towards the grandstand.

A steward in a bowler hat squinted at O'Reilly's badge and waved him through the gate and then another steward who looked about seventy years old asked if he'd mind opening up his case. The police stood watching the twins, their long, lithe legs moving with the grace of thoroughbred racehorses.

"Security, you understand," said the old man apologetically.

A couple of middle-aged women in tweed suits were looking into handbags but the checks were nothing more than a cursory glance. O'Reilly wondered what the hell they expected to find – a black ball with "BOMB" written on it and a burning fuse maybe. The steward in front of O'Reilly rubbed his moustache and smiled and O'Reilly smiled back and put the case on the grass and clicked it open. The old man peered inside.

"Nice equipment," he said approvingly. He looked up at O'Reilly with watery eyes. "I do a bit of photography myself."

"It's a great hobby," said O'Reilly. He took out one of the camera bodies and showed it to the old man. "I always use Nikon," he said. "What about you?"

The man looked pleased about being asked his opinion. "Canon," he said. He handed the Nikon back to O'Reilly. "Enjoy yourself today," he said.

"Got any tips?" asked O'Reilly. He stashed the camera body away, and as an afterthought took the other Nikon from around his neck and put that away, too. He grunted as he picked up the case and slung its strap over his shoulder.

"You could do worse than back Eddery in the third," said the steward. Pity, thought O'Reilly, who wasn't planning to be around for the third race. In fact if everything went the way Fisher had planned it, there wouldn't be a third race.

He bought a race card and walked for a while among the crowds, listening to the plummy voices and girlish giggles. The idle rich at play, he thought. Who else could afford to walk around in thousands of pounds' worth of high fashion and jewellery in the middle of the week? Champagne corks were popping everywhere, and everyone he looked at had the glint of gold on their wrist or around their neck. Some of the women were simply stunning, like the coltish blonde twins he'd seen at the gate, but in the main they were overdressed, overweight and wore too much make-up. They stood in groups, eyeing up the competition, reading the price tags on their outfits every bit as easily as they identified the brand names. They looked fearful, thought O'Reilly. Fearful of what they might lose.

He took his place in the grandstand and scanned the crowds through his binoculars. He spotted a couple of minor starlets who were wearing considerably more than they did in their movies, and several captains of industry who presumably had nothing better to do at the office. There was minor royalty around, too, but he couldn't see any of the heavyweights. He wondered what the chances would be of catching one with the blast but knew that the likelihood was remote. Not that it mattered, the fact that a bomb went off at an occasion attended by the Royal family would be more than enough to guarantee worldwide coverage. He checked out the positions of the television cameras, which were there to cover the crowds as much as the horses. They'd have no problems recording the explosion and its aftermath.

He studied the race card for a while, though he didn't plan on placing any bets. The steward had been right, though, Eddery did look a sure thing in the third race. O'Reilly looked at his watch. Half past one. The aluminium case was under his legs, silently counting off the seconds. Part of him wanted to go now, to get as far away as possible from the bomb before the alarm clock completed the circuit, but he knew that if he left it unattended for any length of time there was a risk that it might be discovered. Fisher had been quite specific about the timing, and, besides, McCormick wouldn't be outside until exactly five minutes before two. He re-read the race card and surveyed the crowds again, anything to keep his mind off the bomb. Once or twice he found himself eaves-dropping on the chatter going on around him but he stopped himself and blocked out the conversations. His neighbours in the stand would be at the centre of the explosion and he didn't want to know anything about them. He didn't want it to be personal.

The minute hand on his watch gradually crept around to ten to the hour and he stood up, stretched, and lifted his case on to the seat. He took off his hat and placed it on top of the case and then moved himself along the row to the aisle, apologising all the way and looking for all the world as if he was on a pre-race visit to the toilet or the Tote. He walked up the aisle, passed the bar and took an escalator down to the ground floor. He slowed down and ambled across the grass to the pre-arranged exit, some way along from where he'd come in so that he wouldn't be recognised by the stewards. The pavements outside were still thronged with racegoers waiting to get in and he pushed through, smiling apologetically.

The green and white Yamaha 750 purred up to the kerb. McCormick was wearing black leathers and had on a white helmet with a tinted visor. A second helmet was attached to the side of the bike and McCormick unclipped it and handed it to O'Reilly. He put it on and fastened the strap under his chin as he slipped on to the seat and found the foot rests. McCormick clicked the bike into gear and drove off towards London. The roads away from Ascot were clear but he stuck to the speed-limit because there were so many police around. Even so, they were still four miles away from the racecourse when the bomb exploded.

Woody was in the office early so that he could hit the phones before Simpson and the rest of the news desk staff arrived. He wasn't surprised that he couldn't get through to Sir John Brownlow himself because the *Sunday World* didn't usually get to the top of the lists of calls to be returned by Members of Parliament. Woody's luck was in, though, because he did get to speak to Sir John's assistant, a pleasant-sounding girl called Ellen. She remembered The Chinaman coming to see her boss, but like Woody couldn't remember his name. He told her that the family name was probably Nguyen and she went off to check the MP's correspondence files. A few minutes later she was back on the line.

"His name's Nguyen Ngoc Minh," she said. "I've got his letter here." She read out the address on the letter and Woody checked it against the address of the Double Happiness Take-Away. They matched. He asked Ellen to spell out Nguyen's full name and he wrote it down in his notebook and then he asked her to read the letter out to him. It was pretty much the same story that he'd told when he visited the *Sunday World*'s office, and there didn't appear to be any information in the letter that would help Woody track him down.

"Can you remember anything else about this Chinaman?" Woody asked. "Anything at all?"

"Well for a start, he isn't Chinese," said Ellen. "He was Vietnamese, that's what he told Sir John. I can't remember if he said he was from the north or the south, but I certainly got the impression he was a refugee. You know, one of the boat people. He has full British citizenship."

"Anything else?"

"I'm sorry, that's all I can remember," she said. "Wait a minute, I've just had a thought. Why don't you try the Home Office?"

"The Home Office?"

"Sure. If he was a refugee then they'd have to have a file on him. It wouldn't matter if he was Chinese or Vietnamese or whatever. There's a hell of a lot of paperwork to go through to get citizenship."

Woody thanked her gratefully and flicked through his contacts book. He'd met a Government Information Officer who worked in the Home Office some years earlier when he'd been chasing up a story on immigration and he'd taken her for a couple of boozy lunches afterwards to thank her. He couldn't recall her name but he'd filed her under "Home Office" in his book. Annie Byrne. She wasn't there when he called but he left a message and he passed the time reading the morning papers and drinking coffee until she called back.

"Woody, long time no hear," she said. She seemed genuinely pleased to hear from him and Woody tried to remember why he hadn't kept in touch with her. He explained that he was trying to get information on a refugee but skipped over the IRA connection. Was there any way that he could get to see the man's file?

"Certainly not officially, no," she said. But she suggested that Woody came round to her office at lunchtime anyway, which Woody took as a good sign.

While Woody was on the phone the news desk drifted in one by one and when he hung up Simpson waved him over.

"You're in early, Woody," he said. "Got much on?"

"A couple of things. I'll let you know when they harden up."

"OK, I've got something here that needs knocking out, something worthy of your talents."

Woody sensed a trap.

"Don't look so nervous, Woody. You're gonna love it. I want you to give me fifty places where you can take the kids over the summer holidays. You know, a guide for the little horrors that the parents can cut out and keep."

"Thanks, mate."

"Come on, Woody, cheer up. A shift is a shift, it's all money in the end."

"Yeah, yeah, yeah," said Woody, and slouched back to his desk.

He left the office just before noon and took the Tube to St James's Park. He'd assumed that Annie was just after a lunchtime drink and a chance to catch up on Fleet Street gossip so he was pleasantly surprised to be shown into her office. She was a short, bouncy girl and she shook him firmly by the hand. She spoke like a head girl and laughed a lot and Woody wondered how long it would be before she was snapped up by one of the Civil Service high-flyers and installed in a country house where she'd breed children and horses. She was a very attractive girl but Woody remembered why he'd never tried to see more of her. She was, he realised ruefully, totally out of his league.

There was a blue cardboard file on her desk and she tapped it with her left hand. An engagement ring glinted under the lights. It was a big diamond. The girl had done well. "Nguyen Ngoc Minh," she said. "I tell you, Woody, this is one damned interesting file. It's just a pity that I can't let you see it. Home Office regulations, you understand. It'd be more than my job's worth. And you know how much my job means to me." She grinned and then looked at her watch. "Golly, is that the time. Look, Woody, I've got a meeting to go to. Can you amuse yourself for a while? I'll be gone for about half an hour. OK?"

"OK. Do you want me to wait outside?"

Annie walked around her desk and patted him on the shoulder as she headed for the door. "No, Woody, you stay where you are. I'll be back."

She closed the door behind her and Woody leant over and picked up the file. It wasn't the first time a civil servant or a police officer had shared information by leaving an open file on a desk, and Woody was sure it wouldn't be the last. At some point in the future he knew Annie would call in the favour. Besides, she'd already read through the file to check that it contained nothing secret or damaging to the Government. He opened it and began leafing through a sheaf of forms and written reports with a growing sense of wonder.

There were reports from the United Nations High Commissioner for Refugees in Hong Kong and from the Hong Kong Government's Security Branch, documents from the US Consulate, photocopies of service records and signed statements from senior American army officers detailing Nguyen's time with the US forces. One of the sheets was a photocopy of the inside of a British passport with Nguyen's photograph and there were photocopies of two awards made to his unit in Vietnam. There was a Meritorious Unit Commendation and a Republic of Vietnam Gallantry Cross Unit Citation, along with a memo from a US colonel recording the fact that Nguyen's unit had the highest body count in Vietnam during the first half of 1973. By the time he'd finished reading the file he was shaking his head in amazement. The man was a bloody war hero, a trained assassin and an expert in jungle warfare.

He went back through the papers, filling his notebook with dates and copying down quotes from the reports. God, it was good stuff. Amazing. The story in the file was award-winning copy in itself. If Nguyen really was after the IRA, it would be dynamite.

It was a very thick file, sheet after sheet. Even in the early eighties, when Nguyen was in a refugee camp in Hong Kong, all incoming Vietnamese boat people were given a thorough grilling to check that they weren't Communist spies or simply criminals on the run. Nguyen Ngoc Minh's story was so complicated, and, Woody had to admit, so frankly unbelievable, that he was interviewed many times. Officials from the UNHCR and the Hong Kong Government's Security Branch had gone over his story again and again, cross-checking and cross-referencing in an attempt to catch him out, until eventually they believed him.

Woody flicked through the file, taking down details of Nguyen's switch to the South Vietnamese and his time with the Long Range Reconnaissance Patrols. The fact that Nguyen had been left behind by the Americans and his time in prison and the re-education camp were detailed in the matter-of-fact reports. Woody could only imagine the horrors the man had endured before he'd finally managed to escape. There were few details of the actual journey to Hong Kong, though it was clear that two of his daughters had died. Nguyen had refused to expand on what had happened and the psychiatrist reckoned that Nguyen was trying to block out painful memories.

Woody wrote quickly. By the time Annie returned to the office the file was back on her desk and Woody was sitting reading through his notes.

"Sorry about that," she said.

"No problem," he smiled.

"I hope you weren't too bored. Right, come on, you can buy me lunch."

Morrison and Kerry arrived at Belfast airport late in the afternoon. Willie O'Hara was there to meet them with the Range

Rover. Morrison got in the front passenger seat while Kerry climbed in the back. She noticed a large black stain on the seat and O'Hara explained that they'd used the car to take Jimmy McMahon to the hospital.

"How is he?" Morrison asked.

"On the mend, thank God. If the bomb had gone off a second later it would've taken his legs off. But it looks as if he's going to be OK. This focking Chinaman is bad news, I can tell you. He was at it again last night."

"He was?"

"Yeah, he set fire to one of the barns. And killed Hennessy's dog."

Kerry leant over the seat. "Jackie? He killed Jackie?"

O'Hara nodded. "Slit its throat."

Kerry slumped back into the seat, her hand over her mouth. To Morrison it seemed that she was more upset about the dead dog than about the man in hospital. They drove in silence down the M2 towards the city. When they passed the ferry terminal Kerry leant forward again. "I'm going to need some things. Can we drive into the city?"

"Yeah, good thinking," said Morrison. O'Hara turned off the motorway and guided the car through central Belfast. They had to pull to one side when a fire engine came up behind, lights flashing and siren blaring. In its wake followed two armoured RUC Land-Rovers. They parked the car and walked to a shopping centre, a pedestrian road sealed off with a metal fence at either end. To get in they had to pass through a turnstile and two surly RUC officers checked through Kerry's handbag and body-searched Morrison and O'Hara. Kerry had said she wanted to go to a sports shop, the sort that sold skiing equipment, and O'Hara took her to one that he knew of.

"I've got to be honest, Kerry, but you're not likely to see much in the way of snow in County Down at this time of the year," said Morrison as she examined a selection of ski-poles. She took one from the rack and held it, feeling its weight. She wasn't satisfied and replaced it with another, slightly longer, version.

"We'll need tracking sticks," she explained. "Walking

sticks will do but ski-poles are the best. You can use them for moving vegetation, and they stop you getting tired. Choose one for yourself, pick one that feels sturdy but not too heavy. This one's fine for me."

Morrison followed her advice while she went over to a display of American baseball caps. When he caught up with her she was looking at herself in the mirror, a blue cap on her head.

"Cute," he said.

"You'll need a hat to shade your eyes from the sun. It makes it easier to follow tracks in bright sunlight. You should get one."

"Whatever you say, Tonto."

By the time he'd found a cap that fitted she was looking at a black squash racket. "Don't tell me," he said, "you use it for filtering soil looking for clues."

She laughed and shook her head. She put the racket back on its stand. "Come on. That's all we need from here. Unless you want to stock up on ski masks for the boys."

Morrison paid for the purchases and followed her out of the shop. "Anything else?" he asked.

She nodded. "Elastic bands, a tape measure, couple of notebooks and pens. And torches."

"I won't ask," he said.

When they'd bought everything that Kerry wanted they went back to the car and continued their journey south.

Fisher and McCormick sat on the leather Chesterfield watching the television. O'Reilly was on the balcony, sunbathing. They each had a can of Guinness and McCormick was smoking. The news came on and the Ascot bombing was the first item. Eight people died, the newsreader said, and fifteen were injured, six of them seriously. McCormick whooped and O'Reilly came inside to watch. There were shots of the dead and injured being carried to ambulances and a shot taken from a helicopter giving a bird's eye view of the damage to the grandstand. Fisher and McCormick clunked their cans together and then both did the same with O'Reilly.

"Great crack," said Fisher. "Those pictures will go around the world."

A senior policeman with a suitably dour expression was being interviewed. The IRA had not claimed responsibility, he said, but there were similarities between this bombing and the previous attacks.

"Yeah," said O'Reilly. "When do we make the call?"

"You can do it now," said Fisher. "But this time don't give a codeword. Just tell them that it was an active service unit of the Provisional IRA, and tell them where and when the bomb was planted. You can also say how much explosive it contained."

"Ten pounds," said The Bombmaker, who was sitting at the dining-table, probing into the laptop computer with a voltmeter.

"Tell them ten pounds of Semtex," said Fisher. "And tell them there will be more bombings until the British Government withdraws its armed forces from Ulster. They'll believe you."

O'Reilly frowned. "Why aren't we using the codeword?"

Fisher waved his can of Guinness in the air. "Change of strategy," he said. "I had a phone call from Ireland while you were out. No codewords from now on."

"Did they say why?"

"Does it matter?" asked Fisher.

O'Reilly grinned. "Not really." He picked up the London street atlas. "Where shall I make the call from this time? How about Barking? I've never been to Barking."

Fisher shook his head. "There are times, O'Reilly, when I wonder if you're quite right in the head."

Hennessy heard the Range Rover crunching down the track and went to the front door to meet it. He was too late, the car had gone round the back to park in the courtyard so he went back through the house and out of the kitchen door. By the time he reached the car Kerry had already got out. She rushed up to him and hugged him.

"Uncle Liam," she said, holding him tightly.

"Kerry, thanks for coming." Over her shoulder he greeted Morrison. "Was your flight OK?" he asked Kerry.

She released him from the hug and stood back, still holding his shoulders. "Uncle Liam, I'm so sorry about Jackie. She was a lovely dog."

"She was that," agreed Hennessy. He'd buried Jackie himself in a patch of rough ground just beyond the vegetable garden. He helped Kerry in with her bag while Morrison carried his own and O'Hara held the ski-poles. Morrison saw the curious look that Hennessy gave the poles and he shrugged. "Don't ask," he said.

Hennessy took Kerry up and showed her the bedroom he'd prepared for her. She'd stayed there many times, especially when she was a teenager. It was a small, pretty room, with pink curtains and pine furniture. She put her case at the foot of the bed and looked out of the tiny window. "Is Auntie Mary here?" she asked.

"No, she's gone to visit Marie in London."

"That's a pity," she said.

"We thought it best. Why don't you freshen up and join Sean and me downstairs," said Hennessy. "I've put some clean towels in the bathroom for you. And you know where everything is."

He went downstairs. Morrison had put his bag in the lounge. "There's a bedroom upstairs ready for you, Sean," Hennessy told him. "Second on the left at the head of the stairs, when you're ready."

"Great, thanks, Liam."

"You know there's been another bombing?"

"Yeah, Willie said on the way in. Blew up your barn, he said."

Hennessy sat down. "No, I mean another bombing on the mainland. At Ascot. Today. Eight killed."

"Has Bromley phoned?" Morrison asked, dropping into an easy chair opposite Hennessy.

Hennessy shook his head. "Not yet."

"I wonder what he's playing at."

"He definitely said he'd go for it?"

"No question about it."

"Then we just have to wait."

"Yeah. I gather The Chinaman was in the house last night. Willie said he was in your room with a bomb."

"Unbelievable, isn't it. Got in and out of the house without anyone seeing him."

"So the fire in the barn was a diversion?"

"I think so, right enough. He said he wanted to talk."

"And?"

"And he's given me three days to find out who's behind the bombings. Then he's going to kill me." The dispassionate way Hennessy described the threat belied his true feelings. "Do you want a drink?"

Morrison shook his head. "No, Kerry says she wants to have a look around while the light is still good. I'd better keep a clear head."

Kerry appeared at the door and the two men got to their feet. She'd changed into jeans and a dark-blue sweatshirt. "You're starting already?" asked Hennessy. "Are you sure you don't want a bite to eat?"

"It's the light, Uncle Liam. The best times to see tracks are early in the morning and late in the afternoon. It's to do with the angle of the sun and the shadows it casts. We've only got an hour or so. Is there someone who can show me where they saw him?"

"Jim Kavanagh knows where the car bomb was triggered. And he can show you where one of our men was attacked."

"Right," she said, rubbing her hands together, "let's get started. Sean, where are the poles and stuff?"

"Willie put them in the kitchen."

"Come on then." She led the way to the kitchen leaving Hennessy and Morrison smiling at each other.

"Looks like she's taken charge," said Hennessy. "I think you might have to watch yourself there."

They walked into the kitchen to find Kerry putting the two poles on the table. She slipped off the discs from the end of each of the poles, the bits that stopped the poles from sinking too deep into the snow. "I forgot to get some binoculars, do you have some?" she asked Hennessy, and he produced a pair in an old leather case from the hall. She opened the case and slotted in a notebook and pencil and the tape measure. She took one of the torches and handed the other, and a notebook and pencil, to Morrison. "Right," she said. "Let's go."

Morrison found Kavanagh at the front of the house and he asked him to show them where The Chinaman had been when the bomb had destroyed the Jaguar. Of the Jaguar there was now no sign, Ryan had towed the wreckage away with one of the tractors and put it in one of the barns, away from the prying eyes of army patrols and low-flying helicopters. The crater had been filled in with soil but was still obvious, like a gaping wound.

"Your hat," said Kerry, holding it out to Morrison as they walked down the track. He took it and put it on.

"Cute," she said.

"That's not a word we normally use to describe Sean Morrison," said Kavanagh, grinning. "But yez right, he does look cute."

"Thanks guys," said Morrison dryly. "Can we just get on with the business at hand."

Kavanagh took them up to the filled-in crater and then led them through the grass. It was trampled down in many places and even to Morrison's untutored eyes it was obvious that a number of men had been there, presumably chasing The Chinaman. Morrison couldn't stop thinking of Nguyen as The Chinaman, even though he knew he was from Vietnam.

"We found a battery here," said Kavanagh, indicating a flattened-down area. "And it's where the wires ended. He lay here until he saw that the car was over the bomb, detonated it, and then ran that way." He pointed towards the hedgerow.

"Ran?" asked Kerry. "You saw him?"

"Well, crawled, I suppose. We didn't see him, not then, but we were too busy trying to get Jimmy out of the wreckage. We saw the wires and guessed that he'd gone that way."

"Where did you first see him?"

"I didn't. We saw some tracks leading to that copse," he

pointed again, "but we didn't know if he'd gone into the trees or run by and gone through the fields. We split up, I went that way, three of the men went into the woods. He attacked one of them and stole his gun, the other two saw him running away, then they lost him again."

"OK, show me which way he went."

Kavanagh led the way, following the trampled grass to the hedge and showing her where the gap was. She examined the broken twigs and the mud by the hedge's roots. "It looks like an army went this way," she said. "They've obliterated any tracks there might have been."

"Hey, we were chasing the bastard, not tracking him!" said Kavanagh angrily. "We'd just seen Jimmy get blown apart, we weren't too concerned about where we were putting our feet."

Morrison put his hand on Kavanagh's shoulder. "OK, Jim, cool down. She wasn't getting at you, she's just trying to help."

"I only meant that it's easier when there's one set of tracks, Jim," she said.

Kavanagh shrugged off Morrison's hand. "Yeah, OK, I'm sorry I snapped at yez. We're all under a lot of pressure, and we didn't get a lot of sleep last night."

"Forget it," said Morrison. "Show us which way he went."

Kavanagh took them through another field, towards the copse he'd pointed at earlier. "I went that way, but three of the men went in to check out the woods." He pushed through some waist-high bushes until they were standing on a pathway that wound through the trees. "The way they tell it, the three of them split up, and one of them, the one that got stabbed, went down the path."

Kerry knelt down and looked at the ground. It was criss-crossed with a multitude of footprints, but she said nothing.

"Where was he stabbed?" asked Morrison.

"In the leg," answered Kavanagh.

Morrison laughed sharply. "I meant where in the woods was he attacked."

"Oh right, I see what yez mean. This way." He took them along the path and showed them. The soil had been flattened and there was a rusty discoloration. Dried blood, Morrison realised.

"Right," said Kerry. "Can you two gentlemen please get the hell off the path?"

Morrison and Kavanagh stepped to one side while she scrutinised the tracks. She walked back down the path a few paces and then squatted down and squinted, moving her head from side to side as she scrutinised the footprints and the place where the man had lain on the ground. She switched on her torch and shone it along the path, altering its angle as she played the light over the soil.

"Any good?" asked Morrison.

She shook her head and stood up. "What happened then?" she asked Kavanagh.

He nodded down the path. "He went that way. One of the others saw him and fired a couple of shots but didn't hear anything. They chased him down the path until one of them got caught in a trap."

"A trap?"

"A hole in the ground with small stakes in it. Smeared with shit, believe it or not."

"How far?"

"A hundred yards or so. But be careful, there could be others. Yez wouldn't want to put yez foot in one of them."

She motioned for them to stay where they were and went down the trail, prodding carefully in front of her with the stick. She came upon the trap and crouched down beside it. There were still too many footprints to be able to tell which belonged to The Chinaman. She continued along the path but found nothing to help her. She did find another trap, though, and she cleared the soil away from it so that nobody would step in it.

She went back to Kavanagh and Morrison and began examining the vegetation either side of the path, using the ski-pole to move brambles aside. "He must have hidden somewhere to have caught your man by surprise," she murmured. "Somewhere where he couldn't be seen but from where he could reach the path quickly – and quietly."

"What are you looking for?" asked Morrison.

"Bruised stems, broken twigs, pebbles that have been moved. It's hard to say, I'll know it when I see it. Problem is, he was here two days ago which means a lot of the traces will have gone. We're lucky that it hasn't rained, but the wind obliterates a lot of stuff and any soil he kicked up will have dried out long ago."

She bent down and looked at the brambles. "Come on, Chinaman, where were you hiding? Where would you feel safe?" She was talking to herself and Morrison could only half hear. She turned round and began searching the opposite side of the path. There was a large spreading oak tree and she scrutinised the brambles at its base.

"Sean, come and look at this."

He stood next to her and looked down at the tangle of thorny strands.

"What am I looking at?" he asked.

She pointed with the end of her pole. "See that bit there, see how it's stuck under that thorn?"

"Yes," he said hesitantly, not sure what she was getting at.

"See how it's under tension," she continued. "It's slightly distorted, it's been pushed into that position and the prickles on that bit are holding it down."

"Which means what?"

She sighed and gave him a withering look. "It means, Sean, that something, or somebody, pushed it into that position. Watch." She used the ski-pole to push the bent strand and it sprang free and wavered in the air like the antenna of a huge insect. Kerry began pushing more of the brambles to the side. "Help me, Sean," she said.

Together they cleared a section of the undergrowth away from the earth. "There! See?" she said. There were two smudges in the soil. "He was walking on the balls of his feet." She held the torch down and shone the light at an angle to the impressions, the shadows highlighting the marks.

"Yes, I see it now. God, you're right. He must have been hiding behind the tree, and attacked our man from behind."

"Come on, we'll go round the tree in the opposite direction, see if there are any better footprints there."

She and Morrison pushed the brambles apart and followed

the curve of the tree around. She found the crack in the trunk and moved aside to show Morrison. In the soft earth were clear signs that The Chinaman had waited there, a number of footprints and a circular indentation which Kerry explained was probably made by his knee. She showed him places on the trunk where he had leaned against it and scraped away parts of the lichen on the bark. She pointed at the best example of a print with her pole. "Now we use our notebooks," she said, opening the binoculars case. She took out her notebook and pencil and with painstaking concentration made a drawing of the print, using the tape measure to ensure that it was an exact copy. She watched as Morrison did the same, correcting him over the shape of the heel of the boot and the pattern of the sole. "We do this so that we'll always know from now on if it's his footprint that we're looking at," she explained. "And when we've finished this we'll draw a print of him walking on the ball of his foot."

When they'd finished the drawings to Kerry's satisfaction, she took the two men along the edge of the path, following the prints of running men past the two exposed traps. After a hundred yards or so the trees thinned out and they were standing in a large field, lush, green grass peppered with daisies and dandelions.

"Question now is which way did he go when he left the woods?" she mused. She pulled the peak of her cap down and scanned the horizon. "Come on, Chinaman, which way would you go? You'd be pretty exposed crossing the field wouldn't you, even if you waited until it was dark. So you'd look for cover, wouldn't you?" She turned to Kavanagh. "Did your men go after him, across the field?"

"No, we reckoned he went to ground somewhere in the copse, but we couldn't find him. We didn't have enough men."

"And were there any animals in the field?"

Kavanagh scratched his head. "I don't think so."

Kerry dropped down low and scanned the field, moving her head slowly but keeping her eyes fixed ahead.

"What are you doing?" Morrison asked curiously. She kept turning her head left and right as she answered. "Changes in colour," she said. "Easier to spot when your eyes are moving. If he went through the grass he'd alter the way the blades lie. The underside of a blade of grass is a bit lighter than the part that faces the sun. You won't notice one or two but you can spot a trail through long grass. That's one of the ways we track deer. Trouble is the grass reorientates itself fairly quickly, just a few hours if it isn't too badly damaged. It depends how tall it is. This is quite long so it could take a while before it reverts to the way it was. Damn, I can't see anything. Come on, walk over here."

She took him a few paces to the left and tried again. She slapped her thigh in frustration. "Damn," she said. She stood up and arched her back, her hands on her hips. "The light's starting to go," she said. "Let me just check the edge of the wood and then we'll call it a day."

She began walking slowly along the perimeter of the copse with Kavanagh and Morrison following behind. She scrutinised the ground and the vegetation overhanging the grass. Several times she stopped and bent down to examine a fallen leaf or a twig, causing the two men to pull up short, but she found nothing to give an indication that The Chinaman had passed that way. Then, just as she was about to give up, she saw a large leaf that had been pressed into the ground. She picked it up and held it out to Morrison. "Yes!" she exclaimed. "See how it's bruised, how it's been crushed across the middle?" she said. "That's a sure sign that it's been trodden on." She turned it over. There were several grains of soil pressed into it. "See that? You can tell by the state the leaf's in that it happened within the last day or two. See how it's still fairly fresh?"

Morrison nodded. "But couldn't it have been an animal?"

"It would have had to have been a fairly large animal, I mean the bruising couldn't have been done by a rabbit or a fox. I reckon this is where The Chinaman came out of the wood. Now, did he go across the field, or did he walk along the edge to that hedgerow?" She scanned the field again with her strange fixed stare. "No, not that way," she murmured. She continued along the side of the copse, pushing straggling vegetation to the side with her pole.

"Got him!" she cried, and waved the two men to come and stand beside her. She grinned and pointed down. At some point in the past a tree stump had been poisoned to kill its roots and the earth for some distance around it was devoid of grass. There, in the soil, were two prints, a left foot and a right foot, less than a metre apart. She took her notebook out and compared the prints to her drawing. They matched.

She slipped two elastic bands on the ski-pole, twisting them around so that they gripped tightly, then held it above the two footprints, parallel to the ground and an inch or so above the soil. She put the tip of the pole above the back of the heel of the front print and slid one of the bands to mark the position of the tip of the toe of the rear print. Morrison watched her, enthralled. Kerry moved the pole so that it ran through the centre of the rear print and she slid the second elastic band down to mark the position corresponding to the rear of the heel, so marking the length of the stride. She stood up and showed her pole to Morrison. "Did you follow that?" she asked, and he nodded. "OK, you have a go then." She watched over his shoulder as he positioned two elastic bands on his own pole.

When he'd finished he got to his feet. "Do you want to tell me what we're doing?" he asked.

"Now we've got a record of the length of his stride, and the length of his footprint. And you can use the stick to get an idea of where the next footprint is when you're following a trail. I'll show you tomorrow."

"You didn't learn that following deer around the Highlands," said Morrison.

"I got it from a book," she said. "A guy called Jack Kearney wrote it. My dad has it in his collection."

"And where did he learn a trick like that?"

"He was a border guard in southern California. He spent more than twenty years hunting down Mexicans who tried to get into America illegally, and he used to help track down missing kids and the like. Come on, I just want to see which way he went when he got to the hedgerow. My bet is that he turned right and headed east." She was right. When she reached the hedge she followed it along and eventually discovered a footprint. "Look, let me show you how to use the stick," she said. She put the two elastic bands on either end of the print. It was a perfect fit. "You can see from the way the heel is slightly deeper than the sole that he was walking, rather than running. So if we put the toe marker on the front of the print, and swing the pole around in an arc, we know that the next print should be within the area it covers. There you are. See?"

Morrison looked and saw the rounded mark of a heel in the ground, not as clear as the first print but definitely there, nevertheless.

Further on the ground sloped sharply down. Kerry held up her hand to stop the two men and she spent a lot of time examining the slope.

"That's interesting," she said, indicating a bluebell that had been crushed against the grass.

"He went that way?" asked Morrison.

"Look at the way it's been trodden on," she said. She sat down on the grass next to it and Morrison joined her.

"I don't follow you," he said.

"The head of the bluebell is higher up the slope than the stalk. That means that whatever squashed it was moving up the slope, not down. If it was The Chinaman, he was coming this way, not going."

"You mean it would be the other way if he'd been going down the slope?"

"Think about it, Sean, picture a foot coming uphill. It'll push the stalk up. And a foot going down would push the stalk down."

"Was it definitely him?"

"Can't say for definite. The grass is too thick and springy, there are no marks in the soil. But if it is him, he's going back the same way he came, he's not just running away. He's returning somewhere." Kerry looked up at the darkening sky. "We might as well go back," she said. "We'll make an early start tomorrow." Morrison stood up and helped Kerry to her feet.

"Shouldn't we go on?" Kavanagh asked.

"We need a good light," she explained. "Otherwise we'll

miss something. We know which way he's headed now, we can pick his trail up at first light."

The three of them walked back to the farmhouse together. Hennessy was waiting for them in the kitchen. Sarah Ryan was there and she rushed over to hug Kerry and kiss her on both cheeks.

"Liam didn't tell me you were coming," she cried. Sarah was a couple of years younger than Kerry and when they were teenagers they had spent a lot of time together during the school holidays, riding and picnicking in the countryside around the farm.

'God, it's been so long," Kerry said.

"I've a few more wrinkles," laughed Sarah.

"Twenty-two years old and you talk about wrinkles, wait until you hit twenty-four!" They hugged each other again.

"Do you want some sandwiches and coffee?" Sarah asked, and Kerry and Morrison both said yes.

O'Hara came in from the hallway as Sarah busied herself with the food. "Any luck?" he asked.

"More than I would have thought possible," said Morrison, leaning his pole against the Welsh dresser next to Kerry's. He held out his notebook.

"Very good," said O'Hara. "By Sean Morrison, aged four."

"It's a drawing of his footprint, you prat," laughed Morrison. He handed it to Hennessy. "Kerry found the spot where he was hiding in the woods. And we think we know which way he went." He took off his baseball cap and dropped it on the table.

"Uncle Liam, do you have a map of the area? A large-scale one," asked Kerry.

"I think so," he said, and went through to the lounge. He returned with several maps including a large one rolled up in a cardboard tube. He popped it open and pulled it out and she helped him spread it over the kitchen table. Morrison used a cruet set to anchor it down at one side and Sarah gave them two knives to weigh down the other side.

Kerry sat down in front of the map while Morrison and Hennessy looked over her shoulder. She traced out the route they'd taken with her finger, down the track, across the field to the copse, around the edge of the trees and to the hedge-row. "We got as far as here," she said, tapping the map. "But the light was starting to go and I didn't want to make any mistakes. We'll start again first thing in the morning. The interesting thing was, Uncle Liam, there were signs that he was going back the way he'd come. As if he had a base some-where, you know what I mean?"

"That's a thought," said Hennessy. "He must be staying somewhere. I suppose I just assumed that he was living rough."

"What about the van?" said Kavanagh. "He'd need some-where to store the stuff he used to make his explosives. And the landlady in Belfast said he drove away in his van."

Kerry took one of the small-scale maps and spread it out on top of the first map. She drew a line on it in pencil. "This is the way he was heading," she said. The line cut across the B8 and B180 and through Dundrum Bay. "That's his general direction, so if we assume that wherever he was heading was twenty degrees or so either side of that line, we're left with this," she said, and drew two more lines either side of the original one, creating two wedge shapes.

"That's still a hell of a lot of countryside," said Kavanagh, unconvinced.

"Agreed, but he's not likely to be travelling too far, not at night. Let's say two hours, six miles maximum. That would put him in this area." She made a curving line that cut across the first three lines.

"That includes a good piece of the Mourne Mountains. And a fair smattering of villages," said Kavanagh.

"He's not likely to leave his van where it would be seen," said Morrison. "He's not stupid. He'll know that the army is all over the place and that they don't take kindly to strange vehicles."

"The van is the key," agreed Kerry. "Assuming he has the van, he must have driven it to where he hid it, which means it can't be too far away from a road. I don't think he'd hide it in the mountains, even if he could drive there. I think we should look for a wooded area with a road nearby. I reckon this is the best bet." She pointed at the Tollymore Forest Park.

Sarah put mugs of coffee on the table and mouthed "See you tomorrow" to Kerry before slipping out of the kitchen door. Kavanagh looked at the map and scratched his head.

"Yez making a lot of assumptions," he said. "The Chinaman could've doubled back, he could've ended up by going west, not east. He might've ditched the van. He could be holed up less than half a mile away, Christ, he could be back in the copse, he could even be watching the house right now."

"You're so bloody defeatist!" snapped Kerry, surprising them all. She realised her show of temper had shocked them so she smiled in an attempt to defuse the situation. "You're right, of course," she said. "But I don't think west is likely. One, because he headed in the opposite direction, and two, because going west would mean crossing the River Bann, either by bridge, where he'd risk being seen, or through the water, which would be perfectly possible but uncomfortable."

"And he did say that he'd be back in three days," said Hennessy.

"Three days?" said Kerry.

"He said I had three days to tell him who's behind the bombings in England," explained Hennessy. "He said that if I didn't have the names by then that he'd kill me."

"Oh God, Uncle Liam. That's terrible."

Hennessy shrugged. "It'll be OK, Kerry. Don't think about it. But the fact that he's given me the deadline means there's no need for him to stay close by. And I don't think he'll dump the van. How else is he going to get away when all this is over? I think you're right, Tollymore looks the best bet. Castlewellan Forest Park is another possibility, but that's a mile or so further away."

"I'm not sure what you're suggesting," Morrison said to Kerry. "I thought the idea was to track down The Chinaman."

She nodded quickly. "Yeah, yeah, but a two-pronged attack doubles our chances. You and I go after him, following his trail as best we can. But at the same time I think you should send some men to check out the forest and come at him from behind."

"But the forest is several square miles," O'Hara protested. "It would take for ever."

Kerry shook her head. "You're forgetting the van," she said. "If we're right and he's hidden the van among the trees, then he must have driven it off the road. All you'll have to do is drive along slowly looking for places where he could have turned off. You've got to think like your quarry, put yourself in his place. It might come to nothing, but it's worth a try. And what's the alternative?"

"She's right," said Hennessy. "Jim, can you take three of the guys tomorrow morning? Use two of the cars and take a run through the forest. No guns, just in case you come across the army. Just the shotguns, we've got licences for them."

"Sure, Liam. Whatever ye says." Kavanagh still sounded decidedly unconvinced.

Kerry sipped her coffee. "Right, that's all I can do tonight," she said. "I'm going to get an early night."

Hennessy raised his eyebrows. "It's only nine o'clock, Kerry."

"When I said we'll make an early start, I meant it," said Kerry. "We'll be up at five."

"Five!" snorted Morrison.

Kerry stood up and grinned at him. "Say goodnight, Sean," she said and leant over to kiss Hennessy on the forehead. "Goodnight, Uncle Liam."

Hennessy reached over and held her hand. "Goodnight, Kerry. And thanks. For everything."

"I haven't done anything yet," she said. "But it's going to be all right, I promise."

The four men watched her go.

"She's one hell of a girl," said Morrison.

"She's her father's daughter, all right," agreed Hennessy. "It must be in the genes."

"Oh yes," said Kavanagh, watching Kerry's hips swing. "It's definitely in her jeans."

"You, Jim, are a sexist pig."

"We all have our faults, Sean."

"If you two children are going to squabble all night I'll leave you to it," said Hennessy, getting up from the table and gathering the maps together. He left the three of them sitting together, drinking coffee and reminiscing about the old days.

Morrison woke to the smell of freshly made coffee. He screwed up his eyes and squinted at Kerry, who was sitting on the edge of his bed holding a steaming mug.

"Rise and shine," she said, and waited until he hauled himself up into a sitting position before handing him the mug. She pulled the curtains open but the sky was just a smudgy grey.

"What time is it?" he asked.

"Four thirty," she said.

Morrison groaned. He gulped down his coffee and gave her back the empty mug. "How come you look so wide awake?" he asked.

"I'm used to it. When we run the executive courses, Dad always gets me to do the night-time marches and stuff like that. It's great fun, we send them to bed at midnight and then wake them up at three in the morning and take them for a six-mile hike. They look like death when they get back."

Kerry looked nothing like death, just then, Morrison thought. Her blue eyes were bright and clear and she seemed to be bursting with energy, her chestnut hair was still damp from the shower and she'd even put on make-up, a little mascara and a touch of lipstick. He doubted that it was for The Chinaman's benefit and he felt suddenly pleased that she'd made the effort for him.

"What are you thinking?" she asked. "You've a wistful look about you, Sean Morrison."

"I was just thinking how dog-tired I am," he lied. "Right, get out of my room and let me wash. I'll be downstairs in five minutes."

"Do you want breakfast?" she asked.

The mere thought of food at that time of the morning made Morrison's stomach lurch and he declined, but said he wouldn't mind another coffee.

When he walked into the kitchen, drying his hair with a blue towel, it was waiting for him. Kavanagh was there, along with three men he'd decided to take with him to the woods: Roy O'Donnell, Tommy O'Donoghue and Michael O'Faolain, all of whom looked totally wrecked. Hennessy was there, too, sitting at the table with a collection of guns and walkie-talkies in front of him. As Morrison sipped his coffee, Hennessy handed him one of the guns, a small automatic. "Be careful," warned Hennessy. "Any sign of the army and dump it fast."

Morrison nodded, more interested in the two other guns on the table. They had short, wide barrels and looked as if they fired just one cartridge. He realised what they were just as Hennessy began to speak. Flare guns. Hennessy was a keen sailor and they were obviously guns for firing distress flares.

"I want you to take one of these, Sean, and let it off if you get close to The Chinaman and need help. You can call in with the radio, but that won't identify your position, so call us up and then fire the flare. I'll give you half a dozen cartridges."

"Do we take the other one?" asked Kavanagh.

"No, I've only got the two and I'll need one here to signal to Sean and Kerry."

"But we'll have the walkie-talkie," said Morrison.

"Yes, but only to call me, you won't be able to leave it on receive in case you get close to The Chinaman and he hears it. If I want to contact you I'll let off a flare and you can call me up on the radio when you're sure it's safe. You'll only use the walkie-talkie if I signal you with the flare or if you've dealt with The Chinaman."

"Dealt with?" said Kerry.

"Captured," said Hennessy. "Or whatever." He held out two of the walkie-talkies to Kavanagh. "You can use these, Jim, keep one in each car. If you catch The Chinaman you call me and I'll contact Kerry and Sean. Does that make sense?"

"It sounds hellish complicated," said Morrison.

"Uncle Liam's right though," said Kerry. "Out there in the countryside sound travels a long way, especially electronic noise."

"And don't forget the army monitors all radio frequencies so we'll have to keep all transmissions to a minimum anyway," added Hennessy. He gave a small canvas haversack to Morrison. "You can use this for the flare gun and the radio," he said.

Kerry picked up the ski-poles from beside the Welsh dresser and stood by the kitchen door.

"What about food, and water?" Morrison asked.

She patted a small rucksack slung over her shoulder. "Here," she said. "And the maps. And torches. And anything else we might need. Come on, Sean, time to saddle up and move out."

"Yes, Tonto," he laughed. He packed the walkie-talkie and the flare gun and slipped the automatic into the inside pocket of his bomber jacket. It was heavy and the jacket bulged.

"This might be more comfortable," said Kavanagh, and slid a clip-on holster across the table. Morrison slotted the gun in and then clipped the holster to the back of his jeans.

"Better?" asked Kavanagh.

"Much," said Morrison. "Good hunting, OK?"

Kavanagh made a gun with his hand and sighted down it at Morrison as he and Kerry went out of the door.

"You lads had better be careful, too," warned Hennessy. "We've got licences for those shotguns but don't go waving them around the Brits, for God's sake. The last thing we need right now is trouble with the army."

"Don't yez worry, Liam, we'll be just fine," said Kavanagh. "We'd better be off." Kavanagh took the three men out into the courtyard and shortly afterwards Hennessy heard the two Land-Rovers start up and drive off. Willie O'Hara, his hair tousled and his eyes bleary, staggered into the kitchen and slumped into a chair.

"What's all the noise, Liam?"

"The lads on the way out after The Chinaman. Do you want coffee?"

"A whiskey'd go down a treat, right enough."

"Aye, you're right. I'll join you."

As Hennessy poured the whiskey into two tumblers, Kerry and Morrison walked across the fields towards the copse. The grass was covered with a sheen of morning dew that glistened in the early light. This time there was no need to walk through the trees so Kerry took him around the perimeter of the copse and along the hedgerow. When they arrived at the slope where they'd examined the squashed bluebell the previous evening, Kerry slowed the pace right down and began walking slowly, her eyes scanning the ground left and right like a fighter pilot scrutinising the sky. Morrison followed behind her and slightly to her left.

"What exactly do I look for?" he asked.

"If we're lucky we'll see a clear sign, like the footprints we saw yesterday, or vegetation that's been trampled. But signs like that'll be few and far between. Generally all we can expect to see are slight changes, small things. It's hard to explain. Sometimes it's just a feeling that something isn't right."

"What sort of changes?"

Kerry prodded the ground with her pole and knelt down to inspect the grass. "Differences in texture or colour of the vegetation, any regular marks in the ground that aren't natural, flattening of leaves or dirt, twigs or stones that have been moved. Anything that he might have dropped. None of those things in themselves prove that he's gone this way but taken together they all add up to a trail." She turned round as she crouched and pointed back the way they'd come. "You can't move across a field without leaving some sort of trace," she said.

Morrison turned and looked. Two lines of footprints were clearly marked in the damp grass stretching back across the fields as far as he could see.

"The obvious signs will disappear as the sun evaporates the dew over the morning, but you see what I mean." She began walking again. "A lot of it is common sense, too," she said. "You've got to think like your quarry. If you come to an obstruction, like a hedge or a river, then you've got to be able to guess what he'll do, whether he'll go to the right or the left, whether he'll go through a group of trees or round them, what he'll do if he comes across a cottage or a farm. In some ways it's easier to follow a man than a deer. A man usually has a reason for going somewhere, unless he's lost, and if he's lost then he's pretty keen to be found. A deer is trying to avoid humans and most of the time it's probably just grazing."

"You've hunted humans before?"

Kerry laughed. "Not with a gun, no. Even the Germans draw the line at deer, but it's a thought, isn't it? We could even arrange for the ears to be mounted."

"Yeah, OK, hunted was the wrong word. Tracked, then."

"From time to time a tourist will get lost in the mountains and the mountain rescue team will call up my dad and ask him for help. I've been with him a couple of times. But like I said, it's one thing to track someone who's hoping to be found, it's quite another to trail a man who wants to hide. And The Chinaman is certainly going to be hiding. At least the weather's going to be good. I suppose you know how the Blackfoot Indians forecast the weather?"

"What?"

"Weather forecasting, Indian-style. Here, I'll show you." She bent down and picked up a small stone and twisted a piece of grass around it so that it was hanging like a conker on a string.

"That's it?" asked Morrison, intrigued.

"That's it," she said. "You hold it in front of you like this, and you watch it. Here, you hold it."

She handed it to him and Morrison studied the stone. "Now what?" he asked.

"Well, first you touch it. If it feels dry, the weather is fine. If it feels warm, it's a hot day. If it turns white, it's snowing. And if it's wet, it's raining. Then you look at it. If it's swinging from side to side, it's windy."

Morrison laughed, realising he'd been taken for a ride.

"And, Sean . . ."

"Yes," he said warily.

"If you can't see it, it's probably foggy." They both dissolved into laughter.

* * *

The telephone rang in the hallway. "I'll get it," said O'Hara, who was sitting closer to the door than Hennessy. He picked up the receiver and then put his hand over the mouthpiece. "It's for you," he called. "Won't give his name."

Hennessy pushed himself up from the table and took the phone from O'Hara. "Liam Hennessy," he said.

"It's Bromley," said a gruff voice. Hennessy reached behind him and closed the door on O'Hara, not wanting him to hear.

"They called?" Hennessy asked.

"They called, but they didn't give a codeword. What's going on, Hennessy?"

Hennessy was confused and he put his hand to his head. "Look, Bromley, if they didn't give the codeword, maybe it wasn't them."

"It was them all right. The Press Association took the call last night. It was a man, Irish accent, and he said there would be no further co-operation with the British security forces and no more use of the codeword system."

"So how do you know the call was kosher?"

"He knew exactly where the bomb had been placed and how much explosive was in it. And with all the other bombs they claimed responsibility within twenty-four hours. We had the normal hoax calls but that was the only one that had enough details to convince us that it was genuine."

Hennessy closed his eyes. This wasn't what he had expected at all.

"Somebody talked," said Bromley.

"That's not possible," insisted Hennessy. "Only two people knew what was happening. Me and the man you met in London, Sean Morrison."

"Well, one of you isn't to be trusted. And only you know which one it is."

"I brought Morrison back from the United States especially for this. He'd been away for two years, so there's no way at all that he could be involved with the active service unit."

"Maybe you talk in your sleep," said Bromley.

"I'll treat that remark with the contempt it deserves,"

replied Hennessy, but something cold ran down his spine and settled in the pit of his stomach.

"So what do you think went wrong? Do you think it was just coincidence, that they decided on a whim not to use the codeword so soon after you changed it?"

"No, of course not. We've changed it twice before this year and each time they've picked it up immediately. No, you're right, they've been warned off. But for the life of me I can't think who it might be. Look, give me a number where I can reach you. I've got some thinking to do."

Bromley read out a number and Hennessy wrote it down. "I can get you there day or night?" he asked.

"If I'm not there, they'll be able to get hold of me."

"I'll call you as soon as I find out what's happening."

"For your sake I hope it's not too late," said Bromley.

"What do you mean?"

He heard Bromley click his tongue as if thinking, and when he spoke again his voice was hesitant. "The climate is changing here, Hennessy. These bombings have been so vicious that public opinion is turning against the IRA in a way that I've never seen before. We're not just talking about right-wing MPs calling for the death penalty or sending in the SAS, this is different. Part of it is the lack of warnings, but a lot has got to do with the choice of targets. When the IRA killed MPs like Airey Neave and Ian Gow you might have been able to justify them as political killings, and the Stock Exchange and the Carlton Club could just about be described as establishment targets, but these latest atrocities, I mean, Bank Tube station, for God's sake. And Ascot. I'll tell you, Hennessy, if much more of this goes on you could find the rules changing."

"What do you mean, rules changing?"

"I mean that, despite what you might think, in the past the IRA has had a relatively easy ride from the British Government."

Hennessy snorted. "Bullshit. The Catholics in Northern Ireland have been ridden rough-shod over in a . . ."

"We're not talking about Catholics, we're talking about the IRA. And all I'm saying is that you and your friends in Dublin, if you're serious about not being involved in these bombings, are going to have to pull your fingers out, or you'll feel a backlash the likes of which you've never known before."

"I hear what you're saying, Bromley. And I've got your number." The line went dead. Hennessy went back into the kitchen, where O'Hara was sitting at the table spooning cornflakes into his mouth.

"Trouble?" he asked, seeing the worried look on Hennessy's face.

"It's OK, Willie. Nothing I can't handle." Oh really? said a voice in his head that sounded disturbingly like Mary's.

Christy Murphy arrived at the farm just before ten o'clock. Hennessy was making coffee when one of the guards knocked on the kitchen door and announced that somebody was driving down the track towards the farm. A few seconds later a car crunched into the courtyard and Murphy let himself into the kitchen.

"Christy, just in time for coffee," said Hennessy, waving the large man to a chair. "Come on, sit down. How's my wife?"

Murphy stood where he was, clenching and unclenching his hands like a prize-fighter about to get into the ring. His big, square face was creased into a frown and for a moment Hennessy feared that something had happened to Mary.

"Mary's all right, isn't she, Christy?"

"She's fine, Liam, but . . ." His voice tailed off.

Hennessy pushed his plate away. "What's wrong, Christy? Cat got your tongue?"

Murphy seemed to be struggling for his words, and although he was normally a quiet man this was something different. He was acting like a small boy who wanted to confess to breaking a window but who was worried about being punished.

"Can I speak to you, Liam. In private?" he said.

"Of course, of course. Come through to the lounge." Hennessy got to his feet and took the big man through the hallway.

As the morning sun climbed higher and higher in the sky, Kerry found it progressively harder to follow The Chinaman's trail. Morrison didn't have to ask why, she'd already explained about the importance the angle of the sun played in defining footprints. Eventually, after it had taken her the best part of an hour to cover a hundred yards, she called a halt.

"I think we should rest for a while," she said. She indicated a leafy birch tree in the middle of a hedgerow. "Let's sit in the shade," she said. They dropped down into the cool grass and she opened her rucksack. She took out a pack of sandwiches and two cans of ginger beer. "I knew we'd be out here for some time," she said.

"How long do you think it'll take?" he asked, helping himself to a sandwich.

"The trail is cold," she admitted. "He's still heading for the forest, by the look of it, and if he is we've a better chance of finding him among the trees. It's harder to move through woods without leaving signs."

"Can't we just go straight there?"

Kerry shrugged. "We could, but we'd be taking a risk. There's still a chance he might turn north or south before we get there, and even if he doesn't we won't know for sure where he went into the trees. You can't take shortcuts, Sean. If we make a wrong call, we might have to spend hours backtracking." She popped open the can of ginger beer.

"You know best," he said. He held up his sandwich. "These are good," he said. "You make them?"

"Yeah, I had plenty of time while you were still in the land of Nod."

They ate together in silence, enjoying the feel of the fresh summer breeze on their faces.

"You live in New York now?" Kerry asked, brushing crumbs from her trousers.

Morrison nodded. "Yeah, raising funds, flying the flag, telling the Yanks where their money is going."

"Don't you miss it?"

"Miss what?"

"The crack. The kick from being in Belfast, where it's all happening." She frowned. "You know what I mean, surely. The fight is in Northern Ireland, not in the States, and certainly not in Scotland." The look of intensity was back in her eyes.

"There are different ways of helping the Cause," he said quietly, aware once again how quickly her temper could flare, how she'd snapped at Kavanagh in the farmhouse.

"Like my dad, you mean. Hiding in Scotland. And keeping me with him."

"Hey, come on now, Kerry. Your father has heard the rattle of soil on too many coffin lids to deserve that. No one has done more for the IRA than Micky Geraghty, you shouldn't forget that."

She shook her head. "I know, that's not what I meant. It's not so much that he's out of it now, it's more that he won't let me get involved. He's so fucking protective."

Morrison looked at her and immediately felt protective towards her himself. Her cheeks were flushing, her chin was up and her eyes flashed fire. She looked as if she was ready to fight the whole world. She was keen, there was no doubt about that, but he also knew that Long Kesh was full of men who had failed to temper enthusiasm with wisdom. "You should be glad you're out of it," he said quietly.

"I'll never be glad until the British are out of Ireland. It's our country, Sean, our country and our religion. You know what I mean, I know you do. You feel the same as I do when you see the black bastards swaggering through the streets in their bowler hats and sashes, their flutes and drums, ramming their religion down our throats. Did it never happen to you, Sean? Being grabbed by the bastard Billy boys and being forced to say 'Fuck The Pope' and 'All Catholics Are Shit'. Tell me that never happened to you. Tell me that your bile doesn't rise when you see an Orange parade."

Morrison said nothing, because he knew she was right.

"I want this Chinaman," she said. "I want to show Uncle Liam what I can do. If I can prove myself just this once, he'll let me do more for the Cause, and it won't matter what my dad thinks."

In the distance to the west a white star climbed into the sky leaving a greyish-blue trail zig-zagging behind it. The star popped with the sound of a bursting balloon.

"That's Uncle Liam!" she said.

Morrison took the walkie-talkie out of the haversack and switched it on. "Are you there?" he said. No names were to be used because the army constantly swept the airwaves.

"I want you back here," said Hennessy's voice. "Now."

"OK, we're on our way. Have you found him?"

"No, I just want you back."

"Understood." He switched off the receiver.

Kerry had heard and she sat forward. "I wonder what's happened?"

"No idea," said Morrison.

"Look, Sean, I think I should stay out here. Uncle Liam said they haven't found The Chinaman yet. And you can see how slowly it's going. I want to keep at it, you can come back here once you've sorted out what he wants."

"How will I know where you are?" he said. "You're the tracker, not me."

"I'm not going to be moving that fast." She picked up a long twig from the hedgerow. "I'll leave sticks like this sticking up every hundred yards or so, and I'll drag the pole through any patches of soil I pass. You'll have no problems finding me again. And I'm not likely to stumble across him, am I? This trail is dead cold. It'll save time."

"I'll have to check with him," said Sean, and switched the receiver back on. "Are you there?"

There was a delay before he heard Hennessy reply. "I'm here."

"I'll come back alone."

"Is that wise?"

"It'll save time later and we are quite sure there's no danger out here. Unless there's a problem."

Hennessy was quiet for a while as he considered Morrison's suggestion. "Be careful," he said eventually.

"Yeah!" said Kerry.

"Any doubt at all and you both come in," Hennessy said to Morrison.

"Understood," he replied, and switched off the receiver again.

"Like he says, be careful," Morrison said. He opened the haversack and took out the flare gun and the cartridges. He handed them, and the walkie-talkie, to her. "You'd better take these," he said.

"What about the gun?" she asked.

Morrison shook his head emphatically. "No, no gun," he said. "Liam was quite clear on that score. And if you think you're getting close and there's any chance of you finding him, then pull back and call me on that." He nodded at the walkie-talkie. "I'll be back once I've found out what it is that he wants."

"It must be important otherwise he'd have told you on the radio what it was," she said.

Morrison thought about that as he jogged back to the farmhouse. Though they had been out for more than five hours they had covered just three miles and it only took him forty minutes to get back.

He was in good condition and he'd barely worked up a sweat by the time he walked into the courtyard to find O'Hara there with two men carrying shotguns. The guns were broken, the barrels pointing down to the ground, but Morrison could see the brass ends of cartridges in place.

"Liam's in the lounge," said O'Hara.

"Everything OK?" asked Morrison, hoping for some clue as to what was going on.

"Fucked if I know," said O'Hara. The two men with shotguns said goodbye to O'Hara and walked across the courtyard towards the cottage. Morrison felt himself sigh with relief. For a wild moment he had thought that they had been waiting for him. An armed escort.

He wiped his feet carefully on the mat by the kitchen door and walked through to the lounge. The door was half open and he walked in to find Hennessy sitting in one of the arm-chairs by the unlit fire. He didn't get up as Morrison entered. "Sit down, Sean," he said. He seemed distant, almost shocked, and the one thought in Morrison's mind was that there had been another bombing. As he went over to the sofa he realised there was somebody else in the room, standing by the door. It was Christy Murphy.

"Christy!" he said, surprised. "When did you get back?"

Murphy looked away from Morrison and seemed ill at ease.

"Christy, you can wait outside," said Hennessy, and Murphy practically ran out of the door so keen was he to get out of Morrison's presence. Hennessy studied Morrison with unsmiling eyes as Murphy closed the door and Morrison began to worry, but the fear was a shapeless, nameless thing, made all the more terrifying by his inability to identify it. He wanted to speak, to ask what was wrong, but felt that to do so would be to imply guilt and that his interests would be best served by keeping quiet. He could feel sweat on the palms of his hands but he resisted the urge to wipe them on his trousers. Liam Hennessy might look like a kindly grandfather but he had the power of life and death and would have no compunction at all about killing somebody who he thought had crossed him. Thoughts of Mary Hennessy flashed into his mind and he felt his cheeks redden.

"The bombers have claimed responsibility for the Ascot bomb," Hennessy said flatly.

Morrison frowned, because that surely was good news, and yet Hennessy said it as if he was announcing the death of a close relative. "And?" he said.

"And they didn't use the codeword. In fact, they said they weren't going to co-operate with the authorities any more and that there would be no more use of the codeword system."

Hennessy looked at Morrison with cold, unblinking eyes and Morrison fought to keep his own steady on the older man's face, trying to stay cool. Eventually he weakened and looked out of the window. The two men with the shotguns were back. He looked at Hennessy again.

"Which means that somebody tipped them off," said Hennessy. He continued to stare straight at Morrison and again

Morrison was forced to avert his gaze. "The problem is, only two people knew about the reason for the change in the code-word. You. And me."

Morrison held up his hands. "I don't know what you're thinking, but I didn't tell anyone, Liam. I knew how important this was. I spoke to Bromley, and that was all. I swear, on my mother's eyes, I swear it."

Hennessy steepled his fingers underneath his chin and studied Morrison as if he was an undecided juror.

"You must have said something to somebody, Sean. Think very carefully."

The two men sat in a silence which was disturbed only by the ticking of a grandfather clock in the corner. Morrison was genuinely bewildered, because he knew that he hadn't broken Hennessy's confidence. He was sure of it. And yet Hennessy seemed so convinced.

Morrison shook his head, not knowing what Hennessy expected to hear.

"Would it help if I told you that I had Christy follow Mary in London?"

Morrison felt as if he'd been kicked in the stomach. He would have been able to face it better if Hennessy had shouted or banged his fist or thrown something at him, but he did none of those things, he simply sat in his easy chair and waited for a reply. It was his quiet acceptance of the facts, an acceptance that bordered on apparent indifference, that made the man seem all the more menacing. Morrison wondered if he was about to die, shot in the back of the head because he'd slept with another man's wife. He thought of lying, of claiming that she had just popped round to the hotel as a casual visitor, but he knew that it wouldn't work. Murphy wasn't stupid, he'd have found out that she'd gone to his room and would have known how long she was in there.

"Liam, I'm sorry . . ." he began to say, but Hennessy held up a hand to silence him.

"I don't want apologies, I don't even want to know what happened in your room. We'll leave that for some other time. All I want to do right now is to establish what went wrong, how they found out what we were up to. I know Mary was in 'your room on Monday morning, what I don't know is what you said to her. What you talked about."

"You don't suspect Mary, surely?" said Morrison.

"At the moment I don't know who to trust, you've quite clearly demonstrated that I'm no judge of character," said Hennessy savagely. "Now don't fuck with me, Sean. Did you or did you not discuss our plan with Mary?"

"No," said Morrison immediately. "I mean yes, sort of. She already knew what you were doing."

"She did not," said Hennessy emphatically. "I told no one. And I mean no one."

"But I'm sure . . ." He lapsed into silence, trying to remember exactly what she'd said as she lay in his arms in the afterglow of their love-making. "She seemed to know already."

"Think carefully about what she said. We spoke on the phone, remember? Could she hear what we were saying?"

It all came back to Morrison with a rush, him lying on his back talking to Hennessy on the phone as Mary made love to him. "Yes, she could hear us," he said. His voice sounded a million miles away. He wondered if Hennessy could see into his mind, if he knew exactly how he'd been betrayed. "And you're right, it was afterwards that she mentioned the codeword."

"She steered the conversation?"

Morrison nodded. "She made it sound as if you'd already told her what was going on. Most of the time I was just agreeing with what she said."

"She is good at manipulating people," said Hennessy, his voice loaded with sadness. Morrison suddenly felt sorry for the man. And guilty. And afraid.

"You think that Mary told the bombers?" asked Morrison. The possibility seemed so remote it was almost laughable.

"Not directly, no. But I think she found out from you what we were planning, and I think that she passed that information on to someone else."

"Who?"

Hennessy fell silent again. He leant forward in his chair, his elbows on his knees. He took a handkerchief from his top pocket and wiped his brow. "Do I trust you, Sean? After the way you've betrayed me, can I trust you?"

"My loyalty to the Cause has never been in question, Liam. The thing with Mary, that's different. I never meant to hurt you, I didn't plan for you to know. We were always very careful."

"You lied to me, you went behind my back. And now I'm supposed to trust you?"

"Liam, I'm sorry. If it makes a difference, it was one of the reasons I went to the States. To put distance between Mary and me. To stop it."

"You mean she wanted to continue the affair?" Hennessy sounded wounded, hurt.

Morrison realised he was making it worse by talking about it. Maybe Hennessy hadn't even considered that the affair had been going on before he went to New York. "We decided it was best," he lied. "Liam, whatever happened is in the past, what matters now is to get these bastards and to put an end to the bombings. To do what we set out to do. We can deal with our personal problems afterwards."

Hennessy nodded and settled back in the chair. "Maybe you're right, Sean. All right, we'll put that to one side. For the moment we'll concentrate on minimising the damage, maybe even turning it to our advantage."

"What do you mean?"

"I had a visitor before you and Kerry arrived. Hugh McGrath. He knew Mary was in London, but there was no way he could have known that."

"Unless she told him?"

"Unless she told him," agreed Hennessy. "She spoke to you, she tricked the information out of you, and then she called him." Hennessy let it sink in, and then twisted the knife. "She used you, Sean." There was bitterness in his voice, a nasty edge which cut through Morrison. He wondered then whether Hennessy really was prepared to put the affair behind them while they sorted out the bombing business. But he knew that Hennessy was right. Mary had bedded him and used him, barely waiting for him to leave before ringing McGrath. Another thought wormed its way into his mind. Maybe she was also McGrath's lover. Maybe she did to McGrath the same things she did to him, gave him her kisses, her passion, her energy, the things he thought she saved solely for him. He thought of her sitting astride McGrath, his hands on her breasts, her riding him until she came, and he felt the anger burn inside and realised for the first time exactly how bitter and betrayed Hennessy must have felt.

"I know she was angry, but I never thought she'd go that far," said Hennessy, almost as if he was talking to himself, or unburdening himself at confession. Morrison couldn't think of anything to say, knowing how easy it would be to provoke the man. "Mary never forgave me for not going after the men who killed her brother."

"They're all in Long Kesh, aren't they?"

"You know as well as I do that we could get to them, wherever they are, H-blocks or no H-blocks. She knew that, too. She never let me forget it. We've been arguing for months. Years."

"Arguing?"

"Mary's always been one hundred per cent behind the Organisation, much more than most people realise. We used to have the most fierce arguments, she couldn't understand why I was trying to take a more conciliatory line with the Protestants. She was always pushing me to gear up the campaigns, to turn the screw, to drive the British out. And that was before Gerry was killed. His death pushed her over the edge, I guess. I should have realised, I should have talked to her more. But by then I suppose we'd stopped talking. Really talking, you know what I mean?"

Morrison nodded, but he was fearful of being forced into the role of confessor. Hennessy was a man who guarded his secrets jealously.

"McGrath was always a possibility, anyway," continued Hennessy. "He makes more money out of the border than anyone else in the organisation, and he has strong links with Gaddafi. It'd also explain why we haven't been able to pin down the active service unit's bombmaker. It could be a complete outsider, someone that McGrath sent to Libya for training without telling us."

"Is that possible?" said Morrison, eager to turn the conversation away from Mary.

"Perfectly. We've always given him a lot of leeway when it came to dealing with the Libyans."

"But why would he have to take explosives and equipment from our stocks? Couldn't he just bring in his own supplies?"

"Some, maybe, but not on any large scale. He'd have to use our established routes to get it into the country and he couldn't do that without us knowing. And he'd know that if he was discovered organising secret deliveries that we'd know what he was up to. He wouldn't want to take the risk. Much safer to take what he needed from existing caches."

"OK, so assuming it is McGrath, what next?"

"He has to tell us where the bombers are," said Hennessy. "We get him here and we get the names from him."

"He's a powerful man, Liam. He carries almost as much influence with Dublin as you do, and he's virtually got his own private army on his farm. We can't just wade in and expect him to open up to us."

"I know, I know. I'm going to speak to Dublin now. And McGrath is going to come to us. I want you to call him and tell him that I've called an emergency meeting of our top officials here at the farm. Tell him it's about a change in our bombing strategy, that should bring him running. Tell him the boys are coming down from Belfast and the meeting is for noon."

"Sure," agreed Morrison. He felt somewhat easier now that Hennessy was concentrating on McGrath but he knew that underneath his neutral exterior the man must be in turmoil. Liam Hennessy was well used to concealing his emotions in the courtroom, and his big advantage had always been that his opponents never knew what he was thinking. He was a difficult man to read, but, no matter how calm he looked, the business over Mary would be gnawing at his insides and at some point it would emerge into the open. Morrison would have to be careful, very careful. One of the men with shotguns was looking into the window and he caught Morrison's eye. The man winked. Morrison didn't feel any better.

Fisher stood on the balcony with half a loaf of stale bread on the table next to him. He picked up a slice and tore it into small pieces and tossed them out into the air. A flock of unruly seagulls sitting on a barge across the river came squawking over and swooped and soared around him. He picked up another slice and ripped it into small bits and threw them one at a time high into the air so that the birds could catch them on the wing.

"You know what I'd like?" said McCormick behind him.

"What's that?" Two of the black-headed gulls collided in mid-air with the sound of a quilt being thumped.

"A twelve-bore shotgun," said McCormick. "Then we could have some real fun."

"You, McCormick, have no beauty in your soul." Fisher tossed out a handful of bread and birds swooped from all directions, beaks wide and wings flapping. When all the bread had been devoured, he went back into the flat.

"It's done," said The Bombmaker.

Fisher sat down and looked at the laptop computer. "It looks so inoffensive, doesn't it?" he said, running his hand along the smooth plastic. "And it works just as it did before?"

"Sure. There's no way of discovering that it's been modified unless it's taken apart. And they won't do that."

"Excellent," said Fisher.

"I've even fixed it so that the time is set by using the keyboard. It's a trick the Libyans taught me, a relatively simple program incorporated into the disk operating system. Once we know when we want it to explode, I call up the program and input the time. The computer does the rest."

Fisher grinned. "I'm impressed," he said. "And it'll get through the X-ray machines?"

"Even the new models. The only drawback is that there's

no room for a barometric device. We can't use altitude to detonate it, so we have to be sure of the timing."

Fisher nodded. "I don't see that being a problem, so long as we stick to a scheduled flight. What about the mule?"

"I've narrowed it down to two. A journalist and a cameraman who works for Thames TV. What about you?"

"There's a girl, an investment banker, who says she'll be going to Paris next week. She always flies British Airways, she says. I think we take the first one to confirm a flight, agreed?"

"Fine by me," said The Bombmaker.

Woody worked flat out to finish the school-holidays feature because he hadn't been told yet whether or not he was working the Saturday shift and the news desk weren't at all happy about his three-hour lunch with Annie. He was determined to keep in their good books, at least until they'd drawn up the weekend rota, but he was suffering. He was all too well aware that he hadn't become a journalist twenty years earlier to end up writing crap like that, but, as usual, he needed the money. He'd cashed two cheques at separate pubs and promised that he'd have enough money in his account to cover them by the end of the following week. He'd been fighting to keep his head above water financially for the last two years but he was getting nowhere. He needed a staff job, but Woody was a realist, his age and his track record were against him. What he needed was a big one, an exclusive story that he could sell for big money and which would restore his tarnished reputation. Yeah, he thought, dream on. Number forty-eight. Take them to the zoo. And feed them to the lions, he typed, and then just as quickly deleted it. It'd be just his luck for something like that to get into the paper.

He finished the feature and as he sent it into the news desk queue the phone on his desk rang. It was Pat Quigley, calling from Belfast.

"Hiya, Woody. I wasn't sure if I'd catch you in, this early

in the week, but I remember you didn't like being bothered at home."

Woody leant back in his swivel chair and put his feet on the desk. "No need for sarcasm, mate. You caught me at a bad time. Anyway, how's it going?"

"Not so bad, Woody. I'm calling about the Hennessy thing."

"Yeah?" said Woody, suddenly interested but trying to conceal it.

"His driver's in hospital. Somebody bombed his car. I'm told by a really good source that it happened on his farm. I started making a few enquiries and it seems that two more of his men are in hospital here in Belfast. One's been stabbed, the other has some sort of strange wounds in his foot. It's bloody curious, Woody, especially after the attack on Hennessy's office. Do you have any idea what's going on?"

"Sounds bloody mysterious to me, Pat. Are you sure it's not the Protestants?"

"Doubtful. There hasn't been much aggro between the guys at the top, not for a while. I suppose it could be starting up again, but it doesn't feel right. There haven't been any other attacks, either on the IRA or the UDA. It looks like a one-off."

"I don't know what to say, Pat. I don't see how I can help."

"You said you'd have a look for the name of the reader who was asking about Hennessy."

"He wasn't asking about Hennessy. He just wanted to write to a few Sinn Fein officials. I really don't think he's your man."

"OK, fine, but can you at least dig out his name for me?"

"I tried, but I can't find it in any of my notebooks. I did look, Pat, honest. It's just one of those things, you know?"

"OK, Woody. Fair enough. I thought I'd check." Woody could tell he wasn't convinced, but there was nothing he could do. Like Woody he was a freelance and dependent upon the paper's goodwill, he couldn't afford to offend anyone, even another freelance, especially a freelance who was doing regular shifts at head office. Quigley rang off.

When Woody went over to the news desk, Simpson was

leaning back in his chair, his immaculate shoes on the desk.

"Good piece, Woody, a classic!" he shouted, giving Woody the thumbs up.

Woody gave him a mock bow from the waist and pulled his forelock before approaching the desk. "About that story idea I had," Woody said.

"Pull up a pew," said Simpson and kicked over a chair.

Woody sat down. "Remember that guy who came to the office trying to offer a reward over the Knightsbridge bombing?"

Simpson screwed up his face like a baby about to cry. "The Chinaman?" he said.

"Yeah, The Chinaman. Only I've found out he's Vietnamese, not Chinese. His wife and daughter were killed in the bombing and he wanted to get the men responsible."

"Thousands of pounds in a carrier bag, right?"

"Right. He rang back a while later, said he wanted to talk to the IRA direct. He wanted names of people high up in the organisation."

"And you gave them to him?"

"Right. Not the IRA, because you know what they'd do to him, but I gave him a few names of the top Sinn Fein people. Now someone is running some sort of vendetta against one of the men, Liam Hennessy. His office has been bombed, his car has been hit and three of his men are in hospital. And the man that came to see me has disappeared."

"Disappeared?"

"He used to own a Chinese take-away in Clapham. He's sold up and vanished."

"And you think he's in Belfast?"

Woody nodded. "If he was crazy enough to offer a reward, he might just be crazy enough to take matters into his own hands."

"But you said Hennessy's office was bombed. You think this Chinaman has got hold of bombs?"

Woody leant forward, his eyes sparkling. "That's the kicker. He's a Vietcong assassin! The bastard can kill with his bare hands, he can make bombs, booby traps, the works."

"Woody, someone's been pulling your chain!"

Woody explained about the Home Office file and Nguyen's life story. When he'd finished, Simpson picked up a ballpoint pen and began chewing the end. "So what are you suggesting, Woody?"

"Let me go to Belfast and sniff around."

"Expensive," said Simpson.

"If the paper'll pay for my flight and cover my expenses, I'll take the fee as lineage. No story, no payment." Simpson agreed. "But if I get a splash, I want serious money. You'll have the best exclusive this year."

"If you're right."

"If I'm right. Is it a deal?" he asked.

"I've got a better idea, a better deal."

"What?" said Woody, warily.

Simpson reached for a letter on his desk and handed it to Woody.

"We've been invited to a conference in Rome. A security conference. All the top guys are going to be there, including David Tucker, the head of Scotland Yard's Anti-Terrorist Branch and a couple of MPs. Some of Europe's top terrorist experts are going to be speaking. It's supposed to be about computerised intelligence systems, but we've been tipped off that they're going to announce a new international database to help in the hunt for terrorists worldwide."

"Government tip?" asked Woody.

Simpson grinned. "Who else? We might show a fair bit of tits and bums but politically we're right behind the Government, and we've got several million readers. The Government wants a big show from this conference, so a few select newspapers have been invited along. They're offering to fly us out on a chartered flight with some of the speakers, all we have to do is cover expenses."

"And report the Government line."

"Don't bite the hand that feeds you, Woody," replied Simpson.

"Perish the thought," said Woody. He waved the letter. "You want me to go to this? You know the flight is tonight?"

"Yeah I know. We were sitting on it but in view of what

happened at Ascot, we'd be crazy to turn it down. I was thinking about sending Williams but he's gone down with the flu. You'll get a bloody good story out of the conference, and you're sure to pick up some juicy stuff behind the scenes. And while you're there you can pick their brains about what's going on in Belfast. I'd be amazed if they hadn't heard something."

Woody nodded his head thoughtfully. It made good sense. "And what about me going to Belfast?"

"Fly straight there from Rome when the conference is over. We'll fix up the ticket for you. Can you fly direct?"

"I dunno, I'll find out. So it's a deal?"

"It's a deal, Woody. Just one thing."

"What's that?"

"Keep off the sauce."

"You know me," said Woody, heading back to his desk.

"Yeah," muttered Simpson. "Too true I do."

Woody went back to his desk just in time to answer his phone. It was Maggie. "Hello, Woody. Do you fancy a drink some time tomorrow?" she asked.

"I can't, I'm afraid. I'm off to Rome tonight. You must be psychic, I've only just been told."

"What time are you going?"

He looked at the letter. "Eight thirty, so I'll have to get to the airport about seven, I suppose. And then I'm going to Belfast."

"Belfast?" she said. Woody explained briefly about the conversation he'd had with Pat Quigley.

"Wow, so you're going after The Chinaman? Hey, if you need any help while you're over there, you should call my cousin, he's a freelance journalist there. God, it's quite a coincidence, he was in London a couple of weeks ago."

"In Belfast? What's his name?"

"Eamonn McCormick, do you know him?"

"No, but it'd be useful to meet up with him. I'll need some help while I'm there. I should even be able to put some money his way, too." It would be best to keep out of Pat Quigley's way when he arrived in Belfast so another contact would be useful.

"Great. He left some stuff with me. You could give it to him when you see him. He's a really nice guy, you'll like him. Look, I tell you what, why don't I pop round and give it to you tonight, before you leave?"

"Lunch would be better." Woody looked at his watch. It was 11.30 a.m.

"I can't, I'm tied up. Why don't I come round to your house? Give me the address."

Woody gave her the address of his bedsit in Fulham.

"What time did you say the flight was again?"

"Eight thirty. It's a special Government charter, high security and all that. I mustn't be late. I'll have to leave the flat by five thirty, just to be on the safe side."

"That's OK, I'll come round about four thirty, maybe five."

"Aren't you working?" he asked.

"I'm supposed to be visiting clients so it's no problem. I might have to sell you an insurance policy, though."

"With my lifestyle, I don't think I could afford the premiums." He laughed and they said their goodbyes. Woody smiled as he replaced the receiver. Maggie was great fun and he was looking forward to seeing her again, even though it was likely to be a fleeting visit. He had yet to get beyond the kiss-on-the-cheek stage, but he lived in hope.

Morrison stood by a window in one of the front-facing bedrooms looking down the track that led to the road. It was just before noon. He saw McGrath's Volvo estate with four men in it and he ran to the door. "He's coming," he shouted downstairs and then rushed back to his vantage point.

Two of Hennessy's men walked towards the car and flagged it down, checking the occupants. Morrison saw the rear window being wound down and then the glint of sunlight off McGrath's glasses. He felt his heartbeat increase and his mouth went dry and he recognised the signs of his body preparing itself for violence. It had been four years since Morrison had killed a man, and then it had been in the heat of a fire-fight at the border near Crossmaglen, but the deaths he was responsible for caused him not one night's lost sleep and he was quite prepared to kill again. He had made the mental switch many years earlier, suppressed the values he'd been taught by the priests and by his teachers at school in favour of the creed of the political terrorist, that violence was justified in the quest for self-determination. When Morrison finally met his maker he would do so with a clear conscience and an untarnished soul, he was sure of that. The death of McGrath, if Hennessy ordered it, would be an added bonus and would go some way to quenching the jealous fire that burned through his mind. As he watched the Volvo bounce down the track and slow to crawl around the filled-in hole that marked the scene of the earlier bombing, images of McGrath and Mary filled his mind again, the two of them naked, enjoying each other, her arching her back and calling out his name.

"Are you OK?" asked a voice behind him, and he turned to see Murphy standing by the door, a large automatic in his hand.

"I'm fine," he said. Morrison was no longer sure how to react to Murphy. They had never been especially close. They were about the same age yet Morrison had gone much further in the organisation, taking a great deal of responsibility at an early age, while Murphy had remained as little more than a bodyguard. Morrison often felt that Murphy begrudged Morrison the access he had to Hennessy and to the other top IRA officials, but now he had something on which to pin his envy. He would never forgive Morrison's betrayal of his employer, and Morrison would forever have to watch his back when the man was around.

Murphy looked at Morrison for a second or two with cold eyes and then nodded, just once. "Liam says he wants us downstairs, in the lounge," he said.

Morrison followed him down the stairs where Hennessy was waiting for them. He took them into the lounge and showed them where he wanted them to stand, just behind the door. The lights were switched on because he'd drawn the curtains so that no one could look in from the courtyard.

"I'll lead him in, you close the door behind him," Hennessy said. "He doesn't normally carry a gun, but I want you to frisk him, and don't be gentle with him. I want him off balance, disorientated, OK?"

The two men nodded.

"If I say hit him, hit him. If I say shoot him in the knee, you do it. No hesitation, no argument. He must know that I am totally serious and that if he doesn't co-operate he will be killed."

"And will he?" Morrison asked.

"Oh yes, Sean. Quite definitely. But we both know that anybody can be made to talk eventually, don't we? Every man has his breaking point. And McGrath is used to giving pain, not receiving it. I think that the mere threat of violence will be enough, but if it isn't he must have no doubt that I mean what I say."

They heard the Volvo drive into the courtyard. "Right, I'll bring him in," said Hennessy and left them. The two men avoided looking at each other and Morrison wondered if Murphy had already been told what Hennessy had planned for him, and if those plans included a bullet in the back of the neck. He shrugged off the morbid thoughts, knowing that there was no point in dwelling on them. Whatever his fate, there was nowhere he could run, Hennessy would have the full backing of the IRA High Command. Morrison was just one man. That thought brought The Chinaman to mind, one man who was taking on the organisation, and who had so far come out on top. He wondered how Kerry was getting on. There were voices in the corridor and then McGrath entered the room, closely followed by Hennessy.

"This is hellish short notice, Liam. When will the rest be getting here?" McGrath said as Hennessy closed the door.

Morrison stepped up behind McGrath and pressed his gun against the man's neck.

"Don't make a sound, Hugh. Don't say a word," said Hennessy.

Morrison moved round in front of McGrath, keeping his gun against his throat, pushing hard so that his head was forced back. Murphy went behind McGrath and kicked his legs apart and then roughly searched him, going through all his pockets and then slapping down his legs and his arms.

"He's clean," said Murphy.

"Now listen to me, Hugh, and listen good. We're going to walk through into the kitchen and we'll stand at the back door. You're going to tell your men that you'll be staying the night and that you'll be going up to Belfast with me tomorrow. Then you and I are going to come back here and have a wee chat. If you try to warn them, they'll be shot. If you try to run we'll shoot you in the legs and then we'll bring you back here and we'll still have a chat, except this time you'll be in a lot of pain. Whatever you do, it's going to end the same way. Do you get my drift?"

"Have you lost your mind?" hissed McGrath.

"No," said Hennessy levelly. "I've lost my wife."

"Is that what this is about? Mary? I don't fucking believe it. I don't know what you're playing at but there'll be all hell to pay when Dublin finds out about this."

Morrison pushed the gun hard into McGrath's throat and made him wince.

"Once your men have gone you can call Dublin and you can speak to whoever you want. But it should be obvious to you that I wouldn't be doing this without their approval. And I'd better warn you, Hugh, they've given me *carte blanche*. Now, are you ready to speak to your men?"

McGrath glared at Hennessy as if about to refuse but suddenly the fight seemed to go out of him and he agreed.

Morrison slid his gun into the pocket of his bomber jacket, making sure that McGrath saw what he was doing. Hennessy opened the door and led the way. Morrison pushed McGrath ahead of him and Murphy fell in behind, his gun held behind his back. They went through the kitchen in single file and Hennessy unlatched the door. McGrath's driver and two bodyguards were in the car, laughing at something. Beyond the car, McGrath saw two of Hennessy's men carrying broken shotguns.

He and Hennessy walked over to the car while Morrison and Murphy remained in the doorway. The window wound down and McGrath put his hand on the roof of the car and dipped his head.

"I'm going to stay over with Liam, and we'll be going up to Belfast tomorrow. You lads can go back to the farm, I'll call you when I get back." His voice sounded to Hennessy as if it was about to break up but his men didn't appear to notice that there was anything amiss. They asked him if he was sure, McGrath insisted, and they started up the car and drove out of the courtyard. Morrison stepped out of the kitchen and around McGrath, shepherding him back inside. Murphy took off McGrath's glasses and threw them on the ground. He stamped on them, grinding the pieces into the ground with his boots, then followed him down the hallway, pushing him roughly in the back.

McGrath tried to talk to Hennessy as the group moved back into the lounge but he was ignored. Morrison recognised the technique of sapping the man's confidence to make him more susceptible to questioning. He took a wooden chair from the kitchen and placed it in front of the fire, facing Hennessy's favourite easy chair. Morrison and Murphy shoved McGrath on to the chair and then stood behind him. He began to turn round but before he did Murphy clipped him a glancing blow with the barrel of his gun. McGrath yelped involuntarily and put his hand to the side of his head. It came away bloody.

"Liam, what the fuck do you want?" He squinted over at Hennessy, trying to focus. The tinted glasses weren't just for show, McGrath was also quite short-sighted.

Hennessy ignored him and went over to the window. He untied two thick cords which were used for holding back the curtains, and he threw them over to Morrison. "Tie his hands behind him, and tie his legs to the chair," he said. Morrison did as he was told while Murphy held his gun against the back of McGrath's head. Hennessy sat down in his armchair.

"Is this about Mary?" asked McGrath. "Is that what that line about losing your wife was about? You're not losing her, Liam. She'll never leave you, she made that clear right from the start."

Anger flared inside Morrison and he stepped forward and smashed his gun across McGrath's face. It cut deep into his cheek and blood spattered across the carpet as Morrison raised his gun again.

"No!" shouted Hennessy. "Leave him be."

Morrison let the gun hang by his side. He was breathing heavily, his heartbeat pounding in his ears.

"We know what you're fucking angry at, don't we, Morrison?" taunted McGrath. Morrison whirled around and slapped him across the face so hard that McGrath keeled over, taking the chair with him and slamming into the floor.

"Sean!" said Hennessy. "You do that again and there'll be hell to pay. Get him up."

Morrison pulled McGrath and the chair back upright. McGrath was dazed and he spat blood on to the floor, groaning and shaking his head.

Hennessy waited until McGrath seemed to regain his senses before speaking again. "This is not about Mary, Hugh. Or at least not in the way you mean. It's about the bombings. The London bombings."

"I don't know what you mean," said McGrath.

"Hit him," Hennessy said to Murphy, and Murphy smacked his gun across McGrath's head.

"This is me asking you nicely," said Hennessy. "In a while I'm going to stop asking you nicely and Sean here is going to blow one of your kneecaps off. He's good at that, is Sean. He's done quite a bit of kneecapping in the past, though sometimes I think he's forgotten where his roots lie. But kneecapping is a bit like riding a bike, once you've got the hang of it you never lose it. And I think we both know that Sean might have personal reasons for enjoying putting a bullet or two in you. In fact, I might have trouble persuading him to keep his aim low. You get my drift, Hugh?"

"Yes, Liam. I get your drift," mumbled McGrath. He seemed to have difficulty moving his lips, and there was blood trickling down his chin. Morrison realised then what a devious, cunning bastard Hennessy was. McGrath was frightened, not just because of the threat of torture, but because he was being put in the hands of the man he'd betrayed most in all the world, the one man who really wanted to kill him with his bare hands, to tear him apart and to eat his raw flesh. McGrath could see the bloodlust in Morrison's eyes and it was infinitely more terrifying than Hennessy's threats.

Morrison was being used by Hennessy almost as cynically as he'd been used by Mary. He knew that, but at the same time he didn't care. He just wanted to see McGrath in pain, and he hoped with all his heart that he'd refuse to answer Hennessy's questions.

"What is it you want to know?" McGrath asked quietly.

"You are behind the bombings?"

"Yes."

"Why?"

"Because I think it's the only way to defeat the British."

"There's more to it than that. There must be."

McGrath shook his head.

"Where did you get the people from?"

"A couple from Scotland, two from Southern Ireland. I got to them before they joined the organisation, told them there was more they could do for the Cause by working directly for me. I sent them to Libya for training, then sent them to London to establish cover stories, to blend into the community."

"Where did the money come from? You couldn't touch IRA funds without it being noticed."

"I used my own money."

"Very noble of you. Hit him, Christy." The gun smashed into the back of McGrath's head again and he moaned and sagged in the chair. Murphy seized him by the hair and pulled his head back. "Where did the money come from, Hugh?" said Hennessy. "I'm about to stop asking nicely."

"Some of it from Libya," said McGrath. "But most of it came from the Iraqis. They channelled the money through Libya."

"You took money from the fucking Iraqis?"

"It's not where the money comes from that counts, it's what we do with it. You know that."

"How much did they pay you?" asked Hennessy.

"I don't know, it was . . ."

"Shoot him, Sean," said Hennessy quietly.

"No!" screamed McGrath. "For the love of God, no. Two million. That's what they paid. Two million pounds." Morrison squatted down and pressed the barrel of his gun behind McGrath's left kneecap. "Get him away, for God's sake get him away." He was screaming and crying and straining against the cords.

"Where's the money?"

"A Swiss bank account. It's yours, Liam, I promise. You can have the fucking lot. Just get him away from me, get him the fuck away from me!"

Hennessy waved Morrison away and he reluctantly took his gun away from McGrath's leg. Hennessy picked up a notepad and a pen. "I want the number of the account, and I want the names and addresses of the bombers."

"What then?" asked McGrath. "I give you the names and then what?"

"I won't kill you," said Hennessy. "You give me the names and I'll take you down to Dublin and you can plead your case to the High Command. That's the only deal you're going to get from me. Now do I get the names?"

McGrath swallowed and coughed, and spat out more bloody saliva. "You get the names," he said.

Despite the sun being almost directly overhead, Kerry began to find the going easier, helped by the fact that The Chinaman appeared to be heading due east, albeit sticking to the hedgerows wherever possible. It would have been harder to follow him if he'd cut across the fields where the grass was thick and springy. As it was she found several good examples of his footprints in muddy places formed where rainwater ran off into the ditches.

It was just after 12.15 p.m. when she came across the B180 and Tollymore Forest Park beyond. She pulled a twig from the hedge and stuck it into the ground like a miniature bonsai as she'd done every hundred yards or so as a signpost for Sean. She took a plastic bottle of water from her rucksack and drank as she planned her next move. He'd obviously crossed the road but it would take some time to find out where. The better bet would be to cross the road straightaway and check the trees where she was more likely to spot evidence of his passing on the forest floor.

"Sean Morrison, where the hell are you?" she said to herself. She wanted to go into the trees immediately, knowing that he'd be certain to be hiding somewhere in there. She felt the same as she did when she got within shooting distance of a deer that she'd stalked for hours, the adrenalin flowed and the desire to get in close was so strong that she could almost taste it. Only one thing held her back, once in the woods she wouldn't be able to see the flare and she'd have to keep the radio off at all times because she'd have no way of knowing if The Chinaman was within listening distance. She could sit down and wait, but she didn't want to. She took out the walkie-talkie and switched it on and pressed the talk button.

"Can you hear me?" she asked, remembering Sean's instructions not to use any names over the air. There was no answer, just static. "Is there anybody there?" she asked. When no one replied to her third attempt she took that as a sign that she was on her own and that Sean Morrison had no one to blame but himself if he couldn't find her. She put the walkie-talkie and the bottle of water back into the rucksack, waited until the road was clear and then dashed across, into the cool, enveloping greenness of the woods.

Hennessy left Morrison and Murphy in the lounge as he went to use the phone. He took the notebook because the four names McGrath had given him were new to him. He dialled the number and it was answered by Bromley himself.

"It's Liam Hennessy," he said.

"Yes," said Bromley. Hennessy heard the sound of a pipe being tapped against an ashtray. The thought suddenly came to him that Bromley probably recorded all his calls, but he'd gone too far now to worry about that. He read out the list of names and gave Bromley the address of the flat in Wapping where McGrath said they could be found. Bromley repeated the names and the address back to Hennessy and then asked if there was anything else.

"Such as?" asked Hennessy.

"Such as the name of the man in your organisation who planned all this?"

"You'll have to leave that side of it to us, Bromley. We'll be washing our own dirty linen."

"You won't even give me the satisfaction of knowing who it was?"

Hennessy laughed harshly. "No, I'm afraid I won't. Just be assured that we'll take care of it."

"Permanently?"

"You have what you wanted, Bromley. Just do what you have to do." He replaced the receiver.

He went back into the lounge.

"What are you playing at?" said McGrath, squinting up at Hennessy.

"Gag him," Hennessy told Murphy.

"Oh for the love of God, Liam, you won't be needing a gag," said McGrath, panic mounting in his voice.

"Gag him," Hennessy repeated. Murphy took a large green handkerchief from his pocket and forced it between McGrath's teeth before tying it behind his head. McGrath grunted and strained, but nothing intelligible emerged. His eyes were wide and frightened, but Hennessy ignored his pleas. "Christy, take him out and shoot him."

Murphy didn't express surprise or argue, he'd killed on Hennessy's orders before, always without question. He moved to untie McGrath from the chair, but the man went wild, thrashing about like a mad thing and trying to scream through the gag. Murphy calmly clipped the butt of his gun against McGrath's temple, knocking him senseless without so much as a whimper.

"Here, let me help you," said Morrison as Murphy slung the unconscious man over his broad shoulders.

"No, Sean, you stay with me," said Hennessy. "Do it in the barn, Christy. You can bury him in one of the fields tonight."

Hennessy waited until Murphy had carried McGrath outside before speaking again. "I want to explain why McGrath is being killed, so that you don't get the wrong idea," he said quietly.

"Wrong idea?"

"Dublin were quite explicit about what they wanted doing. They wanted the bombings stopped and they wanted the man responsible out of the way. I explained that I thought McGrath was the man, and they said that didn't make a difference."

"But you told him he'd get a chance to plead his case."

"That was to encourage him to talk, to give him hope. But they'd already said that if I was one hundred per cent certain then he was to be taken care of here. No appeal, no trial, no publicity. No corpse."

"Why did he do it?"

Hennessy shrugged. "I guess the money helped persuade him. Gaddafi and Hussein have their own axes to grind against the British Government, and someone like McGrath would be a godsend. McGrath earns a small fortune from his smuggling operations, he's been playing the border like a bloody one-string fiddle. But most of that disappeared with the European Community's single market, so recently he's had to depend even more on his other sources of income in Belfast, and they in turn depend to a great extent on the Troubles. He's behind a number of protection rackets in the city. Most of the cash goes into IRA funds, but I doubt if he passed it all on. I'd be very surprised if some of it didn't find its way into his Swiss bank account, along with the Libyan and Iraqi money."

"His men won't be happy."

"Dublin will take care of that. Anyway, that's not the point. The point I'm trying to make, Sean, is that McGrath is being killed because he was a traitor to the Cause, because he betrayed the IRA, not because of Mary."

They heard a muffled pistol shot in the distance, but neither of them showed any reaction to the noise.

"I love Mary," said Hennessy. "Despite everything. We've been together a long time, and sometimes I think I know her better than she knows herself. I'm the rock over which she breaks, if you understand what I mean. I give her stability, a base, security, but she's always needed more than that, more than I can give her." His voice began to falter. "I'm not explaining myself very well," he added.

Morrison felt embarrassed. It wasn't often that Liam Hennessy was lost for words, his oratory skills were legendary in the courts of Belfast. Morrison didn't know what to say and he looked out of the window, hoping that he would finish and he could get back to Kerry and the hunt for The Chinaman, where at least he'd be out doing something. "What I'm trying to say is that you don't have to worry. I'm angry, sure enough, but not to the extent that I'd tell Christy to take you out to the barn. I'm angry at Mary, too, but that's something I'm going to have to work out myself. You've hurt me, Sean, but I've been hurt before and I'll get over it. And your loyalty to the Cause has never been in question. Neither has hers, funnily enough. McGrath might have been doing it for the money, but Mary I'm sure was doing it because she felt it was in the best interests of the Cause. And for revenge, maybe. Because of that I'll try to protect her, though God knows it's going to be hard."

He looked at Morrison, his face unsmiling, but there was no hatred in his eyes, just sadness. In a way, thought Morrison, hatred would have been easier to deal with. Compassion and understanding just made him feel all the more guilty.

"One more thing," Hennessy added. "When all this is over, I'd be happier if you went back to New York, but I guess that's what you'd want, anyway."

Morrison nodded. "Liam, I'm . . ."

"Don't say it," interrupted Hennessy. "I don't want your pity, Sean. Just help me get The Chinaman out of my hair and then go back to the States."

Morrison realised there was nothing more to be said so he went through to the kitchen. Hennessy's walkie-talkie was lying on the kitchen table and he picked it up. He tried to call Kerry but got no reply and that worried him. Surely she wouldn't have left it switched off, not when she was out there on her own? He retrieved his ski-pole and the canvas haversack, checked his gun and stepped into the courtyard. Murphy walked over from the barn. He appeared to be totally impass-ive, no sign that he'd just taken a man's life.

"You're off then?" he said to Morrison, his voice cold.

Morrison wondered what Murphy was thinking, and how he would have reacted if he'd been told to take Morrison into the barn and put a bullet in the back of his neck. He wondered too how much he could actually trust Hennessy now and what would happen once The Chinaman had been dealt with. He would have to be very, very careful.

"Yeah, I've got to catch up with the girl."

"Be careful," said Murphy. Morrison smiled, but he realised as he did so that he had no way of knowing if Mur-phy's words were a genuine expression of concern, or a threat.

Roy O'Donnell was driving one of the Land-Rovers while Kavanagh sat in the passenger seat scanning the roadside. The Land-Rover containing Tommy O'Donoghue and Michael O'Faolain was about a quarter of a mile behind them. They drove slowly and on many occasions impatient drivers had sounded their horns and they'd had to wave them on. At one point a convoy of army vehicles had come up behind them and they'd had to speed up so as not to attract attention. A Lynx helicopter flew low above the army patrol, keeping watch. That had cost them half an hour because when they'd eventually found a place where they could turn off they had had to wait until the convoy was well out of sight before they could drive back along the road and restart the search.

Now they had an excuse to dawdle because ahead of them rumbled a large, mud-covered red tractor. Kavanagh was looking for gaps in the yellow-flowered gorse and the trees, anywhere where a van could be driven. They'd stopped at half a dozen possibilities on the right-hand side and gone into the woods as far as they could but found nothing. Kavanagh's plan was to go all the way through the forest and then to drive back, westwards, checking the other side of the road.

"Slow down," he said to O'Donnell. "Och, too late. Do a U-turn and go back." O'Donnell indicated and pulled hard on the steering wheel. The Land-Rover behind them copied the manoeuvre. "There," Kavanagh pointed.

"I don't see anything," said O'Donnell, screwing up his eyes. "What am I looking for?"

"There's a track there. Look." They drove by a gap between the trees.

"Could be, I suppose," said O'Donnell. "Shall we go down it?"

"Let's give it a go," said Kavanagh. They did another U-turn and this time when they reached the gap O'Donnell indicated a left turn and drove slowly between the trees. When both Land-Rovers were off the main road Kavanagh told O'Donnell to stop the vehicle and he got out. He waved at O'Donoghue and O'Faolain to come over. The four men stood on the track with their shotguns, like a group of country farmers out on a rabbit shoot. Kavanagh looked down at the muddy ground, but he wasn't sure what he was looking for. There were some tyre tracks but he had no way of knowing how long they had been there or what had made them.

"We'll leave the Land-Rovers here and walk," he said. "Spread out and keep your eyes open."

Nguyen heard them coming from almost a quarter of a mile away. He was sitting next to a thick gorse bush by a patch of bluebells eating rice and chicken with his fingers. The first thing he heard was a group of startled birds flapping out of the trees. He put the cartons of food on the ground and stood up. He listened carefully, moving his head from side to side to get a bearing on where they were coming from. Eventually he heard the crunch of a boot on a twig and a sniff from the direction of the track. He couldn't tell how many there were because he was too far away, but he was sure there were more than one. He put the lids back on the foil cartons and packed them in the rucksack next to the pipe bomb. There was no point in using the bomb, for it to be effective it had to be in a confined space. The gun would be better. He checked the magazine before slipping the rucksack on his back and moving in a crouch through the undergrowth towards the track. There was no point in running blindly away, first he had to see who it was. It might be nothing more sinister than a group of forestry workers.

He moved parallel to the track, placing each foot carefully so as to make no noise, stopping and listening every few steps. He took cover behind a leafy horse chestnut and waited for them to draw level with him. There were four of them, three well-built men and a thin youth, all of them carrying shotguns. He recognised one of the men from Hennessy's farm. They were moving slowly, watching the ground more than the forest, and Nguyen doubted that they would fail to find the van, despite the effort he'd made in covering his tracks. None of the men spoke and they were obviously trying to make an effort to move quietly, but to Nguyen they sounded like water-buffaloes. Feet were crunching on twigs, kicking leaves aside, squelching into damp soil. Nguyen could have followed them with his eyes closed.

He crept from tree to tree, flitting from cover to cover like a shadow. The men came to the point where he'd driven the van off the track, and for a moment he hoped that they'd missed it because they continued on, but then the man who appeared to be the leader of the group held up his hand for them to stop. The man knelt down and studied the ground and then went back along the track. He motioned for them to gather around him and then began to whisper earnestly, making small movements with his hand. Nguyen was too far away to hear what he was saying but it was clear that he was telling them that they were to spread out and move through the trees.

Nguyen knew that he had to make a decision now. He could abandon the van and vanish into the woods until the time came to confront Hennessy again, but that would mean that when it was all over he'd have nowhere to go, no way of getting out of the country. He'd be stuck with only what he was wearing and what he carried in his rucksack. And while that was ideal for living rough it would give him a lot of explaining to do when he tried to board a ferry or a plane. But if he killed the men it wouldn't be too long before Hennessy would send more to investigate. And he doubted that he'd be able to conceal four bodies plus whatever transport they had arrived in, not well enough to survive a full-scale search of the woods. He could kill them and then bring his plans forward, go back to Hennessy's farm for the final confrontation. But if he did that then there was a good chance that Hennessy would be none the wiser about the bombings and he'd have to kill him and start all over again with one of the other Sinn Fein names that the London journalist had given him. He'd have to move to a different hiding place, take his van somewhere else. It was possible, he decided. He heard an excited shout and realised that his van had been discovered. He took the safety off the Browning and crept towards them. The leader was standing by the front of the van, pulling away the ferns and branches Nguyen had used to conceal it. He was joined by the red-haired youth and then the two heavyweights came trampling through the undergrowth. They cleared away all the vegetation covering the Renault while Nguyen moved as close as he could without being seen. He hid behind a bush half a dozen steps from the rear doors of the van.

"Open the bonnet, Tommy," he heard a voice say. "And, Michael, check what's in the back."

The gangly youth walked round to the rear of the van. He transferred his shotgun to his left hand and with his right twisted the door handle. It wouldn't move, because Nguyen had locked it. Nguyen put the safety back on and stuck the gun into the waistband of his trousers before slipping the hunting knife out of its scabbard on the rucksack strap. He was reluctant to go in shooting because it was one against four and as soon as they heard a shot they'd all start firing.

He held his left hand up in front of him, his right ready to stab with the knife, because a stab always went deeper than a slash. He took three quick steps, centre of gravity low.

"It's locked," the youth called.

"Well force it," the leader shouted. "Are yez stupid or what?" There was a smash of glass as one of the other men broke the driver's window with the butt of his shotgun.

Nguyen sprang the remaining distance and forced his left wrist across the youth's trachea and simultaneously drove the knife horizontally into the kidney. He twisted the knife to do the maximum amount of damage. The wrist across the windpipe stopped all noise but Nguyen could feel him struggle and tense and then relax and slump as he died. He eased the body on to the ground and put the knife back into its scabbard.

The man who'd smashed the window had opened the door and was looking for the bonnet-release catch. Nguyen took one of his throwing knives and moved to the right-hand side of the van. He risked a quick look and saw that the man had his back to him. Nguyen ducked away, took out the gun and slipped the safety off once more, holding the gun in his left hand.

There was a loud click and the man shouted: "That should do it." Nguyen stepped from behind the van, the knife ready. He was holding the blade about two inches from its tip, the handle upwards. The man closed the van door and as he did, Nguyen had a clear view of the side of his head and his neck and he threw hard. The blade thudded into the man's throat and blood gushed down his chest. Nguyen began moving as the man's mouth opened and closed with no sound because the blade had speared his Adam's apple. He transferred the Browning to his right hand, side-stepped across the rear of the van and moved up the left side. The two men at the front had opened the bonnet and had their heads over the engine. "What do you reckon, pull out the spark-plug leads?" one said.

"Yeah. And let down the tyres. That should fix the bastard."

There was a thud as the man with the knife in his throat fell to the ground, his shotgun scraping against the side of the van.

"What's up, Tommy?" said one of the men.

Nguyen stepped swiftly up to the front of the van, knowing

that the two men would be distracted by the noise of the falling body.

"Tommy?" said the man again, and it was followed by a curse. As Nguyen got to the front the two men had their backs to him as they moved towards their dying friend. Nguyen put the barrel of his gun up against the head of the man nearest to him and fired. The shot was muffled as the bullet smashed through the skull and exploded out of the man's face in a red and pink shower of blood and brains. The other man whirled around but before the shotgun could point at Nguyen he fired the Browning a second time, hitting the man in the dead centre of his chest. He fell backwards, a look of surprise on his face and blood blossoming on his shirt, the shotgun dropping from nerveless fingers.

It had taken less than a minute but all four were dead. Nguyen took no pride in the achievement. When he'd first travelled over to Ireland he'd hoped to get what he wanted without killing anyone. He knew that people would have to be hurt before they'd take him seriously, but he'd taken enough lives during his time in the jungles of Vietnam and he hadn't wanted to add to his body count. They'd forced him into it, he said to himself. It was their fault.

He stood over the body of the last man he'd killed and listened. The forest had gone silent but gradually the birdsong and insect noise returned and when he was satisfied that all was well he turned towards the corpses.

Kerry heard two gunshots, the second louder and more distinct than the first. It sounded as if they came from two different guns. She had gone about eight hundred yards into the forest and was making progress, albeit slowly. She'd found where Nguyen had entered the trees but had lost his trail soon after and had wasted more than an hour doubling back and then searching backwards and forwards in an arc shape until she picked it up again. There was no obvious path for The Chinaman to follow and he had constantly had to change direction to get around large trees or bushes. And her task was made harder by the fact that Nguyen had travelled in both directions. Half the signs that she found were actually made when he had been going west, towards the farm, not into the depths of the forest.

The shots had come from the east, but she had no way of knowing how far away they had been, or even if they had been the result of Nguyen firing a gun or being shot at. If Nguyen was under fire then there was a chance that he'd now be running through the forest in the other direction, putting even more distance between them. If she carried on at her snail's pace she'd never catch up with him. But if she hurried towards the source of the shots and it turned out to be nothing more than poachers or Uncle Liam's men letting off their guns, accidentally or otherwise, then she risked losing the trail.

She tried to think what her father would do. Stick with the tracks or go after the shots? She thought of the tracking expeditions with her father, usually taking rich Germans and Japanese out into the Highlands to kill deer, looking for the spore and the tracks until they were close enough for the kill. Sometimes he'd take shortcuts, ignoring the signs because he felt that he knew instinctively where the deer were. That's how it felt now, she realised. She knew the shots came from Nguyen. She felt it inside. She began to run eastwards, towards where she thought the shots had come from.

Sean Morrison had heard the shots, too. He was almost a mile from the forest, faithfully following the trail Kerry had left for him. He immediately recognised the sounds as coming from a pistol rather than a shotgun or rifle, and guessed that it had been Nguyen. Kavanagh and the boys had taken shotguns and a poacher or farmer wouldn't use a handgun.

He ran for the trees. He saw a twig that Kerry had placed in the gap between two sycamore trees but he ignored it, taking the path of least resistance through the undergrowth. It was never easy to judge how far away a noise like a gunshot was, but Sean didn't reckon it could have been much more than three miles away, possibly closer. He ran for all he was worth because there had only been two shots and whereas Nguyen was armed he knew that Kerry didn't have a gun.

Nguyen dragged the bodies one by one into the undergrowth, putting his arms under their shoulders and letting their heels scrape along the ground. There was no point in going to the trouble of digging graves for them because any serious search would see the disturbed soil, so he made do by hiding them inside a large patch of brambles and covering them with ferns. When he'd finished there were eight wavy lines carved in the mud by their feet and he used a leafy branch to wipe them away.

He went back along the track to find out what transport Hennessy's men had used and came upon the two Land-Rovers. They were blocking the track so he'd have to move them when he wanted to drive the van out, but it made more sense to take them further into the forest right away.

Luckily both sets of keys had been left in the ignition. He climbed into the first and started the engine. His hands began to shake and he gripped the steering wheel tightly, the tension making the veins stand up on the backs of his hands. He struggled to control himself, not sure what was causing the nervous reaction. It could have been delayed shock, but it had never happened to him before after combat, and he had no remorse for what he'd done. He had no doubt at all that the four men would have taken his life without a second thought. So what was the problem? He closed his eyes and felt the vibrations of the diesel engine through his arms, making the bones shudder. He had to regain control of himself, he owed it to his family.

Kerry heard an engine start up and a few minutes later a vehicle growl through the trees. She headed towards the noise and in the distance she saw a Land-Rover. In the driving seat was a small, Oriental man dressed in a camouflage uniform.

"The Chinaman," she said under her breath. She crept forward and hid behind a sycamore tree. She watched as Nguyen stopped the Land-Rover under a spreading horse chestnut at the edge of a clearing and got out. He walked off into the woods and a few minutes later returned with an armful of ferns which he spread over the roof, bonnet and wheels. He then placed branches against the sides of the vehicle before standing back to inspect his handiwork. On his back was a small rucksack, similar to the one she was using to carry her equipment. Stuck into the waistband of his trousers was a large gun and the sight of it reminded her that she didn't have a weapon. Damn Sean Morrison, she thought. Damn him for not leaving the gun. One shot and it would all be over.

Nguyen walked off into the trees again and Kerry followed him. She didn't want to get too close because she was aware that her feet were making a noise as she moved through the undergrowth, no matter how much care she took. She lost him but then heard another engine start up and saw him drive a second Land-Rover along the track. She'd seen it before, parked in the courtyard of her uncle's farm, and with a rising sense of fear she wondered what had happened to the men who'd been driving in the vehicles. Surely The Chinaman couldn't have killed them all? Besides, there had only been two shots.

She crept from tree to tree though with less urgency this time because she knew where he was going. She caught up with him as he was stacking more ferns on the Land-Rover's bonnet and knelt down behind a tree to watch. He walked off into the undergrowth again, presumably for more branches, and he was soon out of sight.

She looked at her watch and wondered where the hell Sean Morrison had got to. The thought suddenly came to her that she hadn't left a trail for him to follow. Would he be smart enough to spot where she'd run through the forest? Had she taught him enough in their few hours together? The only way she had of showing her position was to fire the flare gun, and she couldn't do that without alerting The Chinaman. Her breath quickened at the thought of the flare gun. What if she were to bring in The Chinaman herself? The flare gun would be just as threatening as a pistol. She slid the rucksack off her back and undid the cords at the top. As she put her hand in and groped around for the flare gun she heard a click behind her and found herself looking down the barrel of an automatic pistol.

"Stand up, slowly," said Nguyen. He kept the gun trained on her face as she got to her feet, still holding the rucksack. She clutched it to her chest like a baby. "Who are you?" he asked.

She thought frantically. "I'm a . . . I'm a . . . er . . ." she stammered. "I'm a birdwatcher. Watching birds. My binoculars are in here." She nodded at her rucksack. "Let me show you." Her shaking hand tightened around the handle of the flare gun, but she suddenly realised that it wasn't loaded, the cartridges were loose in the rucksack.

Nguyen held out his hand. "Give me," he said. She handed over the rucksack. "Drop the pole. And move into the clearing," he said, gesturing with the gun. They walked together out of the shade of the trees and he made her stand by one of the Land-Rovers.

"How old are you?" Nguyen asked, frowning.

"Twenty-four," she said.

"I had a daughter who would be twenty-four this year," said Nguyen. He stepped back and put the rucksack on the floor, kneeling down beside it. She wondered if she could rush him, but he never took his eyes off her, using his hands to search the rucksack. He pulled out the case containing the binoculars and opened it.

"Bird-watching," repeated Kerry, willing The Chinaman to believe her. She was finding it hard to breathe and her mouth had gone dry.

Nguyen nodded, placed the case on the ground, and continued to rummage inside the rucksack. He took out the walkie-talkie and examined it and put it next to the binoculars. Again his hand went in like a conjuror looking for the white rabbit, though this time he came out with Kerry's notebook.

Kerry began to say that it was for drawing birds she had seen but Nguyen ignored her and slowly turned the pages.

He saw the sketch she'd made of his footprint and he nodded to himself. "Birdwatching," he mused.

They both heard a crashing noise from the depths of the forest, the sound of a man running. Nguyen looked over his shoulder, then back to the girl, obviously unsure what to do. Kerry knew that The Chinaman was considering shooting her, or maybe using the big hunting knife fastened to the strap of his rucksack. Her stomach turned liquid.

The crashing noise got louder and Nguyen moved away from Kerry, deciding that she was the lesser threat. He ran in a crouch to the edge of the clearing, his gun at the ready. As he ran, Kerry grabbed her rucksack and groped for the flare gun and a cartridge. Her hands were trembling and it took several attempts before she managed to open the gun and force home the cartridge.

She moved to the side so that she could see over The Chinaman's shoulder. He was standing about fifty feet away from her, cocking his head and listening, and then raising the gun as Morrison came into view. Kerry saw him at the same time as Nguyen did, his dark hair waving in the wind and his haversack banging on his hip as he ran. Nguyen ducked behind a tree and Kerry stepped forward, aiming the flare gun with both hands.

Morrison saw her and shouted, and began waving frantically.

"Sean, watch out!" she yelled, as Nguyen moved from behind the tree and pointed his pistol at Morrison.

"Nguyen, it's all right! It's all over!" Morrison yelled, and The Chinaman lowered his gun. As he did, Kerry pulled the trigger.

"Kerry! No! No!" Morrison screamed.

The pistol kicked in her hands but she kept it steady and there was a loud whooshing noise as the flare erupted from the barrel and hurtled through the air leaving behind a trail of white smoke in the still air. It smacked into the rucksack on Nguyen's back. Nguyen whirled round and pointed his gun at Kerry. She flinched, throwing her hands up in front of her face, knowing that he wouldn't miss at that range. Nguyen's finger tightened on the trigger but he couldn't do it, he couldn't bring himself to shoot her. Not a girl. He could smell the burning flare and his ears were filled with the hiss of melting nylon and he knew that she had killed him, that there were only seconds before the heat ignited the bomb in the rucksack. He dropped the Browning and struggled with the straps of the rucksack, yelling at her to get away from him.

Morrison burst into the clearing and saw Kerry kneeling on the ground, her head in her hands. At first he thought that she'd been shot but there was no blood and he hadn't heard The Chinaman fire his gun.

"Go away, go away!" screamed Nguyen. "Bomb! Bomb!"

Suddenly Morrison realised what was happening, why The Chinaman had thrown his gun on the ground and why he was now frantically fumbling with the nylon rucksack. Morrison rushed forward and grabbed one of the straps, forcing it down off his shoulder. The Chinaman was gasping for breath, twisting and turning to get the deadly package off his back. The heat from the flare seared Morrison's hands and he saw the hairs on his wrists shrivel and blacken, then he was hit by a wave of pain that made him cry out. The white light was blinding and he closed his eyes as the rucksack pulled away from The Chinaman's shoulders and he slumped to the ground. Morrison swung the burning mass as hard as he could and let it fly up into the air, hissing and spluttering into the trees, and then he dived over to shield Kerry, falling against her and knocking her to the ground, then lying across her and shouting at her to keep her eyes closed and her face covered.

The explosion came within seconds, the blast deafening and vibrating the ground like a small earthquake, followed by a barrage of twigs and chunks of wood that fell like a tropical rain shower and then stopped just as suddenly. The forest was silent, as if the bomb had killed every living thing for miles. Morrison rolled off Kerry and helped her to her feet. In the distance a bird whistled and was answered by another. Short, nervous calls as if they were testing the silence. Satisfied that Kerry hadn't been hurt, Morrison went over to The Chinaman, who was rubbing his eyes with the knuckles of his hand, coughing and retching.

"Thank you," he said, surprising Morrison with his politeness.

Morrison heard a metallic click and he turned to see Kerry, her hands dwarfed by the big Browning.

"Move away, Sean," she said quietly. "I've got the bastard covered."

"Easy, Kerry," said Morrison. "Put the gun down. He's not going to hurt anyone." The Chinaman showed no fear. He looked at Kerry, his face expressionless.

"I'm going to kill him," she said, her voice oddly flat. Morrison wondered if maybe she was in shock. Her eyes were cold, almost blank, as if she was sleep-walking, but she seemed to have no trouble in keeping the gun pointed at the centre of The Chinaman's chest.

"It's over," said Morrison, holding his hand out for the gun. "We've found out who the bombers are. We know who was backing them. It's finished. We can all go home."

"It's not over!" she hissed. "It won't be over until he's dead."

Morrison looked at The Chinaman. He was standing with his hands loose at his side, his head slightly bowed but his eyes fixed on Kerry's face as if willing her to shoot, as if he wanted her to end it. There was, Morrison thought, a sadness in his eyes, a look that said that there was nothing else they could do to him. Morrison looked back at Kerry, his hand still outstretched.

"Kerry, he could have shot you. He didn't. You can't kill him. He's not armed, he's not a threat." He stepped forward and she took half a step back. "He had a deal with Liam, and we're going to stick to it. It's over. Give me the gun and we can go home."

Her finger began to squeeze the trigger and Morrison knew that she was about to fire. Still The Chinaman stayed rooted to the spot. "Kerry, if you do this you're doing it for the wrong reason. You're not doing it for Liam Hennessy, or for your father, or for the IRA," Morrison said. He took another step forward. "You're doing it for yourself." Another step. The gun was almost within reach. "It'd be on your conscience for ever. It's not worth it. Trust me, I know. It's not worth it."

He moved quickly, bringing down his right hand and forcing the gun to the side, away from The Chinaman, and then he grabbed it and twisted it out of her grasp. She tried to get the gun back but he held it out of her reach. She yelled in frustration, then drew back her hand and slapped him across the face, hard, and began to sob. He stepped forward and took her in his arms, holding her close but being careful to keep the gun where she couldn't grab it, just in case. She put her head against his shoulder and he could feel her body shudder as she cried. He turned with her slowly, as if they were dancing to a slow song, until he was facing The Chinaman.

"Go," said Morrison.

"You said you had the names?"

Morrison told him the names of the bombers, and the address of the flat in Wapping where they were based, and Nguyen repeated them to himself, imprinting the information on his memory.

"Thank you," Nguyen said.

"Don't thank me. Just go."

Nguyen turned and walked into the undergrowth, leaving Morrison and Kerry alone in the clearing. She had stopped crying and he could feel her chest rising and falling in time with her breathing. "I'm sorry, Sean," she whispered. "I'm so sorry."

He smoothed her hair and kissed her on the top of her head.

"It's OK," he said. "Sometimes it gets you like that. The violence. It gets a grip on you without you realising it. It's like a drug, it pulls you along . . ."

She turned her head up and pushed her lips against his, kissing him hard, reaching around his neck with her arms. Her baseball cap fell off and her hair swung free. Her tears wet his cheeks as they kissed and she pressed herself against him. He threw the gun away and then held her with both hands, touching and caressing as her tongue found its way into his mouth, probing, teasing, exciting him until all thoughts of The Chinaman evaporated and he concentrated on her, the feel of her, the smell of her, the taste of her. She pulled him down on to the ground, her hands groping for his belt, her breath coming in small gasps as she said his name over and over again. He made love to her quickly but gently, in the grass, under the trees, next to The Chinaman's gun.

Nguyen couldn't believe that the man would let him go. He was sure that he planned to shoot him as he left the clearing, but there was no gunshot, no thump in the back, he just kept on walking. Once he was sure they really were releasing him he began to run through the forest towards the van. It would only be a matter of time before the four bodies were discovered and when that happened he doubted that Liam Hennessy would be as generous. Nguyen wasn't surprised at how easy it had been to kill the men, he'd always been good at it, all that was required was the mental switch. He'd fought against it when he first started out, but now that he'd killed he knew that he would follow it through to the end. He would avenge his family, he knew that with a diamond-hard certainty. He would do whatever it took, and there would be no remorse, no guilt. Afterwards, when he'd finished, then he'd worry about his own future, but at the moment he could look no further than the flat in Wapping and the IRA bombers.

He opened the back door of the van and quickly threw out all the supplies inside. He stripped off his camouflage gear and changed back into jeans and a pullover, checked that his money was still under the front seat with his passport, and then he drove the van back down the track and on to the main road and headed for the airport.

They travelled in three Range Rovers with a police motorcycle escort, roaring down the outside lane of the M40 at more than ninety miles per hour. The flashing blue lights and the howling sirens forced a clear path through the early afternoon traffic on the motorway, though there were plenty of resentful looks from the company reps in their Sierras and Escorts as the men in the unmarked Range Rovers went by. Pulling over for fire engines and ambulances was second nature, but nobody liked to move out of the fast lane without knowing why, and there was nothing about the vehicles that identified the men inside as belonging to the SAS.

There were four men in each vehicle, tough-looking men with broad shoulders, but as they hurtled towards London they were laughing and smiling and looked no more threatening than a group of miners on a coach trip to the coast. Mike "Joker" Cramer was in the front passenger seat of the first Range Rover, laughing at a particularly foul joke that the driver, Pete Jackson, had spun out over the last two miles. The men were tense as they always were when going into action, but they used humour to keep themselves from worrying.

In the back seat were Sam "Bunny" Warren and Rob "Ginge" Macdonald. Bunny was tapping the back of his hand against the window and he wasn't as quick to laugh at Jacko's joke as the rest were.

Joker, the assault-team leader, was the leanest of the four men, well over six-foot tall, with a thin face that always appeared haggard no matter how much sleep he got. He looked over his shoulder at Bunny, a swarthy, stocky man with piercing green eyes. "Is that Morse code, or what, Bunny?" he said.

Bunny stopped tapping. "Sorry, Joker. Habit."

"You want some gum?" Joker asked, holding out the packet of Wrigley's which he always carried with him now that he'd given up smoking.

"Cheers," said Bunny, taking a piece. "We nearly at the RV?"

"Not far," said Joker. He leant forward and picked up the A to Z map of London. The Colonel had called from London and given them an address in Rotherhithe Street, alongside the Thames, where they were to meet. The convoy left the A40 and they motored along Marylebone Road, along Euston

Road past King's Cross and then they followed City Road to the Thames. The motorcycle riders worked in teams, rushing ahead to hold up the traffic whenever the lights weren't in their favour, then remounting and following up behind like pilot fish busily swimming around prowling sharks. When they reached the river the motorbikes peeled off by arrangement, leaving the three Range Rovers to make their own way across London Bridge to Bermondsey and then left along Jamaica Road to Rotherhithe.

They drove by new wharf-style blocks of riverside flats and then came to the building where the Colonel said they were to meet.

"This is it," said Joker. The three vehicles pulled up at the pavement. Joker climbed out and looked up and down the road. There were no signs that an operation was under way, no police cars, no ambulances, no nothing, just the sound of the Thames lapping against the banks.

The men got out of the cars and stood on the pavement. They were, Joker had to admit to himself, a motley crew. The one thing they had in common was that they were all in the peak of condition and trained to kill. I don't know what they'll do to the enemy, thought Joker, but they scare the shit out of me. He tried to remember who'd said that first, whether it had been Wellington or Napoleon, because he was sure he'd heard it somewhere. Whatever, that's exactly how he felt about the eleven men who began pulling their kit-bags out of the back of the cars.

"Where do we go?" asked Reg Lawrence, another assault-team leader.

"Fifteen B," said Joker. "This one here."

He pushed the button by Fifteen B and a light clicked on. There was a television camera behind a glass panel and a red light came on above it and then he heard the Colonel's voice tell him to come up. The door buzzed and Joker pushed it and the men filed through and followed him upstairs to the third-floor flat.

An intelligence officer in his distinctive green beret had the door open for them.

"The green slime gets here first for a change," jeered a

voice from the back, but when Joker looked to see who it was he was met with blank, innocent faces.

The flat was spacious, white-painted walls and ceilings and polished wood floors, a fully fitted kitchen but no furniture, and there was a "For Sale" sign in one of the bedroom windows overlooking the street.

The Colonel was in the lounge looking through a powerful pair of binoculars mounted on a tripod. A large blackboard was leaning against one wall and, as the men stood around, the intelligence officer began drawing a map of the flat under surveillance in white chalk. The Colonel looked up and nodded at Joker. "Fancy a look?" he asked.

The binoculars were trained on a modern wharf on the north side of the river and when Joker looked through them he saw a large french window and a lounge beyond it, a rectangular room with three men sitting around. The television was switched on but Joker couldn't see what was on the screen. In front of the window was a balcony, twelve-feet square, with a couple of white chairs and a circular table. Joker moved the binoculars sideways. The building was mainly featureless brick wall and double-glazed windows, but two-thirds of the way along the architect had obviously decided to introduce a little variety and he'd staggered the flats so that the one to the left of the flat under observation was about twelve feet further back and the one to the right was an equal distance closer to the river. While it made the building easier on the eye it made it impossible to enter the balcony from either side. There was no flat above the one under observation, but the architect had built a penthouse flat at the right-hand side of the building and its extra-large balcony overlooked it. It was immediately apparent to Joker that the penthouse was the way in. It would be a simple matter to jump down to the balcony below, they wouldn't even have to abseil.

The buzzer sounded from the hallway and the intelligence officer went to open the front door and let in two men from D11, the Metropolitan Police firearms team. They stood at the back of the group of the SAS men, their rifles slung over their shoulders. The Colonel nodded a welcome and went over to the blackboard, chalk in hand.

Woody panicked a little when he opened the door to his bedsit. Clothes were strewn all over the floor, a week's worth of newspapers were piled up under the room's one window, and there was a collection of empty lager cans and a three-quarters empty bottle of Bells by the side of the bed. It looked as if a burglar had wreaked vengeance on the place after finding there was nothing worth stealing, but Woody knew it had been in exactly the same state when he left that morning. He rushed around picking up the rubbish, putting the cans and the papers into an old carrier bag, and was just about to carry them downstairs to the dustbin when there was a knock on the door. He cursed and shoved the bag under his bed and smoothed down the quilt. The knock was repeated as he popped into the alcove where there was a mirror above a small wash-basin. He gave his hair a quick comb and then opened the door. It was Maggie in a dark-green suit, her red hair tied back in a ponytail. She was carrying a black leather briefcase and could indeed have been there to sell him insurance, except the smile she gave him wasn't the professional "have I got the policy for you" type, it was warm and genuine.

He stepped to the side and waved her in. "It's not much," he apologised.

She looked round and nodded. "You're right," she said.

"It's temporary."

"It would have to be," she laughed. "Does it have a bar?"

Woody laughed with her. "Yeah, there's some whisky. Let me wash a couple of glasses." He picked up a glass from off his dressing-table and went back into the alcove. There was another glass on the shelf under the mirror containing his toothbrush and a tube of toothpaste. He tipped them out and washed both glasses, carried them back, and poured them both a drink.

They clinked glasses. "Sit down," said Woody.

Maggie looked around the tiny bedsit. "Where?" she said. There was only one chair and that was covered with a pair of jeans and a couple of shirts that looked the worse for wear. She put her briefcase on the floor by the door.

"It'll have to be the bed, I'm afraid," said Woody.

She smiled and sat down and Woody joined her.

"So, Rome, then Belfast. You get around."

"Yeah, I'm sorry it's such short notice."

"A security conference, you said?"

"Yeah, lots of top guys. And with any luck there'll be a big story, too."

"I'm pleased, you deserve it. Why is it so hot in here?"

"I told you," he said. He tapped the wall behind them. "It's the immersion heater. It's really cosy in the winter."

"I bet, but this is the middle of summer, Woody."

"Let me take your jacket," he said, and helped her slip it off. She opened the top button of her blouse and waved the material back and forth to cool herself. She looked up and caught Woody watching her. She didn't say anything and Woody leaned over and kissed her on her left cheek, close to her mouth.

"Woody, no," she said softly, but she didn't move away so Woody kissed her again, closer to her lips. He reached up and cupped her breast and tried to kiss her on the mouth but she moved her head and his lips brushed her hair.

"Woody, don't," she said, but her hand fell into his lap and stayed there and he could hear her breathing heavily. He massaged her full breast through the soft material of the blouse and he felt her nipple stiffen and when he tried to kiss her again this time their lips met.

He unbuttoned her blouse as they kissed. Her bra fastened at the front and after a couple of attempts he undid that, too. Her breasts fell free and he leant forward and kissed them as she cradled his head in her hands.

"Woody, we don't have time," she said, running her fingers through his hair and kissing the back of his head.

He pressed his fingers against her lips. "Shhh," he said, and kissed her again as he slipped her blouse off her shoulders. She wriggled her arms out of her sleeves and then she helped him off with his shirt and they lay down next to each other, kissing and caressing. Woody broke free and took off his shoes, socks and trousers and then lay down on top of her.

"Woody, we can't," whispered Maggie as he began to push her skirt down her hips. She lifted her backside to make it easier for him and he used his foot to push it the rest of the way down her legs.

"It's all right," he said, kissing her again and running his hands down her legs. She was wearing stockings and they rasped against his fingers. He slipped his hand into the top of her briefs.

"No, it's not," she said. "We can't make love."

He removed his hand and raised himself up on one elbow. "You're not a virgin are you?" he asked.

She collapsed into giggles. "That's very flattering, Woody, but no I'm not." She reached up and linked her arms round his neck and pulled him down on top of her. "It's the wrong time of the month," she whispered into his ear. "I'm sorry."

Not half as sorry as I am, thought Woody. "That's OK," he said, but his voice was heavy with disappointment.

Maggie wrapped her legs around him and held him. She kissed him hard, her tongue probing deep into his mouth and then whispered into his ear again. "Lie on your back," she said. He did as he was told and she lay next to him, her hand moving gently between his legs. He groaned and she moved up the bed slightly so that her breasts were level with his mouth. "Kiss them," she said, while her hand became more insistent, moving faster and harder. "Kiss them while I make you come."

The British Airways stewardess stood to one side to allow the passengers to disembark, a flurry of briefcases and forced smiles. She smiled and said goodbye to an Oriental man in a duffel coat, but he looked right through her. He wasn't carrying any luggage and he was scruffily dressed, jeans and a pullover under the coat. There were streaks of dirt across his face as if he'd washed in a hurry and, not to put too fine a point on it, he stank to high heavens. One of the passengers who had been sitting on the same row had asked to be moved and the stewardess had had to agree. The smell turned her stomach, the bitter aroma of skin that hadn't seen soap and water in a long time. The man had been hungry and had wolfed down the tray of cake and sandwiches put in front of him, keeping his coat firmly buttoned up throughout the flight. She'd pointed the man out to the chief steward but he'd told her not to worry, security checks on the flights between Belfast and London were second to none and he looked more like a man taking his first flight than a potential hijacker. The smell? Well, that was a nuisance, but what could you expect, she was told. Nguyen left the plane at a brisk walk. He had to get to central London before the shops closed.

Woody stretched and looked at his watch. "Christ, is that the time?" he said.

"What time is that?" asked Maggie. She was lying with her back to Woody, her head in the crook of his right arm.

"It's six o'clock. I'm going to have to run." He slid his arm out from under her neck and kissed her shoulder. She turned and kissed him on the lips and his hand went to her breasts again and he moved on top of her. "I wish I could make love to you," he sighed.

"You will," she said. She hadn't allowed him to remove her briefs or stockings but she had made him scream with pleasure with her hands, extending his pleasure until he was exhausted. He'd asked if he could make her come but she refused, saying that she'd rather wait until they could make love properly and fully. "When you get back from Belfast," she'd promised.

Woody sat up and pulled on his underpants, then his socks, then his trousers. Maggie sat up while he went to his wardrobe and took out a clean shirt. She made no attempt to cover herself and Woody turned to admire her breasts while he buttoned his shirt up and put on a tie. She laughed and leant over to pick up her briefcase and swung it on to the bed. She clicked open the case and took out a piece of paper. "Here's the address and phone number of my cousin. I rang him this afternoon and said you'd be coming over and that you'd call him some time."

Woody walked over to take the sheet of paper but as he reached for it she moved it away, catching him off balance. "Ask nicely," she teased. He leant forward and kissed her and she put her arms around his neck, pulling him down on the bed. Woody pulled away and this time she gave him the paper. "And can you give him this?" she said, reaching into the case. She took out a laptop computer and put it on the bed beside her. "He asked me to get it repaired. He bought it in London last year and couldn't get it fixed in Belfast. It's OK now. Do you mind? I know it'll mean taking it all the way to Rome and then back to Belfast, but I don't trust the Post Office."

Woody shook his head. "Of course I don't mind." He picked it up and put it in his overnight bag along with a change of clothes and his washing kit. Maggie made no move to get out of bed so Woody asked her what she planned to do.

"Can I stay here for a while?" she asked. "I'll let myself out."

"Sure," said Woody, looking at his watch again. "Christ, I'm going to have to dash. I'll call you from Rome. What's your home number?"

She grimaced. "My phone's out of order. I'll call you from a call box. What hotel will you be staying at?"

"Hell, I don't know. Call the office, they'll tell you." He picked up his bag and kissed her. He blew her another kiss from the door and closed it behind him.

She lay back in the bed and put her hands over her eyes. She felt sticky and dirty being with the grubby man in his grubby room, relieving him with her hands and pretending to love it. She shuddered. "The things I do for you, Denis Fisher," she said to herself.

She slid out from under the quilt and padded over to the

sink, washing herself as best she could. She caught sight of herself in the mirror and pulled her tongue out. "Whore," she said to herself, and then laughed. She dried herself and put her clothes back on but she still didn't feel clean.

She took the towel and carefully rubbed it everywhere she'd touched, removing all trace of her fingerprints. Only when she was totally satisfied did she pick up her briefcase and let herself out of the room, not forgetting to wipe the door handle.

Woody made it to the airport with time to spare. He could barely keep his eyes open. He'd had a rough drinking session the night before, but it was Maggie who'd sapped his strength. He had no idea as he sat on the bed and tried to kiss her just how enthusiastic she'd turn out to be. He was quite surprised, and pleased. And knackered.

He was met by a Home Office press officer, a colleague of Annie's, a young guy who used to work for the *Daily Telegraph* and who Woody vaguely remembered meeting several years earlier.

"I'm sorry, Woody, there's been a change of plan. The jet we've chartered has had engine problems so we're putting everyone on scheduled flights. I've got you a seat on a plane leaving in forty-five minutes." He handed Woody a ticket. "It's Economy I'm afraid."

"No sweat," said Woody. "Are you going on the same flight?"

The man nodded. "Yeah, and I'll be around to look after you at Rome airport."

"We're not sitting together?"

At least the guy had the grace to look shamefaced as he admitted that he was flying Business Class. They joined the queue to have their overnight bags X-rayed. Woody filled his mind with images of Maggie as he waited.

His turn came and he handed his bag to a uniformed guard who put it on the conveyor and watched it disappear as he stepped through the metal detector. His bag was pulled out by a squat, middle-aged woman with a pointed face and a flat chest and put on one side with half a dozen others. It seemed that they were pulling out one in three bags for hand inspection, which Woody guessed was a result of the bombing campaign. It wasn't so long ago when it was a rarity to have one of the guards go through your luggage and then it was usually because they'd seen something they didn't recognise on the scanner.

A short youth with a pencil-thin moustache and sideburns gave him a crooked smile and asked him if the bag was his. When Woody said it was, the guard put it down on the counter and asked him to open it. Woody did and the boy thrust his hands into it as if he was about to deliver a baby. He pulled out Woody's wash bag, unzipped it and examined his can of shaving foam and toothpaste. He carefully pushed aside Woody's underwear and shirts and then his hands appeared with the computer. He looked at it front and back, peered inside the ventilation grille, and shook it.

"Can you switch this on for me, sir?" he asked.

Woody opened the machine, revealing the screen and the keyboard, and groped at the back where he knew the on-off switch would be. The screen flickered into life. Woody had used portables many times so he had no difficulty getting the computer to flash up a directory. The guard peered at it, and pressed a few keys at random.

"That's fine, sir," he said, allowing Woody to switch it off and put it back in his bag. Woody picked it up and slung it over his shoulder. "Have we got time for a drink before we board?" Woody asked the press officer.

"Probably several."

"You're talking my language," laughed Woody.

Joker stood by the french window and looked over the river towards where he knew the Colonel would be. He couldn't tell which of the many windows the Colonel was behind, but that was to be expected. He'd be well back from the window with the rest of his team. If Joker could see him, the IRA would be able to spot him, too.

As he waited for instructions he hummed to himself quietly. There was nothing else to do. He'd stripped and cleaned his Heckler & Koch MP5, the German-made 9-millimetre machine gun that the SAS favoured, reassembled it and replaced the magazine with its thirty rounds. He adjusted his assault waistcoat, more from habit than because of need, and flicked the safety catch off. Ginge stood by his side, while Bunny and Jacko waited behind. There was only enough space for two of them to jump down on the balcony at the same time so they'd agreed that Joker and Ginge would go first. Bunny and Jacko would follow as back-up.

During the briefing, the Colonel had made it clear that only one four-man team would actually be going into the flat and Joker had held his breath, fearing that he'd be going back to Hereford without seeing action. He needn't have worried, because the Colonel knew that Joker's team had been pulling the best scores in the killing house. The other two assault teams had groaned but knew better than to complain. One four-man team was sitting in a Range Rover in nearby Wapping Lane, parked up and listening on the radio to the Colonel's instructions, ready to give chase just in case something went wrong. The remaining four were in plain clothes, two in Wapping High Street and two down by the river in front of the target flat, but well out of sight.

"Stand by," said the Colonel's voice in Joker's earpiece. "We think we have a clear shot." The two D11 marksmen were the only police representatives Joker had seen, and at first he'd assumed it was because the Colonel wanted to keep the operation low-key and not risk having the terrorists tipped off by too much woodentop activity. During the briefing, however, it became clear that there was another reason for the minimum police presence. The Colonel had stressed that they were not planning to take any prisoners. The operation was to be a hit and run, leaving no martyrs alive in mainland prisons as a focus for future terrorist actions, though the

Colonel had stressed that one of the terrorists had to be interrogated to discover if there were any devices already planted that hadn't gone off yet. The Colonel suggested that The Bombmaker should be left alive, but that it was Joker's call. Obviously if she was armed she'd have to be taken out immediately.

"They've just switched the lights on. There are three men in the lounge area," said the Colonel in Joker's ear. "One sitting at the table, one on the couch, one standing in the hallway. There's still no sign of the girl."

Another voice in Joker's ear, this time one of the men in the Range Rover, cut in. "She's coming. A taxi just pulled up in front of the building. It's her. She's going in."

There was silence for a minute and then the Colonel's voice spoke again. "One of the men is opening the door. Yes, it's her. The two of them are going into one of the bedrooms. OK, stand down. We can't move while two of them are out of sight."

Joker and Ginge went back into the flat to wait.

Fisher took MacDermott in his arms and held her. "Did it go OK?" he whispered.

"It was horrible, horrible. I don't ever want to have to do anything like that again. He was all over me, Denis, like some sort of slobbering animal."

He kissed her ear. "Come on, kid. It had to be done, you know that. And think of the prize. If what he told you is right, that plane is going to be the biggest coup we've ever had. And we get to take out some of our worst enemies. Anyway, it's not as if he was grotesque or anything. He was a good-looking guy."

She pulled away and glared at him. "That's not the fucking point, Denis. I had to spend weeks around him, fending him off, toying with him, waiting for the opportunity to use him. I feel dirty, really dirty."

Fisher held up his hands to calm her down. "OK, OK, I'm

sorry. Don't take me the wrong way. We're all proud of you, really proud. And we know what you went through."

"Do you Denis? Do you really?" She shook her head and there were tears in her eyes. "I'm going to shower," she said, pushing past him.

"Stand by," said the Colonel. "We see the girl, coming out of the bedroom. She's going into the bathroom. The man is out of the bedroom, too, he's walking towards the lounge. OK, we have all three men in view. We'll wait for the girl to come out. Get ready, Joker."

Another voice broke in, this time one of the SAS men on foot. "There's somebody walking along Wapping High Street," he said. "A man. Anyone else see him?"

"We see him," said the watcher in the Range Rover. "He's heading towards the block. No, it's OK, it's a delivery. He's carrying a box. He's a Chink, by the look of it. Yeah, I can see Chinese writing on the box. Somebody's ordered a Chinese take-away by the look of it. Nothing to worry about."

"It can't be for our targets, we saw them eating earlier on," said the Colonel. "Keep an eye on him, just in case."

"He's outside the block," said the man in the Range Rover. "He's going in."

Nguyen hefted the box in his left hand and reached for the doorbells with his right. There were more than twenty individual buttons and he was about to press a few at random to see if anyone would let him in through the security door when he saw movement in the hallway and a second later the door pushed open and a middle-aged man carrying a small terrier went by him. Nguyen caught the door before it swung shut and slipped inside. At the end of the hallway was a lift with its doors open and to the left was a stairway. He headed up the stairs, carrying the box in both hands. He was after Flat 19 but had no way of knowing which floor it was on, so as he reached each landing he quietly eased open the door and checked the numbers of the flats. On the fourth floor he saw a door with 19 on it and he jerked back out of sight. He was almost there. It was almost over.

"Get ready, Joker. The girl is coming out of the bathroom. She's wearing a bathrobe, a white bathrobe, and she's heading for the lounge. This could be it. Where's the guy with the dog?"

"He's well away," said the watcher in the Range Rover.

"No sign of the delivery man?"

"Still inside."

"OK. She's sitting down on the left in the armchair by the television. Hang on, the man at the table appears to have a gun, an automatic, but he's not holding it. It's on the table."

The four soldiers looked to their right at a large drawing of the flat below. The Colonel had copied it from the diagram on the blackboard, including details of where the furniture was. It was pretty much a copy of the flat they were in, though smaller. Joker used the barrel of his gun to indicate where the four terrorists would be. Ginge nodded.

"I'll take the man at the table, and the guy on the couch," said Joker. "The one in the hallway is yours. Don't forget, we try to take the girl alive. We've got some questions for her."

"We think we have a clear shot at the man in the hallway. Stand by," said the Colonel.

"Mine is the couch, yours is the table," corrected Joker.

"Right ho," said Ginge.

"Move out on to the balcony," said the Colonel.

Joker felt the adrenalin surge as he prepared for action. He and Ginge stood side by side waiting for the word. They both cocked the actions of their MP5s, slotting home live rounds into the chamber. They both had their safeties off and their

315

fingers on the trigger guards so that there was no way the guns could go off accidentally when they jumped. There were live rounds in the chambers of their holstered Brownings but they'd kept the safeties on. They were wearing assault waistcoats loaded with stun grenades over black overalls. They had both chosen to wear light body armour and had discarded the high velocity body armour with its tough ceramic plates that they'd brought with them, partly because there was no sign of anything bigger than a handgun in the flat below and because they didn't want to be burdened down with too much weight when they jumped.

"Prepare to jump," said the Colonel. The two SAS men eased themselves over the blue-painted metal railings, facing forward and holding on with one hand. The drop was about twelve feet which was easy enough, but they had to twist through ninety degrees to the right as they jumped so balance would be a problem. Joker would be able to land by the side of the white plastic table and chairs but Ginge would drop behind them so he wouldn't be able to move inside as quickly, he'd have to go round. Bunny and Jacko moved up behind them to stand on the balcony.

Nguyen placed the box on the floor and squatted next to it. He took out the cartons of food, long since gone cold, and stacked them against the wall. At the bottom of the box, in pieces, was a replica of a Kalashnikov AK-47. He'd arrived at the shop minutes before it was due to close, out of breath because he'd run down the Strand, and paid in cash. It was realistic down to the last detail, a perfect copy of the Russian-designed 7.62-millimetre automatic rifle that he'd used in the jungles of Vietnam. He assembled it with an efficiency born of familiarity, screwing home the wooden stock and slotting in the magazine. The weight felt slightly wrong but it looked real enough, and the men he was up against were professionals, they would assume that anyone who moved against them would be using the real thing. He'd have preferred to have used the Browning but he'd left that behind in the forest, and besides, there was no way he could have got any weapons at all through the airport security. Anyway, there was a certain irony in using the AK-47, which is why he'd chosen it over the rest of the range of replica guns the shop had in stock. That and the fact that it was the gun he felt most comfortable with. So long as he kept moving, so long as he didn't give them time to think, they wouldn't realise that it was a replica, they wouldn't notice that the barrel was solid metal and that the gun could never in a million years be used to fire bullets. They'd be off-guard, defensive, and scared, and he'd be able to use their confusion to take their own weapons from them. They'd be sure to have guns, and once he'd taken them from them he'd have no further need of a replica. And if he was wrong, if there were no guns in the flat, then he'd use the knives he'd also bought at the shop.

Nguyen no longer gave any thought to his own future, to what would happen if he should succeed. He didn't care any more. He'd given up any hope of justice being done, all he wanted now was revenge. He wanted nothing less than the death of the four bombers and he had no interest in what lay beyond that. His life was over.

When the weapon was ready he put the cartons back in the box and stood up. He slid the rifle inside his coat, barrel down, and held it in place with his right arm and then picked up the box with his left. It felt awkward, but it wouldn't be for long.

MacDermott ran a towel through her red hair. The shower had helped, she was more relaxed now and the hot water had made her feel a little cleaner, on the outside anyway. She jumped as the doorbell buzzed. Fisher frowned. It wasn't the bell at the entrance to the main security door, it was the doorbell, which meant that whoever was ringing was already inside the building, outside the flat. He motioned to McCormick to pick up the gun as he moved towards the door.

McCormick took the automatic in his hand, clicked off the safety and held it under the table.

Fisher walked down the hallway on tiptoe. He put his eye to the security viewer and a distorted Oriental face looked back, grinning. Fisher saw the man press the doorbell again and it buzzed. The man was holding a box with what looked to be cartons of Chinese food.

"What do you want?" Fisher shouted through the door.

"You order Chinese food?" said the man.

"No, you must have the wrong flat," Fisher shouted back.

"I not hear you," the man said.

"Wrong flat," Fisher repeated, his eye still pressed to the peep-hole.

He could see the Oriental shake his head and step back, looking confused. "I not hear you," he said.

Fisher reached for the lock and turned it. "It's OK," he called to the others. "Some guy trying to deliver a Chinese take-away. He's got the wrong flat, that's all." He unlocked the door and turned the handle, stepping to the side as he did. In the lounge, McCormick relaxed and took his finger off the trigger of his gun. O'Reilly grinned and patted his chest with the flat of his hand.

MacDermott began drying her hair again and then suddenly stopped, her heart pounding as realisation hit her like a kick in the chest. She gasped for breath, her mind whirling as if she was falling from a great height, full of images of Woody's Chinaman, the man on the trail of the IRA, knowing that he was the man outside the door but unable to form the words that she could shout as a warning. All she could think to yell was "No! No! No!" and her screams echoed around the flat, startling them all. McCormick flinched and began to get out of his chair as Nguyen kicked the door open, sending Fisher sprawling across the hallway.

Nguyen threw down his box and grabbed for the Kalashnikov, swinging the barrel up at waist level. He stepped into the hallway and kicked Fisher, knocking him away from the door, keeping him off balance so he wouldn't be able to get a good look at the gun. Over Fisher's shoulder he saw a man at a table, pushing himself to his feet and pointing a handgun towards him. "Drop the gun!" shouted Nguyen, aiming his useless replica at the man's chest and stepping forward. The man looked confused and began to lower the weapon.

"We have another target in the flat," said the Colonel's voice in Joker's ear, calmly and controlled. "I repeat, there are now five in the flat. Three in the lounge, two in the hall." There was a pause, and then he spoke again. "One of the targets in the hallway has an assault rifle. OK, Joker, we have a clear shot at the men in the hall. We'll take them both out from here. Jump on my command." Another pause, enough for three heartbeats. "Go!" said the Colonel. "Go, go, go!"

Joker and Ginge dropped together, and a fraction of a second after they let go of the rail they heard the double crack of two high velocity rounds splitting the air.

To Joker it seemed that time slowed right down as they pushed themselves out and twisted in the air, knees slightly bent to absorb the shock. They hit the ground together and slipped their fingers over the triggers of their MP5s. It took a fraction of a second for Joker's brain to register the scene in the room. There were three of them, two men and a girl, and they all had their backs to the window. The man on the couch was halfway up, the woman was holding a towel over her mouth. The man at the table had a gun in his hand. All were looking at the hallway where a blond-haired man was slumped against the wall, his hand clutched to his blood-smeared chest, obviously just seconds from death. Another man, an Oriental, stood in the hallway with what looked like a Kalashnikov in his hands and blood pouring from a wound in his shoulder. The man's mouth was opening and closing and he had a look of amazement on his face. He saw Joker, saw the MP5 and then looked down at his own gun as if seeing it for the first time. Joker fired instinctively and put three bullets into the man, two in the chest and one in the head, sending him slamming backwards.

The man at the table began to turn but before he could

bring his gun up Ginge hit him with four rounds. Joker took out the man on the couch before he even turned round and he died without knowing what had hit him.

Joker stepped into the room first, followed by Ginge, and Jacko and Bunny dropped down behind them. The girl began to stand up but Ginge pushed her back down. "You fucking Brit bastard!" she screamed, and Ginge slapped her so hard that she was almost knocked out of the chair. A thin dribble of blood ran down her chin. Her eyes blazed and she stood up, her hands hooked like claws, and she lashed out at Ginge's eyes. He swayed backwards, easily avoiding her attack, and prodded her in the stomach with the barrel of his gun. She doubled up, gasping for breath and retching, and Ginge threw her back into the chair.

"Stay where you are you fucking bitch or you're dead!" he warned. He kept the gun trained on her while Joker moved along the hall, stepping over the bodies of the two men, checking the kitchen, bathroom and three bedrooms. Jacko and Bunny moved behind him. They were a well co-ordinated team, they'd spent hundreds of hours training together in the killing house at Hereford, breathing in lead fumes and smoke as they pumped round after round into cardboard cut-outs of Russian storm-troopers. Compared with the killing house, this was a breeze.

"Clear," said Joker when he was satisfied.

"You have the girl?" the Colonel's voice asked.

"Secured," said Ginge.

The Oriental groaned, murmured something in a language none of the men could understand, and then went still, blood seeping from between his lips, his chest a mess of mangled flesh and pieces of ribcage.

The three SAS men joined Ginge in the lounge. Jacko and Bunny checked the bodies while Joker began to search the room, quickly and efficiently. He found the Semtex in a cupboard below a bookcase in the lounge, along with some detonators and several electric clocks. In a walk-in cupboard in the hall, by the front door, he found an empty box that once contained a laptop computer. Inside the box was an instruction manual, still sealed in its polythene wrapping, and pieces of plastic-coated wire. He took it into the lounge and threw it at the girl's feet.

"What's this?" he shouted. "Is this the next bomb, you Irish whore?" His words came out in short, staccato bursts like bullets from his MP5.

The Bombmaker wiped the back of her hand across her mouth, smearing the blood across her lips like a manic clown's make-up. "Fuck off," she said. "And I'm Scottish you ignorant bastard." Joker stamped on her instep and she screamed in pain. As she bent down to rub her foot Joker slammed his fist into her face and she hurtled back into the chair. Tears streamed down her cheeks and she covered her face with her hands. Ginge grabbed her hair and yanked her head back.

Joker put his face up close so that she could smell his breath. "Listen you bitch. We've killed your friends and unless you talk to me you can join them."

He nodded at Ginge and he dragged her by the hair over to where Fisher lay face down in a pool of his own blood. Ginge threw her on top of the body and rubbed her face in the blood. Joker walked over and kicked her in the back, over her kidney where he knew the pain would be excruciating.

"Get her on her knees," Joker said, and Ginge hoisted her up by her hair. Joker stood in front of her and levelled the gun at her mouth.

She shook her head from side to side. "You're too late," she whispered.

"Stand to the side," Joker said to Ginge. "I'm going to blow her fucking head off." Ginge moved from behind her and Bunny and Jacko went to stand by the window.

"There's nobody who'll know that you didn't die when we stormed the flat," he told her menacingly. "There are no witnesses. This isn't going to be another Gibraltar."

"You're too late," she said. "It's set to go off in less than five minutes. They won't be able to land in time."

"A plane?"

"No shit, Sherlock." She cleared her throat and spat down on the floor, not to insult him but because her mouth was filling up with blood and saliva.

"Which plane?"

She was talking now, because she figured that whatever she told him it wouldn't make a difference. She wanted him to know, and to know that there was nothing he could do to stop it. She told him it was a special flight to Rome, that a journalist called Ian Wood was carrying the bomb, and that everybody on board the flight was as good as dead. She began to laugh sourly until Joker hit her on the side of her head with his gun as Ginge began relaying the information to the Colonel.

Woody was on his fourth whisky when the "fasten seatbelt" light went on and the front of the plane dipped down.

"Ladies and gentlemen, this is the captain speaking. There is some turbulence ahead and we are descending to avoid it. Please make sure your seat is upright and your seat-belt is fastened."

Woody frowned. He'd flown often enough to know that the normal procedure was to fly over bad weather, not under it. He fastened his seat-belt and sipped his whisky. Better to drink it rather than to take the risk of spilling it, he decided.

"Would passenger Ian Wood please make himself known to the cabin crew," said the captain. Woody didn't realise at first that it was his name that had been called, but he heard it when the message was repeated. The plane had gone into a steep descent and the stewardesses were briskly moving down the aisles checking that seats were upright and passengers strapped in. Woody could also see that they were scanning the passengers to see if anyone was reacting to the final announcement. He waved to a pretty blonde stewardess. She came over, eyebrows raised.

"I'm Ian Wood," he said. The woman in the seat next to him was openly listening, curious to know what he'd done.

"Mr Wood, do you have any baggage in the hold?" the stewardess asked briskly. Woody could tell from her tone that something was very badly wrong, so he answered immediately, suppressing his first instinct to make a joke.

"No," he said. There was a cold feeling of dread in his stomach.

"Could you give me all the cabin baggage you have, please," she said. She was smiling but he could tell that it was an act to put him at his ease and get his co-operation, the girl was frightened shitless. So was Woody.

"Oh God," he moaned, and reached between his legs to pick up his bag.

The bomb exploded.

Joker and Ginge kept Maggie covered as they waited for instructions from the Colonel. They had made her lie face down on the bloodstained carpet next to Fisher, with her hands clasped behind her neck. She had a good body, thought Joker. Good legs, firm arse, just the way he liked a woman to be. He looked at his watch.

The Colonel's voice spoke in his left ear. "The plane has gone down. We assume with all lives lost. Operation is discontinued. No loose ends. I repeat, no loose ends."

Joker looked across at Ginge to see if he had heard. Ginge nodded and made a small motion with his MP5, his way of saying that Joker could do the honours. Joker fired once into her back, just over where her heart was.

She didn't die straightaway, they never did. In books they often said that people who were shot died before they hit the ground. It never happened that way, Joker knew. Joker had killed people in Belfast, in the Falklands, in the Middle East, and once in Spain, and he'd yet to see anyone die straightaway, no matter where they were shot. If the bullet went through the heart or the lungs then the brain kept sending out messages for up to a minute or so before their eyes glazed over and they finally died. If they were shot in the head and the brains were splattered over the floor, then the heart continued to pump and the limbs twitch for a while until they realised that it was all over. That's what it was like in real life. Not many people knew the difference between death in books and movies and death in real life. But Joker knew.

When the bullet tore through her back and punched a ragged hole in her chest, her arms flailed out and she grunted. Some time after that she died in a pool of blood, her arms and legs drumming against the floor, saliva dripping from her mouth and panic in her eyes. Joker didn't stand over her and watch while she died, he stood with his back to her, looking out over the river as he waited for the banging and wheezing to stop. Slow deaths always embarrassed him.

Jon Simpson stayed late in his office so that he could see the second editions before going home. His own paper wasn't printed for another seventy-two hours but he wanted to see how the dailies treated the bombing of the jet and the SAS operation against the IRA bombers. News of the bombings had broken too late for the papers to do much in their first editions, though most had managed to get in a few pars.

A copy boy came through the double doors with a stack of papers under his arm and dropped them on to the desk. Simpson separated the tabloids from the broadsheets and went through them first: the *Sun*, the *Daily Mirror*, the *Daily Mail*, the *Daily Express*, the *Daily Star* and *Today*. They all had pictures of the wreckage in the sea, and the head-shots of the active service unit. They had all used the girl Bombmaker's photograph big on their front pages because that was the obvious one to go for, and both the *Express* and the *Mail* had used Woody's picture on the front along with the story of how he'd been duped into carrying the bomb.

Yeah, Simpson thought, that's how he'd do it. The bombing, the betrayal, the SAS operation on the front, along with the girl's picture. Inside, backgrounders on the bombing campaign and the SAS, biogs of the bombers and lots of political reaction. A great story, just a pity that it hadn't happened on a Saturday night. The two pictures of Woody looked up at Simpson. Simpson shook his head sadly. "Well, Woody, you finally made the front page," he said to himself. He gathered the papers up and took them home to read in detail.

The call to attend the meeting in Whitehall came as Bromley was reading the morning papers at his breakfast table. The bombing of the jet was on the front of every paper, along with a graphic account of the SAS operation against the bombers in Wapping. From the amount of detail in the reports it was obvious that Ministry of Defence press officers had been hard at work pushing the Government line. There was no mention of The Chinaman in any of the stories. His life, and death, would remain a secret for ever. Another basic fact missing from all of the stories was how the authorities had managed to locate the active service unit. Intelligence, was the nearest thing to an explanation. The press officers knew exactly how to handle the Press, to spoonfeed them with more information than they could handle so that they'd forget to ask the basic questions.

He put his jacket on, kissed his wife on the cheek and went out to the garage to check the underside of his car. He peered through the driver's window to check that the onboard detection device showed that his car hadn't been tampered with and when he was satisfied he took several steps backwards and clicked a small remote-control device that started the car automatically. Only when he was satisfied that his car was safe did he unlock the door and get in. The safety precautions were second nature to him, and had been long before the car-bomb deaths of Airey Neave and Ian Gow.

The early morning phone call meant that he'd have to completely reschedule his day, but a call from the Co-ordinator of Intelligence and Security took precedence over everything else. The Co-ordinator answered to only two higher authorities – the Prime Minister and the Permanent Secretaries Committee on the Intelligence Services. His main role in life was to ensure that all the different intelligence agencies worked together, an uphill struggle at the best of times.

Bromley was one of the last to arrive at the conference room and he eased himself into an empty chair. The room was almost filled by a long, oval table of highly polished mahogany around which sat many familiar faces, several of whom nodded to Bromley. The room itself was typical Whitehall, an ornate fireplace, a smattering of respectable oil paintings in gilded frames and fussy patterned carpets. The man who stood at the head of the table was also typical Whitehall, pin-stripe suit, crisp white shirt, dark-blue tie, neatly combed hair that was greying at the temples, ramrod-straight back behind which were clasped hands with immaculately manicured nails. The Co-ordinator was a career civil servant for whom the fight against terrorism was merely a stepping stone to the knighthood that he regarded as his birthright, but he was every bit as committed to the task as the men who sat waiting for him to speak. They represented, Bromley knew, the cream of the country's anti-terrorism agencies, though he was somewhat surprised to see that there were no heads present, they were all number twos or personal assistants to the chiefs. They were all grim-faced, most had lost colleagues or friends on the doomed flight. He recognised representatives from MI5 and MI6, the Defence Intelligence Staff, several members of his own Anti-Terrorist Branch, and there were men he didn't know. Some were high-ranking police officers, others were men with military haircuts and bearing who he guessed were SAS or SBS.

There were no name-cards identifying those present, nor was there any writing equipment on the table – just a few crystal jugs of water and upturned glasses. There were, he noticed ruefully, no ashtrays.

One or two latecomers filed through the double doors leading to the room, smiling apologies at the Co-ordinator. As they took their places two men in dark suits went out, closing the doors behind them.

"Gentlemen," said the Co-ordinator, "thank you for coming. Let me say first that no notes are to be taken of this meeting, and it must not be the subject of any memos or written reports. You should also not record this meeting in your diaries. This meeting never took place. Is that understood?"

He waited for all the men to nod acceptance.

"Thank you. This is by way of a briefing for the various security and intelligence services, and for those police authorities which will be affected by what I am about to tell you. You are free to verbally brief your superiors on the nature of this meeting, but there is to be no down-the-line transfer of the information. This, as you will appreciate when I have finished, is on a need-to-know basis. And those with a need to know are a very, very select group."

He had the undivided attention of every man in the room now. There was no fidgeting, no coughing, no one looked anywhere except at the face of the Co-ordinator.

"You will all have heard about the horrifying events of yesterday evening. Tragic, absolutely tragic. It did, however, bring about the demise of the active service unit which has been behind the recent atrocities, and for that we are all grateful to Special Branch and to the SAS." He nodded to representatives of both organisations, including Bromley.

"As you know, one hundred and thirty-six people died in yesterday's plane crash. That includes twelve children and three nuns, as well as the Members of Parliament and civil servants who were on the flight. The public backlash against the IRA has already started. Not just in the Press, though obviously all the newspapers are clamouring for something to be done, including the normal misguided calls for the return of the death penalty. It goes beyond that. This time there is a groundswell of public opinion against the IRA, a feeling that something should be done, that something must be done."

He paused again, looking round the table at the men who were hanging on his every word. "Gentlemen, we have here a window of opportunity. Our experts tell us that the reaction against the terrorists will be at fever pitch for the next ten days, possibly two weeks. When the IRA hits a soft target, or kills innocent bystanders, they normally follow quickly with a highly visible attack on a legitimate target. It restores their credibility, as it were. Public opinion is notoriously fickle, but this time they have gone too far. Now, we around this table know that it was a rogue IRA active service unit responsible for the bombing campaign, that in fact it had not been sanctioned by Belfast or Dublin. That information has been kept from the Press. So far as the public is concerned it was an official IRA operation.

"The decision was taken late last night, at the highest level, to take positive action against senior members of the IRA and Sinn Fein. Over the next seven days the top echelons of the organisation will be eliminated, at a time when public opinion will be totally, one hundred per cent, against them. That is the window of opportunity I spoke about. Anything we do now, right now, will have the unqualified backing of the public. This is not, I repeat not, a shoot-to-kill policy. It is a shoot-to-kill operation. A one-off. We have drawn up a list of the twenty-five men, and women, who we see as being the key members of the IRA, without whom we feel the organisation would no longer be a viable terrorist force. A combined, and highly secret, task-force of SAS and SBS operatives will move against them. Wherever possible it will be made to seem like an accident, a car crash, a drugs overdose, a fall downstairs, but if it cannot be done tidily it will be a straightforward assassination made to look as if it is the work of Protestant extremists. Once the operation is over, the IRA will no longer be an effective threat. Then we can take them on using more legitimate methods, including the formation of a new Anti-Terrorist Task-Force, a single national task-force to counter terrorism. That, however, will be the subject of further meetings later this month. Now, are there any questions?"

Most of the men sitting around the table seemed stunned, though Bromley knew that they would all wholeheartedly support the plan put forward by the Co-ordinator. Most of them had privately been pushing for such a policy for many years, determined that the only way to defeat the IRA was to match their ferocity.

"I would appreciate it if you would confine your comments to questions," the Co-ordinator continued. "This is not a discussion forum, there is nothing to be voted on, no consensus is needed. The decision has already been taken at a much higher level. The highest level."

One of the uniformed police officers coughed and raised his hand. "When does the operation start?" he asked.

The Co-ordinator looked at a slim gold watch on his wrist. "It started ten minutes ago," he said quietly.

Another hand went up. One of the MI6 representatives. "Can we be told who is on the list?" he asked.

"Officially there is no list," the Co-ordinator said. "Nothing has ever been put down on paper, there will be no written record. However, I am able to tell you the names of the twenty-five IRA members that we feel the organisation can least afford to lose."

The names were all known to those around the table, so there were no raised eyebrows of surprise, just nods of approval. Bromley put his hand in his pocket and took out his pipe. He tapped the stem against his teeth as the names rolled on. Liam Hennessy came somewhere in the middle. Sean Morrison was the last name to be spoken.